ECHOES
OF THE FINAL WAR

ODYSSEY OF A NEW WORLD

NIELS VANDEN EYNDE

Divine Works Publishing, LLC.
Royal Palm Beach, Florida USA

LLCN Library of Congress Control Number: 2025900365
ISBN-13: 978-1-949105-72-8 (paperback)
ISBN-13: 978-1-949105-79-7 (eBook)

First Edition Published: 01/15/2025
Printed in the United States

Divine Works Publishing books are available at special discounts when purchased in quantity for premiums and promotions and for educational and fundraising use. For details, feel free contact us via email at *books@divineworkspublishing.com* or call the phone number listed below.

Published by:
Divine Works Publishing
Royal Palm Beach, Florida USA
www.DivineWorksPublishing.com
561-990-BOOK (2665)

INDEX

Locations

Artifacts, Objects and Concepts

INDEX

APOCALYPSE UNLEASHED

Amidst the ashes of a world torn asunder, the indomitable spirit of humanity flickers, a testament to our capacity for resilience and renewal. This story, emerging from the depths of our collective ordeal, is a chronicle of that unyielding perseverance. This anticipation, once abstract, materialized into a tangible ordeal, binding the fate of every corner of the world in a shared tapestry of loss and determination. This stark reality, emerging from the shadows of foresight, underscored the fragility of our perceived preparedness and the depth of our collective denial. Dubbed the Final War, this ultimate confrontation was anticipated for ages as the endgame of human conflict, yet its reality caught our generation off-guard, unraveling the world in an inferno of destruction.

Throughout the ages, whispers of such a cataclysmic event circulated, yet few truly believed that our generation would witness the unraveling of the world as we knew it. When the flames of war finally ignited, sparked by a nuclear exchange, the gravity of the situation earned its ominous title. But the war's significance extended beyond its devastating conclusion; its seeds had been quietly sown over time, steadily fermenting until the inevitable eruption.

By the year 3211, the global stage was fraught with tension, marking the onset of a countdown to catastrophe. Over the preceding centuries, the Earth had undergone significant geopolitical shifts. While some traditional nation-states endured, others evolved, dissolved, or amalgamated into new entities. Global power dynamics shifted, driven by fears of emerging technologies, particularly advanced forms of warfare. Despite historical apprehensions about technological progress, such concerns had never before reached the critical point they did at this juncture. This pivot towards an ever-increasing reliance on technology not only reshaped daily life but also redefined the contours of power and conflict on the global stage. To grasp the war's inevitability, we must first understand the intricate political and technological tapestry woven over centuries, setting the stage for disaster.

The geopolitical landscape had been a mosaic of shifting alliances and power struggles, with each faction vying for supremacy in a world teetering on the edge of chaos. The emergence of new superpowers, fueled by technological advancements and economic prowess, added layers of complexity to an already volatile situation. As tensions reached a boiling point, diplomatic channels faltered, and the specter of war loomed ominously on the horizon. As the drumbeats of war grew louder, a palpable dread settled over the globe, pervading homes and public squares alike, where discussions once filled with hopes for the future turned to whispered fears of impending doom.

At that time, the Union of Sovereign Eurasian States (USES), formed through the consolidation of several European and Asian nations, emerged as a dominant global force. Boasting advanced technology, a formidable military, and extensive economic influence, the USES saw itself as the rightful leader of the world, determined to maintain its supremacy at any cost.

In contrast, the Pacific Federation united countries bordering the Pacific Ocean, including the United States, Canada, Australia, Japan, and others.

Advocating for democracy, human rights, and international cooperation, the Pacific Federation forged a robust military alliance to counterbalance USES influence.

Finally, the African Confederation, a union of many African nations after centuries of struggle, pooled resources to combat common challenges like poverty, disease, and environmental degradation. Though lacking military might, the African Confederation wielded diplomatic influence and resource management expertise on the global stage.

A noteworthy development was the global adoption of English as the lingua franca. Slowly integrated into diverse cultures, English's popularity soared until it became the predominant language of international communication and commerce. While exceptions persisted in regions with distinct linguistic heritages, English remained widely spoken, even in areas far removed from the United States.

Before tensions reached their breaking point, the world marveled at the pinnacle of human achievement in technology. The year 3211 stood as an indication of centuries of scientific discovery, technological advancement, and societal transformation. The Internet, a global network of interconnected computers, served as the backbone of modern civilization, facilitating instantaneous communication, seamless access to information, and unprecedented connectivity between individuals and communities across vast distances.

Ironically, it was this very crescendo of progress that sowed the seeds for potential downfall, creating a paradox where our greatest achievements harbored the shadows of our greatest threats. Each innovation, while pushing the boundaries of human capability, also edged us closer to the precipice of self-destruction, weaving a complex narrative of progress and peril.

Before the cataclysmic events of the Final War, technology had reached unprecedented heights, propelling humanity into an era of unparalleled innovation and progress. The year 3211 stood as a showcase to centuries of scientific discovery, technological advancement, and societal transformation, with the world's inhabitants enjoying the fruits of their labor in ways unimaginable to previous generations.

At the forefront of this technological renaissance stood the internet, a global network of interconnected computers that served as the backbone of modern civilization. Spanning the entire globe, the internet facilitated instantaneous communication, seamless access to information, and unprecedented connectivity between individuals and communities across vast distances. Through the internet, knowledge flowed freely, economies thrived, and cultures intermingled in a digital tapestry of human ingenuity and creativity.

Technological marvels abounded in every facet of daily life, from transportation and communication to healthcare and entertainment. Advanced forms of transportation, including high-speed maglev trains and autonomous vehicles, revolutionized the way people traversed the globe, shrinking distances and opening up new frontiers of exploration and commerce. Communication technologies, such as holographic displays and neural interfaces, transcended the limitations of traditional mediums, enabling immersive virtual interactions and instantaneous information retrieval.

In the realm of healthcare, breakthroughs in medical science ushered in an era of personalized medicine, where genetic therapies, nanotechnology, and advanced diagnostics offered tailored treatments for a myriad of ailments. Lifespan extension technologies, coupled with widespread access to preventive healthcare measures, had significantly extended the average human lifespan, allowing individuals to lead longer, healthier lives free from many of the diseases that plagued previous generations.

Entertainment and leisure activities had likewise undergone a transformation in the age of technological abundance. Virtual reality simulations offered immersive experiences that blurred the lines between fantasy and reality, while augmented reality overlays enriched the mundane world with interactive digital content. Artificial intelligence-driven algorithms curated personalized entertainment experiences, from music and movies to literature and gaming, tailored to individual preferences and tastes.

Neural interfaces have become ubiquitous, seamlessly integrating technology with the human mind. These advanced interfaces allow direct communication between the brain and external devices, revolutionizing how individuals interact with technology and each other.

Neural interfaces, once rudimentary prototypes, have advanced into systems of astonishing accuracy, bridging minds and machines in seamless harmony. Yet, for all its wonders, this golden age of innovation cast long shadows, where the very tools that symbolized human ingenuity also sowed the seeds of our greatest peril. In our pursuit of advancement, we teetered on a delicate edge, where the very innovations meant to uplift humanity also harbored the potential to herald its downfall.

The post-war world saw the establishment of an International Technological Ethics Board, an entity charged with evaluating the moral implications of new technologies. This body worked tirelessly to create guidelines that would ensure technological development was aligned with ethical standards, focusing on technologies that could rebuild and rejuvenate without causing harm. Its mandate was clear: to ensure that the tools of tomorrow would serve to unite and heal, rather than divide and destroy. Through a combination of nanotechnology, biocompatible materials, and advanced signal processing algorithms, these interfaces can read neural activity with high precision, allowing for real-time communication between the brain and external devices.

In summary, the technological landscape before the Final War was characterized by boundless innovation, unfettered connectivity, and limitless potential. Humanity had reached a zenith of technological achievement, poised on the precipice of a future limited only by the bounds of imagination and ingenuity. At the height of its technological prowess, humanity stood at the edge of tomorrow, blind to the abyss that their own inventions would unveil. Yet, little did they know that the very technologies that had propelled them to such dizzying heights would also become the instruments of their downfall, plunging the world into darkness and chaos in the wake of the Final War.

As the technological marvels of the pre-war era dazzled humanity with their promise of progress and innovation, behind the scenes, a shadowy underbelly of clandestine operations and covert espionage thrived. While the world marveled at the boundless potential of technology, rumors whispered of darker intentions lurking in the corridors of power. As nations vied for supremacy, intelligence agencies operated in the shadows, weaving intricate webs of deceit and manipulation. The seeds of discord were sown, and the stage was set for a conflict far more insidious than any conventional war—a battle fought not with guns and missiles but with information and deception.

Rumors of clandestine operations and covert espionage permeated the political discourse as nations sought to gain an edge over their adversaries through any means necessary. In the shadows, intelligence agencies operated with impunity, gathering information and sowing seeds of discord in enemy territories. The murky world of espionage became a battleground in its own right, where information was the most potent weapon in the arsenal.

Meanwhile, the global populace watched with bated breath as geopolitical tensions escalated, fearing the inevitable descent into chaos and destruction. Public discourse was dominated by speculation and conjecture, with experts offering dire warnings of the impending cataclysm. Civil society mobilized in a desperate bid to avert disaster, organizing protests and peace rallies in major cities around the world.

As the countdown to war ticked ever closer, a feeling of doom gripped the hearts of millions, who could only watch helplessly as their leaders steered the world towards the brink of annihilation. In the corridors of power, politicians and statesmen grappled with the weight of their decisions, knowing that the fate of humanity hung in the balance.

Decades of simmering tensions between the USES and the Pacific Federation finally boiled over, marking the ignition point of the war. Competition for scarce resources, exacerbated by climate change and environmental degradation, fueled proxy conflicts in Southeast Asia and Eastern Europe. Armed with significant nuclear arsenals, both powers ultimately resorted to their weapons, triggering a catastrophic exchange.

The catalyst for the nuclear war was a territorial dispute over rare-earth minerals between the USES and the Pacific Federation. As nations clashed over earth's dwindling treasures, the first detonations not only razed cities but also extinguished countless lives, leaving a universe of possibilities unfulfilled. Despite international mediation efforts, a series of miscalculations and provocations precipitated a rapid escalation.

With the first nuclear launches, the USES preemptively struck key military installations and strategic targets of the Pacific Federation. In response, the Pacific Federation retaliated, igniting a devastating exchange that spiraled out of control.

On the eve of war, the world held its breath, bracing for the inevitable storm that would soon descend upon them. In the quiet moments before the chaos erupted, there was a palpable sensation of resignation, as if the die had been cast and there was no turning back. The Final War was not just a conflict between nations; it was a battle for the very soul of humanity, a struggle to determine the course of history for generations to come.

As the first bombs fell and the world was engulfed in flames, the true horror of war was laid bare for all to see. The once-prosperous cities lay in ruins, their streets littered with the wreckage of civilization. The cries of the wounded and the dying echoed through the smoke-filled skies, a haunting reminder of the cost of human folly. The inferno of war did not discriminate, erasing not only lives but the very pillars of our cultural and historical identity, leaving a void where once stood monuments to our shared heritage. Every corner of the globe felt the sting of this devastation, uniting humanity not in triumph but in mourning, faced with the shared task of rebuilding from the ashes of despair.

The resulting destruction, loss of life, and environmental devastation were unprecedented. Beyond the physical ruin, the war inflicted deep psychological scars on survivors, eroding the very essence of communal trust and casting a long shadow over the collective human psyche. Entire cities lay in ruins, and the global economy collapsed, ushering in a nuclear winter, famine, and further loss of life. As the dust of conflict settled, a collective resolve emerged from the ruins, a shared commitment to forge a path toward healing and rebuilding, underscored by a newfound appreciation for the fragile bond that unites all of humanity.

In the war's aftermath, surviving nations grappled with rebuilding and cooperation to address humanitarian crises and environmental degradation. The world had irrevocably changed, with the memory of the nuclear holocaust serving as a poignant reminder of the perils of unchecked aggression and the necessity of international cooperation.

In the aftermath, the world bore witness to the true devastation wrought by the war's fury. Cities once teeming with life were reduced to smoldering ruins, their streets choked with rubble and the ashes of the fallen. The wails of the injured pierced the smoke-filled air, a haunting display of the staggering loss of life.

Yet, amidst this all-consuming chaos, embers of hope still flickered in the hearts of its survivors. As the dust settled, the survivors, tempered by loss and fortified by the trials of rebuilding, harbored not just hope for survival but a newfound resolve to forge a world where the scars of the past would pave the way for a future of unity and peace. For while the war had brought humanity to its knees, it had not entirely extinguished the indomitable spirit that had propelled them to such great heights. In the quiet spaces between the echoes of destruction, a new chapter was waiting to be written—one born not of ambition or conquest but of resilience and the unwavering will to rebuild. Among the ruins, beneath the shadow of desolation, seeds of a new beginning quietly sprouted, promising a future forged not from the ashes of war but from the resilience of the human spirit.

In the war's shadow, humanity's remnants grappled with their new reality, a testament to their resilience and unwavering spirit of adaptation. While widespread devastation and high levels of radiation made it unlikely for humanity to fully rebuild and thrive; not all regions were impacted equally. This resilience, an inherent trait of humanity, became the bedrock for the nascent societies emerging from the ruins, where the lessons of the past illuminated the path toward a more hopeful and unified future.

Amidst the chaos and ruin beneath the veil of smoke and ash, subtle currents of change stirred, unseen and unacknowledged by most. The old world crumbled, its once-mighty structures reduced to rubble and dust. Yet, in the quiet spaces between the echoes of destruction, whispers of a distant dawn drifted on the wind.

It was a gradual transformation, imperceptible to those ensnared by the immediacy of survival. Yet for those with eyes to see and minds to ponder, the signs were there. In the cracks of shattered cities and the whispers of windswept plains, the seeds of what was to come lay dormant, awaiting their time to bloom. There are patches around the world that remained relatively safe, shielded from the worst effects of the nuclear exchange by geographic isolation or advanced radiation shielding. Under the scars of the past, a new chapter awaited, its pages yet to be written, hinting at a rebirth from the ashes of the past.

However, the relative safety of these enclaves came at a cost. Isolated from the major centers of technology and infrastructure, the inhabitants of these regions faced numerous challenges. The loss of connectivity severed ties to the global network, including the internet, which had once facilitated instant communication and access to vast repositories of knowledge. This disconnect not only isolated communities but also fragmented the collective human knowledge base, challenging survivors to reimagine ways to rebuild not just their environments but also the information networks that once bound them together. Without this technological lifeline, society was forced to adapt to a world where modern conveniences were scarce and survival often depended on more traditional methods.

Yet, remnants of technology from the pre-war era still existed, scattered among the ruins of civilization. In the face of adversity, these remnants became symbols of hope, ingeniously repurposed to rebuild not just the physical world but also the bonds of community and shared purpose. These artifacts, though functional, lacked the infrastructure and support systems that once sustained them.

In these isolated havens, the remnants of technology became lifelines, repurposed in ingenious ways to purify water, generate power, and reconnect isolated pockets of survivors, embodying the enduring human spirit to adapt and overcome.

As we stood at the threshold of a new era, the dual nature of technological advancement served as both a cautionary tale and a beacon of hope. On the one hand, the remnants of pre-war technology reminded us of the folly of unchecked innovation; on the other, they offered a blueprint for sustainable progress. The challenge lay in navigating this dichotomy, in harnessing the power of technology to heal rather than harm, to unite rather than divide. It was a challenge that was accepted with the gravity and optimism it deserved, shaping the principles that would guide our path forward.

As humanity navigated its recovery, the narrative of technological advancement bifurcated into tales of caution and hope. Technologies once wielded for warfare were now repurposed for healing the earth, restoring ecosystems, and rebuilding societies.

This renaissance of purpose breathed new life into our relationship with technology, framing it not as a harbinger of doom but as a catalyst for global healing and unity.

Innovators and technologists, working with limited resources, spearheaded efforts to retrofit and innovate upon existing technologies, creating sustainable solutions that addressed the immediate needs of survivors while laying the groundwork for future advancements. Without access to the internet, much of the knowledge and expertise of the past began to fade away as experts became increasingly rare and valuable resources dwindled. Modern medicine, engineering, and other fields of study were preserved in fragments, but their full potential remained untapped in the absence of a global network.

As time passed, these isolated communities began to develop their own unique cultures and social structures, shaped by the challenges and opportunities of their environment. With limited access to advanced technology, traditional skills and knowledge became highly valued and passed down through generations as essential tools for survival. Cut off from the digital world, communities turned inward, rediscovering age-old practices in farming, medicine, and governance, crafting a new tapestry of life from the remnants of the old.

The absence of global communication and trade networks forced communities to become more self-reliant, cultivating local resources and forming alliances based on mutual needs and shared values. Determined not to be defined by the tragedies of the past, the survivors embraced a collective vision for the future. Amidst the rubble, international dialogue emerged, fostering collaborations that transcended old boundaries and ideologies. In this crucible of reconstruction, the very notion of governance began to evolve.

Leaders and visionaries debated not just the form but the essence of governance in a world reborn from ashes. The emergency consensus spoke to a governance model that was more decentralized, more collaborative, and yet bound by a universal charter of human rights and environmental stewardship. This vision, however ambitious, underscored a commitment to ensuring that the lessons of the past guide the governance of the future. These discussions planted the seeds for a global initiative focused on reconstruction, environmental restoration, and the establishment of a new world order predicated on sustainable peace and mutual respect.

The global consensus envisioned a governance model imbued with flexibility and resilience, embodying the principles of decentralized authority and participatory decision-making. A global assembly was proposed, leveraging technology for transparent, inclusive governance, ensuring no voice was marginalized in the great task of rebuilding. This model represented a profound shift towards a governance system designed to prevent the failures that led to the Final War, emphasizing sustainability, human rights, and equitable resource distribution as foundational pillars.

This vision, crystallized through shared trials, galvanized a global movement towards rebuilding a world where peace prevails over conflict and unity over division, heralding a new chapter in human history. One that cherishes peace, nurtures resilience and fosters a global community bound by the shared experience of rebirth.

Yet, even as humanity adapted to its new reality, the specter of the past loomed large. The memory of the nuclear holocaust served as a constant reminder of the fragility of civilization and the dangers of unchecked aggression. The war left scars not only on the physical landscape but also on the collective consciousness of what remained of humanity, forever altering the course of history and serving as a cautionary tale for generations to come.

TRANSFIGURATION

The Earth had been ravaged by a catastrophic nuclear war, leaving only a few small human groups scattered across the planet. As the world I knew crumbled, the seeds of a new society were being sown amidst the ruins. This wasn't just the story of one nation or continent; it was a global reawakening, a testament to the resilience of humanity across the shattered remains of Earth.

The thought of emerging into this nascent world, where the remnants of humanity endeavored to rebuild not just buildings but the very fabric of society, filled me with cautious optimism. This vision remained consistent with the scientists' predictions, grounding my expectations in the stark realities of our new world.

As the scientists outlined the probable state of the world I was to awaken in, they painted a picture of vast landscapes altered by the wrath of nuclear fallout, cities reclaimed by nature, and small enclaves of survivors striving to rebuild amidst the ruins. This new world, they surmised, would be both hauntingly beautiful and starkly dangerous, a place where the remnants of old technology would mingle with emergent societies forging new paths forward.

The once-powerful African Confederation was destroyed in the conflict, and only a handful of survivors remained. The African Confederation, once a beacon of unity and progress, fell not just to external forces but to internal strife and resource scarcity, exacerbated by the relentless advance of the war. Meanwhile, in a clandestine underground bunker in Antarctica, a significant scientific organization led by the Russians persists. Their focus was on developing an immortality serum designed to ensure the survival of humans amidst nuclear devastation.

The scientists wrestled with the ethical implications of their work, questioning the morality of playing god with human fate amidst the ashes of civilization.

Each scientist carried the burden of this ethical dilemma, their personal convictions driving them forward despite the profound uncertainties surrounding the outcome of their work. The scientists' quest to defy death itself was not undertaken lightly. Each breakthrough was shadowed by debates on the moral implications of their work. Were they safeguarding humanity's future or meddling with the natural order? This ethical quandary underscored their every action, serving as a reminder of the immense responsibility resting on their shoulders. This serum, named "EterniX," is a groundbreaking scientific achievement developed using advanced biotechnology and nanomedicine. EterniX works by enhancing the body's regenerative capabilities at the cellular level, effectively repairing damage caused by radiation exposure and aging.

The development of EterniX was a monumental task, involving the collaboration of countless scientists and researchers. Their dedication and tireless work underscored the project's critical importance to the future of mankind.

The key components of the serum included nanoparticles. Microscopic nanorobots infused with the serum travel through the bloodstream, repairing damaged cells and tissues with remarkable efficiency.

Telomerase Activation: EterniX activates telomerase, an enzyme responsible for maintaining the length of telomeres, which are protective caps on the ends of chromosomes. This prevents cellular senescence and allows for indefinite cell replication, effectively halting the aging process.

Enhanced Physiology: EterniX enhances the user's physical attributes, including strength, agility, and sensory perception. It also boosts cognitive function and reflexes, giving the user a significant advantage in survival situations and the ability to understand things much more quickly.

Another effect was a mechanism that involved the modulation of synaptic plasticity, the ability of synapses to strengthen or weaken over time in response to neuronal activity. By targeting specific neurotransmitter systems or molecular pathways involved in synaptic plasticity, EterniX could enhance the encoding, storage, and retrieval of memories, giving the user a photographic memory.

Immortality Mechanism: The serum contains a proprietary compound that inhibits apoptosis, the process of programmed cell death. Beyond mere survival, EterniX represented a bridge to the future, a hope to resurrect the virtues of humanity lost in the war's devastation. This ensures that even severe injuries do not result in death, as long as the brain remains intact. The user can only be killed by complete destruction of the brain, such as decapitation.

As I stood on the brink of eternity, I couldn't help but ponder the ethical mazes woven by our pursuit of immortality. Was EterniX a key to humanity's salvation or a Pandora's box that could unleash unforeseen consequences upon the remnants of the world?

The promise of EterniX, while a beacon of hope, also cast a long shadow of doubt within me. What would immortality mean in a world scarred by destruction? Would the essence of what makes us humans survive the test of time, or would we lose ourselves in the quest for survival?

The concept of immortality, once a mere fantasy, now tethered me to an endless future. This endless future stretched before me like an uncharted ocean, its vastness both a promise and a challenge, compelling me to confront the depths of my own humanity. How would the human mind contend with the boundless expanse of time? The prospect both exhilarated and terrified me, offering an eternal stage for humanity's greatest virtues and vices.

My name is Ethan Hawthorne, and I was the recipient of a serum injection for reasons unknown to me. The days leading up to this moment had been a whirlwind, blending rigorous training sessions with long periods of reflection and anticipation. In those moments of introspection, I found myself grappling with the weight of what was to come. The gravity of my upcoming role and the sheer uncertainty of the future began to weigh heavily on my psyche.

This dynamic pacing of events mirrored the unpredictable rhythm of life within the bunker. Despite my lack of exceptional qualities, I was chosen as the subject. This choice was not random, as I later learned; it was my adaptability and resilience in the face of uncertainty that marked me as the ideal candidate—a realization that provided a new perspective on my role in this experiment. My lifestyle was fairly routine: residing alone in an apartment, maintaining a balanced diet, and engaging in regular exercise. My daily routine typically began at 7 a.m., commencing with physical activity at the gym, followed by preparation for my job, which commenced at 9 a.m. Despite the comfort of routine, a nagging feeling of insignificance plagued my mornings, leaving me yearning for something more meaningful than the predictable cadence of daily life. En route, I would typically purchase coffee from Starbucks before proceeding to work.

Employed as a computer scientist for a prominent corporation, my responsibilities primarily entailed the creation of small-scale scripts and tools to support the company's primary applications. While my occupation was mundane, it afforded me the luxury of a standard work schedule without the need for extensive overtime, unlike my more esteemed colleagues. Typically, I concluded my workday at 5 p.m. and returned home to indulge in recreational activities.

Years later, I was granted a promotion where I worked longer hours and had more important duties, such as advanced computer programming, hacking, building high-end computers, and taking care of the servers of our company.

During that time, I lived alone, but I frequently had a woman named Jessica over. Our dynamic could be described as a friend-with-benefits arrangement. However, our relationship was not without its challenges. While I was at work, she often made herself at home in my apartment, helping herself with my alcohol supply.

Jessica had a reputation for being what some might call "a heavy drinker," yet she possessed undeniable beauty.

Despite my attachment to her, I questioned whether she reciprocated my feelings. Our interactions were frequently marred by arguments, often stemming from her financial struggles and my perception that she took advantage of my generosity. In hindsight, I recognize that our relationship was toxic, and I would have been better off without her.

Yet, in the quiet moments away from our disputes, a fragile connection endured, hinting at the possibility of something deeper were circumstances ever to change. Reflecting on my relationship with Jessica, I realized it was a mirror to my own uncertainties and fears—a tempestuous mix of desire for connection and the trepidation of vulnerability that perhaps, at a different time, could have blossomed into something genuinely profound. In my solitude, thoughts of Jessica often surfaced, not as tumultuous waves but as a calm sea reflecting what might have been. These reflections on our shared moments—laughter echoing in empty rooms, silent understandings, and unresolved tensions—served as a poignant reminder of the transience of human connections, intensifying the solitude of my journey ahead.

Our flawed yet genuine moments together became a bittersweet memory, emblematic of human connections that thrive, struggle, and sometimes wither in the face of life's trials. The thought of venturing into the future without the faces that had defined my past—friends, colleagues, even Jessica—stirred a melancholy within me. Among these, the memory of my last day with Jessica—her smile as enigmatic as our undefined relationship—lingered the longest. It was these human connections, flawed yet genuine, that I feared losing most in the expanse of eternity.

Social engagements with friends occasionally punctuated my routine, predominantly conducted through virtual communication channels to avoid the perceived intrusion of face-to-face interaction facilitated by advanced augmented reality interfaces.

However, delving further into my personal life, it becomes apparent that I was an unremarkable individual, seemingly chosen for the serum injection arbitrarily. Nonetheless, I now find myself seated amidst a flurry of activity, surrounded by individuals engaged in unintelligible conversations. While a few have offered partial explanations regarding our current circumstances, much remains shrouded in uncertainty.

And the thing was, I was meant to take this serum. There was only a single dose. Their reason for this, as they explained to me, was that the creation of EterniX required a complex and resource-intensive process, drawing upon advanced biotechnology, nanomedicine, and genetic engineering.

However, the resources necessary for synthesizing the serum were extremely limited due to the scarcity of raw materials and the destruction of critical infrastructure during the nuclear war.

Secondly, the decision to create only a single dose of EterniX may have been deliberate, with the serum intended as a last resort for ensuring the survival of humanity in the event of total annihilation.

By limiting the availability of EterniX, the scientists hoped to preserve its potency and efficacy in the most critical circumstances.

But before that was going to happen, I had a lot of work to do myself, as they told me. When I asked who these scientists were and what their purpose was, they explained to me that the Russian scientists hailed from various scientific disciplines and were likely selected based on their expertise in fields such as biotechnology, nanomedicine, and genetics. Many of them were among the world's top engineers as well. They came together under the auspices of the Russian government, or a secretive organization with access to advanced resources and technology.

The Russian scientists served the interests of their government or organization, which may have its own geopolitical motivations and survival strategies in the aftermath of the nuclear war. Their agenda was likely multifaceted: like other nations, Russia would seek to ensure the survival of its population and maintain its strategic influence in a post-apocalyptic world. By developing EterniX, the scientists aimed to secure a means for humanity to endure and potentially rebuild civilization.

The Russians would also seek to maintain technological supremacy and gain an advantage over rival factions or nations in the post-apocalyptic landscape. The development of EterniX demonstrated its commitment to advancing scientific knowledge and harnessing cutting-edge technology. The Russian survivors remaining in the facility, which they now identified to me as the

"Aurora Genesis Complex," were tasked with documenting their research and the events leading up to the nuclear war.

This indicated a desire to preserve scientific knowledge and historical records for future generations, ensuring that humanity does not lose sight of its past. The motivations driving the Russian scientists included a combination of national pride, scientific curiosity, and a duty to humanity. They viewed their work on EterniX as a demonstration of Russian ingenuity and resilience in the face of unprecedented challenges. Additionally, the desire to preserve human knowledge and ensure the survival of the species were powerful motivators for their actions.

While I was present there, my time was consistently occupied. They imparted numerous survival skills to me—methods for deciphering unfamiliar languages, techniques for combat, and the importance of emotional detachment—as if they aimed to mold me into a psychopath. Alongside this training, I had a small surgery where I underwent a non-invasive procedure to implant a neural interface directly into my brain. This interface consists of tiny electrodes or nanoscale devices capable of interfacing with my neural circuitry and accessing various regions of the brain associated with memory formation and retrieval. Using the neural interface, they uploaded a vast database containing comprehensive records of Earth's history, including texts, images, audiovisual recordings, and scientific data that included all of the scientists' research. This database would be continually updated and curated by AI algorithms to ensure accuracy and relevance. This means I knew the entire history up until now and could regurgitate information when asked about anything.

Throughout my tenure there, I underwent rigorous training in diverse martial arts disciplines under the guidance of multiple instructors within the facility. I mastered techniques from Krav Maga, Brazilian Jiu-Jitsu, Muay Thai, and Jeet Kune Do. This training wasn't just about physical prowess; it was a mental and spiritual preparation, a way to steel myself against the daunting challenges of a world unknown. As my proficiency grew in each, it became evident that they were grooming me for a role akin to that of a super soldier. Each discipline not only honed my physical abilities but also instilled a discipline of mind and spirit, preparing me for the uncertain future that lay ahead.

One training session, in particular, tested my limits like no other. Tasked with navigating a simulated urban wasteland under the cover of darkness, I learned not just to rely on my newly honed skills but to trust my instincts. The challenge culminated in a moment of revelation under the starlit sky—survival was as much about wit and will as it was about physical strength.

The regimen was grueling, not just physically but mentally.

Each session pushed me to my limits, forging not just a warrior's physique but a survivor's resolve. I learned not just how to fight but also how to persevere, adapt, and overcome—essential skills for the uncertain world that awaited me.

In the midst of my daily routine at the facility, the scientists continued to unravel the mysteries surrounding our situation, though much of it remained shrouded in vagueness until the day I crossed paths with Yuri. Among the researchers, one individual stood out as particularly approachable. He sat in a corner, lost in thought. I approached him, curious.

"What's your name?" I inquired.

"My name is Yuri Fedorov," he replied with a smile. "And you are Ethan Hawthorne."

"It seems like my reputation precedes me," I remarked.

"Indeed, you're quite well-known around here," Yuri acknowledged.

"I hadn't noticed; most people don't engage with me," I confessed.

"Well, you're the focal point of this operation; the others are simply absorbed in their tasks," Yuri explained.

"Almost as if they're not humans," I commented. "So, since you're one of the few who actually talk to me, do you care to shed some light on what's really happening here and why I'm at the center of it all?"

"Ah, you're aware of the EterniX injection you're about to receive?" Yuri inquired.

"They didn't spell it out, but after all the training and surgeries, I figured something significant was brewing. Besides, as an outsider here, what else could I be doing?" I mused.

"You're correct, but there's more to the story," Yuri revealed. "Such as?" I probed.

"After the injection, you'll enter a cryo chamber and be in suspended animation for one thousand years," Yuri disclosed solemnly.

The thought of waking in a millennium to a civilization unrecognizable stirred within me a mix of dread and wonder. How much of the world I knew would remain, and what kind of man would I become in its midst?

"Are you serious? I could understand a few years in cryosleep for certain reasons, but a millennium? Why?" I questioned, incredulous.

"There are several reasons. Firstly, it's hoped that society will have sufficiently rebuilt by then, enough for you to reconnect and collaborate with them. Secondly, the radiation will have dissipated to safe levels, making it viable to emerge. Lastly, you could serve as a mentor and guide humanity back to its former glory. The notion of guiding humanity back to its former glory was laden with unknowns. Would the values and ideals of the past still hold weight in a new world, or would I need to forge a new path entirely? Yet, amid Yuri's explanations, I couldn't shake the feeling that unforeseen challenges awaited and that the world of tomorrow might harbor conflicts as yet undreamed of. The best part is that you'll witness it all firsthand. Of course, there's more to it if you choose to pursue it," Yuri elaborated.

"It's quite a long shot, but I see the rationale behind it," I conceded. "But what do you mean by 'if I choose to'?"

"I'm afraid I can't divulge that yet; you'll find out in due time," Yuri replied cryptically.

"Fair enough. And what about the intensive training?" I inquired.

"It's all about preparing you for the challenges ahead. It may seem extreme, but it's to ensure your survival in a potentially hazardous future. And it'll certainly make you formidable. You could become a leader, a beacon of hope for others. I trust your intentions are noble. Ultimately, you're the culmination of years of effort by the Aurora Genesis Complex—a weapon and protector of the Russian government in the post-apocalyptic world. You're too valuable to lose, and your mission is inherently altruistic," Yuri clarified.

"Your explanation sheds some light on the matter. While I'm still not entirely onboard, at least I understand the reasoning behind it, and that gives me purpose," I conceded.

"Having purpose is crucial; without it, existence lacks meaning. And your purpose is monumental," Yuri affirmed.

"I'm still grappling with the specifics of my purpose; it all seems rather vague—save humanity, reunite them, save them, be the hero. I'm not even sure where to begin," I confessed.

"There's more to it than meets the eye. I've heard rumors of a final mission that will shape the future significantly. However, that's all speculation. Only a select few possess the full picture, and unfortunately, I'm not among them," Yuri revealed.

"How am I supposed to navigate all of this?" I sighed. "I shouldn't be telling you this, but a ChronoArchive will provide you with guidance upon awakening from cryosleep. It will outline your duties and offer assistance. But keep this information strictly confidential," Yuri cautioned.

Just to be clear, if you don't know what a ChronoArchive is because you haven't encountered one before, a ChronoArchive can be defined as a sophisticated data storage system designed to preserve and organize vast amounts of information across extended periods of time. Utilizing advanced holographic tape technology, ChronoArchives stores data in a highly durable and compact format, ensuring the long-term preservation of knowledge and historical records. They are intended to last forever. They can be used to wirelessly transfer data from a neural interface to the ChronoArchive, or the other way around. The ChronoArchive, as Yuri detailed, was not just a repository of knowledge but a guidepost for my journey. Its interface, a blend of holographic displays and intuitive controls, offered access to detailed maps, historical data, and survival strategies tailored to the post-apocalyptic landscape. It was to be my compass in a world where traditional navigation points had vanished.

"How did you come by this knowledge?" I inquired. "I happened to overhear a conversation between high-ranking officers. I barely escaped being caught eavesdropping," Yuri confessed.

"I appreciate your candor, Yuri. This newfound clarity will undoubtedly help me make sense of things. And don't worry, I won't breathe a word about what I've learned. I'd probably land myself in hot water," I assured him.

"I must return to my duties now. Until next time, Ethan," Yuri bid farewell.

"Looking forward to it!" I replied with a smile. Yuri waved before exiting the room.

It's important to note that I didn't willingly undergo any of these experiences; rather, I felt coerced into compliance. Threats of violence hung over me, with one individual explicitly stating they'd eliminate me if I didn't comply, readily replacing me with another subject. While I wasn't devoid of a willingness to sacrifice myself to escape, I reasoned that someone else might be subjected to the same fate, leading me to accept my role.

The war had irrevocably changed the face of technology, with survivors cobbling together advancements from the remnants of the old world to address the stark needs of the new.

Before administering the EterniX serum, they outfitted me with an array of tools deemed potentially useful for future endeavors. Their preparation mirrored that of preparing a lone soldier for battle against overwhelming odds. Given the spacious cryo chamber, they packed various tools within a military-grade bag, each requiring explanation due to the unique technological advancements of this era.

Two laser guns: these weapons utilize advanced photonics to generate coherent beams of light capable of cutting through most materials. They are powered by rechargeable energy cells and have a virtually infinite ammunition supply. One of the laser guns was like a handheld pistol with two modes that could be toggled through a switch, one was which was called Nova Strike Nova Strike Shooting one shot at a time, but with a severe and wide area of effect, the other mode called Vortex Burst would evoke a rapid succession of energy blasts swirling from the weapon with reduced impact. I was told the Vortex Burst would almost always be superior unless there were severely large opponents or obstacles to do as much damage as possible in an area of effect, or, of course, if I needed a large area of effect to eliminate multiple enemies at once. This weapon was called a Voltcaster.

Then there was the other weapon, which was a rifle using autofire—less damage than the handheld one, compensated by the incredible speed, and still capable of taking out a target in a single shot. This one was called Fusionizer. Both of these would provide me with great protection in dire circumstances.

A Portable Atmospheric Cleaner is a handheld device equipped with advanced filtration systems and atmospheric scrubbers that can be activated with the press of a button to purify the air and remove contaminants such as pollutants, toxins, and radioactive particles. These portable cleaners provide survivors with clean, breathable air in hazardous environments or contaminated areas.

A Personal Energy Shield is a compact energy shield device worn or carried by users that can be activated with the press of a button. These shields generate a temporary protective energy barrier around the user, deflecting projectiles, absorbing energy-based attacks, and providing temporary protection against physical and energy threats.

Nanomaterial Repair Sprayers are handheld devices loaded with programmable nanomaterials and self-assembling nanoparticles that can be sprayed onto damaged structures or equipment to initiate rapid repairs. With the press of a button, survivors can deploy these repair sprayers to patch leaks, reinforce structures, and restore functionality to essential infrastructure.

An OmniLocator tablet: the OmniLocator is a handheld device designed to find specific objects or custom-programmed items. It utilizes advanced technology to pinpoint the location of desired items, making it a valuable tool for navigation and retrieval in various situations. It could also send out signals and communicate with compatible computers or similar systems.

And finally, a KeyCode Breaker: a cutting-edge lockpicking device designed to bypass a wide array of locks, from standard key locks to keypad-secured entries. This advanced tool boasts the capability to analyze and decode regular locks swiftly, automatically selecting the optimal tool for seamless lockpicking. Additionally, when connected to a keypad, it can be configured to execute brute-force attacks, swiftly deciphering passwords or keycodes with unparalleled efficiency.

Then there was a limited amount of food and water. Thanks to EterniX, I would require less food and water, but I still had a cryo chamber and needed food and water to survive. However, the supplies provided were meant to sustain me until I could establish sustainable sources of food and water in the post-apocalyptic world. These supplies included nutrient-rich protein bars, energy drinks, water purification tablets, and compact emergency rations.

They explained to me that I had to be cautious with my resources and ration them carefully to ensure my long-term survival. They also advised me to scavenge for additional supplies and resources in the environment, such as edible plants, fresh water sources, and abandoned shelters or storage facilities.

Finally, they gave me a first-aid kit in case of minor emergencies. I was supposed to use the injectors only when absolutely necessary. Once again, the kit was not intended for me. My healing abilities would go far beyond what a first-aid kit could do.

One day, when the nuclear war was raging on, EterniX was finally finished, and my training and surgeries were complete. They explained to me that I had to take the serum immediately. A doctor called Dmitri Petrov introduced himself to me. He would lead me through this process, approaching me with a filled needle, his expression a mix of seriousness and reassurance.

In a rare moment of camaraderie, Dr. Petrov shared with me his personal hope that EterniX would symbolize a new dawn for humanity. His reflections offered a rare glimpse into the personal stakes involved in our project. It wasn't just about the survival of an individual, but about carrying forward the spark of hope and humanity. 'We are not just preserving a life,' he said, looking beyond the sterile confines of the lab; 'we are safeguarding the promise of a future where such calamities are mere echoes of a lesson learned.' His words, tinged with both hope and sorrow, offered a glimpse into the burden borne by those who had chosen to play god.

"Well," Dmitri began, "this is it. I am here to inject EterniX and place you in the cryo chamber over there. Before that, though, there is some advice I am supposed to give you."

"Like what?" I asked, my heart beginning to race with anticipation and anxiety.

"When you awaken, we will be gone. Well, we'll still be here, but you won't be able to find us. We won't be alive, of course. But you will be left with a ChronoArchive, which will explain what will have transpired and how to get out of here. We expect the Aurora Genesis Complex to survive over 1000 years, as it cannot be accessed from above ground because of its remote location, being underground, and being less likely to be detected by satellite imagery or aerial surveys.

The entrance will be camouflaged to blend in with the surrounding landscape. It has only a single access point. Further on, no one knows the specific location of the facility, not even our authorities, as was instructed. After you listen to the ChronoArchive that will be left for you, which will clear up everything, you will have to head to what remains of the United

States and assess the situation. By then, you will know what to do. Note that there will be no one to communicate with except for possible locals who might not speak our language, even though English is now a global language. This might evolve, so keep that in mind.

The universality of English had not just simplified global communication before the war; it had woven a tapestry of shared knowledge and understanding. Yet, as Dmitri hinted, the tapestry might unravel in new and unexpected ways, challenging me to adapt once again.

Either way, we are confident that you will do whatever is within your power to succeed."

As Dmitri outlined my journey, the concept of being a beacon of hope in a shattered world felt both grandiose and humbling. The idea that I, Ethan Hawthorne, could play a pivotal role in humanity's rebirth was a mantle I was beginning to accept, albeit with trepidation.

As Dmitri spoke, I started to feel dutiful and determined. I nodded, absorbing his words as if they were a lifeline in the vast unknown ahead.

"So how do I get there? We are in Antarctica after all." I said.

Dmitri looked at me with a questioning look and said, "That too will be explained in the ChronoArchive; for now, not everything is entirely clear even to us, but it will be by the time you wake up."

"Well, that's reassuring, and if it doesn't work, I can always swim my way there, right? Because of my upgrades," I said, trying to inject a bit of levity into the heavy moment.

Dmitri regarded me with a half-smile, his eyes conveying a mixture of amusement and gravity. "Even though you can hold your breath longer than the average person and have increased stamina, you're not incapable of drowning. But I'm assuming you're not serious."

"Right!" I chuckled nervously, feeling the weight of the impending injection pressing down on me.

Dmitri motioned for me to sit down. "Sit down. I'm going to inject you with the serum. Once the serum is injected, you will pass out within a few seconds; this is normal. Then you will wake up in one thousand years. I cannot make any promises, but since there have been no major calamities detected within the next two thousand years, things should be fine. So are you ready?"

"As ready as I'll ever be," I replied, taking a deep breath to steel myself for the unknown journey ahead. In the seconds before the serum took effect, a flood of memories and possibilities raced through my mind. The faces of those I'd known, the world as it once was, and the uncharted future I was stepping into melded into a single, overwhelming moment of transition.

As I drifted into the unknown, questions haunted me. What remnants of our culture, our achievements, and our failures would I find upon awakening? In this new world, would the echoes of our past sins and triumphs still resonate, or would they be lost to time, compelling us to start anew?

At this moment, the weight of my decision pressed heavily upon my soul, not just for the uncertainty of my own future but for the fate of a world I would awaken to—a world I was destined to help rebuild or witness its final downfall.

Carrying the weight of humanity's future, I stood at the precipice of the unknown, a solitary figure tasked with an immense responsibility. The path ahead was shrouded in mystery, and yet within me stirred a resolve to face whatever challenges lay beyond the horizon of time.

Yet, as I stood there, about to cross the threshold into the unknown, a newfound determination took root within me. Despite the uncertainties, I was ready to forge ahead, to play my part in the rebirth of our world.

Jacob approached me with the needle and, with a steady hand, administered the injection. As the serum flowed into my veins, a wave of dizziness washed over me, and the world seemed to spin and blur around me. A cold sense of finality washed over me as the serum's chill spread through my veins, marking the end of my old life and the beginning of an uncertain future. My vision darkened as I slowly lost consciousness.

INTO THE DARKNESS

Darkness enveloped me as I stirred from my slumber, disoriented and chilled to the bone. This awakening was more than a return to consciousness; it felt like a rebirth into a world that had moved on without me, leaving me a stranger in the ruins of the familiar. As the darkness enveloped me, a chill that seeped into my very marrow awakened a primal fear, reminding me of the uncertain world awaiting beyond the cryo chamber's confines. My hands fumbled in the abyss, searching for purchase, but I found only the icy confines of the cryo chamber. Panic clawed at my chest as I grappled with the realization of my entrapment.

A hiss shattered the silence, followed by the grinding of metal as the chamber's door creaked open, admitting a sliver of dim light. Blinking against the sudden brightness, I squinted at my surroundings, taking in the dilapidated chamber and its overgrown walls with a sense of disbelief.

Before me stood a table holding two objects I recognized even in my groggy state: a flashlight, my beacon in the enveloping darkness, and a ChronoArchive, my link to the past and guide for the future. I felt like I had only been asleep for a few hours. I looked around; the walls were cracked, and there were vines and moss growing on them. There was dust everywhere, and it definitely seemed like a long time had passed. As I gazed upon the overgrown ruins of what once was, a wave of surrealism washed over me, blending awe with a deep-seated melancholy for the world lost. I observed an unfamiliar necklace adorning my neck—a piece of jewelry that had not been there previously. I walked towards the ChronoArchive and turned it to play the last message. With a mix of reverence and trepidation, I activated the ChronoArchive, bracing myself for the voice from the past to bridge the chasm of time.

"Hello Ethan, My name is Dr. William Sader. By the time you hear this, you must've woken up from your long sleep. First of all, there are a few things you have to know. After our mission was complete, so was our life's purpose. We were faced with a harrowing decision: to either accept a lifetime of seclusion in the underground facility or take a fast-acting drug called Obliviron that was given to us when we started working in this facility. This drug would bring about a painless and instantaneous state of unconsciousness, leading to death. The choice was not an easy one, but it was presented to us as a final act of sacrifice to prevent the potential misuse or exploitation of our ground breaking research.

In the midst of escalating tensions and the looming threat of a nuclear apocalypse, the Russian government, aware of the ethical dilemmas posed by the immortality serum, enacted a strict protocol to safeguard humanity's future. They recognized the immense power and responsibility associated with controlling access to such advanced biotechnology, fearing the consequences of unchecked proliferation and misuse.

Though the world outside teetered on the brink of destruction, the obligation to protect the serum from falling into the wrong hands remained paramount. By sacrificing ourselves, we upheld our duty to humanity and ensured that the immortality serum would not be weaponized or exploited for personal gain.

In the end, our decision to take Obliviron was a solemn acknowledgment of the greater good, a final act of selflessness in a world on the verge of collapse.

I am the last one alive, and all the others have been buried in special chambers assigned to them.

The year should now be about 4252. Unfortunately, I cannot tell you the state of things outside other than assuming that Antarctica is still the same as it was before. Due to the heavy weather restrictions, it is doubtful anyone has been here. Especially after the fall of society.

Your ticket out of this place is in a hangar concealed behind layers of reinforced steel. In there, you'll find a state-of-the-art aircraft primed for departure.

The path to salvation lies through a labyrinth of decay, with each step guided by the pulsing heart of the complex, urging me toward the concealed hangar and the promise of freedom beyond.

Make your way to the heart of the complex, where the air takes on a faint metallic tang, signaling proximity to the hangar. At the intersection marked by a dimly flickering overhead light, turn sharply to your left. You'll encounter a corridor flanked by rusted piping, leading you deeper into the belly of the facility.

Press forward until you reach a junction where the corridor splits into three divergent paths. Ignore the temptation to veer left or right; instead, proceed straight ahead. The air grows cooler, and the faint hum of machinery echos in the distance—a telltale sign of nearing your destination.

As you press onward, the corridor widens, revealing a massive steel door adorned with intricate engravings—a sentinel guarding the hangar's entrance.

Approach the door and input the access code that has been set to your birthday.

The door should open, granting passage into the cavernous expanse of the hangar. There, you will find the aircraft. This plane is capable of vertical takeoff and landing, harnessing the power of vectored thrust, a concept rooted in the manipulation of airflow. The aircraft, more than a mere vehicle, was my lifeline, equipped with survival kits, communication tools, and scanning devices designed to navigate the uncertainties of the new world. As I laid my hands on its cold, metallic surface, the aircraft felt like the last testament of human ingenuity, a bridge between the world that was and the world that awaited—a silent promise of the journey ahead. At that moment, surrounded by silence, the aircraft wasn't just a machine but a relic of human endeavor, binding me to a world that once thrived on hope and innovation.

Know that its destination is already set. The city of Seattle, Washington, awaits, its coordinates programmed into the aircraft's navigation system. Seattle stood not just as a geographic destination but as a beacon of hope, where the seeds of a new beginning could find fertile ground amidst the ruins of the old world. Chosen for its symbolic resilience and the whispers of a community that might have weathered the apocalypse, Seattle beckoned as a beacon of civilization's persistence against all odds To me, Seattle represented the tangible goal of my odyssey, a point on the map where past and future could intersect, offering the chance to rebuild not just a city but the very idea of community and human connection.

Your journey to Seattle, to the heart of Washington, is drawn from more than mere speculation about its survivability amidst the cataclysm. It was guided by fragmented but compelling whispers of a deeper significance, a purpose etched into the very fabric of its location, hinted at in the remnants of the old world's data archives.

Seattle, as the closest major city that might have evaded the full brunt of the devastation, holds more than the promise of intact structures or the ghostly echo of its once bustling streets. It is believed to be a nexus, a key to unlocking the vast, hidden repositories of knowledge and technology that pre-dated the fall. This city, with its strategic blend of natural beauty and pre-apocalyptic might, is rumored to be the gateway to rediscovering the lost advancements of humanity and perhaps the secrets to its resurgence.

The city's infrastructure—its ports, once teeming with global commerce; its airports, gateways to the skies; and its extensive network of highways—speak of a potential that goes beyond mere survival. These are the arteries through which the lifeblood of a new civilization can flow, offering you the chance to piece together the logistics of rebirth and weave the threads of commerce and connection anew.

Moreover, Seattle's geographical positioning, cradled by coastlines and watched over by the sentinels of mountain ranges, is no accident of urban planning. It is a strategic choice, offering a panoramic view of the challenges and promises of the post-apocalyptic landscape. From this vantage point, you can hope to survey the lay of the land, gauge the movements of friend and foe alike, and scout the pathways to hidden vaults of wisdom and power.

In choosing Seattle, you are not merely seeking refuge or rummaging through the ruins for supplies. You are answering the call of destiny, embarking on a quest laid down by those who have foreseen the fall and prepared for the rise. Seattle is more than a city; it is a beacon, illuminating the path to humanity's salvation and its bold stride into a future reimagined. Hearing Dr. Sader's words, I realized my journey was not just about survival but about carrying the torch of humanity's legacy, a beacon of light in the darkness that awaited beyond these walls.

Once the plane departs, the steel opening through which it exited will seal permanently. The onboard system will then scan the vicinity for a secure landing spot, guiding the aircraft to touch down safely. Upon disembarking, you'll have the capability to track and relocate the plane using the OmniLocator device.

The airplane will be equipped with an Alloyed Charger, a revolutionary motorcycle engineered by our team of experts. Unlike any other, this motorcycle utilizes cutting-edge technology to ensure swift travel. Instead of traditional fuel, it harnesses advanced energy sources derived from innovative materials and systems.

The bike's power source is based on highly efficient energy conversion methods, eliminating the need for constant refueling or recharging. Its frame and components are crafted from state-of-the-art nanomaterials, offering unparalleled durability and resilience against wear and tear.

Equipped with advanced sensors and intelligent algorithms, the bike can seamlessly navigate challenging terrain. Its adaptive suspension systems automatically adjust to the environment, providing optimal stability and control. Losing this invaluable asset is not an option. Its location can also be pinpointed using the OmniLocator.

Upon disembarking, your primary objective is to establish contact with any nearby inhabitants. Keep in mind that language evolution may present communication challenges, but your aptitude for rapid skill acquisition, including language acquisition, remains unparalleled. We trust in your ability to swiftly adapt and establish meaningful communication with the locals.

However, it's possible that no individuals inhabit the immediate area. In such cases, your mission is to journey as far as necessary until you encounter some semblance of civilization. The Alloyed Charger will significantly aid in traversing vast distances efficiently.

Additionally, you can utilize the airplane for reconnaissance missions to locate survivors, although ground searches are imperative for thorough exploration. You have the capability to program the airplane to navigate to specific coordinates.

Lastly, adhere to these final and paramount objectives of your mission without exception, prioritizing them above all else.

Your immediate goal is to ensure your own survival in the post-apocalyptic world.

Then, we have the preservation of knowledge: As one of the few individuals with knowledge of the pre-apocalyptic world and advanced technology, you must seek to preserve and safeguard valuable information for the benefit of future generations. This could involve documenting your experiences, sharing scientific knowledge, and contributing to efforts to rebuild society. This information can be uploaded from your neural interface to a ChronoArchive, sharing your knowledge with anyone and uploading it to any computer. Whatever you do, it is important that this knowledge survives the post-apocalypse.

Next, it is important to connect with people. Over the course of your journey, you must seek to establish connections with the descendants of any survivors of the nuclear war, foster relationships, build alliances, and contribute to the rebuilding of communities. By bridging the gap between the past and present, you can offer guidance, leadership, and hope for the future.

Now there are things you must know more about the necklace you are wearing, as it is essential to your final objective. This necklace is called a BioLock Pendant. This pendant has various important features.

First of all, it features an electrical discharge mechanism.

The BioLock Pendant contains a small, discreet mechanism embedded within the pendant and chain. This mechanism is designed to detect the presence of unauthorized users and deliver a non-lethal electric shock upon contact.

It also has a form of unauthorized access detection, which means that if an unauthorized person attempts to touch the necklace, sensors within the device detect the foreign bioelectrical signature and trigger a response. This activates an electrical discharge circuit that delivers a controlled shock to the intruder's hand or fingers.

The electrical shock delivered by the pendant is calibrated to be non-lethal yet incapacitating. It delivers a high-voltage, low-current pulse designed to temporarily disrupt nerve signals and muscle function, causing the intruder to experience intense pain, muscle spasms, and loss of consciousness.

To prevent accidental activation or misuse, the pendant may incorporate safety features such as a manual override switch, proximity sensors, and fail-safe mechanisms. These ensure that the device only activates in response to unauthorized contact and poses minimal risk to the authorized wearer.

Your primary objective is to locate and activate a hidden network of advanced supercomputers known as the 'Ascendant Matrix.' These supercomputers were developed with the intention of safeguarding crucial data and resources vital for humanity's future resilience. Their activation holds significant importance in shaping the course of events in the post-apocalyptic world, though the true extent of their capabilities remains veiled in intrigue. The intended purpose of the Ascendant Matrix will only be fully revealed upon activation, but for now, it must remain shrouded in secrecy.

However, the Ascendant Matrix was designed to remain dormant until the time was right; it can only be activated by the pendant of the necklace you were given, which has a unique signature. It is built with biometric recognition: the necklace is programmed to recognize the unique bioelectrical signature of its assigned wearer, encoded with the symbol that serves as the key to activating the Ascendant Matrix.

When the authorized wearer touches the necklace, the device remains inert, allowing safe interaction. The Ascendant Matrix has the capability to initiate a global restoration process, utilizing advanced nanotechnology, genetic engineering, and artificial intelligence to rebuild the world and restore ecosystems while also enhancing human physiology and longevity. The necklace can also be located using the OmniLocator should you happen to lose it, though this should never happen.

To continue your mission, you must reach the central command facility where the Ascendant Matrix is housed. The location itself is not known but can be found in a facility called the Nexus Vault, where the location is on a central computer, from which you can upload it to the OmniLocator and then go after the Ascendant Matrix. To find this Nexus Vault, the creators of the Ascendant Matrix have left a number of clues that are located as specified on your OmniLocator. The results of the various clues will provide you with the coordinates of the Ascendant Matrix.

Upon reaching the central command facility, you will encounter a series of complex security protocols and defenses designed to protect the Ascendant Matrix from unauthorized access. Using your enhanced abilities, intellect, and the knowledge you've acquired throughout your journey, you must successfully bypass these obstacles and reach the heart of the facility.

There, you take off the BioLock Pendant, Open a secure access panel, place the pendant in the matching indention, and press the red button next to it to trigger the awakening of the Ascendant Matrix. While challenges remain, the activation of the supercomputers will mark a turning point in the journey toward recovery and renewal, offering hope and opportunity for a brighter tomorrow.

After completing all your missions, your final task is to return to the Aurora Genesis Complex. The entrance, specified by coordinates in your Omni-Locator, is cleverly disguised to blend seamlessly with the surrounding environment. It's covered with snow, ice, and rocks, mimicking the texture and color of the terrain. This natural camouflage makes it virtually indistinguishable from its surroundings, even upon close inspection.

Using the OmniLocator, you'll send a signal to open the entrance hatch. A latch will open, leading downward into a small elevator. Inside, you'll find a single button. Press it, and the elevator will descend until you reach the facility. The OmniLocator will activate all areas and specifics of the facility.

In the central control room, rows of computer terminals line the walls, displaying intricate diagrams and status reports on various systems within the facility. At the main console, a series of labeled buttons and controls await, each corresponding to a different function of the complex. Among them is the 'Self-Destruct' function, marked with a red warning label.

Accessing the self-destruct function requires bypassing several layers of security measures and entering a complex password, a string of known characters found on your OmniLocator. Once inside, you'll be prompted to set a timer in minutes and seconds for the self-destruct sequence. You must input the desired countdown duration.

Once the timer is set, make your way to the elevator, step inside, and press the button to ascend and return to the surface. It's advisable to distance yourself from the area, as the explosion will likely affect the surface area as well. The purpose of destroying the complex is to prevent the technology and knowledge within from falling into the wrong hands. After this, you are now free to pursue your own desires.

That's all you need to know. Once you feel strong enough and the side effects of cryosleep have worn off, you can head to the plane and get your journey started. Farewell. These are my final words before I follow my colleagues into oblivion. Godspeed."

The device made a few beeping sounds and then shut off.

His message conveyed a harrowing truth: the world outside had succumbed to chaos and decay, while I lay dormant in the bowels of the Aurora Genesis Complex. The weight of his words settled upon me—a heavy burden of responsibility and purpose.

I examined the necklace draped around my neck.

The emblem had an overall hexagonal shape. At the center of the hexagon was a stylized eye. The eye could be rendered in a way that looked almost digital, with circuit-like patterns forming the iris, which could also resemble a fingerprint. Encircling the eye were two symmetrical wings that gracefully extended outward. The wings had an angular, mechanical look, giving the impression that they were part of a sophisticated machine or device. Around the outer edge of the hexagon, there was a fine etching of binary code. The emblem was etched onto a smooth, metallic surface that changed color with the light.

I took the flashlight, and with renewed determination, I followed Dr. Sader's instructions, navigating the labyrinthine corridors of the underground facility. Vines snaked through cracks in the walls, reclaiming the sterile environment with nature's relentless embrace.

A surge of vitality surged through my veins, infusing me with a newfound vigor that seemed to emanate from the very core of my being. With each step forward, the shadows of my past seemed to loom larger, not as specters to haunt me but as reminders of what I've lost and what I must strive to rebuild. This journey wasn't just about survival; it was a pilgrimage through the remnants of my own humanity, a quest to find meaning in a world that had discarded it. This physical reawakening mirrored an inner resurgence, a rekindling of hope and purpose amidst the ruins of my former world. Each step felt lighter—not just a stride across the complex, but a march towards a destiny yet unwritten. It was as if I had tapped into an ancient wellspring of energy, rejuvenating me in a way I had not felt in years. With each breath, I felt a sense of invigoration that surpassed any previous experience, as if I had shed the weight of time and emerged anew.

It wasn't a pleasant journey to undertake to reach the plane.

As I ventured deeper into the bowels of the Aurora Genesis Complex, the passage of a millennium had left its unmistakable mark on the once pristine corridors and chambers. With each step, the echo of my footfalls reverberated through the desolate halls, a haunting reminder of the silence that had long since claimed this forsaken place.

My flashlight pierced the darkness like a solitary beacon, casting flickering shadows that danced across the decaying walls. Cracks spiderwebbed across the concrete surfaces, evidence of the relentless march of time and the unyielding grip of nature reclaiming its domain. Vines snaked their way through crevices, their tendrils reaching out like gnarled fingers grasping for purchase in the dimly lit corridors.

Moss and lichen clung to the walls like a shroud, painting the once-sterile environment in hues of sickly green and muted brown. The air was thick with the musty scent of decay, mingling with the metallic tang of rust and corrosion that permeated the stale atmosphere.

Occasional gusts of wind whispered through the corridors, carrying with them the distant echoes of a bygone era. The silence that enveloped the world outside was punctuated only by the distant howl of the wind, a reminder that danger lurked in the unseen corners of this new wilderness. Each moment of reflection was a stolen respite in a journey fraught with unseen threats. It was as if the very walls themselves held the memories of the past, whispering secrets lost to the ravages of time.

Despite the desolation that surrounded me, there was an eerie beauty in the decay. Nature had woven its intricate tapestry amidst the ruins, transforming the sterile corridors into a labyrinth of tangled vegetation and crumbling infrastructure.

With each passing moment, I felt the weight of history bearing down upon me, a tangible presence that hung heavy in the air. Yet, amid the ruins and decay, there was a glimmer of hope amidst the darkness that enveloped the Aurora Genesis Complex.

When I finally reached the plane, after opening the door, three layers of steel opened up and revealed the cold Antarctic sky. I entered the plane and pressed the obviously large green launch button, and the plane went up. Immediately as I exited the facility, the steel roofs shut down again and were already starting to be covered up by snow.

I looked down while approaching Seattle, and there was still definitive evidence of destruction. It did seem that a lot was hidden by sand and plant growth, but here and there you could still see the ruins of what was formerly Washington. And I had no idea what to expect.

As the warning blared, a surge of adrenaline cut through my haze of disbelief, sharpening my resolve to face whatever lay ahead.

Suddenly, the engine started sputtering. A red light on the dashboard turned on, and the plane started talking, "Warning, engine failure. Prepare for an emergency water landing."

I was panicking and looked outside, seeing the plane quickly heading towards nearby water and lowering itself at the same time. Then, above the water, instead of wheels, two large seaplane floats came down from under the wings. The plane dropped rapidly

until it was a few meters above the water when it suddenly slowed down and quietly landed in the water. The plane talked again: "Emergency water landing successful, releasing outboard engine to navigate the water. Current location: Pacific Ocean near Seattle."

I knew from where I was that I had to go eastward. To my surprise, a handle had risen from the top of the tail of the plane and an engine beneath it, so I could drive the plane like a motorboat. So I headed eastward and eventually reached the coast of Seattle.

Stepping out to retrieve the Alloyed Charger, I knew it was more than a vehicle; it was my steed in the quest through this uncharted wilderness, a tangible link to the ingenuity of a world lost to time. I stepped out of the plane and opened the side door to pick up the Alloyed Charger. As I gripped the handles of the Alloyed Charger, I braced myself not only for the wilderness that lay ahead but for the remnants of humanity I would encounter, wondering if they would be friend or foe in this new era. As I prepare to meet those who now inhabit this new world, I wonder whether they will see me as a relic of the past or a herald of a new beginning. My story, like theirs, is one of loss and survival, but shared challenges might yet pave the way for unforeseen alliances.

The Alloyed Charger, my steadfast companion on this journey, was a marvel of engineering, a fusion of advanced materials and cutting-edge technology designed for the world as it stood. Its frame, constructed from a lightweight yet incredibly durable alloy, gleamed under the dim light of the Nexus Vault, and its surface was a tapestry of metallic hues that shifted subtly with the angle of view.

This was no ordinary motorbike; it was a display of human ingenuity, built to navigate the ruins of the old world with ease and grace. Its tires, made from a composite material, were designed to adapt to various terrains, from the cracked asphalt of deserted highways to the overgrown paths that now marked much of the landscape.

The Charger's engine, a silent, electric heart, powered it forward with a smooth acceleration that belied its potent force. The technology that lay dormant around me, the crumbling edifices of a once-thriving civilization, and the overgrown paths that now marked much of the landscape were not mere backdrops to my journey but silent witnesses to the rise and fall of human ambition and folly. It required no fuel in the traditional sense; instead, it was powered by a compact, high-efficiency battery system that never ran out. This feature made it an invaluable asset in a world where conventional fuel sources were a relic of the past.

The controls were intuitive, a blend of tactile buttons and touch-sensitive panels that responded to the lightest touch, offering precision and responsiveness that made navigating through the wastelands a less daunting task. The dashboard, a holographic display projected in front of the rider, provided real-time data on the bike's performance, navigation, and environmental conditions, all without detracting from the view of the road ahead.

But perhaps its most striking feature was its stealth technology. At the flick of a switch, the bike could reduce its acoustic signature to near silence, while a cloaking feature blended it into the surroundings, making it nearly invisible to the unaided eye. This capability was not just for evasion; it was a necessity in a world where threats could come from any direction at any time.

Leaving the plane behind for now, I started my journey into what had now become a jungle where paths were still clear thanks to the ruins of buildings separating different openings through which I could drive. Mounting the Alloyed Charger, I felt the weight of the journey ahead but also an unyielding resolve; this was more than a departure—it was an embarkation on a mission that transcended my own survival. The ignition of the Charger's engine was akin to a heartbeat—a rhythm of life awakening in the midst of desolation, propelling me forward into the unknown. With each mile traversed, I pondered what marks I would leave on this world, aspiring not just to survive but to contribute to a tapestry of human resilience and innovation, weaving my thread into the story of our rebirth. Amidst the desolation, I found within me a flicker of hope, a defiant spark against the encroaching darkness, driven by a resolve to find others who shared this flicker and transform it into a flame that could light the way forward. As I ventured into the remnants of civilization, the road ahead was fraught with unknowns, but within me burned a determination to forge a path through the darkness, to rediscover the light of the human spirit amidst the ruins. As the remnants of the old world loomed around me, I understood that my journey was a testament to the enduring spirit of humanity, ready to face the shadows of the past and forge a path toward a new dawn. The light that once guided humanity has dimmed, but in its flicker, I see the potential for a new dawn. The ruins around me, while symbols of our fall, also offer the foundations upon which we can build anew. In this world of contrasts, I find the strength to carry on, fueled by the hope of what might yet be.

The road ahead was not just a path through ruins but a journey towards legacy, a quest not only for survival but for a renewal of spirit and hope in the ashes of the past.

ECHOES OF DESOLATION

After several hours of travel, I came across a substantial military structure, piquing my curiosity. Memories of my training briefly surfaced, a reminder of the world's reliance on such fortresses in the face of chaos. This structure, however, stood as a silent witness to a downfall it couldn't prevent. The prospect of exploring it held the promise of uncovering valuable information or useful resources. Driven by a mix of curiosity and a desperate need to understand the fate of the world I once knew, I hoped to find clues within these walls. Perhaps in the echoes of this structure's past, I could piece together my own place in this new world order.

Navigating the overgrown pathways surrounding the forsaken edifice, I found myself amidst the remnants of a once-thriving civilization, now obscured by centuries of neglect and nature's relentless reclamation. The silence was a stark reminder of civilization's fragile grip and how swiftly it had been undone by its own hubris and the relentless forces of nature. In these remnants, I saw not just the end of an era but a cautionary tale of what might come again if we do not heed the lessons buried in these ruins. The once-vibrant thoroughfares lay silent, save for the occasional rustle of leaves or the distant cry of a solitary bird.

Inside the vast expanse of the military complex, I found myself surrounded by the remnants of a forgotten era. The corridors stretched out before me. The design and technology spoke of an era teetering on the brink of revolutionary advancements, with relics of both the old world's conventional warfare and the brink of a digital future now stilled in silent testimony to its abrupt end.

Everywhere I looked, there were signs of decay and neglect—rusted metal doors hung precariously from their hinges while crumbling concrete walls bore the scars of time.

As I navigated through the labyrinthine passages, I couldn't help but feel awe at the sheer scale of the complex. Each room held its own, from abandoned barracks to derelict command centers, their silent walls echoing with the whispers of the past.

Despite the desolation that surrounded me, there was a haunting beauty to the decay, a reminder of the sacrifices made in the name of duty and honor. As I ventured deeper into the heart of the building, I couldn't help but wonder what secrets lay hidden within its crumbling walls, waiting to be unearthed.

As I explored the dilapidated compound, the air grew heavy with resilience and decay, mingling with the faint aroma of rust and antiquated machinery. Nature had begun to reclaim the abandoned structures, with vines snaking through cracks in the walls and resilient weeds pushing through crevices in the pavement, evidence of nature's persistent resilience. His reclamation by nature served as a humbling reminder of our transient presence. The ambitions and fears that once filled these halls have faded, yet the earth continues to thrive, embracing and erasing our footprints with impartial grace. Each sprouting weed and nesting bird whispered tales of resilience, offering a somber yet hopeful counterpoint to the omnipresent decay. It was a visceral reminder that life, in some form, perseveres, fueling my own determination to forge ahead.

The main command center, once a bustling hub of activity, now lay in ruins. The roof had long since collapsed, leaving the interior exposed to the elements. Piles of debris littered the floor, scattered among broken chairs and rusted equipment. Faded maps and tattered flags hung from the walls, relics of a time when this place was alive with purpose and ambition.

The barracks were little more than crumbling shells; their windows were shattered, and their doors were hanging off their hinges. Empty bunks lined the walls, their metal frames rusted and sagging with age. The mess hall, once a place of camaraderie and shared meals, now lay silent and empty, its tables overturned and its kitchen equipment rusted beyond repair.

Despite the desolation that surrounded me, there was a somber beauty to the abandoned base, a poignant reminder of the sacrifices made in the name of duty and honor. As I explored the ruins, I couldn't help but feel some reverence for the men and women who had served within these walls, their memories preserved in the crumbling concrete and faded paint. I paused, imagining the echoes of their laughter, the weight of their fears, and the strength of their hopes. Each room told a story of camaraderie, duty, and a world teetering on the precipice of the unknown.

Yet, amidst the decay, there were signs of life—a validation of nature's resilience and the enduring spirit of survival. Birds nestled in the rafters, their chirps echoing through the empty halls. Small animals scurried among the debris, making their homes in the forgotten corners of the base.

As I stood amidst the ruins of the military building, I couldn't help but wonder about the people who had once called this place home. What had become of them in the aftermath of the cataclysm that had befallen the world? Were they still out there, struggling to survive in a world gone mad? Or had they vanished into the annals of history, their stories lost to time?

With these questions weighing heavily on my mind, I pressed on, determined to uncover the possible discoveries within the crumbling walls of the military building.

With a steady breath, I proceeded forward, stepping into the heart of the building with a mix of determination and curiosity.

Crossing the threshold, I couldn't shake the feeling of anticipation of any interesting discoveries.

As I cautiously crossed the threshold of the building, a dim illumination from the windows greeted me, casting eerie shadows along the walls.

I went through one of the open doors, and I found a sleeping area for the military troops. A few of the empty beds still remained. A few windows were also broken. Not much was left, so I left the room. I also entered a few other doors and rooms, but absolutely nothing was left. If there had ever been anything, it would surely have been looted by now. Although that gave me a spark of hope that there would still be people around somewhere, I finally encountered a door with a padlock. I kicked it, and it broke easily.

Inside I saw something of interest this time. There was a single rusted desk, and on the desk was a piece of paper folded twice. I went straight to it, surprised to finally find something that was least likely to survive an apocalypse. And although it was dusty and worn, it was still of decent quality. This map, a tangible link to the world outside these decaying walls, represented more than direction—it was a lifeline, a possibility of connection in the sprawling silence of a broken world.

I unfolded the paper, and once I understood what was on it, it brought me a glimmer of hope. And I almost made a sigh of relief if it weren't for the fact that things had been so desperate up until what I had seen. It was a hand-drawn map rather large in size with a small legend, but the words meant little to me, and it seemed to be about this area as I recognized some roads that matched those I had passed by.

The TechLink Controller, as suggested by the legend, appeared to be a pivotal relic capable of bridging the fractured communication networks of the old world. This map, then, was not just a guide but a beacon leading me toward the hope of reunification in a world torn apart.

Then I even noticed a very small drawing of what must've been this very location. In fact, there was a big blue dot right on top of it. I looked at the legend as I recognized the blue dot on it, and it said "TechLink Controller." It seemed clear to me that the name of this building could not be "TechLink Controller; it had to refer to something else, perhaps something that had been here or some kind of computer. I surmised that the controller might be a keystone in rebuilding communication networks or unlocking other technological resources crucial for surviving and rebuilding in this new era.

Nonetheless, it was a clearly drawn map.

When I continued to study the map, an even greater feeling of hope came over me. At the end of the map was drawn what appeared to be some kind of village. Hoping this map would guide me to some kind of civilization brought me relief that there might finally be other people around.

I took the map with me, rolling it up and putting it in my bag.

I was about to leave the complex when I came upon another door with a keycode. It had a large sign on it with a skull and crossbones, and in large red letters, it spelled "Interdiction: Forbidden Passage.". All of this just made me more curious, and I felt like I had to enter to see what this place might bring. It did seem that the keycode was of old design, and I might be able to brute force my way through it using my KeyCode Breaker.

However, I first had to see if there was a limit to the number of attempts it could make before locking me out. So I tried a few combinations. The combination needed seemed to be about eight numbers, and every time I tried, on the small screen above the keyboard, it turned red and said "Access Denied.". But it appeared there was no limit to how many attempts could be made.

So I tore off the protective casing of the keylock, exposing the wiring and electronics hidden beneath it. There were a few cables neatly put in there. I loosened two of them specifically. I then took my KeyCode Breaker and opened two small hatches, revealing a small chip with circular indents where the wires would fit. I placed each of the two wires in one of the chips and pushed them back in. Then I went into the settings of the KeyCode Breaker and entered the settings to reveal a brute force option for key locks. I set it to start, and immediately the screen turned green and said "Access Granted." I could hear the door unlock. I removed the cables from my OmniLocator.

I opened the door and saw a staircase straight down. It was completely dark, so I took out my flashlight. The air inside was heavy with the scent of age, mingling with a faint metallic tang that hinted at the presence of hidden machinery. With a mixture of curiosity and apprehension, I began my descent down the staircase, each step echoing hollowly in the cavernous space. The air grew colder with each downward stride, sending a chill racing down my spine. At last, I reached the bottom of the staircase, where I reached another door, which I opened.

Before me was a large room, its expanse stretching out into the darkness beyond the reach of the feeble light. Metallic columns rose from the ground like ancient sentinels. My flashlight illuminated the ruins of a long-forgotten era of ancient technology.

In the center of the room stood a pedestal, its surface adorned with strange markings and intricate patterns. Leaving behind the crumbling corridors of the hallway, I ventured deeper into the heart of the basement, guided by the faint echoes of movement that reverberated through the chamber. The dim glow of my flashlight revealed a scene of desolation and decay, where time had taken its toll on what once might have been something more majestic than simply the basement of a military building.

The room stretched out before me. Wires snaked their way across the walls, weaving a tapestry of machinery amidst the ruins. As I pressed onward, the air grew thick with the scent of decay, mingled with the acrid stench of the toxic fumes that filled the room. Vents protruded from the walls, emitting noxious gases that danced and swirled in the dim light, casting eerie shadows that flickered and danced across the room.

At the end of the room, in the center of a door that would lead to the next room, lay a gaping chasm, its depths shrouded in darkness. The floor surrounding the chasm was littered with debris and rubble, remnants of the collapse that had torn the room asunder. Despite the desolation that surrounded me, my eyes were drawn to a faint glimmer of light emanating from the far side of the current. It beckoned me forward, a beacon of hope amidst the darkness.

Moving cautiously through the room, I struggled to push forward, my senses overwhelmed by the toxic gases that filled the air. Frantically searching for a way to escape the deadly fumes, I remembered the atmospheric cleaner I had with me. I took it, turned it on, and the air around me cleared. I could breathe and see clearly.

Now able to perceive the room in its entirety, I observed a network of computers lining the walls, intertwined with a labyrinth of wires. Among them, desks adorned with aging technology occupied the space, with one particular workstation standing out as more modern than the rest. Intrigued, I approached and took a seat.

Despite being initially locked behind a password, I swiftly gained access to the bootloader terminal and reset the security measures. With a few keystrokes, I breached the system and found myself faced with a console prompt, its interface unfamiliar yet navigable. Typing the "help" command provided me with the necessary guidance to navigate the system's functionalities.

After some time familiarizing myself with the interface, I discovered a means to deactivate the defensive mechanisms. The release of toxic gases ceased, rendering my atmospheric cleanser unnecessary. Additionally, a retractable bridge materialized, spanning the chasm that separated me from the far side of the room.

The room sprawled before me, its vast expanse punctuated by towering pillars of metal adorned with faded circuitry. Statues depicting ancient soldiers and robotic sentinels stood stoically at intervals, their weathered visages bearing witness to the passage of time. With each step forward, I braced myself to confront the challenges that lay ahead, prepared to unravel the mysteries concealed within the room's depths.

I realized to myself that this underground location was either rather new in comparison to the military building having been rebuilt or built from scratch, because none of these seemed to fit with what I had seen upstairs and were technologically much more advanced. Also, there wouldn't be any purpose for all of this in a building like this.

In the center of the chamber, a dais rose up from the floor, its surface adorned with intricate patterns and symbols that seemed to pulse with a faint inner light. At its center stood a pedestal, upon which rested a single, strange device in the form of a rectangular block turned sideways and held up by mysterious forces as it seemed to float on its lower corner.

Despite the desolation that surrounded me, there was a haunting beauty to this room, a poignant reminder of the grandeur that once was, now preserved only in the fading echoes of a distant past.

Standing in the center and still in a trance by the magnificence of this room, suddenly a latch from the roof opened and dropped some kind of mechanical drone. The drone seemed to be a formidable robotic entity, standing roughly seven feet tall. It possesses a sleek and angular design, with metallic limbs resembling bipedal robots. Its exterior is coated in a gunmetal gray material, giving it a formidable and imposing appearance.

The drone was equipped with articulated arms, each ending in robotic hands similar to those of a human. At the center of its chest cavity was a pulsating energy core encased in a protective housing. This core seemed to serve as the drone's power source.

Before I could even make a move, the drone headed straight in attack formation towards me. One of its robotic arms pulled a large knife from its back. It held me with one hand by my shoulder, and using the knife, it prepared to stab me. Immediately, I responded by kicking the drone as hard as I could at its very center. It flew backwards, crashing right into the wall, rubbles of the wall flying everywhere, and when the drone dropped to the ground, a large black dent with cracks all around it was left where it had hit the wall, pieces of debris still falling from it.

Unfortunately, it had not phased the drone, as it stood back up unharmed and ready to attack me again. In an intense fight using all the combat techniques I had learned, I fought the drone, which applied a custom fighting style yet unknown to me. Though fast as it was, we seemed to be equals in combat, and the fight raged on, each dodging each other's strikes and kicks until, finally, in a moment of lapse, the drone was able to make a move in which it struck me with the knife, cutting me in my arm, leg, and chest and tearing through my clothing and skin. I retreated to the entrance of the room, and out of my bag, I grabbed the Voltcaster.

Heart racing, I grappled with fear and determination in equal measure. Each move against the drone was a dance with my own mortality, a stark reminder of the fine line between survival and obliteration in this new world. I then shot straight at the drone. A large explosion went off, and the drone was knocked back. In the fleeting moments of our skirmish, I calculated the drone's possible weaknesses, leveraging my knowledge of machinery and combat tactics. My mind raced through potential strategies, settling on exploiting the brute force of the Voltcaster as a last resort. The walls were damaged, and more debris dropped from the walls and ceiling, but the drone remained unarmed. I switched out the Voltcaster for the Fusionizer and started circling the drone while releasing fire upon it again and again, but it seemed to be all for nothing.

As the drone closed in, I evaded its lumbering movements, circling around it while unleashing a barrage of energy blasts.

Despite the ferocity of my assault, the drone's thick armor proved impenetrable, deflecting each shot with ease.

Frustration mounted as I realized that brute force alone wouldn't bring down this mechanical monster. With a quick mental recalibration, I focused on its vulnerabilities, recognizing the exposed wiring and joints as potential weak points.

Taking calculated shots, I targeted these vulnerable areas, aiming to disrupt the drone's internal systems. With each hit, sparks flew and circuits fizzled, causing the drone to finally stagger momentarily. Encouraged by this progress, I pressed on, intensifying my assault in a bid to weaken its defenses further.

Finally, the drone was knocked down. And I wasted no time, so I speeded towards it and grabbed, with both hands, the energy core's protective housing. Adrenaline surged through me; I felt my strength increase, and with all I had within me, I pulled as hard as I ever had before, and I heard the housing cracking.

This motivated me to keep going, and with even more effort, I pulled. Bolts flew off the drone until finally it loosened up and came off so hard that it smashed into the ceiling, causing pieces of the ceiling to come off. It then went down and dropped with a loud clanging sound. I looked at it, and it was part of the protective housing that had been torn off. Not completely, but enough to expose the energy core.

As the drone retracted its hands into its arms, energy weapons materialized in both appendages, and it resumed its assault, unleashing a barrage of energy blasts in my direction. Reacting swiftly, I evaded each shot with nimble footwork, narrowly dodging the projectiles that tore through the walls upon impact. My advanced reflexes allowed me to anticipate the drone's movements, enabling me to avoid its attacks with relative ease. So I seized the opportunity to strike at its core.

Picking up the Fusionizer with precision and determination, I directed a relentless barrage of energy blasts at the exposed energy source nestled within its chest.

A deafening roar filled the chamber as the energy core erupted in a shower of sparks and flames, signaling the drone's defeat. With a final surge of triumph, I watched as the mechanical monster faltered and fell, its once formidable frame now rendered inert.

With the drone vanquished, a wave of relief washed over me, mingled with a profound feeling of accomplishment. In the quiet that followed, the echoes of the battle lingered, a haunting chorus that underscored the solitude of my quest. It was a victory, yes, but one that bore the weight of solitude and the unending road ahead. This encounter was a brutal reminder of the challenges that lay ahead. Yet, as I stood among the remnants of my adversary, I recognized a growth within myself—a melding of human resilience and technological prowess. It emboldened me, fortifying my resolve for the uncertain journey ahead. As I surveyed the aftermath of the battle, I knew that this victory marked a significant milestone in my quest for survival amidst the ruins of a world ravaged by chaos and destruction.

As I stood amidst the remnants of the battle, I felt a renewed resolve and was determined, knowing that each obstacle I overcame brought me closer to achieving my purpose. I looked at my wounds, and they were already partially healed.

Among the spoils of his triumph, I discovered a cache of advanced technological components salvaged from the defeated drone. These components included high-grade alloys, advanced circuitry, and rare energy cores, all of which possessed extraordinary potential for further experimentation and innovation.

With these resources at my disposal, I could enhance my own equipment, develop new technologies, and fortify my defenses against future threats. Furthermore, the remains of the drone itself provided me with valuable salvageable materials, such as reinforced armor plating and specialized actuators.

These components could be repurposed and integrated into my arsenal. In essence, my victory not only granted me valuable knowledge and experience but also tangible assets that would empower me to face the challenges ahead with greater confidence and capability.

I put as much of it as I could into the bag. If I had to deal with these types of powerful enemies, I would have to build a suit out of the materials I had ascertained for protection against such battles. Even though this made my bag significantly heavier, my enhanced strength still allowed me to carry the whole pile of stuff on me. But eventually I had to find a place to store my stuff, as I could not afford to be hindered by a large bag filled with heavy materials in the long run.

In the room, the rectangular block sat atop a pedestal, seemingly the object the drone had guarded. With trepidation, I cautiously lifted the box from its perch, half-expecting some calamity to ensue—a seismic upheaval or the sudden appearance of another menacing drone. Yet, to my relief, nothing untoward occurred.

Upon closer inspection, I realized that the block was not a solid entity but rather a box held together by magnetic forces. Gently prying open its lid, I discovered an intricate piece of technology nestled within. It was a compact device that had to be opened by sliding the front cover upwards, adorned with enigmatic symbols arranged in a manner reminiscent of a numeric keypad. Each symbol emitted a soft glow as my fingers grazed over them, fading away once released. Clearly, it was a sophisticated keypad for a purpose yet unknown to me—a groundbreaking find awaiting further exploration.

Could this enigmatic device be the fabled TechLink Controller mentioned on the map? The possibility ignited a spark within me, a flicker of anticipation for the connections it could rebuild and the secrets it might unveil. It held the promise of a bridge to a world I thought I had lost. In my hands lay not just a tool, but the hope of piercing the veil of isolation that enveloped this world. It was a chance to reach out across the void and find others who might share this fight for a new dawn. I mused, pondering its significance as I carefully slid back the cover once more and tucked it into my pocket.

I made the decision to depart from the eerie confines of the military complex, feeling as though I had gleaned the most crucial insights it had to offer. Time, which once marched to the steady rhythm of clocks and calendars, now flows unbound by human constructs. Here, amidst the relics of a world paused in mid-breath, the future stretched out undefined, like a canvas waiting for new stories to be etched upon its surface. With each step away from the remnants of the past, I felt a resolve hardening within me, a silent vow to carry forward the legacy of those who had fallen and to forge a path toward a future they could only dream of. A thought came to me as I was about to head up the stairs, reminding me of the drone's successful strikes. My shirt and pants were still torn, but when I looked at the location of the wounds, I noticed they were gone completely, as if they had never been there. It felt odd having these healing capabilities; it almost felt that no matter the challenge, I would be able to overcome it thanks to my upgrades. But I also feared getting cocky; the fight with my first enemy definitely wasn't a walk in the park, and I had to remain prepared.

As I ascended the stairs, I noticed the encroaching darkness beyond the building's threshold, signaling the lateness of the hour.

Realizing my own exhaustion after several sleepless days, I ventured outside and collected some wood, igniting a fire within the shelter of the building. Crafting a rudimentary bed from branches and leaves, I succumbed to weariness and drifted into slumber within moments. It was the first restful night since emerging from the cryochamber, yet it brought with it the most vivid and unsettling dreams.

In my sleep, I found myself immersed in a dystopian vision of a world ravaged by a second apocalypse, where life itself seemed an impossibility. The landscape was a desolate expanse of blackened earth, interspersed with rivers of molten lava and punctuated by erupting volcanoes. In this barren wasteland, devoid of flora, fauna, or civilization, I stood alone amidst the chaos, gazing skyward at a canopy of ash-laden clouds and distant stars.

Suddenly, I was jolted awake, drenched in sweat, just as a towering wave of fiery liquid surged toward me in my dream. Shaken by the intensity of the vision, I struggled to shake off its lingering impact, eventually regaining my composure as the light of dawn filtered through the building's windows.

With no means of measuring time in this post-apocalyptic world, I marveled at the oversight of not bringing a simple timekeeping device from before my cryosleep. Nonetheless, I trusted my body's internal clock to gauge my rest.

Within hours of leaving the military complex behind, the land began to change. Fields once green and fertile were now barren, scattered with the twisted wrecks of what once was.

Navigating this landscape, I encountered pockets of radiation and the aggressive overgrowth of mutated flora, challenges unforeseen yet tackled with a blend of ingenuity and caution. Each obstacle overcome was a testament to the adaptability required to survive here.

Venturing outside once more, I consulted the map I had acquired, locating the nearest settlement marked with a green dot and labeled "Twilight Crest" in the legend.

Within hours of leaving the military complex behind, the land began to change. Fields once green and fertile were now barren, scattered with the twisted wrecks of what once was.

Navigating this landscape, I encountered pockets of radiation and the aggressive overgrowth of mutated flora, challenges unforeseen yet tackled with a blend of ingenuity and caution. Each obstacle overcome was a testament to the adaptability required to survive here.

Though unsure of the map's scale, its relative accuracy instilled a measure of confidence as I prepared to journey toward the village on my Alloyed Charger, apprehensive yet determined to make contact with whatever remnants of humanity remained. Yet, beneath the resolve, a knot of apprehension tightened. How would those who survived beyond these ruins perceive me? As a friend, a foe, or a relic of a world best forgotten? The answers lay at Twilight Crest, shrouded in the uncertainty of this new era.

After days of journeying, with the shadows of Twilight Crest finally on the horizon, I decided to examine the TechLink Controller more closely. Under the faint light of my campfire, the device came to life, revealing its true capabilities. It was not just a tool for navigation; it held the key to accessing forgotten networks, a way to bridge the vast silences of this new world. With a mixture of awe and determination, I realized that this device could be the catalyst for rebuilding what was lost.

As the horizon beckoned, a tapestry of emotions wove itself within me—hope intertwined with uncertainty and courage, shadowed by the specter of solitude. The Twilight Crest symbolized not just a destination but the promise of new beginnings, of stories yet to unfold, and of destinies yet to be forged. The solitude that enveloped me was both a shield and a shadow, a constant companion along the paths I walked. Yet, within the depths of silence, I harbored a quiet hope for kinship, for faces to share in the light of the fire and voices to break the monotony of the wind. The Twilight Crest held more than the promise of survival; it whispered the possibility of connection in a world reborn from the ashes.

With the map as my guide and the remnants of hope as my companion, I set forth on a journey not just of distance but of discovery—toward a destination where the past and future might converge in the shadow of Twilight Crest. The path ahead, veiled in the mists of the unknown, promised trials and encounters that would test the very essence of my being. In this moment of departure, the remnants of the past melded with the possibilities of tomorrow, imbuing me with a sense of purpose as profound as the ruins around me. It was no longer just about survival but about carrying the torch of humanity forward, into the shadows, and towards the light of a new dawn.

Yet within my heart, a flame of resolve flickered bright, fueled by the yearning to reclaim a semblance of the world we once knew and to carve a place within this reshaped reality.

SHADOWS OF RESILIENCE

As I trekked toward the village marked on the map, the dense forest enveloped me in its cool embrace, the towering trees stretching toward the sky like ancient sentinels. The path wound its way through the undergrowth, a narrow ribbon of dirt softened by layers of fallen leaves.

Halfway to my destination, I decided to take a much-needed break beneath the shade of a towering oak tree. I unpacked some rations from my bag and began to eat, relishing the quiet solitude of the forest. I still had enough rations for a while, so I had some time to begin scavenging for my own food.

Suddenly, the tranquility was shattered by the sound of snapping twigs and rustling leaves nearby. I tensed, my hand instinctively reaching for the Volt-caster strapped to my side.

Emerging from the undergrowth, I spotted a wounded creature limping into view—a magnificent new species with a deep gash across its flank. It stood tall, its body covered in sleek, iridescent scales that shimmered in the dappled sunlight filtering through the canopy above. Its eyes, large and intelligent, held a mix of pain and apprehension as they met mine.

Its iridescent scales, a marvel of natural evolution, hinted at its role within the forest's delicate balance. The gash on its flank is a stark reminder of the ongoing strife between the remnants of humanity and the natural world, struggling to heal from past recklessness.

Moved by compassion, I set aside my meal and cautiously approached the injured creature. Despite its wariness, the creature allowed me to draw closer, as if sensing my intentions.

With gentle hands, I inspected the wound and assessed its severity. The creature winced in pain but made no attempt to flee, as if trusting me to help.

Drawing upon my rudimentary knowledge of wilderness medicine, I retrieved a first aid kit from my bag and began to clean and dress the wound. I worked methodically, my hands steady despite the adrenaline coursing through my veins.

As I tended to the creature's injuries, I marveled at its unique physiology. Its scales, though damaged in places, retained their vibrant hues, reminiscent of the gems that once adorned the crowns of ancient kings. Its tail, long and flexible, swayed gently as it watched me with wary eyes.

After applying a makeshift bandage to the creature's wound, I stepped back and watched as it slowly rose to its feet, its gaze filled with gratitude. With a graceful nod of its head, the creature turned and disappeared into the depths of the forest, leaving me alone once more.

Watching the creature disappear, I pondered the fragile web of existence binding us all. In saving it, perhaps I was also saving a part of myself, a reminder that even in ruin, there's room for compassion and renewal.

Though my encounter with the wounded creature had delayed my journey to the village, I felt fulfillment knowing that I had been able to make a difference in the life of another living being.

As the creature vanished into the thicket, a sense of kinship washed over me, stirring memories long buried. I recalled a time when the world was whole, and my biggest concern was not survival but mundane daily tasks. How drastically the world has changed, and with it, me.

With renewed determination, I set off once more, my heart lighter and strengthened by the bond forged in the depths of the forest. Clutching the worn photo in my pocket, a relic from a world now lost, I felt a surge of resolve. This journey was not just about survival; it was a quest to restore a semblance of the peace depicted in that faded image.

Amidst the dense foliage, my thoughts drifted to the ruins of the city I once called home, a stark reminder of the resilience needed to navigate this new world. It was there, among the crumbling remnants of civilization, that I first learned the true value of compassion and the importance of fighting for a cause greater than oneself.

This moment of unexpected compassion amidst the wilderness forced me to reconsider my own journey. This was not just a quest for survival, but a path toward understanding the fragile interdependence between all living beings in this new world.

When I had finished eating, I put everything back and resumed my journey. Though the meeting with this new type of creature wouldn't be my only encounter on my path,.

As I ventured deeper into the heart of the forest, the verdant canopy overhead formed a natural tapestry, filtering the sunlight into a mesmerizing dance of light and shadow on the forest floor. Shafts of golden sunlight pierced through the dense foliage, creating intricate patterns that shifted with the gentle sway of the trees in the breeze.

In the evenings, gathered around flickering fires, the villagers shared tales of lost loved ones and dreams of reclaiming their future. Each story, a thread woven into the fabric of our shared resolve, reinforced my commitment not just to my mission but to the people who had become my unintended kin.

The tranquility of the woodland enveloped me, wrapping me in a cloak of serene solitude. The forest's air, thick with the scent of pine and damp earth, filled my lungs, grounding me in the moment. Every step unleashed a symphony of sounds: the crunch of leaves, the whisper of the wind through the branches, and the distant call of wildlife, painting a soundscape of serene wilderness. Each step I took stirred the fallen leaves underfoot, releasing a faint earthy scent that mingled with the crisp freshness of the forest air. The only sounds that dared to disturb the peaceful silence were the occasional rustle of small creatures scurrying amidst the underbrush and the melodious trill of unseen birds perched high in the treetops.

As I wandered further into the depths of the forest, I found myself immersed in a symphony of nature's own making. The soft murmur of a nearby brook added a gentle rhythm to the tranquil melody, its clear waters babbling over smooth stones as it meandered through the woodland glade. The distant call of a lone owl echoed through the trees; its haunting cry was a manifestation of the wild and untamed beauty that lay hidden within the heart of the forest.

Despite the vast expanse of greenery that surrounded me, I felt profound peace and belonging amidst the ancient trees and lush undergrowth. The pristine wilderness, untouched by the scourge of conflict, contrasted sharply with the worn faces and dilapidated homes of Misty Hollow, each telling a silent story of endurance in the face of adversity. Every leaf that quivered in the breeze seemed to whisper secrets of the forest's storied past, while the dappled sunlight danced upon my skin like a gentle caress from nature itself.

In this tranquil oasis, far removed from the hustle and bustle of the outside world, I found solace in the simple beauty of the natural world. With each passing moment, I felt myself drawn deeper into the embrace of the forest, captivated by its timeless allure and enchanted by its whispered secrets.

Suddenly, without warning, a low growl echoed through the trees, making my flesh crawl. Instinctively, I tensed, preparing myself for whatever threat lurked nearby.

Emerging from the undergrowth, a sleek, leopard-like creature bounded into view, its eyes gleaming with predatory intent. Its fur was a mottled blend of earthy tones, perfectly camouflaged amidst the forest backdrop. I immediately jumped off my bike and took a few steps backwards.

Without hesitation, the creature lunged at me, claws extended and teeth bared in a ferocious snarl. Drawing upon my combat training and enhanced reflexes, I swiftly sidestepped its attack, narrowly avoiding its slashing claws.

With each new adversary, my ability to predict and counteract evolved. No longer was I merely reacting; I was anticipating, melding instinct with strategy, each confrontation a step towards mastery.

Despite the creature's relentless onslaught, I maintained my composure, waiting for the perfect opportunity to strike back. With a swift and well-timed counterattack, I delivered a powerful blow to its side, causing it to stagger and retreat momentarily.

Taking advantage of the opening, I pressed the attack, driving the creature back with a series of rapid strikes and well-placed kicks. With each blow, I could feel the tide of the battle shifting in my favor.

Finally, after a fierce exchange, the creature faltered, its movements growing sluggish as fatigue set in. Seizing the opportunity, I delivered a decisive blow, incapacitating the creature and sending it crashing to the forest floor with a resounding thud.

As the creature lay defeated at my feet, I couldn't help but feel pride in my abilities. Though the encounter had been intense, I had emerged victorious, relying solely on my own skills and instincts.

With the immediate threat neutralized, I took a moment to catch my breath, my heart still racing from the adrenaline of the encounter. Though the forest remained fraught with danger, I knew that I possessed the resilience and determination to overcome whatever challenges lay ahead on my journey to the village.

Once again, I continued my journey, the path ahead winding like a ribbon through the heart of the forest. The dense foliage stretched out before me, casting dappled shadows that danced across the forest floor. The air was alive with the hum of insects and the occasional trill of a bird, creating a symphony of nature that enveloped me as I pressed onward.

As I drove, my mind wandered, reflecting on the events of my journey thus far. Memories flickered like candle flames in the recesses of my mind—encounters with strange creatures, the thrill of exploration, and the quiet moments of solace beneath the canopy of trees. Each step brought me closer to my destination, yet the path ahead remained veiled in mystery, its secrets waiting to be revealed.

The forest seemed to breathe around me, its ancient heart pulsing with life and energy. As I navigated the forest, I noted the subtle signs of its inhabitants: the fleeting shadow of a deer and the intricate web of a spider glistening with dew, each a testament to the resilience of nature amidst chaos. I marveled at the intricate web of life that surrounded me, from the delicate ferns that carpeted the forest floor to the towering giants that reached for the sky. It was a world teeming with vitality, an affirmation of the enduring power of nature.

As the sun dipped lower in the sky, painting the forest in hues of gold and amber, I quickened my pace, eager to reach my destination before nightfall. The air grew cooler, and a gentle breeze rustled through the leaves, carrying with it the scent of pine and earth.

Finally, as the last rays of sunlight filtered through the trees, I emerged from the depths of the forest and into a clearing. Before me lay the village of Twilight Crest, nestled in a valley between the mountains. Smoke rose lazily from chimneys, and the sound of voices drifted in the breeze.

I paused for a moment, taking in the sight before me. The village appeared peaceful and idyllic, a sanctuary amidst the wilderness. Yet, beneath the surface, I sensed a tension—an undercurrent of unease that whispered of hidden dangers lurking in the shadows.

With a determined stride, I made my way down the winding path that led into the heart of the village. As I walked, I passed quaint cottages with thatched roofs and neatly tended gardens. The streets were quiet, save for the occasional passerby, their faces etched with lines of worry and concern.

At last, I reached the village square, where a bustling market was in full swing. Merchants were hawking their wares, and villagers bustled about, their voices mingling in a cacophony of sound. I took a moment to soak in the sights and sounds of the market.

With renewed intent, I set off to find someone who could point me in the direction of the village Elder. In the village square, I shared a pouch of dried berries with a group of wide-eyed children, their laughter a fleeting reprieve from the shadows that lingered over Misty Hollow. It was a simple gesture, but one that wove me tighter into the fabric of this community. It was time to begin my quest in earnest, to unravel the mysteries that lay hidden within the heart of Twilight Crest.

As I stood in the village square, surrounded by the hustle and bustle of the market, I couldn't help but marvel at the quaint charm of Twilight Crest— or rather, Misty Hollow, as I soon would learn it was called. The village, though small, exuded an air of resilience, with its inhabitants going about their daily lives amidst the remnants of destruction that lingered like ghosts of the past.

I spotted a figure making their way through the crowd towards me, their gait purposeful yet cautious. As they drew nearer, I caught sight of the determined set of their jaws and the glint of curiosity in their eyes.

"Holō, hwo yu bi?"[1] said the figure greeting me in a language unfamiliar to my ears; their words had a melodic cadence that danced on the breeze.

Perplexed, I furrowed my brow, trying to make sense of the strange sounds that fell from their lips. Sensing my confusion, the figure raised their hand in a gesture of greeting, their fingers forming a peace sign.

Taking the cue, I returned the gesture and replied in the only way I knew how: "Hello, I'm Ethan. I come in peace."

"Holō, Ethan. Wɛlkəm. Yu kʌm in pis, yu sɛ?"[2] the figure responded, their voice tinged with warmth and hospitality.

I nodded in understanding, recognizing the gesture of peace they had offered. It was a sort of evolved variant of English.

"What's your name?" I inquired, pointing towards the figure before me.

"Ay, mi neɪm bi Kael Ravenscroft. Wat bi jɔrz?"[3] Kael replied, returning the gesture and pointing to me as well.

"My name's Ethan. It's nice to meet you, Kael," I said, offering a warm smile in return.

"A Pleʒər, Ethan. If yu nid ɛniθɪŋ els, jʌst æsk,"[4] Kael said, their words a reassuring promise of assistance.

I observed him smoking something resembling the vaporizers of our past. I recalled the existence of cigarettes, a once-popular but unhealthy and addictive habit from the sixteenth to the twenty-first century. The scene closely mirrored images I accessed through my neural interface, depicting humanity's historical habits.

He took a drag and blew out the smoke, which emitted a soothing aroma characterized by a delicate blend of floral, herbal, and earthy notes. The scent was reminiscent of a serene garden after a gentle rain.

"Can I ask what it is you're smoking?" I asked.

"Is dis ðə fɜrst tajm juv sin sʌmwʌn smokɪŋ?"[5] He asked, "Wel, tə sʌmrə,rajz, wat aɪm smokɪŋ spəsɪfɪkli ɪz kɔld 'Bətænɪkl Hɑr'məni', ɪts med ʌv seɪdʒ, pɛpərmɪnt, lʌvəndər ənd kæmə,mil. ɪt 'moʊstli hɛlps mi rɪ'læks ænd 'foʊkəs. wi doʊnt ɔl smok ðə seɪm hɜrbz əv kɔrs."[6]

I didn't fully grasp his words, so he patiently broke them down into smaller parts, using ample gestures to illustrate.

Eventually, I understood that he was smoking an herbal cigarette. He mentioned they were known as "herbal haze sticks, although commonly referred to as herbsticks.

"May I give it a try?" I inquired, prompting him to pass the herbal stick to me. As I indulged, I felt a calming effect wash over me, clearing my thoughts. I returned it to him, grateful for his kindness. I expressed my thanks before voicing my purpose for coming to Misty Hollow. "So I've been looking for a village called Twilight Crest. Is this it?"

"Nō, this is Mistiholō, o ōr lāst ov it. The Twilightcrest is a symbōlik kī nidid tu ōpēn ðə templ at ðə top ov ðə mōntenz. Wī ōnd ðə Crest bʌt it wuz stōlən frəm ʌs rēsəntli,"[7] Kael explained, their gestures punctuating their words with clarity.

Listening intently, I absorbed Kael's explanation, piecing together that this place was not called Twilight Crest but Misty Hollow, and the Twilight Crest was a key symbol for a temple at the top of the mountains and that it had recently been stolen.

I frowned, processing the information. "Why would they steal something that seems to hold no value beyond something symbolic?"

"Dat's jʌst it,"[8] Kael explained, shaking his head. "Dɛ bɪliv ðə templ hoz grɛt rɪtʃɪz, bʌt ɪts nʌθɪŋ mɔr ðæn ə mɪθ. ðə templ ɪz ə seɪkrəd pleɪs, jɛs, bʌt ɪts tru vælju laɪz ɪn ðə hɪstəri ænd nɑlɪdʒ ɪt həʊldz, nɑt mətɪrɪəl wɛlθ."[9]

At this point, I realized that Kael could understand what I was saying very well. And I was able to piece together his expressions, gestures, and the format of the language to understand what Kael was talking about. Although his messages frequently required clarification in segments,. His intention was to convey that while the bandits harbor aspirations of untold riches within the temple, reality paints a different picture. He articulated that the temple's significance lies not in its material opulence but rather in its rich history and reservoir of knowledge and wisdom.

As we walked through the desolate streets of Mist Hollow, Kael delved deeper into the lore surrounding the bandit stronghold. "Ðə fɔrtrəs ðe kɔl hom,"[10] he began, his voice tinged with a mix of caution and apprehension, "ɪz ə pleɪs ʌv dɑrknɪs ænd dɪsper, ɪnhæbɪtɪd baɪ bændɪts ænd aʊtlɔz hu preɪ əpɑn ðə wik ænd dɪfɛnslɪs."[11]

Kael expounded on the subject of the bandit stronghold, depicting it as a foreboding enclave inhabited by nefarious individuals. He elucidated how its shadows conceal acts of cruelty perpetrated against the vulnerable and defenseless.

I listened intently as Kael paused, searching for the right words to convey the grim reality of the situation. "ɪts nɑt ʤʌst ə fɔrtrəs, 'iθən. ɪts ə bæstjən ʌv lɔlesnəs, wɛr 'ɑnli ðə strɔŋ sə'vaɪv ænd ðə 'mɛrsɪlɪs 'θraɪv."[12]

Delving deeper into his discourse, Kael underscored that the fortress transcends mere physical structure; it embodies a lawless realm where brute strength reigns supreme and compassion finds no place.

My expression darkened as I absorbed the meaning of what he said, my eyes narrowing with understanding. "So, it's more than just a base of operations for them. It's a symbol of their power.

"Aɪ," Kael confirmed, nodding solemnly. "bʌt ɪts 'ɑɫso ə fɔrtrəs bɪlt ɑn fɪr ænd ɪntɪmə'deɪʃən. aɪv hɜrd telz ʌv ɪts 'taʊərɪŋ 'geɪts, 'fɔrtə,faɪd wɪθ 'reɪzər 'waɪr ænd gɑrdəd baɪ 'ruθləs 'sɛntɪnəlz hu ʃoʊ noʊ 'mɜrsi tu ðoʊz hu dɛr tu ə'proʊʧ."[13]

Kael's demeanor suggested concurrence as he painted a chilling portrait of the fortress, emphasizing its ominous and perilous nature. He recounted tales of formidable barriers fortified with razor wire and manned by merciless sentinels.

As we walked, Kael painted a vivid picture of the stronghold's imposing facade and its chaotic interior. "wɪðɪn ɪts 'wɔlz, 'keɪɑs reɪnz sə'priːm,"[14] he continued, his voice carrying a note of unease. "kruːd 'ʃæntiz ænd 'ræm,ʃækəl 'strʌktʃərz 'lɪtər ðə 'lænd,skeɪp, ə'dɔrn wɪð ðə 'trafiz ʌv pæst 'kɑnkwɪsts ænd ðə spɔɪlz ʌv wɔr."[13]

Kael meticulously delineated the fortress's appearance, both internally and externally, portraying it as a disheveled bastion strewn with the spoils of aggression. He described a chaotic landscape, marred by plundered remnants of others' misfortune.

Further elaborating, Kael depicted an environment of disarray within the fortress, where hastily erected structures betray a lack of order. He detailed how these edifices, adorned with the ill-gotten gains of their occupants, serve as grim reminders of the bandits' ruthless exploits.

Kael's words painted a vivid picture of the challenges facing Misty Hollow—a stronghold encampment inhabited by bandits and outlaws, driven by the misguided belief that the nearby temple held untold wealth. Their presence had wreaked havoc upon the village, leaving behind a trail of destruction and the depletion of vital provisions.

As Kael spoke, his gestures underscored the gravity of the situation, each movement punctuating the harsh reality of their plight. I struggled to grasp the full extent of their predicament, needing clarification on several occasions before the pieces finally fell into place.

In essence, Misty Hollow was under siege, its inhabitants held captive by the tyranny of those who sought to plunder their resources and exploit their vulnerability. It was a dire situation, one that demanded immediate action and unwavering determination to overcome.

"I will help you not just to bring the crest back but also to bring you the food you need, but before I do, I want to be completely familiar with your language, so I can question the locals and possibly negotiate with the thieves," I declared, my resolve firm as I pledged my assistance to Kael and his fellow villagers.

"Nəu, I wɪl bi fɔrevər in yor dept, I wɪl tītʃ yu awr langwɪj and I nō sʌmwʌn hʊ kæn šo yu haw tu get tu ðə bandit fort,"[16] Kael responded, his gratitude evident as he accepted my offer of aid. It was a pact sealed in mutual understanding and shared purpose, a bond forged in the crucible of adversity.

With Kael's guidance, I would learn their language, bridging the gap between us and the villagers of Misty Hollow. Together, we would unravel the mysteries of the Twilight Crest and confront the looming threat of the bandit stronghold, united in our quest for justice and redemption.

During my three-day sojourn in Misty Hollow, I delved deep into the fabric of the village's existence, observing its daily rhythms and uncovering the intricate web of relationships that bound its inhabitants together. Although I had swiftly grasped the nuances of their language upon my arrival, it was through keen observation and candid conversations that I truly began to understand the heart and soul of this resilient community.

As the sun dipped below the horizon, casting long shadows over the desolate landscape, a trio of bandits emerged from the dense forest surrounding Mist Hollow. Mounted atop rugged steeds, they rode with an air of authority, their presence heralded by the thundering hooves of their mounts.

The leader, a towering figure with a mane of unkempt hair cascading down his broad shoulders, exuded an aura of command and intimidation. His muscular frame was clad in weather-beaten leather armor, adorned with the insignia of his bandit clan. Scars intersected his rugged features, a showcase of a lifetime spent in pursuit of wealth and power.

At his side rode a lean and wiry bandit, his calculating gaze fixed on the humble village before them. Despite his diminutive stature, there was a dangerous glint in his eyes, a silent promise of the chaos he could unleash with his cunning and ruthlessness. Clad in tattered rags and patched leather, he exuded an air of cunning and deception, his every move calculated to further his own ambitions.

Bringing up the rear was the third member of the trio, a towering brute of a man whose hulking form seemed to dwarf even the largest of horses. Clad in crude chainmail and wielding a massive warhammer with ease, he was a fearsome sight to behold. His face was obscured by a tattered hood, leaving only his piercing eyes visible beneath the shadowy depths.

Together, they formed a formidable trio, their presence casting a dark shadow over Mist Hollow as they rode towards the beleaguered settlement with a proposition. As they approached the village gates, the leader called out to the wary villagers, his voice booming with authority.

"Gud pipel ov Mistiholō!"[17] he bellowed, his words echoing through the stillness of the night. "Wī kam not az konkerərz, bʌt az kolektərz ov ðə deɪli tribjut oʊd tʊ əs. Brɪŋ fɔrθ ðə wan rɪsponsəbəl fɔr ðə kəlekʃən, and lɛt ʌs ekspidajt ðɪs trænzækʃən."[18]

They were essentially claiming that they were not here to conquer or attack the village but rather to collect the daily tribute that they believe is owed to them. They're demanding that the person responsible for collecting these taxes be brought forward so they can swiftly carry out this transaction.

His words hung heavy in the air, and the villagers exchanged nervous glances as they reluctantly obeyed the bandits' demands. Misty Hollow, once a thriving community of artisans and farmers, is now teetered on the brink, its resources dwindling under the bandits' relentless demands. Previous attempts at resistance had been met with brutal retribution, leaving the village caught between the specter of starvation and the tyranny of submission. With some feeling of resignation, the village Elder emerged from the crowd, a small pouch of precious medical supplies clutched tightly in his trembling hands.

With a menacing smile, the leader gestured for The Elder to approach, his eyes gleaming with greed as he eagerly accepted the meager offering. "Yor komplajəns bi noted, Oðɛr,"[18] he sneered, his voice dripping with contempt. "Sē ðæt ðɪs tribjut kontɪnjuz tu floʊ, lɛst yu fes ðə kənsɪkwɛnsəz ʌv yor dɪfaɪəns,"[19] the bandit leader warned, his voice laced with menace.

"Next tɪm, wīl ɛkspekt ʌ sʌplaɪ ʌv Vɜrdant Zɛfər, əlɔŋ wɪð ʌ saɪzəbl ʌmaʊnt ʌv fud."[20]

He basically expected the tributes to be coming and specified what he wanted the next day. It had already occurred to me that there was a different tribute each day. And this time it was a sizable amount of food and a supply of Verdant Zephyr.

Verdant Zephyr is a delicately crafted alcoholic beverage. It is made from a blend of fermented fruits, herbs, and botanicals, carefully selected for their aromatic qualities and flavor profiles. The beverage undergoes a meticulous fermentation process, transforming the raw ingredients into a symphony of flavors.

Verdant Zephyr had become a cherished beverage in what would now be the equivalent of wine in the post-apocalyptic world.

This was definitely an expensive tribute because Verdant Zephyr was rare and took time to make. I had tasted it before, and it was without doubt superior to regular wine.

As the bandits rode off into the night, leaving Mist Hollow in their wake, the villagers watched in silence, their hearts heavy with the burden of their daily tribute. In the harsh world of these days, survival often came at a steep price, paid unwillingly to those who held power over them.

Despite the palpable tension that hung in the air, the people of Misty Hollow carried on with stoic resolve, their daily routines a demonstration of their unwavering resilience. Walking through the village, I noticed a young child clutching an empty bowl, his eyes wide with longing as he gazed at the sparse offerings in the market. It was a silent testament to the heavy toll the bandits' demands had taken on the villagers' ability to sustain themselves.

As the echoes of the bandits' departure faded, a heavy silence fell over Misty Hollow. The villagers' fleeting glances spoke volumes of their fear and desperation, a daily torment that I could no longer ignore.

Women tended to their homes and children with quiet determination, while men toiled in the fields or mines from dawn till dusk, their labor a vital lifeline in the face of adversity.

Amidst the rustic charm of the village, pockets of modernity emerged like beacons of hope amidst the darkness. A solitary blacksmith plied his trade with skill and precision, forging tools and implements essential for the village's survival. Nearby, a pharmacy, doctor, and hospital stood as bastions of healing, their shelves stocked with medicines and remedies gleaned from a bygone era—a confirmation of the enduring resilience of the human spirit.

Yet, amidst the semblance of normalcy, I felt foreboding lingered in the air. The village militia, though valiant in their defense of Misty Hollow, stood as a dwindling bulwark against the ever-present threat of banditry. Led by a steadfast captain, their numbers had been decimated by relentless attacks, leaving the village vulnerable to further assaults.

And yet, amidst the uncertainty and turmoil, a glimmer of hope flickered on the horizon. Though the bandits held sway over Misty Hollow through fear and intimidation, the villagers' indomitable spirit remained unbroken. Through acts of solidarity and resilience, they stood united against the encroaching darkness, determined to carve out a future of peace and prosperity amidst the chaos of the world.

As I wandered the winding streets and shadowed alleys of Misty Hollow, I bore witness to the indomitable human spirit that thrived amidst adversity. Each conversation, each interaction, served to witness the resilience of the human spirit—a beacon of hope in a world shrouded in darkness. And though the path ahead was fraught with peril and uncertainty, I knew that together, the people of Misty Hollow would overcome whatever trials lay in their path, emerging stronger and more united than ever before.

I went to The Elder to discuss the issue of the bandits. Among Kael's belongings, I stumbled upon a torn page from a bandit's journal, its scribbled notes hinting at desperation and a twisted sense of justice. It seemed the line between villain and victim was blurred by survival. A villager pointed out my way to his house, and I knocked on the door. He opened the door, and I looked at him. He had weathered features that bear the marks of a life well lived.

His face was lined with age, but his eyes sparkled with a sharp intelligence and deep insight that came only from years of experience.

He had a commanding presence, standing tall and proud despite the passage of time. His hair, once dark and vibrant, now streaked with silver, frames a face that carries the weight of countless stories and lessons learned.

Dressed in practical attire, The Elder wore garments that were both functional and symbolic of their role in the community. He wore a cloak or shawl made from weather-beaten fabric, adorned with symbols of wisdom and authority. Around his neck hangs a pendant, or amulet.

Despite his age, The Elder moved with grace and strength that commanded respect. He was smoking an herbstick.

"Yes, hwo mæi ai bi ov asistɛns?"[21] inquired The Elder, his voice tinged with hoarseness.

"I've come to address the bandit issue," I responded.

"Wat æspekt wud yu laik tu diskʌs?"[22] he inquired further. "It's rather straightforward, really; the current situation must cease. You're not indebted to these bandits, certainly not with a daily, costly tribute," I explained.

"Aɪ dɒnt dɪsəgriː, bʌt aʊr rɪˈsɔrsɪz ænd strɛŋθ ɑr lɪmɪtɛd ɪn kənˈfrʌntɪŋ ðɛm,"[23] he acknowledged.

"Then I intend to take matters into my own hands," I asserted.

As I prepared for my encounter with the bandits, I couldn't help but wonder about the circumstances that led them to this path. Were they driven by desperation, or was it the allure of power?

Understanding their motives could be key to finding a peaceful resolution or, failing that, predicting their next move.

"Wɑt kæn yu æˈtʃiv əˈlon ðæt wi ˈhævnt ˈmænɪd?"[24] he questioned skeptically.

"In essence, I believe I can put an end to the bandit threat," I declared, "be it through diplomacy or by force. I'm confident I can ensure that these outlaws never trouble anyone again."

"Aɪm ɪksidɪŋli ˈdaʊtfl. Yul bi ˈsaɪnɪŋ yor oʊn dɛθ ˈwɔrənt. Ar yu ˈtruːli prɪˈpɛrd fɔr ðæt?"[25] he inquired.

"I'm prepared for anything," I asserted. "That's precisely why I'm here—to resolve issues like these. I refuse to stand idly by while this village continues to be plundered. And mark my words, once you're unable to meet their demands, these outlaws will surely ravage what's left of your town."

"ın ðæt keıs, aı woʊnt ˈhındər yu."[26] The Elder conceded.

"Aım nɑt wʌn tu dıkˈteıt ˈpipəlz ˈækʃənz, ısˈpɛʃəli ðoʊz frəm ˈaʊtsaıd. aı ˈoʊnli ˈhændəl ˈkɒnflıkts ænd ˈpɜrsənl ˈmætərz. bʌt doʊnt seı aı ˈdıdənt wɔrn yu; rıˈtɜrnıŋ meı pruv tə bi ə ˈʧælındʒ, ıf æt ɔl."[27]

"One thing I'm curious about is what we're up against with these bandits. Kael provided ample details about their fortress, but do you have any additional insights?" I inquired.

Aım əˈfreıd nɑt,"[28] The Elder replied, "Nʌθıŋ yu laıkli ɑːrn't alˈrɛdi əˈwer ʌv. ðıs pərˈtıkjələr ˈbændıt grup ız noʊˈtɔriəsli ˈvaıələnt, dıˈstrʌktıv, ænd əˈverıʃəs. ðeər ˈɒrıdʒınz rıˈmeın ʌnˈnoʊn tu ʌs. aı noʊ ðeı hæv ə ˈliːdə, ænd ıf yu kæn pərˈsweıd hım, ˈpɜrhæps yu wıl stænd ə ʧæns. haʊˈɛvər, ıf hiːz ˈeniˌθıŋ laık ðə wʌnz wi hæv ınˈkaʊntərd, aı ˈhaıli daʊt yu wıl bi ˈeıbl tu ˈriːzn wıð hım. mɔrˈoʊvər, yu wʊd hæv tu rıʧ hım fɜrst, ænd ˈgıvən ðer ˌdıspəˈzıʃən, aı ænˈtısəˌpeıt ðeıl ʃʊd yu ɒn saıt."[29]

Once more struggling to grasp his words, he elaborated that the bandit faction was notably brutal, led by a figure whom reaching and swaying would present a daunting challenge. Even if approached, convincing him would prove arduous. Moreover, overcoming the hurdle of reaching him alone posed a significant obstacle.

As I left The Elder I immersed myself deeper into the daily life of Misty Hollow, I found myself navigating between the realms of NeoAnglish and English with ease, seamlessly transitioning between the two languages as the situation demanded. While NeoAnglish served as the lingua franca of the era, a demonstration of the ever-evolving nature of language, English remained my steadfast anchor amidst the swirling currents of change.

In the tapestry of my narrative, English emerged as the thread that bound together the disparate strands of my experiences, weaving a cohesive tale that resonated with clarity and resonance. With each word penned in my native tongue, I found solace in the familiarity of expression, drawing upon the rich tapestry of my linguistic heritage to convey the depths of my thoughts and emotions.

Yet, the choice to write my story in English extended beyond mere linguistic preference—it was a deliberate act of preservation, a homage to the cultural legacy that transcended the boundaries of time and space. English, with its storied history and global reach, stood as a display of the enduring power of communication, bridging the divide between past and present with effortless grace.

Moreover, English served as a bridge between worlds, offering a gateway to the treasures of antiquity for generations yet unborn. In the ever-shifting sands of linguistic evolution, English remained a steadfast beacon of continuity, its roots reaching deep into the annals of history while its branches stretched forth to embrace the boundless possibilities of the future.

And so, as I penned my tale in the language of my forebears, I did so with the knowledge that each word carried with it a weight of meaning, a connection to a rich tapestry of human experience that spanned the ages. In the end, it was not merely a story I sought to tell but a legacy—evidence of the enduring power of language to transcend the barriers of time and space and unite us all in the shared journey of the human experience.

While it's feasible to decode and comprehend both language formats with some effort, for individuals proficient in a single one of the languages, I shall henceforth render the dialogue in conventional English for the sake of consistency and convenience. However, I may still opt for NeoAnglish in certain instances where it seems more appropriate.

On the third day of my stay in Misty Hollow, I resolved to seek out Aeridian Thornbrook, the enigmatic recluse rumored to possess knowledge of the bandit encampment's whereabouts.

Following Kael's directions, I made my way to Aeridian's secluded abode, a modest dwelling nestled amidst the verdant embrace of the village outskirts.

Approaching the weather-beaten door, I rapped my knuckles against its weathered surface, the sound echoing through the stillness of the surrounding woods. Silence greeted my initial summons, prompting me to repeat my plea for entry. After a tense moment, the door creaked open, revealing a figure cloaked in shadow.

"What in the world do you want? Can't you tell I want to be left alone?" The gruff voice came from within, tinged with a note of irritation.

Steeling myself, I met Aeridian's gaze with earnest determination. "I'm sorry, sir, but I need information only you could provide me," I ventured, hoping to appeal to his altruism.

An opening appeared in the door, revealing Aeridian's weathered countenance. "You're new; I'll help you because you're new and don't understand the rules yet, one of which is to not bother Aeridian," he grumbled, begrudgingly conceding to my request.

Entering the dimly lit interior, I surveyed the cluttered space, taking note of the eclectic array of books and scrolls that adorned the shelves. Antiquated wisdom permeated the room, emanating from the trove of knowledge that lay within Aeridian's grasp.

"So what exactly are you here for?" Aeridian inquired, his tone laced with skepticism.

"I need to find the way to the bandit fortress," I replied, meeting his gaze with unwavering resolve.

"Why would you want to go there? Do you have a death wish?" Aeridian scoffed, his incredulity palpable.

"Quite the contrary, I'm here to help the people of your village," I asserted, hoping to assuage his doubts.

"Bah, there's a reason no one else is allowed to know their location: these poor bastards, thinking they're heroes, would run straight up there and get themselves killed," Aeridian retorted, his cynicism undiminished.

"Well, I'm going over there trying to negotiate, and if that doesn't work, take the fort by force!" I declared, determined to see my mission through to its conclusion

"You and what army?" Aeridian quipped, his skepticism unabated.

"Trust me, I can do it," I insisted, my confidence unshaken by his doubts.

"I'm not convinced, but I'll give you the location; maybe you can do what others can't. Though I doubt it, if you want to kill yourself, go ahead," Aeridian relented, begrudgingly agreeing to divulge the information I sought.

Aeridian, with his gruff exterior and guarded secrets, had once led the village's defenses against the first bandit raids, his knowledge of the wilderness unmatched. Yet, the weight of losses had pushed him into seclusion, and his wisdom is now a beacon sought only in desperate times.

"I do have a map here; maybe you can point it out," I suggested.

"Show me," Aeridian replied, his tone begrudging yet curious.

Carefully, I unfurled the map on the table before him, its aged parchment crinkling softly beneath my touch.

"Ah, yes," Aeridian murmured, scrutinizing the map with a practiced eye. "Well, that map isn't complete. These days, we've only got maps of specific areas you see. Your map is basically some sort of treasure map that encompasses a specific area. But as you can see, our village is located near the top of the map, and upwards is where you're going to go."

With a deft motion, Aeridian traced his finger over the assorted books and scrolls lining the shelves until he located the desired item. Retrieving a weathered scroll crafted from cloth, he unfurled it upon the table, revealing a series of crude drawings denoting key locations "Here!" he declared, indicating an empty spot on the map. "I don't see anything there," I admitted, peering closely at the map's surface.

"That's because the map is older than the encampment. They've only been here for a few months, and from there, they've been robbing people on the roads, specifically us," Aeridian explained, his voice tinged with a hint of bitterness.

"How far is it?" I inquired, eager to gauge the distance to our destination.

"Well, I don't know about your way of transportation, but on a horse, it would take you about a day," Aeridian estimated.

"Ah, so just a few hours for me then," I mused aloud, momentarily forgetting the disparities in our modes of travel.

"What?" Aeridian queried, puzzled by my statement. "Nevermind," I dismissed, realizing the futility of explaining my capabilities to him.

"You can borrow the map, but make sure to bring it back after. Preferably, slide it under my door," Aeridian instructed, begrudgingly offering his assistance.

"Thanks for your service; do you happen to know a place where I can store my supplies?" I inquired, hoping for a solution to my logistical dilemma.

"Not here!" Aeridian snapped, his patience wearing thin. "Do you know of a place?" I persisted, undeterred by his brusque demeanor.

"No, now get out of here; you got what you wanted." Aeridian dismissed me curtly, already engrossed in a tome.

Gathering the maps, I made my exit, the door closing softly behind me as I left Aeridian to his solitary pursuits.

I sought out Kael, eager to secure a safe location for my supplies.

"Yes, at my place, I've got a large empty chest with a solid padlock, and I'll give you the key," Kael offered generously.

"That's very kind of you. Do you think it could hold the bag I've been carrying?" I inquired, hoping for a solution to my burden.

"Easily," he assured me, his confidence putting my worries to rest.

Together, we made our way to Kael's abode, where he revealed a hidden compartment beneath the floorboards perfectly suited for the sizable chest.

"The chest is stuck in there; it's too heavy to get it out, but it's a safe location anyway," Kael explained as he accessed the concealed space.

I felt relief when I removed the weighty burden of technology that I deemed unnecessary for the journey ahead. I only took the Fusionizer with me. Securing my belongings within the chest, I closed it firmly, feeling the weight lift from my shoulders.

Kael handed me the key to the padlock, and I locked it securely in place. As he deftly replaced the tile over the compartment, concealing any evidence of its existence, I expressed my gratitude and bid him farewell.

With my supplies safely stowed away, I made my way outside, where my Alloyed Charger awaited. As I prepared my Alloyed Charger, a relic of a bygone era, I couldn't help but reflect on the irony of my journey. Here I was, reliant on the pinnacle of lost technology, yet increasingly drawn to the raw, untamed wisdom of the natural world. It was as if each mile traveled on this mechanical beast brought me closer to understanding the delicate balance of life that technology had once sought to dominate. The Alloyed Charger, more than just a vehicle, was a beacon of the world before—a piece of lost technology that bridged the gap between the past and my journey into this uncertain future. Its silent hum was a constant reminder of the fragile balance between what was and what could be.

As I prepared to leave Misty Hollow, a reflection caught my attention. The man staring back at me from a puddle wasn't just a survivor; he was a guardian of these new bonds and memories. The compassion and resolve in his eyes were new, sculpted by the hands of every soul I'd encountered on this path.

As I delved into the nuances of their language, I realized that words were more than mere communication; they were the bridge between souls, the first stone in rebuilding the ruins around us. Taking one last glance at the map to confirm my destination, I embarked on my journey with newfound determination.

As I revved up my bike, the hum of its engine resonated through the forest, propelling me forward on my journey. The dense canopy above gradually thinned, and the lush greenery gave way to barren patches of earth. Despite the dwindling vegetation, I pressed on, guided by the insatiable curiosity driving me deeper into the unknown. As I set off into the unknown, a part of me wondered what unforeseen challenges lay ahead. Would the decisions I make in the name of compassion and justice always hold true in the face of desperation? The world had changed, and with it, the nature of right and wrong seemed more ambiguous than ever.

[1] "Hello, who are you?"

[2] "Hello Ethan. Welcome. You come in peace, you say?"

[3] "Yes, my name is Kael Ravenscroft. What is yours?"

[4] "A pleasure, Ethan. If you need anything else, just ask."

[5] "Is this the first time you've seen someone smoking?"

[6] "Well, to summarize, what I'm smoking specifically is called 'Botanical Harmony'; it's made of sage, peppermint, lavender, and chamomile. It mostly helps me relax and focus. We don't all smoke the same herbs, of course."

[7] "No this is Misty Hollow, or at least what's left of it. The Twilight Crest is a symbolic key needed to open the temple at the top of the mountains. We owned the Crest, but it was stolen from us recently."

[8] "That's just it."

[9] They believe the temple has great riches, but it's nothing more than a myth. The temple is a sacred place, yes, but its true value lies in the history and knowledge it holds, not material wealth."

[10] "The fortress they call home."

[11] "is a place of darkness and despair. Inhabited by bandits and outlaws who prey upon de weak and defenseless."

[12] "It's not just a fortress, Ethan. It's a bastion of lawlessness, where only the strong survive and the merciless thrive."

[13] "But it's also a fortress built on fear and intimidation. I've heard tales of its towering gates, fortified with razor wire and guarded by ruthless sentinels who show no mercy to those who dare to approach."

[14] "Within its walls, chaos reigns supreme."

[15] "Crude shanties and ramshackle structures litter the landscape, adorned with the traces of past conquests and the spoils of war." [16] "Now, I will be forever in your debt, I will teach you our language and I know someone who can show you how to get to the bandit fort."

[17] "Good people of Misty Hollow!"

[18] "We come not as conquerors, but as collectors of the daily tribute owed to us. Bring forth the one responsible for the collection, and let us expedite this transaction."

[19] "See that this tribute continues to flow, lest you face the consequences of your defiance."

[20] "Next time, we expect a supply of Verdant Zephyr, along with a substantial amount of food.

[21] "Yes, how may I be of assistance?"

[22] "What aspect would you like to discuss?"

[23] "I don't disagree, but our resources and strength are limited in confronting them,"

[24] "What can you achieve alone that we haven't managed?"

[25] "I'm exceedingly doubtful. You'll be signing your own death warrant. Are you truly prepared for that?"

[26] "In that case, I won't hinder you,"

[27] "I'm not one to dictate people's actions, especially those from outside. I only handle conflicts and personal matters. But don't say I didn't warn you; returning may prove to be a challenge, if at all."

[28] "I'm afraid not,"

[29] "Nothing you likely aren't already aware of. This particular bandit group is notoriously violent, destructive, and avaricious. Their origins remain unknown to us. I know they have a leader, and if you can persuade him, perhaps you'll stand a chance. However, if he's anything like the ones we've encountered,

I highly doubt you'll be able to reason with him. Moreover, you'd have to reach him first, and given their disposition, I anticipate they'll shoot you on sight."

THE LION'S DEN

With each passing mile, the landscape transformed before my eyes. Here, in the stark contrast between the dying natural world and the remnants of a once-advanced civilization, lay the cautionary tale of humanity's quest for progress—a relentless pursuit that ultimately led to its downfall.

As I ventured deeper into this forsaken landscape, my thoughts lingered on the delicate interplay between destruction and resilience. It wasn't merely a journey across a ravaged land but a profound exploration of what it means to persist in the face of insurmountable odds.

This reflection served as a grim reminder of my own part in this saga, not just as a witness but as a participant whose actions could either echo past mistakes or forge a new path forward. Trees became sparse, their gnarled branches reaching towards a sky tainted with the ominous hues of decay. Yet, as I pressed on, the air grew heavy with the scent of desolation, a stark reminder of the world's fragile balance. This desolation mirrored my own transformation, from a life once vibrant to one shadowed by survival.

In this desolation, I saw a mirror of my own journey—from a life once filled with purpose to one burdened by survival. The decaying world around me wasn't just a backdrop for my mission; it was a constant reminder of what was at stake.

Arriving at my destination, I surveyed the scene before me. Halfway between forest and wasteland, the land lay in a precarious state of transition. Clumps of hardy vegetation clung to life amidst the encroaching decay—an assertion of nature's resilience in the face of adversity. Yet, I knew that beyond this point, the landscape would succumb entirely to the wasteland's embrace.

I was shrouded in the shadow of impending doom. There stood a fortress that struck fear into the hearts of all who dared to venture near it. This fortress was not a bastion of hope or a beacon of light, but a grim stronghold of darkness and despair, ruled by ruthless bandits who preyed upon the weak and defenseless. The fortress, a stark silhouette against the twilight sky, stood as a monument to desolation. It was a stark reminder of the fragility of civilization, now reduced to a stronghold of despair amid the wilderness.

The journey to the fortress's gates felt like a descent into the belly of the beast. Each whispered warning from the earth and each ominous message on the walls heightened the sense of an impending reckoning, as if the fortress itself were a living entity, aware of my every move. With each step, the air grew thicker, charged with an unspoken warning. It was as though the very earth beneath my feet whispered cautions, urging me to tread lightly upon its scarred surface.

As I approached the fortress, warning signs scrawled in crude graffiti adorned the walls, their ominous messages serving as a dire proclamation to all who dared to trespass. "Tûrn awæ drims, wandərerz, hre holts noɔt bʌt šadøz" one inscription wwarned,which meant "Turn away dreams, wanderers, here holds naught but shadows", while another declared, "Onlē aʊtloz, skəm, θivz, an bændɪts mē pæs, ɛl ʌðɛrz, bəwɛr!" which meant "Only outlaws, scum, thieves, and bandits may pass, all others, beware!"

In addition to those, there were several traffic signs indicating restrictions or prohibitions. One, in particular, displayed a skull and crossbones symbol.

Each stone and scrap told a story of downfall, a testament to what happens when humanity's reach exceeds its grasp.

The outer walls of the fortress bore the scars of countless battles and raids; their once proud facade is now marred by bullet holes and scorch marks. Razor wire coiled along the perimeter, a grim reminder of the fortress's intent to repel intruders by any means necessary.

Atop the towering gates, two archers stood sentinel, their eyes scanning the horizon with cold, calculating precision. Clad in tattered leather armor and wielding crude bows fashioned from scavenged materials, they watched over the fortress like silent sentinels, ready to rain death upon anyone who dared to approach.

Within the fortress, chaos reigned supreme. Crude shanties and ramshackle structures dotted the landscape, their walls adorned with the trophies of past conquests and the spoils of war. Scavenged vehicles lay abandoned in the courtyard, their rusted frames serving as a grim reminder of the fortress's violent past.

As I gazed upon the fortress from a safe distance, this was no place for the faint of heart or the weak of spirit, for within its walls, only the strong survived and the merciless thrived. I approached the gate cautiously, only to be met with a sharp command from one of the archers perched high above. "Halt! Who goes there? State your business!" he bellowed, his voice echoing across the barren wasteland.

Unperturbed, I squared my shoulders and replied, "My identity is inconsequential. I seek an audience with your leader or whoever holds authority in this stronghold."

Their laughter echoed, a harsh reminder of how far humanity had strayed. Yet beneath their scorn, I sensed a flicker of curiosity—a testament to the enduring spark of humanity, even in the darkest corners of the world.

A derisive chuckle erupted from the archer's lips as he retorted, "You must be daft if you think we'd grant you entry, let alone an audience with our boss. What reason could you possibly give us to consider such a request? Our leader would sooner take our heads than allow an outsider to enter uninvited."

"I come bearing an offer of peace, initially with Misty Hollow, but also to persuade you to cease your pillaging of innocent travelers and settlements," I countered, my tone firm and resolute.

Laughter rang out from behind the fortified gates, and a sneer crept across the archer's face as he regarded me with thinly veiled contempt. "Your proposal is laughable, stranger. You're deluded if you think anyone here would entertain such notions," he scoffed.

Undeterred, I stood my ground. "I refuse to accept rejection," I declared firmly.

With a signal to someone below, the archer's demeanor shifted, his expression turning sinister. "Kill him!" he commanded.

In an instant, arrows whistled through the air, aimed straight at my heart. But to their astonishment, I deftly caught each projectile mid-flight, my movements fluid and calculated. With a flick of my wrist, I dispatched one arrow back towards its sender, the sharp tip embedding itself just above his head.

"Now, will you grant me entry?" I taunted, a smirk playing on my lips.

Silence greeted my challenge, broken only by the creaking

of the gates as they slowly began to open. But before I could step forward, three formidable warriors emerged, forming a barrier between me and the fortress beyond.

Their armor was crafted from scraps of junk and remnants of the wild, and was a patchwork of scavenged metal plates salvaged from the husks of abandoned vehicles and torn from the wreckage of ancient buildings. Each piece bore the scars of its previous life, dented and rusted from years of neglect and decay.

Yet, despite its crude appearance, the armor provided essential protection.

Interwoven with the metal plates were strips of animal hide and fur, harvested from the creatures that roamed the desolate landscape. Thick layers of leather provided additional padding and insulation.

Under the armor, warriors wore garments fashioned from roughspun fabrics and reinforced with strips of canvas and burlap. These makeshift garments offered further protection against the elements and the hazards of battle, while also serving as a canvas for the intricate markings and symbols that adorned them.

Across their chests and backs, warriors bore the sigils of their clans and factions, painted in bold strokes of blood-red and midnight black. These symbols served as a reflection of their allegiance and their willingness to fight and die for their cause, whatever it may be.

Their helmets were equally makeshift, fashioned from salvaged motorcycle helmets, welding masks, and other discarded headgear. Horns and spikes adorned the helmets, adding to their menacing appearance and striking fear into the hearts of their enemies.

As the warriors marched towards me, their armor clanking and rattling with each step, they were a fearsome sight to behold. Clad in their makeshift armor, they were the embodiment of the post-apocalyptic ethos: survival at any cost and strength in the face of adversity.

Each warrior brandished a formidable shield and a gleaming battle axe, their imposing figures exuding an aura of raw power and primal ferocity. Conversation was not their forte; instead, they communicated through guttural grunts and growls, punctuated by terse, monosyllabic words that conveyed their intent with chilling clarity. Faced with their looming threat, I called upon every ounce of my training, prepared to turn their aggression into their downfall.

Here, at the entrance of the fortress, amidst the boundary where verdant forests reluctantly yielded to encroaching decay, I found myself confronted by these three formidable adversaries: bandit warriors whose very presence spoke of untamed strength and unyielding ferocity, their eyes ablaze with primal determination.

With the weight of an impending battle heavy upon me, I steeled myself for the clash ahead. With every fiber of my being attuned to the imminent conflict, I awaited their advance, acutely aware of the subtle shift in the surrounding landscape—from lush forest to foreboding wasteland, where the echoes of nature's resilience mingled with the whispers of encroaching decay.

As the first warrior surged forward, his axe raised high, I moved with the fluid grace of a predator, sidestepping his assault with uncanny agility. With a swift and decisive motion, I launched a barrage of strikes, my fists and feet blurring in a flurry of motion as I engaged him head-on.

Simultaneously, the other two warriors closed in, their weapons raised in tandem as they sought to overwhelm me with sheer brute force. But I was ready.

With lightning-fast reactions, I deflected their blows with precision; each strike met a calculated counterattack that kept them at bay. As the battle raged on, I danced between them with unmatched agility, my movements a symphony of grace and power as I engaged them in a deadly dance of combat.

With every strike, I felt the weight of my opponent's determination, their attacks growing increasingly desperate as the tide of battle turned in my favor. But I remained steadfast, my resolve unyielding, as I pressed forward, determined to emerge victorious against all odds.

In a final, decisive moment, I unleashed a devastating assault, my blows landing with pinpoint accuracy as I incapacitated each of my opponents in turn. With a resounding crash, they fell to the forest floor, defeated but unbowed, their weapons clattering against the earth as the echoes of battle faded into the stillness of the surrounding wilderness.

As the skirmish drew to a close and the last echoes of battle faded into the stillness of the surrounding wilderness, I found myself standing amidst the scattered remnants of our conflict. Triumphantly, I knew that whatever challenges lay ahead, I would face them with the same unwavering resolve that had carried me through this trial by nature's design. Turning my attention towards the imposing fortress looming before me, I steeled myself for the next phase of my mission. With each step towards the entrance, the weight of an impending confrontation hung heavy in the air, and my senses heightened as I prepared to confront the leader of these lawless outlaws.

I went to the gate, kicked it open, and looked around. As I entered the front gate of the bandit fortress, I was greeted by a scene of organized chaos. The courtyard bustled with activity as bandits went about their daily routines. To my left, I saw a makeshift market where stolen goods were traded and bartered. Tents and lean-tos lined the perimeter, serving as shelter for the bandits and their families.

Directly ahead, a large bonfire crackled in the center of the courtyard, casting flickering shadows on the surrounding walls.

Bandits gathered around the fire, sharing stories and laughter as they cooked meals over the flames. The scent of roasting meat mingled with the acrid smell of smoke, creating an atmosphere both enticing and foreboding.

To my right, I noticed a training area where bandits sparred with each other, honing their combat skills in preparation for future raids. Wooden targets stood at the far end of the yard, pocked with arrows from countless practice sessions.

Above it all loomed the imposing fortress itself, its walls constructed from salvaged junk and remnants of the post-apocalyptic world. Guard towers made from repurposed vehicles and scrap metal rose high into the sky, offering vantage points for the fortress's defenders. Guards patrolled the ramparts, keeping a watchful eye on the bustling activity below.

At that moment, all activity came to a standstill as every eye in the vicinity fixed on me. They were aware of the confrontation at the gates, causing them to refrain from approaching me. Instead, their stares bore into me, treating me like a nuisance needing eradication from the earth.

In a commanding voice, I demanded, "Where is your leader? I require his immediate attention!"

The onlookers remained motionless. After a brief pause, a slender figure rose to his feet. Dressed in a black leather suit with a matching cloak that shrouded his head, he sported gray fingerless gloves and boots fastened with hooks. A gray mouthcap completed his attire, casting a stark contrast to my worn jeans and jacket with visible tears. The absence of my lost hat, whisked away by the wind on my bike, hardly fazed me.

Adorned with a slender, elongated sword strapped to his back, his fierce gaze hinted at his prowess, suggesting he was one of the formidable fighters in the vicinity. His sleek physique exuded strength, emphasizing the advantage a nimble fighter held over a cumbersome warrior weighed down by cumbersome armor and a massive axe.

Confidently advancing towards me, he announced in a gravelly voice, "I'll escort you to him."

Leading the way through a concealed entrance at the rear of the stronghold, I followed him into a spacious chamber where the leader held court on his imposing throne.

The leader's room commands attention from the moment one steps inside, its spacious expanse filled with an eclectic array of furnishings and decorations. Dominating the chamber is a throne crafted from salvaged scraps of metal and jagged pieces of broken machinery, towering over the room like a twisted monument to power and authority.

The throne itself is a marvel of ingenuity and brutality, fashioned from welded-together pieces of rusted metal and adorned with spikes and jagged edges that serve as a stark reminder of the leader's ruthless nature. Despite its crude construction, the throne exudes an undeniable aura of dominance, its imposing presence casting a long shadow over the room.

Along the walls, shelves and tables are cluttered with an assortment of curiosities and trophies, each one a manifestation of the leader's prowess and ambition. Mounted animal skulls leer down from their perches, their empty eye sockets seeming to follow visitors with an unnerving gaze.

Behind the throne, a large banner hangs from the wall, emblazoned with the symbol of the leader's band of outlaws. Tattered and worn from years of use, the banner serves as a grim reminder of the group's violent history and unwavering loyalty to their enigmatic leader.

Despite the room's ominous atmosphere, there are glimpses of luxury and extravagance scattered throughout. A large fur rug covers the stone floor beneath the throne, providing a touch of warmth and comfort amidst the cold, industrial surroundings.

In one corner of the room, a small alcove houses a makeshift bed, piled high with furs and blankets for the leader's rest. Nearby, a crude wooden desk serves as a workspace, cluttered with maps, charts, and other documents detailing the bandit leader's plans and ambitions.

Overall, the leader's room is an illustration of his status as a formidable and enigmatic figure, a place where power and brutality reign supreme amidst the harsh realities of the post-apocalyptic world.

A huge guy was sitting on it, clad in a fearsome ensemble crafted from the spoils of the wilderness. As the colossal figure rose from his throne, his presence seemed to fill the room, not merely with his physical size but with an aura of unchallenged authority. Here stood a man who had carved out a kingdom from chaos, a leader who wielded fear and respect with equal proficiency. His armor, though a patchwork of conquests, was worn not as protection but as a testament to his dominion over both man and nature. His helmet, adorned with a menacing visage, sports a formidable arrangement of bear skin and bone, unmistakably fashioned from the formidable creature's head.

His chest armor boasts a rugged construction of overlapping pieces, each intricately etched with symbols of power and dominance. The centerpiece of his attire is a breastplate fashioned from thick plates of hardened leather, reinforced with metal studs and rivets for added protection. Across his shoulders, he wears a mantle of fur, a validation of his prowess as a hunter and survivor in the unforgiving wilderness.

His arms were encased in vambraces crafted from the same resilient leather as his chest armor, intricately tooled with patterns reminiscent of ancient tribal markings. Under these protective layers, sinewy muscles ripple with every movement, a manifestation of years of physical exertion and combat prowess.

As for his lower limbs, the leader wears greaves fashioned from thick layers of leather and metal plating, offering vital protection to his shins and calves. Strapped securely to his boots are spurs, adorned with jagged spikes that serve as both a deterrent to adversaries and a symbol of his authority among his band of outlaws.

In sum, the leader's attire exudes an aura of primal strength and savage cunning, reflecting his status as a formidable warrior and master of the untamed wilderness.

When I finally stood in front of the bandit leader, he looked at me with a mix of curiosity, suspicion, and perhaps even a hint of respect. The door creaked open slowly, revealing the bandit leader in his full, menacing regalia. His presence was not just announced by his imposing physique but also by the palpable shift in the air, a mix of fear, respect, and the undeniable mark of leadership. As he stood, his stature alone commanded the room, a stark silhouette against the dimly lit backdrop. His armor, a mosaic of battles won and lost, was more than protection; it was his story, written in steel and scars. His gaze sized me up with a calculating stare, trying to assess my intentions and capabilities.

His expression conveyed wariness, as I represented an unknown variable in their world of survival and conflict.

Overall, the bandit leader's look at me was a complex blend of scrutiny, assessment, and the beginning of a tentative interaction that could shape the future dynamics between us. The leader's stern gaze hinted at a tumultuous past, suggesting that his path to power was as fraught with hardship as it was with conquest.

"What do you want?" he inquired, a hint of begrudging admiration tainting his words. "I've seen what you're capable of out there. Dodging arrows,

I took down three of my best fighters simultaneously. I must admit, I'm impressed."

Unfazed by his acknowledgment, I pressed on. "I understand if you're not inclined to agree," I replied calmly. "But it's worth a shot. Here's my proposition: cease your harassment of Misty Hollow and the travelers on our roads. Return the Twilight Crest and all that you've pilfered from our people. And to sweeten the deal, throw in a generous supply of food. If you agree, I'll return to town and organize a group to transport everything back on horseback."

His response was laced with amusement. "You've got guts," he remarked, gesturing for me to accompany him outside.

As we stepped into the open air, the bandit leader's voice boomed with authority. "Whoever kills this guy gets a promotion to my second in command and can take whatever they desire from our spoils!"

As tension rippled through the crowd, every person rose to their feet, and the archers swiftly drew their bows. Even those who had been inside moments ago emerged, swelling the ranks of outlaws and bandits gathered before me.

Before drawing my weapon, I paused, considering a different kind of warfare—one fought with words and wits. "Consider the benefits of peace," I suggested, locking eyes with the bandit leader. "Your strength and resolve could be invaluable in rebuilding what's been lost. This is your chance to shape a legacy beyond mere survival." My words hung in the air, a gambit aimed not only at disarming his hostility but at sowing seeds of doubt among his ranks. Alas, it had no effect.

Before launching into action, a fleeting moment of reflection arrested my thoughts. With every adversary that fell before me, I couldn't help but ponder the cycles of violence that had come to define our existence. Was I a liberator in this desolate world, or had I become indistinguishable from those I sought to overcome? It wasn't just the potential loss of life that weighed heavily on me but the realization that with each life taken, a piece of the world's already dwindling humanity was extinguished. This battle was not just for survival but also for the soul of what remained of our world. Had the line between my own actions and those of the bandits begun to blur? In this lawless world, power asserted through violence seemed the only currency, yet I wondered if, in exercising such power, I was losing a part of myself.

Then I launched into action. A swift kick to the leader's stomach caused him to recoil momentarily, but he quickly recovered, brandishing his axe with intent. Evading his clumsy swing with practiced ease, I seized the opportunity to break his arm, wrenching the weapon from his grasp in the process. Despite his futile attempt to restrain me, a well-placed knee to his vulnerable point thwarted his efforts. As he staggered sideways, I swiftly delivered a fatal blow, the axe cleaving through flesh with a sickening crunch, sending blood spraying in all directions.

Raising my gaze, I found myself encircled by the bandits, their faces contorted in battle cries as they closed in on me. Despite their relentless assault, I fought back valiantly, felling one foe after another. Dodging swinging axes and swords, I shattered shields and deftly evaded the hail of arrows aimed in my direction. Yet, despite my skill, I was not immune to their onslaught, sustaining wounds from arrows and other weapons amid the chaos. Despite the bloodshed, the bandits persisted in their attack, their determination unwavering.

"Enough!" I yelled. They all responded by stopping and apparently hoping I would walk away. But then I grabbed the Fusionizer off my back, and a lot of them looked at me curiously, not sure whether to continue or to wait.

Survival hinges on your departure! Leave now, or face certain demise!" My voice boomed with authority, punctuating the urgency of the situation. Ignoring their cries for battle, I unleashed a relentless barrage of lethal energy bolts, swiftly incapacitating anyone who dared to challenge me. With each discharge, the area surrounding me expanded, prompting many of the bandits to reconsider their defiance and retreat.

Amidst the chaos, I pinpointed the archers who continued to launch arrows in my direction, swiftly dispatching them before they could pose a significant threat. Despite sustaining a few hits myself, I remained steadfast, determined to prevail. As the skirmish drew to a close, only a handful of adversaries remained standing, their resolve waning in the face of an inevitable defeat.

"Cease your resistance; we accept your surrender!" pleaded one of the bandits, while the rest echoed his sentiment through gestures of acquiescence. His plea for mercy echoed in the silence, a stark reminder of our shared humanity even in this desolate world. In sparing him, I sought not only information but a chance to break the cycle of violence that had ensnared us all.

The decision to spare him was not borne out of mercy but from a strategic need for information. Yet, as I stared into his eyes, I saw not an enemy but a fellow survivor, caught up in the same cycle of violence that defined our existence.

"Depart from this place and do not return," I commanded sternly, simultaneously restraining one of them as the others dispersed.

"What fate awaits me?" the captive implored, desperation evident in his voice.

"Your fate is of no concern to me," I replied calmly. "I seek only information."

"What knowledge do you seek?" he inquired, his tone tinged with apprehension.

"I want to know the whereabouts of the Twilight Crest," I demanded forcefully. My demand for the Twilight Crest's whereabouts was more than a mission objective; it was a test of the bandit leader's honor, a gauge of his willingness to part with power for the promise of peace. In this new world, where every day was a battle for survival, could trust be built on the precarious foundation of mutual necessity?"

"I am unaware of such an object; however, if it held value to our leader, it would likely be concealed behind his throne," he offered in response.

"Very well," I conceded, releasing my hold on him.

Approaching the throne, I discovered a concealed compartment at its rear, housing not only the Twilight Crest but also an assortment of treasures: an amulet, a key, a map, and a golden hunting knife. The items laid before me were not mere artifacts but symbols of a forgotten time when the world was whole. The Twilight Crest, in particular, seemed to hum with ancient energy, as if awakening from a long slumber. Pocketing them all, I swiftly exited the fortress.

Scanning the surroundings, I located the largest bag available and meticulously packed it with provisions for food until the bag could hold no more.

Observing the abundance of resources within the fortress, including clothing, food, and medicine. As I surveyed the fortress's resources, a plan began to take shape in my mind. These supplies, hoarded from countless raids, could serve as a lifeline for Misty Hollow. But more than that, they represented a bridge of understanding, a potential pathway from conflict to coexistence. My actions now bore the weight of countless futures, each hanging in the balance of my next decisions. After laboriously transporting everything to a secluded corner, I camouflaged the cache beneath a heap of scrap, rendering it indistinguishable from ordinary debris.

Confident in my resolution of the bandit situation, I made my way to where I had stationed my Charger, only to be met with astonishment when I found it missing. Despite securing it with a lock and ensuring it wouldn't operate without unlocking, its absence perplexed me, especially given its substantial weight. Realizing I had left my Omnilocator back in the village compounded my dismay.

Fortunately, luck was on my side, as I discovered several horses still housed in the stables. Without hesitation, I selected one and rode back to Misty Hollow. The journey back was a contemplation of the day's victories and the battles that lay ahead. With every hoofbeat against the earth, I felt a growing resolve to not just survive this world but to reclaim it. A sense of purpose solidified within me. This was more than a return; it was a proclamation of my commitment to change, to fight not just against the bandits of the world but against the despair that had taken root in the heart of humanity.

As the horizon bled with the hues of dusk, my resolve hardened. Misty Hollow was not just a destination; it was a beacon of hope in a world starved for redemption. There, I would rally the survivors, forge alliances, and together, we would carve out a sanctuary in this desolate world.

The fading light of day cast long shadows, intertwining with my thoughts of what lay ahead. This journey had not only been a confrontation with the darkness that pervaded our world but also a beacon of hope for what we could rebuild. The battles fought today were not just for survival but for the promise of a dawn where such strife was no longer our only reality.

A sense of purpose solidified within me. This was more than a return; it was a proclamation of my commitment to change, to fight not just against the bandits of the world but against the despair that had taken root in the heart of humanity.

THE TEMPLE OF KNOWLEDGE

iding back through the wilderness, I could really feel the difference in speed compared to the Charger. As I rode back through the forest on horseback, the dense canopy above cast dappled shadows on the winding path. Rays of golden sunlight filtered through the canopy, dappling the forest floor with patches of luminous greenery and painting a mosaic of light and shadow across the foliage. This wilderness, with its unyielding beauty and stark reminders of what once was, echoed the duality of my own journey. As the light filtered through the trees, casting shadows that danced with the whispers of the wind, I saw parallels in my own path—a blend of light and dark, hope and despair. It wasn't just a passage through nature, but a journey through the remnants of a world lost to time, urging me to look beyond the desolation for the seeds of renewal. The rhythmic clip-clop of the horse's hooves echoed softly against the earth, blending with the rustle of leaves and the gentle murmur of a nearby stream.

The scent of pine mingled with the earthy fragrance of damp soil, invigorating my senses as I navigated through the wilderness. Shafts of light danced across the forest floor, creating a mesmerizing play of light and shadow that shifted with the swaying branches overhead.

Occasionally, a small creature darted across the path, disappearing into the underbrush with a fleeting rustle of leaves. The horse's steady gait carried me forward, each stride bringing me closer to my destination. Despite the tranquility of the forest, there was an underlying tension in the air, and I felt it was urgent to drive onward.

As I rode, I couldn't shake the feeling of being watched, as if unseen eyes followed my every move from the depths of the forest. This sensation, akin to a shadow flickering at the edge of vision, stirred within me a resolve born from countless trials. Each glance back into the silent depths of the forest served as a stark reminder of the isolation my path necessitated—a lone sentinel against the encroaching darkness of forgotten realms. Yet I pressed on, my determination unwavering, as I rode through the verdant wilderness.

In these moments of solitude, amidst the untouched beauty of the wilderness, the weight of my mission pressed heavily upon me. Not just a quest for survival, but a pursuit of redemption for the world we had lost. Each step forward was a step toward the hope of rebuilding and turning back the tide of desolation that had claimed our civilization.

As I rode through the desolate landscape, the rhythmic beat of my horse's hooves echoed in the stillness of the night. The moon cast an ethereal glow upon the world, illuminating the path ahead with its silvery light. Despite the tranquility of the night, I felt unease gnawing at the edges of my consciousness.

About halfway to my destination, I decided to pause and take stock of my surroundings. Pulling gently on the reins, I brought my horse to a halt, allowing him a moment of respite. The darkness seemed to stretch on endlessly, broken only by the occasional glimmer of starlight.

As I dismounted from my steed, I felt a chill run down my spine. The air was heavy, as if the very land itself held its breath in anticipation of what was to come.

This palpable tension between the serenity of nature and the remnants of human folly served as a stark reminder. It whispered of nature's resilience, of its capacity to endure and reclaim spaces once scarred by human ambition.

In this balance, I found a reflection of my own quest: a battle not against the wild but alongside it to restore a semblance of harmony to the shattered tapestry of our world. It was a call to arms, not of weapons but of will—a test of whether one could be both the sword and the shield against the impending void.

In this quietude, I found a resolve not just to witness but to mend, to contribute to this cycle of renewal. I couldn't shake the feeling of being watched—the sensation of unseen eyes following my every move.

Seeking solace in the familiar routine of camp, I tethered my horse to a nearby tree and unpacked my provisions. A green apple and a bowl of stew awaited me, their comforting warmth a welcome sight in the cold night air. Sitting down by the makeshift campfire, I savored each mouthful, the taste of home offering a brief respite from the trials of the road.

As I ate, my thoughts turned to the treasures I had acquired from behind the Bandit Leader's throne. The silver necklace, with its intricate spider web design, seemed to pulse with an otherworldly energy. Was it merely a trinket, or did it hold some deeper significance? Only time would tell.

Examining the key, I puzzled over its inscription: "Cæpyard Synapso," meaning "Junkyard Junction." The words seemed to echo with a sense of history. Alongside the text, there was a symbol etched into the aged metal, a complex intertwining of letters and decorative lines.

The symbol was a fusion of the letters of the words themselves, with ornate loops and swirls connecting them in a mesmerizing pattern. From the central point where the letters intersected, delicate lines branched out like tendrils, weaving a tapestry of intricate designs that seemed to dance across the surface of the key.

As I traced the lines of the symbol with my fingertips, I marveled at the skill and artistry that had gone into its creation. Each curve and flourish was meticulously crafted, imbuing the symbol with a sense of elegance and grace.

With a sense of reverence, I pocketed the key, feeling its weight against my palm. Whatever mysteries awaited us beyond the door, I knew that this symbol would guide us somewhere, perhaps leading us ever closer to some truth to be discovered.

Turning my attention to the map I had acquired, I traced the familiar landmarks with my finger. The bandit fortress loomed large in the center, its ominous silhouette a stark reminder of the challenges that lay ahead. Yet, amidst the desolation, I spotted a distant structure marked on the map—a lone building standing amidst the wasteland.

Could this be Junkyard Junction, the place I sought? I wondered about the possibility of hanging tantalizingly in the air. I resolved to uncover the truth behind this enigmatic location.

Gazing at the golden hunting knife, I marveled at its craftsmanship. The blade gleamed in the firelight, evidence of the bandit leader's wealth and power. Yet its true purpose remained a mystery, their secrets hidden behind a veil of uncertainty.

As the fire crackled and danced, casting long shadows across the barren landscape, I knew it was time to press on. I had a purpose that was driving me forward. I mounted my horse once more and set off into the night.

It seemed like a long night still, but eventually, by daylight, I finally arrived back at Misty Hollow. I went straight to the village Elder to show him my haul of food I had brought and the Twilight Crest.

The return to Misty Hollow was a surreal experience, with the familiar sights and sounds of the village now imbued with a deeper significance. Each greeting from the villagers, each smile that met my eyes, felt like threads weaving me tighter into the tapestry of this community. It was a poignant reminder that my journey was not just a solitary endeavor but a shared struggle, with each victory bringing not just personal satisfaction but hope to those who had dared to dream of a better tomorrow alongside me.

The Elder stood in awe at the sight of the abundance of food before him.

"Your generosity knows no bounds," he exclaimed. "Did you manage to retrieve these provisions from the clutches of bandits?"

I nodded, a hint of weariness in my voice. "The situation unfolded quite differently than anticipated. I managed to eliminate their leader, after which I found myself facing the entire camp, and after a fierce battle, only a handful were able to flee."

The Elder's eyes widened in disbelief. Seeing the disbelief in the Elder's eyes, a flicker of loneliness crossed my heart. 'Yes, I alone,' I thought, the reality of my solitude dawning anew. This power, while a boon in combat, set me apart from those I aimed to protect, casting me as the other in a world I desperately wanted to belong to. "You, alone, vanquished such a formidable force? We struggle to contend with even a few of them. Please enlighten me on your methods."

I paused, considering how best to explain. "It's a long story," I began. "But it boils down to this: I've been augmented with advanced technology, granting me abilities beyond the ordinary."

These augmentations, remnants of a world teetering on the brink of technological singularity, endowed me with capabilities far beyond human norms. Born of necessity in a world ravaged by war, they were not just enhancements but a bridge between what was and what could be, a hope for humanity's resurgence. What may appear insurmountable to others is merely a minor hurdle for me. And this," I said, revealing the Fusionizer on my back, "is a relic of my origins."

Perplexed, The Elder inspected the weapon. "What manner of device is this?"

"It harnesses the power of the technology from whence I came," I elucidated. "Its energy bolts can dispatch multiple adversaries with a single shot. It's akin to the force of a hundred swords striking at once."

"Is it akin to a firearm?" he inquired.

His familiarity with weaponry that was more advanced than traditional swords and axes caught me off guard. "Yes, precisely. It's a sophisticated type of firearm," I confirmed. "And it never exhausts its ammunition, or in this instance, energy bolts. But I'm intrigued by your knowledge of firearms. I haven't encountered any in these lands or elsewhere."

"I possess knowledge of certain things that others do not," The Elder elucidated. "Knowledge that I believe is best kept hidden. If the concept of firearms were to spread among the populace, imagine the havoc it could wreak. I am well-versed in the history of weaponry, the wars, and the atrocities of the past."

He paused, deep in thought, before continuing. "However, the role of firearms in those events is a topic of debate. The discourse surrounding gun control has persisted for generations. Yet, for now, I view it as a risk not worth taking. There may indeed be firearms in circulation once more, but I prefer they remain unknown to the common folk. Even the monks would concur with my stance, particularly since neighboring communities are similarly unaware."

"Wait a moment. Monks? Other communities? What are you referring to?" I interjected, seeking clarification.

"Ah, I neglected to mention. Within the temple, there is a particular sect of monks. They dedicate their lives to unraveling the temple's vast reservoir of knowledge, undertaking arduous studies for extended periods. Their aim is to utilize this knowledge for the betterment of our world, hence the absence of firearms. And due to the potential misuse of the knowledge contained within, only a select few are permitted entry to the temple," The Elder elaborated.

"I understand. But what about these other communities?" I inquired with keen interest.

"To our knowledge, there exist three other communities," The Elder explained. "Two of them are akin to ours in structure. While we are aware of each other's existence, meaningful interactions are infrequent. Typically, we maintain a respectful distance, preferring not to meddle in each other's affairs. The third group comprises a bandit encampment. However, unlike the ones you've encountered thus far, they tend to keep to themselves, venturing out only for essential raids to replenish their supplies.

Regrettably, they've raided one of the neighboring villages before, albeit sparingly engaging in highway robberies due to the scarcity of travelers. It could also be the vast distances separating them from our settlements that deter frequent interactions. Nevertheless, they exhibit a level of self-sufficiency and resort to aggression only in dire circumstances. Nonetheless, they pose a problem that requires resolution."

"I can see that," I acknowledged. "But what exactly are the distances we're talking about?"

"Well, the closest community is approximately four days' journey away if you travel on a swift horse. If you're headed towards the bandit fortress you recently encountered, you'll need to continue north. The second community lies two weeks' travel to the east from this village. Beyond that village, the bandit camp is another week's journey to the north. I have a map that you can borrow; it contains the locations of all the communities and the paths leading to them," The Elder explained.

"Then my aim is to bring all of you together!" I declared. "I believe it's feasible and would offer numerous advantages, such as resource sharing, defense and security, exchanging skills and knowledge, and many other benefits that would enrich everyone."

"And how do you propose to accomplish that? While we are relatively close in proximity, the distances still pose a significant challenge, among other obstacles we'll face," The Elder pointed out.

"I'll find a way; just allow me some time to strategize," I assured. "For now, I'll bid farewell and prepare myself for the journey up the mountain to the temple. Could you guide me on the route from here?"

"Embarking on the path to the temple is considered a rite of passage for those seeking its wisdom. Along the ascent, you'll encounter several checkpoints, each presenting a riddle to guide you to the next. It's a test of worthiness," The Elder elucidated.

"I'm skeptical, but I'll follow your guidance and attempt to unravel the mysteries. Before I depart, there's one more favor I'd like to ask," I added.

"Anything," The Elder replied.

"I'm in need of some new clothing and armor, preferably leather," I stated, gesturing to my worn attire. "As you can see, my current garments have seen better days."

"Indeed," nodded The Elder. "I will fetch them for you." "Thank you," I replied. "While you do that, there are some matters I need to attend to. I'll meet you at your door shortly."

With that, we parted ways. I made my way to Kael's place to access my OmniLocator. Upon arrival, Kael greeted me warmly, and I explained my need to access my inventory. I began by scanning all the maps I possessed, consolidating them into one unified map on the OmniLocator. Though the resulting map was somewhat vague and inaccurate, it provided a clearer view of the available paths.

Next, I used the OmniLocator to locate my Alloyed Charger, discovering it was a day's journey away from the bandit fortress.

Despite this, I decided to prioritize visiting the temple of knowledge first. I stowed my Fusionizer, anticipating it wouldn't be necessary for the journey, but ensured to bring the OmniLocator along to access and upload any available information within the temple.

Upon returning Aeridian's map, I made my way back to The Elder's dwelling. Just as I reached the door, he emerged, and together we entered his abode. Inside, he presented me with the new clothing, which bore a striking resemblance to my previous attire, almost as if he had intentionally selected them to maintain continuity. Swiftly, I exchanged my worn garments for the fresh attire, then donned my armor over the newly acquired clothing.

The leather armor incorporated strategic metal components for enhanced protection. Crafted from the finest hides and reinforced with carefully forged metal plates, this armor offers a formidable defense against both physical and elemental threats.

The leather torso piece boasted a sturdy framework of interlocking metal plates, seamlessly integrated with supple leather panels to provide optimal flexibility and resilience. Gleaming steel rivets secured the layers in place. Across the shoulders and chest, polished steel pauldrons offered additional protection.

Metal bracers adorned the forearms, intricately etched with arcane symbols and fastened securely with leather straps. Under his boots, steel greaves safeguard his lower legs. It was embossed with ornate patterns and embellished with subtle engravings.

I returned The Elder's map, and we went outside. There, he pointed out the route I had to take to reach the mountain's trailhead. I bid The Elder goodbye, and he wished me good luck. I then headed towards the trail that would lead me up the mountain.

It was a crisp autumn morning when I set out on my journey, following the village Elder's instructions to seek wisdom at the ancient Temple of Knowledge. The winding path led me into the looming mountain range, towering peaks draped in ethereal mists.

After a few miles of trekking through the dense forest, I stumbled upon a large, flat stone resting in a small clearing. Etched upon its weathered surface was the first riddle:

"Beneath the boughs where sunlight filters,

Among the roots that earth's soil tillers,

Seek the path that winds 'round steady,
Your next step awaits when you're ready."

I studied the words carefully, scanning my surroundings for any clues. Nearby, I noticed a trail spiraling around the thick trunk of an ancient oak. Trusting my instincts, I followed the winding path.

The way was not easy, as gnarled roots burst through the earth, threatening to ensnare my feet with each step. Swarms of biting insects pursued me relentlessly until I stumbled into a murky marsh. After struggling through the sucking mud, I finally emerged, caked in filth, to find the second stone amidst a cluster of towering ferns.

This riddle read:
"Where waters rise from unseen fonts,
And mossy sculptures, like sentinels, hunts,
Climb past the mists that ghostly swirl,
To reach the heights that the world unfurls."

My gaze lifted towards the distant peaks, where wispy tendrils of fog coiled around the craggy outcrops. I noticed a narrow trail ascending through the low-hanging clouds and set off in that direction.

The air grew thin as I scrambled over loose shale, every breath a labor. Suddenly, the clouds parted, revealing a breathtaking vista of soaring granite spires. It was there, perched precariously on a jutting ledge, that I found the third stone inscribed with another enigmatic verse:
"Where talons grip unyielding stone,
And winds whisper in plaintive tone,
Let sharp eyes guide unwavering feet,
For a mistaken step would be defeat."
I realized I would have to traverse along the dizzying precipice, avoiding even a sidelong glance into the dizzying depths.

With slow, calculated movements, I inched across the narrow path, fingertips clinging to every slight protrusion and nook.

Finally, I reached the other side, trembling but victorious over the perilous traverse. A short distance away rested the fourth stone, sheltered by a shallow overhang. But there was a greater obstacle between me and the stone.

An enormous, grotesque creature lumbered into view around the next switchback. At first, it resembled a bear, but there were...abnormalities. Wicked spines protruded along its hunched back, oozing a viscous fluid. Its musculature strained against the mottled, tumor-riddled hide. But worst of all were the four lean, sinewy limbs that stretched far too long, each tipped with hooked talons that gouged deep furrows in the frozen earth.

The mutated beast's nostrils flared as it caught my scent. A guttural roar ripped from its fanged maw, echoing across the stark alpine slopes. That's when it charged, jaws unhinged and snapping.

While a normal human would surely have frozen in sheer terror, my enhanced physiology allowed me to react with unnatural speed. I sidestepped the beast's initial attack with feline grace, the ground shuddering as it thundered past.

The mutant bear skidded to a halt, pivoting with shocking agility for its grotesque size. It issued another bone-chilling bellow before lunging once more.

This time, I stood my ground, tensing my body in preparation. As those gnarled, serrated claws swiped towards me in a deadly arc, I dropped into a sidekick, my booted foot slamming into the outstretched limb with the force of a battering ram.

Even with my amplified strength, I felt the jarring impact reverberate through me, but the sickening crunch announced the bear's ruined foreleg. It reared back with an anguished roar.

Before the beast could recover, I pounced, driving my armored fists into its gnarled flank, savaging the mutated flesh. In the heat of battle, time seemed to slow, offering a moment of clarity.

Each blow I dealt was a testament to the training that had honed my instincts, yet it was the cause I fought for that sharpened my resolve. Beyond survival, this was a fight for the future, a declaration that we would not go gently into the night. Fetid blood and ichor sprayed from the rents I tore.

Yet the beast's tenacity was unbelievable. It twisted with terrifying speed, those jagged fangs clamping onto my shoulder. I grunted in pain, feeling those piercing teeth punch through skin and muscle as if they were so much wet tissue. The bear thrashed its mighty head, aiming to rip my entire arm from its socket.

Capitalizing on the brief opening in its defenses, I slammed my palm against the monster's skull in a percussive strike, followed by a relentless barrage of blows that cratered its bulbous skull like wads of dense putty striking solid rock. At last, its ferocious jaws went lax, its fangs relinquishing their grip on my mangled flesh.

The mutated bear toppled sideways, crimson gushing from its ruined head, its flesh already knitting itself back together. Even so, I didn't relent in my onslaught until the beast's thrashing ceased, and those soulless black eyes stared lifelessly.

For several minutes, I knelt there, hot blood pulsing over my shredded coat, soaking the pristine snow. My heightened metabolism grappled furiously to mend the damage. But despite the unnatural resilience the EterniX had imbued me with, such traumatic injuries couldn't simply be hand-waved away.

The icy winds seemed to grow even more punishing in their ferocity, with knife-like needles assaulting my exposed wounds. In this moment of raw exposure, a fleeting doubt crept into my resolve. The relentless forces of nature, indifferent to human struggle, mirrored the cold void left in the aftermath of our societal collapse. This vulnerability, though fleeting, was a stark reminder of the fragility of existence, pushing me to ponder the true extent of my capacity to effect change in this vast, indifferent world. My breath came in ragged gasps, each exhale spawning billowing clouds of vapor. I would need to find shelter—some refuge from the relentless elements—to complete my regenerative cycle.

Near the switchback, a craggy overhang provided a shallow alcove in the mountainside. It was not ideal, but it had to suffice. For the next two agonizing hours, I remained hunkered there, shudders wracking my body as the serum worked feverishly to repair my ravaged flesh, knitting muscle and resculpting shattered bone.

At last, the wounds had closed, and the constant ache of healing was fading. I rose stiffly, stamping some feeling back into my legs, now numb. As the numbness faded, replaced by a throbbing reminder of the ordeal, a wave of introspection washed over me. This pain was a testament to the sacrifices required on this journey—not just of flesh and blood, but of the soul itself. Each scar was a narrative of survival, a badge of honor in the relentless pursuit of a cause greater than oneself. With a final glance at the mutant bear's corpse rapidly being consumed by the insatiable snows, I squared my shoulders and resumed my way towards the stone. The riddle etched there gave me pause:

"Where silence shrouds in hushed domain,

And still, waters, their depths contain,
Seek the road 'neath the watcher's breadth,
Whose gaze defies the shadow's stretch."
My eyes were drawn upwards to the sheer cliff towering

above, where a single shaft of light pierced through a narrow cleft, like a vigilant sentinel keeping watch over the secluded hollow below. Carefully, I circled the base until I found the narrow crevice hinted at by the riddle. Pulling myself through the tight fissure, I emerged into a wondrous grotto, the far side opening to reveal a sunlit glen.

There, amidst a swaying grove of aspens, stood the fifth and final stone.
"When aspen leaves in zephyrs swayed,
Find peace within the verdant glade.
Flecked shadows flee the sinking sun.
journey's end has at last begun."

With a sense of reverence, I followed the sunbeams filtering through the quaking trees. Until cresting the final rise, I beheld an awe-inspiring sight— the ancient Temple of Knowledge, hewn from the very rock itself. Ornately carved pillars framed the arched entrance, beckoning the seekers of enlightenment.

As I slowly approached the sacred edifice, I felt a profound sense of humility, for the path had demanded every ounce of my perseverance, wisdom, and courage. Though my body ached from the toils, my spirit felt renewed with the promise of revelations to come. With a steadying breath, I stepped through the threshold into the inner sanctum, ready to receive the temple's guarded truths.

The Temple of Knowledge emerged from the swirling mists like a sentinel of wisdom. Perched atop the jagged peak, its grand silhouette loomed against the backdrop of the frozen landscape, evidence of the enduring power of knowledge.

Carved from the frost-kissed stone of the mountain itself, the temple's imposing facade rose defiantly against the elements. Its towering spires reached towards the frosty heavens, their edges etched with intricate patterns that shimmered in the pale light of the sun.

I approached the temple's grand entrance, a massive gateway framed by columns of ice that sparkled like diamonds in the crisp mountain air. The heavy wooden doors, adorned with ancient runes and symbols of knowledge, stood sentinel, their icy surfaces glistening with a veneer of frost.

As I stood before the entrance, a chill wind whispered through the mountain pass, carrying with it the faint scent of ancient knowledge and the promise of enlightenment. The temple seemed to pulse with an otherworldly energy, beckoning me to step inside and unlock its secrets.

As I reached out to push the doors open, a surge of anticipation coursed through me. However, upon attempting to open the doors, I encountered resistance. It dawned on me that I needed to insert the Twilight Crest into the indentation on the wall adjacent to the door. As I did so, a distinct clicking noise resonated throughout the chamber. With the task complete, I returned to the door once more. With a heave, I applied pressure to the heavy wood, feeling the resistance give way gradually. The door groaned in protest, as if reluctant to reveal the secrets held within.

With a final push, the doors swung open, revealing a dimly lit chamber beyond. A rush of cold air greeted me, carrying with it the musty scent of ancient parchment and the promise of hidden knowledge.

Taking a deep breath, I stepped over the threshold and into the heart of the temple, eager to uncover the mysteries that awaited within its icy halls.

Inside, the temple unfolded into a vast labyrinth of corridors and chambers, each one filled with the accumulated knowledge of ages past. Towering shelves lined the walls, stacked high with scrolls, tomes, ChronoArchives and artifacts from civilizations long forgotten. Shafts of sunlight filter through stained-glass windows, casting kaleidoscopic patterns of color upon the ancient tomes that line the shelves.

The air is thick with the scent of parchment and dust, mingling with the faint aroma of incense that wafts through the air. Soft candlelight flickers in alcoves, casting dancing shadows upon the walls and illuminating the intricate carvings that adorn every surface.

As seekers wander through the temple's labyrinthine corridors, they encounter chambers devoted to every imaginable field of study. Astronomy, philosophy, history, alchemy—the temple holds the sum total of human knowledge, preserved for eternity within its hallowed halls.

As I explored the temple, I was struck by the abundance of knowledge that surrounded me. Each scroll unfurled, every tome perused, felt like peeling back layers of time, revealing the cumulative wisdom and folly of civilizations past. This treasure trove of human achievement and error was both a beacon and a warning.

The weight of this knowledge bore heavily upon me, a solemn reminder that our future hinges not just on the preservation of this wisdom but on the wisdom to discern its lessons.

Hours slipped away as I delved into scrolls, books, and the vast repository of data stored within the ChronoArchives. Much to my surprise, a significant portion of the information was in English rather than NeoAnglish, prompting speculation about the linguistic landscape of this society. Despite the presence of a distinct alphabet, NeoAnglish materials were plentiful, hinting at its prevalence in everyday communication.

Among the wealth of resources, I stumbled upon a trove of maps that offered glimpses into the geography of Washington. While they spanned different epochs, primarily predating the war, each map provided unique insights into the region's evolution. Despite discrepancies arising from temporal disparities, I meticulously scanned and cataloged them using my OmniLocator, gradually piecing together a comprehensive overview of the area.

These maps, now unified in my OmniLocator, were not just a record of the past but a beacon for the future. They illuminated the potential for connections between scattered survivors, hinting at a network of alliances and shared knowledge. This was the groundwork for a new civilization, one that could rise from the ashes of the old, bound by shared purpose and newfound unity. Though not entirely accurate, these maps afforded me valuable insights into the layout of villages, buildings, and other landmarks, laying the groundwork for my future endeavors.

Various gaps in historical records were evident across the ChronoArchives, prompting me to diligently upload missing information to my neural interface. Among my discoveries was the revelation of the duration of my cryosleep—a staggering 700 years elapsed before radiation levels subsided to tolerable thresholds. The widespread deployment of cobalt bombs contributed to this prolonged period of environmental hazard, rendering vast swathes of the world inhospitable for an extended duration.

Cobalt bombs, encased in cobalt-59, underwent transmutation to cobalt-60 upon exposure to the intense neutron flux of nuclear detonations.

Emitting gamma radiation with a half-life of approximately 5.26 years, cobalt-60 poses significant health risks due to its ability to penetrate tissues and induce cellular damage.

During this tumultuous era, global affairs remained eerily tranquil as radiation-stricken zones lay desolate and uninhabited. Isolated pockets of humanity, spared from the devastation, found themselves severed from the modern world, their technological prowess limited by dwindling resources and environmental constraints. Despite their best efforts, technological relics such as

ChronoArchives and radiant illuminators endured, their longevity an indication of human ingenuity. However, as centuries passed, knowledge of their operation waned, and dwindling supplies hastened their obsolescence, consigning them to the annals of history.

Yet, amidst the challenges of post-apocalyptic existence, humanity persisted, drawing upon resilience and adaptability to navigate the harsh realities of their environment. Though the vestiges of their once-great civilization faded into obscurity, the indomitable spirit of humanity endured, forging a path toward a new dawn.

Despite the challenges posed by the post-apocalyptic landscape, remnants of valuable knowledge persisted in the form of salvaged books and documents, offering insights into diverse subjects ranging from construction techniques to medical practices. This juxtaposition of survival against the backdrop of a world that once teemed with innovation and progress painted a poignant picture. It was a reminder that the essence of humanity's legacy lay not in the ruins but in the resilience to rebuild, to learn from the ashes of the past and forge a new narrative of hope and reconstruction Armed with this fragmented wisdom, survivors ingeniously fashioned rudimentary tools and implements, leveraging their ingenuity to adapt to their new reality.

As radiation levels gradually stabilized over time, brave pioneers began to venture into the once-forbidden territories, cautiously reclaiming the desolate landscapes for habitation.

However, the arduous process of rebuilding civilization proved daunting, and the inhabitants found themselves grappling with the harsh realities of their environment. Though strides were made in establishing semblances of community and infrastructure, the arduous journey toward reclaiming their former world remained a distant dream, forever obscured by the shadows of a bygone era.

My quest for information regarding the enigmatic Ascendant Matrix yielded frustratingly scant results; not a single mention of it graced the tomes and scrolls I diligently combed through.

This void of information only fueled my determination, turning the quest into more than a search for answers—it became a challenge to the shadows of oblivion that threatened to engulf the remnants of our world. This journey, fraught with peril and shadowed by the remnants of a fractured world, has been a crucible for my transformation. Beyond the physical trials, it has been the internal journey—a reshaping of my beliefs, desires, and fears—that has marked the true passage. Each step forward has not only been a stride towards my goals but also a step in the evolution of my own identity, from a solitary wanderer to a beacon of hope for those scattered souls striving towards a dawn yet unseen Yet, within this resolve lay a silent battle—a tug-of-war between the drive to uncover the mysteries of the past and the fear of what truths they might unveil. This internal conflict was my constant companion, sharpening my focus yet casting long shadows of doubt that danced just at the edge of my consciousness. The Ascendant Matrix was not merely a tool or a weapon; it was a beacon of hope, a key to unlocking a future where the darkness of the past no longer held dominion over the survivors However, amidst the troves of data, I stumbled upon a ChronoArchive containing encrypted records, alluding to the existence of the elusive Nexus Vault. Though the contents remained beyond my grasp, I possessed a glimmer of hope—a tantalizing fragment of the puzzle awaiting decryption.

Undeterred by this setback, I immersed myself in mastering an array of practical skills essential for survival in the unforgiving wilderness. From honing crafting techniques to refining repair skills, from mastering the art of hunting to acquiring rudimentary medical knowledge, each skill acquired represented a crucial step towards self-sufficiency in this harsh new world.

With my thirst for knowledge partially quenched and my repertoire of skills expanded, I bid farewell to the hallowed halls of the temple, took back the Twilight Crest, and embarked on the journey back down the mountain. As I prepared to leave the temple, a newfound sense of connection to the scattered communities of survivors emerged within me. This connection, forged not just by shared history but by shared hardship, strengthened my resolve. It was a silent vow, a promise made in the silent halls of ancient knowledge, that I would not rest until the fragments of humanity were united.

This quest transcended personal salvation; it was a covenant to mend the broken world, to stitch together the fabric of human society that had been torn apart. et, as the familiar contours of Misty Hollow came into view, a niggling sense of unease tugged at the edges of my consciousness. Unseen challenges lurked on the horizon, their shadows mingling with the light of a new dawn, promising that my journey was far from over.

With the twilight crest securely in my possession and the echoes of ancient wisdom guiding me, I set my sights on the daunting task ahead: uniting the disparate strands of humanity into a single tapestry, vibrant with the promise of a reborn world.

The shared heritage housed within these stone walls was a testament to our common past and a potential foundation for a unified future. The notion that I could play a role in weaving these disparate threads into a cohesive tapestry filled me with a purpose that transcended mere survival. Guided by newfound proficiency and aided by the serene tranquility of the weather, my descent unfolded with remarkable ease, hastening my return to the foothills below. As I navigated the winding path down the mountain, the crisp air carried the scent of pine and the distant sounds of the awakening valley below, a symphony of nature that soothed the weariness in my bones and kindled a fire of determination in my heart.

TRIUMPH AMIDST ADVERSITY

Returning to Misty Hollow, despite having discovered the whereabouts of Junkyard Junction through the temple maps and recognizing its significance, I remained steadfast in my commitment to uniting the communities. With a solid plan in mind, I made my way to The Elder's residence, eager to discuss my strategy with him.

Upon knocking, the door swung open, revealing not The Elder but a burly figure clad in yellow shorts and a snug shirt, accentuating his muscular frame with only two straps intersecting his torso. Just as the door opened, I took a moment to adjust to the unexpected sight before me. A figure stood as a stark contrast to the environment I had come to associate with The Elder. His presence, marked by his attire and build, hinted at a story yet untold, a narrative intertwined with the fate of Misty Hollow.

"Who might you be?" I questioned.

"I am Enzo Russo," came the reply.

"Could you enlighten me as to the reason for your presence here? And where might I find The Elder?" I inquired further.

"The Elder is unwell; I am attending to his care," Enzo explained.

"Is there a particular ailment troubling him? Perhaps there's some assistance I could offer?" I offered.

"Regrettably, The Elder's condition signifies his imminent departure from this world," Enzo somberly stated.

"Departure? You mean… he's passing away?" I sought clarification.

"Yes, he is in his final moments," confirmed Enzo. "May I have a word with him?" I pleaded urgently.

"Certainly, please come inside. He rests behind the curtains to the left of his bed," directed Enzo.

I entered the room and approached The Elder's bedside. "Elder, is it true? Are you truly departing from this life?" I inquired softly.

"Yes, I have come to terms with it. My time here draws to a close," The Elder responded.

"Who will assume your responsibilities once you're gone?" I pressed.

"I have a daughter named Elena. She will shoulder the burden in my absence," he disclosed.

Elena's eyes held a depth that spoke of countless untold stories, a testament to the resilience woven into the fabric of Misty Hollow. As she spoke of her father and the legacy he left behind, a fleeting shadow of vulnerability crossed her face—a reminder of the personal stakes she held in the fate of their community.

"Elder, I came here to tell you about a plan to unite the four communities," I revealed.

"You should discuss this matter with Elena," he suggested. "I have briefed her about you. She will be receptive to your proposals. Now, if you'll excuse me, I wish to spend my remaining moments in solitude."

The Elder's voice was a whisper, a gentle breeze carrying the weight of a lifetime. "My journey ends, but yours has only just begun. Remember, the strength of Misty Hollow lies not in its past but in the promise of its future. You, Ethan, are a beacon of that future.

Feeling a pang of sorrow at the looming loss of The Elder, I sought out Enzo and inquired about Elena's whereabouts.

"She's outside, lending aid to the villagers," Enzo replied. "You'll recognize her by the flowing robe of finely woven fabric, cinched at the waist with a belt, and the sturdy leather boots she wears. Her hair is tied back in a ponytail, and she wears a golden circlet on her head."

"Thank you for your guidance," I expressed my gratitude. "I shall go to her immediately."

Stepping out into the village, I wandered until I spotted her assisting an elderly woman with her groceries. Seizing the opportunity, I approached her.

"Whenever you have a moment, I'd like to speak with you," I conveyed.

"Of course, I'm free now; I just finished up," she responded. "I am Ethan; The Elder mentioned he had briefed you about me," I introduced myself.

As I introduced myself to Elena, the weight of the responsibility I was about to assume pressed heavily upon my shoulders, a tangible reminder of The Elder's faith in me and the expansive legacy I was poised to inherit.

In my voice, I tried to convey the weight of my journey and the burdens I carried, not just for myself but for the future of Misty Hollow. My travels had not only been a quest for knowledge but a deep, personal pilgrimage to understand the role I was to play in the tapestry of our interconnected fates.

"Ah, Ethan, the hero of Misty Hollow! I heard you journeyed to the Temple of Knowledge. How was your experience?" She inquired with enthusiasm.

"It was enlightening," I said. "I've gained invaluable knowledge and wisdom from the visit. Information that will undoubtedly aid me on my path."

The air seemed to hold its breath as I spoke, carrying the weight of my words to Elena. Her eyes, a mirror to the resilience and hope of Misty Hollow, reflected back at me the shared understanding of our significant roles. This was more than a mission; it was a calling that bound us, a silent vow made amidst the echoes of our forebears and the whispering wind.

"I trust it was not an easy journey; it seems your armor bears a significant tear. You should have it seen to by the blacksmith," she advised.

"Thank you; I'll see to it. However, my purpose here today is to discuss a matter I intended to bring up with The Elder, but unfortunately, his health has declined," I explained.

"Yes, I was saddened to hear of my father's illness. Now, it falls upon me to manage his duties in addition to my own. But what did you wish to discuss?" she inquired. As Elena spoke of her father, her voice carried a blend of sorrow and resolve. "Inheriting his duties is not just about continuing his work; it's about building on his legacy, ensuring that Misty Hollow thrives not just in body, but in spirit. And I believe, with your plan, we can achieve just that.

"Well, I have devised a plan to amalgamate the four communities into one cohesive unit. The aim is to foster consistent collaboration, paving the way for a unified future," I explained.

"Yes, my father mentioned your intentions. It's certainly ambitious. Do you have a concrete plan?" Elena inquired.

"Indeed, it comprises several steps, all geared towards envisioning the potential of collective effort when initiated now," I replied.

"Please enlighten me. How do you propose to achieve this?" Elena pressed.

I proceeded to outline my plan: "Firstly, communication is paramount. All communities must establish a means to converse, facilitating discourse on important matters and everyday occurrences. To this end, I will construct radios and provide training to village leaders on their usage. These devices will form a network, enabling communication among the villages. Additionally, I will extend this network to travelers journeying to and from your settlements.

Once communication is established, we turn to checkpoints.

These will serve as trading posts, fostering commerce among the communities. Over time, these checkpoints will evolve into independent hubs, complete with militias for defense, traders, travelers, and necessary amenities. Each checkpoint will also be equipped with a radio for inter-checkpoint communication.

Depending on the distance, multiple checkpoints may be erected along each route to expedite travel.

Furthermore, diplomatic missions will be organized to visit each community, promoting goodwill and initiating discussions on collaboration and alliance-building. While radio communication suffices for most exchanges, face-to-face meetings will be essential for crucial discussions.

A council will be formed to oversee community leadership, comprising village leaders and selected representatives.

Cultural exchange programs will further strengthen bonds, fostering understanding, trust, and camaraderie among diverse groups.

Lastly, joint projects requiring collaboration, such as infrastructure development, resource management, or defense initiatives, will be undertaken to foster interdependence and cooperation.

By implementing these strategies and demonstrating an unwavering commitment to unity, the communities can overcome geographical barriers. To bring this vision to life, we'll start small, focusing on building trust and demonstrating the tangible benefits of our collaboration. Success in these initial endeavors will be crucial for gaining widespread support and momentum.

Undoubtedly, the most challenging aspect will be soliciting assistance from each village. Convincing the bandit camp may pose a particular challenge, but I believe showcasing the benefits and superiority of cooperation over their current ways may sway them.

Their formidable fighting strength could make them valuable allies in forming a militia. My role in the plan will focus on setting up communications. Your task will involve handling other aspects, such as establishing checkpoints and fostering collaboration among the various communities. Managing those matters isn't something I can take on. It's essential that you all learn to work together effectively, and that responsibility rests with you." I concluded.

That's an impressive plan, indeed. I can envision its success, although rallying everyone to collaborate will be the real challenge," remarked Elena.

"Are you willing to be the pioneer community in this endeavor, forming alliances?" I inquired eagerly.

"Yes," affirmed Elena, "I'm onboard with working alongside you on ta shared. Do you need anything from me?"

Elena's agreement was a beacon of hope, a testament to the strength found in unity. In the quiet that followed Elena's agreement, a torrent of thoughts washed over me. For so long, I had walked a path shadowed by solitude, my goals as distant as the horizon. Now, amidst the ruins of a world clinging to the threads of unity, I found myself weaving a tapestry of connections that stretched beyond mere alliances. Elena's faith, mirroring that of her father's and the villagers, grounded me. It was a mirror to my own evolution, from a lone seeker of knowledge to a pillar upon which the hopes of a fractured community could lean. This journey was shaping me, not just as a leader but as a part of something greater than myself—a testament to the power of unity in the face of adversity.

It reminded me that the foundation of any lasting change is cooperation and a shared vision. In her willingness to stand with me, I saw the first real glimmer of a united future, a community that could rise above its fragmented past and forge a path of collective resilience and mutual support.

"Not at the moment; I'll begin by constructing the initial four radios. Afterward, I'll chart the most strategic course for each community, visiting them individually and endeavoring to persuade them," I explained.

I headed to the blacksmith's workshop to address my armor's repairs. He assured me the task would be completed within a day, prompting me to return for the newly refurbished gear.

Following the blacksmith's visit, I made my way to Kael's residence. Spotting him lost in thought by the left window, I approached and exchanged greetings.

"Salutations, my friend. Your exploits and ventures, especially your pilgrimage to the Temple of Knowledge, must have left you with much to ponder," Kael remarked.

"Indeed, the temple provided invaluable insights," I replied. "I come seeking your aid on several matters."

"In what way may I assist you?" Kael inquired.

"Firstly, I require a space to construct four radio devices," I explained. "Would you be amenable to offering a guest room for this purpose?"

"Certainly, you're welcome to utilize one, provided you tidy up afterward," Kael consented.

"Secondly," I continued, "I seek to retrieve my bag, containing salvaged technological components from past endeavors essential for the construction of the radios."

Lastly, I broached the topic of companionship on my forthcoming journeys, inviting Kael to join me. After elucidating my plan to unite the communities, he agreed to accompany me.

"Very well," I concluded. "We shall embark once the radios are complete. However, I still lack some materials necessary for their construction. So it might take some time."

Venturing to the marketplace in search of specific components, I found some but realized more were needed. The marketplace was just beginning to awaken, stalls slowly coming to life under the soft morning light, a testament to the community's resilience and the simple continuity of daily life despite the looming shadows of greater quests.

The marketplace in Misty Hollow buzzed with activity, a vivid tapestry of colors and sounds. Stalls laden with goods from all corners of the community showcased the diversity and resourcefulness of its people, from intricately woven fabrics to hand-forged tools, each item telling a story of tradition and innovation.

Determined, I sought assistance and bumped into' a mysterious individual known as "The Seeker," who had overheard my talk with Kael and claimed he could lend a hand in my quest.

"So, I know of' a place called TechForge Citadel," The Seeker told me. "It's a spot of which I've heard many tales. One of' the yarns that was spun to me was that it was some kind o' electronics manufacturing haunt; whatever that might mean, I'm certainly talkin' 'bout a place where electronics could be found and be what ye may seek."

The TechForge Citadel, a behemoth of the old world, stands as a silent testament to the duality of progress—its innovation birthed from ambition, yet its abandonment a reminder of hubris. As we stepped into its shadow, the air around us thickened with the scent of ancient metal and the whispered echoes of a bygone era. Light filtered through broken windows, casting fragmented shadows that danced along the debris-strewn corridors, guiding us into the heart of forgotten sagas etched in rust and silence. As we navigate its forsaken corridors, every echo tells the story of a civilization reaching for the stars, only to fall into the shadows of its own making.

"That sounds interesting; do you happen to know the directions there?" I asked.

"Aye, I've skirted 'round the place a time or two, but never ventured inside. I've only peeked at its edges because, nearby," said The Seeker, "I spotted all sorts o' queer critters. They looked like colossal buzzing bugs with wings as wide as me arms, but these weren't yer ordinary bugs. Their bodies shimmered with metallic hues, and their stingers were like jagged spears, glinting' danger-ously in the sunlight. They sported a grayish color with dark metallic tinges, like silver in the moonlight. I wasn't keen on gettin' too close. I didn't want to get too close; they seemed hungry and ready to pounce. Not to mention, it was downright menacing.

But I do know the way; on horseback, it's 'bout three days from here. I'll lead the way, but ye best be preparin' yourself with weapons, 'cause I reckon these critters'll be quite the trouble, and we'll surely have to face 'em."

"Aren't you scared to go there and confront them?" I inquired.

"Aye, but that's what I've got ye for, aye? From what I've heard, 'bout ye, ye could handle 'em, I reckon, and with me perhaps limited aid, we might just be able to fend 'em off," said The Seeker.

"Maybe you're right. But perhaps we could use some extra help. I know someone who might be willing to join us. Let's plan to leave tomorrow around noon. We'll meet up in front of The Elder's house as our rendezvous point. Make sure you've got a horse, decent armor, a weapon, and enough food to last a few days," I suggested.

"Sounds like a plan, boss," drawled The Seeker.

"Boss?" I surprisingly asked.

"Sure thing. I might be the one pointin' us in the right direction, but ye're the one makin' the calls and gettin' things done, ain't ye? Seems mighty fittin'," he responded.

"My name is Ethan; you can call me by my name or whatever you fancy; I'm not an authority figure," I said.

"Sure thing, boss," said The Seeker.

"Right," I said.

I returned to Kael's place and greeted him once more. I outlined our plan to visit the TechForge Citadel and the risks involved with the creatures there. Despite the dangers, I asked if he'd consider joining me and The Seeker on our journey, knowing his skills could prove invaluable. He agreed, and we discussed the departure details.

"Lastly," I said, handing him the Voltcaster, "I want you to have this weapon."

After explaining its use, Kael appeared to grasp its significance. It seemed he, like myself, understood the gravity of my mission to unify the communities and the measures required to achieve it.

As the sun dipped below the horizon, I wandered towards a bustling corner of the village where folks were gathering around a bonfire.

The air was alive with the sounds of music, with drums and tambourines setting the rhythm, while voices rose in harmonious chants, creating a pleasant evening ambiance. People mingled, chatting, feasting, and enjoying themselves, some engrossed in lively board games. Amidst the festivities, I struck up a conversation with a woman named Aria Sterling, who kindly offered to mend the tear in my vest and shirt. Gratefully accepting her offer, I noted the location of her house for our meeting in the morning, eager to avail myself of her expertise as an experienced tailor.

I made my way to Kael's residence, finding him already lost in slumber. With a sigh, I settled onto the guest bed, succumbing to the embrace of sleep. Hours passed in the quiet of the night until a glimmer of dawn began to edge its way into the room, rousing me from my rest. Kael still slept soundly, so I slipped out into the burgeoning morning.

As darkness reluctantly yielded to the soft hues of dawn, I felt a sense of eager anticipation wash over me. The gradual transition from night to day seemed to stretch time itself, caught in a delicate balance between the past and the future. Though morning approached, it felt as if I stood suspended in a timeless moment, poised on the threshold of a new day.

With each passing moment, my impatience grew palpable, manifesting in restless fidgeting and aimless pacing. I busied myself with trivial tasks, rearranging my supplies or meticulously inspecting my gear in a futile attempt to ward off the creeping sense of unease that accompanied the pre-dawn hours. The world outside remained shrouded in an eerie half-light, casting long shadows that seemed to dance and sway with a life of their own.

Despite my best efforts to distract myself, my thoughts inevitably drifted back to the impending dawn. It loomed on the horizon like an unspoken promise, beckoning me forward into the uncertain embrace of a new day. Yet, for now, I remained trapped in the in-between, suspended between the fading darkness of night and the tentative light of morning.

As the first hints of sunlight began to streak across the sky, my anticipation reached a fever pitch. With each passing moment, the promise of morning grew more tantalizing, drawing me ever closer to the threshold of a new day. And so I waited, yearning for the moment when the dawn would finally break and the world would awaken anew.

Wandering nearby Aria's house, I noticed her standing in front of the door, smoking an herbstick.

"What are you doing up so early?"

"I'm usually up earlier than this. I find that I work best in the early hours of the morning. I was just taking a break right now."

"Sounds good to me; I'm ready to get those tears fixed," I said.

"Once I finish my break, dear," she said. "Could I have a drag, then?" I asked.

"Sure," she said as she handed the herbstick to me. I took a breath and felt a sense of calm wash over me, as I did when I first tried it, accompanied by clarity of thought. The soothing aroma and herbal blend induced a relaxing sensation, helping me unwind and focus my mind.

"Where do you get such an herbstick anyway?"

"Didn't you know?" Aria asked? Next to the pharmacy, there is a woman who deals in herbs, botanicals, and wraps. You can make your own combination, or you can just buy the herbstick itself. Just give her something shiny or seemingly valuable."

"I'll keep it in mind, thank you," I said.

"Now let's get those clothes fixed, shall we?" Aria said.

Within a short matter of time, she had sawn my shirt and jacked it back together thoroughly, making sure it would stay fit.

"Thank you," I said. "What do I owe you?"

"Just consider it a gift. You can repay me with a dance whenever you're around in the evening," she giggled.

"Sure thing, just give me a nudge when we're both there," I said, smiling.

Before joining my companions, I followed her advice. I fetched one of the energy cores I had stored. These cores, gleaned from the vanquished drone, were modest in size, akin to half a baseball. They paled in comparison to the colossal core nestled within the drone's chassis, dwarfing them sixfold.

Nonetheless, they possessed considerable potency, akin to compact yet formidable batteries.

Next, I sought out the domicile purportedly housing the purveyor of herbal wares. I rapped on the door but received no immediate response. Undeterred, I knocked once more. From within, a woman's voice called out, groggily pleading for patience. At last, the door swung open, revealing a disheveled figure cloaked in a nightgown, her hair awry, and her eyes heavy with sleep.

"I'm sorry, did I wake you up?" I asked somewhat nervously. "Did you wake me up? Did you make me up? Isn't it

obvious? People around here know I'm never up yet around this time; why did you need to wake me?" The woman replied.

"I'm profoundly sorry, ma'am," I said. "I'm an outsider, and I was just here to buy an herbstick."

"Herbstick, really? I'd really wish you would've come by later, but since I'm awake now, what do you want?" she asked.

"Well, do you know Aria Sterling?" I asked, "I tried one of hers, and I found those especially pleasant. I'd like the same blend as her, if you remember."

"Yes, yes, I know what you mean; she comes by often enough. How do you intend to pay for it, though?" she asked.

"Well, I have this," I said as I showed her the energy core.

Her eyes suddenly opened wide, as she had been immediately shocked awake.

Certainly," she said, "that is quite a rarity. In fact, I've heard of these things. A while back, a wanderer was in town specifically looking for what he described as what you have there. Supposedly, it's some device that, in his words, stores, generates, or distributes energy. If you give me that, I'll give you a daily supply of herbs and even new sticks whenever you want. now on, no strings attached. Come back any day, and you'll have your herbstick for as long as you want. But only if you come by noon. And days you aren't here won't add to the next day. It's simply fifteen a day. Is that agreeable?"

"Definitely, yes, that would be perfect for me," I said.

"Then hand it over, and for the first day, I'll supply you with a large supply of herbs. Aria was supposed to drop by today, but since you've roused me from my slumber so early, I can whip up a fresh batch before she arrives," she said, a hint of annoyance creeping into her voice.

"Well, it's not that early," I muttered.

"Another rule for scoring these sticks is to mind your tongue around me. It's too early for sass," she retorted, her frustration evident.

"Very well, it's a deal," I acquiesced.

She disappeared briefly into her abode, rummaging through her stores before returning with a sachet of herbs, the stick itself, and a pocket of matches.

"Here you go, sir. Now, if there's nothing else you need, I'd like to get myself ready for the day," she said briskly.

"That's all. Thank you!" I replied.

With a sharp click, she shut the door, leaving me to stow the sachet safely in my vest pocket.

I reckoned it was now an appropriate time to rendezvous with my companions and embark on our journey.

After waiting a bit at our rendezvous point, my companions arrived. We greeted each other and departed for our journey.

As we left, the sky was filled with hues of pink and gold. My steadfast companions Kael, The Seeker, and I embarked on our arduous three-day journey to the Techforge Citadel. With supplies strapped to our horses and determination etched on our faces, we set out from our campsite nestled amidst towering pines, ready to face whatever challenges lay ahead. Before we left, I lit up my herbstick and enjoyed it's aroma and the calmness and focus that went over me.

The path ahead was rugged and unforgiving, winding through dense forests, treacherous mountain passes, and vast plains. We navigated through winding valleys and across rushing rivers, overcoming obstacles such as hostile wildlife and unpredictable weather. Our journey tested not only our physical endurance but also our resolve and camaraderie.

"By the stars above, them wolves were fierce today," exclaimed The Seeker, his voice carrying a hint of amusement despite the danger we had just faced. "But we showed 'em who's boss, didn't we?"

"Aye, that we did," agreed Kael, his gaze scanning the horizon for any signs of further danger. "But we best keep moving if we want to reach the citadel. before nightfall."

And so we pressed on, our spirits undeterred by the challenges we faced. Along the way, we shared stories of past adventures and dreams of what awaited us at our destination. Despite the fatigue weighing heavy on our shoulders, our determination to succeed only grew stronger with each passing mile.

As we traversed deeper into the wilderness, the landscape shifted, giving way to vast plains and rolling hills. Here, we faced new challenges, navigating treacherous terrain and unpredictable weather. Torrential rains lashed at us, threatening to wash away our progress, while fierce winds threatened to topple us from our saddles. But through it all, we remained resolute, our spirits undaunted by the trials we faced.

"Weather's got a mind of its own, it seems," remarked The Seeker, his words punctuated by a gust of wind that nearly knocked us off our horses. "But we'll weather this storm, just like we've weathered everything else."

With each passing mile, the landscape grew increasingly unfamiliar, and the air tinged with the scent of smoke and ash as we drew closer to our destination. As the shadows of the citadel rose before us, a moment of stillness fell over our group. Kael, usually so steadfast, glanced at me with a hint of uncertainty, while The Seeker's usual banter quieted. 'What if what we find changes everything?' I mused aloud, more to myself than to them. The question hung in the air, a specter of the unknown challenges that lay ahead. 'Then we face it together,' Kael responded after a moment, his voice firm. 'And we adapt, as we always have.' His words, simple yet profound, echoed the sentiment of our collective journey. Our mission was more than just a quest for unity; it was a test of our resolve, our ability to confront the unknown and, perhaps, to redefine the future of Misty Hollow.

At long last, the Techforge Citadel loomed on the horizon, its towering spires proof of the ingenuity and craftsmanship of its creators.

But as we approached, we were met with a formidable obstacle—a towering cliff face that barred our path. Undeterred, we devised a plan, scaling the sheer rock walls with the skill and agility of seasoned climbers.

With ropes secured and muscles straining, we ascended ever higher, our determination unwavering in the face of adversity. At last, we reached the summit, greeted by the sight of the sprawling citadel spread out before us.

But our journey was not yet complete, for within its walls lay untold dangers and mysteries waiting to be uncovered. "Looks like we made it, lads," I said, a note of relief in my voice as I surveyed our surroundings. "But we best stay on our guard. Who knows what awaits us within those walls?"

"Hey, that's the attitude," said Kael with excitement in his eyes. "There's nothing quite like some adventure to get your heart racing, right?"

The Seeker's eyes widened with apprehension as he surveyed the terrain below. "By the stars above, Ethan, ye best keep yer wits about ye," he cautioned, his voice hushed with a touch of unease.

"Down yonder, I spied creatures the likes of which I've come across afore," The Seeker mused, his tone carrying the weight of experience. "Massive they were, with wings spread wider than the branches of an ancient oak. But these weren't your run-of-the-mill woodland critters, no sir."

I cocked an eyebrow, remembering our previous banter about these enigmatic beings. "You've tangled with them before?" I inquired, intrigued by The Seeker's nonchalant demeanor.

"Aye," he confirmed with a nod, his eyes twinkling with a hint of mischief. "Their bodies gleamed with an otherworldly sheen, like they'd been kissed by the forge of the gods themselves. And their stingers, Ethan, are sharper than a serpent's tooth and twice as lethal. A queer gray hue draped 'round 'em, laced with veins of dark metal, as if they'd been born from the heart of a mighty mountain. I tell ye, I felt a shiver down me spine just layin' eyes on 'em. They weren't lookin' for a friendly chat, that's for certain."

I exchanged a glance with my companions, a silent understanding passing between us. We may have reached our destination, but our journey was far from over. With the area around the citadel swarming with these menacing creatures, we knew we would need to proceed with caution if we were to uncover the secrets hidden within the Techforge Citadel. And so, with hearts full of determination and minds sharp with anticipation, we prepared to face whatever challenges lay ahead.

"We'll have to figure out whether they're actually hostile," I said. "Maybe we can pass just by them."

"Well, you go ahead and see," said the seeker. "Ain't no way I'm getting close to those things first."

"If they're hostile, you'll have to fight them as well, you know," I said.

"Well, reckon that might be true, but why don't you go take a gander and see if they're dangerous, huh?" remarked The Seeker in his usual manner.

I went closer, and as the creatures sensed our presence and began advancing towards us with alarming speed, a sense of urgency washed over us.

With a quick exchange of glances, we knew we had to act swiftly to fend off the impending threat.

I gripped the Fusionizer tightly in my hand, its energy core pulsating with anticipation. Drawing upon its power, I unleashed a barrage of searing energy bolts towards the approaching creatures, aiming to create a barrier of intense heat to deter their advance. The bolts crackled and hummed through the air, casting an ominous glow as they streaked towards our adversaries.

Beside me, Kael wielded the Voltcaster, its energy reservoir crackling with power. He fired a steady stream of energy bolts towards the creatures, each bolt arcing through the air with deadly precision. The crackling energy sizzled and popped as it struck its targets, causing the creatures to recoil in pain.

Meanwhile, The Seeker, his bow in hand, took aim with practiced ease. I watched in amazement as he notched an arrow onto his bowstring and drew it taut. With unwavering precision, he released the arrow, and it sailed through the air, finding its mark amidst the chaos and striking true.

As our combined onslaught rained down upon the creatures, they faltered and stumbled under the barrage of attacks. Their metallic forms sizzled and smoked as they recoiled from the relentless assault, their advance momentarily halted by the ferocity of our counterattack.

Surprised by The Seeker's remarkable marksmanship, I couldn't help but marvel at his skill. His arrows found their targets with uncanny accuracy, each shot hitting its mark with deadly precision. It was as if he were a natural-born marksman, his aim true and unwavering even in the heat of battle.

Emboldened by The Seeker's prowess, we pressed our advantage, redoubling our efforts to drive back the creatures and force them into retreat. With each blast of energy, crackle of power and tthe twangof the bowstring, we fought with unwavering determination, united in our resolve to emerge victorious against the encroaching threat.

And as the last of the creatures fell before our combined might, we breathed a collective sigh of relief, our hearts pounding with the exhilaration of triumph. Though battered and weary, we stood tall in the aftermath of the battle, our weapons still crackling with residual energy as an assertion of our hard-won victory.

Amidst the wreckage of our hard-won victory, a sea of lifeless forms lay scattered around us, an attestation to the ferocity of our battle. As we caught our breath and surveyed the aftermath, a sense of relief washed over us, knowing that we had proven ourselves capable of standing against the relentless horde.

"Those Mantara Hornets sure put up a fight, but we showed 'em who's boss, eh, boss?" The Seeker chimed in, his tone laced with a hint of pride.

"Mantara Hornets?" I queried, raising an eyebrow at the peculiar name.

"Yeah, well, seemed fitting, didn't it? Can't just go around callin' 'em 'creatures' all the time. Gotta give 'em a proper name, like. Makes it easier to talk about 'em," The Seeker explained, a mischievous twinkle in his eye.

"I suppose you have a point," I conceded, nodding in agreement.

The TechForge Citadel stands as a towering relic of industry amidst the desolation of the post-apocalyptic world. Once a thriving electronics factory, its towering smokestacks now stand silent against the ashen sky, devoid of the plumes of industry they once exhaled.

Surrounded by rusted barbed wire fences and crumbling concrete walls, the Citadel exudes an aura of desolation. Its exterior, adorned with faded signage and weather-worn logos, speaks to a bygone era of technological prowess and innovation, now lost to the annals of time.

Within its dilapidated halls, rows of long-abandoned assembly lines gather dust, their machinery frozen in time like relics of a forgotten age. Conveyor belts, now rusted and broken, lie dormant amidst the cavernous chambers, silent witnesses to the passage of years.

Despite the silence, echoes of past industry linger within the citadel's empty corridors. Ghostly whispers seem to emanate from the rusted machinery, a haunting reminder of the bustling activity that once filled these halls. In the quiet aftermath of our skirmish with the Mantara Hornets, I found myself reflecting on the TechForge Citadel's haunting beauty—a poignant reminder of nature's reclaiming power and the delicate balance between creation and decay.

Amidst the decay, shadows dance in the dim light that filters through broken windows, casting eerie shapes on the dusty floors.

The air is heavy with the scent of rust and decay, mingling with the faint aroma of ozone that permeates the abandoned complex.

Within the citadel's crumbling walls, the legacy of mankind's technological prowess lies dormant, waiting to be rediscovered by those brave enough to venture into its depths.

The landscape transformed as we neared the TechForge Citadel, the once verdant expanses giving way to a stark, almost alien terrain. Shadows of towering structures loomed like specters of a bygone era, their steel skeletons ensnared by nature's relentless grasp. The air, tinged with the metallic scent of rust and decay, whispered secrets of the old world, carried on the winds that swept through the desolate grounds. This threshold between the natural and the man-made world served as a poignant reminder of the fine balance between progress and preservation. Here, at the edge of civilization's remnants, we stood as witnesses to the enduring battle between the creations of mankind and the inexorable forces of nature.

As we ventured deeper into the building, I took a moment to outline the specific items we needed to scavenge. With a shared understanding of our objective, my companions set off to search while I kept an eye out for anything of value. After a thorough exploration, we managed to unearth a handful of promising pieces of technology that could aid in our endeavor to construct the radio devices. Despite our progress, it was evident that we still lacked sufficient resources to complete the task at hand.

However, our search led us to a partially open door, revealing a staircase descending into darkness. Curiosity piqued, and we made the unanimous decision to explore further, eager to uncover what lay beyond. With cautious steps, we descended into the depths below, our anticipation mounting with each passing moment. Eventually, we found ourselves standing in a vast chamber, the air thick with anticipation as we surveyed our surroundings.

The room teemed with frenetic energy, an incessant hum filling the air as Mantara Hornets darted to and fro in a symphony of motion. Everywhere I looked, the walls pulsed with life, the surface alive with the intricate patterns of their honeycomb-like hives. Each hexagonal cell pulsed with activity, housing the larvae and pupae of the colony, tended to with meticulous care by the worker hornets.

The walls themselves seemed to throb with life, the organic structure of the hives intertwining with the crumbling architecture of the abandoned factory. Strands of glistening resin dripped from the honeycombs, coating the surrounding surfaces in a sticky web of amber. Everywhere I turned, the air was thick with the scent of honey and wax, an overpowering sweetness that hung heavy in the stagnant air.

Amidst the labyrinthine chambers of the hive, Mantara Hornets scuttled about their duties with single-minded determination. Some busied themselves with the construction of new cells, while others ferried pollen and nectar from the outside world, their abdomens swollen with the precious cargo. Above it all, the queen Hornet presided over her domain, a regal figure ensconced within the heart of the hive.

But beneath the surface of industry, danger lurked amidst the bustling activity of the Mantara colony. The Hornets were fiercely territorial; their buzzing formed a constant reminder of the peril that surrounded us. Any false move could provoke their ire, unleashing a swarm of angry insects upon unwitting intruders.

As I gazed upon the bustling hive, I couldn't help but feel a sense of awe at the intricate web of life that unfolded before me.

Here, amidst the ruins of mankind's once-great achievements, nature had reclaimed its rightful place, weaving a tapestry of beauty and danger amidst the decaying remnants of civilization.

The queen hornet stood as a mesmerizing fusion of technology and biology, a creature of unparalleled complexity and power. Her form, once that of a mere insect monarch, had transcended its natural limitations, melding seamlessly with the surrounding technology to become something altogether more formidable.

From her sleek metallic carapace to the pulsating veins of circuitry that threaded through her body, every aspect of the queen hornet bespoke a union of man and machine. She exuded an aura of raw energy; her very presence was an indication of the boundless potential of symbiosis between organic life and artificial intelligence.

Gone were the frailty and vulnerability of her insectoid kin; in their place stood a being of unmatched resilience and strength. No longer bound by the constraints of mere flesh and exoskeleton, the queen hornet had become impervious to all but the most potent of attacks.

Even the most powerful attacks would glance harmlessly off her armored form, their potency nullified by the intricate web of defensive mechanisms that now shielded her from harm. She moved with a grace and fluidity that belied her immense size, each movement an affirmation of the seamless integration of man and machine.

But perhaps most unsettling of all was the intelligence that burned behind her multifaceted eyes—a cold and calculating intellect that spoke of eons of evolution and adaptation. She was no mere insect queen; she was a living manifestation of the inexorable march of progress, a harbinger of a new era where the boundaries between man and machine blurred and merged into one.

As I looked further around, I saw that beneath the towering structure of the hornet queen, the room stretched out, its walls adorned with a myriad of technological wonders. Shelves lined the periphery, laden with an array of devices and tools, each one an affirmation of the ingenuity of those who once inhabited this place.

Among the shelves, intricate machines hummed softly, their screens dark and silent in the absence of power. Yet despite their dormancy, they exuded an air of latent potential, their sleek surfaces gleaming dully in the dim light that filtered through the chamber.

Clusters of cables snaked across the floor, connecting various consoles and terminals in a tangled web of wires and circuitry. Here and there, faint glimmers of light flickered sporadically, the remnants of a bygone era where electricity flowed freely and machines thrummed with life.

Amidst the technological marvels, tools of every shape and size lay scattered haphazardly, their surfaces dulled with age and disuse.

The eerie silence of the TechForge Citadel was a stark reminder of the world that once was—a world where technology promised a brighter future. Now, as we ventured through its forgotten halls, it felt like walking through a dream of the past, with the shadows of innovation lingering in the air.

From precision instruments to heavy-duty machinery, each item spoke of a time when this room buzzed with activity.

As I peered further into the depths of the chamber, my gaze fell upon the sprawling expanse beneath the towering structure of the hornet queen. The room seemed to stretch endlessly, its walls adorned with a myriad of technological wonders that whispered tales of a bygone era. Shelves lined the periphery, laden with an array of devices and tools, each one a witness to the ingenuity of those who had once inhabited this place.

Among the shelves, intricate machines hummed softly, their screens dark and silent in the absence of power. Yet despite their dormancy, they exuded an air of latent potential, their sleek surfaces gleaming dully in the dim light that filtered through the chamber. It was as if they were merely biding their time, waiting for the spark of electricity to bring them back to life.

Clusters of cables snaked across the floor, connecting various consoles and terminals in a tangled web of wires and circuitry. Here and there, faint glimmers of light flickered sporadically, the remnants of a bygone era where electricity flowed freely and machines thrummed with life. It was a stark contrast to the stillness that now pervaded the chamber, a silent demonstration of the passage of time.

Amidst the technological marvels, tools of every shape and size lay scattered haphazardly, their surfaces dulled with age and disuse. From precision instruments to heavy-duty machinery, each item spoke of a time when this room buzzed with activity. Now, however, they lay dormant, their once-potent capabilities reduced to mere relics of a forgotten age.

I noticed various devices and tools we would be able to use for the purpose of constructing radios. In fact, I believed if we could access them, we would have enough to build plenty of the radio devices needed. But somehow we needed to get to the things first.

"The things we need are here," I said, a glimmer of hope igniting within me. "Let me try something."

With cautious steps, I approached a box of antennas, my eyes scanning the surrounding area for any signs of danger. As I reached out to open the box, I couldn't shake the feeling of unease that prickled at the back of my neck. And then, with a sudden burst of movement, the hornets descended upon us, their wings buzzing with fury as they prepared to defend their queen at all costs.

"Now you've done it," said The Seeker, his voice tinged with resignation as he notched an arrow onto his bow.

As the hornets swarmed towards us, their numbers seemed endless, a dark cloud of fury descending upon us with relentless determination. Undeterred, we met their onslaught with unwavering resolve, our weapons raised, and our hearts filled with the fire of battle.

Kael, his Voltcaster crackling with energy, unleashed a storm of firepower upon our foes, each bolt finding its mark with deadly accuracy. With each shot, he carved a path through the mass of hornets, his determination shining like a beacon amidst the chaos of battle.

Beside him, The Seeker stood firm, his bow drawn taut as he let fly a volley of arrows that sang through the air like a chorus of vengeance. With unerring precision, his shots found their mark, piercing the hearts of our adversaries with pinpoint accuracy.

But even as we fought valiantly against the tide of hornets, the queen herself remained a formidable foe, her massive form looming over us like a dark specter. With a deafening buzz, she launched herself into the fray, her wings beating with a thunderous roar as she descended upon us with lethal precision.

Despite our best efforts, her augmented form seemed impervious to our attacks, with her metallic exoskeleton deflecting our blows with ease. With each strike, she shrugged off our assault, her eyes glowing with an otherworldly gleam as she met our gaze with unyielding defiance.

Yet still, we fought on, our determination unbroken as we pressed forward against overwhelming odds. With each passing moment, the intensity of the battle only grew, and our resolve tempered in the crucible of combat as we refused to yield to the queen's relentless onslaught.

In desperation, I scoured the chamber for any sign of weakness, my eyes darting frantically across the chaotic landscape of battle until they finally alighted upon a cluster of exposed wires dangling from the ceiling. With a surge of inspiration, I realized that our only hope lay in disrupting the queen's connection to the machinery that surrounded her, severing the lifeline that sustained her formidable power.

"Kael, the wires!" I shouted, my voice cutting through the clamor of battle like a clarion call. "We need to disrupt her connection to the machinery!"

My companions, ever attuned to my intentions, sprang into action without hesitation. Kael, his eyes gleaming with determination, adjusted his aim with practiced precision, directing his energy bolts towards the exposed wires with unwavering accuracy. The Seeker, his bow drawn taut and his arrows poised for action, mirrored Kael's movements with uncanny synchronicity, his movements an attestation to his unparalleled skill as a marksman.

As their combined assault rained down upon the exposed wires, sparks flew in a dazzling display of pyrotechnics, the crackling energy dancing like a symphony of chaos amidst the dimly lit

chamber. With each strike, the wires sizzled and smoked, their once formidable integrity faltering under the relentless barrage of our attacks.

With each shot, the queen's metallic form convulsed violently, her augmented exoskeleton writhing with spasms as the crackling energy surged through her body like a tempest unleashed. The electrical currents danced across her once impervious defenses, searing through her metallic hide with an intensity that belied our unwavering determination.

As the relentless barrage of energy bolts continued to rain down upon her, the queen's movements grew increasingly erratic, her once calculated strikes devolving into wild, desperate flails as she struggled to maintain her footing amidst the maelstrom of chaos that engulfed her. With each passing moment, her once-indomitable resolve wavered, her strength ebbing away like the dying embers of a fading flame.

And then, with a final burst of effort, we unleashed a concentrated barrage of energy bolts, directing our combined firepower towards the queen's weakened form with a ferocity born of desperation and determination. The air crackled with tension as our onslaught intensified, our weapons blazing with an incandescent fury that illuminated the darkness of the chamber with a blinding radiance.

With a deafening explosion that reverberated through the chamber like the roar of a mighty thunderstorm, the queen's metallic form convulsed violently before collapsing to the ground in a smoldering heap, her once formidable presence reduced to nothing more than a lifeless husk. The air crackled with residual energy as the echoes of battle faded into the ether, leaving behind a palpable sense of triumph amidst the wreckage of our hard-won victory.

As the acrid scent of burnt metal and ozone filled the chamber, we stood amidst the aftermath of our triumph, our breath ragged and adrenaline still coursing through our veins like molten fire. The weight of our exertions hung heavy in the air, a tangible reminder of the trials we had endured and the sacrifices we had made in the pursuit of victory.

With weary but determined eyes, we surveyed the scene before us, taking in the sight of the fallen queen and the scattered remnants of her once formidable army. The chamber lay in disarray, its walls scarred by the ferocity of our battle, yet amidst the chaos, there was a sense of newfound motivation and resolve that filled the air like a beacon of hope in the darkness.

For in that moment of triumph, we knew that we had faced our greatest challenge and emerged victorious, our bonds forged in the crucible of battle stronger than ever before. And as we stood amidst the wreckage of our hard-won victory, I couldn't help but feel a surge of pride and gratitude for the companions who had fought by my side; their unwavering courage and steadfast loyalty were an indication of the indomitable spirit of humanity in the face of overwhelming adversity.

Navigating through the dense, sticky web spun by the hornets proved to be quite a challenge. With our weapons in hand, we carefully carved our path through the intricate strands, mindful not to damage any of the valuable technology surrounding us. After some effort, we finally acquired the components essential for constructing multiple radio devices. Despite being partially ensnared in the sticky residue, we departed the room and ascended the stairs back to ground level. Amidst the relics of the TechForge Citadel, a sealed envelope caught my eye, its seal intact despite the years of decay.

The sealed envelope, its contents unknown, felt heavy in my pocket—a mystery wrapped in aged paper. Its presence was a silent reminder of the depth of history and secrecy that enveloped Misty Hollow. I vowed to myself that once the immediate dangers were behind us, I would seek the solitude and quiet necessary to unveil their secrets. Whatever knowledge or truths it held could be the key to understanding the past's hold on our present endeavors and perhaps guide our path forward.

As I pocketed the sealed envelope, a strange sense of inevitability settled over me, as if the faded seal were not just a marker of the past but a key to unlocking futures untold. I refrained from breaking the seal, allowing the envelope to rest heavy in my pocket. Its presence was a silent sentinel, guarding secrets that could unravel the tightly knit threads of our understanding. 'This could change everything,' I thought, a shiver of anticipation running down my spine. The mysteries of Misty Hollow were deep, its secrets buried in the shadows of time. This envelope, innocuous as it seemed, held the potential to cast light on forgotten truths or reveal new paths forward. It was a reminder that our journey was intertwined with the past and that understanding it could be the key to securing our future. Though tempted to open it, I pocketed the envelope, a decision that would later unfold the secrets of Misty Hollow's past and reveal unexpected alliances. While there were several alternative routes available downstairs, I didn't even consider venturing through them.

Once we were back on solid ground, relief washed over us like a warm blanket, soothing our frayed nerves and weary bodies. But the calm was short-lived. Before us loomed a sight straight out of a nightmare—a sentinel drone, its metallic frame gleaming ominously in the dim light.

"What in tarnation is that?" The Seeker blurted out, his voice a mix of awe and apprehension.

"I know exactly what it is," I replied, my disappointment palpable.

"Then spill the beans, Boss. Friend or foe?" The Seeker pressed, his curiosity getting the best of him.

"It's a sentinel drone, an incredibly formidable and perilous adversary. I've encountered one before, and let me tell you, it's impervious to most attacks and can even swap out its appendages for weapons. Defeating it once was an immense challenge, requiring my utmost effort. This presents a serious obstacle for us."

"Well, boss, if you've tamed that beast solo, reckon we can wrangle it with three cowboys in the ring!" The Seeker exclaimed optimistically.

"I surely hope so," I replied, my tone tinged with uncertainty. "Facing another one of these alone would be quite a daunting prospect, I must admit."

"I'm with ya, Boss! Ain't no metal monstrosity gonna stand in our way!" Kael chimed in, his confidence unwavering.

With resolve in our hearts and weapons in hand, we squared our shoulders and prepared to face the mechanical menace standing between us and victory.

As we stood before the sentinel drone, its metallic form casting an eerie glow in the dim light, a sense of trepidation settled over us like a heavy fog. The memories of my previous encounter with such a formidable adversary flooded back, reminding me of the immense challenge that lay ahead.

With a resolute nod, I rallied my companions, steeling ourselves for the battle to come. "Alright, let's stay focused and work together. We've faced tough odds before, and we'll overcome this obstacle just like any other."

The Seeker, ever the optimist, cracked a grin and offered his quirky take on the situation. "Don't you worry, boss. With our combined grit and gumption, we'll have that tin can singing a different tune in no time!"

Kael, his confidence unwavering, chimed in with his own brand of reassurance. "You got it, Ethan! Ain't no hunk of metal gonna stand a chance against us!"

With our spirits bolstered by camaraderie and determination, we sprang into action, each of us poised to play our part in the impending showdown. As the drone advanced, its menacing presence looming ever closer, we unleashed a coordinated barrage of attacks, our weapons flashing in the dim light of the chamber.

Energy bolts crackled through the air as Kael unleashed the power of his Voltcaster, while The Seeker's arrows flew true, finding their mark with unerring precision. I, armed with the Fusionizer, focused on targeting the drone's exposed vulnerabilities, aiming to disrupt its internal systems and weaken its defenses.

The drone, undeterred by our assault, retaliated with a ferocity that matched our own, its mechanical limbs moving with lethal precision as it sought to overwhelm us with its firepower.

Dodging and weaving through its relentless onslaught, we pressed on, refusing to yield to the overwhelming odds stacked against us.

With each passing moment, the intensity of the battle escalated, the chamber echoing with the clang of metal and the crackle of energy as we traded blows with our mechanical adversary. Sparks flew and circuits sputtered as our weapons found their mark, slowly but surely chipping away at the drone's formidable defenses.

As the battle raged on, with each volley of energy bolts and flurry of arrows, the drone's armor began to show signs of wear and tear. Amidst the chaos of combat, a well-placed shot from Kael's Voltcaster caused a critical breach in the drone's defensive plating, exposing a vulnerable section of its chassis.

With a keen eye for opportunity, I seized upon this momentary vulnerability, directing a concentrated barrage of energy blasts towards the exposed area. Each shot struck true, gradually chipping away at the protective casing surrounding the drone's energy core.

As the protective housing weakened under the relentless assault, cracks began to form, allowing glimpses of the pulsating energy core within. Sensing an opportunity, I redoubled my efforts, focusing my firepower on the exposed core with unwavering determination.

With a final surge of power, the protective housing gave way, shattering into fragments that scattered across the chamber floor. In a shower of sparks and flames, the energy core lay exposed, its once impenetrable defenses now compromised.

Seizing the moment, I pressed the attack, directing a final barrage of energy blasts towards the vulnerable core. With a deafening roar, the energy core erupted in a brilliant flash of light, signaling the drone's ultimate defeat.

As the echoes of battle faded, we stood victorious amidst the wreckage, our hearts filled with a sense of triumph and relief. The silence that followed their victory over the sentinel drone was eerie, almost unnatural. It was a stark reminder that in the shadows of the TechForge Citadel, danger lurked at every turn, each step forward a dance with the unknown.

In the end, it was our perseverance and determination that led us to victory, overcoming even the most formidable of adversaries.

But it was not until we recognized a pattern in its movements that our fortunes began to turn. Seizing upon a momentary lapse in its defenses, we launched a coordinated assault, targeting its exposed energy core with relentless precision.

As our combined firepower converged upon the drone's weakened form, a deafening roar filled the chamber, signaling the moment of triumph. With a final surge of effort, we watched as the drone faltered and fell, its once formidable frame now reduced to a lifeless heap of metal and circuitry.

Our breath was ragged, and adrenaline was still coursing through our veins. The battle was not just a test of strength but also of will. As we stood united against the drone, it became clear that our resolve, forged in the fires of adversity, was our greatest weapon. In this moment of conflict, we were more than allies; we were a testament to the enduring spirit of humanity. With a shared sense of relief and accomplishment, we knew that no obstacle could stand in the way of our unwavering resolve and unbreakable bond.

In the quiet aftermath, as the echoes of our confrontation faded into the stillness of the TechForge Citadel, a moment of reflection washed over me. Each victory on this path wasn't merely a notch in our belts; it was a testament to the strength of our bonds and the righteousness of our cause. With every challenge we overcame, the dream of a united Misty Hollow felt less like a distant hope and more like a tangible future. The weight of this journey, with its burdens and uncertainties, felt lighter in the company of allies who had become more like brothers. Their unwavering support was a beacon in the darkness, guiding me forward.

Both The Seeker and Kael were panting like a pair of old hounds after a fox chase. Me? I was feeling chipper as a sparrow in springtime, but I figured I'd let the dust settle before hitting the road.

"Well, well, well, would ya look at that? It seems the time has come to mosey on back," drawled The Seeker, his voice as crooked as a river's path.

As I rode on horseback, I recalled the herbal sticks I had brought along. Lighting one, I savored its soothing effects.

In the heart of Misty Hollow, where the tales of old whisper through the leaves, each of us carries a legacy—a burden from the past shaping our steps forward. My journey, intertwined with those of Kael and The Seeker, is more than a quest; it's a path to understanding the true essence of unity and resilience.

As the sun dipped below the horizon, casting long shadows across the rugged landscape, our trio made camp for the night.

Amidst the crackling of the campfire, we shared a simple meal of dried fruits, jerky, and hardtack, the flames dancing in the darkness, casting flickering shadows on our faces.

In the simplicity of our shared meal and the warmth of the fire's glow, there lies an unspoken bond, a silent acknowledgment of the hardships faced and the challenges yet to come. It's in these moments of togetherness that the true strength of our fellowship is forged, not just in the battles fought but in the quiet support we offer each other. As the fire crackled, I pondered the journey ahead, realizing that the quest to unite the communities was not just about mending the fabric of a fractured society but also about healing the scars of his own past, a journey from isolation to belonging.

With the night air cooling and the stars twinkling overhead, I decided it was time to open up to my companions. Sitting around the fire, I recounted my entire history, from the moment I discovered my abilities to the mission I was now embarking on. I laid bare my fears, my doubts, and my hopes for the future, seeking their understanding and support.

To my relief, both Kael and The Seeker listened intently, their expressions a mix of curiosity and empathy. When I finished my tale, I looked to them, awaiting their response.

"I'm in," Kael declared without hesitation, his eyes reflecting a newfound determination.

The Seeker nodded in agreement, his gaze lingering on the flames. ""Throw me into the mix, boss," he said, his voice quiet but resolute.

Encouraged by their unwavering support, I felt a weight lift from my shoulders, knowing I wouldn't have to face the challenges ahead alone. As I shared my story with Kael and The Seeker, the warmth of the fire mirrored the warmth growing within me, fueled by the bond of shared purpose and mutual trust. Their silent attentiveness was a balm to my soul, a silent affirmation that I was no longer a solitary wanderer but part of a fellowship. In their eyes, I saw not just comrades but brothers-in-arms, ready to face whatever lay ahead with unwavering support and steadfast courage.

By the crackling fire, we bantered and reveled in each other's company, passing around an herbstick for a mellow vibe. As the night wore on, both Kael and The Seeker drifted off into slumber, leaving me alone with my thoughts. I watched the embers dance in the darkness, occasionally taking a drag from the herbstick, its soothing effects calming my restless mind. The dance of the embers at our campfire, like the journey of life, is transient yet mesmerizing. Each spark, a fleeting moment of brilliance against the night's canvas, mirrors our own struggles and triumphs in the vast tapestry of existence.

Eventually, exhaustion caught up with me, and I too succumbed to sleep, albeit briefly. As the embers of the campfire died down and the stars watched over us, I couldn't help but reflect on the journey that had led me here. With each step and each battle, I had not only found allies but had also discovered a part of myself. I was ready to face the uncertainties of the future, knowing that I was no longer alone.

When I awoke, the others were still lost in dreams. I busied myself by organizing our gear, checking our supplies, and silently contemplating the journey ahead until the first light of dawn painted the sky. In these quiet moments before dawn, I often find myself reflecting on the weight of my mission. The solitude of the early morning is a rare chance for introspection, to question and reaffirm my resolve. It's not just the fate of Misty Hollow that weighs on my mind, but the lives intertwined with its destiny. Every decision and every acton, is a ripple in the pond, affecting not just my future but the future of all who call this place home.

As dawn breaks, painting the sky with hues of promise, I find my thoughts wandering to the crossroads of destiny and choice. The paths we've chosen, entwined by fate and resolve, have led us here, to the brink of a new horizon. In this moment of quietude, the realization dawns upon me—our journey is not merely about the destinations we seek but about the discoveries we make within ourselves and each other.

Eventually, we all stirred awake, ready to resume our journey.

During the journey, amidst the rhythmic hoofbeats of our horses, I turned to The Seeker, curiosity tugging at my thoughts. "Hey, Seeker," I began, "how did you come by that nickname?"

The Seeker chuckled softly, his eyes glinting with amusement. "Well, it's really simple," he replied, his tone cryptic. "I earned it through my skills with a bow. Always searching, always seeking."

Intrigued, I pressed further. "But what's your real name?" I asked, hoping to learn more about my enigmatic companion.

The Seeker's expression turned serious, a shadow passing over his features. "Some things are better left unknown, Ethan," he replied evasively. "Let's just say the past is behind me, and I prefer to focus on the journey ahead."

As the group resumed their journey back to the village, the landscape stretched out before them in a serene expanse of rolling hills and verdant meadows. The path they followed wound its way through dense forests, alive with the chatter of birds and the rustle of leaves in the gentle breeze.

Underneath the canopy of trees, dappled sunlight danced on the forest floor, creating patterns of light and shadow that seemed to shift with every step. The air was cool and fragrant, carrying the scent of pine and earth.

Occasionally, they passed by clear streams babbling over smooth stones, offering a refreshing respite from the warmth of the day. The Seeker paused now and then to scoop up handfuls of crystal-clear water, quenching his thirst with a satisfied sigh.

Kael led the way with a steady stride, his keen eyes scanning the surroundings for any signs of danger or disturbance. Despite the tranquil surroundings, his instincts remained sharp, attuned to the slightest shift in the natural rhythm of the forest.

I followed close behind, his mind abuzz with thoughts of the mission that lay ahead. The weight of responsibility hung heavy on his shoulders, but for now, he allowed himself to be swept away by the beauty of the wilderness surrounding them.

As they trekked onward, conversation flowed freely between them, punctuated by laughter and the occasional shared observation of their surroundings. They spoke of their past adventures, their hopes for the future, and the bonds that had formed between them during their time together.

Though the journey was uneventful, each step brought them closer to their destination and the challenges that awaited them in the days to come. But for now, they walked in companionable silence, content in each other's company, as they made their way back to the village they called home.

REFLECTIONS AND RESOLUTIONS

Upon returning to Misty Hollows, I wasted no time and delved into the task of crafting radio equipment. While Kael and The Seeker opted to linger in the village, relishing their homecoming, I made my way to Kael's house. In the guest chamber, I found a suitable bureau ideal for assembling the devices, illuminated by the flickering glow of a lantern that cast playful shadows upon the walls.

The flickering light of a lantern casts dancing shadows on the walls. With meticulous care, I laid out the components before me, each piece gleaming softly in the dim light.

My hands moved with practiced precision, and my fingers deftly soldered wires and connected circuits. The air was filled with the faint smell of burning flux as I meticulously aligned each component, my focus unwavering as I worked to bring the radios to life.

Time seemed to blur as I immersed myself in the task at hand, my mind buzzing with thoughts of connectivity and communication. With each solder joint made and each wire carefully routed, the radios began to take shape, their form emerging from the jumble of parts before me.

As I neared completion, my excitement grew, and my anticipation mounted with each passing moment. Finally, with a satisfying click, I connected the last wire, and the radios hummed to life, emitting a soft crackle of static before tuning into the first clear signal.

With a triumphant grin, I tested each radio, ensuring they were functioning flawlessly. Satisfied with my handiwork, I leaned back, the lantern's glow casting a warm light across my face as I marveled at the fruits of my labor. Hours had melded into the night, a testament to the focus and precision that the task demanded.

Time slipped by unnoticed as I was focused on other tasks.

It wasn't until Kael was already bustling around the kitchen, preparing a meal, that I realized how much time had passed. Joining him, I asked about his trip to town. The aroma of spices and the warmth of the hearth filled the kitchen, creating a comforting backdrop to our conversation about the journey ahead.

"Great," he replied, stirring a pot. "Nice to catch up with a few folks, though I had to explain my plans to follow in your footsteps."

"I hope leaving your friends behind wasn't too tough," I remarked.

"Nah," Kael waved off. "I doubt they'll remember me after a few days."

"If you ever reconsider, just say the word," I offered.

"No turning back for me," Kael affirmed. "Adventure's calling louder than village life."

"Got it," I nodded. "The radio's ready, so we can head out tomorrow toward Willowbrook, the closest stop."

"How long a trek is that?" Kael asked.

"About four days north," I answered.

"A decent journey already; we'll need to stock up," he noted. "Absolutely. We'll have to make a short stop on our way to Willowbrook to retrieve my Alloyed Charger along the way, meaning we'll have to leave a horse behind once we reach the camp."

"It'll find its way back, I'm sure," Kael reassured me. "I agreed.

"Have you thought about that bandit camp I've heard rumors of? That one might take some convincing," Kael remarked. "I'm aware. But if they're entrenched there, they'll need to be integrated eventually. It's our last stop, so we have to give it a shot," I replied.

"Fair point. Let's aim for negotiation rather than annihilation this time," Kael suggested.

"I'll do my best," I said with a hint of jest.

After sharing a meal with Kael and bidding him farewell, I made my way to The Elder's house and knocked on the door. Enzo, The Elder's attendant, answered.

"What do you need now?" he grumbled.

"Firstly, I'd like to inquire about The Elder's well-being," I stated.

"He's passed on to a better place," Enzo informed me. "Ah, that's saddening news. He was a good man," I reflected.

"Indeed. You missed the funeral," Enzo chided. "Is there anything else?"

"Is Elena available? There are some matters I'd like to discuss with her," I requested.

"She's in the living room. Come in," Enzo said, stepping aside.

I found Elena seated at a table, surrounded by documents likely related to The Elder's affairs or his passing. "Hello," I greeted. "Do you have a moment?"

"Sure, what do you need?" she replied.

"I'm here to discuss the idea of uniting our communities," I explained. "I've prepared enough radios for each community, including yours. These will enable communication once they're distributed."

"It's great that you've got the radios ready," she acknowledged. "What's the next step?"

"I'll journey to the nearest community, propose the idea of unity, and gauge their interest. If they agree, you'll soon be in touch with them via the radio once it's operational," I outlined.

I proceeded to detail how the radios functioned for inter-community communication.

The radios, forged from the remnants of a civilization that thrived on connectivity, now served as our beacon through the silence that had befallen the world. Modified to harness the long-forgotten frequencies of the old world, they stood as a testament to resilience—a bridge over the chasms that divided humanity. 'In an age where digital whispers have faded into silence, these devices are our voice across the void,' I explained. 'A remnant of past ingenuity, repurposed for our shared hope. Through these, we weave a new web of unity, one frequency at a time.'

After some further discussion, I bid her farewell and left to relax and engage in recreational activities.

As the evening unfurled its embrace, the air was filled with the melody of music, the rhythm of dance, and the warmth of shared laughter. Feeling drawn to the lively atmosphere, I decided to join the festivities, hoping to lose myself in the joyful ambiance.

Amidst the swirl of dancers, I found myself face-to-face with Aria once again. With a playful glint in her eyes, she approached me and uttered those enchanting words, "How about that dance you owe me?"

Feeling a flutter of nerves, I confessed, "I must admit, I'm not exactly a master of dance."

But she simply smiled, her gaze filled with understanding. "No need to worry," she reassured me, her voice as melodious as the music surrounding us. "Just let yourself be swept away."

With her hand in mine, we moved closer to the flickering glow of the campfire. As we swayed to the music, I found myself captivated by her grace, unable to tear my gaze away from her mesmerizing eyes.

Aria's beauty was unmistakable, even in the ruggedness of the world we traversed. She possessed an ethereal quality, as if she had stepped out of the remnants of a more graceful era into the harsh reality of our current existence. Her eyes, a striking shade of hazel, seemed to capture the very essence of the landscapes we journeyed through, reflecting the verdant greens of the forests and the stark blues of the winter skies with equal depth.

Her hair, a cascade of dark curls, fell around her shoulders, framing her face with an effortless elegance that belied the challenges we faced daily. The sun seemed to weave gold into her strands, highlighting a natural luster that no hardship could dull. Her skin, despite the relentless exposure to the elements, retained a softness and a subtle glow, as if lit from within.

Aria moved with a grace that was captivating, each gesture an expression of a resilience that had been honed in the fires of adversity.

In an unexpected moment of intimacy, she drew nearer, wrapping her arms around me, and tenderly pressed her lips to mine.

I was caught off guard and momentarily stunned, unsure of how to respond. Sensing my hesitation, she pulled back, her expression tinged with concern. "I apologize," she murmured softly. "Was that too forward?"

Though my mind was reeling with uncertainty, I couldn't deny the flutter of warmth that spread through me at her touch. "Not at all," I managed to reply, my voice barely above a whisper.

With her hand in mine once more, we continued to dance beneath the starlit sky, each step infused with a newfound sense of closeness. But as the night began to wane, reality beckoned, and Aria reluctantly announced her departure. As Aria winced in pain, a realization dawned on me. Her suffering mirrored the world's plight—fractured yet fiercely resilient. In her resilience, I saw not just personal defiance against her agony but a collective whisper of hope amidst despair. This world, ravaged and torn, was still capable of healing, just like Aria. And perhaps our journey was more than a quest for survival; it was a pursuit of redemption, for the world and for ourselves.

As she cast me a lingering glance, a tender smile gracing her lips, I couldn't help but return the sentiment. "Until we meet again," I murmured softly.

Alone amidst the gentle crackle of the fire, I settled back, taking a moment to savor the lingering traces of her presence. Lost in contemplation, I pondered the significance of that fleeting kiss, wondering if it held the promise of something more profound.

As the dawn light crept through the window, I found myself pondering not just our personal entanglements but the practical implications of Aria's injury on our mission. Seated around a crudely made wooden table, I looked at each of my companions in turn. "Aria's bravery last night saved us, but it has also left her injured," I began, my voice carrying a mix of gratitude and concern. "We must consider how this affects our approach to Pinecrest Camp. Aria, do you feel up to the task of negotiation, or should we adapt our roles to ensure your safety and recovery?"

Aria, her shoulder bandaged and her expression determined yet touched by a shadow of pain, nodded slowly. "I appreciate your concern, Ethan. While I may not be at my full strength, I can still contribute significantly. Perhaps I can focus more on strategy and less on the front lines. Let's not forget, our unity and adaptability have always been our greatest strengths."

Kael chimed in, his tone pragmatic. "Aria's right. We've faced challenges before and adapted. This is no different. We'll adjust our roles as needed. Ethan, you and I can take the lead on more physical tasks. Aria, your insight and tactical acumen will be invaluable from the back."

This conversation, though brief, solidified our resolve and adaptability. It was a testament to our bond, forged through adversity—a bond that would carry us through the uncertainties of Pinecrest Camp.

After finishing the herbstick, I decided to head over to Kael's place and relax on the guest bed for a bit. The odd thing about needing less sleep these days was that there wasn't much to occupy my time during the night. I found myself grappling with boredom more frequently than ever before. Back in my era, we had video games, television, and the internet to keep us entertained for hours on end. I couldn't help but reminisce about those simpler times and realize how much I missed the comforts of a normal life.

However, I knew deep down that things would never return to the way they were before. It was a reality I had to come to terms with. So, instead of dwelling on the past, I resolved to make the best of the present situation.

Lost in my thoughts, I drifted into a state of contemplation, not quite asleep but not fully awake either. As time passed, the soft light of dawn began to filter through the windows, signaling the start of a new day. Curious about what was happening outside, I decided to step out and see for myself.

After sharing the potent Ironbrew with my companions, a moment of silence befell us, a rare pause in our relentless journey. It was during this quiet interlude, amidst the clamor of the inn's morning bustle, that I found the courage to voice a thought that had been haunting me. 'You know,' I began, my voice barely above the whisper of the wind outside, 'in all our adventures, amidst the chaos and the quests for survival, I've come to realize something profoundly simple yet infinitely complex. We are not just survivors in this shattered world;

we are the keepers of stories, the custodians of the light that once was and might be again. Our journey is not solely about the destinations we seek or the dangers we face. It's about the moments we share, the memories we create, and the hope we kindle along the way. Maybe, just maybe, our true mission is to weave these threads of light into a tapestry that speaks of resilience, of a world reborn from the ashes of its despair.' The words hung in the air, a soft echo of a dream daring to take flight. In their eyes, I saw the reflection of that dream, a shared vision of what could be, binding us together with a purpose deeper than survival.

After sharing the potent Ironbrew with my companions, a moment of silence befell us, a rare pause in our relentless journey. It was during this quiet interlude, amidst the clamor of the inn's morning bustle, that I found the courage to voice a thought that had been haunting me. 'You know,' I began, my voice barely above the whisper of the wind outside, 'in all our adventures, amidst the chaos and the quests for survival, I've come to realize something profoundly simple yet infinitely complex. We are not just survivors in this shattered world; we are the keepers of stories, the custodians of the light that once was and might be again. Our journey is not solely about the destinations we seek or the dangers we face. It's about the moments we share, the memories we create, and the hope we kindle along the way. Maybe, just maybe, our true mission is to weave these threads of light into a tapestry that speaks of resilience, of a world reborn from the ashes of its despair.' The words hung in the air, a soft echo of a dream daring to take flight. In their eyes, I saw the reflection of that dream, a shared vision of what could be, binding us together with a purpose deeper than survival.

The Seeker came sauntering over, a wild glint in his eyes. "Boss, we've hit a snag!"

"A snag? Did something befall the horses or our stash?" I inquired.

"Worse, there's this lass itching to hitch a ride with us," he declared.

"Well, more hands on deck could prove beneficial, especially in matters of negotiation," I mused.

"But she's a woman?" The Seeker balked. "What of it?" I shrugged.

"Ah, you see, we're all blokes here, and it might throw off the vibe, you know?" he rambled.

"No issue there; is she awake? Lead the way," I directed. "Aye, she's over yonder, lounging under that tree, puffing on an herbstick."

As I drew near, disbelief washed over me. It was Aria. What drove her to seek our company?

I caught her eye, and she approached. "Salutations!" she chirped.

"Hello, Aria," I greeted. "The Seeker mentioned your desire to tag along on our escapades; pray, enlighten me as to why?" "Just yearning for adventure," she replied. "I've wandered these roads before, and the call of the unknown beckons once more. Your motley crew seemed as good a company as any."

"Not a qualm from me, but you'll be our final addition. Can't have the gang getting too crowded," I said. "What talents do you bring to the table?"

"I'm a whiz with dual blades, throwing knives, and hand-to-hand tussles," she boasted.

"Well, that sounds mighty handy!" The Seeker interjected. "Agreed. Once Kael rouses, we'll set course for Willowbrook," I decided.

Eventually, Kael emerged from his abode, and we relayed the plan, with Aria now part of the entourage. He concurred, seeing the merit in bolstering our ranks.

With provisions and steeds in tow, we set our sights northward.

As we set out from Misty Hollow, my companions—Kael, The Seeker, and Aria -—d I embarked on our journey across the desolate post-apocalyptic wilderness. Mounted on our sturdy horses, we traversed through rough landscape, navigating rocky outcrops and dusty trails under the relentless sun. The landscape stretched endlessly before us, an assertion to nature's resilience in the face of adversity. Throughout the day, we encountered various challenges typical of the wilderness - s:ep inclines, narrow ravines, and the occasional encounter with wildlife. Yet, with our combined skills and determination, we pressed onward, driven by the urgency of our mission.

As dawn broke on the second day of our journey, our spirits remained high, despite the challenges ahead. With the halfway point looming on the horizon, we continued our trek across the untamed wilderness. The landscape shifted subtly, transitioning from rocky foothills to open plains, offering fleeting glimpses of the rugged beauty of the post-apocalyptic world. Along the way, we encountered obstacles that tested our resolve: unpredictable weather patterns, treacherous terrain, and the ever-present threat of danger. However, with Aria's expertise in combat, Kael's resourcefulness, and The Seeker's keen intuition, we navigated through these challenges with ease. As we approached the designated rendezvous point, anticipation filled the air. With the Alloyed Charger awaiting us, we pushed forward, eager to reclaim our invaluable asset and continue our journey toward the town of Willowbrook.

The Alloy Charger sat atop a dilapidated cart, its sleek frame juxtaposed against the rustic backdrop of the broken-down vehicle. One wheel lay discarded nearby, a silent manifestation of the trials it had endured. Whether the cart had fallen victim to an attempted robbery, an animal's relentless assault, or simply succumbed to the weight of its burden, it remained a mystery. Regardless, I wasted no time hoisting the Charger from its makeshift perch, activating its dormant systems with a familiar touch.

As the hum of the Alloyed Charger filled the air, a sense of familiarity washed over me; its reassuring presence was a welcome sight amidst the desolate landscape. With a determined stride, I set out on foot, leaving behind my trusty steed to navigate the harsh terrain at a slower pace. Mindful of my companions on horseback, I adjusted the Charger's speed accordingly, ensuring that we traveled together as a cohesive unit on our journey forward.

As we resumed our journey towards Willowbrook, the landscape unfolded before us in a patchwork of rolling hills and winding trails. The air carried a crispness that invigorated our spirits, promising adventure with each step forward.

With the Alloyed Charger leading the way, its metallic sheen glinting in the sunlight, we forged ahead with renewed determination. The path ahead was rugged and unforgiving, yet we pressed on undeterred, fueled by the promise of reaching our destination.

Throughout the day, we encountered a myriad of obstacles, from fallen trees obstructing our path to treacherous ravines that tested our agility and resolve. Yet, with each challenge overcome, our bond grew stronger, a confirmation of the camaraderie that united us on this quest.

As the sun dipped below the horizon, casting long shadows across the land, we made camp for the night. Amidst the crackling of the campfire and the soft murmurs of conversation, we found solace in each other's company, drawing strength from the shared experiences that bound us together.

With the dawn of a new day, we set out once more, the town of Willowbrook looming ever closer on the horizon. Though the journey had been arduous, we knew that our perseverance would soon be rewarded as we ventured forth towards our final destination, united in purpose and resolve.

As we approached the town, we noticed sturdy stone walls encompassing it, boasting two entrances—one at the front and one at the back. The remainder of the town appeared shielded from the outside world, a reassuring sight indicating safety from potential threats. While not overly expansive in size, the town appeared cozy and inviting, hinting at a promising haven for inhabitants seeking refuge in these uncertain times.

As we approached the town gates, two guards stood sentinel, their eyes sharp and vigilant. One of them, a burly figure with a rugged demeanor, stepped forward, addressing me with a hint of curiosity in his voice.

"Well, well, whatcha all doin' 'round here?" He inquired, his words colored with a distinct southern drawl.

"We've come to discuss matters concerning the union of several communities across different towns. We seek an audience with your leader," I replied, my voice steady and resolute.

The guard paused, his brow furrowing as he considered my words carefully before nodding in acquiescence. "Alright then, come on through," he said, gesturing for us to enter, his accent lending a unique charm to his words.

As we approached the outskirts of Willowbrook, the landscape gradually transitioned from rugged wilderness to quaint countryside. Nestled amidst rolling hills and lush greenery, the town exuded a rustic charm that welcomed weary travelers with open arms.

The main thoroughfare, flanked by quaint cottages and bustling storefronts, bustled with activity as townsfolk went about their daily routines. A gentle breeze carried the scent of freshly baked bread from the local bakery, mingling with the earthy aroma of the surrounding farmland.

At the heart of Willowbrook stood a stately town square, adorned with a weathered fountain that served as a gathering place for locals and visitors alike. Surrounding the square, vibrant gardens bloomed with colorful flowers, adding a touch of natural beauty to the quaint surroundings.

Streets lined with towering oak trees led to quiet residential neighborhoods, where charming houses with picket fences stood in neat rows, each one bearing the mark of a proud homeowner.

Children played in the streets, their laughter echoing through the air, while elderly residents sat on their porches, exchanging stories and gossip.

Despite its modest size, Willowbrook exuded a sense of warmth and community that was palpable to all who passed through its streets. From the friendly smiles of its inhabitants to the picturesque scenery that surrounded it, the town embodied the timeless allure of small-town living, a haven of peace and tranquility in an ever-changing world.

As flecks of snow drifted gently from the sky, I couldn't help but ponder the passage of time in this post-apocalyptic world. It felt like I had been navigating its desolate landscapes for months now, each day blending into the next in a haze of survival and uncertainty.

"Hey, do you guys still measure the seasons?" I asked my companions, curiosity tingling my voice as I glanced around at Kael, The Seeker, and Aria.

The Seeker responded in his own peculiar way. "Well, ya see, we mostly separate winter from summer now, Ethan. Makes it easier to keep track of things in this topsy-turvy world, ya know?"

His words resonated with a strange kind of logic, and I nodded in understanding. But then my gaze shifted back to the falling snow, and I couldn't help but voice my concern. "Is this a sign that winter is coming?"

Kael and The Seeker exchanged a knowing glance before Kael spoke up, his voice carrying a sense of resignation. "Usually around this time, winter starts to rear its icy head."

I grimaced at the thought, imagining the journey ahead becoming even more arduous under the weight of winter's chill. "That's going to make things much harder for us," I remarked, my tone heavy with apprehension.

But Aria said reassuringly, "It won't be that bad, Ethan. We're only at the start of winter. The worst of it won't hit for a few months yet."

Her words provided some reassurance, and I felt a flicker of gratitude for her unwavering optimism.

I shivered, both from the thought of the cold and the foreboding sense of uncertainty that hung in the air. As the snow continued to fall around us, I couldn't help but wonder what other challenges lay ahead because of the coming winter. Even though they reassured me, I had a bad feeling about it.

In the village, we sauntered over to what looked like a militia gathering and asked about the whereabouts of the town's leader.

After a bit of back and forth, one of them gestured for us to tag along.

We wandered through an opening in the stone wall into a room decked out with a desk, a chair, and various knick-knacks, including paintings plastered on the walls. Perched on the chair was a hefty figure dressed in leather with a fur collar, donning gray boots, and a mop of long, flowing brown hair.

"Sir," the militia member addressed him, "these folks would like a word with you."

"Alright, send 'em in," he rumbled in a deep, gravelly voice, his accent thick as molasses.

"Thank you for seeing us so promptly, sir," I began. "Please call me John. I'm John Wilson," he stated.

I proceeded to lay out our proposal, detailing our plans regarding the radio devices.

"Well, you've got big dreams; I'll give you that," John mused, considering the situation. "But it ain't gonna be easy to get things rollin'."

"Yes, indeed, it's a long-term project. Our aim is to unify our communities through hard work, building something lasting and beneficial for all," I explained.

"You make a compellin' case, but I can't shake my concerns about them bandits. Don't trust 'em one bit," John remarked, his accent thickening with each word.

"I understand your apprehension, but cooperation with the bandits isn't a must. If they aren't interested, we'll manage without them. And I reckon they'll see the advantages of joining forces over their old ways soon enough," I assured him.

"You're right indeed; this isn't just a few day's work. I can't deny that. But I see the long-term benefits for our communities. My only concern is that you include those bandits in your plan. I don't trust 'em, you know?"

"I can see your issue, but if they don't want to cooperate, then I won't include them. And I'm sure they'll see the benefits as well. It'll be much more advantageous for them to join us than to keep to their old ways, I believe."

"Just hope they don't double-cross us. That's my worry," John admitted, his voice tinged with skepticism.

"Listen here, mister, you know what happened over by Misty Hollow with them bandits? They refused to cooperate, and guess what? Our buddy here wiped 'em out single-handedly. True story. If those rascals ain't keen on playin' nice, they best be ready for the consequences," The Seeker chimed in.

"Really? Heard rumors 'bout that, but one man takin' on a whole fortress? Hard to believe," John remarked, impressed. "But if that's the case, reckon those bandits'll think twice 'fore causin' trouble. Aye, I reckon that'll give 'em enough reason not to cross ya.

But whether they'll join is a whole different kettle of fish, ya see," said John, his voice thick with a rugged accent.

"That's right, mister," drawled The Seeker. "Y'all best steer clear of our friend here, else he'll give ya a whuppin' so hard, yer rear ends'll be flyin' all the way to outer space. Yessir, them bandits'll be doin' some serious second-thinkin' 'fore messin' with us; that's a fact."

Let's hope for the best, then. Now, there's something I'd like to propose, if you're game, John," I interjected.

"What's that, then?" he inquired, intrigued, his accent lending a rugged charm to his words.

"I have something I'd like to try, John," I said. "Wot would tha' be?" he asked curiously.

"Well, I've told you about the radio devices, right? I've got one right here for you. And I'll show you how it'll help us in matters of communication," I explained.

Explaining the workings of the radio to him, I put one right in front of his face and said, "Try it; if there's someone on the other line, you'll be sure to get a response."

"What do I say?" John asked.

"Just say hello or something. It doesn't really matter," I said. John held down a button and said, "Hello there."

To his surprise, a voice came from the device: "Hearing you loud and clear, who am I speaking to?"

John remained dumbstruck fer a moment. Then he said, "This 'ere's John, leader o' Willowbrook. Ethan gave me this device fer communicatin' purposes. Am I speakin' to someone from Misty Hollow?"

"That's right, my name's Enzo; our leader Elena put me in charge of this device in case something came through. It looks like it's working."

"It sure does; I was downright flabbergasted. That's a major leap forward to be able to gab with other communities. A giant step toward bringin' our folks together as Ethan's schemed, I'd reckon," said John, his accent ringing loud and clear.

"Is there any matter you would like to inform us of?" said Enzo.

"Only thing's, Ethan and his bunch rolled into town, got that radio cookin' up. If y'all need any more info, reckon I'll give ya' a holler," John conveyed.

"Very well. Good to hear from you, John; we're all looking forward to working together soon," said Enzo.

"Indeed, ya'll hear from me later, when we got business to chew on. Lookin' forward to it," said John, his words laced with a colorful twang, his demeanor exuding a quirky charm that was uniquely his own.

"Right, I hope to hear from you soon. Also, if you ever need to talk to Elena, let me know, and I'll make sure she's here," said Enzo.

"That's good to hear," said John. "I reckon we'll have a heap of chin-waggin' ahead; bye."

"Goodbye," replied Enzo.

The connection closed, and John was delighted to say to Ethan that he now really believed in his ability to make a difference. John, Ethan, and the companions talked a bit more about the matter, and then they noticed the day making room for dusk.

Looks like the sun's takin' a rest," said John. "Why don't you find yerself a cozy nook for the night? Tomorrow's a new day, and before ya hit the trail, stock up. It's all on the house; just tell 'em ol' John sent ya. And if they ain't buyin' it, send 'em my way, I'll sort 'em out. I appreciate yer efforts, son. I'm puttin' my trust in yer mission.

Don't let me down, lad. Once this kerfuffle's over, yer deeds will be etched in the annals of our townsfolk."

My companions and I rested until dawn, waiting for the shopkeepers to open. We stocked up on supplies for the journey ahead and prepared to depart. Unexpectedly, the villagers had already heard about our meeting with John, and they approached us with curiosity, asking questions and engaging in conversation.

Eventually, we had to bid them farewell and set out on our long journey towards Greendale.

As The Seeker, Aria, and I embarked on our journey from Willowbrook to Greendale, we traversed through rugged terrain, winding through dense forests and sprawling plains. The path ahead stretched out before them, promising both adventure and peril.

The journey proved to be arduous, with the companions encountering a myriad of obstacles along the way. Harsh weather conditions tested their resolve, with sudden storms and biting winds slowing their progress. Despite the challenges, my enhanced abilities, coupled with The Seeker's precision with the Voltcaster energy gun and Aria's skill with dual blades and throwing knives, allowed them to press on with determination.

As we ventured deeper into the wilderness, we found ourselves confronted by dangerous mutated wolves, their snarling forms lurking in the shadows. These fearsome creatures, twisted by the effects of radiation and genetic mutation, posed a formidable threat to the travelers. With their razor-sharp claws and feral instincts, the wolves launched relentless attacks, seeking to tear apart anything in their path.

The mutated wolves resembled beasts from nightmares, their once sleek fur now matted and discolored, patches of sickly green and pulsating purple marring their coarse coats. Their eyes glowed with an unnatural intensity, gleaming like molten amber in the darkness, filled with an insatiable hunger for blood.

But it was not just their appearance that marked them as abominations; protruding from their backs were rows of jagged bones, twisted and gnarled like the spines of ancient predators. These bone-like structures jutted out at odd angles, adding to their menacing silhouette and giving them an even more formidable presence.

Undeterred by the grotesque sight before them, The Seeker, Aria, and I fought valiantly against the onslaught of mutated wolves. I unleashed bursts of energy from his Fusionizer rifle, each blast searing through the air with blinding intensity, striking down the wolves with deadly accuracy.

The Seeker's Voltcaster discharged bolts of crackling energy, each blast striking the mutated wolves with searing intensity. These energy bolts sizzled through the air, leaving trails of light in their wake as they found their marks. Upon impact, the bolts momentarily stunned the wolves, buying precious moments of respite for his companions as they continued their valiant defense against the relentless predators.

Together, the three of us formed a formidable team, our skills complementing each other as we fought tooth and nail against the relentless assaults of the mutated wolves. With every blow we struck, we edged closer to victory, determined to emerge triumphant against the horrors that lurked in the heart of the wilderness.

Despite the ferocity of our foes, we stood our ground, our determination unwavering in the face of adversity. Through skillful coordination and unwavering teamwork, we emerged victorious against the mutated wolves, their resolve unbroken as we continued our journey.

As the sun dipped below the horizon, casting the wasteland in a blanket of darkness, we made camp for the night. Amidst the crackling of the campfire and the soft murmurs of conversation, Kael and The Seeker had already succumbed to the embrace of sleep, their rhythmic breathing providing a comforting backdrop to the scene.

Yet, Aria and I remained awake, sitting side by side beside the flickering flames. The air was alive with the gentle rustle of leaves and the distant chirping of crickets, a soothing symphony that seemed to echo the rhythm of our hearts.

In the quiet stillness of the night, with the stars twinkling overhead like distant beacons of hope, I stole a glance at Aria. Her silhouette was bathed in the warm glow of the fire, casting a soft radiance upon her delicate features.

Unable to resist the pull of her presence, I reached out to brush a stray lock of hair from her face, my fingers lingering against her skin as if seeking solace in the touch. Aria turned to meet my gaze, her eyes reflecting the myriad emotions swirling within her.

In that moment, with the world around us fading into the background, I leaned in, capturing Aria's lips in a tender kiss. The warmth of her lips against mine sent a jolt of electricity coursing through my veins, igniting a fire within that burned brighter than any flame.

As we pulled back, our breaths mingling in the cool night air, I found myself lost in the depths of Aria's eyes. In her gaze, I saw a reflection of my own desires, a silent understanding that transcended words.

With a smile that spoke of a thousand promises, I took Aria's hand in mine, our fingers intertwining as we sat beneath the blanket of stars. In this moment of quiet intimacy, amidst the chaos of the world around us, I couldn't help but feel a glimmer of hope that perhaps, just perhaps, our bond could withstand the trials yet to come.

As the first light of dawn broke through the darkness, I found myself stirring from a restless slumber, my mind still lingering in the realm of dreams. Beside me, Aria slept peacefully, her features softened by the gentle light of morning. Our fingers remained intertwined, a silent reflection of the connection that bound us together.

Despite my lack of sleep, I couldn't help but savor every moment, cherishing the quiet intimacy of the morning. The rhythmic rise and fall of Aria's chest, the warmth of her hand in mine—it was a moment of pure serenity amidst the chaos of our journey.

Gently disentangling my fingers from hers, I rose from my makeshift bed, careful not to disturb her peaceful slumber. With a soft smile lingering on my lips, I watched as Aria slept on, her breathing steady and calm.

As I tended to the morning chores, the events of the previous night played over in my mind, each moment etched into my memory with crystalline clarity. Despite the uncertainty of our path ahead, I couldn't help but feel a sense of optimism, knowing that no matter what trials awaited us, we would face them together.

As we pressed onward, we knew that more challenges awaited us on the road ahead. Yet, with our bond forged in battle and their spirits undaunted, we remained steadfast in their quest, ready to confront whatever obstacles lay in our path as we journeyed towards our destination.

As the sun dipped below the horizon, casting the wasteland in a blanket of darkness, we pressed on through the unforgiving terrain. The distant howls of the wind echoed in the night, serving as a grim reminder of the dangers that lurked in the shadows.

The trail grew narrow, forcing us to abandon our horses, including my trusty Alloyed Charger, and proceed on foot.

Our path was fraught with obstacles—rivers of toxic sludge, towering rock formations, and treacherous ravines—all of which threatened to impede their progress. Yet they forged ahead, their determination unyielding as they navigated through the desolate landscape.

As they encountered each obstacle in their path, we pooled their skills and resources to overcome them.

When we reached the toxic sludge rivers, I used my knowledge of survival to fashion makeshift bridges from fallen debris, allowing us to traverse the hazardous terrain safely. Aria's agility proved invaluable as she leaped across gaps and crevices, securing ropes and footholds for her companions to follow. Meanwhile, The Seeker utilized his Voltcaster to create electromagnetic fields that repelled the noxious fumes emanating from the sludge, providing us with a clear path forward.

As we approached the towering rock formations, I relied on my strength to clear away debris and create a passable route through the labyrinthine maze of stone. As we faced the obstacles on our journey, The Seeker's resourcefulness and ingenuity proved invaluable. Drawing upon his keen intellect and intuitive understanding of nature, he devised clever solutions to bypass the obstacles that blocked our path. Instead of relying on technology and engineering, he utilized his knowledge of the natural world to harness the power of the elements.

With a keen eye for the environment, The Seeker identified natural features that could be leveraged to our advantage. He found sturdy vines that could be fashioned into ropes, allowing us to climb over towering rock formations and navigate treacherous ravines. In place of pulleys and levers, he improvised with branches and roots, creating makeshift mechanisms that helped us ascend to higher ground.

With each obstacle we encountered, The Seeker's innovative approach offered evidence of his adaptability and resourcefulness. Through careful observation and creative problem-solving, he led us safely through the rugged terrain, proving that sometimes the most effective solutions are found in the simplicity of nature itself.

Aria's keen eyes and sharp reflexes helped us navigate the precarious ledges and narrow passages, ensuring we stayed on course despite the unforgiving ground.

When we encountered treacherous ravines, I led the way, using my experience in wilderness survival to find safe paths through the tough terrain.

The Seeker instead tapped into his innate instincts and survival skills to assess the terrain ahead. With a keen eye for detail and a deep understanding of the natural world, he scanned the surroundings, picking up subtle cues and signs of potential hazards. Employing age-old tracking techniques passed down through generations, he navigated the treacherous landscape with a wisdom born of experience, guiding his companions safely through the rugged landscape.

Meanwhile, Aria's unyielding resolve and fearless demeanor spurred us onward, infusing us with renewed determination to overcome whatever challenges lay in their path. Her sharp intuition and honed instincts allowed her to anticipate obstacles before they arose, charting a course through the wasteland with precision and grace. With each step forward, she led our group with confidence, her steady hand and unwavering spirit serving as a beacon of hope in the face of adversity.

Together, we faced each obstacle with courage and determination, our bond growing stronger with each challenge they overcame. And as we continued our journey through the wasteland, we knew that no matter what lay ahead, we would face it together, united in our quest to reach our destination.

With each step, we drew closer to our destination, our resolve unwavering despite the challenges that lay ahead. We relied on one another for support, offering words of encouragement and assistance as we braved the perils of the wasteland together.

The air was thick with tension, with every rustle of the wind and distant rumble sending shivers down our spines. Shadows danced ominously in the flickering light of their torches, casting eerie shapes upon the barren ground.

Despite the darkness that enveloped us, we pressed on, and our senses heightened as they scanned the horizon for any sign of danger. Our muscles ached with exhaustion, and our minds were weary from the constant vigilance required to navigate the treacherous landscape.

Yet, amidst the desolation, there was a sense of camaraderie—a shared understanding that we were not alone in their journey. Together, we faced the challenges of the wasteland head-on, with each step bringing us closer to our goal.

And so, under the cover of darkness, we continued our journey, our spirits undaunted by the trials that awaited us. We knew that only by pressing forward could we hope to overcome the obstacles that stood between us and our goal.

As we ventured through the unforgiving ground towards Greendale, we soon found ourselves stalked by these biomechanical beasts. The scraphounds were a fusion of organic and mechanical components, their metallic bodies gleaming in the dim light as they prowled through the ruins and forests.

With razor-sharp claws and advanced sensors, the scraphounds hunted with a predatory precision that made them formidable adversaries. Their mechanical limbs allowed them to traverse the landscape with ease, while their augmented senses enabled them to track their prey with deadly accuracy.

We quickly realized that traditional weapons and tactics were ineffective against these biomechanical predators. Bullets ricocheted off their armored hides, and blades barely left a scratch on their metallic surfaces. Even Aria's expert knife skills seemed futile against the scraphounds' reinforced exoskeletons.

As we pressed forward, we found ourselves engaged in a desperate battle for survival against the relentless scraphounds. My Fusionizer energy rifle discharged bursts of energy, momentarily staggering the mechanized beasts, while The Seeker's Voltcaster unleashed bolts of energy, temporarily disrupting their circuitry.

Meanwhile, Aria danced nimbly around the scraphounds, her agility allowing her to evade their lunges and strikes. With each well-aimed throw, she targeted vulnerable joints and sensors, seeking to disable the creatures long enough for her companions to deliver the finishing blow.

Despite our best efforts, we soon realized that we were outmatched by the relentless onslaught of the scraphounds. With our strength waning, we knew that we needed to find a way to outsmart our mechanical adversaries if we were to have any hope of surviving the journey to Greendale. With danger lurking around every corner, we steeled ourselves for the challenges ahead, determined to overcome the odds and emerge victorious against the biomechanical beasts that hunted them.

As we ventured deeper into the untamed wilderness, we encountered a series of narrow gorges flanked by towering cliffs and dense foliage. The rocky terrain offered limited visibility, providing ample opportunity for ambushes from the biomechanical beasts that lurked within.

With each step, the ground trembled beneath our feet as the mechanical monstrosities closed in on us with unnatural speed. These creatures, known as Scrapstalkers, were towering constructs of metal and sinew, their glowing eyes scanning the surroundings for prey.

We prepared our weapons, ready to face the relentless onslaught of the scrappers. My Fusionizer hummed with energy, crackling with power as I aimed it at the approaching horde. The Seeker's Voltcaster whirred to life, unleashing arcs of electricity that crackled through the air. Aria twirled her dual blades with practiced precision, her keen eyes tracking the movements of their adversaries.

With a deafening roar, the Scrapstalkers lunged forward, their metal claws slashing through the air with lethal precision. I unleashed a barrage of energy bolts from his Fusionizer, each shot finding its mark and sending sparks flying as it struck the mechanical beasts. The Seeker's Voltcaster emitted a blinding flash of lightning, illuminating the darkness as it arced towards the Scrapstalkers, sizzling against their metallic hide.

Aria darted between the towering beasts, her blades flashing in the dim light as she danced with unmatched agility. With each strike, she severed cables and connections, rendering the Scrapstalkers momentarily incapacitated before they could retaliate.

Despite our formidable foes, we fought with unwavering resolve, our skills complementing each other as they worked in unison to fend off the relentless assault. With each scrapstalker that fell, our confidence grew, fueled by the knowledge that we fought not just for survival but for the safety of all who called the wasteland their home.

As the last of the Scrapstalkers crumbled to the ground,we stood victorious amidst the wreckage of our fallen adversaries.

Though weary from battle, our spirits remained unbroken, strengthened by the bonds of camaraderie forged in the heat of combat.

As we pressed onward through the unforgiving wasteland, our journey to Greendale tested our resilience and determination at every turn. Despite the myriad challenges we encountered, from treacherous terrain to unpredictable weather, we persevered, driven by their shared goal and unwavering camaraderie.

After days of arduous travel, with the sun setting on the horizon, we finally caught sight of the sprawling settlement of Greendale in the distance. Its sturdy walls and bustling streets offered a beacon of hope amidst the desolation of the wasteland, promising safety and respite after our long and perilous journey.

As we drew closer, the gates of Greendale swung open to welcome us, the guards recognizing our weary but determined expressions. Stepping through the threshold, we were greeted by the bustling sights and sounds of the settlement, the air alive with the chatter of traders and the clatter of hooves on cobblestone streets. Seeking out the local inn, we found refuge for the night, eager to rest our weary bodies and replenish our supplies before embarking on the next leg of their journey. Over a hearty meal and steaming mugs of ale, we shared stories of our adventures and toasted to our success, grateful for each other's steadfast companionship in the face of adversity.

As the night wore on and fatigue finally caught up with them, we retired to our rooms, with the promise of a new day and fresh opportunities awaiting us in the bustling settlement of Greendale. With a sense of accomplishment and anticipation for the adventures yet to come, my companions drifted off to sleep, ready to face whatever challenges lay ahead in this newfound haven amidst the wasteland.

As the night wore on and the adrenaline of battle faded into a silent, heavy air, I found myself alone with my thoughts, the soft breaths of my companions the only sound in the quiet rooms. Lying in the darkness, the day's events replayed in my mind like echoes in a vast canyon—a mixture of victory and vulnerability, of bravery and fear. Aria's brave act, taking the blow meant for me, etched itself deep into my consciousness, a stark reminder of the fragility of our existence in this shattered world. It brought forth a surge of emotions I hadn't anticipated, a tumultuous sea of concern, gratitude, and an unnamed feeling that bordered on something deeper, more profound. As I lay there, the line between day and night blurring into insignificance, I grappled with the realization that our mission, while paramount, was intricately woven with the threads of our personal lives. Our quest for unity, for a semblance of peace in this post-apocalyptic wasteland, was not just about the communities we sought to bring together but about the unity within our own ranks—the unspoken bonds that had grown between us, strong and unyielding. And in that moment of introspection, I understood that these bonds were our true strength, the beacon that would guide us through the darkness. With the first light of dawn creeping through the window, casting a soft glow on the room, I rose, my resolve strengthened, ready to embrace the day and whatever it might bring, with my companions by my side.

In the quiet moments before daybreak, as I sat alone with my thoughts, I reflected on the journey that had led us here. From the solitary days of wandering through the ruins of the old world to finding a semblance of family in my companions, I had grown in ways I could never have anticipated. The world around us was a harsh, unforgiving place, yet it was our shared struggles that had shaped me the most.

Leadership, I realized, was more than just making decisions; it was about understanding the hearts and hopes of those who follow you. Friendship was not just about companionship; it was about the unspoken bond that forms in the face of adversity, a promise of solidarity against all odds. And survival? It was about finding moments of humanity and warmth in the coldest of places.

These lessons, learned not through words but through actions, would guide me as we continued our quest.

As the first rays of sunlight pierced the darkness, casting a soft glow on the dilapidated walls of our temporary refuge, I knew it was time to face the day. With a sense of purpose renewed, I rose to my feet, ready to reunite with my companions and continue our journey together, whatever it might hold.

That night, sleep eluded me once again, a familiar occurrence to which I had grown accustomed. Lost in my thoughts, time seemed to slip away unnoticed, until the first light of dawn pierced through the darkness. Lying awake, the events of the past days replayed in my mind like a relentless tide, each wave bringing with it a mix of resolve, doubt, and the raw edge of vulnerability. "Are we mere pawns in the grand scheme of things, or do our actions truly shape the world around us?" I pondered. The darkness before dawn seemed to hold its breath, offering no answers, only the echoing reminder of the delicate balance between fate and free will. In those quiet hours, I confronted my own doubts, realizing that to lead is not to be unshakable but to walk forward despite the tremors of uncertainty.

It felt like a restless state of semi-consciousness, but I'd learned to manage.

While my companions slumbered on, I took the opportunity to inquire about the whereabouts of the camp's leader and whether I could arrange a meeting with her. The locals assured me that she was always receptive to visitors and granted the guards permission to enter. They gestured toward a distinctively prominent house in the vicinity, indicating that it belonged to her.

The house, though constructed with primitive means, exudes an air of grandeur befitting its esteemed occupant. Rising proudly from the snow-covered landscape, its sturdy walls stand tall and imposing, crafted from thick logs and reinforced with salvaged metal plating. Each timber, weathered and worn from the elements, bears the scars of its journey, evidence of the resilience of those who built it. Outside, a sprawling courtyard extends from the rear of the house, enclosed by sturdy wooden palisades that offer protection from potential threats.

Once I caught sight of the others exiting the inn, I hurried over to join them and brief them on our next destination. Together, we made our way toward the town leader's residence, only to be intercepted by vigilant guards stationed at the entrance.

"Halt! State your purpose," one of them demanded.

"We're here to discuss pressing matters regarding the unity of neighboring communities," I replied.

"Very well. You may proceed, but your weapons stay with us," he instructed.

Reluctantly, we handed over our weapons, causing the guard to gape at the unfamiliar arsenal before him. After a brief moment of hesitation, he accepted them and granted us entry, gesturing toward the leader's abode.

As we stepped inside, we found ourselves awestruck by the sight that greeted us. Within the main hall, a massive hearth dominated one wall, its roaring fire casting a warm glow that banishes the chill of the outside world. Above it, a vast cauldron hangs from a sturdy iron chain, perpetually bubbling with hearty stews and savory soups that nourish the town's inhabitants.

Beyond the main hall lie chambers reserved for the town leader and their family, each one spacious and lavishly appointed despite the scarcity of resources. Thick fur pelts line the floors, offering comfort and insulation against the cold, while handcrafted wooden furnishings provide a touch of rustic elegance to the interior decor.

In the town leader's private chamber, a massive canopy bed occupies the center of the room, its towering frame draped with richly embroidered fabrics and plush cushions. A small writing desk sits nearby, littered with scrolls and parchments detailing the town's affairs, a constant reminder of the responsibilities that come with leadership.

For now, the town leader was located in the main hall, standing near a small table, going through a pile of documents.

The town leader, despite her youth of what looked to be 21 years of age, possesses a countenance that belies her tender years. Her visage carries the weight of experience far beyond her age, marked by a serene confidence and a piercing intellect that commands respect from all who cross her path.

Standing tall and resolute, she exudes an aura of authority tempered by compassion, her every gesture reflecting a deep-seated determination to protect and nurture her community. Her eyes, keen and observant, betray a wisdom that speaks volumes of the trials she has faced and overcome in her brief yet eventful life.

Her attire, though simple, speaks volumes about her role as a leader. She wears a practical yet dignified ensemble, consisting of a sturdy leather tunic cinched at the waist with a thick belt adorned with intricately carved symbols of her station. Over this, she dons a weathered cloak, its deep indigo hue bearing the insignia of her town—a symbol of her unwavering dedication to its prosperity and well-being.

"Hello," I said, feeling a bit overwhelmed by her youthfulness and the intensity in her eyes.

"Hello to you too," she replied, her voice soft but confident. "I'm Anna. And who do I have the pleasure of speaking with?"

"I'm Ethan," I answered, gesturing towards my companions. "This is The Seeker, Kael, and Aria. We've come to talk to you about something important."

"Whoa, hold up! Aren't you a tad young to be running a whole town?" The Seeker interjected, his tone laced with his typical brand of quirky curiosity.

"I am indeed young," Anna began, her voice carrying a sense of maturity beyond her years, "My father, the previous town leader, passed away unexpectedly, thrusting the responsibilities of leadership upon me at a young age. Despite my youth, I have proven capable of managing the daily affairs required to lead a town. Now, what is this proposition you speak of?"

Ethan once again outlined our plan to unite the various towns, starting with the use of radios. Both Anna and I dove into the details, demonstrating how we could communicate with Greendale and Misty Hollow. While impressed by the presentation, Anna expressed doubts about the feasibility of our plan.

"What concerns you about the plan?" I inquired.

"It's the distance," Anna replied thoughtfully. "I understand your intentions to establish checkpoints for trading, but I'm uncertain about whether it will work and if the other towns will uphold their agreements. Trust doesn't come easily to me, and I find it difficult to envision the outcome you propose."

"I appreciate your skepticism," I acknowledged. "It's wise not to place blind trust in promises. However, I believe that with collective determination, we can make it happen. The other communities are eager to collaborate, and they trust me to lead this initiative. While I cannot guarantee the future, I refuse to let uncertainty deter us from striving for progress."

"You make a compelling argument," Anna conceded, "but I still harbor doubts. However, I'm willing to give it a chance under one condition: the other communities must prove their commitment to us. I will observe their progress, and if they demonstrate their ability to work with us, then we can proceed together."

"If that's what it takes," I agreed, "then I accept your terms.

However, I urge you to convey your mindset to the other communities over the radio. I believe they will agree to the same terms."

"Very well," Anna concluded, "if there's nothing else to discuss, you are free to come and go as you please. I assume you'll be leaving now. Until we meet again, whether in person or over the radio."

"Agreed, I'm confident things will work out," I replied with a nod, bidding farewell as my companions and I exited the house, retrieving our weapons from the guard stationed outside.

"Um, pardon my curiosity, but what exactly are those things you've got there?" the guard inquired, eyeing our gear with fascination. "I've been wondering about them, though I'm too cautious to touch them."

"I'm afraid the story behind these items is rather lengthy," I explained, "but they're advanced technology and formidable weaponry. However, delving into where they came from would require a considerable amount of time to explain. I hope you understand."

"Ah, yes, of course," the guard nodded understandingly. "Curiosity can be a tricky thing."

"Alright, strap in, 'cause here comes the wild ride." The Seeker drawled in his characteristic accent, his words tinged with a Southern twang. "So, y'see, Ethan here? Dude's been frozen solid for a good thousand years, and when they thawed him out, bam! Suddenly, he's all decked out in this fancy gear from the pre-war days. And get this—superpowers! They jabbed him with some serum that makes him practically immortal, and-"

"Enough," I interjected sharply. "That's not something I care to share publicly, if you catch my drift."

To our surprise, the guard burst into laughter, tears streaming down his face. "You got me good, sir!" he exclaimed between laughs. "I haven't had a chuckle like that in ages. You've got quite the sense of humor!"

"Meh," muttered The Seeker, unimpressed.

With that settled, we retraced our steps back to the heart of the town, and our curiosity piqued about what awaited us in this unfamiliar place. Having journeyed for what felt like an eternity, I reasoned that it might be worthwhile to linger for a while and explore the offerings of this town before resuming our travels.

As night descended upon the peaceful town of Willowbrook, whispers of unease echoed through the frost-kissed streets. For weeks, a shadowy figure had prowled the darkness, stealing into homes under the cover of night and pilfering valuables from unsuspecting residents. As rumors spread of the elusive thief's exploits, a sense of fear and mistrust gripped the once-tranquil community.

Determined to put an end to the reign of terror, I rallied my companions—Aria, Kael, and The Seeker—for a nighttime patrol, our senses keen and our resolve unwavering. With stealth born of necessity, we traversed the winding alleyways and silent thoroughfares, vigilant for any sign of the elusive intruder.

Yet, despite our best efforts, the thief remained elusive, slipping through our fingers like a wisp of smoke. Hours passed in fruitless pursuit, the chill of the night air gnawing at our bones as fatigue threatened to cloud our judgment. Frustration mounted with each passing moment, our determination waning in the face of our adversary's elusiveness.

It was then, amidst the depths of our despair, that a glimmer of hope emerged—a villager, his face etched with concern, approached us with an offer of assistance. "I've heard tell of a robotic dog designed to sniff out intruders and track their movements," he explained, his voice tinged with urgency. "If anyone can help you catch this thief, it's that mechanical marvel."

Grasping at the lifeline offered by the villager, we wasted no time in seeking out the robotic dog, its sleek metallic form gleaming in the moonlight. With a renewed sense of determination, we set forth once more, the mechanical hound leading the way with unerring precision.

Hours stretched into eternity as we followed the robotic dog through the labyrinthine streets of Willowbrook, our senses attuned to the slightest disturbance in the night. At long last, our perseverance was rewarded—a shadowy figure, cloaked in darkness, emerged from the depths of an alleyway, its form shrouded in mystery.

Without hesitation, we sprang into action, confronting the thief with steely resolve. But to our astonishment, the figure was no mere mortal—it was a robotic opponent, its movements fluid and precise, its eyes glinting with malice.

With lightning speed, the thief drew a titanium katana, its blade shimmering in the pale moonlight as it struck with lethal precision. We fought valiantly, our weapons clashing with the metallic clangor of steel on steel, but the robotic foe proved a formidable adversary, its speed and strength surpassing our own.

The battle raged on, with each blow exchanged with fierce intensity as we struggled to gain the upper hand. But no matter how we attacked, the thief danced effortlessly out of reach, its movements a blur of calculated precision.

As the minutes stretched into eternity, a sense of desperation took hold, with our exhaustion threatening to overwhelm us. But even in the face of seemingly insurmountable odds, we refused to yield, our determination burning brightly within our hearts.

As the battle with the robotic thief raged on, our options dwindled in the face of its lightning-fast movements and unyielding strength. However, amidst the chaos, The Seeker, with his keen intellect and resourcefulness, spotted a vulnerability in the thief's defenses.

With a shout of determination, The Seeker devised a plan to exploit this weakness, leveraging each of our unique skills to execute a coordinated attack. Drawing upon our collective strengths, we positioned ourselves strategically, ready to strike when the moment presented itself.

As the thief lunged forward with blinding speed, Kael unleashed a barrage of distracting projectiles, forcing the mechanical foe to momentarily divert its attention. Seizing the opportunity, I unleashed a powerful energy blast from my Fusionizer rifle, aiming for a critical juncture in the thief's armor.

Simultaneously, Aria sprang into action, her dual blades flashing in the moonlight as she aimed for the thief's joints, seeking to disable their mobility. With precision and grace, she danced around the mechanical adversary, her movements fluid and precise.

However, despite our coordinated efforts, the thief proved a formidable opponent, with its defenses holding strong against our relentless assault. It retaliated with swift counterattacks, its titanium katana slashing through the air with deadly accuracy.

In the midst of the chaos, tragedy struck—Aria, in a moment of split-second decision, leaped in front of a devastating blow aimed at me, sacrificing herself to protect her comrade. The thief's blade struck true, slicing through Aria's shoulder with a sickening crunch.

The impact sent Aria reeling, a cry of pain escaping her lips as she staggered backward, clutching her injured shoulder. A cold shiver of fear coursed through me at the sight, my mind racing with worry for her well-being beyond the immediate danger.

Blood seeped from the wound, staining her clothing crimson as she fought to maintain her footing amidst the onslaught.

Despite the agony coursing through her body, Aria refused to yield, her determination unshaken by the pain. With gritted teeth and unwavering resolve, she pressed on, her blades flashing with renewed ferocity as she continued to engage the mechanical thief.

In the quiet moments that followed the battle's end, as I tended to Aria's wound, the reality of our situation pierced through the adrenaline-fueled haze. Her injury, a stark symbol of our vulnerabilities, also underscored the depth of our commitment to one another. In the flickering shadows, our conversations meandered between light-hearted jests and solemn promises, each word a balm to the unseen wounds we carried. Aria's resilience, in the face of physical pain, mirrored the indomitable spirit of our group, a beacon guiding us through the darkness.

As the battle reached its climax, our coordinated assault finally began to take its toll on the robotic adversary. With a final, decisive blow, The Seeker targeted the thief's power source, delivering a disabling blast that sent sparks flying in all directions.

With a mechanical whirr, the thief stumbled, its movements growing sluggish as it struggled to remain upright. Sensing an opportunity, we launched a final, concerted attack, overwhelming the now-vulnerable foe with a barrage of strikes.

With a resounding crash, the thief collapsed to the ground, its metallic form crumpling in defeat. We stood victorious over our fallen adversary, the echoes of battle fading into the night as we caught our breath, our hearts heavy with the memory of Aria's sacrifice.

The silence that enveloped us was more than the aftermath of combat; it was a moment of reflection on the sacrifices that bound us together. "True unity," I realized, "is forged in the moments when we stand not just alongside each other, but for each other." Aria's act of bravery was a stark reminder that our mission was grounded not just in the hope of rebuilding what was lost, but in the unspoken vows we made to protect and uplift one another, even against the gravest of odds.

In the aftermath of our confrontation, as we left the battlefield behind, a contemplative silence enveloped us. Each step away from the debris was a step inward, into the recesses of our minds. 'What cost comes with our survival?' I pondered, the echoes of our victory ringing hollow in my heart. 'In our battle against the shadows of this world, are we safeguarding our humanity, or are we losing pieces of it along the way?' It was a moment of introspection, a brief respite where the soul weighed more than the sword, reminding us that our journey was not merely about the destinations we aimed for but about the individuals we were becoming in the process.

As the dust settled and the echoes of battle faded into the night, we stood victorious over our fallen foe, its metallic form lying motionless at our feet.

After the intense battle with the robotic thief, amidst the scattered remains of its metallic form, we discovered a small, intricately engraved emblem—a logo etched into one of the thief's components. It was a distinctive symbol, unfamiliar yet unmistakable in its design.

"Oi, what's this then?" exclaimed The Seeker, squinting at the emblem. "Looks like some sorta fancy doodle. But I reckon it's more than just that."

Examining the logo closely, The Seeker's keen eye recognized it as a mark of craftsmanship—a signature, perhaps, left by the creator of the mechanical adversary.

"By the gears of Gadzooks! This 'ere symbol ain't just for show," he declared. "It's a clue, mates! A clue to who's behind all this tomfoolery."

Intrigued by The Seeker's revelation, we pondered the significance of the emblem, our minds racing with possibilities.

"Hey, do you think that tinkerer guy on the outskirts could be behind this?" I mused, recalling rumors of a skilled inventor in the area.

"Aye, could be," nodded The Seeker. "But there's only one way to find out. We gotta pay ol' gadget man a visit and see if he's been cookin' up trouble in his workshop."

Driven by the need for answers and justice, we set off to confront the recluse inventor, determined to unravel the mystery of the mechanical menace that had plagued our town.

Upon reaching the inventor's humble abode, we were met with skepticism and reluctance.

"I haven't done anything wrong, I'm telling you!" protested the inventor, his voice trembling with apprehension. "My inventions are meant for good, not mischief."

But when presented with the evidence—the emblem found among the thief's remains—the truth could no longer be denied.

"Oh, bloody hell! That's my emblem, alright," confessed the inventor, his facade crumbling under the weight of guilt. "But I swear on my gears, I didn't mean any harm. I was coerced, I was!"

As we searched the inventor's workshop, we discovered a cache of stolen belongings hidden among his possessions—a damning revelation that confirmed his complicity in the crimes that had plagued our town.

With the truth exposed, we seized the stolen goods and returned them to their rightful owners, bringing closure to those who had been wronged by the mechanical thief.

In the aftermath of the ordeal, the town rallied together, united in their gratitude for our efforts to protect and defend their community. Our bond was strengthened by adversity; we stood as guardians of justice, ready to face whatever challenges the future might hold. And though the scars of battle remained, they served as a reminder of the resilience and courage that defined us as heroes of Greendale.

As we gathered the stolen goods, ready to return them to their rightful owners, a sense of accomplishment filled the air. Yet, the encounter with the robotic thief lingered in our minds, a puzzle begging to be solved. Back at the inn, our gathered group leaned into a huddle, the day's events casting a long shadow over our conversation.

"Do you think there could be more out there?" Kael asked, breaking the silence. "More creations like that thief lurking in the shadows?"

"It's a possibility we can't ignore," I admitted, the weight of leadership pressing down on my shoulders. "This encounter has shown us there are forces at work we don't fully understand. As we head to Pinecrest Camp, we need to be prepared for anything."

Aria, still nursing her injury but with a fire in her eyes, added, "Let's take this as a lesson. We've faced what we thought was impossible and came out stronger. No matter what lies ahead, we'll face it together. Our mission hasn't changed, but our resolve must be stronger than ever."

In the brief silence that followed, the weight of Aria's words hung heavily in the air. I looked at her, seeing not just the warrior and ally she had become but also the depths of her own story that had led her to this moment. "Each of us carries scars, some visible, others not," I thought to myself. "Aria's resilience, born from a past punctuated by loss and survival, mirrors the very essence of what our journey embodies. As we prepare to face the uncertainties of Pinecrest Camp, it's not just the physical challenges we must overcome but also the shadows of our pasts that shape our resolve.

Nods of agreement circled among us. The night had tested us, but it had also reaffirmed our commitment to our cause. With the stolen goods in tow, we stepped out into the fading light of day, ready to make amends and continue our journey. Our spirits, tempered by the night's ordeal, were now unbreakable—forged in the fire of adversity, ready to confront whatever challenges lay ahead with a unity that had become our hallmark.

I led Aria to a quiet corner of the town, away from prying eyes, where I could tend to her wounds in privacy. My heart raced with worry as I saw Aria bleeding from her shoulder, but I tried to keep my composure as I quickly retrieved the medical supplies we needed. With gentle hands, I began to clean the wound, my movements careful and precise as I worked to stop the bleeding.

As I tended to her, a whirlwind of emotions stirred within me. Seeing Aria injured sparked a fierce protectiveness I hadn't realized I possessed, mingled with a deep affection that bordered on love. Each bandage applied felt like a connection, drawing us closer in ways I couldn't quite explain.

Once her wound was properly cared for, I sat beside Aria, our shoulders touching as we gazed at each other in the dim light. The tension between us was palpable, an unspoken acknowledgment of the feelings that lingered between us.

"It scares me, you know," I admitted softly, my voice barely above a whisper. "The thought of losing you."

Aria met my gaze, her eyes reflecting a mix of understanding and uncertainty. "I know what you mean," she replied quietly. "The world as it is... it's unpredictable. And the idea of losing you is equally terrifying."

Our conversation drifted into uncertain territory, with the weight of our feelings hanging heavy in the air. We both knew there was something undeniable between us, a connection that transcended mere friendship. But the reality of our situation made us hesitant to fully embrace it.

"I wish things were different," I murmured, my voice heavy with regret. "That we could just be... without worrying about what might happen."

Aria nodded in agreement, her expression mirroring my sentiment. "But we can't ignore the risks," she added softly. "We have to be realistic about what we're facing."

Our words hung in the air, a silent acknowledgment of the complexities of our situation. Despite the uncertainty, there was an undeniable truth that lingered between us: we loved each other. But whether that love could withstand the challenges of our world remained to be seen.

Before we parted ways, I took Aria's hand in mine, squeezing it gently as I met her gaze. "Thank you," I said softly, my voice filled with emotion. "For taking that hit for me. Even though I would've healed on my own, the gesture meant more to me than you'll ever know."

Aria smiled sadly, her eyes shimmering with unshed tears. "I'd do anything for you," she whispered, her voice barely audible above the faint rustle of the wind. "Just know that."

With a final squeeze of our hands, we parted ways, each lost in our own thoughts as we returned to the group. The uncertainty of our relationship lingered, but so did the undeniable truth: we loved each other, and that was enough for now.

The day crept by slowly, and my mind was still tangled with thoughts of Aria. Yet, I knew I had to press on, so I busied myself with preparing the horses and gathering supplies for our trek to Pinecrest Camp, the home of the bandits. Convincing this community to join us would be our toughest challenge yet.

Nightfall descended, and my companions and I retired to the inn for some much-needed rest. Alone in my thoughts, I pondered the uncertain future, reminiscing about Aria and contemplating the paths that lay ahead for us after our mission was complete. Where would destiny lead me next? How could I unearth more clues about the elusive Nexus Vault? The enormity of the world loomed before me, daunting and vast, with the vault potentially hidden anywhere.

I needed guidance, a beacon to steer me towards my objective. Wandering aimlessly through abandoned buildings and ruins in search of answers wasn't sustainable. There had to be a more strategic approach.

Lost in my musings, I lost track of time, only to awaken to the bustling morning. I noticed my companions were already up and about, following the rhythm of the sun's ascent. Perhaps it was time to embrace the timeless tradition of marking time by the sun's movement.

Rising from my bed, I felt as if I had indulged in a long, uninterrupted slumber, a luxury I hadn't experienced since before the war. An insatiable craving for a jolt of energy propelled me downstairs to the inn's common area, where I sought out a cup of coffee.

"Cawfee, what in the 'eck is cawfee? Nevah 'eard of it, mate. You lookin' for anythin' specific then?" the bartender queried, his words tinged with curiosity.

Perplexed by the unfamiliarity with coffee, I inquired further, "What do you folks typically indulge in upon awakening, in need of a pick-me-up?"

"We 'ave various roasted grain beverages; they ought to do the job if ya lookin' for somethin' to get ya goin', ya know. That's what people usually drink in the mornin'. An' mushrooms, but we don't serve that 'ere," the bartender explained in his gruff voice, gesturing towards the assortment of drinks behind the counter.

"Just give me one of those, whatever's the strongest you've got," I requested, eager to kickstart my morning.

"One cup o' Ironbrew comin' right up, mate!" the bartender replied with a nod, disappearing momentarily to prepare the concoction.

He returned with a sizable black cup, its contents resembling murky water. Despite its unappetizing appearance, I took a hesitant sip, immediately regretting it as the potent brew hit my taste buds with full force. Determined to power through, I forced myself to finish the entire cup, feeling a surge of alertness coursing through my veins. The intensity of the beverage left me trembling slightly, but I couldn't deny its efficacy as a wake-up call.

"What do I owe you?" I inquired, mentally preparing to settle the bill.

"Tell the innkeeper, yer mates 'ad a few drinks yesterday as

well, an' the nights you've stayed 'ere. I've 'eard it all 'asn't been paid for. So ya better talk to 'im before ya get outta 'ere or ya probably won't be comin' back inside," the bartender warned, his tone firm but not unkind.

Grateful for the generosity, I sought out the innkeeper to settle my debt. "You've done enough for this town already, mate. This one's on me," he insisted with a smile, refusing payment.

"Oh, and one more thing," the innkeeper said, "Anna has arranged for several horses for your journey. We noticed you arrived on foot, so they're all set and ready. And don't worry about the cost—they're free considering everything you've done for us."

"I appreciate that; I'll be sure to visit once I come here again," I replied, though I knew deep down that such a return visit was unlikely. With a sigh of contentment, I stepped outside, eager to reunite with my companions and continue our journey.

I stumbled upon Kael and Aria engaged in conversation, their voices hushed as I approached, casting a momentary silence over their exchange.

"Did I interrupt something?" I inquired, sensing a shift in their demeanor.

"No, well, actually, yes, kind of," Kael admitted, his tone betraying a hint of awkwardness.

"And what's that supposed to mean?" I prodded, a twinge of curiosity coloring my words.

"To be honest," Aria confessed, "we were discussing you and the conversation we had yesterday. I just sought some advice from Kael, that's all," she explained, her words tinged with sincerity.

"I can't say I'm thrilled about not being included in that conversation, Aria. But fair enough. I'm not here to dictate your actions. So, what's the conclusion?" I inquired, masking my unease with a semblance of composure.

"We simply agreed that it's a complex situation," Kael chimed in, offering his perspective. "I mean, if you two were to pursue a relationship, that'd be wonderful. However, considering your ongoing mission, it might put Aria at risk. I'm sure you're not willing to compromise your objectives, so perhaps this doesn't have to be defined in concrete terms. Think of it as a unique kind of companionship. That's the best compromise we could come up with," he suggested.

"That's pretty much it," Aria confirmed, her gaze meeting mine with a mixture of understanding and uncertainty.

"I suppose that arrangement works for me," I acquiesced, though a tinge of ambivalence lingered beneath my words. "At least, as fine as such a situation can be defined,. Anyway, are we ready to depart? Where's The Seeker? I need to have a word with him."

"That's a different matter altogether," Kael interjected, his expression sober. "It's best you speak with him directly. I believe he'd prefer to explain himself."

"Well, then I'll track him down," I resolved, determination lacing my tone. "Where can I find him?"

"He's likely roaming the market, last I heard," Kael replied, his gaze drifting towards the bustling marketplace beyond.

So I made my way through the bustling market, scanning the colorful stalls and weaving through the crowd until I finally spotted The Seeker rummaging through a rack of clothes.

"Hey Seeker," I called out, approaching him amidst the myriad of fabrics and textures. "Ready to hit the road, or are you planning on setting up shop here for the day?"

"I'd say the latter," he replied with a mischievous twinkle in his eye.

"Wait, you're going to spend the day browsing clothes?" I asked with a hint of disbelief in my voice.

"Nah, not exactly," he began, his tone laced with his usual eccentric charm. "The thing is, I've decided to stay behind. I fancy the idea of sticking around for a while. Had my fill of wanderin', you know?"

His decision caught me off guard, but I respected his choice. After all, we couldn't expect our companions to accompany us indefinitely.

"Well, if that's what you want, then I won't stop you," I replied, masking my surprise with understanding.

"Listen, boss," he continued, his accent thick and jovial. "It's nothing personal, see? I just need some time to myself. Gonna soak up the town life; maybe lend a hand here and there, ya know?"

"Yeah, I get it." I nodded, accepting his explanation. "So I guess this is goodbye for now?"

"Aye, something like that," he replied, a touch of nostalgia in his voice. "Maybe our paths will cross again, depending on where I end up. But for the foreseeable future, I'll be sticking around these parts. Farewell for now, boss. Safe travels to ya."

"Thanks," I said, extending my hand for a shake. A pang of loss tightened around my heart as I realized the journeys shared and the battles fought had forged bonds that were not easily broken. His departure left a void, a silent echo of his presence that would travel with us. "You take care of yourself."

As I walked away, the weight of The Seeker's absence settled over me. Our journey had been fraught with challenges, each of us carrying our own burdens yet finding solace in our shared purpose. The Seeker's quirky humor and unyielding spirit had been a constant amidst the chaos, and his departure was a stark reminder of the personal paths we each must tread. Though our mission pressed on, the echoes of his laughter would remain with us, a testament to the bonds formed in the face of adversity.

With a final wave, we parted ways, and I made my way back to my other companions.

Before the chaos, I had a life filled with the mundane and the extraordinary alike,' The Seeker shared, his gaze distant. "Ah, ye see, there be a family, dreams, an' a snug little home that stood firm against the whispers o' the wind. But when the world crumbled, so did the foundation o' me existence. This place it be a reminder of what once was an' what could be again. Perhaps, jest perhaps, it be time to seek not what's beyond the horizon, but what's right in front o' me, ya see." His confession unveiled a layer of sorrow veiled by his jovial facade, a poignant reminder of the personal odysseys entwined with our shared journey.

As dawn painted the sky with hues of gold and crimson, we set forth towards Pinecrest Camp, each step carrying the weight of our past victories and the shadows of our uncertainties. The road ahead promised no respite, each horizon a new challenge to overcome. Yet, in the silence of the morning, a profound truth resonated within me: it was not the destination that defined us, but the journey itself. With Aria by my side and the memory of those we had lost etched in our hearts, we rode forward, not just in search of the Nexus Vault but in pursuit of a legacy that would echo through the ages, a testament to our resilience, our hopes, and the indelible mark of our shared humanity.

Before the chaos, I had a life filled with the mundane and the extraordinary alike,' The Seeker shared, his gaze distant. 'A family, dreams, and a home that stood firm against the whispers of the wind. When the world crumbled, so did the foundation of my existence. This place is a reminder of what once was and what could be again. Maybe, just maybe, it's time to seek not what's beyond the horizon, but what's right in front of me.' His confession unveiled a layer of sorrow veiled by his jovial facade, a poignant reminder of the personal odysseys entwined with our shared journey.

"Ready to hit the road?" I asked them, eager to continue our journey.

They nodded in agreement, and together we mounted our horses and rode towards the exit of the town, bidding farewell to the guards as we embarked on the next leg of our adventure.

BENEATH BITTER WINDS

As the bitter winds swept through the desolate landscape, rattling the occasional window and sending swirls of dust dancing in their wake, Aria, Kael, and I continued our journey towards Pinecrest Camp, our next destination in this unforgiving land. The land around us, once teeming with life, now lay silent, a testament to the resilience required to navigate through what had become a tapestry of survival and forgotten echoes.

Each silent echo beneath our feet whispered stories of what was and what might never be again, urging us forward not just in body but in spirit as we sought new horizons beyond the scars of yesteryear. With each step, the echoes seemed to merge with our own, crafting a chorus of determination that resonated with the promise of a future reclaimed from the ruins. Each echo, like the remnants of a forgotten song, seemed to carry the weight of our past journeys, whispering of battles won and lost and of friendships forged in the heart of adversity. It reminded us that, just like these echoes, our actions and choices would resonate long into the future, shaping the legacy we would leave behind in this new world.

"The weather seems to be getting worse," Kael remarked, his voice barely audible over the howling wind. "We should find shelter soon."

I nodded in agreement, my gaze scanning the horizon for any sign of refuge amidst the desolate landscape. "We'll keep an eye out for any abandoned buildings or caves," I replied, my words carrying a note of urgency. "We can't afford to get caught out in the open during a snowstorm."

Aria glanced around nervously, her fingers tightening around the reins of her horse. This nervous glance was more than a momentary fear; it was a window into Aria's evolving resolve. Each challenge faced on our journey did not just test her; it forged her courage in the fire of adversity, shaping her into a beacon of hope and strength for us all.

"I don't like the look of those clouds," she said, her voice tinged with concern. "We should find shelter before the storm hits."

"Just as we have before, we'll weather this storm together," I said, recalling the nights we huddled together under scarce shelter, stories and shared warmth binding us closer. "Each storm faced, each challenge overcome, has only made our bond unbreakable."

The terrain, though not marked by the ruins of civilization like many other places we had passed through, still bore the scars of the world that had once been. These scars, etched into the very earth, were not just markers of loss but beacons of resilience, guiding us through the wilderness with silent stories of endurance.

In the quiet spaces between the howling winds, the land seemed to breathe out stories of yore, a mute witness to the resilience of nature and mankind alike. It served as a solemn reminder that while civilizations may crumble, the earth endures, bearing the marks of its past with a silent dignity.

Its sparse vegetation and barren expanses spoke of a world forever changed by the ravages of time and war. In this desolation, however, there lingered a silent testament to resilience, echoing the indomitable spirit of life that endures amidst ruin. This landscape, battered by the whims of fate, stood as a stark reminder of the persistence required not just to survive but to thrive in a world reborn from the ashes of its former self. It was in this crucible of destruction that the true essence of hope and resilience shone brightest, illuminating paths forward where none seemed to exist.

In the darkest nights, our shared stories became beacons, guiding us through uncertainty with the promise of dawn's light. This journey, etched with trials, taught us that hope's true power lies not in erasing shadows but in teaching us to navigate through them.

Yet, despite the desolation that surrounded us, there was a sense of resilience that permeated the air, an indication of the enduring spirit of those who roamed these lands.

Leaving behind the familiarity of our previous campsite, we set our sights on the open road ahead, our horses picking their way carefully through the debris-strewn pathways. The landscape stretched out before us, a vast expanse of barren wasteland punctuated by the occasional cluster of skeletal trees and crumbling structures.

"We should keep an eye out for any signs of trouble," Aria suggested, her eyes scanning the horizon for any movement. "We don't know what dangers lurk out here."

Kael nodded in agreement, his hand resting casually on the hilt of his blade. This gesture, simple yet profound, was an indication of Kael's emerging role as more than a fellow traveler but as a pillar of guidance and wisdom. In the silence that often followed our conversations, a new understanding began to take root among us, revealing the depth of our bonds and the unspoken trust that had begun to define our journey together.

It was as if our shared silences spoke louder than words ever could, weaving a bond of solidarity that grew with every step taken together through the forsaken lands. His readiness to confront whatever lay ahead, with a hand on his blade and a steady gaze, marked the birth of a leader amongst us, quietly assuming the mantle of responsibility.

"Agreed," he replied, his voice steady despite the tension that hung in the air. "We can't afford to let our guard down."

As the hours stretched into days, the monotony of the journey was broken only by the distant howl of a pack of feral dogs. Yet, despite the solitude of our surroundings, there was a sense of determination that drove us forward—a shared determination to reach Pinecrest Camp and the safety it promised.

"And if we stick together, we'll make it through anything," I added, trying to inject a note of optimism into our conversation.

"We've faced worse odds before."

With each passing mile, our spirits remained high, buoyed by the knowledge that we were not alone in our struggle. Together, Aria, Kael, and I would face whatever challenges lay ahead, united in our quest to survive in this unforgiving post-apocalyptic world. Yet, this unity was not without its tests. The road to Pinecrest Camp reminded us that division, both within and beyond our group, lay as much in wait as the unity we sought. Every step taken was a step towards bridging divides, challenging the notion that survival was a solitary endeavor in this fractured world.

As we rode through the snow-covered wasteland, the skeletal trees stood stark against the backdrop of the wintry landscape, their branches stripped bare of leaves by the biting cold.

This wintry landscape, though barren, was alive with the whispers of the past, telling tales of a world that once flourished here. As we traversed this silent symphony of loss and renewal, the resilience of the world around us lent strength to our own resolve, whispering of cycles of decay and rebirth that mirrored our journey. The skeletal trees, standing as silent sentinels, served as reminders of nature's cycle of rebirth and decay, a cycle we found ourselves a part of in our quest for survival and unity.

"These trees look like they've seen better days," Aria remarked, her gaze lingering on the twisted forms of the skeletal trees. "It's like they're reaching out for something."

Kael nodded in agreement, his eyes scanning the desolate landscape for any signs of movement. "Let's keep moving," he suggested, his tone cautious. "We don't want to linger out here longer than we have to."

Our journey, marked by silent vows of perseverance, wove through the remnants of a world holding both peril and promise.

Each mile traversed, each obstacle overcome, didn't just bring us closer to Pinecrest Camp; it deepened our understanding of the world we navigated, a world demanding not just physical endurance but an unwavering resolve to see the journey through. Snowstorms raged around us, threatening to engulf us in their icy embrace, while the biting cold gnawed at our bones with relentless persistence.

"We need to find shelter," I called out over the howling winds, my voice barely audible above the din. "We won't last much longer out here in the open."

Aria nodded in agreement, her teeth chattering from the cold. "I spotted a building up ahead," she replied, pointing towards a dilapidated structure barely visible through the swirling snow. "It might provide some cover from the storm."

With renewed determination, we urged our horses forward, pushing through the snowdrifts towards the shelter of the old building. But little did we know that danger lurked within its crumbling walls—an ominous presence that would test our courage and resolve like never before.

"Is everyone okay?" Aria asked, her voice shaking slightly as she surveyed the aftermath of the battle.

"I'm fine," Kael replied, his voice steady despite the weariness etched into his features. "Just a few scratches."

I nodded in agreement, my heart still pounding in my chest as the adrenaline of battle began to fade. "We were lucky," I said, my voice hoarse from exertion. "That could have ended much worse."

But our victory was short-lived, as we soon found ourselves faced with yet another challenge—the crumbling ruins of the building itself. As we ventured deeper into its decaying halls, we soon found ourselves confronted with a myriad of obstacles that threatened to impede our progress at every turn.

"Watch your step," Kael warned, his voice echoing softly in the dimly lit corridor. "These floorboards don't look very stable."

Aria nodded in agreement, her eyes scanning the ground for any signs of weakness. "We need to be careful," she cautioned, her voice tinged with apprehension. "One wrong move, and we could end up falling through."

I swallowed hard, the weight of our predicament settling heavily on my shoulders. "Let's stick together and watch each other's backs," I suggested, trying to sound more confident than I felt. "We'll get through this together."

Rotted floorboards groaned beneath our weight as we made our way cautiously through the decaying structure. Every step was a gamble, each creak of the wood sending a shiver down my spine as I prayed that it wouldn't give way beneath us.

Crumbling walls leaned precariously overhead, their mortar crumbling away to reveal the skeletal framework of the building beneath. With each passing moment, it felt as though the entire structure was poised to collapse around us, a constant reminder of the danger that lurked within its decaying walls.

But despite the peril that surrounded us, we pressed on, our determination unwavering as we continued our journey through the treacherous corridors of the old building. With each obstacle we overcame, our resolve only grew stronger, fueled by the knowledge that our survival depended on our ability to persevere in the face of adversity.

As we ventured deeper into the heart of the building, we encountered other obstacles that sought to hinder our progress. Each barrier, whether a fallen beam or a collapsed wall, challenged us not merely as obstacles but as testaments to our resolve, demanding we adapt, overcome, and forge ahead.

Fallen debris littered the hallways, creating makeshift barriers that forced us to find alternate routes through the maze-like structure.

"We'll have to find another way around," Aria observed, her eyes scanning the debris-strewn corridor for any signs of a path forward. "This way is completely blocked."

Kael nodded in agreement, his gaze focused on the crumbling walls ahead. "There might be a way through over there," he suggested, pointing to a narrow gap between two collapsed sections of wall.

With no other options available to us, we cautiously made our way towards the gap, our hearts pounding in our chests as we squeezed through the narrow opening. This passage, fraught with uncertainty and danger, was a stark metaphor for our journey itself—navigating through the narrow gaps of survival, inching towards hope with every step, despite the omnipresent shadow of peril.

Every movement was fraught with tension, with each shift of the debris threatening to bring the entire structure crashing down around us.

But despite the danger, we pressed on, our determination driving us forward even in the face of overwhelming odds. With each obstacle we overcame, our bond grew stronger, united by a shared purpose and a common goal.

The anticipation of reaching Pinecrest Camp grew with each step, not just as a destination but as a milestone in our journey. The relenting storm mirrored our own transition from struggle to hope, from battling the elements to glimpsing the possibility of respite and renewal.

And then, as if by some miracle, the weather began to relent, the snow giving way to clearer skies as we approached our long-awaited destination. The air grew warmer, and the biting cold that had gripped us for so long began to dissipate, replaced by a sense of renewed hope and optimism.

As we rode onwards, the landscape around us began to change, the barren wasteland slowly giving way to a more verdant terrain. This transformation beneath our feet served as a silent testament to the power of unity; just as the land healed and blossomed anew, so too did our collective spirit, bound by shared purpose and a common destiny.

This transition was more than a shift in the scenery; it was a symbol of our journey's evolution. The emerging verdancy spoke of life's resilience, of the possibility that even in a world scarred by the past's calamities, growth and renewal could find a way. As we observed the budding greenery, a symbol of the land's relentless spirit, we too felt a kindred stirring within us—a renewal of hope and purpose on our shared path.

Trees stood tall and proud, their branches heavy with snow, while patches of vibrant green grass peeked out from beneath the melting snowdrifts. It was a sight to behold, a stark contrast to the desolation that had surrounded us for so long, and it filled us with a sense of wonder and awe as we continued our journey.

With each passing mile, our anticipation grew, fueled by the knowledge that our long and arduous journey was finally drawing to a close. We could almost taste the sweet relief of reaching our destination and finding safety and shelter within the walls of Pinecrest Camp. And though we knew that our trials were far from over, we took comfort in the knowledge that we had faced every obstacle that had been thrown our way with courage and determination, and that we had emerged stronger for it.

And so, with hearts full of hope and determination, we rode onwards towards our final destination, ready to face whatever challenges lay ahead with unwavering resolve. In the silence of our march, our hearts spoke volumes, promising to each other that no matter the darkness ahead, the light within us, fostered by unity and shared dreams, would guide our way. We knew that no matter what trials awaited us, we would face them together, united in our quest to survive.

Upon reaching Pinecrest Camp, we surveyed our surroundings and beheld a vast expanse enclosed by a formidable wooden wall, encompassing a collection of diverse buildings and outposts. As we advanced toward the imposing gates, we noticed two guards stationed at the entrance.

One of them was wearing a weather-beaten leather duster, adorned with frayed edges and patched-up bullet holes that billowed around the wearer like a cloak of defiance against authority. Its deep brown hue has faded over time, bearing the scars of countless skirmishes and daring escapes.

Under the duster, the outlaw wore a faded denim shirt, its once vibrant blue now muted by the dust and grime of the road. The shirt is open at the collar, revealing a glimpse of a scarred chest and a hint of the rugged individualism that defines the wearer.

Tattered black trousers, reinforced with strips of worn leather at the knees and thighs, provide protection against the hazards of the wilderness while allowing for freedom of movement in combat. A wide leather belt cinches the waist, adorned with an assortment of pouches and holsters for storing weapons and ammunition.

On the outlaw's feet are scuffed leather boots, their soles worn thin from countless miles of travel. Spurred heels jingle with each step, an expression of the wearer's readiness for action at a moment's notice.

Topping off the ensemble was a wide-brimmed hat, whose once pristine surface was now weathered and stained from exposure to the elements. The hat casts a shadow over the wearer's face, concealing their identity from prying eyes and adding an air of mystery to their presence.

The other one wore a patchwork coat of mismatched fabrics and scavenged materials draped loosely over the raider's shoulders, its various colors and patterns an illustration of the wearer's resourcefulness and adaptability. Ragged edges flutter in the breeze, adding a sense of movement to the ensemble.

Underneath the coat, the raider sported a faded flannel shirt, its sleeves rolled up to reveal a network of tattoos that snaked across weathered skin like a roadmap of their past exploits. The shirt is open at the collar, allowing for easy access to the weapons and tools strapped to the wearer's chest.

Sturdy cargo pants, reinforced with patches and reinforced stitching, provide ample storage space for pilfered goods and supplies. Bulging pockets bulge with the weight of ammunition, while straps and buckles secure knives and other implements of destruction.

Heavy boots, caked with mud and grime from countless forays into the wilderness, stomp defiantly against the earth with each step. Steel-toed caps provide protection against the hazards of combat, while thick treads offer traction on treacherous terrain.

Perched atop the raider's head is a makeshift helmet, fashioned from salvaged metal and adorned with spikes and studs for added intimidation. A strip of cloth is tied around the wearer's face, concealing their identity and adding an air of menace to their presence.

As we approached the camp's entrance, tension hung in the air, a stark contrast to the unity we had fostered among ourselves.

The juxtaposition of our forged unity against the camp's wary defenses served as a vivid reminder that trust was not just earned but also a fragile bridge between the known and the unknown. It was in this moment of uncertainty that we were confronted by the camp's guardians, their skepticism evident in their stance.

"What brings you all the way here?" one of the bandits grumbled.

"We've traveled quite a distance," I replied. "Our purpose is to discuss forging an alliance between neighboring communities to unite as one."

"Are you serious?" scoffed the bandit. "Why would we bother getting involved with those folks? We'd rather relieve them of their valuables than join forces. What's the benefit for us?"

Kael stepped in: "Let's be realistic. Those villages are too remote to simply plunder. I know you're in need of essentials like food and supplies, not just riches. It's scarce out here, especially nowadays. Drop the tough act and let's have an honest conversation."

"Fair point," the bandit conceded, "but the final say rests with Blackhawk, the boss around here. I'm just a grunt."

"Can we speak with him?" I inquired.

"If they let you through, sure. I'll open the gates, but don't expect any guarantees about what happens next," the bandit replied.

As the gate creaked open, we stepped into the camp.

Suspicious eyes followed our every move as we entered, wary of unfamiliar faces. As the gates of Pinecrest Camp closed behind us, a moment of reflection washed over me. The bandits' skepticism and their harsh reality of survival stood in stark contrast to the vision of unity and hope we carried. It was a reminder that the path to change was not just about overcoming the wilderness outside but also the wilderness within hearts hardened by too many winters. Eventually, one of them approached us.

"Why are you strangers here? You don't belong," he stated. "The guard at the entrance allowed us in. We're here to meet Blackhawk and discuss a plan I have," I explained.

"Hmm, can't say I trust any of you. You seem like the type of person we'd usually relieve of their belongings. But since you're here, there's not much you can do to us. Follow me; I'll take you to him."

And so we were led to Blackhawk's presence.

Nestled amidst a collection of ramshackle tents and makeshift structures, the bandit leader's quarters stood out, showcasing their status within the camp. Perched atop a raised platform of weathered timber, the leader's tent was adorned with tattered banners bearing the insignia of their gang, fluttering defiantly in the breeze.

Surrounded by a motley assortment of guards and henchmen, the leader's tent served as the focal point of the camp, a hub of activity and intrigue where deals were struck and plans were made. Flanked by roaring bonfires and illuminated by flickering torchlight, the tent cast a warm and inviting glow amidst the darkness of the surrounding wilderness.

Inside, the tent was adorned with all manner of ill-gotten spoils and trophies, from stolen riches and plundered artifacts to grisly mementos of past conquests. Rich tapestries lined the walls, depicting scenes of battle and glory, while piles of treasure and crates of supplies were stacked haphazardly in every corner.

At the center of the tent stood the bandit leader's throne, a crude and imposing chair fashioned from scavenged timber and adorned with the skulls of fallen foes. Draped in furs and silks of stolen finery, the leader reclined regally upon their seat, a commanding presence amidst their retinue of loyal followers.

Surrounding the leader's throne were a collection of maps and charts, detailing the gang's territories and marking potential targets for future raids. A table strewn with scrolls and parchment served as the leader's desk, where they oversaw the day-to-day operations of the camp and issued commands to their underlings.

Outside the tent, the sounds of revelry and merriment echoed through the camp as the bandits caroused and celebrated their latest victories. Bonfires blazed brightly, casting long shadows across the clearing as the bandits danced and drank beneath the watchful gaze of their leader.

In the distance, the silhouettes of armed guards patrolled the perimeter, their watchful eyes scanning the darkness for any sign of trouble. Beyond the camp, the wilderness stretched out in all directions, a vast and untamed landscape teeming with hidden dangers and untold treasures, ripe for the taking by those bold enough to seize them.

The bandit leader cut an imposing figure, standing tall and proud amidst his followers, exuding an aura of authority and command. Clad in a weather-beaten leather coat, adorned with intricate stitching and patches, his attire spoke of rugged individualism and a life lived on the edge of society.

Under the coat, he wore a tattered shirt of faded denim, its sleeves rolled up to reveal a network of tattoos that snaked across his weathered skin like a roadmap of his past exploits. Around his waist, a wide leather belt cinched the fabric, adorned with an assortment of pouches and holders.

His trousers were sturdy and practical, reinforced with strips of worn leather at the knees and thighs, providing protection against the hazards of the wilderness while allowing for freedom of movement in combat. Scuffed leather boots, caked with mud and grime from countless forays into the wilderness, adorned his feet, their soles worn thin from years of travel and adventure.

On his head, he wore a wide-brimmed hat, whose once pristine surface is now weathered and stained from exposure to the elements. The hat cast a shadow over his face, concealing his features from prying eyes and adding an air of mystery to his presence.

Around his neck, he wore a necklace adorned with trinkets and talismans, each one a symbol of his status and power within the bandit camp. His eyes gleamed with fierce intensity, reflecting the firelight as he surveyed his domain with a mixture of pride and determination.

Overall, the bandit leader's appearance was rugged and formidable, a reflection of his life as a survivor in the harsh and unforgiving wilderness. He commanded respect and fear in equal measure, his presence alone enough to send shivers down the spines of even the bravest of men.

"Quite the establishment you've got here," remarked Kael. "Indeed, we like to display our spoils from various ventures to showcase our prowess. But enough about us; what brings you here? Our guards don't just let anyone through without reason," Blackhawk inquired.

"That's precisely why we've come," I replied. "What value do all these trophies hold if you lack the essentials like food and clothing?"

"And what's your proposal?" Blackhawk pressed.

"We're offering a solution. Imagine having access to vital resources without resorting to theft and plunder," I explained.

"Interesting proposition. We've struggled with scarce resources for some time now. What exactly do you suggest?" Blackhawk queried.

"In the long run, you could have all the resources you need, provided you abandon your bandit lifestyle," I proposed.

"That's easier said than done. Robbing and plundering are our way of life," Blackhawk hesitated.

"But it doesn't have to be. What good are trinkets if you lack sustenance? Resources would serve you far better," I reasoned.

"Even if that were true, why should I trust you? What proof do you have?" Blackhawk challenged.

"A fair point. Allow me to demonstrate," I replied, placing a radio before him.

"What in blazes is this contraption, and how does it benefit me?" Blackhawk questioned.

"Allow me to show you," I said confidently.

I powered up the device, initiating communication with the various towns, all of which expressed agreement with my proposal. The chorus of distant voices, each affirming their support, felt like a tapestry of hope being woven in real-time, a testament to the power of unity over division.

The bandit leader's skepticism waned as voices from across the region chimed in through the radio, affirming their support for the alliance. It was a turning point, not just in our conversation but potentially for the fate of Pinecrest Camp itself, as the prospects of unity and cooperation began to overshadow the isolation of a bandit's life. This moment of consensus, fleeting yet pivotal, held the promise of a new dawn, one where unity could pave the way for a reimagined world.

Then, I elucidated my entire plan to him. The bandit leader appeared skeptical, his gaze fixed as if contemplating two paths, each with its own advantages. Finally, he posed a crucial question: "And if I agree to all of this, no more robbing or plundering?"

"That's the essence of the deal. Trust me, embracing this change is in your best interest. Consider not only yourself but also your comrades in this camp. They require sustenance and resources. While the benefits may not be immediate, in the long run, once everything runs smoothly, you'll be better off. Moreover, think about your stance toward the other communities. They're now unified, posing a formidable challenge if you were to consider them adversaries," I reasoned.

"I can't deny it; you've made a compelling case. However, just because I hold some sway in this camp doesn't mean convincing others will be a walk in the park. It's more of a democracy here; easier said than done," he noted.

"What if I join forces with you? Together, we can present a united front to them. Even if they resort to aggression, I'm not one to be easily intimidated. I've faced off against fiercer bandits before," I proposed.

"What do you mean by that? Have you encountered bandits in the past?" Blackhawk inquired.

"Yes, outlaws, thieves, and various other miscreants. Not far from here, there used to be a fortress inhabited by a particularly hostile group. They eventually regretted crossing paths with me," I recounted.

"Wait, that was you?" Blackhawk's eyes widened. "Single-handedly tackling an entire fortress of bandits? I'd heard rumors, but I never believed them. Now, you're telling me it's true, and you're the one behind it all?"

"Certainly, it's the truth, and I'm indeed the one responsible," I affirmed.

"How did you manage it?" Blackhawk inquired, his curiosity palpable.

"Well, let's just say I possess enhanced physiology and access to advanced technological weaponry. I won't delve into the details, but suffice it to say, despite the odds, I had the advantage," I explained.

"I'm astounded," Blackhawk admitted. "Knowing that, I'd think twice before crossing paths with you."

"Shall we inform your men about our discussion?" I proposed.

"Let's proceed," Blackhawk agreed.

And so, we ascended a platform and summoned all the bandits to address the issue. While some voiced dissent, a significant number threatened to depart from the camp if changes weren't made.

"Listen, everyone," I began, addressing the gathered bandits. "Consider what your current lifestyle has truly provided you. Yes, you may have stolen food and supplies in the past, but how sustainable is that in the long run? With dwindling resources and no one left to plunder, how will you survive, especially during this season? And if you leave, where will you go? Is that truly a better option? Think about the potential benefits of joining a unified community. Imagine Pinecrest Camp not as a bandit stronghold but as one of four communities working together for a brighter future. I urge you to reconsider and embrace the opportunities this alliance presents."

Despite some individuals choosing to depart with their supplies and horses, the majority seemed to embrace the notion I presented. It appeared that the people of this camp were ready to shed their bandit label and become integral members of a thriving community.

Blackhawk and I retreated to his tent to further discuss our plans.

"Do you trust me now?" I inquired.

"You've certainly convinced me," Blackhawk affirmed. "Then inform the other communities of our success today. I won't be returning to continue my journey for the time being. There's much left to do, and I can't afford to spend more time wandering these lands. However, I will return eventually to check on our progress. For now, I'll need to use the radio a bit longer to communicate with the other villages," I explained.

"Of course, feel free to use it as you see fit," Blackhawk consented.

I proceeded to communicate with each village individually through the radio, detailing the process for creating their own radios once they established outposts at the designated checkpoints. This way, communication could extend throughout the entire region. I also informed them of my intention to depart and continue my mission, promising to return to check on their progress.

In a private conversation, Elena informed me that they had decided to name their united communities "The Concord Alliance" and bestowed upon me the title of "The Champion of Concord." She even offered to send one of their finest warriors along with a bard to spread the tales of my adventures and achievements to other travelers and distant communities. Initially hesitant about titles and accolades, I eventually accepted their offer with gratitude.

Next, I contacted Willowbrook and requested that they retrieve my Alloyed Charger from where I had left it once the roads were deemed safe. I instructed them on how to operate it and navigate back to their village, eventually arranging for it to be transported to Junkyard Junction, my next destination. They agreed to assist, and with the absence of the charger and the necessity to continue my journey, I set out on horseback.

I made the decision to journey towards Junkyard Junction, considering it was not too far from our current location. However, before I could depart, Kael approached me with a solemn expression.

"I regret to inform you, my friend, that I've also decided to remain here at Pinecrest Camp," Kael said. "I believe it's crucial to ensure that everything proceeds as planned. I still harbor doubts about the bandits honoring their part of the agreement, and I feel compelled to stay and oversee things for the time being."

"If that's what you deem necessary, I won't object," I replied.

In Kael's resolve, I found a poignant reminder of the sacrifices we each must make, a testament to the depth of his commitment to our shared cause.

"Just know that you'll always be a valued friend to me. Let's bid farewell for now, with hopes of meeting again someday."

I further elaborated that he could retain the VoltCharger as a token of appreciation, as my Fusionizer alone would suffice for our protection. Kael graciously accepted the gift with heartfelt gratitude.

As we prepared to part ways, I found a moment of quiet beside Aria, the campfires casting long shadows in the twilight. 'It's strange,' I confessed, 'how decisions once made in solitude now ripple through the lives around us.' Aria nodded, her hand finding mine in the dim light. "We're woven into a larger tapestry," she mused, "each thread as crucial as the next."

In that moment, the silent understanding that passed between us was as tangible as the warmth of a fire in winter, a reminder that our shared journey had intertwined our destinies in ways that transcended mere companionship.

It was a moment of vulnerability, a shared understanding that our journey was not just about survival but about the connections that bind us and the choices that define us. This realization that our intertwined destinies were a source of strength, not vulnerability, emboldened us, reminding us that together, we could face the darkest storms and emerge stronger on the other side.

We exchanged an emotional goodbye before I set out towards my next destination. That farewell, heavy with unspoken words and shared memories, marked not an end but a milestone in our journey, a poignant reminder of the bonds forged in adversity and the resilience of the human spirit.

Before turning away, Kael caught my arm, determination in his eyes. 'I'll start by mapping out a plan,' he said, 'organizing the camp, setting up defenses, and reaching out to nearby communities. It's about building, not just surviving.' His resolve was palpable, marking the beginning of his leadership in transforming the camp, a testament to the person he had become. Now accompanied only by Aria, we embarked on our journey with a single horse, hopeful that the path ahead would be smooth.

As we ventured forth, the echo of our first steps toward Pinecrest Camp mingled with the anticipation of the roads ahead, a symbolic passage from the trials behind us to the unknowns that lay before.

When we set our course toward Junkyard Junction, rumors of its vast scrapyard landscapes and territorial disputes filled our conversation.

As Junkyard Junction awaited, intercepted static-filled transmissions hinted at unrest within its walls—talk of contested resources and power struggles. 'It seems we're heading into a storm of a different kind,' I noted, the radio crackling ominously in my hand.

The uncertainty of what awaited us there lingered like a shadow, a stark reminder that the peace we sought was not just a destination but a path fraught with choices that would test our very ideals.

With each step towards Junkyard Junction, a silent resolve settled over us, a pact made not in words but in shared glances and the steady beat of our hearts.

The silhouette of Junkyard Junction, emerging on the distant horizon, was like a beacon in the twilight, promising new challenges and opportunities, yet shrouded in the uncertainty of what lay ahead. We knew the road ahead would demand everything we had to give, and we were ready to answer that call. This looming shadow, however, did not dampen our spirits but sharpened our resolve, as we knew that the worth of our quest was not in the absence of adversity but in the strength and unity we found in facing it together.

Each mile closer to Junkyard Junction layered our resolve with a quiet tension, as if the very air whispered of the challenges that lay ahead. Yet, within this anticipation, there existed a silent promise—a vow that, together, we would navigate the storms on the horizon, united in purpose and spirit.

With each step closer to Junkyard Junction, our shared resolve solidified, transforming apprehension into a steadfast commitment to navigate whatever challenges lay ahead together.

As the crackle of the radio melded with the silhouette of Junkyard Junction on the horizon, a sense of foreboding settled over us, hinting that the true test of our convictions lay not in the battles fought but in the choices yet to be made amidst the shadows of old ruins and new beginnings.

The horizon was a tapestry of juxtapositions, where the raw beauty of nature met the scarred remnants of industrial might. The silhouette of Junkyard Junction, with its tangled mazes of metal and shadow, stood as a monument to both human ingenuity and its folly. The air carried a tang of rust and forgotten stories, whispering of relics hidden within the metal graveyard that awaited our exploration.

Aria met my gaze; her resolve was firm. "Together, we've weathered much," she said, "and whatever awaits in Junkyard Junction, we'll face it as we always have: united." Her words, firm and resolute, echoed the unwritten oath between us, a promise not merely of companionship but of a shared destiny, woven from the trials we faced and the dreams we dared to dream. It was a promise, not just to each other, but to the future we were determined to shape.

"They say it's a place where the past and present collide,' Aria remarked, her gaze lost in the distance. A maze of history is waiting to be navigated.

In these reflective moments, the stories of our past, the trials we've overcome, and the dreams we've dared to dream wove together, creating a tapestry of our collective journey that stretched beyond the horizon. This moment of introspection served not just as a pause in our physical journey but as a bridge to the internal voyages we each had undertaken, reshaping our perspectives in ways we had yet to fully comprehend. In the quietude that enveloped us, our thoughts meandered through the tapestry of our experiences, each thread a narrative of transformation and revelation, painting us not as mere survivors but as architects of our fates.

This tapestry, woven from moments of despair, resilience, and triumph, draped over us like a mantle of complexity, each thread a testament to the indelible mark the journey had imprinted upon our souls.

In the silence that stretched between us, filled with the soft crackling of the radio and the distant murmur of the wind, there lay an unspoken acknowledgment of our intertwined fates. As we stood on the brink of the unknown, it was not just the physical distance we had traversed that dawned upon us, but the vast emotional journey we had navigated, from solitude to solidarity, from individual quests to a shared destiny. This realization did not weigh us down but instead lent us a sense of purpose, a collective strength fortified by every trial faced and every victory earned together.

It was as if the nearing of our destination urged us to look inward, contemplating the paths we had traversed, both physically and emotionally.

The journey lent us time, and with it, Aria began to unravel her past to me. Her revelations, intertwined with the landscapes we traversed, painted a vivid tableau of resilience and dreams rekindled amid ruins, urging us to ponder the legacies we wished to create in this reshaped world.

"I never imagined a life beyond the hollows of where I grew up," she shared, her voice soft against the backdrop of our traversing. This confession from Aria not only pulled back the curtain on her inner world but also served as a poignant reminder of our shared humanity. In a landscape marked by survival, dreams and aspirations found a way to echo louder, challenging the silence of desolation with whispers of hope.

As Aria shared her reflections, it dawned on me that our journey was not just a passage through the wilderness but a journey through the realms of possibility, reshaping our visions of what could be amidst the remnants of what was.

In these moments of shared reflection, the boundaries between past and future blurred, and our mission transcended mere survival, evolving into a quest to redefine what it meant to live and thrive in a reborn world. This evolution of purpose, from surviving to thriving, marked not just a change in our circumstances but a profound shift in our very beings, a dawning realization that we were part of something greater than ourselves.

This realization brought a newfound clarity, casting our past struggles and victories in a transformative light as stepping stones toward a future where the scars of our world could forge not just survivors but pioneers. In this light, every hardship faced and every victory earned was not an end but a beginning, a first step on the path to not just mend the world's scars but to redefine the very landscape of our future.

This journey, marked by both darkness and light, had not only shaped the landscape around us but had also sculpted the very essence of our beings, merging our individual stories into a collective saga of endurance and hope 'But now, seeing the world changing, I wonder what mark I'll leave.' Her contemplation stirred a silent echo within me, a reflection on the fleeting nature of hope amidst the ruins of certainty. 'Change,' I pondered aloud, 'is the only constant in this vast, reborn world. Yet, it's not the change itself that defines us, but the scars we choose to heal and the paths we dare to forge through the uncharted.' This musing served as a bridge between our past endeavors and the uncertain future awaiting us, a reminder that while the world around us evolves, so too do our dreams and the legacy we aspire to leave behind.

Aria's gaze met mine, a spark of understanding flickering in her eyes as she absorbed the weight of my words. "Yes,' she whispered, her voice carrying a mix of determination and vulnerability," 'and in forging our path through this uncharted world, we create our legacy, not by the scars we carry but by the lives we touch and the world we dream of building.' Her affirmation, soft yet resolute, was a testament to the depth of her evolution from a solitary wanderer to a visionary dreamer.

Kael, ever the stoic guardian, nodded, his usual reserve giving way to a rare glimpse of agreement. "Every step forward," he added, his tone carrying an unspoken pledge, "is a step towards that future, a future we shape not alone but together." His words, few as they were, echoed the sentiment of unity and shared purpose, reinforcing the bond that had been forged through trials and triumphs alike.

Her words offered a glimpse into her soul—a woman not just following a path but seeking to forge her own in this new world. The thought of navigating through both the literal and metaphorical remnants of a bygone era added a layer of anticipation to our journey.

Yet, my past experiences have reminded me that such optimism is often unfounded. A chill that had little to do with the cold air settled over me. The landscape around us, bathed in the eerie glow of twilight, seemed to hold its breath, as if anticipating the challenges that lay hidden in the shadows. This world, scarred by the remnants of a civilization long gone, whispered secrets of resilience and despair, urging us to tread cautiously yet boldly into the unknown.

"This place," I murmured, more to myself than to Aria or Kael, "holds secrets and challenges we have yet to uncover. Our journey, it seems, is poised to enter a new chapter, one that will test us in ways we can scarcely imagine." This reflection was not born of fear but of a sobering respect for the unpredictability of our path.

Aria, sensing the shift in my mood, offered a quiet nod, her resilience shining through. There was a steely resolve in her eyes, a silent declaration that no matter the darkness that awaited us, the light of our shared determination would pierce through the shadows. Her journey, once a solitary fight for survival, had transformed into a quest for something greater—a search for meaning in a world reborn from the ashes of its past.

"No matter what lies ahead," she affirmed, "we've proven that we're more than the sum of our pasts. Together, we'll face whatever Junkyard Junction has in store for us."

Her words, echoing in the chill air, were a beacon of hope, illuminating the strength of our bond. This beacon, shining through the veils of uncertainty, became our guidepost, reminding us that together, we had the strength to face the unknown, to transform every challenge into a step toward the future we envisioned.

In that moment, our shared laughter broke through the lingering shadows, a reminder of the light we carried within us. Our laughter, echoing across the barren expanse, was more than a brief respite; it was a declaration of our inner strength, a sign of the emotional fortitude we had forged from the fires of adversity. This laughter, a harmonious blend of relief and resolve, became our silent anthem, carrying us forward with an unspoken vow to meet the future with open hearts and unwavering courage.

'We've become more than allies; we're kin forged through fire,' I said, the warmth in my voice mirroring the warmth in their smiles. This journey had intertwined our fates, binding us with invisible threads stronger than any steel, ready to face the unknown together.

In the fabric of our shared journey, each challenge weaved tighter threads of camaraderie and trust, crafting a tapestry rich with the colors of resilience and undying hope.

Kael, in his characteristic manner, simply tightened his grip on his weapon, a silent vow of protection and perseverance. Kael's gaze briefly met mine, a rare vulnerability flashing in his eyes. "In the silence of the night, amidst the whispering winds, I've pondered the weight of the path we tread," he started, his voice low but clear. "To stand guard, to protect, is a role I've embraced, yet I find myself at a crossroads of purpose. The camp, with all its turmoil and potential, beckons not just my strength but my spirit to forge a semblance of order from chaos. It's a challenge I accept not out of obligation but a deeper call to shape a legacy beyond the battles fought—a legacy of peace, perhaps, in a world accustomed to strife."

This path, fraught with uncertainty, demands not just vigilance but a profound sense of duty to those who look up to us. The road to peace is paved with trials that test our spirit and resolve, shaping us into leaders we never anticipated becoming.

His words, laden with the weight of a newfound resolve, resonated deeply within me. As I turned to leave, the finality of the moment hung heavy between us. Yet, in this farewell lay not an end but a promise—a vow of reuniting on a path forged by our collective efforts toward a future reborn from the ashes of the old. With a last look back, I stepped into the unknown, the echoes of our past endeavors fueling the journey ahead. Each step forward was a step into a new chapter, not just of our journey but of the legacy we hoped to build.

Looking back, I realized our footprints on this desolate land were more than mere marks of survival; they were the imprints of a legacy we were carving with each decision and each act of courage. Each step, each decision, wove us into the fabric of this new world, not as forgotten footnotes in its history but as architects of its future, shaping a legacy of hope that would endure long after our journey ended. Our legacy, I understood, would not be measured by the obstacles we overcame but by the trails we blazed for those who would follow.

As custodians of this new dawn, our every action carved a path not just through the wilderness before us but through the annals of time, setting a course for generations yet unborn. In forging this legacy, we became not just survivors of a forgotten world but pioneers of a new one, laying the foundations for a future where unity and resilience shine brighter than the shadows of our past.

I paused, allowing myself a moment of reflection under the star-studded sky. 'Our journey,' I mused, 'is a tapestry of light and shadow, each thread a story of resilience, hope, and the relentless pursuit of a dream.' This realization, both humbling and empowering, reaffirmed my resolve. Our legacy would not be defined by the hardships we faced but by the hope we inspired in the hearts of those who heard our tale.

The horizon, alight with the first rays of dawn, served as a reminder that in every ending, there is a new beginning. And in the heart of every challenge, there lies an opportunity to forge a path that will echo through the annals of time, a testament to the enduring spirit of those who dare to dream.

It was a poignant reminder that our journey was not just about surviving the chaos of a fractured world but about reimagining the very essence of what it meant to live within it. In Kael's determination, I saw the outline of a future where our battles gave way to bridges, connecting the scattered fragments of humanity in a shared quest for peace. His actions spoke as loudly as any words, a reminder that our bond was forged not just in shared hopes but in the unspoken commitments we made to each other.

JUNKYARD JUNCTION

The journey from Pinecrest Camp to Junkyard Junction stretched ahead of us like an uncharted path through the wilderness, with two days of travel on horseback looming before us. Aria and I set out together, sharing a single horse as we embarked on the next leg of our adventure.

The first day of our journey was marked by the rhythmic clip-clop of hooves against the hard-packed earth and the steady cadence of our progress echoing through the tranquil landscape. As we rode side by side, the silence between us was companionable, our thoughts drifting like clouds across the vast expanse of the sky.

This silence wasn't born of discomfort but of a deepening bond, an unspoken understanding that comforted more than words ever could.

Occasionally, we would pause to rest and refresh ourselves, taking advantage of the brief respites to savor the simple pleasures of the journey—a cool sip of water from our canteens, a handful of trail mix to stave off hunger, and the gentle touch of the breeze against our faces.

As the sun dipped below the horizon, casting the world in shades of dusky orange and violet, we made camp for the night, the soft glow of our campfire warding off the encroaching darkness.

Sitting side by side beneath the starlit sky, we shared stories and laughter, with the warmth of the fire drawing us closer together.

I gazed into the flickering flames, watching as they danced and cracked in the cool night air. "Do you remember the first time we met?" I asked, turning to Aria with a smile.

Aria's expression softened, but I could see a hint of hesitation in her eyes. This hesitation, a flicker of vulnerability in Aria's otherwise stoic demeanor, hinted at the depth of experiences and emotions she carried within her, each layer waiting to be unveiled.

"Of course," she replied quietly, her voice tinged with uncertainty.

I felt a pang of unease at her response, wondering if perhaps I had overstepped some invisible boundary. The fragility of our growing connection, a delicate thread in the vast tapestry of our shared journey, seemed all too apparent in that moment. This moment of doubt revealed a facet of my character that I seldom acknowledged—my fear of isolation and my deep-seated need for the connection that Aria and I shared, fragile though it might be.

"I hope it wasn't too awkward for you," I said, trying to lighten the mood.

Aria shook her head, a small smile playing at the corners of her lips. "No, it wasn't awkward," she admitted. "Just unexpected."

I nodded, relieved by her answer but still uncertain about the tension I sensed between us. "I know things have been...

complicated lately," I began hesitantly, searching for the right words to express what I was feeling.

Aria's gaze flickered away from mine, her expression guarded. "Yeah, they have," she agreed quietly, her voice barely audible above the crackling of the fire.

I reached out tentatively, wanting to reassure her but unsure of how to proceed. "But that doesn't mean we can't... you know, enjoy each other's company," I said, my voice trailing off uncertainly.

Aria met my gaze, her eyes searching mine for answers. "I just don't want things to get too complicated," she admitted softly, her words hanging heavy in the air between us.

I nodded in understanding, my heart sinking at the thought of losing the fragile connection we had forged. "I don't want that either," I confessed, my voice barely above a whisper.

For a long while, we sat in silence, the crackling of the fire the only sound breaking the stillness of the night. The fire's warmth did little to dispel the chill of uncertainty for our future, a shadow that lingered despite the flames.

The second day dawned crisp and clear, with the promise of a new adventure beckoning us forward. With renewed determination, we set out once more, the landscape unfurling before us like a tapestry woven by the hand of nature.

As we rode, our conversation flowed freely, weaving through topics both trivial and profound. Aria shared stories of her childhood adventures, while I recounted tales of my travels before our paths converged.

"It's funny how life has a way of bringing people together," Aria mused, her eyes scanning the horizon.

I nodded in agreement, a smile playing at the corners of my lips. "Yeah, it's like we were meant to meet," I replied, feeling a sense of gratitude for the serendipitous encounter that had led us here.

We spoke of our hopes and dreams, our fears and uncertainties, and our words formed a bridge that spanned the distance between us. "I've always wanted to see the world," Aria confessed, her voice tinged with longing. "To explore new places and experience different cultures."

I listened intently, captivated by her words. "Me too," I admitted, feeling a sense of kinship with her desire for adventure. "There's so much out there to discover."

Junkyard Junction emerged before us, a haunting testament to abandonment and decay. Surrounded by a crumbling perimeter of weathered concrete and rusted metal, its entrance gate hung askew, besieged by weeds and thorny vines. Tattered banners and faded signs clung to the skeletal remains of buildings, each boarded-up doorway and broken window narrating the settlement's slow succumb to obscurity. As we approached, the mingled scents of rust and decay intensified, underscored by the silhouettes of discarded junk and scrap metal that sprawled across the landscape, a stark reminder of what was left behind.

Despite its derelict appearance, there was a haunting beauty to be found amidst the ruins of Junkyard Junction. We allowed ourselves a moment to absorb this eerie beauty, a brief respite in our relentless journey, underscoring the stark contrast between the rush of our quest and the stillness of the world we traversed. Stray beams of sunlight filtered through the gaps in the clouds, casting an ethereal glow upon the desolate landscape.

As Aria and I ventured into the desolate interior of Junkyard Junction, we were met with a scene of eerie desolation and decrepitude. The once bustling settlement now lay in ruin, its streets littered with debris and detritus from years of neglect and abandonment.

Dilapidated buildings lined the narrow thoroughfares, their crumbling facades adorned with faded graffiti and shattered windows. Piles of rusted scrap and discarded machinery lay strewn about haphazardly, casting long shadows in the dim light filtering through the overcast sky.

The air was thick with the scent of decay and rust, a tangible reminder of the settlement's gradual decline into obscurity.

This scent carried stories of forgotten days, of laughter, and of life now surrendered to time's relentless march. In this decay, there was a silent testament to resilience; amid the rust and ruin, nature reclaimed what once was hers, weaving a tapestry of life amidst desolation. Everywhere we looked, signs of past life lay buried beneath layers of dust and neglect, their silent echoes haunting the desolate streets.

Despite the pervasive sense of abandonment, there was an eerie beauty to be found amidst the ruins of Junkyard Junction. Stray beams of sunlight pierced through the gloom, casting ethereal shafts of light upon the weathered structures and broken pavement.

Occasionally, we would come across traces of human habitation—a makeshift shelter fashioned from salvaged materials or the remnants of a long-abandoned campfire. These fleeting glimpses of life amidst the desolation served as a stark reminder of the settlement's former inhabitants, now lost to the ravages of time.

As we navigated the labyrinthine streets of Junkyard Junction, a sense of unease settled over us, fueled by the oppressive silence and pervasive sense of abandonment. Our steps became more cautious, the pace of our exploration slowed by the oppressive atmosphere, and each corner turned, revealing another layer of the town's forgotten stories. Yet, amidst the ruins, there was also a glimmer of hope—a faint reminder that even in the darkest of times, the human spirit endures, resilient and unyielding. The anticipation of uncovering Junkyard Junction's secrets lent a surreal edge to our approach, as if we were about to step through the pages of history into a tale long forgotten.

As Aria and I approached the desolate expanse of Junkyard Junction, a sense of trepidation settled over us like a shroud. The eerie silence enveloped the abandoned town, broken only by the occasional creak of a decaying structure in the wind. Rows of dilapidated buildings stretched before us, each one a reflection of neglect and decay, their weathered facades telling silent tales of a forgotten past.

Uncertainty gnawed at my gut as I surveyed the scene before us. The buildings all seemed to blur together in a haze of disrepair, lacking any distinguishing features to guide our search.

Without a clue or intuition to rely on, we stood at the threshold of the ghost town, unsure of where to begin.

Aria and I exchanged wary glances, silently acknowledging the daunting task that lay ahead. "This place gives me the creeps," Aria whispered, her voice barely audible over the sound of the wind rustling through the abandoned buildings.

I nodded in agreement, my gaze sweeping over the row of dilapidated structures lining the abandoned street. "Yeah, it's like something out of a nightmare," I replied, my voice tinged with unease.

"We need some sort of direction," Aria remarked, her brow furrowed in concentration. "A way to figure out where to go."

With a heavy sigh, I reluctantly selected a building from the row of decaying structures. Its façade, adorned with cracked bricks and weather-worn wood, blended seamlessly with the surrounding decay. "This one," I said, gesturing towards the crumbling structure. "It looks as good as any."

As we approached, the wooden door creaked open, revealing a darkness that seemed to swallow the feeble rays of sunlight struggling to penetrate the gloom. Aria hesitated, casting a wary glance over her shoulder. "Are you sure about this?" she asked, her voice tinged with uncertainty.

I swallowed hard, trying to ignore the knot of fear that had formed in the pit of my stomach. "We have to start somewhere," I replied, my voice steady despite the tremor of doubt that lingered beneath the surface. "Let's see what we can find."

Upon entering, a chorus of neglect enveloped us; the musty air, laced with the scent of decay, whispered of years forsaken. Our steps stirred dust motes into a ghostly dance through spaces where cobwebs adorned neglected corners. What lay before us was not merely a building but a monument to decay, its interior a testament to time's unyielding march, with each room revealing the scars of abandonment under the dim caress of fading light.

Moving cautiously through the building, we explored room after room, each one revealing a snapshot of the past frozen in time.

In one room, faded curtains fluttered in the breeze, their once-vibrant colors now muted by years of exposure to the elements. In another, shelves lined with dusty books stood as silent witnesses to the knowledge that had long since been forgotten.

Despite our efforts, each building we entered seemed to offer more questions than answers. Yet, we pressed on, driven by a determination to uncover the truth hidden within Junkyard Junction. With each new building we explored, we remained ever vigilant, searching for the elusive clue that would finally lead us to our destination.

Room after room revealed nothing but decay and emptiness, each one a dead end in our search for answers. The walls, once vibrant with life, now stood as silent witnesses to the passage of time, their peeling paint and cracked plaster echoing the forgotten stories of those who had once inhabited this forsaken place. Dust motes danced in the stale air, swirling in the dim light like ghosts of the past.

With each empty room we encountered, doubt tightened its grip on my heart, threatening to suffocate the flickering flame of hope that had guided us this far. The weight of our mission pressed down upon us like a leaden cloak, each step forward feeling more futile than the last. Was this journey destined to end in failure, our efforts wasted in a futile quest for redemption?

As the minutes stretched into hours, fatigue gnawed at our bodies, sapping our strength and resolve. Aria's footsteps faltered beside me; her brow furrowed in frustration as we trudged onward through the labyrinth of decay. How many more rooms would we have to search before admitting defeat and acknowledging that our quest was nothing more than a fool's errand?

In a sudden and startling twist of fate, a colossal figure materialized in the midst of the desolate street, its towering form commanding attention and instilling a primal sense of awe. It stood before us, an imposing sight to behold, reminiscent of the formidable drones we had faced in our previous encounters, yet distinctly different in its sheer magnitude and formidable presence.

Standing in the shadow of the towering behemoth, a knot of apprehension coiled in the pit of my stomach. Its colossal frame rose to dizzying heights, dwarfing us beneath its imposing presence. Each limb was thickly muscled, resembling the sinewy coils of some ancient serpent, while its metallic exterior gleamed with an otherworldly sheen.

The Behemoth's body was a patchwork of jagged edges and angular plates, giving it the appearance of some fearsome creature forged from the very depths of the abyss. Its massive head was crowned with a crest of razor-sharp spikes, while its glowing red eyes burned with a malevolent intelligence that sent shivers down my spine.

As it moved, the Behemoth emitted a low, rumbling growl that reverberated through the chamber like the roar of a distant thunderstorm. Each step sent tremors rippling through the ground, shaking the very foundations of our resolve.

But it was not just its size and strength that inspired fear; it was the aura of primal power and ancient menace that seemed to radiate from every inch of its massive form. In its presence, I felt as though I stood on the brink of some unfathomable abyss, staring into the gaping maw of oblivion itself.

As the Behemoth loomed over us, its towering form casting a long shadow across the chamber, I knew that we faced our greatest challenge yet. But with courage in our hearts and determination in our souls, we would stand our ground and face this fearsome foe head-on.

"What in the world is that?" Aria gasped, her voice barely above a whisper, her eyes wide with disbelief.

"That, my dear Aria," I replied solemnly, "is what nightmares are made of."

Aria's eyes widened in alarm, her gaze fixed on the hulking monstrosity before us. "How are we supposed to take down something like that?" she asked, her voice tinged with uncertainty.

"We'll have to find a way," I assured her, though doubt gnawed at the edges of my confidence. "We've faced tough odds before, and we've always come out on top. We just need to stay focused and work together."

As the Behemoth advanced, its heavy footsteps reverberating through the street, I could feel the weight of its presence bearing down upon us. Its towering form seemed to blot out the very light from above, casting us into a shadowy realm of uncertainty and fear.

"We're going to need a bigger plan," Aria muttered, her voice tinged with apprehension.

I nodded in agreement, my mind racing as I scanned the chamber for any signs of weakness in our formidable foe. "We'll have to hit it hard and hit it fast," I replied, my voice steady despite the rising tide of fear within me.

With weapons drawn and hearts filled with determination, we prepared to face our most daunting challenge yet. The Behemoth loomed before us, a colossus of steel and fury, but we refused to back down.

As the battle commenced, the place erupted into chaos, with the clash of metal and the crackle of energy filling the air. The Behemoth unleashed a relentless barrage of attacks, its massive limbs swinging with devastating force as it sought to crush us beneath its formidable bulk.

But we refused to yield, dodging and weaving through its onslaught with practiced skill and determination. With each passing moment, we chipped away at its defenses, exploiting every opportunity to strike at its vulnerable points.

As the battle against the Behemoth raged on, our resolve was tested to its limits as we faced a foe of unparalleled strength and ferocity. With each strike, the Behemoth seemed to grow more formidable, its metallic frame absorbing our attacks with chilling efficiency.

Aria, wielding her dual blades with unparalleled skill and precision, danced through the chaos with a grace that belied the danger that surrounded her. With lightning-fast strikes, she carved through the air, her blades flashing in the dim light as she sought out vulnerabilities in the Behemoth's defenses.

Meanwhile, Ethan, armed with the Fusionizer, unleashed a relentless barrage of energy blasts upon the towering monstrosity. With each shot, the air crackled with raw power as beams of energy streaked towards their target, impacting with explosive force against the Behemoth's armored hide.

But the Behemoth was no mere machine; it was a relentless adversary, its massive form shrugging off our assaults with unnerving ease. With a thunderous roar, it retaliated with a devastating counterattack, its massive limbs swinging with bone-crushing force as it sought to crush us beneath its colossal weight.

Caught off guard by the Behemoth's ferocity, we found ourselves pushed to the brink of exhaustion as we fought tooth and nail to keep ourselves alive. Aria, her blades flashing like silver in the dim light, narrowly dodged a sweeping blow from the Behemoth's massive arm, her reflexes pushed to their limits as she danced out of harm's way.

Ethan, his Fusionizer blazing with fiery intensity, fired shot after shot at the Behemoth's armored hide, each impact sending sparks flying as the creature's defenses held firm against his onslaught. With each passing moment, the strain of the battle began to take its toll, our bodies aching with fatigue as we struggled to keep pace with our relentless adversary.

But even as our strength waned and our resolve faltered, we refused to back down, drawing upon reserves of courage and determination we never knew we possessed. With a defiant cry, we launched our final assault, channeling every ounce of energy and skill we had into one last, desperate bid for victory.

Aria, her blades a blur of motion, danced through the chaos with unparalleled grace, her strikes finding their mark with deadly accuracy as she sought out weaknesses in the Behemoth's armor. With each blow, she chipped away at the creature's defenses, her relentless assault driving it ever closer to the brink of defeat.

Meanwhile, Ethan, his Fusionizer blazing with raw power, unleashed a relentless barrage of energy blasts upon the Behemoth's massive form. With each shot, the air crackled with electricity as beams of energy streaked towards their target, impacting with explosive force against the creature's armored hide.

But the Behemoth was not so easily defeated; with a thunderous roar, it unleashed a devastating counterattack, its massive limbs swinging with bone-crushing force as it sought to crush us beneath its colossal weight. Caught off guard by the ferocity of the onslaught, we found ourselves pushed to the brink of exhaustion as we struggled to keep pace with our relentless adversary.

Yet even as our bodies screamed for respite, we refused to yield, drawing upon reserves of courage and determination we never knew we possessed. With a defiant cry, we launched our final assault, channeling every ounce of energy and skill we had into one last, desperate bid for victory.

Aria, her blades flashing like lightning in the dim light, danced through the chaos with a grace that defied description. With each strike, she carved through the air with lethal precision, her blows finding their mark with deadly accuracy as she sought out weaknesses in the Behemoth's armor.

Meanwhile, Ethan, his Fusionizer blazing with fiery intensity, unleashed a relentless barrage of energy blasts upon the Behemoth's massive form. With each shot, the air crackled with electricity as beams of energy streaked towards their target, impacting with explosive force against the creature's armored hide.

But the Behemoth was not so easily deterred; with a deafening roar, it retaliated with a devastating counterattack, its colossal limbs thrashing about with lethal precision as it sought to overpower us with sheer brute force. Aria's blades flashed in the dim light as she deftly parried the Behemoth's strikes, her movements a blur of calculated grace amidst the chaos of battle. Meanwhile, Ethan's Fusionizer hummed with charged energy as he unleashed a relentless barrage of shots, each blast aimed with deadly accuracy at the Behemoth's armored exterior.

As the battle wore on, the Behemoth's onslaught grew increasingly relentless, its massive frame shaking the very ground beneath our feet with each thunderous blow. Despite our best efforts, its defenses held firm, and the layer of reinforced steel protecting its energy core proved to be an impenetrable barrier against our attacks.

With every passing moment, the odds seemed to stack higher against us, the Behemoth's unyielding resilience testing the limits of our endurance. Aria's blades flashed and danced in a desperate flurry of strikes, each blow aimed at weakening the Behemoth's defenses and exposing its vulnerable core, while Ethan's Fusionizer spat forth a relentless stream of energy blasts, each shot fueled by sheer determination and unwavering resolve.

But as the battle raged on, disaster struck; a thunderous blow from the Behemoth sent Ethan crashing to the ground, his body wracked with pain as he struggled to rise to his feet. Blood trickled from his wounds, staining the ground crimson as he fought to keep the darkness at bay. With each passing moment, his strength waned, the pain threatening to overwhelm him as he battled to stay conscious amidst the chaos of battle. In these moments of vulnerability, the depth of our companionship was revealed, not just in battle, but in the quiet strength drawn from one another's presence.

Desperation gripped us as we fought to turn the tide of battle in our favor, our every move fueled by a fierce determination to emerge victorious against all odds. With a final surge of adrenaline, Aria launched herself at the Behemoth with renewed ferocity, her blades striking true as she sought to breach its formidable defenses and expose its vulnerable core.

And then, in a moment of sheer determination and unyielding courage, Ethan rallied despite his injuries, his Fusionizer roaring to life with renewed intensity as he joined Aria in their final assault. With a deafening roar, the chamber erupted into chaos as the Behemoth staggered and fell, its once mighty form reduced to a smoldering wreck as its energy core finally succumbed to their relentless onslaught.

Aria rushed to Ethan's side as he collapsed to the ground from his injuries.

"How bad is it?" she asked, concern etched on her face. "It's bad," Ethan replied, grimacing. "But thanks to my rapid healing, I should be fine within a few hours. Help me over to the wall of one of the buildings. While I heal up, you should continue searching the buildings."

Ethan retrieved a key from his bag and showed it to Aria. "See this symbol here on the key? Look for it. I'm sure it signifies something important, something that will guide you to the right place."

"No!" protested Aria. "I'm staying with you until you're healed. I'm not leaving you alone out here; not a chance."

"Don't worry about me; I'll be fine. Just go," Ethan insisted. "I refuse to leave you alone," Aria declared firmly. "Say what you want, but I'm staying put. Is that clear?" "Yes, ma'am," Ethan acquiesced.

As Ethan began to heal slowly but steadily, Aria watched him with a sense of worry in her eyes. It was almost as if her heart was breaking. She kept gazing into his eyes, and then, unexpectedly, she leaned in and pressed her lips against his. She cupped his cheeks with her hands and held them there.

"I don't want to lose you," she whispered. "I don't care about the dangers of our journeys or what the world is like. All that matters to me is you, right here, right now."

I smiled at her, understanding the depth of her feelings and the significance of her words. Despite the desolate world we inhabited, the ruins surrounding us held no weight in her eyes anymore. The sight of me injured made her realize that she wanted to cherish every moment with me, whether it was in the safety of a village or amidst the perils of abandoned cities and treacherous landscapes. She would rather face the dangers of our journey together, risking everything, than never have experienced our bond at all.

"Better to have loved and lost than never to have loved at all" is something she heard once, and this moment epitomized that sentiment perfectly. She sat beside me, our shoulders touching, and took my hand, our fingers intertwining. With her eyes closed, she drifted off to sleep, finding solace in the midst of uncertainty.

As I watched her sleep, I couldn't help but find her occasional snore endearing. Closing my own eyes, I allowed myself to rest, feeling the fatigue dissipate as I drifted into slumber. When I woke up, I found her still beside me, peacefully asleep. Feeling refreshed, I glanced down at my armor and noticed the extent of the damage it had sustained. In contrast, Aria wore serpent skin armor, a reflection of her agility and skill as a fighter. Despite the scratches and tears adorning her armor, she appeared unharmed, a silent guardian by my side.

Her hand had slipped from my cheek, finding its place on my lower arm. Despite the temptation to let her continue her peaceful slumber, I knew I had to rouse her before any potential threats emerged.

"Wake up," I murmured softly, careful not to startle her.

Gently, I rubbed her cheek and shook it lightly, coaxing her back to consciousness. Slowly, her eyelids fluttered open, revealing sleepy eyes that met mine.

"You've been sleeping for quite a while," I remarked, concern evident in my voice. "Are you okay?"

With a yawn, she responded, her voice tinged with drowsiness. "I'm fine, just a bit groggy."

Glancing outside, we both noticed the encroaching darkness, illuminated only by the full moon and the twinkling stars overhead—a breathtaking sight amidst the desolation.

"We should find a building to take shelter in for the night," I suggested, wary of potential dangers lurking in the darkness. "I'd rather not face any threats in the dark, especially not some black roach or whatever else lurks in these ruins."

"But are you sure you're okay?" she inquired, her concern palpable. "You were badly injured, and now you seem to be completely healed. Your enhanced healing is remarkable. How does it work?"

"I forgot to mention," I admitted, recalling our conversation with The Seeker and Kael. "I explained everything to them, but you weren't there yet. I'll fill you in once we're settled somewhere safe, alright?"

"Okay," she agreed, scanning the area for a suitable shelter. "How about that building over there?" she suggested, pointing toward a structure that appeared relatively intact, offering cover under its roof.

"Sounds good," I replied, rising to my feet. As we stood up, I realized our hands were still intertwined, a comforting connection amidst the uncertainty. With a reluctant sigh, I released her hand and led the way to the chosen building, her presence beside me reassuring in the dim light. Drawing my flashlight, I illuminated our path as we ventured into the building's sheltering embrace.

The interior of the building was a haunting tableau frozen in time, bearing the scars of neglect and decay. As we stepped through the weather-worn doorway, the musty scent of dampness and decay assailed our senses, mingling with the faint aroma of rust and dust that hung heavy in the stale air.

Inside, the space was cloaked in darkness, and the broken windows were boarded up. The walls, once adorned with peeling wallpaper and faded paint, stood bare and barren, their surfaces marred by stains and streaks of grime.

The floor beneath our feet was littered with debris and detritus, the remnants of years of neglect and abandonment. Piles of discarded junk and broken machinery lay scattered about, their rusted forms casting eerie shadows in the dim light.

Amidst the clutter, we caught glimpses of forgotten relics from a bygone era—a tattered poster clinging to the wall, its colors faded and edges frayed; a rusted metal filing cabinet, its drawers hanging open as if in silent protest; a broken chair, its wooden frame splintered and worn.

The silence of the abandoned building was broken only by the occasional creak of shifting timbers or the distant sound of debris tumbling to the ground. Each step echoed through the empty space, a solemn reminder of the desolation that surrounded us.

Despite its dilapidated state, there was a sense of eerie beauty to be found within the abandoned building, a haunting reminder of the passage of time and the inevitable march of decay. As we explored further, each room revealed new secrets and hidden treasures. If you can call them treasures, as they were mostly intriguing trinkets from an era long ago.

We fashioned a makeshift campfire in one of the rooms, salvaging the remnants of chairs to create a makeshift seating arrangement. Side by side, we settled down, and I embarked on recounting my entire history, much as I had done with The Seeker and Kael.

"Does this change things between us?" I ventured, a hint of uncertainty in my voice.

Her response was swift and reassuring. "No, not at all," she affirmed. "It's certainly an unusual tale—your existence spanning over a thousand years, witnessing the era before the final war. But what matters to me is who you are, not where you've been or what you've endured. Your physical enhancements are undeniably advantageous. Without them, we might have faced a different outcome today. In fact, I might not even be here if not for those enhancements."

Our conversation meandered through various topics, delving into the intricacies of my identity and existence. Eventually, a comfortable silence settled between us, punctuated only by the crackling of the fire and the soft glow of moonlight filtering through the window.

As we gazed out at the moon and stars, wrapped in each other's embrace, the night slowly surrendered to the approaching dawn. With the first light of morning, the surroundings gradually became visible, revealing the neglected and desolate landscape.

Amidst the layers of neglect, my gaze fell upon a faint etching on the decaying wood of the doorframe—a familiar symbol, reminiscent of the key I held in my hand. A surge of recognition swept over me, and I couldn't contain my excitement.

"Look!" I exclaimed, holding up the key for her to see. "It's the same symbol. Can you believe it?"

"Yes, we've finally found it, or at least I hope so," she remarked, a note of cautious optimism in her voice. "But let's replenish our energy first before venturing further. We have no idea what lies ahead, and we might find ourselves confined for an extended period."

We savored the simple pleasure of a meal, relishing the faint glimmers of light filtering through the boarded windows and the gentle caress of the early spring breeze.

As the meal concluded, we turned our attention to the door, its formidable presence imposing a tangible barrier to our progress. Constructed from graphene, it stood as an impregnable fortress, barring entry without the proper key.

With a mixture of anticipation and trepidation, I ran my fingers along the surface, tracing the intricate markings etched into the material. Each stroke filled me with a renewed sense of resolve and a fervent hope that this would be the culmination of our quest.

With a steady hand, I inserted the key into the designated slot, feeling its weight in my palm. As I turned it, the mechanism responded with a soft click, echoing through the silent chamber.

A series of mechanical sounds reverberate through the abandoned corridor. The door emitted a low hum as unseen mechanisms engaged, preparing for the momentous opening.

With a sudden burst of energy, the door began to move, its massive form shifting with a sense of purpose. Slowly at first, then picking up speed, the graphene panels glided smoothly along hidden tracks, revealing the passage beyond with a spectacular flourish.

As I descended into the depths of the underground facility, Aria's voice echoed softly behind me, her tone laced with a mix of awe and apprehension.

"This place is incredible, Ethan," she murmured, her eyes wide with wonder as she took in the futuristic machinery surrounding us. The sheer scale of the underground complex was staggering, with towering consoles and sleek panels stretching as far as the eye could see.

I nodded in agreement, my gaze sweeping over the intricate designs and pulsating lights that filled the chamber. "It's like stepping into another world," I replied, my voice barely above a whisper as I reached out to touch one of the buttons on the control panel. The sensation of cold metal beneath my fingertips sent a shiver down my spine, a tangible reminder of the advanced technology that lay dormant within these ancient walls.

As Aria and I stood amidst the intricate machinery, I couldn't help but marvel at the resilience of the technology surrounding us. "This technology must have persisted for ages," I remarked, awestruck. "It's unbelievable that it hasn't been affected by the chaos and destruction outside. It's quite impressive."

Aria stepped closer, her curiosity piqued by the sight before us. "Do you think it's still functional?" she asked, her fingers trailing along the surface of a nearby monitor. Her touch seemed to awaken the dormant machinery, as lights flickered overhead and monitors hummed to life, displaying streams of data and information.

Before I could respond, the room suddenly came to life with a symphony of mechanical sounds. The air was filled with the hum of generators and the whir of cooling fans, while panels slid open to reveal hidden compartments and access points. Lights flashed in intricate patterns, casting the chamber in an eerie glow that danced across the walls.

Aria's eyes widened in amazement as she took in the spectacle before us. "It's working!" she exclaimed, her voice tinged with excitement as she moved closer to examine the flashing screens. Each monitor displayed a different aspect of the facility's operations, from power distribution to environmental controls, painting a vivid picture of the complex network of systems that powered the underground facility.

I couldn't help but smile at her enthusiasm, my own sense of wonder growing with each passing moment. "It looks like we stumbled upon something pretty remarkable," I remarked, my gaze lingering on the array of advanced technology surrounding us. The sheer complexity of the machinery was staggering, with countless buttons, switches, and screens demanding our attention.

As we delved deeper into the facility, Aria's questions flowed freely, her insatiable curiosity driving our exploration. Together, we marveled at the ingenuity of its design and the sophistication of its technology, each discovery sparking new questions and theories. We moved from room to room, uncovering hidden chambers and secret passageways, our footsteps echoing through the labyrinthine corridors.

And amidst the whirring machinery and flashing lights, our shared sense of adventure bound us together, forging a connection that transcended the boundaries of time and space. In this hidden underground labyrinth, we were explorers on a journey of discovery, united by a common purpose and an unbreakable bond. With each new revelation, our determination grew stronger, propelling us ever deeper into the heart of the facility and the mysteries that lay hidden within.

As Aria and I ventured deeper into the underground chamber, the air grew heavy with anticipation. The dim light cast eerie shadows across the labyrinth of machinery that surrounded us, while the soft hum of electrical currents filled the cavernous space. The pristine technology stood as a remarkable demonstration of human ingenuity and technological prowess, but beneath the surface, something sinister lurked.

"My, oh my," Aria whispered, her voice barely audible over the thrum of machinery. "This is like stepping into a different world."

I nodded in agreement, though a sense of unease prickled at the back of my mind. The technology seemed out of place in the abandoned underground chamber, its pristine condition contrasting sharply with the surrounding decay.

But before we could delve further into the mysteries of the facility, a sudden surge of electricity crackled through the air, causing the machinery to flicker and spark with newfound life. Alarms blared in the distance, their shrill cries echoing off the metal walls as the chamber erupted into chaos.

"We need to find a way out of here," I shouted over the deafening din, my heart pounding with fear. But as we turned to flee, the doors slammed shut with a resounding clang, trapping us inside the chamber with no means of escape.

Panic surged within me as I frantically searched for an exit, my hands trembling as I tried to override the security systems that held us captive. Aria stood by my side, her expression a mix of determination and fear as she scanned the room for any sign of hope.

And then, just when it seemed all hope was lost, a flicker of movement caught my eye—a hidden panel nestled among the rows of machinery, its surface adorned with glowing symbols that pulsed with an otherworldly light.

"There!" Aria exclaimed, pointing towards the panel with a sense of urgency. "That must be our way out."

With renewed determination, I rushed towards the panel, my fingers flying over the controls as I inputted the sequence needed to override the security protocols. The chamber trembled as the doors slowly creaked open, bathing us in blinding light as we stumbled out into the safety of the corridor beyond.

As we caught our breath, I couldn't shake the feeling that we had narrowly escaped something far more sinister than mere malfunctioning machinery. The technology down there held secrets beyond our wildest imagination.

As we ventured further into the depths of the underground facility, my eyes scanned the array of advanced technology surrounding us. Each room held the promise of discovery, and I was determined to uncover the clues that would lead us to our next destination. Beside me, Aria shared my excitement, her eyes alight with anticipation.

"It looks like we've stumbled upon something intriguing," Aria remarked, her voice echoing softly in the cavernous chamber as she surveyed the high-tech machinery lining the walls.

I nodded in agreement, though my thoughts were clouded with uncertainty. "It's definitely a find, but I can't shake the feeling that there's more to this place than meets the eye," I replied, my voice tinged with cautious optimism.

Suddenly, my attention was drawn to a peculiar console tucked away in a secluded alcove. Its surface was adorned with intricate symbols and glowing buttons, hinting at its significance in the grand scheme of the facility's operations. Intrigued, I approached the console, Aria following close behind.

"What do you think it does?" Aria asked, and her curiosity piqued as she examined the mysterious device.

"I'm not sure," I replied, my fingers tracing the ancient runes etched into the metal surface. "But there's only one way to find out."

As I touched the symbols, the console sprang to life beneath my fingertips, emitting a soft hum as its screens flickered to life. Lines of text scrolled across the monitors, revealing fragments of information that hinted at the true purpose of the underground facility. Aria and I exchanged curious glances, unsure of what secrets the console held.

Together, we delved deeper into the console's interface, uncovering encrypted files containing enigmatic messages. Each file was a puzzle waiting to be solved, a riddle that teased at the possibility of something greater beyond. It was a daunting task, one that filled me with both excitement and trepidation, but I knew that Aria and I were in this together.

And then, amidst the sea of data, I stumbled upon a message unlike any other. Buried deep within the files was a cryptic clue—a faint whisper of something hidden in the shadows. It was a single mention of the Nexus Vault, elusive and mysterious yet tantalizingly close. Aria and I exchanged surprised glances, the gravity of our discovery sinking in.

"We've found something," Aria exclaimed, her voice filled with excitement. "But what does it mean?"

I shook my head, my mind racing with possibilities. "I'm not sure," I admitted, my voice barely above a whisper. "But it's definitely a clue. And if there's one thing we've learned on this journey, it's that every clue brings us one step closer to the truth."

With anticipation coursing through my veins, I hesitated only briefly before initiating the download, transferring the enigmatic inscription onto the same ChronoArchive I had acquired from the Temple of Knowledge, along with the encoded data about the Nexus Vault. As the data streamed into my device, I couldn't shake the feeling of excitement mingled with apprehension. This digital artifact held the key to unlocking the secrets of the Nexus Vault, but deciphering its cryptic message would require both skill and patience.

The quest for the Nexus Vault isn't just a search for forgotten knowledge; it's a race against time to prevent the resurgence of forces that once brought the world to its knees. Unraveling its secrets could mean the difference between salvation and the resurgence of an age-old catastrophe.

Continuing my exploration of the chamber's technological marvels, my attention was captured by a peculiar device nestled amidst a cluster of futuristic machinery. Unlike the other consoles, this one radiated an aura of significance, with its sleek design and illuminated display hinting at advanced capabilities.

Approaching cautiously, I narrowed my eyes in recognition as I examined the intricate interface before me. The device bore a striking resemblance to the deciphering computers I had encountered on previous expeditions, its configuration and layout reminding me of the ancient artifacts used to unlock long-lost secrets.

Driven by a sense of ambition, I instinctively reached out, my fingers hovering over the touch-sensitive surface as if pulled by an unseen force. I tapped into the device's power source, awakening its dormant systems with a soft hum of activation.

As the display flickered to life, my suspicions were confirmed. This was indeed a deciphering computer, a tool crafted by a long-forgotten civilization to unlock the mysteries of hidden enigmatic inscriptions.

Filled with a mix of excitement and trepidation, I prepared to interface with the device, aware that its insights could hold the key to deciphering the cryptic messages downloaded onto my ChronoArchive.

The first translated message said: "Vénčr tu ðə fɚgɒtn rʊ'ɪnz hwɛɚ 'ʃædoʊz 'lɪŋgɚ, ænd ðɛɚ, bɪ'niθ ðə 'enʃənt triz ɪm'breɪs, sik ðə ki tu ən'lɑk ðə 'geɪtweɪ tu ˌɛtɚ'nɪti."[1] and the second message said: "Climb þe hýst plácn hwǽr ðæt sky tǽccoð ðæt éorð, and ðǽr, midst þe swýrling windas, þe wǽg to ðæt Nexus Vǽlt shal bǽon rǽvǽlad."

This meant I now had two clues to the Nexus Vault, which, to me, signified considerable progress.

piqued.

"What do those messages mean?" asked Aria, her curiosity

"I'm not sure yet. I need more clues, but these will guide me

to the Nexus Vault," I replied, contemplating the cryptic messages. "I really hope you'll be able to figure it out," Aria said, her concern evident.

"I have no choice. It's part of my main mission. The Nexus Vault will lead me to the Ascendant Matrix, and then I'll have finally completed the most difficult parts of my tasks," I explained, determination in my voice.

"It all seems rather complicated. This Ascendant Matrix better be worth it," remarked Aria, her skepticism showing.

"I can only agree. All this effort would be for naught if it wasn't. But it has to be. There's a reason for the changes they made to me, and then they put me on ice. I'm sure they'd have a good reason for that," I reasoned, hoping for a satisfactory outcome.

I disassembled the computer that decrypted the mysterious messages and was capable of turning it into a handheld form, so I could take it with me and manually decrypt further messages. I dubbed it the "Cryptex Decoder.". This Cryptex Decoder was more than a tool; it symbolized the bridge between past knowledge and our future discoveries, a beacon guiding us through the darkness of forgotten lore.

"What did you just do?" asked Aria in shock.

"I turned the computer into a handheld device; from now on, we'll be able to decrypt messages whenever we encounter them," I said.

"Oh, that should be useful," she said.

At this crossroads, uncertain of our next direction, I turned to Aria; her insight was a guiding light in the maze of our journey.

"I'd just continue forward; all we can do really," suggested Aria, her pragmatism shining through.

"Sounds as good of an idea as any, but first I'd like to check something," I said, a plan forming in my mind.

As we prepared to leave the underground chamber behind, a faintly illuminated map caught my eye, nestled among the myriad of screens. It displayed a constellation of nodes spread across the land, each potentially holding a piece to the puzzle of the Nexus Vault. 'Our journey is far from over,' I mused aloud, the map etching itself into my memory. 'These nodes might just be the breadcrumbs leading us to the heart of the mystery. Guiding the horse towards the entrance of the city, I found what I was looking for: my Alloyed Charger.

When Aria noticed it, she exclaimed in great surprise, "How in the world did that thing get here already?"

"Well, considering that it's twelve times faster than the fastest horse you can imagine, and we've been away for quite a while now, I was hoping it was already here. Although I honestly didn't count on it,. It was brought here remarkably fast," I explained, impressed by the efficiency of the delivery.

"Wow, if you don't mind, I'd really like to try that thing." Aria said it in amazement.

"Well, at full speed, it can actually be quite dangerous. I'll let you try it one day. But for now, you can jump in at the back," I offered, eager to share the experience with her.

"There's a place for two?" Aria asked, and her excitement was palpable.

"Sure is. We'll leave the horse behind and get going. We'll be at our next destination, whatever that might be," I declared, ready to embark on the next leg of our journey with Aria by my side. As we prepared to depart, I paused, turning to Aria with a sense of resolve. 'Whatever lies ahead,' I said, 'we face it together. Not just as companions, but as partners in this journey of discovery and

challenge.' Aria nodded, her expression one of determination and warmth. 'Together,' she echoed. The path forward might be fraught with unknowns, but with our combined strength and courage, we were ready to confront whatever mysteries and dangers awaited us.

[1] "Venture to the forgotten ruins where shadows linger, and there, beneath the ancient tree's embrace, seek the key to unlock the gateway to eternity."

[2] "Climb the highest peak where the sky touches the earth, and there, amidst the swirling winds, the path to the Nexus Vault shall be revealed."

SHELTERED SHADOWS

Leaving the streets of Alloy City behind us, Aria and I embarked on the next leg of our journey through the desolate wasteland. The winter's chill hung heavy in the air, casting a pall of frost across the barren landscape as we rode on, our Alloyed Charger carrying us swiftly through the frozen expanse.

As we ventured further into the abandoned wilderness, the remnants of civilization faded into the distance, replaced by snow-covered ruins and skeletal trees. The air was crisp, and still, the only sound was the crunch of snow beneath our Charger's metal feet.

Navigating through the snow-laden streets and icy winds, we remained vigilant, scanning our surroundings for any signs of life or clues that might lead us closer to our goal. Each twist and turn of the road brought new challenges and uncertainties, but we pressed on with unwavering determination under the cold winter sky.

Despite the biting cold and desolation that surrounded us, there was a sense of unity between Aria and me, a silent understanding forged through shared experiences and the trials we had faced together. Side by side, we rode on, our bond growing stronger with each passing mile.

As the day wore on, we eventually came upon a crossroads, the path splitting off in different directions. With no clear indication of which way to go, we paused to consider our options, seeking shelter beneath the skeletal remains of a frozen structure.

In the distance, a glimmer of light caught our attention, beckoning us towards its mysterious allure. Intrigued by the prospect of discovery, we decided to follow the elusive vision, hoping it would lead us to answers or aid in our quest.

With renewed resolve and the winter's chill biting at our heels, we urged our Alloyed Charger forward, its mechanical legs trudging through the snow-drifts. Whatever lay ahead, we faced it together, ready to confront the challenges of the frozen wasteland under the unyielding gaze of the winter sun.

Suddenly, we had to stop abruptly as a mysterious figure stood before us. The figure appeared weather-beaten, with a rugged appearance indicative of a life spent surviving in the harsh conditions of the wasteland. He was clad in layers of tattered clothing, patched together from various scraps and salvaged materials. A worn leather duster hung loosely from his shoulders, its once-dark hue faded by exposure to the elements. Under the duster, he wore a threadbare flannel shirt, its vibrant colors dulled by years of wear and tear. Tattered denim jeans, reinforced with patches and stitching, provided protection against the biting cold. His feet were encased in scuffed leather boots, their soles worn thin from countless miles of travel through the snow. Despite his rugged appearance, there was a sense of resilience and determination in his weathered features, hinting at the hardships he had endured and the secrets he held.

"Whoa, what in the world!" exclaimed Ethan. "Why are you blocking our path? Move out of the way so we can pass."

"Just hold on a moment," the figure replied calmly. "I'm here with a proposition."

"And what might that be?" inquired Aria.

"I come from a shelter beneath a nearby rocky area. We can offer you shelter, food, and a warm bed to rest on," the figure explained.

"Nothing comes without a cost," Ethan interjected. "What do you need from us in return?"

"Well, you see, we've been grappling with an illness spreading among our people. I was hoping you could lend us your assistance," the figure responded.

"I'm not entirely certain." Ethan hesitated. "While I have some medical knowledge, diagnosing an illness is a different beast altogether. Nonetheless, I'll do what I can. I can't make any guarantees, though."

"Ethan, are you sure about this? I don't want us to fall ill," Aria expressed her concern.

"It's our responsibility, Aria. We can't abandon these people without at least attempting to aid them," Ethan asserted.

"I suppose you're right. Alright then, but I'm not versed in medicine, so I'll rely on your guidance," Aria consented.

"Of course," Ethan reassured her. "Feel free to ask me anything if you have questions."

"Follow me," the figure beckoned.

We trailed behind them until we reached an overhead formation of rocks, fused together over time. A sizable opening revealed everything within.

"Welcome to Havenrock Refuge," said the figure.

Within the shelter, a sense of bustling activity filled the air as residents went about their daily routines, their collective efforts aimed at maintaining a semblance of normalcy amidst the challenges they faced. The interior was dimly lit by flickering torches and lanterns, casting dancing shadows across the rough-hewn walls and makeshift furnishings.

At the heart of the shelter, a central gathering area served as a communal hub where residents came together to socialize, share meals, and seek solace in one another's company. A sturdy wooden bar, weathered with age and well-worn from years of use, stood as a focal point, its surface polished by countless hands and adorned with a collection of mismatched mugs and tankards.

Surrounding the bar, a scattering of tables and chairs provided seating for the shelter's occupants, offering a place to rest weary limbs and enjoy moments of respite amidst the chaos of their surroundings. Some tables were occupied by groups engaged in lively conversation or games of cards, their laughter and camaraderie echoing off the walls.

In one corner of the room, a small play area had been set up for the shelter's youngest residents, with colorful toys and games scattered about to keep them entertained. Children darted to and fro, their laughter ringing out as they chased one another in carefree abandon, momentarily oblivious to the hardships that surrounded them.

Nearby, a group of adults could be seen huddled together, deep in discussion, as they strategized and planned for the days ahead. Some were engaged in tasks such as cooking, cleaning, or tending to the sick, their faces etched with determination as they worked tirelessly to keep the shelter running smoothly.

Throughout the space, the scent of home-cooked meals wafted through the air, mingling with the earthy aroma of the shelter's rustic surroundings. A sense of warmth and camaraderie pervaded the atmosphere, fostering a sense of belonging and unity among the shelter's diverse inhabitants Despite the challenges they faced, there was an undeniable sense of resilience and hope that permeated the shelter, an emblem of the strength and spirit of its residents as they came together to weather the storm and support one another in their time of need. "Feel free to grab a seat wherever suits you best. On the right side of the cave, you'll find an opening leading to some beds if you're feeling weary. But if you're hungry or thirsty, we've got plenty of drinks and food to go around. And when you're ready, the area through the opening on the left is where you'll find the sick folks. By the way, my name's Harper Morgan, so if you ever need anything, just give me a shout. I'll be at your service," Harper offered.

"Not particularly hungry, but a drink sounds good," I replied. "Afterward, we'll check on the sick."

"Sounds good," Aria agreed.

"What's on the menu? Any chance you have beer?" I inquired.

"Beer, huh? Don't know what that is exactly; what's it like?" the bartender asked.

"It's yellow, a bit bitter, and has a kick to it if you overdo it. The more you have, the better it gets," I explained.

"Ah, gotcha," the bartender nodded, placing a pint of brownish liquid in front of me.

"What's this?" I asked.

"That's about as close as we've got to what you described. It's not yellow, but it fits the bill otherwise. We call it Dustbrew. Give it a try and let me know what you think," the bartender said.

I took a few sips, trying to recall the taste of beer.

Surprisingly, it wasn't too bad—not nearly as awful as I anticipated. "Close enough!" I remarked. "Aria, why don't you order something too? You've been quiet for a while."

"Lost in thought, huh?" she said. "Well, I suppose you don't happen to have Verdant Zephyr around here?"

"I'm sorry, but we can't get that stuff so isolated from society. We do have something different, though. It's made from apples and oranges, similar to how they make Verdant Zephyr. It's not that close, but it's the closest to it," the bartender explained.

"That'll have to do," Aria replied.

As she tasted it, she seemed quite content with the flavor and expressed her intention to have more.

"Don't get yourself wasted," I cautioned. "After we visit the sick, we'll come back, and you can get as drunk as you want. But first, we'll have to remain sober."

"I intend to get wasted for sure. I need a moment of respite and to escape from reality for a bit, you know?" she replied.

"I can understand that," I said, turning to the bartender.

"Now, I have to mention something you said before. You mentioned you are isolated from society. What exactly do you mean by that? You're saying that there's a whole society out there?"

"Yes, sir. It depends on what you mean by society, but yes, there are people out there," the bartender confirmed.

"But what kind of society? Do you mean like a village or something?" I inquired further.

"I wouldn't call it a mere village; it's more of an entire city. Thousands of people live there. They've done a good job of rebuilding the place, I tell ya. They call it Apex City for a reason. I lived there once but decided to go on an adventure. Little did I know I'd end up here as a bartender. Not that it's so bad, except for the sick people and all," the bartender elaborated.

I stood there, struck by the revelation. An entire city existed out there with people, and I knew nothing about it. I felt a surge of eagerness to go there.

"So, where might this place be?" I asked.

"It's about thirty-three thousand miles to the east. Then, if you follow the road for a few hours, you'll start to encounter a path that leads to a stone-gravel area. If you continue, you'll eventually end up in the city," the bartender explained.

"Do you happen to have a map or something?" I inquired. "Of course I do. I wouldn't have gotten here if it weren't for me having a map now, would I?" The bartender quipped.

"Could you lend it to me for a few minutes?" I requested. "Sure thing," she replied.

She disappeared into the bedroom area and returned with a large piece of paper.

"Here it is," she said, handing it over.

I immediately retrieved my OmniLocator from my bag, scanned the document, marked it as Apex City, and stowed it away again.

"Thanks!" I said.

"What did you do there?" she asked.

"I scanned the document. Now it's stored in my OmniLocator. It's a device that can locate specific things and recognize maps, among other things," I explained.

"Aw heck, that would've been convenient if I had one of those. Where do I get those things?" the bartender inquired.

"Unfortunately, it's one of a kind. You aren't going to find any of those anywhere," I replied.

"Ah, that's too bad. Sure, I could've used one of those, but if there ain't more of those, then so be it," she shrugged.

"Well, at least I know my next location," I remarked.

Aria nodded and said, "Looks like we have a goal now, don't we?"

"We sure do. Who knows what we'll find out there?" I mused.

I sat there for a while, staring and thinking about the city.

Then, my mind returned to the present, and I started to empty my pint.

After we finished our drinks, I grabbed my first aid kit, and we made our way to the room where the sick people rested on their beds. We were taken aback by the sheer number of sick individuals. Coughs filled the air, mingling with the sound of labored breathing and occasional moans.

Feeling a few foreheads, it was evident that they were all suffering from extreme fever.

"I don't think my first aid kit is going to cut it," I remarked. "Can you go to the bartender and get as many wet towels and handkerchiefs as you can?"

Aria hurried back and returned with a huge pile of towels and assorted pieces of cloth.

"Yes, that'll do," I said as I grabbed two boxes of painkillers. "So, we'll split this task in half. I want you to fold everything you have there in a way that it'll fit on their heads. Then, I want you to place it over their heads and give them one of these pills."

Handing her a box of painkillers, I took the pile from her hands and spread it out on the floor.

"Just take a few and move on to the next person. Got it?" I instructed.

Aria nodded. Together, we distributed the towels and painkillers, doing what little we could to alleviate their suffering. Once we were finished, we gathered up the remaining towels and cloth and returned to Harper.

"We've done what we can to reduce their pain, but I'm afraid it won't cure the sickness," I admitted.

"What would it take to cure them?" Harper inquired.

"If I'm correct, and I'm not entirely sure I am, they're suffering from bacterial pneumonia. If that's the case, then they'll need antibiotics. Something I don't have," I explained.

"Where would we get those types of things?" Harper asked. "I don't know. We need to find a pharmacy and hope there's anything left after all these years," I replied.

"Well, I do know of a place where you might find medicine," Harper offered.

"What? Where?" I asked eagerly.

"To the west. If you follow the left path and keep going, you'll eventually reach several warehouses. One of them is specifically for medicine. At least, that's what I've heard. I can't guarantee there's anything left, but it's your best chance," Harper explained.

"Well, it looks like we're headed there," I decided.

Aria nodded, but her silence was too much for me to bear. "Aria, you've been quiet all day. Now tell me what's up, because I won't put up with it anymore," I said, frustration creeping into my voice.

Tears welled up in her eyes. "I'm so sorry, Ethan. I didn't mean to offend you. I just can't stop thinking about those sick people," she confessed.

"It's okay," I said gently, pulling her into a comforting embrace. "You're just an empathetic person. I'm not mad at you. I understand."

"Thank you, Ethan, for understanding. I'll talk more if you want me to," Aria offered.

"You don't have to if you don't feel like it. It's okay. We'll help those people as best we can. Once we find the medicine they need, they're going to be fine. It's going to take some effort, but we'll do it," I reassured her.

Aria and I wasted no time in making our decision to depart without delay, our determination fueled by the urgency of the situation. With each passing moment, the gravity of the task ahead weighed heavily on us, driving us to expedite our journey with all possible haste.

As Aria and I embarked on our journey to the warehouses, the desolate landscape stretched out before us, barren and unforgiving. The winter chill hung heavy in the air, biting at our exposed skin as we trudged onward.

Our path led us through rugged terrain, littered with the remnants of the old world. We navigated through rocky outcrops and overgrown brush, our footsteps crunching on the frozen ground beneath us.

After navigating the dense underbrush and the tangled maze of Washington's wilds, we encountered a seemingly unremarkable cavern nestled beneath the verdant canopy.

As we sought refuge for a brief respite, the cavern's hidden entrance beckoned to us, promising shelter and a moment's peace. The secrets it held felt almost tangible, like whispers from the earth itself, guiding us to its depths. With dusk painting the sky in shades of purple and gold, I began to gather what dry branches and foliage I could find, building a campfire at the cavern's mouth. Its welcoming glow soon pushed back the chill of the evening, and Aria and I settled beside the warmth, allowing the fire's crackle to fill the silence between us.

The cavern, with its walls illuminated by our small fire, seemed to come alive, its shadows dancing in harmony with the flames. It was in this tranquil haven, where the world outside felt both close and miles away, that he made his presence known. Stepping from the shadows with a quiet deliberation, he moved as if he were part of the natural world around us, his approach almost imperceptible until he was simply there, beside the firelight, a silhouette emerging from the dim.

"Mind if I share your fire?" His voice, melding seamlessly with the night, carried the gentle rustling of leaves and the distant calls of nocturnal creatures. There was an ease to his introduction, a sense of mutual respect among those who navigated the wilds.

"I'm Marcus," he offered, extending a hand not just in greeting but as an invitation to share in the knowledge he carried. Introducing himself as a historian dedicated to the preservation of knowledge and truths long buried, Marcus embodied the spirit of a seeker, drawn to the cavern by the same threads of curiosity that guided us.

Our conversation unfolded naturally, as if destined. In the company of Marcus, our brief interlude by the campfire became a meeting of minds. He spoke with passion about Washington's unique role as a sanctuary for the wisdom of the ages, illuminating the depth of his scholarship and the significance of our path.

In Marcus's company, beneath the ancient gaze of the cavern, our moment of rest transformed into a pivotal encounter. His introduction, far from abrupt, felt like the revelation of a guidepost, a moment of clarity and connection on the long and winding road that lay ahead.

Marcus, with a gaze that seemed to pierce the veils of time, shared his insights into the significance of our location and, by extension, the entirety of Washington. "Ethan," he began, his voice echoing softly in the confines of the cavern. "Washington is not just the backdrop to our journey by mere coincidence. It is a land chosen by visionaries, a cradle for the rebirth of civilization."

He spoke of hidden vaults filled with the seeds of future knowledge, artifacts of immeasurable power, and libraries safeguarding the cumulative wisdom of ages—each embedded within the landscape, protected by nature and by technologies beyond our current grasp. "These sanctuaries," Marcus explained, "were woven into the fabric of Washington, hidden in plain sight, awaiting those with the foresight to seek them out."

As the fire crackled and popped, Marcus's tale unfolded—a narrative of premeditated resilience, of zones where the fabric of reality thinned, and of a network of safeguards meant to guide humanity through its darkest hour. "Each step we take," he concluded, "brings us closer to unlocking the legacy left behind by the architects of rebirth, guiding us towards a future they dared to envision."

Our conversation, illuminated by the fire's dying embers, left me with a profound sense of purpose. The path before me, I realized, was charted with intentions far greater than my own. It was a pilgrimage through a land imbued with the legacy of those who had prepared for humanity's second act.

As Marcus disappeared into the night as mysteriously as he had arrived, leaving me to ponder the weight of our encounter, I understood that my journey was not merely one of survival but a quest to uncover the beacons of hope and renewal hidden within the heart of Washington.

Feeling invigorated by our brief respite in the cavern, we resolved to press onward with our journey. With time slipping away and darkness enveloping the world outside, we knew we could not afford to linger any longer. The chill of the night air served as a reminder of the urgency driving us forward. Despite the lack of warmth, we pressed on, our determination unwavering in the face of adversity.

Occasionally, we came across the skeletal remains of abandoned vehicles, rusted and broken by the passage of time. Each one served as a somber reminder of the world that once was, now lost to the ravages of the apocalypse.

As we journeyed further, the landscape grew increasingly desolate, with only the occasional patch of hardy vegetation breaking up the monotony of the barren wasteland. As I ventured deeper into the heart of Washington, the true extent of its significance began to unfold before me like a well-kept secret whispered across generations. The journey was not just a path through physical space but a dive into the layered complexities of history, nature, and the boundless ambition of human innovation.

In the solitude of my travels, I often found myself pausing to reflect on the remnants of a bygone era—structures and machines that seemed out of place amid the wild, untamed landscapes. These were not merely relics; they were markers of a deliberate symbiosis between nature and technology, an attestation of Washington's role as a sanctuary for human achievement.

One evening, as the sun dipped below the horizon, casting a fiery glow across the sky, I stumbled upon a series of worn, half-buried markers leading to a hidden cavern. Inside, protected from the elements, lay a cache of documents and digital recordings—echoes of the past that shed light on Washington's pivotal role.

I activated an old, dust-covered playback device, its screen flickering to life with the image of a scientist whose name had been lost to time. "Washington," the figure began, "was chosen not merely for its natural beauty but for its strategic advantages. Its varied landscapes, from dense forests to towering mountains and vast waterways, provided unparalleled protection against external threats."

The scientist spoke of technological anomalies—areas where the fabric of reality seemed thinner and where the laws of physics bent in ways that defied explanation. "These anomalies," they continued, "attracted the brightest minds, drawn by the potential to push the boundaries of science and technology."

As I delved deeper into the archives, I found references to projects that blended seamlessly with the natural environment, their locations chosen for their ability to harness Washington's unique geological and climatic conditions. Hydroelectric facilities hidden within mountain gorges, research labs nestled in valleys shielded by dense forests, and data vaults buried beneath ice and rock—all designed to ensure that the heart of human knowledge would endure the tests of time and conflict.

One recording, more personal and reflective, caught my attention. A voice, weary yet hopeful, recounted the days leading up to the final war. "We knew that what we were building had to last beyond us, beyond our conflicts and our shortsightedness.

Washington was our fortress, our library, and our laboratory. We embedded our hopes in its soil, in the belief that one day someone would uncover them and carry forward the torch of enlightenment."

These discoveries, hidden away for generations, underscored the duality of Washington's identity: a place of natural splendor and a crucible of human aspiration. It was here, amid the ruins of the old world and the burgeoning life of the new, that the future of humanity was quietly being shaped.

Reflecting on these revelations, I realized that my journey was more than a search for survival or even understanding. It was a pilgrimage to the heart of human resilience, a quest to reconnect with the dreams and ambitions of those who had dared to imagine a future beyond the end of the world.

And so, as I left the cavern behind, the words of the forgotten scientist echoing in my mind, I looked upon Washington with new eyes. It was not just the setting of my journey but the keeper of our legacy—a beacon of hope that, even in the darkest of times, refused to be extinguished.

The silence of the wilderness enveloped us, broken only by the sound of our own breathing and the crunch of snow underfoot.

Despite the harsh conditions, we remained focused on our goal, our minds consumed with thoughts of the antibiotics we so desperately needed. With each step, we drew closer to our destination, driven onward by the hope of finding a cure for the sickness that plagued our friends back at the shelter.

Finally, we reached our destination: a vast expanse, the ground beneath us a patchwork of crumbling asphalt and encroaching nature, signaling the end of winter's grip. The remnants of snow clung stubbornly to the earth, the last vestiges of a season relinquishing its hold.

While surveying the area, we noted the uniformity of the surrounding warehouses, which were indistinguishable from one another. Thankfully, Harper's instructions had been clear, guiding us to the exact location we sought.

Approaching the designated warehouse, we found its entrance firmly secured and impenetrable without the proper means of access. Unfazed, I wielded my Fusionizer, unleashing a volley of energy bolts at the door's center. With persistence, the door yielded, allowing us to pry it open and discover an abundance of medical supplies within—evidently untouched for ages. It struck us how fortunate we were to be in a region spared the direct devastation of the bombs. Had it been otherwise, the landscape, along with the villages and shelters we'd encountered, might have been mere memories.

Amidst this contemplation, I couldn't help but ponder the fate of areas less fortunate, now reclaimed by nature and potentially ripe for resettlement in the wake of diminished radiation levels.

Aria, attempting to speak, was suddenly overtaken by a severe coughing fit. After a tense moment, her coughing eased, and she voiced concerns about a sore throat and headache.

Fearing she might have contracted the illness we'd encountered, I reassured her of our likely proximity to a cure. Our search through the dust-covered supplies was interrupted by Aria's excited shout, having discovered a cache of antibiotics.

"You've found it," I affirmed with a sense of achievement. "Well done."

Aria suggested a thorough search for additional resources, leading us to unearth a treasure trove of medical essentials:

painkillers, antiseptics, antivirals, and more, all invaluable in our current world.

Convinced we had gathered enough, I called to Aria, only to find her collapsed, feverish, and barely conscious on the floor. My concern for her surged as I administered antibiotics, hoping for a swift recovery. As she regained awareness, her weakened state was evident.

With Aria in dire need of care, I prepared to carry her to safety, only to be confronted by the imminent threat of two sentinel drones. I carefully placed Aria on the ground, bracing myself for the confrontation ahead.

Under the open sky, the warehouses around us whispered tales of a bygone era, their silent stories overshadowed by the impending threat. The first Sentinel Drone emerged from the shadows, its sleek, angular form cutting a formidable silhouette against the dimming light. Moments later, its twin joined, standing side by side with an air of mechanical menace. I had faced one of these behemoths before, a lone sentinel in a dance of death. The memory of that battle weighed heavily on me, a stark reminder of the challenge they presented.

Their gunmetal gray exteriors gleamed ominously, each movement synchronized in a chilling display of coordination. As they advanced, their energy cores pulsed—a vivid, threatening glow that served as a harbinger of the battle to come. The first drone brandished a large knife, moving with unsettling speed for its size. It grabbed me with a robotic hand, the cold metal a stark contrast to the warmth of human touch I so missed. With agility born of desperation, I dodged its initial strike, feeling the air shift as the knife sliced through where I had been moments before.

My mind raced, analyzing and planning. The drones, while formidable, were not invincible. Their design favored strength and armor, but I had found their Achilles' heel in my last encounter: the precise targeting of joints and wiring. Yet, with two drones and without my Voltcaster, the dynamics had changed. I needed to adapt, to outmaneuver them, and to fight smarter.

The battle that ensued was a maelstrom of motion and steel. The drones were relentless; their attacks were coordinated and efficient. But for every strike they aimed at me, I countered, dodging and weaving with every ounce of my enhanced agility. The ruins around us bore witness to our deadly ballet, the sound of clashing metal echoing off their ancient walls.

I focused on evasion, biding my time, and looking for an opening. It came in a fleeting moment when one drone misjudged its strike, embedding its knife into the ground. Seizing the chance, I launched myself at the other, targeting its exposed wiring with a barrage of blows from the Fusionizer. Sparks flew as my hits found their mark, but the drone was quick to retaliate, its companion freeing itself to join the fray once more.

Their armor was nearly impervious to the Fusionizer's blasts, a fact that hammered home with each futile strike. Frustration mounted, a dangerous distraction in the heat of battle. It was then, amidst the chaos, that I remembered the protective housing of their energy cores. It had been a vulnerability before; it could be again.

With renewed focus, I aimed not to destroy but to disarm. I danced around them, a shadow flickering in and out of their reach, until I saw it: a momentary gap in their defense. The drone I had struck first had a slight, almost imperceptible loosening in its armor near the energy core.

Channeling all my strength and precision into a single, decisive moment, I struck, targeting the gap with a barrage from the Fusionizer. The drone staggered, its movements erratic, as the integrity of its protective housing was compromised. Encouraged, I pressed on, dodging the other drone's attempts to protect its counterpart, focusing all my firepower on that one critical point.

Finally, with a sound like the world itself tearing apart, the housing shattered. The energy core, exposed and vulnerable, was a beacon of victory in the dim light. Without hesitation, I directed every bit of energy I had left into a final, devastating blow.

The explosion was blinding—a brilliant release of energy that rocked the very ground beneath us. When the light faded, one drone lay inert, its core extinguished. But victory was short-lived; the second drone, undeterred by the fate of its counterpart, advanced with renewed aggression.

Pain and exhaustion clouded my senses, but the sight of the fallen drone reignited a spark of determination within me. I couldn't falter now, not when I was so close. Leveraging the debris from the destroyed drone, I fashioned a makeshift spear, a primitive weapon against a technologically superior foe. It was a desperate plan, but desperation had become my closest ally.

As the second drone charged, I feigned weakness, staggering back as if on the verge of collapse. It saw its chance, closing in for the kill. But at the last moment, I pivoted, channeling every bit of my remaining strength and speed into a single, piercing thrust.

The spear found its mark, penetrating the drone's armor and piercing its energy core. The light in its mechanical eyes flickered, then died as it crumpled to the ground, a heap of lifeless metal.

Breathing heavily, I surveyed the aftermath of the battle.

The ruins around me were scarred by the conflict, a physical indicator to the struggle for survival in this forsaken world. My body ached with every beat of my heart, each wound a reminder of the drone's lethal precision. Yet, standing amidst the wreckage of my foes, I felt an overwhelming surge of triumph. The victory was not just mine but a symbol of human resilience—the indomitable spirit that refuses to yield even in the face of insurmountable odds.

As the adrenaline began to wane, the reality of my situation settled in. I was alone, far from any semblance of civilization, with only the ruins and the fallen drones for company. The silence that followed the battle was deafening, a stark contrast to the chaos that had preceded it. I took a moment to collect myself and bandage my wounds as best as I could with the limited supplies in my bag. The injuries were severe but not life-threatening, thanks to my enhanced healing capabilities. Still, they would need time to fully recover.

Despite the urgency of the moment, it was imperative that I took Aria and returned to Havenrock Refuge without delay. Her well-being was my priority, and the health of those suffering depended on the antibiotics we had secured. I harbored hope that this would be the remedy we needed.

Guiding the Alloyed Charger with Aria carefully positioned behind me, I felt a mix of concern and urgency. Aria, battling bacterial pneumonia, had already taken a dose of antibiotics at the warehouse, offering a glimmer of hope amidst the gravity of her condition. As we embarked on our journey back to Havenrock Refuge, the motorcycle's seamless navigation through the wilderness was an indicator of its advanced design, providing a steady and reliable passage through the remnants of winter's touch.

The landscape around us bore the scars of the season's end, with small patches of snow scattered like forgotten memories across the earth. The Charger's adaptive suspension made light work of the terrain, with its intelligent algorithms ensuring a ride as gentle as possible for Aria.

The journey, underlined by the quiet hum of the bike and the soft rustling of nature waking around us, was momentarily peaceful until a sudden shift in Aria's posture signaled distress. Pulling the bike to a gentle stop, I quickly turned to assess her condition. To my relief, Aria was conscious, albeit weak, of her earlier dose of antibiotics, beginning to wage war against the infection that had claimed her strength.

"I'm okay," she murmured, her voice weak but steadied by the medicine's initial effects. "Let's keep going. I don't want to stop now." Her determination, even in the face of her illness, was a beacon of strength. Assisting her back into position, we resumed our journey with renewed purpose, the Alloyed Charger carrying us swiftly through the wilderness.

As we navigated the landscape, the Charger's efficiency cut through the remnants of winter, a symbolic gesture of our own struggle to overcome the adversity of Aria's illness. The journey back to Havenrock Refuge was marked by moments of silent solidarity and the unspoken bond that adversity had forged between us.

Aria's improvement, though subtle, was a promising sign that the antibiotics were taking effect. With each mile that passed beneath us, the heaviness of my worry lightened, replaced by cautious optimism for her recovery and the well-being of those we were rushing to aid back at the shelter.

The silhouette of Havenrock Refuge appeared on the horizon, like a lighthouse guiding weary travelers home. As we approached the shelter, the sense of relief was palpable, not just for the safety it promised but for the hope that Aria's recovery could begin in earnest within its walls.

As we pulled into the refuge, the sense of urgency that had propelled us gave way to a quiet resolve. We had made it back, not just with the medicine that promised healing for Aria and the sick within the shelter.

As we approached, Harper spotted us from afar.

"Did you find it? Did you find the medicine?" he inquired eagerly.

"Yes, we did, and it should do the trick," I confirmed. "Aria was infected too, but the antibiotics cleared her up. I can't guarantee everyone will pull through, but most should see improvement."

Handing over a bottle of pills to Harper, I added, "Make sure everyone gets one of these, and they should be alright."

"Thank you so much. I can't express how grateful we are," Harper exclaimed. "Finally, a cure for our people who've been suffering for so long. I don't know how to thank you enough."

"The satisfaction of helping is a reward in itself, isn't it, Aria?" I remarked.

"Indeed, but any token of appreciation is welcome," Aria replied.

"Well, I do have one thing to offer," Harper revealed. "It's a ChronoArchive I stumbled upon in the ruins of an abandoned building. It took some digging, but it's yours now. I couldn't think of a better gift, although I can't vouch for its value."

As I examined the ChronoArchive, I was astounded to find another encoded message pointing towards the Nexus Vault.

"Thank you," I said genuinely. "This is more than I could have hoped for."

"Really? I'm glad it's of use to you. At least now I feel like I've given something valuable in return for all you've done," Harper responded.

Placing the ChronoArchive on my Cryptex Decoder, a new message emerged: "Fólou ðə rívərz wájndɪŋ pæθ əntɪl ɪt kənvərjəz wɪð ðə éjnʃənt trí, hwær ʃædoʊz dæns ɪn ðə múnlaɪt rivílɪŋ ðə éntrəns kí."[1]

"I think we're getting closer," I remarked. "It won't be long before we uncover the location of the Nexus Vault."

"I'm not so sure," Aria countered. "We still don't know where to begin searching. If we did, we might stand a chance."

"You're right," I admitted. "We need a way to pinpoint the exact location described in those clues."

"Let's hope we stumble upon a clue that leads us there," Aria suggested.

"For now, our best bet is Apex City," I concluded.

"But how long will it take us to get there?" Aria inquired. "With the Alloy Charger, we could make it in two weeks at most if we maintain a speed of about one hundred miles per hour," I estimated.

"Then let's not waste any time. We should start preparing to leave," Aria urged.

"Agreed. We'll need to gather supplies and acquire new armor and clothes before we set out," I replied. "Harper, can you assist us with these provisions, and what will it cost?"

"For what you've done for us? It's on the house. We have skilled artisans who can craft armor and clothes, and I'll make sure you're stocked up for your journey," Harper assured us.

"Thank you, Harper. Your generosity is greatly appreciated," I expressed my gratitude.

"It's the least I can do after everything you've done for us," Harper replied sincerely.

They provided us with new clothes and new armor.

I got a heavy-duty, weather-resistant jacket with a removable insulated lining. The jacket featured multiple pockets, including hidden ones for valuable items, a hood with a reinforced brim, and reinforced cargo pants made from a tough, rip-stop fabric with pockets and secure closures to keep items safe. Knee patches and a gusseted crotch ensure durability and ease of movement.

Aria received a long-sleeve, fitted pullover made from a technical fabric that retains heat but releases sweat, with a half-zip front for temperature regulation. Heavy-duty, yet flexible, trousers with reinforced stitching and a water-resistant coating. Cargo pockets for extra storage and articulated knees for mobility.

As for my armor, the base layer consisted of high-quality, treated leather, chosen for its toughness and flexibility. The leather was dyed in a dark, earthy tone to blend with various environments and to minimize visibility during stealth movements. Key areas of the armor, including the shoulder guards, parts of the chest plate, gloves, and the tips and heels of the boots, were reinforced with silver graphene. This advanced material is known for its exceptional strength-to-weight ratio, offering unparalleled protection without sacrificing mobility. The silver sheen of the graphene parts provided a striking contrast against the dark leather, which gave the armor a rugged yet futuristic appearance. The knuckles and back of the hands were covered with graphene plating, offering protection during hand-to-hand combat without impairing dexterity.

Aria's armor utilized serpent skin, prized for its natural resilience and flexibility. The skin was treated with a proprietary technique to enhance its protective qualities while retaining its lightweight nature. The armor adopted the serpent skin's natural patterns, giving it an organic, camouflaged appearance that seamlessly blends into its natural surroundings. Matching gloves and boots were made from the same serpent-skin material, designed for tactile sensitivity and a firm grip. The boots featured reinforced soles for durability and traction across varied terrains.

"Looking sharp, you two," he remarked. "All set for a fresh venture, I gather."

"It appears so," I replied gratefully.

"Well, if you're setting off now, then I suppose this is farewell. Wishing you both the best of luck on your journey."

We expressed our gratitude and bid him farewell before embarking on our journey towards Apex City, ready to embrace the adventures that lay ahead.

[1] "Follow the river's winding path until it converges with the ancient tree, where shadows dance in the moonlight, revealing the entrance key."

BLUEPRINTS OF DESTINY

Traversing the labyrinthine forests of Washington, my journey had taken me through remnants of the old world and whispers of the new. It was on a day, cloaked in the mists of an early dawn, that I stumbled upon a secluded settlement, its inhabitants a group of survivors who had carved out an existence amidst the chaos of the post-apocalyptic landscape. It appeared that we weren't heading to Apex City just yet, as I sensed that this place warranted further investigation.

As we approached, wary of their intentions, we were met not with hostility but with a cautious curiosity.

As we strolled through the settlement, our path led us to an intriguing establishment, beckoning with its partially open door.

Stepping inside, I found myself enveloped in darkness, save for the faint flicker of candlelight casting eerie shadows upon the walls. The interior was adorned with an eclectic array of oddities: an antique pocket watch, its hands ticking backward as if counting down to some forgotten event; a mesmerizing collection of enchanted marbles, shifting hues in response to nearby emotions and emitting whispers when touched; and a weathered tome bound in ancient leather, its pages inscribed with arcane symbols and long-lost rituals.

Perched atop shelves were an assortment of dangling charms and baubles crafted from bones and beads, swaying gently as if moved by some unseen force. The air was filled with the soft clinking of chimes, their melodies weaving through the dimly lit space like echoes of forgotten rituals.

A chill ran down my spine as I surveyed the scene, a sense of otherworldly tranquility washing over me. "This place is... unsettling," remarked Aria, her voice tinged with unease.

"I know what you mean," I replied, my gaze lingering on the mysterious artifacts. "There's something about this place that I can't quite grasp."

"We shouldn't linger," suggested Aria, her discomfort palpable.

"But we must explore," I insisted, drawn to the mysteries concealed within.

Moving further into the shop, we approached a glass desk adorned with more curious trinkets. Behind it stood an elderly figure, weathered by the passage of time—a guardian of secrets in this enigmatic realm.

"Hail, wanderers, I be Azrel, a guide in these realms of mystery. What be yer needs?" the man inquired, his voice carrying the soft whisper of ancient winds.

"My name's Ethan, and this is Aria," I introduced, casting a curious glance around the shop. "We stumbled upon your store and couldn't help but be intrigued by the array of oddities you've got here."

"Spy any treasures catchin' yer eye, do ye?" Azrel inquired, his gaze lingering on the curious artifacts scattered about the room.

"We're new to town and haven't had the chance to chat with many folks yet. Could you perhaps shed some light on what makes this place tick?" I inquired, hoping for some insight into the town's secrets.

"Ah, this ain't yer ordin'ry hamlet, lads. 'Tis a place where secrets dwell, guarded by those who've seen the world's very dawn," Ezra explained, his words laced with the weight of forgotten ages.

"I've come across my fair share of places brimming with ancient knowledge, delving into histories long forgotten. What sets this town apart?" I probed, eager for enlightenment.

"Aye, there be many spots where the whispers of ancients linger. But not all hold the same depth of knowin' as our folk do," Ezra remarked, his tone tinged with the solemnity of ancient rites.

"And what sort of wisdom might that be?" I pressed, keen to uncover the mysteries hidden within.

"What goods have ye to barter for the wisdom ye seek?" Ezra questioned, his eyes piercing with a knowing gaze.

"I've got some potent pain relievers on offer, with a bonus kick of euphoria. But mind you, they're not to be trifled with they are highly addictive if overused or taken for the wrong reasons. Will that suffice?" I offered, hoping to strike a deal.

"V'ry well, these here pills I can sell, for they hold little value to me," Ezra conceded, his demeanor bearing the weight of untold wisdom. "But the knowledge ye seek lies in a sacred lib'ry of boundless lore. Yet its whereabouts elude me. Instead, seek out Suzi, an elder in our village. She holds the key to further enlightenment."

"Many thanks for the guidance. We'll seek her out." I nodded appreciatively, acknowledging the path laid before us.

"Ready to make our exit?" Aria inquired, eager to depart. "Absolutely," I agreed, satisfied with our newfound knowledge. "I reckon we've gathered what we came for."

We left the store and went through the town, getting acquainted with the area. Then we asked around for a woman called Suzi, and lots of them knew about her, but no one seemed to know about her whereabouts.

We visited an inn and ordered for us both some water, as I was out and we were pretty thirsty. We also asked a few to take the road. We listened to the surroundings; there seemed not much going on. A lot of people were there on their own, and those in groups had rather quiet tones of voice, so we couldn't overhear anything interesting.

Slowly, the day made way for the evening, as we were still wandering around town. Then we could see a group of people sitting around a fire, and we went closer to look at what they were doing.

Invited to share the fire and the meager warmth it offered, we were introduced to an elder of the group, a woman whose eyes held the weight of knowledge and sorrow.

It appeared that we had finally found the woman we sought, Suzi. She seemed receptive to our presence, engaging us in conversation for some time. Eventually, we broached the topic of the library Ezra had mentioned to us.

She spoke of the library, a repository of wisdom hidden deep within the mountains, protected from the ravages of time and conflict. It was a place that held records of ancient prophecies, etched in stone and preserved through generations.

Sensing my skepticism, she handed me a worn, leather-bound map, its edges frayed but the paths clearly marked. "The library," she said, "holds the key to understanding the cycle of destruction and rebirth. The prophecies it contains were known to our ancestors, who foresaw the fall of civilizations long before the first bombs fell."

"Are there any dangers we should be aware of?" I asked. "Not that I know of; it might be a bit of a journey, but the library is safely located within the mountains," she said.

"You have my thanks," I said. "We will head off in the morning."

After talking for a bit more with Suzi and the group, we eventually decided to get back to sleep and spend the night together.

Aria and I were together in a room, and we were talking about the various things we had seen in the village and what was ahead of us.

"What do you think we'll find in that library?" Aria asked. "Ancient wisdom, or something alike," I said. "I don't expect more information than what I've seen in the Temple of Knowledge, but I do think I might learn something new; there's something about it that tells me to go there."

"I suppose you should follow your instinct; it has gotten you this far already," said Aria.

"Exactly!" I said.

After a bit more talking, we decided to go to sleep, preparing for the following morning to head towards the mysterious library.

The quest for the hidden library took Aria and me across the rugged expanse of Washington, where the whispers of ancient secrets and the promise of undiscovered knowledge spurred us forward. With dawn's first light painting the sky in hues of gold and crimson, we embarked on our journey, the Alloyed Charger humming beneath us as we ventured into the wild unknown.

The map, a relic of a bygone era, sprawled across our laps, its lines and markings a cryptic guide through the wilderness. It was not just a map but an indication of the determination of those who had charted these lands before the fall, those who had hidden the library away from the ravages of time and the greed of men.

As we drove, the landscape around us shifted, from dense forests where sunlight struggled to penetrate the thick canopy above to rugged cliffs that offered breathtaking views of the valleys below. Aria, with her keen eye, pointed out paths that seemed to disappear into the foliage that might have once led to secrets now reclaimed by nature.

Our journey was as much a battle against the elements as it was a quest for knowledge. Storms descended upon us with little warning, turning streams into raging torrents and paths into mudslides. We sought shelter under the boughs of ancient trees, their trunks as wide as houses, marveling at the resilience of nature and its capacity for both destruction and renewal.

In these moments of enforced pause, Aria and I found solace in each other's company. We shared stories of the lives we had led before the world changed, of the dreams we had harbored, and of the losses we had endured. It was in these conversations, lit by the flickering flames of our campfire, that I saw the strength in Aria's resolve, the depth of her compassion, and the fierce spirit that drove her forward.

The terrain grew more challenging as we neared our destination. Mountains loomed before us, their peaks shrouded in mists, their slopes steep and treacherous. We abandoned the Charger, continuing on foot, our progress measured in the slow, steady climb towards the summit. Every step was an expression of our determination, and every breath was a defiance of the odds stacked against us.

As we climbed, the world seemed to open up around us.

Vistas of untamed beauty stretched to the horizon, valleys and rivers carving through the landscape, a reminder of the world's enduring majesty. It was a humbling experience, one that put our quest into perspective, reminding us of our place in the tapestry of life.

Our arrival at the library's hidden entrance was not marked by fanfare or revelation. It was a quiet moment, a pause in the rhythm of our journey. The entrance, concealed from view by nature's own design, was a door not just to knowledge but to understanding—the understanding that our quest was but a part of a larger journey, one that connected us to the past and to the future.

The library's interior unfolded before Aria and me like a sanctuary carved from time itself. As we crossed the threshold, the air shifted, heavy with the scent of aged paper and the silent presence of countless tomes that had witnessed the passage of centuries. The dim light that filtered in through the narrow windows high above cast the vast space in a soft, reverent glow, illuminating the dust motes dancing in the air.

Row upon row of towering shelves stretched into the distance, their wood aged to a deep, rich hue, cradling volumes whose spines bore the marks of hands long gone. These were not merely books but vessels of knowledge, each one a portal to worlds both vast and intimate, spanning the spectrum of human thought and beyond.

Intricate carvings adorned the pillars that supported the high, arched ceiling, their motifs a homage to the pursuit of knowledge—a tree whose branches reached towards the sky, a river that flowed endlessly from source to sea, and the figure of an owl, silent guardian of the wisdom housed within these walls.

As Aria and I moved through the library, the silence around us felt like a presence, a keeper of secrets that whispered of the power of knowledge to change the world but also of its fragility, its susceptibility to the forces of time and neglect.

"So did you find anything interesting yet? It's all so overwhelming," said Aria.

"I found a lot of things I was already aware of, but some things I didn't know. It would take too long to go through everything," I said.

We kept on searching, and I discovered records of prophecies that spoke of a great calamity, a fire that would consume the world and give birth to a new era. These were not mere myths but warnings, etched into the fabric of time by those who had understood the cyclical nature of human folly and hubris.

But it was not just the wisdom of the ancients that I found within those hallowed walls. Documents, once hidden by the government and corporate entities, lay bare the truth of their awareness and exploitation of these prophecies. Washington, with its natural fortifications and strategic significance, had been chosen as the epicenter for projects of monumental importance—efforts to safeguard the future of humanity, influenced by legends and guided by the hands of those who sought to control destiny.

As Aria and I delved deeper into the labyrinthine aisles of the library, the air thick with the scent of ancient knowledge, a trove of information about Washington began to unfold before us.

As I scanned the shelves, my fingers trailed over countless books and scrolls, each holding its own piece of knowledge. Yet, it was when my touch fell upon a tome titled "The Washington Codex: Charting Humanity's Path" that I paused. The title alone sparked my interest.

"Well, this sounds intriguing," I remarked. "Which one are you referring to?" Aria inquired.

"This one," I replied, indicating the book with my finger. "It seems significant."

"That's quite the title. You should definitely take a closer look," Aria suggested.

I carefully extracted the dusty tome from the shelf, its pages fragile and yellowed with age but remarkably preserved.

"This could be something," I murmured, opening the book to a page adorned with detailed maps and ancient texts. Aria leaned over my shoulder, her interest piqued by the discovery.

"What is it?" she asked, her voice a soft echo in the vast silence of the library.

"It's a blueprint... No, it's more than that. It's a strategic plan that spans centuries," I replied, my eyes scanning the documents.

"Washington wasn't chosen by chance. It's part of a deliberate design."

Aria's eyes widened as she absorbed the revelation. "So, all this time, the forests, the mountains... they weren't just barriers but part of a larger plan?"

"Exactly," I said, my gaze fixed on the ancient texts as I absorbed their profound implications. "But what we've uncovered extends even beyond these immediate discoveries." My finger hovered over an intricate map of a hidden complex nestled within Washington's untamed wilderness.

"These are not mere shelters or archives. They're beacons of humanity's enduring spirit, designed not just to preserve the past but to serve as catalysts for a new beginning," I explained, my voice a mixture of awe and realization. The documents detailed a series of enclaves, each a crucible of preservation and innovation, meticulously hidden yet pivotal to an envisioned future.

"These sites," I pointed to a designation marked 'Project Phoenix Array', "arethey're earmarked for pivotal roles in a post-recovery era. It's as if they were preparing not just to survive the apocalypse but to leapfrog into a future brimming with possibilities."

Aria leaned closer, piecing together the grandeur of the plan. "They foresaw a renaissance, a rebirth through the ashes, using the collective wisdom and technological marvels of ages past."

As we delved deeper, a series of letters caught my eye.

These were not mere correspondences; they were the confluence of visions and fears, of hopes and strategies.

"Listen to this," I said, unfolding a letter that spoke of an unprecedented conclave of minds, unified in their resolve to anchor the future's resurgence to Washington's land.

"'In the twilight of this era, we seed the dawn of the next.

Washington, with its natural fortifications and its troves of knowledge,

will be the nexus from which civilization will rise anew,'" I read aloud, the words resonating in the hallowed silence.

Aria's gaze met mine; her expression was a mix of realization and determination. "Our journey, our survival... it's a thread in the tapestry of a much larger design. We're not just remnants of the past; we're harbingers of the dawn."

The revelation imbued our quest with a new dimension. "Exactly," I agreed, the pieces of the puzzle aligning in my mind.

"We're guardians of this legacy, custodians of the blueprint for the rebirth that awaits."

She nodded, her resolve mirrored in her eyes. "Our task is clear. We must safeguard this knowledge, ensuring that the vision for a world reborn is not lost but flourishes, heralding the advent of a new civilization."

In the confines of that ancient library, amid the echoes of past epochs and the whispers of the future, our mission crystallized. Our path was not merely a struggle for survival but a voyage towards a promise—a promise of a world rejuvenated by wonders unseen, of a society propelled into a new age of enlightenment and progress.

Washington, with its concealed sanctuaries and silent witnesses, was not just the backdrop of our survival; it was the crucible of humanity's next great leap. Our journey had evolved, transforming from a fight for existence to a quest to unlock the doors to an unprecedented era of human achievement and harmony.

The revelation that my quest was entwined with a purpose recognized by both ancient wisdom and modern conspiracy was a burden and a blessing. It lent a sense of gravity to my journey, connecting my path to a legacy that spanned millennia.

Armed with our newfound knowledge, we departed from the library and made our way back to the settlement, eager to share our discoveries. Throughout the journey, our minds were preoccupied with the implications of what we had uncovered. Were we destined to fulfill an ancient prophecy, one that might have been foretold long before my time? These thoughts swirled in our heads, suggesting the existence of concepts and ideas that could serve as a reset button for human civilization and evolution.

Both of us remained silent during our journey, lost in contemplation as we navigated the challenging terrain. Despite the rugged landscape presenting its usual difficulties, we encountered little trouble along the way. Eventually, we arrived safely back at the settlement, ready to disseminate the revelations we had unearthed.

There, with the map and the secrets of the library in my possession, I shared my discoveries with the elder and her people. Our conversation, long into the night, bridged the gap between past and present, between prophecy and action.

The knowledge I had gained was a beacon, illuminating the path ahead. Washington, with its hidden vaults and whispered secrets, was more than just the backdrop to our survival; it was the stage upon which the future of humanity would be decided, guided by the echoes of ancient prophecies and the shadows of government and corporate conspiracies.

In this revelation, my mission found its true depth, linking the struggle for survival with a deeper, ancient purpose that had been woven into the very land upon which we walked. It was a call to action, a charge to fulfill a destiny that had been foretold long before the world had been torn apart.

Despite the weight of our newfound knowledge, we resolved to press on with our journey as originally intended. With unwavering determination, we set our course for Apex City, determined to forge ahead despite the revelations that lay heavy on our minds. Despite the weight of our newfound knowledge, we resolved to press on with our journey as originally intended. With unwavering determination, we set our course for Apex City, determined to forge ahead despite the revelations that lay heavy on our minds.

"As we prepare for the next leg of our journey, I can't help but feel the enormity of the task that lies ahead," I said, breaking the silence that had enveloped us since leaving the library. The fire crackled in response, its light flickering across Aria's face, revealing a mix of determination and apprehension.

Aria nodded, her eyes reflecting the flames' dance. "It's overwhelming, Ethan. The knowledge we've uncovered, the responsibility it entails... it's not just about survival anymore, is it? It's about fulfilling a destiny that's been laid out before us, long before we ever took our first breaths in this new world."

I took a deep breath, feeling the cool night air fill my lungs. "No, it's not just about survival. We've been given a glimpse into a plan far greater than either of us could have imagined. And with that knowledge comes a choice—to walk away and focus solely on our own lives or to accept the role that's been bestowed upon us and strive to make a difference for the future."

The fire's warmth seemed to grow as we sat in contemplation, its glow battling the night's chill. "I choose to make a difference, Ethan. No matter how daunting the path may be, I believe in the vision laid out in those ancient texts. I believe we can be the architects of a new dawn for humanity," Aria said, her voice steady and resolute.

Her words bolstered my own resolve. "Then together, we'll walk this path. We'll carry the burden of this knowledge not as a curse but as a beacon—a beacon to guide us and, hopefully, others towards a future where the mistakes of the past are lessons learned, not repeated."

With that shared commitment, the enormity of our journey didn't seem quite as insurmountable. Together, we faced not just the road to Apex City but the journey towards a destiny that was intertwined with the very fabric of this new world.

As the night deepened, we allowed ourselves a few hours of rest, the fire's embers casting a protective glow around us. In the morning, we would set off towards Apex City, carrying with us the hopes and dreams of those who had dared to envision a brighter future amidst the darkest of times.

APEX CITY

We mounted the Alloyed Charger with a mix of apprehension and resolve. The journey to Apex City promised to be arduous, traversing landscapes that had been scarred by the cataclysm that reshaped our world. Yet, the prospect of reaching a thriving city sparked a flicker of hope in our hearts.

Our journey took us through what we dubbed the Scorched Forests, an expanse that bore the scars of a past not solely defined by its encounter with fire but shaped by an enduring environmental anomaly. Decades ago, the area was at the epicenter of a massive chemical spill, a calamity whose effects have lingered far longer than anyone could have anticipated. The chemicals, which are highly toxic and resistant to natural degradation, seeped into the soil and groundwater, creating a zone where traditional plant life struggles to survive.

As we ventured into this blighted landscape, the sight that unfolded was one of stark desolation. Trees, once abundant and teeming with life, now stood as lifeless husks, their forms twisted and blackened, not by flames but by the pervasive toxicity that enveloped the area. The ground itself was a patchwork of barren earth and brittle, contaminated soil, supporting only the hardiest of invasive species—plants that could withstand the harsh chemical residues but did little to restore the once-vibrant ecosystem.

Navigating this chemical wasteland presented its own set of challenges. The Charger's path was illuminated by its lights, casting an eerie glow on the decaying vegetation and the occasional pools of stagnant, contaminated water. The air carried a faint, acrid tang, a constant reminder of the invisible threat that lingered in the soil and water. We had to be cautious of the ground we traversed; areas that appeared solid might conceal pockets of weakened earth, compromised by the ongoing chemical reactions below the surface.

This section of our journey was quiet; the usual sounds of wildlife were eerily absent. Only the crunch of dead vegetation underfoot and the distant, unsettling sound of shifting earth broke the silence. It was a landscape that had not only been scorched in a literal sense but had been thoroughly scarred by human error, a stark reminder of the long-lasting impact our actions can have on the natural world.

A bridge that spanned the Cratered Divide presented a formidable challenge. Its once-sturdy expanse was now a precarious path of rotted planks and rusted cables. Halfway across, the bridge faltered under our weight. The planks beneath us groaned ominously before giving way, leaving us teetering on the brink of disaster. With quick thinking and trust in the Charger's capabilities, we managed a daring leap across the chasm, landing with a jarring thud that echoed in the silent air. Our hearts raced in unison, adrenaline surging through our veins—a shared triumph over the abyss that had sought to claim us.

Our passage through the desolate Wastes of Desolation was not just a test of endurance but of will. This treacherous expanse, a crucible for the lost and the forsaken, became the stage for an unexpected confrontation that would push us to our limits. The ambush sprang upon us with a ferocity that was bone-chilling, raiders cascading down the rocky outcrops with predatory eagerness. The initial flurry of projectiles zipped dangerously close, their presence announced by the menacing whistling that cut through the chilling silence of the desolate landscape.

"Leave this to me," Aria proclaimed, her voice embodying a blend of unwavering resolve and tranquility. With swift, practiced movements, she drew her dual blades, the metal catching the faint light, signaling her readiness for the onslaught.

I offered her a nod, a silent acknowledgment of her prowess. "I've got your back," I declared, stepping down from our ride to confront our adversaries directly. The Fusionizer in my grasp buzzed to life, a beacon of power ready to be unleashed against those who dared to challenge us.

The raiders' advance was relentless, a disordered ballet of violence and mayhem. Aria was a whirlwind of deadly precision, her blades an extension of her will, severing the air and our foes with equal finesse. I provided suppressive fire, the Fusionizer's potent blasts carving paths through the enemy ranks, and its luminous energy bolts a harbinger of doom for those caught in their wake.

"Behind us!" Aria's urgent call redirected my focus in the nick of time, allowing me to counter a raider's aerial assault with a direct hit from the Fusionizer, sending him sprawling into the barren dust.

The conflict intensified, the air thick with the electric charge of battle. Side by side, we moved as one, an indomitable force amidst a sea of desperation. Our assailants' numbers dwindled, yet their aggression seemed only to amplify, each fallen raider fueling the resolve of the survivors.

In a brief respite, Aria's voice sliced through the momentary calm. "Ethan, watch the left!" she warned. Her alert allowed me to unleash a concentrated volley from the Fusionizer, decimating another wave of foes that thought to flank us.

When the final adversary lay defeated, an oppressive silence settled over the battlefield. Aria and I, standing among the remnants of our foes, were a stark reminder of the savagery required to traverse this unforgiving world. The solemnity of our survival resonated deeply, a heavy realization of the perilous journey that lay ahead.

Surveying the landscape, littered with the consequences of our defiance, the weight of our skirmish was palpable. We had stood firm against the chaos, a unified front against those who would see us undone. In the aftermath, as we collected ourselves amidst the silence, the reality of our existence in this fractured world was ever-present—a stark reminder of the fragile thread upon which life and death balanced in the post-apocalyptic expanse.

"That was too close," I admitted, holstering the Fusionizer and surveying the damage. "You okay?"

Aria nodded, sheathing her blades. "Yeah, just another day in paradise," she replied, her voice laced with irony.

As the adrenaline faded, the weight of exhaustion settled upon us. We sought refuge in a nearby alcove, the fire we built offering scant warmth against the chill of the wasteland night.

Sitting beside the fire, the flickering flames casting shadows across Aria's face, I found the courage to breach the silence. "Aria, back there... you were incredible."

She looked away, a modest smile playing on her lips.

"We're incredible," she corrected gently. "We survive because we have each other."

Her words, simple yet profound, struck a chord within me. In the harshness of this world, it was our bond, our shared will to survive, that kept us moving forward. The fire between us seemed to burn brighter at her words, a beacon of hope in the vast darkness.

As the night deepened, we shared tales of the past and dreams of a future, our voices a defiant whisper against the desolation that surrounded us. It was in these moments, between battles for survival, that we found our strength, not just in arms but in the shared solace of our company.

"Aria," I said, my voice barely above a whisper, "whatever lies ahead, we'll face it together. You and me, against the world."

She reached out, her hand finding mine in the space between us. "Together," she agreed, her voice steady and sure.

That night, under the vast expanse of stars, amidst the ruins of a world long lost, we found solace in each other's presence. It was a quiet affirmation of our journey, a promise made without words but understood in the heart. In the face of desolation, we had each other, and in that, we had everything.

In the aftermath of our skirmish, without wounds to tend to or damages to the Charger to repair, an unexpected calm enveloped us. Under the expansive canvas of stars, untainted by the glow of a civilization now just whispers of the past, Aria and I found a moment of peace amidst the turmoil of our odyssey. She reached for my hand; her touch was a gentle contrast to the harsh reality we faced daily.

"Ethan," she whispered, her voice a soft melody in the hush of the night. "I don't know what the future holds, but I'm grateful for every moment with you."

Her words, sincere and raw, struck a chord within me. The world around us may have been shattered, but in that instant, amidst the ruins and the starlight, we found solace in each other's presence. It was a connection forged not in the heat of battle but in the quiet spaces between, a bond that promised hope amidst despair.

With revitalized determination, we resumed our journey at dawn, the horizon stretching before us with the promise of challenges and discoveries yet to come.

With revitalized determination, we resumed our journey at dawn, the horizon before us promising a tapestry of challenges and discoveries yet to unfold. The dawn's light cast a serene glow over the land, its beauty a stark contrast to the hardships we had faced and those still lurking on our path to Apex City.

Our surroundings gradually transformed, the desolation giving way to a landscape teeming with life. It was a reminder of nature's resilience, its capacity to flourish amidst the remnants of a world once dominated by humanity. The Alloyed Charger, ever reliable, carried us through this changing terrain, its steady hum a constant beneath the symphony of the waking world.

Aria's strength had visibly returned, her spirit buoyed by the prospect of new horizons. There was a quiet determination in her gaze, a reflection of the resolve that had carried us this far. Despite the journey's uncertainties, moments of beauty and tranquility pierced the veil of survival, offering glimpses of a world reborn from the ashes of its past.

In one such moment, as the day's heat began to wane, we found a clearing bathed in the soft light of the setting sun. Deciding to rest, we dismounted, the silence around us a rare reprieve from the constant motion of our journey. The scene was idyllic—a world untouched by the chaos that had once reigned.

It was there, in the tranquility of nature's embrace, that Aria approached me. The golden hour cast a warm glow over her, highlighting the depth in her eyes, a mirror to the soul that had faced adversity with unwavering courage. "Ethan," she began, her voice a gentle melody in the quiet of the evening, "do you ever wonder what life will be like once we reach Apex City?"

I looked into her eyes, finding there a reflection of my own hopes and fears. "I do," I admitted. "But I believe that whatever we find, we'll face it together, just as we've done with every challenge that's come our way."

Her smile then, tender and true, bridged the distance between us, erasing any uncertainty. She stepped closer, her presence a comfort, her warmth a balm to the weariness that shadowed our journey. In that moment, there was no Apex City, no relentless pursuit of survival—there was only us, Aria and Ethan, two souls intertwined by fate and bound by a journey that had shaped our very beings.

Without a word, she reached up, her fingers tracing the contours of my face with a delicacy that belied the strength within her. And then, as naturally as the sun gives way to the night, our lips met in a kiss that sealed our bond, a promise of togetherness amidst the uncertainty of the world beyond.

The kiss was a manifestation of our journey, a symbol of the love that had blossomed in the face of adversity. It was a moment of profound connection, a harbinger of the hope and challenges that lay ahead as we continued our path to Apex City.

With the dawn of a new day, we set forth once more, our resolve strengthened by the bond we shared. The journey to Apex City was not just a quest for a destination but a journey of the heart, a journey that, no matter its end, had already defined us.

The road ahead stretched on endlessly, winding through valleys and scaling rocky ridges as we pressed onward toward the distant promise of Apex City. Each day brought new challenges and discoveries, testing our mettle and fortifying our resolve as we ventured deeper into the heart of the wilderness.

Our path led us through dense forests teeming with life, where sunlight filtered through the canopy in dappled patterns, casting an ethereal glow upon the forest floor. We marveled at the intricate web of life that surrounded us, from the delicate ferns that carpeted the forest floor to the majestic redwoods that towered overhead, their branches reaching toward the heavens like out-stretched arms.

But amidst the beauty of the wilderness, danger lurked in every shadow. We encountered fearsome predators that prowled the underbrush, their keen senses attuned to the slightest movement.

We learned to tread cautiously, our senses alert to the ever-present threat of danger that lurked just beyond the edge of our vision.

As we journeyed onward, we crossed vast plains where the wind whispered secrets of ages past, carrying with it the scent of distant horizons and the promise of new adventures. We rode through rolling hills cloaked in golden grasses that swayed in the breeze, their undulating waves a reflection of the timeless rhythm of the natural world.

Yet, for all its beauty, the wilderness could be unforgiving, testing our resilience at every turn. We weathered fierce storms that swept across the plains; their fury unleashed upon us with relentless intensity. We sought shelter in the lee of towering rock formations, huddling together beneath makeshift shelters as lightning danced across the sky and thunder rumbled like the roar of some ancient beast.

But through it all, we persevered, our determination unyielding in the face of adversity. Together, we forged ahead, our spirits undaunted by the trials that lay before us. For we knew that beyond every storm lay the promise of clearer skies and brighter days, and that with each step forward, we grew stronger, more resilient, and more alive.

And so we continued our journey, our hearts filled with hope and our eyes fixed on the horizon. In this moment of awe, the seeds of a new beginning were sown in our hearts, whispering of possibilities in a world waiting to be reborn under our careful stewardship.

For though the road ahead may be long and fraught with peril, we knew that as long as we walked it together, we would overcome whatever obstacles stood in our way. And eventually, as the city's silhouette grew on the horizon, a mix of anticipation and resolve filled us.

The landscapes we traversed, the challenges we overcame, and the moments of unexpected beauty all led to this. We approached Apex City not just as survivors but as bearers of a newfound hope, a hope nurtured in the wilds and sealed with a kiss beneath the setting sun.

The city emerged as a veritable haven amidst the desolation of the post-apocalyptic world, guarded by several walls and defenses. We approached a grand door where a guard, dressed in a red uniform with black shoulder pads, belt, boots, and gloves, stood beside it. He remained indifferent until we reached for the door, at which point he quickly sprang to attention, inquiring about our purpose.

"We've traveled a great distance to reach this place," I explained. "Seeking answers to questions that have haunted us across the desolate lands. We hope to find some of what we're looking for here."

"Hmm, well, that's reason enough to permit your entry, especially if you're just visitors," the guard responded. "We've already got plenty of people here. Nonetheless, everyone is welcome, as long as they're not bandits or raiders. They've been attempting to breach our defenses, but none of them have succeeded yet. Nevertheless, you're welcome to enter."

With a slow creak, he swung open the gates, revealing a sight that exceeded our wildest expectations.

Towering structures stood unscathed by the ravages of time, defying the decay that typically marked such environments. Streets bustled with activity, with inhabitants clad in pristine attire, betraying no hint of the harsh realities outside. It was as though this urban landscape had arisen from the ashes, a phoenix of civilization amidst the remnants of a shattered world. Neon lights flickered atop buildings, casting an ethereal glow, while street lamps illuminated the thoroughfares evenly.

Lush greenery adorned every corner, meticulously tended gardens, and flourishing trees, contrasting starkly with the barrenness of the journey thus far. These were not mere survivors from the journey, but vibrant specimens nurtured with care. The cityscape boasted an array of establishments—stores, eateries, and unfamiliar buildings—eager to welcome visitors, evoking a sense of a bygone era.

Parks dotted the landscape, vibrant with the laughter of children and the hum of activity. Here, amidst the modern amenities, youngsters reveled in the simple joys, engaging with the abundance of recreational facilities available.

Apex City truly was the zenith of post-apocalyptic urban development, a beacon of civilization's resilience amidst the ruins of the old world. Emerging from the ashes of global catastrophe, this city stood as a manifestation of human ingenuity, a fusion of advanced technology, and the indomitable human spirit.

Situated strategically to harness the natural resources of its surroundings, Apex City was surrounded by high walls made of reinforced, weather-resistant materials, standing as a bulwark against the dangers of the outside world. The cityscape was a blend of green zones and architectural marvels, with buildings designed for sustainability, incorporating vertical gardens, solar panels, and wind turbines into their structures.

The heart of Apex City pulsed with life, powered by renewable energy sources and governed by a council of wise and just leaders who emerged from the remnants of humanity. The city's infrastructure was advanced, featuring efficient waste recycling systems, purified water supply networks, and a transportation network of electric vehicles and magnetic levitation trains, minimizing the ecological footprint.

Technology in Apex City was both a tool for survival and a bridge to the past. Community hubs were equipped with digital archives, preserving the knowledge of the old world and facilitating education for new generations. Health care was enhanced by nanomedicine and regenerative therapies, extending lifespans and improving quality of life.

Despite its technological advancements, Apex City was not just a place of machines and cold steel. It was a vibrant community where art, culture, and nature intertwined. Public spaces were filled with greenery, with parks and communal gardens providing residents with spaces to reconnect with nature. Art installations and museums celebrated human creativity, while marketplaces buzzed with the exchange of goods and ideas, showcasing the diverse heritage of their inhabitants.

Security was paramount, with a defense system that combined surveillance technology and a well-trained militia to protect against external threats. Yet, the city's essence lay in its community-focused approach, promoting inclusivity, education, and well-being, ensuring that despite the harshness of the outside world, within its walls, humanity could thrive.

In essence, Apex City was a symbol of hope, a place where the future was forged by learning from the past's mistakes, embracing diversity, and uniting towards a common goal of survival and prosperity.

"This is incredible," remarked Aria, her voice filled with awe. "You're right," I agreed, marveling at the scene before us.

"It's even more remarkable than I had imagined. Complete buildings, bustling streets, and such advanced technology for this era. I never fathomed such advancements were still possible. I'm not quite sure where to begin our search, but I'm confident we'll find a lead somewhere."

We approached several people, hoping to glean some information, but most of them seemed to disregard us, treating us as though we were mere beggars.

"Look over there!" exclaimed Aria, pointing towards a distant building with the word "library" emblazoned in large letters—"Láibreri," it read.

"Brilliant idea!" I exclaimed. "If there's anywhere we can uncover information, it's there."

With haste, we made our way to the building and stepped through its doors.

Inside, towering shelves lined with books greeted us, with a dedicated section for ChronoArchives. At the front, a clerk stood behind a counter. We approached her, inquiring about the Nexus Vault or the Ascendant Matrix.

"I'm afraid I don't know anything about that," she responded curtly. "And as for the ChronoArchives, I've already cataloged everything, so you won't find what you're looking for here. Most of these books predate the era of ChronoArchives."

"Is there anywhere else we might find this type of information?" I pressed.

"Your best bet would be the large tower where the mayor resides," she suggested. "If anyone knows about such matters, it would be him."

"And where might we find this tower?" I asked.

"It's on the east side of town. You can't miss it—it's the largest building in the city and stands out prominently," she explained.

"Thank you for the information," I acknowledged.

"Save your thanks until you've met the fellow. He's not the friendliest person around. So, mind your manners, but don't expect too much from him," she cautioned.

"We'll give it a shot regardless. Thanks," I replied. "No problem," she responded.

Exiting the library, we scanned the surroundings and spotted the distant tower looming in the skyline. That was our destination.

"What do you reckon we'll find there?" Aria inquired. "Hopefully, the mayor," I quipped.

"In a building that large, there's bound to be more than just him, right?" she pondered.

"Perhaps, but I'm not holding my breath," I admitted.

As we meandered through the streets and alleys, we encountered various intriguing establishments along the way. One of them was a shop adorned with a sign proclaiming it to be a purveyor of technological marvels.

"Oh, can we go in there?" Aria pleaded.

"Sure, but I'm not sure what you're expecting to find," I remarked.

Inside the shop, an array of gadgets greeted us, although they weren't as advanced as one might anticipate. Nevertheless, Aria appeared captivated by the assortment of items. Her attention was particularly drawn to a pair of dual blades with intricate markings.

She picked them up and carried them to the counter.

"What are these for, exactly? Do they possess any special capabilities?" she inquired with curiosity.

"Ah, indeed, young lady," the shopkeeper replied. "These aren't your ordinary dual blades. They're equipped with two unique magnetic energy fields. They're devices designed to be worn on the palms, and once thrown, they will eventually return to the owner's hands."

"I hope it's not the sharp parts that are attracted," I joked. "Of course not; only the handles are drawn to the energy fields. You can throw them quite a distance before they return. Quite convenient in combat, I assure you," the shopkeeper assured us.

"Oh, Ethan, can I please have these?" she pleaded.

"That depends," I replied. "What are you willing to trade for them?"

"Well, anything of equal value. Any kind of technology that's the same price or more, I'd trade you for it," she proposed.

"Alright," I agreed, reaching into my bag and retrieving one of the energy cores I had remaining.

"What about this?" I offered.

The shopkeeper's eyes widened, and after a moment's consideration, he exclaimed, "Sold!"

I handed over the energy core, and in return, the shopkeeper produced two bands with a small patch of steel at the center.

"Now, make sure to keep the center of these circles—the small steel areas—within your palms," he instructed. "Those are the energy fields that will attract the blades back towards your hand. So, keep them securely in place, or you might end up getting hurt."

"I understand," Aria chimed in, her excitement palpable as she admired her newly acquired weapons and her eyes sparkling as she looked at me.

"That'll be all," I stated, and we exited the shop.

Without hesitation, Aria secured the bands around her hands, grabbed one of the blades, and tossed it into the air. True to the shopkeeper's words, the blade swiftly returned to her hand, poised for further action if necessary.

"Oh, thank you, Ethan," she exclaimed, planting a kiss on my cheek.

"It's no trouble at all, as long as you're careful with those," I cautioned.

"I will be, I promise," she assured me.

And so, we proceeded towards the large building on the east side of town, passing by various houses, shops, and picturesque areas adorned with greenery or bustling with people in parks.

Finally, we reached the building. Pushing open the heavy door, we entered an entrance hall bustling with several individuals. We approached the woman behind the counter and inquired if we could see the mayor.

"I'm sorry, do you have an appointment?" she inquired. "No, but we still need to speak with the mayor," I replied. "The mayor isn't available at the moment," she informed us. "Then what is he doing?" I pressed.

"He's busy," she replied curtly.

Growing increasingly frustrated, I exclaimed, "I'd like to speak with the mayor right now. Either you call him up, or I'll go up to every floor and make some noise until he comes down himself."

"Please wait," she said, picking up the phone and explaining the situation. After a brief wait, she instructed us, "The mayor is ready to see you now. Go up three flights of stairs and ring the bell next to the door."

"Thank you," I said.

We ascended the stairs until we reached the third floor, where I knocked loudly on the door.

A rather short man in a suit opened the door and inquired, "What is all this commotion about?"

"We were told to come here. Are you the mayor?" I asked. "Yes, I am. And you're that persistent individual from the desk below, I presume?" he replied. "That would be me," I confirmed.

"So, what brings you two here?" he inquired.

"We're here to inquire about some information," I stated. "Information? Couldn't you have handled that at the desk below?" He questioned me impatiently.

"No, we were told you were the person to ask," I explained. "Alright, come on in," he relented.

He sat behind a desk and asked us what information we needed.

"We'd like to know about the Nexus Vault or the Ascendant Matrix. We were told if anyone knew about that, it would be you," I explained.

"Hmm," he mused, appearing to delve deep into thought. "Hmm, hmm," he continued to hum.

"Are you singing or actually thinking?" I quipped. "Patience; the thought process of a wise man takes time,"

he retorted.

"Hmm, yes, the Ascendant Matrix?" he finally inquired. "Yes, what do you know about it?" I prompted. "Nothing," he declared.

"What?" I exclaimed.

"I've never heard of it," he stated.

"So, you don't know anything?" I prodded. "Hold on, I didn't say that," he clarified. "Then what do you know?" I asked.

"I know something about the Nexus Vault," he revealed. "And what might that be?" I inquired.

The mayor proceeded to divulge information about the Nexus Vault, describing it as a contingency plan to preserve human civilization in the face of annihilation. Within its walls lay lost technologies, extinct flora seeds, and digital remnants of human culture. However, he cautioned that the vault was protected by challenges intended to assess the worthiness of those seeking its secrets. It was designed to be found only when humanity was ready to rebuild, not merely survive.

"I thought the Ascendant Matrix was responsible for those things," Ethan remarked.

"Hmm, I can't tell you about this Ascendant Matrix of yours, but that is what I heard about the Nexus Vault," the mayor concluded, "which is more than a treasure trove of the past; it's a test. A test of strength, wisdom, and heart. It's a crucible through which humanity must pass if it ever hopes to reclaim its glory."

Confused, I pondered to myself about what the Ascendant Matrix could be if the Nexus Vault was all about that.

"And do you have any information about the location of the Nexus Vault?" I inquired.

"Well, I do have a ChronoArchive with some cryptic information that references the Nexus Vault. You can have it. I wouldn't know what to do with it, honestly," he offered.

Another ChronoArchive, I mused. It seemed luck was on my side to acquire so many in such a short time. However, it still wouldn't pinpoint the exact location of the vault.

"Alright, I'll take it and get out of your hair," I acquiesced. "Great idea!" the mayor agreed.

He rummaged through various drawers, producing a mishmash of items, including pencils, pieces of paper, a few ChronoArchives, and a stack of pre-war magazines in surprisingly good condition, leaving me to wonder where he had found them. Finally, he retrieved another ChronoArchive.

"Here you go. Enjoy it or whatever you intend to do with it, and do what you promised," he said, placing the ChronoArchive in front of me.

"What did I promise?" I asked.

"To get out of my damn hair. I have business to attend to, so please leave me be. And next time, make sure to get an appointment before you come barging in here and demanding to speak to me," he admonished.

"Nonetheless, I thank you for your help. You've been of great assistance," I acknowledged.

"Yes, that's what I'm known for," he remarked. "What do you mean exactly?" I inquired.

"My generosity. Now, are you still here? Get out!" he exclaimed.

Aria and I quickly exited the place, returning to the streets below.

"Well, do you think there's anything useful on that thing?" Aria asked.

"Let's find out," I said, scanning the message with the Cryptex Decoder: "Beníð ðə gæz ov Libertiz wéstərn sístər, hwær ðə sájlənt séntənl wəns stʊd gɑrd ovər Pújɪts æʒʊr dépθs, lájz ðə kí, nésləd bítwin ðə rʊts ov ðə wərld ribɔrn."

"It's another clue," observed Aria.

"It is indeed, but yet again, what does it mean exactly?

These messages are so cryptic; it's hard to make sense of them," I remarked.

"Don't worry about that; we'll figure it out. I bet we almost have all of them. Then we'll just have to figure out where we'll have to go," reassured Aria.

"Let's hope so," I said.

"I'm sure we're another step closer!" Aria exclaimed.

"So, what's our next move?" I inquired. "We can't just depart from this incredible place yet. There's still so much left to explore."

"Absolutely," Aria concurred. "Let's wander around the city and see what we stumble upon."

"Sounds like a plan," I agreed.

As we strolled through the city, we were captivated by its splendor. The lush greenery and enchanting ambiance held us spellbound for hours. Eventually, we stumbled upon a group of individuals playing a game with balls and bats in a park beneath the shade of trees. Intrigued, we approached them to inquire.

One of them, identifying himself as Mason Williams, explained that they were engaged in a game called PulseBall and extended an invitation for us to join. Both Aria and I accepted.

"Before we join in, could you explain the rules?" I requested.

"No problem," said Mason. "First of all, you'll need PulseBats, which are lightweight, durable bats integrated with a low-intensity pulse emitter at the tip. The pulse gently vibrates to indicate when a player should swing to hit the incoming ball optimally. Don't worry, we'll provide all the equipment.

Then we have something called EchoBalls, which are small, soft balls equipped with a responsive core that emits a soft, pulsing glow when hit, making it easier to see in dim conditions and adding an extra layer of challenge and excitement. There are two goal posts: simple, portable posts installed at each end of the playing area, serving as targets for scoring Each of the teams take a turn at bat and field. The batting team aims to hit the EchoBall and knock over the goal posts at the fielding team's end to score points, while the fielding team tries to catch the ball and return it to stop the batting team's progress.

Each player on the batting team has a chance to hit the EchoBall and run between the goal posts to score points. Points are awarded for each successful run and for knocking over a goal post.

The fielding team can end a player's run by catching the EchoBall or tagging the runner with it before they return to the starting post.

A standard game consists of two innings, with each team batting once per inning. The team with the most points at the end of both innings wins."

"I'm not entirely sure I grasp it," Aria admitted.

"Don't fret," Mason reassured her. "You'll pick it up as we go. It's all in good fun, so don't worry about making mistakes."

As the game commenced, it seemed daunting at first.

However, with time, I grew more confident and began to understand the mechanics.

"Mason, where should I position myself?" I asked as the game started.

"Start near the goal post, Ethan. You've got a good eye. Call the plays as you see them," Mason suggested, clapping me on the shoulder before darting off to his position.

The game unfolded with a rush of energy. My first swing at the ball was a hit, more luck than skill, sending the EchoBall arcing beautifully across the field. "Run, Ethan!" Aria cheered, her laughter ringing out as I sprinted between the goal posts, scoring our first point. The team erupted in cheers, with Mason leading the applause. "Nice hit! You're a natural," he exclaimed.

Aria was a whirlwind on the field; her agility was unmatched. When it was her turn, she swung the PulseBat with precise timing, the ball zooming low and fast. Her runs were swift, each one earning our team valuable points. "Aria, you're amazing!" Mason shouted, his voice full of genuine admiration.

Laughter became a constant backdrop to our plays, especially after a particularly comical moment where I managed to chase my bat instead of the ball. "Guess I need to work on my grip," I joked, retrieving the errant bat, my cheeks warm with embarrassment but my heart light with laughter.

The game's highlight came when a high-flying EchoBall threatened to earn the opposing team a hefty score. "Ethan, boost me!" Aria called out, a daring plan sparking in her eyes. I nodded, crouching down as she ran towards me. With a push, I lifted her into the air, her hand closing around the ball just in time. We landed in a tumble, laughter and cheers mixing as our teammates rushed to congratulate us.

"Mason, did you see that?" Aria gasped between breaths, her eyes shining with exhilaration.

"That was incredible! You two are full of surprises," Mason laughed, helping us to our feet. "What a play!"

A defining moment of teamwork came when the opposition sent the EchoBall soaring high, its pulsing glow a beacon against the evening's dim light. The ball's trajectory, aimed beyond our reach, promised our rivals a significant lead. Yet, with unspoken agreement, Aria and I devised a plan on the spot. As the ball descended, I crouched, bracing myself, then propelled Aria into the air at the crucial moment, boosting her high enough to snatch the ball from its flight. The catch was more than just a play; it was a triumph of our unity and adaptability. As we landed, the look we shared spoke volumes of our shared pride and exhilaration. Our teammates' cheers enveloped us, their embrace embodying the true spirit of PulseBall—unity, joy, and collective achievement.

As the game wound down and twilight settled over the park, our group gathered, the day's excitement still buzzing in the air. "You two brought some fresh energy to the game. It was great having you on the team," Mason said, clapping me on the back and giving Aria a high-five.

"Yeah, thanks for showing us the ropes, Mason. Today was more fun than I've had in a long time," I admitted, feeling a camaraderie I hadn't realized I'd been missing.

Aria nodded in agreement. "And that catch, Mason, you should've seen your face! Priceless!" She teased, and we all burst into another round of laughter.

As Aria and I eventually made our way out of the park, the echoes of our laughter lingering behind, I realized that this game, this moment of shared joy and teamwork, had offered us a glimpse into the heart of human connection.

"Today was a good day," I said, looking over at Aria, who nodded, her smile a mirror of my own feelings.

"Yeah, it was," she agreed, and we stepped into the evening, the memory of our day at the park with Mason and the PulseBall game a bright spot in our journey through Apex City.

Eventually wandering through the streets with the city lights illuminating the streets, we could see a place with large neon text above it stating "Zénəth Dájnɪŋ", illuminated by soft, ambient lighting that bathed the surrounding area in a gentle radiance. The stylish lettering shined brightly against the night sky, beckoning diners to step inside and experience the culinary delights within.

Its exterior transformed into a captivating sight. The warm glow from the restaurant's interior spilled out through the large windows, casting a welcoming aura onto the sidewalk.

The awnings or canopies over the entrance were softly illuminated from above, casting a warm glow over the sidewalk below. The decorative planters filled with greenery took on a magical quality in the evening, their foliage bathed in the soft light that spilled out from the windows.

Aria and I looked at each other and were impressed by the captivating sight. We had to take a look inside to see what was going on. We entered the room. The place transformed into a cozy retreat. Soft lighting and flickering candles cast gentle shadows across polished floors and exposed brick walls. Guests savored gourmet dishes amidst the soothing ambiance, accompanied by the smooth melodies of a live jazz band. Plush seating and elegant décor created an intimate yet vibrant atmosphere where laughter and conversation flowed freely, creating unforgettable memories in the heart of the city.

We scanned the restaurant, noting the abundance of vacant tables. Eventually, we settled on a cozy table for two and took our seats. Engrossed in conversation about the day's events, we were interrupted by the arrival of a waiter at our table.

"What can I get for you?" the waiter inquired.

"We're hungry and thirsty, but what do you accept as payment?" I queried.

"Anything of value you have on hand will do. Show me what you've got, and I'll make some suggestions," the waiter replied.

Rummaging through my bag, I retrieved a collection of technological components leftover from my encounters with drones. Displaying them to the waiter, I asked, "Will these suffice?"

After a thorough inspection, the waiter nodded. "Indeed, these are quite rare and valuable. I can offer you both a plate of Radiant Roast, paired with Earth's Bounty Stew and Wild Harvest Platter. Additionally, you can choose any drink from our selection. How does that sound?"

"Sounds perfect to me. What about you, Aria?" I turned to her. inquired.

"Yes, and do you have any Verdant Zephyr to drink?" she "We do. And for you, sir?" The waiter turned to me.

"I'll have a pint of quality Dustbrew," I replied.

"Very well. Your dinner and drinks will be out shortly," the waiter assured us before departing.

As we waited, Aria and I continued our lively discussion, reminiscing about our day and sharing laughter over our adventures in Pulse Ball. We also exchanged amusing anecdotes about the eccentricity of the mayor, who, despite his stature, proved to be an entertaining character.

Soon, the waiter returned with our meals and drinks, and we expressed our gratitude as we dug into the delicious food. The Dustbrew surpassed my previous experience, and Aria marveled at the unique preparation of the Verdant Zephyr.

As Ethan and I savored our meal in the intimate glow of the place, the soft candlelight cast a warm aura around us, enveloping us in a cocoon of tranquility. Our conversation flowed effortlessly, punctuated by shared laughter and stolen glances that spoke volumes.

In a moment of quiet connection, I reached out and took Aria's hand in mine, feeling the gentle warmth of her touch send shivers down my spine. With a tender smile, I expressed my admiration for her, my words carrying the weight of my affection.

As our eyes met, I saw a spark of emotion reflected in hers, a silent acknowledgment of the bond that had formed between us. In a bold move, Aria leaned forward, her lips brushing softly against my cheek in a gesture of unspoken affection.

Caught off guard by the sudden intimacy, my heart raced with anticipation, my breath catching in my throat as I returned her tender kiss with a gentle caress of her cheek. In that fleeting moment, I was surrounded by the soft glow of the restaurant and the hushed murmur of conversation.

Once our meal concluded, we left the restaurant in search of lodging for the night. Eventually, we stumbled upon a hotel where Aria and I shared a bed, finding solace in each other's embrace.

Despite my usual struggle with sleep, the warmth of her body brought a sense of calm, enveloping me in tranquility. With the break of dawn, we arose from our slumber, eager to embark on another day of exploration in the city.

We dedicated ample time to thoroughly explore every corner of the city, marveling at its technological wonders and visiting notable landmarks and points of interest. During our exploration, we stumbled upon a gathering where individuals shared personal anecdotes and recounted the city's origin story.

The narrative was captivating, detailing how a resilient community of survivors banded together to establish their home amidst the ruins and remnants of a bygone era. What once lay in disarray was now a thriving city, an attestation to their resilience and determination to rebuild amidst the remnants of the past.

Despite the initial devastation, the area proved to be abundant in resources, offering an ideal haven shielded from external threats. Gradually, the inhabitants embarked on a mission to clear away debris and stabilize the ruins, mitigating the risk of structural collapse. Salvaging valuable materials, they repurposed them to construct sturdy shelters, surpassing the dilapidated buildings that once littered the landscape.

A significant portion of the populace consisted of engineers and builders, leveraging their expertise to harness available technology and implement innovative machinery. Their collective efforts breathed new life into the remnants of the city, transforming it into a hub of ingenuity and progress.

They embarked on the monumental task of restoring the buildings to their former glory, gradually attracting more visitors who were enticed by the burgeoning community. With newfound manpower, they undertook extensive renovations, gradually erasing the scars of ruin from the cityscape. Over the course of several years, every building was meticulously restored, and new structures emerged to accommodate the growing population drawn to the area.

In the interest of safety, they commenced construction on a formidable wall encircling the city, bolstered by an array of advanced weaponry and manned defenses. As the city expanded, former buildings were repurposed into shops, restaurants, and various other establishments, enriching the urban landscape and fostering a vibrant atmosphere of commerce and culture.

As time passed, the construction of the wall reached its culmination, fortified by sturdy gates at each cardinal point, rendering the city impervious to external threats. A substantial contingent of individuals underwent rigorous training to assume roles as militia and guards, stationed at strategic points along the perimeter. Their primary objective was to vigilantly monitor the gates, scrutinizing all newcomers to prevent any individuals harboring ill intentions from infiltrating the city's sanctum.

As the settlement flourished, a governing body emerged, comprised of a council democratically chosen to oversee the affairs of the city. Their primary mandate was to foster communal harmony and ensure the administration of justice, although instances of crime were rare as the residents generally lived in harmony with one another.

Architecturally, Apex City became a blend of necessity and vision. Buildings were constructed with sustainability in mind, utilizing renewable materials and incorporating green spaces to not just inhabit but also enrich the environment. Technology evolved through experimentation and adaptation, leading to advancements in energy, agriculture, and communication tailored to the new world's challenges.

As physical needs were met, the city's focus shifted to cultural and social reconstruction. Art, music, and literature flourished, drawing from the old world's remnants and the new experiences of post-apocalyptic life. Festivals and communal events solidified a sense of identity and purpose, celebrating the city's resilience and the collective journey of its inhabitants.

Over time, the burgeoning society attracted migrants from far and wide, swelling its population to thousands and earning renown among travelers. Despite its fame, the city remained somewhat isolated, its distance deterring all but the most determined visitors. As the years passed, the city faded from the collective memory of distant communities, yet for those who remembered, it remained a symbol of hope and resilience—a symbol of humanity's ability to rebuild amidst adversity in the post-apocalyptic world.

After hearing about the history of the city, someone else came and spoke about a distant place from the city called the Verdant Expanse. This place would be a sprawling wilderness that had reclaimed vast swathes of land from the old world. It would be a region where nature had flourished unchecked, creating a dense, lush environment that's both beautiful and perilous. This area was rumored to be home to a community known as the Greenwardens, a group of survivors who had adapted to live in harmony with the new wilderness, becoming custodians of the natural world and its secrets.

He continued to share tales of the area's mysteries, many of which seemed far-fetched. Yet, we sensed there was something worth exploring there.

Returning to the library, we approached the clerk. "Do you have any information on a place known as the Verdant Expanse?" I inquired.

"Indeed, I do," she replied, her voice carrying a hint of intrigue. "There's a brief document and a map that could guide you there, should you wish to venture."

"Absolutely," I responded eagerly.

She led us through the maze of shelves to a secluded corner cluttered with ancient scrolls and documents. After a brief search, she produced two items. "This document offers some insights into the Expanse. It's succinct, but it might pique your interest. And this map," she added, unrolling a parchment, "shows it's about ten thousand miles from here—a formidable journey, though I suspect you two are up for it. Please examine them, but ensure they are returned to their place."

"And that is...?" I asked, amazed by her ability to navigate the chaos.

"Just here," she indicated, indicating a now-empty spot on the shelf.

"Understood," I acknowledged.

As she returned to her desk, I discreetly used my Omnilocator to scan the document, securing the map's information without needing to physically take it with us. I then turned my attention to the document she had handed us. It detailed a hidden community within the wilderness, surrounded by dense flora, and a community known as the Greenwardens. They lived apart from society, shrouded by the forest's towering trees.

The expanse was vast and wild, a place few would dare tread unknowingly, for it concealed many dangers beneath its lush canopy. The document described a journey starting across an open wasteland, leading to a dense jungle that rose abruptly, marking the entrance to a realm of verdant life.

It spoke of the wildlife thriving there, some of which was marked as perilous. Yet, the Greenwardens had made a home amongst them, a signification of their resilience. While much of the document dwelled on the ever-changing landscape and the elusive location of the community—information that seemed mutable with time—it provided us with a solid foundation for our exploration.

As the city faded into the distance behind us, Aria and I shared a moment of contemplative silence. The hum of the Alloyed Charger beneath us was a steady reminder of the journey ahead. 'You know,' I started, glancing over at Aria, 'every step we take feels like we're walking further into the pages of a story yet to be written.' She nodded, her eyes fixed on the horizon. 'And in that story, I think we're about to turn a very interesting page.' Our laughter mingled with the wind as we sped towards the Verdant Expanse, hearts buoyed by the promise of discovery. Whatever secrets the Greenwardens and their lush sanctuary held, we were determined to uncover them. Together, we were not just survivors but seekers on the cusp of unraveling the mysteries of a world reborn from the ashes of the old.

After a second review of the document, confirming we had gleaned all necessary details, we thanked the clerk for her assistance and bid farewell. As we stepped outside, the reality of our next adventure dawned on us. We made our way back to where we had parked my Alloyed Charger, the steadfast vehicle awaiting our return.

Mounting the bike, we set off on the Verdant Expanse, ready to uncover the secrets it held and to meet the Greenwardens who called it home.

[1] "Beneath the gaze of Liberty's western sister, where the silent sentinel once stood guard over Puget's azure depths, lies the key, nestled between the roots of the world reborn."

BENEATH VERDANT CANOPIES

Our departure for the Verdant Expanse unfolded at dawn, with the silhouette of Apex City softening into the morning light. Aboard the Alloyed Charger, Aria and I embarked with a blend of anticipation and resolve, with the vast journey ahead promising a fusion of discovery and unforeseen challenges.

The initial stretch of our journey was navigated on deserted highways, a stark departure from the life teeming within Apex City. These roads, marred by neglect, wound through a landscape silently bearing the scars of time. Come midday, a sudden storm besieged us, the winds howling their ancient grievances. Seeking shelter, we nestled the Charger under an abandoned overpass, watching as the tempest transformed the path ahead into treacherous streams of mud.

"Patience, in the face of nature's fury, is its own kind of strength," Aria remarked, her voice nearly lost amidst the storm's cacophony.

With the storm's rage spent, we ventured into the remnants of towns once vibrant, now reduced to silent testimonies of what was. While searching for supplies amid these ruins, we faced the dual challenge of scarcity and the occasional distrustful gaze of survivors who had chosen solitude over communal survival. A surprising obstacle—a makeshift barrier—blocked our path in one town. Dismantling it demanded a careful strategy, lest we attract unwanted attention. Our efforts were later rewarded in a deserted store, where we found just enough provisions to replenish our dwindling supplies.

The landscape presented a formidable adversary on the third day: a wide, vigorous river asserting its dominion over the land. The remains of a bridge, now useless, stood as a mute witness to the river's might. Our passage necessitated a makeshift raft, cobbled together with the debris of the past. Halfway across, as our raft threatened to disintegrate beneath us, Aria and I fought desperately against the current, our unity and resolve tested by the river's relentless flow. Soaked yet unbroken, we continued on, the wilderness around us growing denser with each mile.

The eve of our arrival at the Verdant Expanse tested us with terrain both wild and unwelcoming. The undergrowth concealed dangers beneath its verdant facade; a misstep nearly cost Aria a serious injury. We made camp at the boundary of a vast wasteland, beyond which lay our destination, a verdant wall signaling the end of desolation and the beginning of an untamed world.

Traversing the wasteland aboard the Charger, we witnessed the gradual embrace of life. What began as barren soil slowly surrendered to persistent greenery, heralding our entry into the Expanse. The air, once arid, now teemed with the vitality of a world reborn.

The Verdant Expanse, with its majestic trees and chorus of wildlife, welcomed us into its depths. The transition from mechanical horsepower to the power of raw, unbridled nature was stark. Here, the Charger was not just a vehicle but a vessel, carrying us from the world of man into the heart of the earth's resurgence.

Navigating through the towering trees and dense foliage, we realized that our journey to the Verdant Expanse was a passage through the layers of survival, adaptation, and the enduring pulse of life. This wilderness, vast and unyielding, awaited with its untold mysteries, ready to challenge, change, and ultimately reveal the essence of existence post-calamity. And so, with the Alloyed Charger humming softly beneath us, we delved deeper into the green abyss, each turn, each clearing, bringing us closer to the heart of the unknown, to the secrets guarded by the Greenwardens, and to the truths about ourselves and the world we sought to understand.

As we moved forward, the landscape suddenly opened up, revealing a vast field scattered with bones. Human skulls and the remnants of what I assumed were once mighty predators—tigers, wolves, bears, and lions—covered the ground. Despite the eerie sight, we decided to press on quickly.

But before we could resume our journey, a volley of arrows flew toward us. We swiftly dismounted the bike and dodged the incoming arrows. One arrow aimed directly at my head, but I managed to catch it mid-air and drop it to the ground.

"Oh heavens, I thought they got you there for sure," Aria said, amidst the shower of arrows.

As the arrows continued to rain down, though more sparsely, we found ourselves without cover. Resorting to the bones on the ground, we used them to deflect the arrows until the attack ceased. We braced ourselves for more, but instead, figures began to emerge from the underbrush.

I caught a snippet of their conversation. "Dese people, they dodge them arrows as if it were nothin'."

"Maybe if you talked to us first, then there wouldn't be any need for an attack like that," I yelled back at them.

"Ye folks, welcome ye ain't," declared one. "We've had more than our share of visitors and shadows in their hearts, and we've long since closed our paths to wanderers."

"Well, considering what's scattered all around here, we'd still like to pass through. Can we speak to one of you in person?" I asked.

The figures retreated back into the foliage. We prepared for another onslaught, but instead, a single person stepped forward. He was dressed in layers of green and brown, made from woven plant fibers and animal hides. His dark skin, broad nose, and bald head stood out, his eyes twinkling in the sunlight like stars in the night sky.

"What is it ye seek from us?" he queried.

"Are you the Greenwardens?" I asked in return.

"Aye, we are. Now, ye must share yer tale," he responded. "We were led here, in a manner of speaking. It's known that many are aware of you folks, with documentation and maps about this place existing out there. We were expecting a warmer welcome," I explained.

"Ah, 'tis the tales and maps that bring the greedy and the wicked, thinking we hide riches. Once, our arms were open wide, but the days of welcome have faded into the mist," he acknowledged.

"Wouldn't shooting at visitors on sight contribute to that change?" I inquired.

He took a moment before saying, "Ere we stood watch with arrows, the road brought naught but trouble. There's another way, for those bearing light, not shadows."

"We weren't aware of any other route. Had we known, we would have taken it. We mean no harm," I assured him.

"And what wind blows ye to our door?" he inquired with a keen eye.

I explained our journey, mentioning the Nexus Vault and the Ascendant Matrix, and how our travels had taken us from village to village until we arrived in Apex City.

"Wait now, be ye the Hero of Concord?" Respect tinged his voice as he pieced together our story.

"That I am, though it was a title given to me some time ago," I said. "How did word of that reach you?"

"In these deep woods, tales fly fast and far. Your deeds have echoed with us. In light of this, our hearts are yours," he offered warmly.

"Thank you," I responded.

"Come, follow my steps to where we make our stand. For the chill welcome, my apologies. These days, caution is our companion. Jabari, I'm called. Not a leader, but a guide amongst our folk. Orders, we follow not," he led the way, weaving through the natural tapestry to their dwelling.

Jabari guided us deeper into the wilderness, which soon revealed itself as their village. It wasn't a village in the traditional sense but rather an extension of the wilderness itself, with huts and trees ingeniously arranged to create habitable spaces. A grand rock opened to reveal a communal area descending into the earth, surrounded by circular tables uniquely designed with central holes, each encircled by a singular, expansive bench.

The village buzzed with life; individuals donned in garb similar to Jabari's moved about, children played freely, and many were engaged in tasks that seemed aimed at enhancing their living environment.

"Here, take a seat." Jabari motioned towards the gathering space. "Let's exchange tales."

Gathering around one of the tables, we awaited insights from Jabari, hoping for guidance or knowledge.

"This place you've entered, welcome you are. Yet, the mysteries you chase, answers I hold not," Jabari began, his tone a blend of regret and openness. "Our focus has been on rooting ourselves anew. A tempest past laid our former homes to waste, and here we endeavor to rebuild, as you see."

"So, we journeyed here only to find empty hands?" I couldn't hide my disappointment.

"Nay, empty not your journey ends. Behold yonder," Jabari pointed to a distant structure, a statue weathered by time yet imposing. "There lies a gate to yesteryears' secrets. We've tread its threshold, yet beyond that, darkness deters our steps. Perhaps therein lies what you seek."

His words ignited a spark of hope. "Then our path leads to these ruins," I resolved.

"Hasten not as night approaches. Underneath this stone, sustenance and rest await. The morrow shall grant passage to your quest. Speak to our kin, learn of our ways; insights unforeseen may yet reveal themselves," Jabari advised.

Pondering his counsel, I turned to Aria and asked, "Should we embrace this pause and delve into the tales and wisdom of this place before our venture tomorrow?"

Aria nodded, her curiosity piqued. "Indeed, this place holds a charm unseen. To acquaint ourselves with its people and their stories would be a journey in itself."

Out of nowhere, a woman clad in attire echoing Jabari's style approached, her outfit reminiscent of a bikini crafted from similar materials. She handed each of us a cup of water, casting a playful wink in my direction before departing. As I was about to quench my thirst, Aria's intense gaze caught me off guard.

"What's the matter?" I inquired, puzzled by her reaction. "Did you think I missed that little exchange?" Aria's tone was laced with warning. "It seems I'll need to watch you more closely here."

"I assure you, I have no sway over the actions of others here," I responded, attempting to diffuse the tension.

"Indeed," she retorted, her annoyance palpable. "But should such antics persist, there might be consequences."

"Let's not dwell on it," I suggested, hoping to reassure her. "It's inconsequential."

Jabari, having overheard our exchange, chimed in, "I see you two share a bond. Pay the waitress no mind; her actions bear no ill intent."

"She better not," Aria replied, her irritation still evident. "Aria," I sought to lighten the mood, "I hadn't pegged you for the jealous sort."

"Perhaps for you, I am," she admitted, her words softening. "That's endearing." I smiled.

"Enough with the jests," she cautioned, a hint of a smile betraying her feigned sternness.

"In all seriousness," I continued, "Jabari, could you direct us to where we might find a meal?"

"Beneath the rock, seek out the waitress; she'll assist you," Jabari directed.

Taking the initiative, Aria rose and made her way to inquire about food.

"We'd like some food, if you could," Aria requested upon finding the waitress.

"O' course," the waitress responded, eager to accommodate. "For two, aye?"

"That would be perfect," Aria confirmed.

After a short while, the waitress returned bearing two plates laden with the bounty of the wilderness—wild fruits, berries, nuts, seeds, and a portion of fish for each.

"Will this serve?" she inquired, presenting the meal. "It looks wonderful," I remarked, genuinely impressed. "Yes, this is perfect; thank you," Aria concurred.

We settled back at one of the outdoor tables to enjoy our meal.

"This is truly a taste of the wild," I observed, savoring the first bite.

"It's different from what we've experienced in Apex City, but it's nourishing and flavorful," Aria noted, appreciating the meal before us.

As we dined, a Greenwarden approached, taking a moment to silently observe us with a discerning gaze.

"Is there something you need?" I queried as he scrutinized us, seemingly to gauge our essence, before finally articulating, "Nah, it's more like, can I be offering you aid?"

"And how would that be?" Aria probed, her curiosity piqued. Jabari's been whispering 'bout some fresh faces. Word is, you're aiming for the ruins 'round these parts, true?" Tano's inquiry came with a hint of excitement.

"Possibly," I acknowledged, "but why's it concerning you?" "Well, see, I've had my eye on exploring their depths for quite some time now. Venturing solo, though, seems like a path fraught with peril. Hearing of your intent, I figured I might lend my stride to yours if you're venturing that way."

"If we choose to embark, you're welcome to join. What name do they call you by?" I inquired.

"Names Tano have been a part of this wilderness longer than most. I reckon I've got skills and know-how that could serve us well on this journey," he declared, confidence lacing his voice.

Taking a moment to absorb his presence, I noted the distinctive blend of traditional and personal elements in his attire. His cloak, crafted from the silk of forest spiders, was both durable and light, colored in shades that whispered of the forest's depth and mystery. Embellished with glowing symbols, it told stories of his achievements and standing among the Greenwardens.

His belt, an indication of both utility and past victories, bore various tools and weapons, each essential to his survival and role. The staff he carried was a marvel of craftsmanship, smooth and adorned with symbols and runes that glowed softly in the twilight, signifying his deep bond with the land.

Resting upon his back is a crossbow of elegant design, its construction a harmony of forest materials and ingenuity, promising swift and deadly precision. The crossbow, alongside Tano's staff, marked him not only as a guardian but as a warrior adept in both ancient traditions and the necessity of defense.

Tano's appearance, from his intricately braided hair adorned with tokens of the wilderness to his rugged yet wise demeanor, spoke volumes of a life intimately woven with the tapestry of the Verdant Expanse. His skin bore the kiss of countless suns and storms, while his eyes, reflecting the hues of the forest, held a vigilance born of respect and a profound connection to his home.

In Tano, the wilderness had not just a defender but an embodiment of its untamed spirit and enduring resilience.

"You definitely look like a skilled warrior, especially from the looks of that impressive crossbow. How do we know we can trust you, though? We don't know enough about your people to know if we can trust you," I said.

"Trust in me, ye can, sure as the stream flows to the river," Tano reassured. "My people, we walk in peace, no shadows in our heart. Only when the wind whispers threats do we stand tall. In our hands, the land rests gentle; our strength is its shield."

"That's easy for you to say, but our welcome was marked by arrows. Without our quick thinking, we'd be nothing but shadows among the bones that litter your forest floor," I countered.

"Ah, the sorrow for that welcome sits heavy on my spirit, like dew upon the morning leaves," Tano expressed regretfully. "The path you tread, it's watched by eyes guarding against the night, not expecting those who walk in daylight."

"Tell that to the people who had a unique way of greeting us; if it wasn't for our ability to deal with a volley of arrows, we wouldn't even be here but rotting away among the rest of the cadavers we encountered when we arrived at the forest."

"That truth pierces deep, like the thorn among the roses. To Jabari, this wisdom I'll carry, hoping to find a new way that welcomes the dawn without fear," Tano contemplated.

"What about those innocents caught by your arrows? Their stories ended before they could even begin," said Aria, pressing the point.

"Your words strike true, a call to heed the lessons of the leaf and the stream. Shadows are cast where they shouldn't darken the soul. With my kin, these thoughts I will share, seeking a path that harms none, welcoming the morrow with hands open, not fists clenched," Tano vowed with sincerity.

"That's all we ask of you," I acknowledged, appreciating his understanding.

In our continued conversation, Tano wove tales of the Greenwardens' genesis and life amidst the verdant cloak of their forest home. Born of the wilderness, nurtured by its bounty and challenges, the Greenwardens stood as vigilant protectors, their existence a harmony of nature's raw beauty and its untamed perils.

They continued building their community by assigning individual tasks, such as caring for buildings, clearing the environment, and training many warriors. The warriors underwent a final ritual where they had to hunt down powerful and dangerous creatures of the wilderness, presenting their heads to the leader of the warrior clan to prove their strength and ability. Consequently, many became formidable fighters, while even those not officially part of the warrior ranks developed impressive self-defense skills due to the inherent dangers of the wilderness.

Their weaponry primarily consisted of spears and bows, and a select few wielded carefully crafted crossbows for added protection. Their intensive training surpassed the capabilities of most warriors outside the wilderness in the post-apocalyptic world, making them formidable adversaries. Few would dare challenge even a single member of their community.

Leadership in the community differed from traditional structures, relying instead on elders and guides to assist the people and resolve disputes according to their customs. Crimes like theft and murder were punished according to the principle of "an eye for an eye," where the affected family member was allowed to seek retribution, often resulting in a deadly confrontation. Such forms of justice ensured order within the community, with individuals relying on their unique ways of handling situations.

Reflecting on these customs, I pondered whether their decentralized governance might have been superior to the ineffective governments of the past. Given the catastrophic consequences of past world events, their way of life seemed to offer a viable alternative. The idea lingered with me long after our conversations, prompting contemplation on the potential benefits of such a society.

"As the day's light begins to fade, 'tis time we seek the embrace of slumber," Tano observed, watching the horizon.

"But the sun's not even down completely. It can't be that late."

"In these parts, the sun lingers above like a watchful guardian, bestowing light longer than one might reckon. We lay ourselves down now, for come dawn, the world awakens in full glory," he shared, his voice echoing the rhythm of nature.

"Well, I don't know if that counts for me; I require a little sleep myself," I mentioned.

"Come, let me lead ye to a haven of rest," Tano offered, guiding us to a humble shelter. "Here, the beds of wood and leaf await, woven by the hands of those who dwell beneath the canopy's watch. Fear not the chill, for warmth is the forest's promise, save for the winter's brief whisper."

Aria and I wished goodbye to Tano as he left the hut. "This really is an amazing place," mentioned Aria.

"It is," I said, "very different from what I've seen so far, but I think I like it here, away from the desolation and ruins of the world as it is out there."

"That's certainly the case; I wouldn't mind staying here for a long time," I said.

"Unfortunately, we'll have to move on at some point; we can't stay put in one place when you have a mission to complete, can we?" said Aria.

"You're right, of course," I said.

As the moon cast its gentle glow through the cracks in the wooden walls of the rustic hut, Aria and I found ourselves sitting on the makeshift beds crafted from sturdy branches and adorned with soft leaves. The ambiance was serene, with the only sounds being the gentle rustle of the leaves outside and sounds of various animals Our conversation flowed effortlessly, weaving between stories of our past adventures and dreams for the future.

"You know," I said softly, "I never imagined finding myself in a place like this, surrounded by nature's beauty and with you by my side."

Aria smiled, her eyes flickering. "It's moments like these that make all the challenges worth it," she replied. "To be here with you, sharing this quiet intimacy, it's everything I've ever wanted."

With a tender gaze, I reached out to gently tuck a loose strand of hair behind Aria's ear, my touch sending shivers down her spine. "You are my everything," I whispered, my voice barely above a breath.

Aria's heart swelled with affection as she leaned closer, our breaths mingling in the intimate space between us. "And you are mine," she murmured, her fingers tracing the lines of my jaw.

In that moment, time seemed to stand still as our eyes met, speaking volumes without uttering a single word. And then, as if drawn together by an invisible force, our lips met in a soft, lingering kiss that ignited a fire within our souls.

Our embrace deepened, hands intertwining as we melted into each other's arms. "I never want this moment to end," I whispered against her lips, my voice filled with longing.

"Nor do I," Aria replied, her voice a mere whisper in the stillness of the night.

In the quiet of the night, we found solace in each other's presence, finding comfort and belonging in the depths of our love.

At night, Aria was fast asleep, occasionally emitting cute snores. Restlessness overcame me, prompting me to grab my flashlight and venture out for a walk. As I wandered deeper into the wilderness beneath the moon's glow, I found myself captivated by the serene surroundings. Enthralled, I felt almost entranced, surrounded by the symphony of nature's nocturnal orchestra.

The rustling of leaves and creaking branches accompanied my footsteps, blending harmoniously with the melodic hooting of an owl, the soft churring of nightjars, and the rhythmic chirping of crickets. It was as if the night itself was serenading me, and I was completely lost in its enchanting melody.

As I continued my wanderings, a sudden growl pierced the stillness, emanating from beneath a thick cluster of leaves.

Instinctively, I directed my flashlight toward the source, revealing the menacing silhouette of a panther poised to pounce, its eyes gleaming with predatory intent.

The creature's fur was unusually thick and patchy, with sections of fur appearing discolored or matted. It was quite sizable for a panther; it had muscles visibly bulging beneath its fur. Its eyes glowed with an eerie luminescence, casting an otherworldly glow in the darkness. I noticed enlarged claws and strange abnormal bone structures.

With every muscle tense and ready, I prepared to defend myself against this creature of the night. As it lunged towards me with a guttural growl, I sidestepped its attack with lightning reflexes, narrowly avoiding its razor-sharp claws.

Despite its ferocity, I could sense a hesitation in its movements, a weakness born of its mutation. Seizing the opportunity, I countered with a swift strike, my fists and elbows becoming deadly weapons in the darkness.

The panther roared in pain, but still, it fought on, unleashing a flurry of strikes that I deftly parried. With each exchange, I could feel the tide of battle shifting in my favor, my movements becoming more fluid and precise.

But the panther was relentless, its primal instincts driving it forward even as its strength waned. With a final, desperate lunge, it sought to end the battle in one last, desperate bid for victory.

Yet, as its claws raked the air, I saw my opening. With a decisive blow, I struck true, delivering the finishing blow that would end the conflict once and for all.

As the panther fell to the forest floor, defeated but not forgotten, I couldn't help but feel a sense of awe at the raw power of nature.

I decided I had wandered far enough now and went back through the route I came from. At last, upon arriving back at the hut, instead of laying on my own bed, I put myself behind Aria next to her in her own bed and put my arms around her. For a second, she awoke, looked at me, smiled, and fell right back to sleep. I savored the moment I held her in my arms and fell into a state of trance, lost in the thoughts of both of us and our adventures together.

In the morning, as she stirred awake, I rose from my makeshift bed.

"Did you sleep well?" I inquired.

"Yes, especially when you joined me," she replied, her voice tinged with shyness.

"I hope I didn't disrupt your rest," I said.

"Not at all. I had a wonderful night," she assured me. "Now, are we ready to head to those ruins?"

"Absolutely. I just need to check if Tano is up and ready," I replied.

Upon reaching Tano's place, I found it empty. Spotting him a short distance away engaged in conversation with a woman, I approached them with a polite interruption.

"Apologies for the interruption, Tano, but Aria and I are preparing to depart for the ruins. Will you be joining us?"

"Indeed, I shall find my way to you," Tano assured us with a nod.

"Are you sure we'll be there within less than an hour? Are you sure you'll make it in that time?"

"Fret not on my behalf," he added with a calm smile, "for my steps are sure, and the forest whispers its paths to those who listen."

"Alright," I confirmed, returning to Aria to signal our readiness to depart on the Alloyed Charger.

"But what about Tano?" she inquired. "He assured me he'd be there," I replied.

"But how?" Aria pressed for more details.

"I'm not sure; he just said he would," I admitted.

"Okay then, let's hope he keeps his word. I'm not keen on waiting around for him," Aria remarked.

"I'm sure he'll figure something out," I reassured her.

And so we set off towards the ruins, speeding through the wilderness with determination. The journey seemed to blur by, and before we knew it, we arrived at the ancient ruins, where Tano stood waiting for us.

"Looks like you got here already," I said, filled with curiosity. "I must know; how did you do? I need to know."

"If you seek knowledge, then knowledge I shall impart," Tano responded. "I traversed the skies upon a glider of my own making."

"A glider?" I asked.

"Indeed, fashioned from the resilient fibers of our verdant realm and the steadfast wood of ancient trees," Tano explained.

"Crafted with care by the skilled hands of our Greenwarden brethren, it allowed me to soar upon the breath of the wind, guided by the gentle whispers of the forest."

"Impressive, so you basically took the way in a straight line and very quickly," I said.

"Aye, compact and portable, borne upon my back as I ascended a towering sentinel of the woods," Tano continued. "Once unfurled, it caught the currents of the heavens, carrying me aloft upon the wings of the breeze, aided by the earth's own thermal currents rising from below."

"Well, if I had that, maybe I wouldn't even have any need for my Alloyed Charger, then again, there aren't many tall trees left in the wasteland. Shall we move on?" I asked.

"Indeed," Tano affirmed with a nod, his demeanor earnest yet tinged with anticipation. "It appears we stand upon the precipice of a discovery both wondrous and profound."

The structure looked very intimidating. It was a wide block of stone with an opening at the center. On top of the block was an enormous structure that reminded me of what I remember looking like the statues on the Easter Islands. Though whether they were still there was doubtful.

"There's the entrance," said Aria, pointing at the opening. "Let's go," I said.

When we neared the entrance, we saw a set of stairs leading straight down into a room made entirely of the same type of stone as we had seen on the outside.

The interior of the room exuded an aura of antiquity and mystery. The walls, adorned with faded murals and intricate carvings, told tales of a bygone era. Sunlight filtered through cracks in the ceiling, casting ethereal beams that danced across the dusty floor.

In one corner, a crumbling stone altar stood as a silent sentinel of the room's past purpose, its surface adorned with offerings long since decayed. Nearby, weathered pillars rose towards the ceiling; their once grandeur now faded with time, yet still retaining an air of majestic resilience.

Across the room, ancient relics lay scattered haphazardly, remnants of a forgotten civilization. Ceramic urns adorned with faded glyphs, weathered scrolls nestled among the debris, and rusted weapons spoke of battles long past.

From the center of the room, two corridors extended like beckoning pathways into the unknown. Each corridor held its own secrets, promising untold discoveries and dangers alike. The air was thick with anticipation as I stood at the threshold.

"What are these scrolls all about?" asked Aria.

"Let us not waste our time with those," Tano advised, gesturing dismissively towards the worn and indecipherable scrolls. "Others before us have delved into this chamber and shared their findings. The true mysteries lie beyond, waiting to be unveiled by our own hands."

"It looks like we'll have to pick a corridor," I said, "and I sure as hell don't end up intending on splitting up. So which one will it be?"

"How about the right one? Left means unlucky or something, right?"

"It doesn't matter to me," I said. "Let's go."

As we followed the corridor, things got darker, and I grabbed my flashlight to see better. The floor looked like it was about to collapse, but it was on solid ground, so we knew it wouldn't.

The air grew noticeably colder, sending shivers down their spines despite the warmth of the outside world. The walls, once adorned with intricate carvings, now bore the scars of time, their surfaces marred by cracks and fissures.

Dim torches lined the corridor. I lit one of the torches with a match. I grabbed one and used it to light the remaining torches. They cast flickering shadows that danced eerily along the walls. Strange symbols etched into the stone seemed to pulse with an otherworldly energy, adding to the sense of unease that permeated the air.

As they pressed forward, the companions began to hear faint whispers echoing through the corridor, like the murmurs of long-forgotten spirits. The whispers grew louder with each step, their words indiscernible yet undeniably unsettling.

Soon, they reached a chamber bathed in an ominous glow, the source of which remained unseen. Within the chamber, shadows stirred and shifted, coalescing into sinister forms that seemed to watch the intruders with malevolent intent.

Though the dangers lurking within the corridor were not immediately apparent, the sense of foreboding that hung in the air served as a warning of the perils that lay ahead. It was clear that this path was fraught with unknown terrors, and the companions would need to proceed with caution if they were to emerge unscathed.

As we stepped into the chamber, shafts of sunlight streamed in through narrow crevices in the ceiling, casting golden beams that illuminated the space. Aria let out a soft gasp of wonder, her eyes wide with awe.

"This place is incredible," she murmured, her voice barely above a whisper.

Tano nodded thoughtfully, his gaze drawn to the intricate symbols adorning the chamber's walls. "Though their purpose eludes me, they undoubtedly played a pivotal role in the ancient rites performed within these hallowed halls."

I couldn't help but feel a sense of anticipation building within me as I surveyed the room. "Let's take a closer look," I suggested, my voice echoing softly against the ancient stone walls.

We moved further into the chamber, drawn towards the weathered stone altar that stood at its center. Aria reached out to touch the smooth surface, her fingers lingering on the cool stone.

"What do you think this was used for?" she wondered aloud, her eyes scanning the intricate carvings that adorned its sides.

Tano shrugged, his gaze fixed on the ornate symbols that covered the walls. "Casting my gaze upon this relic, I am left to ponder its purpose," Tano reflected, his voice laced with uncertainty. "Though shrouded in mystery, I envision it as a pivotal component of the ancient rites once practiced within these sacred walls."

As we explored further, we discovered a collection of artifacts and relics scattered about the chamber—each one offering tantalizing glimpses into the past.

"Come hither!" Tano exclaimed, stooping to retrieve a weathered amulet from the ground. "Behold this marvel of craftsmanship."

Aria nodded in agreement, her eyes sparkling with curiosity. "And what about this dagger?" she asked, holding up a ceremonial blade that gleamed in the sunlight.

I couldn't help but feel a sense of reverence as I surveyed the treasures before us. "Perhaps these objects hold the key to unlocking the secrets of this place," I said, my voice filled with awe.

I collected as many relics as I could and divided them among the three of us, ensuring each of us had enough to fill our pockets.

"Let's hope these will prove useful," I remarked. "Otherwise, we'll be lugging this stuff around for nothing."

"Perhaps they hold some value for trade, regardless," Aria suggested.

"Good point," I conceded.

As we continued, our attention was drawn to another solitary corridor, hinting at the possibility of yet another room beyond.

"Our path lies through yonder passage," Tano remarked, his voice resolute yet tinged with uncertainty.

We proceeded down the dark corridor, illuminating our path with torches. Suddenly, toxic fumes began seeping from the cracks in the walls, disorienting us and making it difficult to discern our direction. Despite the challenge, we pressed onward, eventually entering another expansive chamber.

The noxious fumes hung heavy in the air, obscuring our vision and making it hard to breathe.

"Press your hands against the walls and follow along," Aria advised, her voice muffled by the thick haze. "We might find an opening."

We complied, feeling our way along the rough stone walls. Inadvertently, I stumbled into another corridor, but the toxic gases still permeated the air. Undeterred, I continued to trace the wall with my hand, eventually finding myself in a small, dead-end chamber.

Using my torch to illuminate the dim space, I scanned the walls for any signs of interest. On the back wall, a series of symbols caught my attention, faintly glowing when I touched them. Coughing from the fumes, I attempted various combinations, hoping for a breakthrough, but to no avail. However, a nagging sense of familiarity gnawed at me as I studied the symbols.

It all clicked into place, a familiar realization washing over me: the Tech-Link Controller. With a surge of hope, I retrieved it from my pocket and confirmed my suspicions—the symbols on the wall matched those on the device. Without hesitation, I pressed a button on the controller corresponding to the first symbol, and both symbols lit up in response.

Despite the haze of toxic mist obscuring my vision, I persisted, using my torch to illuminate the symbols on the wall as I pressed the corresponding buttons on the controller. Gradually, the symbols began to glow in unison, guided by the sequence dictated by the TechLink Controller.

Occasionally, I encountered resistance, needing to press certain buttons twice to activate the symbols on both the wall and the device, which turned a teal color as a result. Despite my efforts, however, nothing seemed to change—the chamber remained unchanged.

With only one symbol remaining unpressed on the TechLink Controller, I hesitated, unsure of what lay ahead. Summoning my courage, I pressed the final button, bracing myself for the unknown.

Suddenly, mechanical noises reverberated through the chamber—beeping, cracking, and the unmistakable sound of a large mechanism in motion. As vents positioned at the top and bottom of the room sprang to life, sucking the toxic gases out into the void, a sense of relief washed over me.

The release of any more gases ceased, replaced by a profound silence broken only by the sound of a large stone door opening. Though I couldn't see it, the unmistakable sound signaled a breakthrough.

Exiting the chamber and corridor, I was met with Aria's urgent voice piercing through the lingering echoes of mechanical noises. "What did you do? Did you fix it?" she called out, her words carrying a mix of anxiety and anticipation.

I displayed the Techlink Controller to Aria with a triumphant grin. "Apparently, I had a device all along that would help us!" I cheered.

"That's good, but Tano is hurt," she replied, her tone tinged with concern.

Without hesitation, I rushed over to where Tano lay on the ground, his breathing heavy and labored. "Is he conscious?" I asked, my voice betraying my worry.

"I don't think so," Aria responded.

"Alright, let me try a few things," I said, determined to help our injured companion.

I attempted to rouse Tano by shaking him gently and tapping his cheek, but received no response. Concerned for his airway, I carefully tilted Tano's head back and lifted his chin to open his airway, listening intently for any signs of breathing. Thankfully, I could hear him breathing clearly now.

Taking quick action, I placed Tano in a recovery position to keep his airway clear and prevent any potential complications. With his head tilted back and supported by his hand, I continued to monitor his breathing and pulse, relieved to find them both steady and normal.

"Okay," I reassured Aria, "he seems to be fine physically; he just lost consciousness." Determined to help Tano regain full consciousness, I retrieved my first aid kit and some smelling salts.

Breaking one in half, I held it under Tano's nose.

Within seconds, Tano startled back to consciousness, his eyes blinking open in confusion.

"You saved him!" Aria exclaimed, her relief palpable.

"Where doth my journey lead? Am I yet among the living?" Tano inquired, his voice tinged with uncertainty.

"Yes, you're fine. I think you just passed out," I said, offering reassurance to Tano.

"Ah, fortuitous indeed! When I felt the encroaching darkness, I feared my journey had come to an end," Tano admitted. "Pray, how did you halt the noxious vapors?"

"Look," I said, displaying the Techlink Controller to Tano. "On the left side of the room, there's another small room with a wall covered in all kinds of symbols. I recognized them from the controller, so I pressed the buttons according to the symbols on the wall. That seemed to fix it," I explained.

"Whence did you acquire that relic?" Tano queried, his curiosity piqued.

"I found it in a military complex some time ago. Who could've imagined it would be the solution to something in a place like here?" I said, reflecting on the unlikely source of the Techlink Controller.

"Maybe it's for multiple purposes, one of which is a situation like this," Aria suggested, her voice tinged with curiosity.

"I guess that must be it. There must be a greater meaning to these symbols than I thought," I agreed, my mind swirling with thoughts about the mysterious connection between ancient symbols and advanced technology like the Techlink Controller.

"Look yonder!" Tano exclaimed, pointing towards a previously unnoticed doorway. "Though obscured from view, its presence is undeniable."

"There was already another open door on the right side of the place," Aria noted, her voice echoing softly in the dim chamber. "I felt it when I was passing along the walls. I entered it, and it led to a collapsed chamber. The air was surprisingly clear in there, perhaps explaining why I remained conscious. There's another opening hidden behind some debris. I believe that's where we're meant to go."

"Hold on," I interjected, feeling a surge of curiosity. "I want to investigate the door that opened first. There must be something in there."

"Yeah, alright, we'll do that first then," Aria agreed.

We approached the door and entered another chamber.

As I stepped into the secret room, a shiver ran down my spine, a palpable sense of mystery enveloping me. The space was shrouded in darkness, but torches affixed to the walls offered flickering illumination, casting dancing shadows across the rough-hewn stone walls.

In one corner, an altar stood adorned with wilted flowers and dried herbs, its surface etched with enigmatic symbols lost to time. On the opposite wall, shelves sagged under the weight of ancient tomes and crumbling scrolls, their secrets waiting to be uncovered.

At the center of the room, a weathered wooden table held a jumble of papers, vials, and mysterious instruments. The air was heavy with the scent of herbs and chemicals, mingling with the musty odor of age and decay.

Overall, the room exuded an aura of secrecy and intrigue, with its hidden treasures and forgotten knowledge beckoning to us.

Among the various objects in the room, we found some intriguing items, including a peculiar compass, assorted vials, and a potion belt adorned with flasks filled with a strange black liquid.

As I sifted through the ancient tomes and scrolls, deciphering what little remained readable, I stumbled upon a revelation: the potion belt was purportedly effective against a mythical entity known as the "Enigmatic Guardian," although the details remained elusive. Nevertheless, I decided to don the potion belt and pocket the compass, anticipating their potential usefulness in future encounters.

Turning to Tano, I handed him the vials and explained their contents, ensuring he was informed of their potential significance.

Despite our thorough search, the room yielded little else of note, save for several cumbersome artifacts too heavy to carry.

"It seems we've exhausted our discoveries here. Are you ready to move on?" I inquired, eager to continue our exploration.

"Certainly," Aria replied, her voice echoing with determination.

And so, we pressed forward, leaving the enigmatic chamber behind as we ventured deeper into the labyrinthine depths of the collapsed building. With each step, the sunlight streaming through the fractured roof illuminated our path, guiding us through the debris-strewn corridors and towards the next doorway. Beyond lay another small chamber, beckoning us further into the heart of the ancient structure.

The room enveloped us in darkness, save for the faint glimmer seeping from the stairwell above and the beam of my torch slicing through the obscurity.

"Creepy," Aria muttered, her voice barely audible over the silence that hung heavy in the air.

I ignited the torches one by one,, scattered throughout the chamber. Their flickering flames danced, revealing the eerie sight before : - a grand burial site with four imposing sarcophagi neatly arranged.

"Well, this just got interesting," Ethan remarked, his tone a mix of excitement and apprehension.

Entering the burial chamber felt like stepping into another realm entirely. The solemnity of the space was palpable, a reverence that seemed to echo through the ages.

"These murals recount tales of epochs long past," Tano observed, his fingers tracing the intricate designs etched upon the chamber's walls.

The vibrant hues of blues, greens, yellows, and reds brought the ancient scenes to life, weaving a tapestry of myth and belief before our eyes.

"Each sarcophagus is a work of art," I observed, awestruck by the craftsmanship evident in every detail.

Surrounding the sarcophagi were shelves holding canopic jars, whose contents, once vital organs, are now preserved for eternity. Offerings of food, jewelry, and pottery lay scattered about, an indication of the reverence paid to the deceased.

"It's like they believed in a life beyond death," Aria whispered, her voice tinged with wonder.

As we stood amidst the relics of a civilization long gone, the weight of history bore down on us, a reminder of the timeless quest for immortality and the mysteries that lie beyond the realm of the living.

"Other than the beauty, there's not much to find here," Aria remarked with a hint of disappointment. "Let's move on."

And so, we continued our journey, navigating through countless chambers and winding corridors. Along the way, we encountered numerous traps, from spikes rising ominously from the floor to spears piercing through the walls. With quick reflexes and steady nerves, we managed to evade each perilous obstacle unscathed.

After enduring the trials of the labyrinth, we finally stumbled upon something of interest.

A courtyard stretched out like a forgotten kingdom reclaimed by nature's gentle embrace. Its circular expanse was encased by stately stone pillars, standing tall and proud like guardians of an ancient realm. As we approached, the intricacies of the carvings etched into the pillars became more apparent. Symbols and motifs, weathered by time but still retaining their enigmatic allure, adorned the surfaces.

"Look at these carvings," I remarked, my voice filled with wonder. "It's like they're telling a story."

Tano nodded in agreement, his eyes lingering on a particularly elaborate depiction. "Aye, I ponder the significance of these symbols and the rites they represent."

Aria traced her fingers along the rough surface of a nearby pillar, her eyes alight with curiosity. "It's fascinating to think about the people who built this place. What were their lives like?"

The sunlight filtered through the canopy above, dappling the courtyard floor with patches of golden light. The grass beneath our feet swayed gently in the breeze, whispering the secrets of a bygone era.

"It's like stepping into another world," Aria murmured, her words barely audible over the rustle of leaves.

I couldn't help but agree. The courtyard felt like a sanctuary, a refuge from the chaos of the outside world. Here, surrounded by the remnants of a forgotten civilization, time seemed to stand still.

As we continued to explore, our eyes scanned the courtyard for any signs of the past waiting to be unearthed. Among the pillars and patches of grass, our attention was drawn to a single object of undeniable value: a magnificent golden amulet nestled amidst the foliage at the base of the ancient tree.

"Look at that!" I exclaimed, my voice barely concealing my excitement as I pointed towards the gleaming artifact.

Aria gasped, her eyes widening in awe. "It's beautiful."

Drawing closer, Tano's expression betrayed a mixture of wonder and reverence. "Never have I beheld such wonders."

Carefully, I reached out to retrieve the amulet, marveling at its intricate design. Etched into the golden surface were symbols and glyphs, each one an affirmation to the skill and craftsmanship of its creators. It seemed to pulsate with a faint energy, as if infused with the wisdom of ages past.

"What do you think it signifies?" Aria wondered aloud, her fingers hovering over the surface of the artifact.

"I'm not sure," I replied, my mind racing with possibilities. "But I have a feeling it holds the key to unlocking the secrets of this place."

"Imagine the stories this place would tell," I mused, carefully examining a piece of intricately crafted jewelry.

"It is as though we tread upon the footsteps of history," Tano mused, his eyes alight with excitement.

With each step, the courtyard revealed more of its secrets, drawing us deeper into its enigmatic embrace. And as we stood amidst the ruins of a forgotten kingdom, I couldn't shake the feeling that we were on the brink of uncovering something truly extraordinary.

At the center of the courtyard, towering above the surrounding pillars and artifacts, stood a majestic tree—an ancient sentinel that seemed to have witnessed the passage of time itself. Its gnarled branches reached skyward, as if yearning to touch the heavens, while its sprawling canopy provided a sanctuary from the relentless glare of the sun. Under its protective embrace, the courtyard was transformed into a haven of tranquility.

The tree's leaves rustled softly in the breeze, creating a symphony of whispers that echoed through the open space. Each rustle seemed to carry with it the wisdom of centuries, a gentle reminder of the resilience of life even in the face of decay and destruction.

As we stepped closer to the tree, the ground beneath our feet shifted from ancient stone to lush green grass—a vivid carpet that seemed to stretch out in all directions. Its verdant hue provided a stark contrast to the weathered stone that surrounded it, infusing the courtyard with a sense of vitality and renewal.

"It's like stepping into a realm of enchantment," Aria marveled, her voice filled with wonder as she gazed upon the vibrant landscape before us.

I nodded in agreement, my senses heightened by the sights and sounds of this hidden oasis. Here and there, delicate flowers peeked out from between the blades of grass, their petals adding splashes of color to the otherwise muted palette of the ruins. It was as if nature itself had reclaimed this forgotten corner of the world, breathing new life into its ancient bones.

"Marvel at the beauty that persists amidst decay," Tano breathed, his gaze sweeping over the courtyard with a sense of awe.

As we stood amidst the verdant oasis of the courtyard, surrounded by the relics of a bygone era, I couldn't help but feel a sense of gratitude—for the opportunity to witness such beauty and for the chance to uncover the secrets hidden within these ancient walls. And as the gentle breeze caressed my skin and the leaves above whispered their ancient secrets, I knew that our journey was far from over.

"It's like a hidden oasis," Aria marveled, her voice filled with awe as she surveyed the scene before us. The courtyard seemed to exist outside of time, a tranquil sanctuary untouched by the passage of centuries.

I couldn't help but agree. Despite the passage of countless centuries, the courtyard retained an otherworldly beauty, a confirmation to the craftsmanship of its long-forgotten creators.

"Behold these ancient glyphs," Tano remarked, indicating the intricate markings that adorned the chamber's walls. "Their meaning eludes us, yet they speak volumes of a forgotten era."

As we approached the tree, its ancient branches swayed gently in the breeze, as if whispering secrets of the past. The allure of the treasures scattered around its base was irresistible, drawing us in like moths to a flame. Jewels glinted in the sunlight, their brilliance reflecting the stories of generations long gone. Ancient artifacts lay strewn amidst the grass, each one a silent witness to the passage of time.

"What do you think they were protecting here?" Aria wondered aloud, her voice tinged with curiosity as she surveyed the courtyard for any clues. We exchanged speculative glances, pondering the significance of the artifacts that surrounded us.

Lost in contemplation, our attention gradually shifted towards the stone wall at the far end of the courtyard—a weathered sentinel standing guard over the mysteries hidden within. At its center, a single opening beckoned us forward, its darkened depths promising untold secrets beyond its threshold.

As if drawn by an unseen force, we found ourselves inching closer to the opening, the anticipation of discovery coursing through our veins. Though reluctant to leave the tranquility of the courtyard behind, the lure of the unknown was too strong to resist.

"Shall we continue?" I asked, my voice tinged with excitement as we stood on the cusp of a new adventure. With hesitant steps, we crossed the threshold of the opening, each one filled with anticipation for the mysteries that awaited us beyond.

After the spectacular view we just experienced, wandering through the various chambers and corridors became boring, we surely came upon interesting places such as chapel for prayer, or another burial chamber but nothing of interest could be found there and we just kept moving on.

We eventually came to a closed door, next to it was a circular indentation. Surrounding the indentation were various

symbols. The top one was a bird, it looked like a toucan and it was facing straight downwards, the right one was a line and a half circle, it seemed to represent a sunset; the bottom one was obviously a snowflake; and the left one was a stylized depiction of an eagle in flight, facing towards the right.

I was lost in thought for a while until Aria mentioned something: "It looks like those represent specific directions."

"What do you mean?" I asked Well, look at it; the top one is a bird aiming down, which is south. The right one is like a sunset, and the sun sets in the west, right? Then there's the bottom one, representing a snowflake, meaning somewhere it's cold and snowing, so it means north. And the last one is an eagle facing to the right, which is east."

"You're right, I said," amazed by her wit.

It said south, west, north, and east. But why, and what does it signify then? Then he came to me. The compass. I took the compass, and it fitted perfectly. I then turned so each direction matched the ones representing the symbols. The door started to slide open with a resonant rumble, echoing through the chamber.

There were a few steps down, but I was afraid to step down because of what I saw.

Before us, the shadows of the chamber coalesced into a towering colossus, a formidable adversary that bore the grandeur of ancient royalty and the foreboding air of a cursed pharaoh's tomb. The statue, dark as a moonless night and wide as the Nile at its broadest, came to life with a presence that was both awe-inspiring and terrifying.

Its surface, though hewn from the darkest onyx, was enlivened with a kaleidoscope of colors that had no place in the realm of the living. The gold that wrapped its limbs seemed to pulse with a malignant power, and the gems adorning its headdress glinted with an inner fire that spoke of otherworldly origins. The once silent lips, now touched with the gold of a conqueror's spoils, parted to let out a sound that was the lament of aeons, a war cry that threatened to bring down the cavern around us.

As the behemoth moved, each gesture was an elegant threat, a prelude to the destruction it was sworn to unleash. It stood ready, not as a guardian of history's treasures but as the final sentinel over a tomb that was never meant to be opened. The robes of stone, painted in the vibrant hues of life, now seemed to mock our mortality, flowing with a supernatural grace that chilled the blood.

We stood united, a band of companions whose journey had led us to this moment, this confrontation with a legend that sprung from its eternal slumber. We knew then that our quest could not advance without overcoming this ancient power, a force that had waited patiently for those brave or foolish enough to challenge the old gods.

And so, with weapons drawn and resolve steeled, we prepared to fight. Not just for survival, but for the countless stories that would end if this creature of myth and stone were to claim victory over us. The air grew thick with the magic of the past and the palpable tension of the impending battle as the colossus stepped forward, ready to defend its dominion over the threshold of time.

As the last light waned, casting long shadows across the ruins, the colossus before us stirred—a giant wrought from epochs past. Its stone limbs, imbued with an otherworldly palette, moved with a life that should not have been. We stood, three against a legend, knowing that the coming moments would test our very existence.

My hands tightened around the Fusionizer rifle, the familiar hum of its charging cells a comfort against the looming dread. Beside me, Aria's fingers danced over the hilts of her dual blades, and Tano stood resolute, his staff in one hand and the crossbow that had felled many a beast in the other.

The battle erupted without warning; the colossus's first move was a shockwave that threatened to cleave the earth beneath our feet. I fired, energy bolts searing the air, their brilliant arcs seeking the creature's heart. But it was like striking the mountainside, the impacts leaving scars that healed too quickly.

Aria leapt with a grace that belied the gravity of our plight, her blades a blur. They found their marks, slicing through ancient stone, her throws so precise, the blades returning to her palms as if they possessed a will to fight alongside us. Yet the colossus seemed unfazed, its counterstrikes swift and brutal.

It was then that we remembered the potions, discovered in a hidden chamber within the ancient structure we'd explored days before. Reaching for my belt, I drew forth a small vial, the liquid inside pulsating with a vibrant glow. Not just any concoction; these were ancient alchemist's brews, designed to amplify the inherent properties of our weapons—a necessary edge against an opponent of this magnitude.

With deliberate care, I applied the potion to the Fusionizer's energy matrix, its hum deepening, signaling a surge of potentized force. Aria, recognizing the shift, anointed her blades with her potion, their edges gleaming with a deadly luminescence.

Tano, with a solemn nod, consumed his potion, designed to bolster his strength beyond the limits of mortal men. His stance solidified, an aura of raw power radiating from his being as he gripped his staff tighter, ready for the renewed onslaught.

Tano moved like the wind through the leaves, his staff a thunderous beat against the colossus's advances, his crossbow bolts finding their way through the thinnest of the creature's defenses. I could hear him chanting a low song of the earth that gave rhythm to our defiance.

"We are the unbroken chain, the children of the new dawn!" I cried out, rallying against the hopelessness that clawed at the edges of my resolve.

The colossus's eyes, deep wells of ancient fury, turned upon me, and I felt the weight of centuries in its gaze. It moved, a limb as wide as the Nile swinging with the force of a tempest. My shield flickered as the blow descended, the energy field absorbing the impact that would have ground me to dust.

Aria danced closer to the edge of death with each pass, her blades cutting deep but never deep enough. She was poetry in motion—every step, every thrust, a stanza in the saga we were writing. Her laughter, tinged with the thrill of the fight, rang clear even as blood began to paint her path in crimson.

The battle raged—fierce and unforgiving. We wove between the colossus's legs like shadows chased by the sun, our attacks mere annoyances to the ancient behemoth. Aria, swift as the desert wind, struck from every angle, her blades a silver flash against the dark stone. Tano's bolts, each one sung from the crossbow with a prayer, thudded into the colossus's hide, leaving deep scars that smoldered with energy.

In the chaos, a pattern revealed itself—a rhythm to the colossus's movements, a telltale pause as it gathered its strength for each thunderous assault. It was in those fleeting moments of stillness that our opportunity lay—a vulnerability not of body but of time.

"Tano, Aria, the joints!" I shouted above the din of battle. "When it pauses, aim for the joints!"

Tano nodded, understanding flashing in his eyes as he reloaded. Aria didn't respond; she didn't need to—her next throw aimed with precision at the joint where the creature's arm met its shoulder. The blade sank deep, and for the first time, the colossus roared in pain, its arm hanging limp.

Encouraged, we pressed our advantage. Tano's bolts flew, now targeting the joints with the precision of a surgeon. But it was not enough. The creature was wounded, yes, but far from defeated. It lashed out blindly, its remaining arm sweeping across the ruins in a devastating arc.

As the last light waned, casting long shadows across the ruins, the colossus before us stirred—a giant wrought from epochs past. Its stone limbs, imbued with an otherworldly palette, moved with a life that should not have been. We stood, three against a legend, knowing that the coming moments would test our very existence.

My hands tightened around the Fusionizer rifle, the familiar hum of its charging cells a comfort against the looming dread. Beside me, Aria's fingers danced over the hilts of her dual blades, and Tano stood resolute, his staff in one hand and the crossbow that had felled many a beast in the other.

The colossus's first move, a shockwave that threatened to cleave the earth beneath our feet, was met with our defiance. Aria leapt, her blades slicing through ancient stone, while Tano's bolts found their way through the creature's defenses. But it was like striking a mountain—the impacts left scars that healed too quickly.

"In the names of the old gods and the new, we defy you!" I cried, my Fusionizer blazing with energy.

The colossus retaliated, sweeping its arm across the ruins. In that moment of impending doom, instinct took over. I activated the Energy Shield, enveloping us in a protective dome as the colossus's blow descended. The ground beneath us shuddered, but we were unharmed, our spirits unbroken.

Amid the chaos, I noticed the glow from the colossus's chest—a core that pulsed with life. "Aria, Tano, cover me!" I shouted, charging forward. They answered with a barrage of attacks, diverting the colossus's attention.

The battlefield became a blur as I focused on the core, the source of the colossus's power. With a cry of determination, I fired the Fusionizer. The bolt struck true, piercing the core, and the colossus exploded in a cascade of light and sound, its form crumbling to dust.

But victory was short-lived. As the dust settled, I found Aria, struck down by a shard from the colossus—a final, spiteful act. Her life ebbed away as I held her, her smile fading with the setting sun.

"We did it, Ethan," she whispered, her voice a mere echo of her vibrant self.

The pain of her loss was a chasm that swallowed me whole.

In her final moments, we shared a kiss, a promise of a love that would endure beyond death. And then she was gone, leaving a void that could never be filled.

Tano and I bore her from the battlefield, the weight of our sorrow as heavy as the setting sun. That night, under a blanket of stars, I made my vows— to remember, to honor her legacy, and to carry on the fight for a future she believed in.

Our victory was pyrrhic; the cost was engraved upon our hearts. Aria, the fiercest of us all, had fallen. And in the aftermath, I was changed, driven not just by duty but by the memory of her unyielding spirit.

Tano stood at a distance, his head bowed. No joy could be found in our hollow victory. His staff and crossbow, once proud tools of the Greenwardens, now seemed heavy with the weight of our loss. He approached slowly, respect and sorrow etched deep in his face.

"Ethan," he said, his voice carrying the somber tones of the ancient woods, "the spirits of the wildlands weep with you. She was... truly remarkable."

I could barely hear him through the haze of my grief. The edges of the world blurred; time stretched and twisted, each second an eternity without Aria. The chamber where we had fought so valiantly seemed to close in around us, the walls whispering of the relentless march of time, indifferent to the living and the dead.

In my arms, Aria was still, too still, her vibrant spirit extinguished. The echoes of our battle rang mockingly in the silence that followed, the dust settling around us like a shroud. I was dimly aware of Tano's hand upon my shoulder, a gesture meant to comfort me, yet nothing could reach me in the depths of my despair.

"We must honor her," Tano spoke again, his voice a steady presence amid the chaos of my thoughts. "She fought with the heart of a lioness, with the grace of the gazelle. Her memory will walk with us, her strength will bolster our resolve, and her courage will light our path."

But his words were a distant rumble of thunder against the storm of my grief. I clung to Aria, her name a mantra on my lips, a futile plea for her return. In the silence that followed, there was a solemn understanding that we would carry her with us, not just back to the light of the world, but in every step we took from this day forward.

Tano finally guided me to my feet; his support was the only thing keeping me from collapsing into the dust. Together, we bore Aria out of the ruins, her form shrouded in the cloak that had once billowed behind her as she fought.

As we emerged into the fading light of day, the sun dipped below the horizon, casting a closing eye on the world that had irrevocably changed. In the twilight, we walked, a procession of two, carrying a warrior whose light had been snuffed out too soon.

That night, as the stars blinked awake, I whispered promises into the void. Promises of remembrance, of vengeance, of a legacy that would not be forgotten. And when the dawn finally broke, it found me changed. What I had once fought for out of duty, I would now fight for in the name of love—a love that had burned bright and fierce, a love that had died in my arms under the cold gaze of history come to life.

After the battle, amidst the debris and echoes of their struggle, I discovered a sophisticated device that, at first glance, appeared out of place amidst the ancient ruins. At the back, it said Tactical Multi-Tool (TMT).

The TMT was compact, sleek, and felt robust; its surface was a mesh of matte black and metallic gray, with an intuitive interface that lit up upon touch.

In a hidden compartment of my TMT, I discovered a thin, durable sheet—a field manual of sorts, providing a rudimentary guide to the tool's features. While much of it was in technical jargon that required time to fully comprehend, it offered invaluable insights into the more complex functionalities, such as the environmental analyzer and the medical scanner's full diagnostic suite.

The Tactical Multi-Tool was an amalgamation of advanced technology, designed for immediate use in a wide array of situations, particularly useful for someone like me, who finds herself often in the thick of danger and exploration. It comprised several key features:

Advanced Scanning Capability: With a flick, I could deploy a holographic display that scanned the environment. It was capable of identifying structural weaknesses in buildings, finding salvageable materials within a certain radius, and even detecting life forms. This feature proved invaluable for navigating dangerous territories or finding resources in desolate landscapes.

Communication Relay: The TMT could intercept, decrypt, and send communications across various frequencies, making it possible for me to tap into forgotten networks or stay one step ahead of adversaries by eavesdropping on their plans.

Medical Scanner and Basic Field Aid: It included a medical scanner that could diagnose injuries with recommendations for immediate treatment using available resources. Coupled with a compartment containing essential first-aid supplies, it became a critical tool for survival.

Energy Blade: Concealed within was a retractable energy blade that, while not as powerful as dedicated weaponry, could cut through metal, clear obstructions, or be used in close combat. Its versatility made it a reliable backup when conventional weapons were not an option.

Environmental Analyzer: the TMT could assess atmospheric conditions, detect toxins, and filter water, making it indispensable for ensuring my survival in hazardous environments.

Sonic Cipher Decoding: The apparatus had the capacity to decipher concealed messages within diverse sounds, adeptly discerning virtually any genre of music and unraveling their significance.

I wasted no time in utilizing the device, eager to uncover any potential means of escape from our current predicament. Upon activating it, the advanced scanner immediately pinpointed a significant feature in the chamber—an inconspicuous block of stone nestled at the chamber's rear, along with a set of stairs leading upward. With a determined resolve, I decided to press the button.

A symphony of ancient mechanisms sprang to life, filling the chamber with a cacophony of mechanical whirring and clicking. The door, a massive slab of stone and metal, began its slow ascent, accompanied by the haunting echoes of creaks and groans from the archaic hinges and pulleys.

As the door lifted, a rush of displaced air filled the chamber, accompanied by a faint hiss as it broke free from its ancient seal.

The sudden movement cast eerie shadows across the chamber, heightening the sense of anticipation and foreboding.

Ascending several flights of stairs, we finally reached a small hatch above, through which we emerged into the wilderness beyond.

"Tano, do you know a way back to the initial structure?" I inquired, my gaze turning towards our guide.

"Come, gaze upon this sight," Tano beckoned. "Even from here, its presence is unmistakable."

Without further ado, I set off towards the ancient structure, determined to find our way back.

"Take heed of serpents and other dangers," Tano cautioned, his words laced with concern.

I nodded in acknowledgment, my focus unwavering as I forged ahead towards our destination.

For the rest of the journey, Tano kept quiet. He had realized I had no desire to talk.

When we arrived, Tano, without saying a word, climbed a high tree and left in his glider. I grabbed the Alloyed Charger and took off as well.

When I arrived at the village, I saw Jabari heading towards me.

"How went it?" He asked, "Found any revelations?"

"I did find out a lot," I said, "but there were many dangers in our path. In the end, we lost Aria. She was the one thing I truly held valuable."

"My heart aches to hear that. Is there aught I can offer?" Jabari said.

"I just want to be left alone. I'm going to leave this place behind and continue on to my next destination," I said.

"And what's yer plan then?" Jabari asked. "I don't actually know," I said.

"Can I make a suggestion?" Jabari asked.

"Sure," I said.

"I've heard tale of a spot called the Whispering Plateau, nestled 'neath the Skyreach Mountains' shadow. 'Tis said to be touched by the ancients themselves," said Jabari, "'Tis a place of myst'ry, where the wind carries echoes from the yesteryears and the ground holds truths hidden from the unworthy. Atop the plateau, rumor speaks of a monolithic structure shrouded in vines and forgotten by time, dubbed the 'Singing Stone.' They say it sings with voices of the old world."

"I'm not sure if I believe in that kind of stuff, but if there's something out there, I might as well investigate it.

"Keep in mind that it might not be safe; there are tales of the place that would be fraught with dangers, from treacherous terrains to guardians of the old world meant to deter the unworthy.

However, it's said that those who are pure of heart and resolute in their quest can awaken the Singing Stone and decipher its secrets." said Jabari.

Well, I guess that's where I'm going. I don't have any other ideas, so I might as well. Thank you for the advice. Do you know which way I have to go?"

Jabari explained the entire route very well, and his information was enough to make it there as I already had an area on my OmniLocator that was very nearby. It would take a day to travel at maximum speed.

"Well, I wish ye fortune, and again, my condolences. I can't fathom yer sorrow. But mayhaps ye'll find a fresh path ahead." said Jabari.

"I have my goal set out in front of me; I just need to find out where I can find the answer to my questions," I said.

We told each other goodbye again. And I left for the Whispering Plateau.

As I set my sights on the Whispering Plateau, the weight of my journey pressed heavily upon my shoulders. The loss of Aria, a constant ache in my heart, served as a stark reminder of the stakes of my quest. Yet, amidst the sorrow, a spark of determination ignited within me. The mysteries of the ancient world, the secrets whispered by the wind, and the promise of uncovering truths long buried fueled my resolve. The road ahead was fraught with uncertainties and dangers, yet the quest for knowledge and the pursuit of my mission propelled me forward. I could not allow Aria's sacrifice to be in vain; her spirit, a guiding light, pushed me to seek answers that might change the course of this shattered world. As the landscape began to blur beneath the steady hum of the Alloyed Charger, I embraced the solitude of the journey, each mile a step closer to unraveling the mysteries of the Singing Stone and, perhaps, a step toward understanding my own place in this reborn world.

WHISPERS AND SHADOWS

As I embarked on my journey to the Whispering Plateau, the weight of grief hung heavy upon me, like a dark cloud obscuring the path ahead. The loss of Aria, my steadfast companion and the love of my life, echoed through my heart with each turn of the Alloyed Charger's wheels. Memories of our adventures together danced before my mind's eye, each one a bittersweet reminder of what once was.

The landscape stretched out before me, a desolate expanse of ruined cities and barren wastelands, scarred by the remnants of the nuclear devastation that had torn the world apart a millennium ago. With Aria's spirit as my guide, I steeled myself against the desolation, the Alloyed Charger carrying me forward into the unknown. The air was thick with the stench of decay, and the sky above was tinged with an eerie glow, a haunting reminder of the lingering radiation that still plagued the land.

As I rode onward, the Alloyed Charger tearing through the desolation with unmatched speed, I found myself lost in a whirlwind of emotions. Anguish and despair gnawed at my soul, threatening to consume me whole, yet beneath the weight of my sorrow, a flicker of determination burned bright. I knew that I must press on, for Aria's sake, and for the hope of finding solace amidst the whispers of the ancient plateau.

"With Aria's spirit as my guide, I steeled myself against the desolation, the Alloyed Charger carrying me forward into the unknown."

The journey was arduous and fraught with peril and uncertainty at every turn. I faced dangers both natural and man-made, treacherous terrain, and crumbling ruins. Yet through it all, I clung to the memory of Aria, her presence a guiding light in the darkness that threatened to engulf me.

I encountered a band of raiders emerging stealthily from the rocks and trees behind me. With their bows aimed at me, they demanded I surrender my belongings. The forest fell silent once more, the chaos of battle giving way to solemn contemplation of the journey that lay ahead. Unwilling to comply, I surged forward toward the nearest raider, delivering a decisive blow to his jaw. As arrows whizzed past, I skillfully evaded each one, systematically incapacitating my assailants. My rage fueled my actions as I unleashed a barrage of strikes, swiftly incapacitating my foes one by one. Despite the option to utilize my Fusionizer, I chose to confront them head-on, channeling my fury into each blow. Gripping one raider by the throat, I thrust him forcefully into a nearby tree.

"What is your purpose here? Are you seeking to rob me of my possessions, the few remaining items of value to me? Not today. You've chosen the wrong adversary at the wrong moment," I declared before forcefully slamming his head against the tree trunk. With only a handful of raiders left, attempting to flee, I retrieved my Fusionizer and dispatched them from a distance.

The forest fell silent once more, the chaos of battle giving way to solemn contemplation of the journey that lay ahead.

My anguished cry echoed through the forest, startling the birds into flight. Collapsing to my knees, tears streamed down my cheeks as I grappled with the intensity of my emotions. Moments passed as I sat, head bowed in anguish. Eventually, I rose to my feet, mounting the Alloyed Charger once more, determined to press on.

After ensuring no further threats remained, the forest fell silent once more, the chaos of battle giving way to solemn contemplation of the journey that lay ahead. This silence wasn't just the absence of noise; it was a heavy, poignant stillness that seemed to acknowledge the weight of what had transpired. In that quiet, with the echoes of my own actions reverberating through the trees, I found a moment of clarity amidst the turmoil of my quest.

With renewed resolve, I swiftly traversed the remaining distance, finally arriving at the base of the Whispering Plateau.

Exhaustion weighed heavily on my weary frame, yet a sense of quiet resolve filled my heart. As the last rays of the sun kissed the horizon, I ventured into the heart of the plateau, its secrets veiled in twilight shadows. For here, amidst the whispering winds and the echoes of a forgotten world, I hoped that I would find the answers I sought and perhaps a measure of peace for my shattered soul. For here, amidst the whispering winds and the echoes of a forgotten world, I hoped that I would find the answers I sought and perhaps a measure of peace for my shattered soul.

I truly felt tired for the first time since my cryosleep. It was like the world's gravity had increased. Everything felt heavy, even my feet, which I almost had to drag behind me. The sun was slowly setting, and I was looking for shelter. I looked around to see what the place was like.

The Whispering Plateau had been a place of ethereal beauty, marked by its vast expanse of gently rolling hills that rose and fell like the breath of the earth itself. Towering ancient trees, their branches heavy with the weight of centuries, had created a canopy so dense that sunlight trickled down only in soft beams, illuminating patches of the verdant underbrush below. These trees, witnesses to ages past, seemed to murmur secrets on the wind—a constant, soft whisper that gave the plateau its name.

A thick mist had often lingered in the air, especially at dawn and dusk, wrapping the landscape in a mysterious veil that transformed the familiar into the realm of enchantment. Amidst this mist, the ruins of old structures had peeked through the foliage, their stones covered in a patina of moss and lichen, suggesting a history intertwined with nature, abandoned by its creators yet embraced by the earth.

Streams, fed by hidden springs, had meandered across the plateau, their clear waters bubbling and laughing over rocks, adding a musical quality to the whispering winds. Here and there, clearings had opened up to reveal breathtaking views of the valley below, where the land stretched out to the horizon in a quilt of forests and meadows.

At the heart of the plateau, a singular, ancient tree, larger and more majestic than the rest, stood as a sentinel. Its roots delved deep into the earth, while its branches reached for the sky, as if connecting the land to the heavens. This tree had been the centerpiece of many legends, said to be the oldest on the plateau and a keeper of the land's deepest secrets.

The Whispering Plateau had not been just a location; it had been a living, breathing entity, filled with the echoes of the past and the whispered promises of the future.

Dotting the edges of the plateau were stone huts, their walls thick and sturdy, covered in moss and climbing vines. These structures, built from the very rock upon which they stood, offered a basic but solid shelter against the elements. Inside, the remnants of fire pits and simple stone benches suggested they once served as homes or waystations for travelers of old.

I peered into one of the huts, finding nothing but a cold stone bench. Disheartened, I returned outside, collecting natural materials to fashion a makeshift bed. As I lay down, the day's burdens weighed heavily on my mind, ushering me into a restless slumber filled with echoes of the past. With determination, I transformed the hard bench into a more comfortable resting place, arranging my belongings before finally lying down. Exhaustion washed over me, and before I knew it, sleep claimed me, granting me respite from the relentless ache in my heart.

In my slumber, I found myself wandering through a magnificent garden where vibrant flowers bloomed in abundance. Roses, tulips, and daisies—their colors danced in the sunlight, filling the air with their sweet fragrance. Towering trees cast comforting shadows, and amidst it all stood a grand house, beckoning me with its mysterious allure. Yet, no matter how hard I tried, the door remained closed to me.

"It's not your time yet," a gentle voice echoed from behind.

Turning, I beheld Aria, her presence both comforting and surreal. "Aria," I breathed, overwhelmed by a flood of emotions. "I've missed you more than words can express. The pain of your absence has been unbearable."

"Don't mourn for me, Ethan," she said softly, her gaze filled with compassion. "I am at peace now, in a place where pain and sorrow no longer hold sway. But you must find solace in our memories and in the love we shared. I will always be with you, nestled within the depths of your soul."

"But how can I go on without you?" I pleaded, my heart heavy with grief.

"You are stronger than you realize," Aria reassured me, her voice tinged with unwavering love. "Embrace our love, cherish the moments we shared, and let them guide you forward. Your mission awaits, and with each step, you draw closer to your destiny. Trust in yourself, Ethan, and know that my love will be your guiding light, now and forever."

Tears welled in my eyes as I reached for her hand, our surroundings fading into an ethereal haze. "I love you," I whispered, holding onto her presence for as long as I could.

"And I love you, Ethan," she replied, her form gradually fading from view, leaving behind only the echo of her words and the warmth of her love.

Don't leave me again," I pleaded, my voice filled with desperation.

"I'm sorry, Ethan, but my time here is over. It's time for you to wake up," Aria's voice echoed softly.

"Wake up..."

As consciousness returned, I found myself drenched in sweat, the morning sun casting its warm glow upon the world outside. The remnants of my dream lingered, stirring something deep within me. A newfound determination coursed through my veins, urging me to press forward on my quest. With Aria's presence still lingering in my heart, I emerged from the hut, ready to explore the unknown. As I gazed upon Twilight Crest, I contemplated the road ahead. The loss of Aria and the desolation of the Plateau were behind me, but the quest for survival and purpose in this new world was just beginning.

I scoured every corner of the area, and my senses heightened as I searched for any sign that would point me towards the elusive Singing Stone. Yet, despite my efforts, I found myself at a loss, with the vastness of the landscape offering no clear direction.

Then, like a whisper in the wind, I heard it—a faint melody drifting through the air, beckoning me towards its source. Following the ethereal sound, I came upon a towering ruin, its ancient stones reaching towards the heavens.

Ascending the crumbling stairs, I reached the pinnacle of the tower, where a scene of mystical wonder awaited me. At its center stood a round table, upon which rested a gazing ball, emanating an otherworldly aura. As I approached, a surge of energy pulsed through the air, drawing me closer to its enigmatic allure.

With trembling hands, I reached out to touch the gazing ball, a surge of electricity enveloping me in its embrace. In that moment, as the currents of power coursed through my being, I knew that my journey was far from over. The mysteries of the Singing Stone awaited, and I was determined to uncover their secrets, no matter the cost.

I found myself enveloped in a world shrouded in darkness, where the only illumination came from a swirling, purple path beneath my feet. Above me, a silent thunderstorm raged, with flashes of lightning casting eerie shadows across the glass-like surface below.

As I followed the path, it led me to a surreal scene—a floating platform adorned with the semblance of a home. Within its walls, frozen in time, I glimpsed fragments of a life once lived. A woman stood in the kitchen, her movements suspended in a timeless dance of food preparation. Nearby, a child played amidst a sea of toys, his innocence preserved in the stillness of the moment.

Yet, behind their tranquil facades, I sensed a lingering sadness—a longing for something lost to the ravages of time. And as I gazed upon the familiar faces before me, I realized with a pang of nostalgia that this was my past—a world untouched by the scars of war.

Memories flooded my mind of days filled with laughter and love, before the shadows of conflict descended upon our lives. I remembered the ache in my heart for a father long gone, his absence casting a pall over our once vibrant home.

But amidst the bittersweet yearning for days gone by, I also felt a stirring of hope—a longing to reclaim the innocence of youth, to recapture the magic of a simpler time. And as the scene faded into darkness once more, I knew that my journey was far from over.

With renewed resolve, I pressed onward, guided by the beckoning glow of the purple path.

As I traversed the path, I stumbled upon yet another platform, where a scene from my teenage years unfolded before me. There, amidst the familiar setting of high school hallways, I saw myself walking alongside my best friend, Jason. Memories flooded back as I recalled our shared struggles in a world where acceptance seemed elusive and bullies lurked around every corner.

The hallways were lined with rows of rectangular lockers, each one a portal to a world of books, binders, and hidden treasures. I could almost hear the metallic clang of the locker doors as they swung open, revealing their cavernous depths. The floor beneath our feet was a checkerboard of black and white tiles, illuminated by the warm glow of overhead lights.

As I focused on our younger selves, I overheard snippets of conversation—a plan forming, a pact being sealed. My younger self, fueled by a sense of righteous indignation, spoke of retribution against our tormentors and a desire to strike back and reclaim our dignity.

"I don't know, Ethan." Jason's voice echoed in the hallway, a note of caution tingeing his words. "We could get in trouble, you know."

But my younger self was undeterred, his determination unwavering. "We have to stand up to them," he insisted. "Show them we won't be pushed around anymore."

As I continued along the winding path, the scene shifted once again, transporting me to a time in my life tinged with both nostalgia and pain. Here, in a cramped and dilapidated apartment, the walls adorned with peeling wallpaper and the air heavy with the scent of dust, I witnessed a poignant reunion between my father and me.

Amidst the worn furniture and dimly lit room, my father stood before me, clad in the uniform of a soldier. The sight of him stirred a flood of emotions within me—a mixture of longing, resentment, and ultimately, forgiveness.

As I focused on our embrace, I heard snippets of conversation, fragments of a dialogue that had shaped our relationship. My father spoke of his absence and the painful choice he had been forced to make in the wake of my parents' divorce. He recounted his time in the army and the years spent in distant lands, far from the comforts of home.

I listened, my heart heavy with understanding, as he shared the harrowing details of his service—the rigorous training, the camaraderie forged in the crucible of conflict, and the scars, both physical and emotional, that he bore as a witness to his sacrifice.

In that moment, clarity washed over me like a soothing balm, and I realized the depth of my father's love and the sacrifices he had made on my behalf. With tears in my eyes, I embraced him once more, a silent acknowledgment of our shared journey and the bond that endured despite the trials we had faced.

His name was James—not just a war veteran, but a beacon of strength and resilience, a hero in the truest sense of the word. And as we stood there, lost in the embrace of our shared history, I knew that his legacy would live on in the echoes of our memories and the strength of our enduring bond.

Life had taken a difficult turn for me. When I first ventured out on my own, I had a modest sum of money to my name, but employment proved elusive. Despite my best efforts, I found myself unable to secure steady work, relying instead on the generosity of others to make ends meet.

Fortunately, I managed to secure lodging in exchange for serving as a caretaker, a role that provided me with a roof over my head and a modest stipend to cover my basic needs. However, sustenance remained a constant struggle, and more often than not, I found myself relying on the kindness of strangers or scavenging for scraps just to put food on the table.

But now, with my father's return, there was a glimmer of hope on the horizon. His promise to support me and ensure my well-being offered a ray of light in an otherwise bleak existence. With his guidance and assistance, I dared to believe that I might finally find stability and the chance to live a life of dignity and purpose once more.

As the swirling path led me forward, I found myself standing in the solemn midst of a funeral procession. The air was heavy with grief, and the weight of loss hung palpably in the air. It was my father's burial, a somber occasion marked by the presence of only a handful of mourners—his fellow comrades from the army and myself.

My heart ached with a pain that seemed to reverberate through every fiber of my being. Tears streamed down my face unchecked, the depth of my sorrow laid bare for all to see. The loss of my father had left an indelible scar upon my soul, a wound that throbbed with an ache that refused to be quelled.

Surrounded by the solemn silence of the graveyard, I stood beside his final resting place, grappling with the enormity of my grief. The sight of his comrades standing stoically by his graveside served as a poignant reminder of the profound impact my father had made during his lifetime.

In the hushed stillness of the graveyard, surrounded by the silent sentinels of stone, we stood gathered around the freshly turned earth of my father's final resting place. The solemnity of the moment weighed heavily upon us, a somber acknowledgment of the irrevocable passage of time.

Before us stood the priest, a figure of solemn reverence amidst the solemnity of the occasion. His voice, low and resonant, carried across the quiet expanse of the graveyard, each word imbued with a weighty significance that seemed to echo through the ages.

"Ladies and gentlemen, today we gather to honor the life of a true hero, a devoted father, and a cherished member of our community. As we lay to rest our beloved James Hawthorne, we are reminded of the immense sacrifices he made and the profound impact he had on all of us.

James was not just a soldier; he was a beacon of courage, selflessness, and unwavering dedication. His valor on the battlefield exemplified the highest ideals of service and sacrifice. He fought not for glory or recognition but out of a deep sense of duty and love for his country and fellow citizens.

Beyond his role as a warrior, James was a loving father who instilled in his son the values of integrity, kindness, and resilience. He leaves behind a legacy of love and guidance that will continue to inspire generations to come.

Today, as we bid farewell to James, let us not mourn his passing but celebrate the extraordinary life he lived. Let us remember his laughter, his kindness, and the countless lives he touched with his compassion and generosity.

Though he may no longer walk among us, James Hawthorne will forever remain in our hearts as a shining example of bravery, honor, and sacrifice. May his spirit soar free, knowing that he will always be remembered as a hero of the people.

Rest in peace, dear James. Your legacy will live on in the hearts of all who knew and loved you."

In the solemn company of my father's comrades, I beheld a collective sorrow that mirrored the depths of my own grief. Each face bore the weight of shared loss, their expressions etched with the silent anguish of farewell.

As I gazed upon their somber countenances, a wave of desolation washed over me, engulfing me in a sea of sorrow from which I felt powerless to escape. In the presence of their silent solidarity, I found myself consumed by a profound sense of emptiness, a gnawing void that seemed to devour the very essence of my being.

My father's passing had cast a pall of darkness over my soul, plunging me into the depths of despair where even the simplest tasks felt like insurmountable burdens. The weight of his absence bore down upon me like a leaden shroud, suffocating me with its suffocating embrace.

In the midst of my despair, I felt utterly lost, adrift in a sea of sorrow with no beacon to guide me home. Every moment without him felt like an eternity, each heartbeat a painful reminder of the void he had left behind.

But amidst the darkness, a flicker of hope began to stir within me—a fragile ember of resilience that refused to be extinguished. Though the pain of his absence may linger, I knew that my father's spirit would forever dwell within me, a guiding light in the darkness, urging me to press on in the face of despair.

And so, with his memory as my anchor and his comrades as my companions, I resolved to honor his legacy with every breath I took, to carry his spirit forward in my heart, and to find solace in the knowledge that though he may be gone, he would never truly leave me.

Once more, the world around me dissolved into shadows, ushering me along the ethereal path of memories yet unspoken. As I traversed the winding azure trail, I found myself confronted with another fragment of my past—a haunting tableau of desolation and despair.

There, in the dim recesses of a forgotten alley, I beheld a spectral reflection of myself, shrouded in the tattered remnants of my former life. Clad in threadbare jeans and a weathered red hoodie, I sat hunched and defeated, my weary form a witness to the trials I had endured.

It had been years since I had been cast adrift from the sanctuary of my father's care, expelled from the comfort of home for my perceived failures as a caretaker. Left to fend for myself amidst the unforgiving streets, I had become a ghost among the shadows, a solitary figure lost in the labyrinth of urban decay.

In those desolate alleys, I had walked a precarious tightrope between survival and oblivion, navigating a treacherous landscape fraught with peril at every turn. The company I kept was as varied as it was dangerous—fellow outcasts and desperate souls, each one a potential threat or ally in the harsh crucible of street life.

But despite my best efforts to remain vigilant, I found myself vulnerable and defenseless against the predations of those who would prey upon the weak. Malnourished and sleep-deprived, I was ill-equipped to withstand the onslaught of violence and exploitation that lurked around every corner.

In the depths of my despair, I felt the weight of my own frailty bearing down upon me, a suffocating burden that threatened to crush my spirit beneath its oppressive weight. Yet even in my darkest moments, a flicker of resilience burned within me, a stubborn refusal to surrender to the shadows that sought to engulf me.

And so, with each passing day, I clung to the fragile hope that someday, somehow, I would find my way out of the darkness and into the light. For despite the trials that lay ahead, I knew that within the depths of my soul, the spark of resilience still burned bright, a beacon of hope amidst the encroaching shadows of despair.

A memory I wished to cast aside, yet it persisted, an unwelcome echo of a time fraught with hardship and uncertainty. Determined to forge ahead, I followed the winding path until it led me to a place of solace—a sanctuary amidst the chaos of life's tumultuous journey.

Here, in the hallowed halls of an office, I found refuge and purpose as a computer scientist. Surrounded by friendly faces and willing mentors, I immersed myself in the intricacies of my craft, honing my skills through hours of dedication and hard work.

With perseverance and determination, I mastered the nuances of my profession, earning a fair wage and securing the means to provide for myself. No longer shackled by the chains of poverty, I embraced the opportunity to build a better life—a life filled with stability, comfort, and the promise of a brighter tomorrow.

As I sat at my desk, gazing out at the snowfall beyond the window, I savored the warmth of camaraderie and the sense of belonging that permeated the air. Across from me, my colleagues engaged in lively conversation; their laughter and banter were a welcome respite from the rigors of the day.

In this moment, surrounded by the familiar sights and sounds of the office, I reveled in the simple joys of everyday life. And though the shadows of my past still lingered on the periphery of my consciousness, I refused to be defined by the struggles that had come before. In this place of newfound opportunity, I had discovered the strength to overcome adversity and embrace the promise of a brighter future.

"So, Tommy, how was your weekend? Visit any strip clubs again?" inquired Rick, a mischievous grin playing on his lips.

"Nah, man. Money's tight these days. I have been splurging on useless stuff lately. And those strip clubs? They're a black hole for your wallet," replied Tommy with a wry chuckle.

"You have to learn to budget, friend. I always have some cash left at the end of the month. It's doable," I said.

"Yeah, well, I'm not surprised you're good with money," teased Rick. "What shady dealings are you up to in secret? Maybe running a clandestine operation in your basement?"

"Cut it out, Rick. That's not funny," admonished Tommy, his tone serious. "Ethan's a smart guy. He knows how to handle his finances better than you."

"Apologies, Ethan. Just a jest," conceded Rick sheepishly. "Well, it didn't land," retorted Tommy, unamused.

"No worries, guys," I interjected, trying to diffuse the tension. "Let's focus on work, shall we?"

"Touché, Ethan," quipped Rick. "Back to the grind before the boss catches wind of our little chat," agreed Tommy, steering the conversation back to work.

The scene shifted once more after I traveled another twirling path, this time about fifteen years into the future. I found myself in a cozy apartment with sleek gray tiles adorning the floor. The kitchen area seamlessly blended into the living room, where a snug square table was surrounded by an 'L'-shaped couch. Beyond the living area lay my sanctuary—the bedroom and bathroom.

Despite the passage of time, I remained in the same job, albeit with a significant promotion and increased workload. However, the perks included a substantial raise, affording me a comfortable lifestyle. I felt content.

Sharing my space was Jessica, a woman with whom I maintained a somewhat ambiguous relationship. While not officially dating, we were more than friends, often indulging in the benefits of companionship without the commitment. Jessica frequently stayed over, enjoying the comforts of my home, particularly the plentiful food and beer. She was undeniably attractive, making it challenging for me to resist her allure. Yet I couldn't overlook her penchant for alcohol, often taking advantage of the drinks stocked in my house.

As I focused on our interactions, I could hear the echoes of our arguments.

"How much longer are you planning to keep this up, Jessica?" I inquired, my frustration evident in my tone.

"What do you mean, Ethan?" she responded innocently. "You're practically living off my dime. You spend more time here than I do, and you consume the money I work hard to earn," I explained, trying to keep my voice steady.

"Come on, you know you love having me around, babe," she countered with a playful smirk.

"I do, but not when you're intoxicated, especially when I'm not even home. You need to find a better-paying job. Then maybe I could visit you more often and raid your stash of booze," I retorted, growing more exasperated by the minute.

"Don't give me that nonsense. Here's your key back. Take it if you want me gone for good," she challenged, holding out the key to my apartment.

I couldn't deny that letting go of her was challenging. She was like a nagging toothache, impossible to ignore. You knew you needed to see the dentist, but you kept postponing it. Yet, I sensed that things would soon change.

Once more, the surroundings plunged into darkness, and I continued along the path. Suddenly, I found myself atop the roof of my apartment complex, next to a chopper. It was three years later. A group of Russians had barged into my place, seizing me by the neck, and ushered me upstairs. They were wearing a tactical military outfit that included a full-body uniform, typically utilized for special operations. The ensemble was primarily in a dark, black color. The uniform was equipped with various pockets and pouches for carrying essential gear and ammunition.

They were also wearing a ballistic helmet with a full-face visor, offering significant protection and anonymity. On their torso, they were outfitted with a bulletproof vest layered with additional storage compartments. The arms of the uniform had reinforced elbow pads, and the gloves seemed to be of a rugged design.

On the lower end, there was a utility belt tightly secured around the waist, which appeared to be holding additional equipment. The pants had carit hado pockets and were tucked into sturdy, combat-ready boots, suitable for various terrains. Knee pads were also visible, suggesting an emphasis on protection and mobility for potentially high-impact activities.

As I focused on the situation, I could recall it vividly, as if it happened yesterday.

"Alright, Mr. Hawthorne, jump on in; we need to get going as fast as possible," one of them said.

"What's this all about?" I asked.

"We're not at liberty to tell you anything. All you need to know is that you'll have to come with us immediately," another one stated firmly.

"Where are we going?" I inquired. "Antarctica," the man replied bluntly. "What? Why?" I pressed for answers.

"Like I said, it's not our job to provide you with any information. Just do as you're told, and everything will be fine," he insisted.

Feeling like I had no other choice, I reluctantly jumped into the helicopter. The others followed suit, and soon we were airborne. I watched as the chopper lifted off from the rooftop of the apartment building. And then, once more, everything faded away.

Once more, I traversed the subsequent violet path, arriving at a platform within an underground laboratory. There, I observed myself seated in a chair, poised to undergo an injection. The events beyond this juncture need no recounting, as I have previously detailed their unfolding.

Moving forward to the subsequent and concluding scene, I bore witness to a recent event etched in my memory. There, I beheld Aria, struck by a deadly shard, her life slipping away as I cradled her in my arms, her radiant smile slowly fading. "We did it, Ethan," were her final words as we shared one last kiss—a moment seared into my heart with unbearable sorrow. Surveying the desolate surroundings—a landscape of ancient ruins overrun by encroaching grass—I found myself consumed by overwhelming grief, leaving no space in my mind for anything else.

Unable to endure any further, I pressed on along my path until I reached a door. Upon opening it, a brilliant light enveloped me, drawing me back into the harsh reality from which I sought escape.

Standing atop the tower on the Whispering Plateau, I found myself clutching a shattered orb in both hands. Uncertain of its significance or the meaning behind my experiences, I couldn't shake the feeling of enlightenment coursing through me. It was as though I had undergone a therapeutic journey, reliving pivotal moments of my past. Descending the stairs, I felt a weight lifted from my shoulders, yet I couldn't discern what internal transformation had taken place within me.

I observed that a fierce storm raged outside, its powerful winds threatening to topple me, while the deluge of rain obscured my vision. Amidst the chaos, thunder roared and lightning crackled dangerously close. Knowing I needed refuge, I hastened downstairs in search of shelter.

As I scanned the surroundings, my gaze fell upon a descending path leading underground. Without hesitation, I ventured into the depths, where I discovered a labyrinth of caverns.

The entrance to these caverns was marked by intricately carved stone arches, half-hidden by overgrowth. Inside, the air was cool and still.

In these caverns, I felt the weight of ancient rites and the whispers of the long-departed envelop me as I traversed the underground tombs and chambers. These were the resting places of a civilization that had vanished into the mists of time, leaving behind only their honored dead.

The air around me was heavy, thick with the scent of earth and that indefinable fragrance of things long buried. The silence of the caverns was profound, disturbed only by the soft sound of my footsteps. I moved cautiously, the beam of my torch casting eerie shadows against the walls adorned with elaborate carvings and hieroglyphs. They told stories of life and death and of beliefs in a world beyond this one.

The caverns opened into larger burial chambers, where sarcophagi of stone rested in solemn rows. They were decorated with precious stones and the remnants of offerings, tokens of a journey beyond the mortal coil. I saw murals depicting the interred's achievements, alongside scenes that I presumed illustrated their conceptions of the afterlife.

I discovered that each chamber had its own tale, evident in the size and grandeur of the tombs and the complexity of the artwork. The grandest were surely meant for royalty or esteemed heroes, while the simpler ones belonged to common folk, their love and memories just as palpable.

I found artifacts—weapons, jewelry, and scrolls—placed as grave goods alongside the sarcophagi. These relics spoke of a belief in an afterlife where the dead would need such items. I tread lightly among these treasures, feeling a deep sense of respect and an unwelcome shiver of trepidation at the thought of disturbing the peace of the caverns.

The Burial Caverns were more than a silent repository of the past; they were a test of one's spirit. The omnipresent shadows seemed to watch, and the air itself felt charged with history. I couldn't shake the feeling that the spirits might not rest as peacefully as the art suggested.

As I meandered through the silence of the Burial Caverns, the air grew denser, and a chill clung to my spine. The torch in my hand sputtered, casting long, dancing shadows on the walls lined with silent watchers—statues of warriors long dead, their stone gazes fixed in an eternal vigil.

Without warning, the ground beneath me gave a treacherous tremble. Instinctively, I leapt back just as a section of the stone floor collapsed, revealing a gaping pit that promised a swift, brutal end. My heart pounded in my ears, the echo of the fall resonating through the hollows of the cavern.

With the path behind me now blocked, I pressed forward, only to trigger another, more sinister mechanism. A soft click reverberated off the walls, and suddenly, arrows whistled through the air from hidden alcoves, seeking my flesh with deadly precision. I darted and weaved, using the statues as shields, but the relentless volley followed my every step. It was a dance with death, orchestrated by the ancient protectors of the tomb.

Then came a grinding noise, and from the shadows emerged a figure cloaked not in flesh but in malice and armor—an automaton of the ancients, a guardian wrought from bronze and sorcery. Its single glowing eye fixed on me, and it advanced with a menacing purpose. The torchlight glinted off its polished surface, revealing intricate inscriptions that seemed to pulse with dark energy.

With nowhere to run, I readied my weapon, but the automaton proved a relentless adversary. Its limbs moved with a grace that belied its form, each blow it delivered ringing with the might of bygone wars. My shots seemed to merely graze its metallic hide, sparks showering with each impact but no sign of faltering in its stride.

A direct confrontation would be futile. Recalling the environment scanner built into my Tactical Multi-Tool, I activated it mid-duel, desperate for any advantage. The device hummed to life, and a holographic display painted the cavern with light, revealing structural weaknesses in the architecture and the automaton's arcane power source—a glowing core seated within its chest.

Seizing my chance, I feigned a direct attack to draw the guardian's strike, then rolled aside, targeting the exposed power core with a precise shot. The automaton staggered, its movements becoming erratic as I unleashed a barrage of energy bolts at the core, each one bringing a flash of disruption to its ancient systems.

Finally, with a resonant boom that echoed the hollow cries of the tomb, the automaton crumpled to the ground, its light extinguished. The cavern fell silent once more, save for the faint whispers of dust settling back to rest on the ancient stones.

I stood there, breathing heavily, the weight of the encounter pressing down on me. But in the stillness that followed, I felt a grim satisfaction. The traps and the guardian—mechanisms of a forgotten age—had tested me, and I had prevailed, my path forward clear but uncertain, leading ever deeper into the enigmatic heart of the Burial Caverns.

As the automaton lay silent, defeated by my hands, I allowed myself a brief moment of respite. The dormant construct was a sign of the lost artistry of its creators. Even in its stillness, it exuded a bygone power—a sentinel of a long-forgotten epoch.

I pressed on through the Burial Caverns, feeling a sense of solemnity as I moved through this repository of the dead. The dim glow of my torch cast shadows over the rows of sarcophagi, the interred occupants now mere memories carved in stone.

The silence was oppressive, a tangible presence that seemed to absorb the sound of my footsteps. I could feel the weight of countless generations watching me from the darkness. Each step took me deeper into the heart of the caverns, where the air grew thick with the smell of ancient stone and the whisper of secrets.

The path before me branched like the roots of a great tree, a sprawling network of passages that wormed their way into the earth. The carvings on the walls became more intricate, telling stories of valor and defeat, of lives lived fiercely and ending all too soon.

I continued cautiously, mindful of the traps that were likely hidden in the shadows. It was not long before my caution was rewarded—or punished. A series of stone slabs on the floor lay innocuously enough before me, but as I stepped upon one, it depressed slightly under my weight. A click echoed ominously through the cavern, the sound of a mechanism triggered after centuries of silence.

In an instant, darts tipped with ancient poison hissed through the air from hidden alcoves. I threw myself to the ground, rolling behind a sarcophagus for cover. The darts embedded themselves into the stone with lethal precision, leaving no doubt about their intended purpose. Cautiously, I surveyed the area, looking for patterns in the trap's design and any signs of safe passage.

My study revealed a path, marked subtly by the arrangement of tiles slightly different in color than the rest. With careful steps, I navigated the deadly mosaic, each movement a calculated risk. The traps seemed almost alive, hungry for the carelessness of intruders. But not for me—not today.

Beyond the gauntlet of traps lay a chamber, the central heart of the Burial Caverns. The ceiling here was vaulted, supported by columns entwined with carvings of vines and flowers, a tribute to life within a chamber of death. At the far end of the room, a grand sarcophagus stood, larger and more ornate than the rest. This was the resting place of someone of great importance, a leader or a hero whose name had been lost to time.

The sarcophagus bore no traps, only a silence that felt like a held breath. I approached, examining the cryptic symbols that adorned the lid, symbols that seemed to resonate with the ones I held in my memory. My hand traced the cold stone, and to my astonishment, the lid began to shift. A stairway opened beneath, leading down into darkness.

This was no ordinary burial site; it was a gateway, and I knew instinctively that this was the path I had been seeking. With a torch in hand, I descended the stairs, which spiraled down into the very bones of the earth.

Down, ever down, the stairway took me until it ended abruptly at a small, subterranean dock where a boat bobbed gently on an underground river. The water flowed quietly in the dark, leading away into a tunnel that bore the promise of an exit—an escape from the cavern's labyrinthine grasp.

I climbed aboard the vessel, pushing off from the dock with a sense of finality. The river carried me through the mountain's roots, an undulating serpent of water that knew the way out better than any map. Time became meaningless in the enveloping darkness, and eventually, I emerged from the cave's mouth into the light of a new dawn.

The river had delivered me to the other side of the mountain range, sparing me the journey back through the perilous caverns. As I looked back at the path I had traversed, I understood that the Burial Caverns were more than a tomb; they were a crucible, a test of one's mettle. I had emerged not just alive, but reborn with a newfound purpose.

With a deep breath, I turned away from the caverns and set my sights on the horizon, where my journey would continue.

I returned to my humble abode to seek solace and rest. As I reclined and surrendered to the embrace of sleep, I found myself abruptly awakened in the heart of night. The moon, resplendent amidst the celestial tapestry, cast its radiant glow upon the land, illuminating the glade with an ethereal radiance. The bioluminescent flora, alight with spectral hues, danced in the nocturnal breeze, casting enchanting shadows that cloaked the surroundings in a tranquil yet disquieting stillness.

Amidst this nocturnal symphony, the whispers, once faint, now beckoned with an urgent call, guiding me towards their elusive source. Following their elusive trail, I stumbled upon a vessel brimming with crystalline water, its presence seemingly tied to the enigmatic murmurs that surrounded it. Yet, as I grasped the jug, the whispers, capricious as the night itself, darted away to distant realms, leaving behind naught but a lingering echo.

Undeterred, I pursued the elusive whispers, each step a pilgrimage towards revelation. Eventually, I arrived at the precipice of the forest, where a majestic willow tree stood sentinel amidst the shadows. Its branches, reaching skyward, and roots, intertwined with the earth, bespoke an ancient wisdom that transcended mortal comprehension. Bathed in the moon's luminous embrace, the tree pulsed with a gentle energy, resonating with the primordial forces that governed the glade.

Though its presence seemed a manifestation of the moon's ethereal grace, the whispers persisted, their sibilant chorus a manifestation of the mysteries that lay concealed within the arboreal guardian. And as the night whispered its secrets to the wind, the willow tree, the sentinel of the shadows, swayed in silent communion, a harbinger of secrets untold.

Instinctively guiding my hand, I uncorked the jug and poured its contents upon the gnarled roots of the willow, the whispers fading into silence as if appeased by the offering. With a sense of reverence, I returned the vessel to its rightful place and beheld a wondrous sight: the earth beneath the ancient tree began to stir, parting like a veil to unveil a hidden passage.

Stepping forth upon this newfound path, I felt the dense foliage of the forest recede, replaced by the radiant splendor of the Luminous Glade, a realm bathed in an otherworldly luminescence. Amidst this surreal tableau, I chanced upon a monolithic stone, its surface adorned with inscriptions that spoke of arcane wisdom:

To approve thy worthiness and claim "The Singing Stone," thou must face the Trial of the Guardian Spirits. This trial shall assay thy courage, wisdom, and connection to the natural world around thee, demanding a demonstration of reverence and comprehension towards all forms of life. There be four steps to prove thyself:

The Path of Thorns: You shalt first journey the path of barbs that doth enshroud the glade. This perilous way, quickened with hidden powers, doth respond to the intents of the venturesome wanderer. Only by treading with reverence and mindfulness, embodying thy accord with the veiled domains of nature, canst thou unravel the elusive path through the tangled mystery without awakening its ancient slumber.

The Circle of Guardians: Upon entering the sanctified glade, thou shalt find thyself encircled by statues of spectral guardians, each embodying mysterious aspects of the natural order—tthe shadowed hunter for loyalty and lineage, the shrouded sage for enlightenment and concealed truths, the dormant colossus for resilience and sanctuary, and the spectral doe for serenity and intuition.

Thou must offer homage to each guardian, presenting not material tributes but echoes of past deeds or whispers of untold secrets shared with the sentinels of the unseen.

The Dance of Light and Shadow: The Dance of Shadows: As twilight cloaks the realm, the bioluminescent flora begin to pulsate with ethereal hues, beckoning thee to partake in a dance that mirrors the eternal interplay of light and darkness, creation and oblivion. By moving in symbiotic cadence with the enigmatic rhythms of the glade, thou must unveil thy cognizance that within the shadows lie hidden truths, and amidst the radiance reside profound mysteries, each essential for the equilibrium of existence.

The Whisper of the Stone: Having traversed the veiled veils of the earlier stages, thou shalt be drawn by an ethereal luminescence to the heart of the glade, where "The Whispering Stone" rests upon a pedestal of entwined branches. As thou drawest near, the stone shall stir, resonating with a melody that echoes the harmonies of the arcane realm. To claim the stone, thou must evoke a counter-point, a melody sung with a voice that echoes thy reverence for all that dwells within the veiled mysteries of creation.

As I ventured forth, I beheld a narrow passage leading to a vast chamber teeming with verdant life. Yet, these were no ordinary plants; they bristled with myriad thorns, presenting a formidable barrier that I must overcome.

Recalling the cryptic words of the initial riddle, I pondered: "Only by treading with reverence and mindfulness, embodying thy accord with the veiled domains of nature, canst thou unravel the elusive path through the tangled mystery without awakening its ancient slumber."

Realization dawned upon me; these thorns were not mere obstacles, but sentient beings attuned to the delicate balance of the glade. With the utmost care and deference, I approached the living maze, eschewing any notion of brute force or coercion. Instead, I observed the subtle ebb and flow of the breeze, discerning its gentle influence on the labyrinth.

Guided by the harmonious rhythm of nature, I discerned a pathway that yielded to my respectful demeanor, parting like a silent guardian to grant me safe passage. In this act of communion with the living essence of the glade, I affirmed my reverence for the natural world and earned my right to progress further along the enigmatic journey.

Pressing onward, I arrived at the fabled "Circle of Guardians," a place shrouded in mystery and veiled in enigma. This riddle posed a formidable challenge, its meaning eluding my grasp like elusive shadows slipping through eager fingers.

"The shadowed hunter for loyalty and lineage," I mused, grappling with the cryptic words that cloaked the true intent of the message. At first, my mind conjured images of a human hunter lurking in dim forests, bound by ancestral ties and steadfast loyalty. Yet, as clarity dawned upon me, I discerned the deeper significance hidden within the riddle's embrace.

The shadowed hunter was none other than the elusive wolf, a symbol of unwavering loyalty and ancestral lineage. Casting my gaze upon the statues encircling me, I beheld the silent sentinels embodying the essence of nature's guardians: the wolf, the owl, the bear, and the deer.

Recalling the guiding words etched upon the stone, I understood my task: "Thou must offer homage to each guardian, presenting not material tributes but echoes of past deeds or whispers of untold secrets shared with the sentinels of the unseen." With newfound clarity, I embarked upon the solemn duty that lay before me, ready to unveil the hidden truths and forge a bond with the ethereal guardians that watched over the realm of secrets untold.

Before the stoic wolf statue, I bowed in reverence, my hand pressed solemnly against my chest. I recounted a tale of tempestuous trials and of venturing through raging storms to procure medicine for an ailing comrade, showcasing my unwavering loyalty and the depths of my devotion to my kin.

Turning my gaze to the next guardian, veiled in the cloak of wisdom and veiled truths, I recognized the sage concealed within the guise of an owl. Standing in silent contemplation before the watchful owl statue, I closed my eyes, allowing the stillness of the moment to envelop me. With a deep breath, I delved into the depths of memory, recalling a night spent beneath the vast expanse of the starlit sky. In the hushed embrace of nature's secrets, I learned the profound lessons of silence, discovering the inherent wisdom that resides within the unspoken truths of the universe.

The third guardian stood as a dormant colossus, symbolizing resilience and sanctuary—the bear. With unwavering resolve, I approached the towering bear statue, channeling its strength within me. I recounted a moment of fierce protection, where I stood steadfast against bullies to shield a younger sibling.

Through courage and a resolute spirit, I embodied the bear's essence, demonstrating that true defense arises from the depths of the heart.

As for the final guardian, there was no hesitation, for only one remained—the spectral doe, embodying serenity and intuition. Before the gentle deer statue, I extended my hand with care, stopping just shy of touching the ethereal form, mindful of its presence. I shared a memory of nurturing an injured bird, guided by an intuitive understanding of its needs, until it could soar once more. My actions mirrored the doe's grace and intuitive compassion, an expression of life's delicate yet resilient nature.

Upon completing the previous trial, a new doorway unveiled itself, beckoning me forward to face the next challenge: "The Dance of Light and Shadow." Here, I was tasked with partaking in a dance that mirrored the perpetual dance of light and darkness, creation and oblivion.

Observing the bioluminescent flora, I discerned a pattern in their pulsing—not haphazard, but in harmony with the moon's glow and the shadows cast by the surrounding trees. With deliberate movements, I began to sway, syncing my steps to the rhythmic interplay of light and shadow. In this dance, I embraced both elements as integral facets of existence. My movements embodied the delicate balance between joy and sorrow, life and death, demonstrating my profound understanding of the interconnectedness of all things. Through this harmonious expression, I sought to convey to the guardian spirits my wisdom and equilibrium.

Another portal unveiled itself, and with haste, I made my way towards it, driven by the anticipation of reaching my ultimate objective: the Singing Stone. There it stood, resting atop a pedestal entwined with branches, poised in the center of a tranquil pool. As I drew near, the water in the pool shimmered, emitting a luminous glow that echoed a melody resonant with the harmony of nature.

Recalling the enigmatic riddle, "To claim the stone, thou must evoke a counterpoint, a melody sung with a voice that echoes thy reverence for all that dwells within the veiled mysteries of creation," I knew what was required of me.

Standing before the reflective pool, I began to hum a melody that encapsulated the essence of my journey—the trials endured, the wisdom gained, and the unity forged with the natural world. My song, sincere and earnest, reverberated through the Luminous Glade, its echoes intertwining with the very fabric of existence.

As my melody filled the air, the surface of the pool began to radiate with newfound brilliance, and from its depths emerged the Singing Stone, its own ethereal tune blending seamlessly with mine.

In that moment, as the stone offered itself to me, I knew that I had proven myself worthy, attuned to the intricate harmonies of creation.

And so it came to pass that I finally held within my grasp that which I had sought for so long—the mythical Singing Stone. But what significance did it hold? As I pondered, the stone's radiance intensified, enveloping the glade in a gentle, harmonious glow.

Sensing the completion of my trial and my deepened connection with the natural world, the Guardian Willow facilitated my swift return.

Before I knew it, I stood once more at the spot where the Guardian Willow had stood, yet it was no longer there. I glanced at the sky and realized that the sun now hung high above, marking the passage of time. Though my sojourn within the Glade seemed to last a few hours, I must have been absent longer than I had perceived.

Contemplating the meaning behind the stone's melodic resonance, I recalled the TMT device. Utilizing it to capture the stone's song, I watched as a pattern emerged on the screen.

Eventually, the TMT succeeded in deciphering the recurring notes and sounds, translating them into a coherent message: "Ʊndər ðə watʃ ov ðə ɛvərgrin gardiənz, hwær ðə lænd kısız ðə si, sik ðə wıspərz ov hıstəri æt ðə pɔınt hwær ɛkoʊz ov lıbərtiz pramıs ænd ðə sɛntınəlz saılənt vıjıl kənvərdʒ, ðær ðə ki weıts, ʃrəʊdıd ın ðə mısts ov taım."[1]

It was a clue—another piece of the puzzle leading to the Nexus Vault. The connection between the stone and the location became apparent, or perhaps someone had manipulated the melody to convey the hint. With this new revelation, I now possess five clues in total. Would this be sufficient to unlock its true significance? I realized that I needed assistance in deciphering its meaning and resolved to seek out someone knowledgeable on the matter.

Understanding the stone's significance and the potential attention its powers could attract, I decided to create a secure and fitting place for it. Drawing on the lessons learned in the Luminous Glade, I chose a location that resonated with natural harmony and was shielded from those who might seek to misuse the stone's abilities.

From what I had learned, I knew that I now had the ability to connect to the natural world in this place and communicate with the animals, plants, and environment. So I called upon nature, and I enlisted the help of the local wildlife, asking them to watch over the sanctuary and alert him to any disturbances.

"As I settled the Singing Stone within its new sanctuary, surrounded by the guardians of the wild that I had called to its defense, I couldn't help but feel a shift within me. The trials of the Luminous Glade, the echoes of my past it conjured, and the melody of the stone had woven a complex tapestry that seemed to stretch beyond the confines of my own story. With every beat of the stone's song, I felt more connected to the world around me, more attuned to its whispers and secrets.

The message encrypted within the melody was a beacon, guiding me toward an unseen horizon. The Nexus Vault, a term that once held no meaning, now pulsed with the promise of untold revelations. Yet, the path to deciphering its secrets remained shrouded in mystery, a puzzle that demanded not just the wisdom of one but the shared knowledge of many. The realization that I needed help and that my journey was not meant to be a solitary quest was both humbling and invigorating.

As the first light of dawn crept across the sky, painting the world in hues of hope and renewal, I knew that the road ahead was fraught with uncertainty. Yet, the Singing Stone, with its enigmatic message and the power it represented, had ignited a flame of determination within me. I was ready to face whatever lay ahead, armed with the lessons of the past and the promise of the future.

And so, with the sanctuary secured and the stone's song echoing in my heart, I set out at dawn's light. The Nexus Vault called, its secrets beckoning from beyond the veil of the known. The journey ahead was unclear, but my resolve was steadfast. I was not just a seeker of truths hidden in the shadows of history; I was a guardian of a legacy that bridged worlds and times. With the Singing Stone as my guide, I stepped into the day, ready to uncover the mysteries that awaited, knowing that each step taken was a step closer to understanding the essence of existence itself.

I also established a simple, yet powerful, ritual that must be performed to open the sanctuary and awaken the stone's song. This ritual involved a sequence of natural offerings and melodies, ensuring that only I, or someone with a true understanding of harmony and nature, could access the stone.

[1] "Under the watch of the evergreen guardians, where the land kisses the sea, seek the whispers of history at the point where echoes of liberty's promise and the sentinels' silent vigil converge; there the key waits, shrouded in the mists of time."

PATHS WOVEN IN STARLIGHT

I consulted my OmniLocator in hopes of uncovering any noteworthy locations in the vicinity. The OmniLocator, a compact device engineered from the remnants of pre-war technologies, combined satellite mapping and ancient digital archives, offering a beacon of guidance in a world where the old pathways had been obscured by time and neglect.

Although my current whereabouts weren't mapped, the device allowed me to approximate my position. Among the listings, one entry caught my eye: "The Adventurer's Guild." It seemed like an auspicious starting point for my quest, where I could potentially find someone adept at deciphering the clues I possessed.

With a rough sense of direction in mind, I mounted my trusty Charger, knowing it would be a day's ride to reach my destination. As I set out, the Charger's hum became a comforting constant, its seamless navigation through changing landscapes a tribute to the marvels of the old world. The journey ahead promised not only the pursuit of the Nexus Vault but a deeper exploration into the remnants of a past civilization and, perhaps, a better understanding of Aria's legacy within this world.

With determination fueling my journey, I set off on the path ahead, eager to unravel the mysteries that awaited me at the Adventurer's Guild. Each turn of the Charger's wheels carried me further from the life I had known, propelling me into a world teeming with the unknown. With each passing mile, I shed the remnants of my past, drawn ever onward by the whispers of destiny and the shadow of a promise made beneath starlit skies.

As I embarked on my journey towards the Adventurer's Guild aboard the Alloyed Charger, I found myself traversing through a myriad of landscapes, each presenting its own unique challenges and captivating wonders.

Setting out from the edge of the known world, I pedaled through dense forests alive with the chorus of wildlife, their calls echoing through the canopy overhead. The Alloyed Charger glided smoothly along the winding paths, its alloy frame absorbing the uneven terrain beneath me as I ventured deeper into the wilderness.

As the day unfolded, the scenery transitioned from verdant woodlands to expansive meadows adorned with vibrant wildflowers swaying in the gentle breeze. With each pedal stroke, I felt a sense of exhilaration and freedom, surrounded by the beauty of nature unfolding before me. For a moment, I allowed myself to imagine Aria beside me, her eyes alight with the joy of discovery, finding beauty in these wild expanses. 'She would have loved this,' I whispered to the breeze, letting my heart hold onto the memory of her smile.

Each mile traversed was a mile further from where Aria and I had dreamed together, yet closer to fulfilling a promise made in her memory. The thought of her smile, a beacon in my darkest moments, spurred me on, imbuing my quest with a purpose that transcended the mere discovery of ancient vaults.

As the sun began its descent towards the horizon, casting long shadows across the landscape, I found myself traversing rocky trails that led through rugged terrain. The Alloyed Charger's robust tires gripped the uneven ground with ease, propelling me forward with determination as I navigated the challenging landscape.

With dusk approaching, I pedaled on, guided by the soft glow of distant lanterns that marked the path ahead. The air was filled with the scent of pine and earth, mingling with the sounds of nocturnal creatures stirring from their daytime slumber.

As night fell and the stars emerged in the velvety sky above, the Adventurer's Guild came into view on the horizon, its sprawling silhouette illuminated against the darkness. With a sense of anticipation and excitement, I quickened my pace, eager to reach my destination.

In a world slowly piecing itself back together, the Adventurer's Guild stood as a symbol of human resilience, a fortress against the oblivion that had once threatened to consume us all. It was here, among the remnants of civilization, that adventurers and seekers of truth congregated, drawn by the lure of discovery and the bonds of shared purpose.

The Adventurer's Guild stands as a grand edifice amidst the surrounding landscape, its imposing structure commanding attention from afar. Rising tall and proud, it resembles a fortress from a bygone era, with sturdy stone walls encircling its vast expanse.

At the heart of the guild is a central courtyard, bustling with activity as adventurers from far and wide converge upon its hallowed grounds. The courtyard is lined with towering pillars adorned with intricate carvings depicting legendary heroes and mythical creatures, their tales woven into the very fabric of the guild's history.

Surrounding the courtyard are numerous wings and annexes, each dedicated to a different aspect of the adventurer's life. There are training grounds where aspiring adventurers hone their skills under the watchful eye of seasoned mentors and workshops where craftsmen ply their trade, forging weapons and armor fit for the most daring quests.

Tall spires rise from the guild's roofline, their peaks reaching towards the heavens as if reaching for the stars themselves. These spires serve as beacons for weary travelers seeking refuge and camaraderie within the guild's walls, their warm glow casting a welcoming light across the surrounding landscape.

The Adventurer's Guild is more than just a place of rest and respite; it is a bustling hub of activity, a melting pot of cultures and backgrounds united by a common purpose. Here, adventurers gather to share tales of their exploits, forge alliances, and embark on epic quests that will leave their mark on the annals of history.

I roamed through the crowd, observing the assortment of travelers and adventurers, hoping to chance upon someone with a hint of wisdom or knowledge. Eventually, I succumbed to the need to inquire and approached a random individual.

"Excuse me, may I have a moment of your time?" I asked politely.

"Certainly, what can I do for you?" the man replied. "I've been searching for someone who might be able to assist me in deciphering some textual clues. Do you happen to know anyone who fits the bill?" I inquired.

"Well, you might want to head inside and ask around.

There's an older fellow in there. I can't say for sure if he'll be of any help, but it's worth a shot," he suggested.

Grateful for the guidance, I thanked him and made my way into what appeared to be a tavern. Inside the tavern, the air buzzed with tales of distant lands and echoes of battles fought. It was here, amidst adventurers and scholars, that I hoped to find a piece of the puzzle that had eluded me. Each face in the crowd held a story—a potential key to the vault that called me forward.

Inside, the atmosphere was lively, with a large bar at the center, surrounded by small chairs. The walls were adorned with

paintings and various decorations, including animal trophies. Round tables with chairs scattered around occupied the rest of the space. A distinct aroma of alcoholic beverages mixed with the scent of aging wood permeated the air.

Among the patrons, I spotted an older man seated at the counter, sipping from a pint glass filled with a mysterious blue liquid. Bald with a long, pointed white beard, he sported sunglasses and a simple yellow shirt adorned with flowers, shorts, and sandals.

Despite his unconventional appearance, I felt compelled to approach him. However, before I could initiate a conversation, the bartender approached me.

What'll it be?" The bartender inquired.

"I'll have the same as him," I replied, nodding toward the older gentleman.

"With what are you paying?" the bartender questioned.

I reached into my bag, fumbling around until I retrieved a small emerald.

"Will this suffice?" I asked.

"With that, you can buy about twenty drinks of your choice," he informed me.

"Excellent, can I have my drink now?" I requested. "Certainly, one Blueberry Breeze coming right up!" he announced.

As I took a sip, the concoction of honey, blueberries, and alcohol danced on my palate, leaving a delightful sensation behind.

The drink, a surprising blend of sweetness and warmth, seemed to momentarily lift the weight of solitude from my shoulders. It was a reminder of the simple pleasures to be found, even on a journey fraught with unknown dangers and solitary quests.

Turning to the older man, I broached the topic I had been pondering.

"I was wondering if you could help me." I began. "What do you need?" he inquired.

"I have several lines of text that seem to point to a specific and important location. I need someone who can decipher their meaning," I explained.

"I'm afraid that's not my area of expertise, but I know someone who might be able to assist you," he responded.

"Who might that be?" I pressed.

"They call him the Cartographer. If anyone can unravel those clues, it's him." His eyes flickered with recognition and a glint of familiarity. "You're the Ethan that's been the talk of the far lands, aren't you?" he mused, his question weaving my reputation into the fabric of this journey he revealed.

"Well, where can I find this Cartographer?" I inquired eagerly.

"I'm not entirely sure," he admitted.

"You have no idea? Can't you at least point me in the right direction?" I persisted.

"I've heard he's a bit of a hermit, living off the grid. But perhaps someone else in town might know more," he suggested.

"The Cartographer?" The bartender interjected suddenly. "I know someone who's well-versed in such matters."

"Who? And where can I find him?" I inquired.

"I'm not entirely sure. I think he resides nearby, but I can't say for certain. His name is Will Duke. He's made a few appearances here, but I wouldn't count on him returning anytime soon," the bartender responded.

"Alright, I understand. It seems I'll have to find another way," I conceded.

Pausing at the threshold, I took a deep breath, the air thick with anticipation and the scent of adventure. This tavern, with its stories and secrets, was but a waypoint. Ahead lay the true test of my resolve. "For Aria," I murmured, stepping into the twilight, my heart set on the enigma of the Nexus Vault. I finished my drink before departing from the bar.

As I made my way out, a thought struck me, and I remembered my TMT. Although I had lost my last radio device, the TMT was equipped to pick up and transmit radio signals. I configured it to transmit and attempted to reach out to my old friends at Misty Hollow.

waves.

"Hello, is anyone there?" I called out through the radio "Yes, this is Enzo. Who's this?" came the response. "It's Ethan," I replied.

"Ethan! It's a pleasant surprise to hear from you. Would you like me to fetch Elena?" Enzo offered.

"Well, unless you happen to know anything about a Will Duke or a man called The Cartographer, then yes, please," I answered.

"Alright, I'll go fetch her for you," Enzo agreed before the radio fell silent once more.

The radio fell silent for a moment, then a familiar voice echoed through the static: "Ethan, is that really you? We haven't heard from you in ages. How have you been?" Elena's voice filled the airwaves.

"Well, things could be better at the moment, but I'm hanging in there," I replied.

"At least you're alive," Elena remarked with a hint of relief. "I'm curious, Elena, how are things on your end? Has the plan worked out as expected? Are your communities cooperating smoothly?" I inquired.

"Absolutely, it's like we've become one cohesive community now," Elena responded. "The checkpoints have transformed into thriving hubs of activity, just as you predicted. Trade has flourished, and we sailed through the winter without a hitch, all thanks to these changes. The former bandits from

Pinecrest have even established their own village and have become integral members of our society. Many of them now serve as security and defenders for our outposts."

"That's fantastic news. I always had faith in you all," I said warmly.

"So, what prompted this call?" Elena asked, curiosity evident in her tone.

"I've been searching for someone knowledgeable in cartography. I need to have certain clues examined that point to a specific location. Does the name Will Duke ring any bells? Or perhaps you've heard of a man who goes by the name of The Cartographer?" I inquired.

"Not personally, but let me reach out to the other members of the council. One of them might have some information," Elena replied.

"Thanks," I said, waiting patiently as the radio fell silent once more. After what felt like an eternity, a response finally came through.

"There were no leads on The Cartographer, but John mentioned a man named Will Duke. Apparently, he's an old friend of his," Elena relayed.

"And do you have any idea where I can find him?" I asked eagerly.

"Reportedly, he resides in a modest cottage on the outskirts of a town called Fairhaven, nestled in the countryside," Elena informed me.

further.

"Do you happen to know the way to Fairhaven?" I inquired

"Yes, John provided some directions," Elena confirmed, guiding me through the path to the town, which fortunately wasn't too far from the Adventurer's Guild. With this newfound information, I made up my mind to head there without delay.

As I rode towards the village of Fairhaven, the sun dipped low on the horizon, its golden rays painting the sky in hues of crimson and gold, a breathtaking backdrop to my journey. The road stretched out before me, a ribbon of earth winding its way through the picturesque countryside, bordered by fields of swaying grass and dense patches of woodland that whispered secrets to the passing breeze.

With each turn of the pedals, I drew closer to my destination, the allure of progress and discovery propelling me forward. Yet, just as the village of Fairhaven came into view on the horizon, an unexpected obstacle loomed before me, threatening to derail my progress: a gaping chasm, carved deep into the earth, severed the path in two.

The broken remains of a once-sturdy bridge spanned the divide, its fractured timbers serving as a stark reminder of the forces of nature that had torn it apart. I paused at the edge of the chasm, surveying the treacherous gap with a furrowed brow, my mind racing with thoughts of how to proceed.

But I was not one to be easily deterred. With a determined glint in my eye, I set about devising a plan to overcome this unexpected hurdle. While searching the surrounding landscape, my gaze fell upon a fallen tree, its gnarled branches reaching out like the fingers of an old friend.

With a strength born of necessity, I hoisted the fallen trunk onto my shoulders, the weight of it pressing into my muscles as I carried it towards the edge of the chasm. Sweat beaded on my brow as I worked, the rhythmic thud of my footsteps echoing in the stillness of the evening.

At last, I reached the edge of the gap, my heart pounding in my chest as I carefully positioned the tree across the divide, its sturdy form bridging the chasm like a lifeline to the other side. With a sense of satisfaction, I tested the makeshift bridge, my breath catching in my throat as it held firm beneath my weight.

With a final glance back at the village of Fairhaven, now tantalizingly close on the horizon, I took a deep breath and stepped onto the makeshift bridge, my resolve unwavering as I forged ahead towards my destination, ready to face whatever challenges lay in wait on the other side.

The village of Fairhaven held a captivating allure as I approached. From afar, my gaze fell upon a sizable section of the town enclosed by sturdy wooden logs, hinting at a protective perimeter. Dominating the skyline was a towering structure, its stature surpassing that of any other building in the vicinity.

Though the houses within the walled area were visible, their interiors remained out of reach due to the formidable barrier. Despite this, the village exuded charm, with houses seamlessly integrated with vibrant flower gardens that added to its picturesque allure.

Even at a distance, the rhythmic clang of a blacksmith's hammer echoed through the air, a reflection of the village's industrious spirit.

Beyond the protective enclosure sprawled a landscape dotted with villages and farms, where the diligent efforts of the inhabitants were evident in their agricultural pursuits. People could be seen tending to livestock, working the fields, and nurturing lush gardens, while taverns and inns offered respite both within and beyond the protective walls.

Navigating the terrain proved uncomplicated, as the open expanse outside the walls allowed for easy traversal. With no knowledge of Will Duke's whereabouts, I embarked on a quest for information, seeking out locals for guidance. After querying several individuals, one gestured toward a residence near the perimeter. With determination, I made my way to the indicated location and rapped on the door, anticipation coursing through my veins.

The door creaked open, revealing a peculiar figure with a cap askew atop his head. Clad in a checkered shirt and sturdy overalls, his presence exuded a sense of rustic charm.

"How can I assist you?" he inquired, his voice tinged with curiosity.

"I'm in search of a man known as The Cartographer, and I've been told you might be able to point me in the right direction," I explained.

"Aye, The Cartographer," he mused, his gaze wandering into the distance. "He's a solitary soul, dwelling in his remote cabin deep within the woods, far from the bustle of civilization."

"And which woods might that be?" I pressed.

He gestured behind us, towards a dense expanse of trees shrouded in darkness. "Right yonder."

Indeed, looming before us was a sprawling forest, its tangled canopy obscuring any glimpse of what lay within.

"How deep into the forest does he reside?" I inquired. "Quite a ways," Will replied cryptically.

"But how do we locate him, then?" I pressed for more details.

"Press on straight ahead, I reckon. That's all I can offer," Will replied with a shrug.

"Thank you for your assistance," I replied, realizing I could employ the TMT to scan the area for The Cartographer's abode.

As I ventured into the depths of the forest, darkness enveloped me like a heavy cloak. Armed with both my TMT and flashlight, I cast their beams into the impenetrable gloom, hoping to pierce through the obscurity. Despite the TMT's extensive range, its signals failed to yield any trace of the Cartographer's cabin. I wandered aimlessly, my footsteps echoing in the silent expanse of the woods.

As I ventured deeper into the forest, the trees closed in around me, their branches intertwining like twisted fingers in a macabre dance. The dense canopy above blocked out the sunlight, plunging the forest floor into an oppressive darkness. Every step forward felt like a struggle against the suffocating embrace of the trees.

In this pitch-black labyrinth, every sound seemed amplified, echoing through the gnarled branches and tangled undergrowth. The rustling of leaves became whispers of unseen threats, and the creaking of branches sounded like the ominous warnings of an ancient guardian.

As I pressed on, the air grew thick with a palpable sense of dread. Shadows danced at the edge of my vision, and I could feel unseen eyes watching my every move. It was as if the very forest itself was alive, its malevolent presence palpable in the oppressive darkness.

Abruptly, the TMT sprang to life with a soft hum, its sensors scanning the surroundings for any hints of unusual activity or concealed threats. To my astonishment, the device registered a mysterious presence nearby, its readings suggesting the existence of an unidentified figure concealed within the shadows.

Suddenly, I stumbled upon a clearing, and in its center stood a solitary figure cloaked in shadow. His presence filled me with a sense of unease, but as he stepped forward, his features became clearer, and I realized that he was not an adversary to be feared but rather a mysterious presence in this forsaken place.

His eyes gleamed with an enigmatic intensity, and I could sense a depth of knowledge and experience in his gaze. He spoke in a voice tinged with mystery, offering cryptic words of wisdom and guidance that only deepened the intrigue surrounding him.

At that moment, I realized that the figure in the cloak was not a foe or a friend, but a mystery waiting to be unraveled. He was an enigmatic stranger in the heart of the forest, his true identity shrouded in secrecy amidst the darkness.

"Who are you?" I asked, my voice tinged with uncertainty and a hint of fear.

"Weren't you looking for me?" he responded. "The Cartographer!" I exclaimed, recognizing him.

"That I am, and you are Ethan. I've heard of you and your travels, Champion of Concord," he acknowledged.

"I was hoping you could help me investigate some clues I found," I explained.

In his eyes, I saw a glimmer of curiosity, the kind born of countless hours of poring over maps and ancient texts. It was clear he was no stranger to the mysteries of this world, perhaps even those that lay beyond.

"Certainly, follow me to my house," he invited.

As we traversed through the dense forest, I couldn't help but inquire, "How do you find your way in this place?"

"I have my ways," he replied mysteriously.

Finally arriving at his abode, I observed a cluttered desk adorned with various papers, walls lined with shelves brimming with books and ChronoArchives, a crackling fireplace nestled at the back, and a large rug draped over the floor. Positioned in the center was a sturdy table, upon which lay an assortment of trinkets, scrolls, and tools. We stood on opposite sides of the table, facing each other.

"Now tell me, what are the clues you seek to answer?" he prompted.

"I am seeking a place called the Nexus Vault. The clues I have point me in that direction, but I don't understand their meaning," I confessed.

"Show me the clues," he instructed.

Gathering all the clues into a single ChronoArchive, I displayed the various texts on its screen.

He was able to explain the meaning behind each of the texts.

The first clue was: "Venture to the forgotten ruins where shadows linger, and there, beneath the ancient tree's embrace, seek the key to unlock the gateway to eternity."

"This clue suggests a location that is historically significant yet abandoned and features a notable tree. The "ancient tree's embrace" could symbolize a singular, well-known tree or a natural landmark known for its old growth," he said.

He then read the second clue: "Climb the highest peak where the sky touches the earth, and there, amidst the swirling winds, the path to the Nexus Vault shall be revealed."

"This likely refers to reaching the summit of a location. The 'highest peak' could metaphorically refer to the top of something, which offers a vantage point where the 'sky touches the earth.' The mention of 'swirling winds' may indicate the windy conditions often experienced at the top. Therefore, the clue suggests that by ascending to the top, the path to the Nexus Vault will become evident or revealed," he said.

Next, he read the third clue: "Follow the river's winding path until it converges with the ancient tree, where shadows dance in the moonlight, revealing the entrance key."

"This indicates a mountain or a high elevation point 'where the sky touches the earth.' The "swirling winds" highlight its exposed, possibly lofty nature. This clue points towards a natural viewpoint or landmark known for its height and perhaps its challenging climate or atmosphere," he explained.

Clue four was: "Beneath the gaze of Liberty's western sister, where the silent sentinel once stood guard over Puget's azure depths, lies the key, nestled between the roots of the world reborn."

"Liberty's western sister" refers to a replica or a monument related to the Statue of Liberty, suggesting a location that has a lesser-known connection to this iconic symbol, perhaps a park or public space with a view of such a statue.

The "silent sentinel" could hint at a military fort or observation post that historically served as a lookout over Puget Sound, a body of water adjacent to Seattle. This place, once bustling with activity, now stands quiet, perhaps abandoned or transformed by nature.

The 'key' being 'nestled between the roots of the world reborn' suggests that the entrance or clue to finding the Nexus Vault is hidden in a natural setting, possibly in an area that has undergone significant natural growth or ecological recovery, blending the remnants of human history with the resilience of nature.

Together, the message implies that to find the Nexus Vault, one must look near a location in Seattle that offers a view of a Statue of Liberty replica, near an area with historical military significance, where nature has overtaken a place once marked by human vigilance." He concluded.

Then the final clue: "Under the watch of the evergreen guardians, where the land kisses the sea, seek the whispers of history at the point where echoes of liberty's promise and the sentinels' silent vigil converge; there the key waits, shrouded in the mists of time."

"This clue points to a location where several key elements intersect, suggesting a place of natural beauty and historical significance near the water, specifically within or near Seattle, considering the previous clues.

'Under the watch of the evergreen guardians' suggests a location surrounded by lush, evergreen trees, indicative of the Pacific Northwest's iconic landscapes.

'Where the land kisses the sea' identifies a coastal area or a point where landform meets the water, likely along the shores of Puget Sound or a similar body of water in the region.

'Seek the whispers of history at the point where echoes of liberty's promise and the sentinels' silent vigil converge' hints at a place of historical importance, potentially related to the concept of freedom or guarded by historical 'sentinels,' which could be interpreted as military forts or historical markers. The mention of 'liberty's promise' could further narrow it down to a location with a monument or marker symbolizing freedom or the Statue of Liberty replica, aligning with previous clues.

'There the key waits, shrouded in the mists of time.' This part of the clue reinforces the idea that the sought-after Nexus Vault or its key is hidden in this historically and culturally significant place, waiting to be uncovered by those who can interpret the signs." The Cartographer noted.

He then concluded: "Considering the elements together, this clue likely directs the seeker to a specific, scenic location along the coastline near Seattle, possibly at or near Discovery Park, where historical military sites like the West Point Lighthouse exist and evergreen landscapes meet the sea. This area, known for its natural beauty and historical depth, would align with the themes of liberty, guardianship, and the convergence of natural and historical elements mentioned in the clue."

"So you're saying the location is at West Point Lighthouse within Discovery Park?" I inquired, seeking confirmation.

"Exactly!" The Cartographer affirmed with a nod.

"So that's the solution; that's what I've been looking for all this time; for so long, I've finally found it!" I exclaimed, feeling a surge of elation.

"Indeed, you've done a great job collecting these clues," The Cartographer commended.

"Now tell me how to get out of here; I have business to attend to," I requested, eager to move forward.

"I'll guide your way," The Cartographer assured me.

With the Cartographer's words echoing in my mind, I stepped out of the shadowy embrace of the forest, feeling the cool evening air against my skin. For a moment, I paused, allowing myself to absorb the profound journey that had led me here. It wasn't just the physical distance I had traversed, but the emotional and spiritual journey that had shaped me along the way. From the heartache of loss to the resilience found in pursuit of a promise, each step had been a testament to the strength I had gathered, inspired by Aria's memory and fueled by the mysteries of the Nexus Vault. Now, as I prepared to mount my Alloyed Charger once more, it wasn't just the anticipation of uncovering ancient secrets that drove me forward, but a deeper quest for understanding—of the world, of Aria's legacy, and of my own place within this vast tapestry of life. With a renewed sense of purpose, I knew that whatever awaited me at the lighthouse would be another chapter in a journey that was far from over.

With his guidance, I navigated out of the dense forest, my mind already racing ahead to the next steps. As soon as I reached my Alloyed Charger, I wasted no time in speeding towards the lighthouse.

The path to the lighthouse, illuminated by the setting sun, stretched before me like a ribbon of destiny. This was not just a journey across land, but a voyage through the layers of history and the very essence of human endeavor. With the wind at my back and Aria's spirit in my heart, I rode towards the culmination of my quest, where the past would meet the present in the shadow of the Nexus Vault.

As the forest gave way to open skies, I couldn't help but feel a sense of departure, not just from the woods but from an old part of myself. Each step towards the Nexus Vault was a step into the unknown, a challenge to the limits of my courage and determination.

THE NEXUS VAULT

After a considerable ride, I reached West Point Lighthouse. Surprisingly, the structure stood largely undamaged, as though someone had diligently cared for it in the aftermath of the war. Despite the passage of time, the building remained whole, though adorned with cracks and the lush growth of moss and vines.

The area that had surrounded the lighthouse was a verdant, tranquil landscape, showing signs of serene abandonment.

Overgrown grass and wild shrubbery had blanketed the ground, revealing a once-tended path now reclaimed by nature. A series of old, weathered wooden steps, hinting at previous foot traffic, had led towards the lighthouse.

The vegetation was lush, with the greenery swaying gently in the sea breeze, interspersed with wildflowers that had added splashes of color.

On either side of the path, derelict and moss-covered wooden beams and broken-down fences peppered the landscape, remnants of what might have been a bustling area or a structured approach to the lighthouse. Sparse trees had dotted the area, their trunks standing tall against the sky, and some branches had reached out over the scene as silent observers of time's passage.

The sea had loomed in the background, its vast expanse meeting the horizon, while above, a dynamic sky had hosted clouds that ranged from the fluffy and white to the heavy and storm-laden. The light from the setting or rising sun had bathed the scene in a warm, ethereal glow, casting soft shadows and creating a tranquil, almost otherworldly atmosphere. Birds could have been seen in the distance, contributing to the sense of peaceful isolation as they traversed the open skies. The overall impression had been one of serene desolation and the enduring beauty of nature.

I pushed open the weather-beaten door and stepped into the lighthouse, greeted by a surprisingly well-preserved interior.

Inside the lighthouse, the atmosphere was one of quiet grandeur and historical resonance. The interior exuded an air of nostalgia and adventure, with weathered wooden beams and aged stone walls bearing the marks of time. As you stepped inside, you were greeted by the faint scent of saltwater lingering in the air and the gentle creaking of the floorboards beneath your feet.

The main chamber boasted tall ceilings adorned with intricate designs, while large windows allowed sunlight to filter in, casting soft beams of light across the space. Antique furniture and artifacts lined the walls, telling stories of seafaring adventures and maritime history.

A spiral staircase led to higher levels, offering panoramic views of the surrounding landscape and the vast expanse of the sea beyond. Overall, the interior of West Point Lighthouse Discovery Park was a captivating blend of rustic charm and coastal elegance, inviting visitors to explore its rich heritage and timeless beauty.

Near the stairs leading to the lighthouse's summit, I spotted a weathered yet oddly futuristic keypad. Its presence contrasted sharply with the antiquity of the surrounding structure, hinting at a different era altogether. However, my focus lay on reaching the pinnacle of the lighthouse, so I ascended the stairs without dwelling further on the keypad's curious appearance.

From the top of the lighthouse, I was treated to a breathtaking panoramic view of the surrounding landscape. To the east, the cityscape of Seattle stretched out, with its iconic skyline punctuating the horizon. To the west was the vast expanse of Puget Sound, shimmering in the sunlight, once dotted with sailboats and ferries traversing its waters. To the north and south, dense forests and greenery extended as far as the eye could see, blending into the distant horizon. The view from this vantage point offered a stunning blend of natural beauty, making it a memorable experience for any visitor.

In the center of the lighthouse's summit, a pedestal caught my eye, adorned with a solid stone bearing unfamiliar symbols.

Curious, I turned to my TMT, hoping it could decipher their meaning. The scan yielded a series of numbers, resembling a code of sorts. Suddenly, it clicked—I recalled the keypad downstairs and realized this must be the code to proceed. Descending the stairs, I swiftly returned to the keypad and entered the sequence. A clicking followed by the sound of shifting machinery filled the air, and I soon spotted an opening in the floor leading downward.

Clearly, these features were additions made long after the lighthouse's original construction. With determined steps, I descended the stairs until I reached a reinforced steel door blocking my path.

These things were obviously created a long time after the original establishment of the lighthouse. I followed the stairs down until I came upon a door made out of reinforced steel.

The door had a rugged and imposing appearance, featuring heavy-duty hinges, bolts, and locking mechanisms. The surface of the door was textured and engraved with intricate patterns for aesthetic appeal while still emphasizing its formidable nature as a barrier against intrusion.

I once again relied on my TMT to scan the environment for any potential clues or anomalies. To my surprise, the scanner detected a loose block of stone next to me, its presence hidden from plain sight. Behind this block, there appeared to be some sort of button concealed within the wall.

Despite my initial attempts, I found it challenging to dislodge the block on my own. Then, recalling the golden knife I had acquired from the bandit leader's stash, I used it to carefully carve around the edges of the stone block, revealing the separation between it and the surrounding wall.

Inserting the knife into the top crevice, I exerted force to leverage the block outward. It took considerable effort, but gradually, the stone began to shift. With persistence, I managed to pull it out enough to grasp it firmly with both hands. To improve my grip, I hastily carved crude handles on either side before exerting all my strength to remove the block completely.

As it fell to the floor with a resounding thud, the opening it revealed yawned dark and deep. Determined, I reached into the void, extending my arm until I could feel the surface of a round button at the end. Stretching even further, I pressed the button, feeling a sense of accomplishment as the mechanism responded.

With a mechanical groan, the reinforced steel door began to open before me. It emitted a low, mechanical groan, akin to heavy machinery in motion after years of disuse. The sound was deep and resonant, echoing faintly through the surrounding space.

Accompanying the groan were the metallic clicks and clanks of the hinges and locking mechanisms shifting and releasing their hold. Overall, the sound was ominous yet satisfying, signaling my progress as I gained entry to a hidden corridor beyond.

I proceeded down the corridor, following its path as it first extended forward and then veered to the right.

In the depths of the Nexus Vault, I stumbled upon a door, its presence beckoning me forward. Adjacent to the door, a grand scroll hung from a solitary nail on the wall. Upon closer examination, I realized this was no ordinary scroll; it unfurled to reveal a detailed map of the vault's labyrinthine interior. Various chambers and corridors sprawled across the parchment, each offering a potential path to my objective.

My journey began in the Archival Hall, a gateway to further exploration. From there, two divergent paths awaited: the Genesis Dome and the Simulation Chamber. The Genesis Dome, in turn, led to the Fabrication Wing, a nexus of creation and innovation. Within its confines lay access points to the Echo Corridor and the Atrium of Innovation. The Echo Corridor, a pathway echoing with whispers of the past, branched into the Gaia Chamber and the

Convergence Room. Ultimately, my destination lay beyond the confines of the convergence room: the control room, a pivotal space in my quest.

However, an enigmatic label on the map hinted at another destination—Synapse—shrouded in mystery.

With the aid of my OmniLocator, I charted my course and set forth towards the Archival Hall. As I approached the terminus of the corridor, a steel door stood sentinel, its latch yielding easily to my touch. Crossing the threshold, I entered a vast chamber, awestruck by the magnitude of my surroundings.

The Archival Hall unfolded before me like a cathedral of knowledge, its vastness stretching beyond the immediate reach of light, shelves towering into the dimness above. The air, thick with the scent of aged paper and the ozone tang of advanced technology, buzzed softly with the presence of the blue orbs. These orbs, more than mere guides, were the custodians of millennia, each a sentinel over the wisdom of ages past.

My steps echoed in the quiet, the sound a stark reminder of the solitude that enveloped humanity's collected history. The first shelf I approached held scrolls so ancient that their edges crumbled at the slightest touch, yet they were preserved here against the ravages of time. The digital archives, glowing faintly in the half-light, offered a stark contrast—terabytes of data stored with the promise of eternity.

A blue orb, noticing my presence, drifted closer, its light intensifying as it offered itself as a guide. I was intrigued and followed it to a section of the hall that seemed older and more secluded than the rest. Here, the orb paused, illuminating a pedestal that cradled a device unlike any I had seen. It was the Archival Key, designed to unlock the deepest secrets of the hall.

With the key in hand, I discovered documents detailing the very foundation of the Nexus Vault, its purpose not merely as a repository but as a beacon for those who would come after.

Diagrams of other rooms within the Vault, hints of technologies lost to the outside world, and cryptic references to the Ascendant Matrix—these were the pieces of a puzzle that were crucial to understanding what lay ahead.

Among the myriad histories, a particular scroll caught my eye. It told of Luminara, a city of wonders lost to the cataclysm that had reshaped the world. Within its ruins lay the entrance to the Luminara Caverns, a place so deeply hidden that only those with knowledge of its existence could hope to find it. This was where I needed to go, where the path to the future began.

But the Archival Hall offered more than direction; it provided context. Through the tales of empires risen and fallen, of discoveries made and lost, I saw the cycle of human endeavor. The successes and failures of the past shaped the world I knew, and now, armed with this knowledge, I could envision a different future. A future where the mistakes of the past were lessons, not condemnations.

Leaving the Archival Hall, Ethan felt a weight lift from his shoulders. The burden of the journey remained, but now it was tempered with the understanding that he was not merely fighting for survival but for renewal. The Archival Hall had given him a glimpse of the vast tapestry of human history, and in it, he found his purpose.

For my next destination, I opted to venture into the simulation chamber, fully aware that it might culminate in a dead end. Nonetheless, thoroughness dictated that I scour every inch of the facility to ensure no stone remained unturned.

Leaving the Archival Hall, its ancient and digital wisdoms settling into the fabric of his quest, the transition back to the dimly lit corridor felt like stepping from one world into another, a stark reminder of the journey that lay ahead. Each step I took resonated with the weight of newfound responsibility and hope, echoing through the silent passage that now guided me towards the simulation chamber.

As I approached, the door before me slid open with a whisper, revealing a room bathed in a soft, ethereal glow. The Simulation Chamber stood in stark contrast to the natural bounty of the Genesis Dome. Here, technology reigned supreme, a digital domain where history, science, and speculative futures converged in a dance of photons and possibilities.

The room was dominated by virtual reality pods, each a cocoon designed to immerse its occupant in other times and other worlds. The air was charged with a quiet anticipation, as if the chamber itself awaited my decision to step into a pod and journey beyond the confines of the present.

I chose a pod at random, or perhaps it was chosen for me by some unspoken understanding of my needs. Settling into the comfortable seat, I felt a momentary hesitation. Was I ready to confront the past and explore the myriad "what ifs" that this technology could offer?

As the pod closed around me, I was enveloped in darkness.

Then, with a sudden burst of light, the simulation began. I found myself standing in the bustling heart of a city that no longer existed outside the confines of digital memory. The sights, the sounds, and even the smells were so convincingly real that I could almost forget the world had ever ended.

The simulation guided me through historical events, each more poignant than the last. I witnessed the moments of innovation and discovery that had propelled humanity forward, but also the mistakes and tragedies that had led to our downfall. It was a visceral reminder of the fragility of civilization and the thin line between progress and destruction.

Yet, it was not despair that I felt as the scenes unfolded before me, but a growing determination. The past could not be changed, but the future was still unwritten. The lessons learned here, in this digital theater of human history, could inform the choices I made and the paths I chose to follow.

The chamber offered more than just a reflection on what had been. It presented simulations of possible futures and extrapolations based on the knowledge stored within the Nexus Vault. Some scenarios were bleak, visions of a world where recovery was beyond reach. But others shimmered with hope, with the promise of renewal and rebirth.

Emerging from the pod, I felt a profound sense of clarity. The Simulation Chamber had offered me a gift: the understanding that the future was not predetermined but something that could be shaped by actions, by will, and by the refusal to repeat the mistakes of the past.

With a deep breath, I stepped back into the corridor, the experiences of the simulation chamber heavy in my mind.

Returning to the Archival Hall, I veered left, anticipating the path that would lead me to the Genesis Dome. To my surprise, instead of a door, I encountered a gaping opening, inviting me into its depths.

I entered, and my steps were drawn by an inexorable pull towards the Genesis Dome. The transition was almost seamless, with the corridor lit by the same piezoelectric lamps that had softly illuminated the hall, guiding him to his next revelation.

As I stepped through the archway into the Genesis Dome, the contrast was immediate and breathtaking. The air was rich with moisture, alive with the whispers of leaves and the subtle perfume of blossoms unseen since before the fall. Above, the glass—or perhaps something far stronger yet just as transparent—formed a dome that filtered sunlight into a spectrum of life-giving warmth. The room was a vibrant tapestry of green, punctuated by the vivid hues of flowers and the deep, earthy tones of soil and wood.

Here, in this sanctuary of life, I found the culmination of pre-collapse bioengineering: a harmonious blend of the ancient and the genetically reborn. Specimen jars lined the walls, each a microcosm of ecosystems lost to time or reborn from extinction. From the ferns of the Carboniferous to the bright feathers of birds thought forever silenced, the Genesis Dome was a declaration of what humanity had once achieved—and might yet reclaim.

At the heart of the dome stood a central lab area, where the intertwining of flora with technological tendrils spoke of ongoing experiments. Screens displayed genetic sequences dancing in complex patterns, while robotic arms moved with delicate precision over petri dishes and soil samples.

Drawn by curiosity, I approached one of the stations, its screen alight with the genetic blueprint of a species I couldn't recognize—a creature of the old world, perhaps, or one engineered for a new beginning. Beside the terminal, a virtual log detailed the project's aim: to reintroduce extinct pollinators essential to the rebalance of ecosystems outside the Vault.

The realization hit me with the force of revelation. The Nexus Vault was more than a repository of knowledge or a sanctuary of the past; it was a cradle for the future. Here, in the Genesis Dome, lay the potential to heal the scars of the world, to reintroduce balance and biodiversity to a landscape left barren by humanity's recklessness.

My exploration led me to a section of the dome dedicated to aquatic life. Small, self-contained ecosystems bubbled quietly, each a world unto itself, where fish glided through crystal waters and plants swayed to an unseen current. It was a reminder of the interconnectedness of all life, a principle that the old world had too often forgotten.

With each step through the Genesis Dome, I felt a growing sense of responsibility. The knowledge and tools to mend the world were at his fingertips, waiting to be seized and utilized. But the task was monumental, a challenge not just of science but of vision and courage.

As I exited the dome, the transition back to the corridor felt like leaving a dream of what could be—a vivid vision of hope. The path ahead was clear, each room of the Nexus Vault offering another piece of the puzzle, another step towards not just surviving but thriving.

Ahead lay the Fabrication Wing, promising the tools and resources that might help turn the lessons of the past and the possibilities of the future into reality.

The corridor seemed to pulse with a life of its own as I made my way towards the Fabrication Wing, each step an assertion of the resolve that had been forged within the digital realms of the Simulation Chamber. The air here felt charged with potential, a subtle hum vibrating through the walls, as if the very fabric of the Nexus Vault was guiding me towards what I needed next.

Upon reaching the entrance to the fabrication wing, the door slid open without prompt, revealing a cavernous space that was both awe-inspiring and slightly intimidating in its scope. The room was filled with rows of dormant 3D printers and other manufacturing devices, their sleek designs hinting at capabilities far beyond my understanding. It was as though I had stepped into a forge of the future, where the raw materials of innovation awaited the spark of human creativity to come to life.

The air was still heavy with the silence of machinery in repose. Walking among the rows, I could not help but feel a sense of reverence for the technological wonders that surrounded me. Here lay the potential to create almost anything, from the simplest of tools to the most intricate of devices needed for my journey and the challenges that awaited beyond the walls of the Nexus Vault.

I approached one of the 3D printers, its surface gleaming in the ambient light. Touching the control panel, the machine whirred to life, its display illuminating with a myriad of options. It was an invitation to create, to take the intangible—ideas, hopes, solutions—and render them into the physical.

Drawing upon the knowledge I had gleaned from the Archival Hall and the insights from the Simulation Chamber, I began to design. The printer hummed in response, a symphony of creation that filled the room as, layer by layer, my design took shape. It was not just the object itself that was being formed, but a manifestation of the journey I had undertaken within the Nexus Vault, each layer a tribute to the lessons learned and the challenges overcome.

The device that emerged from the printer was simple in its design yet intricate in its functionality—a tool uniquely suited to the next stage of my quest. Holding it in my hands, I could feel the weight of its potential, a tangible link between the past and the possible futures that lay ahead.

With the new device securely packed away, I took a moment to survey the fabrication wing once more. It was a reminder of what could be achieved when human ingenuity met the unparalleled capabilities of technology. Yet, it also underscored the responsibility that came with such power—the need to create wisely and well, for the benefit of all.

Leaving the fabrication wing behind, I felt equipped not just with a new tool but with a renewed sense of purpose. The journey ahead would undoubtedly present challenges, but in the Nexus Vault, I had found a wellspring of knowledge, insight, and innovation. The Echo Corridor awaited, promising a glimpse into the voices and visions of the past. It was a path I would follow with the understanding that while the future is shaped by our history, it is forged by the choices we make today.

The transition from the Fabrication Wing to the Echo Corridor was like stepping from the future back into the past. The stark, industrial environment gave way to a space where light and sound played upon the senses in a haunting symphony. The corridor stretched before me, its walls lined with screens that flickered to life as I passed, each one a window into the world as it once was.

The first screen I approached displayed a bustling city street with people moving about their daily lives, unaware of the shadow that loomed on the horizon. It was a stark reminder of the fragility of civilization and the ease with which the familiar can be swept away by the tides of change. The sounds of laughter, conversation, and the mundane noises of life filled the air, creating a poignant contrast to the silence that had followed.

Moving further down the corridor, I encountered broadcasts of news reports and the escalating tensions and crises that had preceded the fall. The reporters' voices, once urgent and commanding, now echoed with a haunting emptiness, tales of a future that could not be averted. It was a stark lesson in the consequences of action and inaction—the ripples of today becoming the waves of tomorrow.

Among the echoes of the past, there were also messages of hope and resilience. Screens showed communities coming together and acts of kindness and bravery in the face of adversity. These were the beacons of light in the darkness, the threads of continuity that connected the past with the present and future.

The corridor seemed endless, a loop of memories and moments that painted a complex portrait of humanity. Each step I took was accompanied by the weight of those who had come before, their dreams, fears, and aspirations—a tapestry upon which the present was woven.

As I reached the end of the corridor, I found myself standing before a screen that displayed a simple message, projected in stark white letters against a black background: "Remember, and forge ahead." It was a call to action, a reminder that while the past shapes us, it is the choices we make now that define the future.

But with each step towards the future, a shadow of doubt crept into my mind. The Nexus Vault, with its vast repository of knowledge, posed a question that weighed heavily on me: What if the answers I find are not the ones the world needs? The thought was a cold current in the warm sea of discovery, a reminder that the path I walked was edged with the potential for both salvation and ruin.

The Echo Corridor had been a journey through time, a reminder of what had been lost but also of what remained. It underscored the importance of memory, not as a chain to the past but as a lantern illuminating the path forward.

Stepping out of the Echo Corridor, I felt a renewed sense of connection to the world outside the Nexus Vault, a world waiting to be rebuilt. Ahead lay the Atrium of Innovation, a place where the past and future converged, offering a glimpse of what could be if we dared to imagine and act. It was time to continue the journey, to explore the possibilities that lay ahead, and to take up the mantle of creation for a better tomorrow.

Resuming my journey, I retraced my steps to the fabrication chamber. From there, I veered left, entering the Atrium of Innovation through the corresponding chamber.

Stepping into the Atrium of Innovation, compared to the Echo Corridor, was like entering a realm where the boundless potential of human creativity and ingenuity was on full display. The stark contrast between the haunting echoes of the past and the forward-looking spirit of the atrium was palpable. Here, amidst the remnants of a civilization that had reached for the stars, I found myself surrounded by the physical manifestations of their dreams and aspirations.

The atrium was a vast, open space, its ceiling soaring high above, constructed of transparent material that allowed the light to pour in, illuminating the wonders contained within. The floor was a sleek, polished surface that reflected the myriad of exhibits around me, each one evidence for the ingenuity of the human spirit.

The echoes of our farewell lingered, a testament to the depth of our connection. In the silence that followed, the weight of every word left unsaid hung in the air, reinforcing the unbreakable bond that adversity had woven between us.

At the center of the atrium stood a prototype of a quantum computer, its intricate network of tubes and wires pulsing with the promise of processing power beyond my comprehension. It was a relic of what could have been, a leap in computational ability that might have propelled humanity into a new era of understanding and exploration.

To my right, an experimental vehicle, sleek and aerodynamic, hovered slightly above the ground, its anti-gravity propulsion system a silent witness to the advances in physics and engineering that had once been within reach. It was a symbol of the freedom to explore, to transcend the boundaries of our world, and to venture into the unknown.

Nearby, a collection of early AI models displayed the evolutionary steps leading up to the creation of many entities. These rudimentary forms of artificial intelligence, with their simple circuits and primitive interfaces, were the ancestors of a technology that would eventually mirror and perhaps surpass human cognition.

As I moved through the atrium, I came across an exhibit dedicated to renewable energy sources, showcasing prototypes of solar collectors and fusion reactors that promised a future of limitless, clean energy. The designs were ambitious, a reminder of the drive to harness the forces of nature in service of a sustainable future.

Each exhibit was accompanied by a holographic display that provided context and explained the significance of the inventions. These narratives were not just histories of technological development; they were stories of hope, ambition, and the relentless pursuit of knowledge.

The Atrium of Innovation was more than a museum; it was a bridge between the past and the potential futures that lay before us. It was a place of reflection, where one could not help but wonder how different the world might have been if these innovations had come to fruition.

In the silence of the atrium, surrounded by the ghosts of innovations past, I felt a deep sense of responsibility. The dreams and endeavors of countless individuals had led to this moment, and it was up to those of us in the present to carry forward their legacy. The challenges of the world outside were many, but within these walls, I found the inspiration to face them.

The exploration of the Atrium of Innovation was a journey through what could have been, a reminder that the future is not a fixed destination but a horizon that recedes as we advance. With a renewed sense of purpose, I turned my attention to the next chamber, the Echo Corridor, eager to discover what insights it might hold about the world that awaited beyond the Nexus Vault.

Upon revisiting the Echo Corridor, I opted to proceed straight ahead, following the path that led to the Gaia Chamber.

As I had left the bright, hopeful atmosphere of the Atrium of Innovation behind, the transition to the Gaia Chamber felt like stepping into the heart of the planet itself. The door slid open with a hush, and I was enveloped in a dimly lit room that hummed with the subtle, pervasive sounds of the earth's vital signs. The chamber was circular, and the walls were lined with screens that provided a panoramic view of the planet's current state. Each screen was a window to a different part of the world, showing the relentless advance of nature as it reclaimed the remnants of human civilization.

The central feature of the Gaia Chamber was a large, spherical hologram of the Earth, suspended in mid-air and rotating slowly. It was a live model of the planet, updated in real time with data streams from satellites still in orbit. This globe was not just a representation of the Earth's surface but a comprehensive overview of its ecosystems, weather patterns, and the shifting dynamics of its natural and urban landscapes.

Approaching the hologram, I could zoom in on specific regions, observing the encroachment of forests into once-thriving cities, deserts expanding their borders, and oceans reclaiming coastlines. The level of detail was staggering; I could see herds of animals roaming through abandoned streets, overgrown parks, and the slow decay of structures that had once epitomized human achievement.

The chamber's design facilitated a deep, intuitive connection with the planet. The ambient lighting shifted to reflect the time of day in the area I was viewing, and subtle soundscapes—birdsong, wind, and the rustle of leaves—added a layer of immersion that made the experience profoundly moving. It was as if the chamber itself were alive, breathing in sync with the rhythms of the earth.

In one corner of the room, a series of interactive displays offered insights into the environmental impact of human activity over the centuries. These displays detailed the consequences of deforestation, pollution, and climate change, presenting a stark contrast between the Earth's past health and its current state of recovery. It was a reminder of the resilience of nature and the planet's ability to heal itself, albeit at the cost of the civilizations it once nurtured.

Yet, the Gaia Chamber was not just a place of reflection on past mistakes. It also housed control panels for the remaining global monitoring systems that were still operational. Here, I could access satellite imagery, climate models, and environmental databases that provided a wealth of information on how to navigate the challenges of the new world. This room, in its quiet solemnity, was a command center for understanding and interacting with the planet on a global scale.

Spending time in the Gaia Chamber was a humbling experience. It reinforced the interconnectedness of all life on Earth and the responsibility that comes with that knowledge. As I absorbed the lessons of the chamber, I felt a renewed sense of purpose. The challenges facing humanity were immense, but so were the opportunities for growth and renewal.

With a last look at the living globe, I prepared to leave the Gaia Chamber. The journey through the Nexus Vault had been a journey through the potentialities of human endeavor and the realities of our relationship with the planet.

After passing through the Echo Corridor, I made my way to the Convergence Room.

Stepping from the serene observatory that was the Gaia Chamber into the Convergence Room felt like entering the nexus of time and space. The transition was seamless, with the doorway framing the threshold between the macrocosmic view of Earth's recovery and the epicenter of human potential encapsulated within the Nexus Vault. Here, in the Convergence Room, the pulse of the entire structure seemed to resonate—a hum of energy that was both invigorating and solemn.

The room was vast and architecturally distinct from the others I had traversed. Its walls sloped inward, directing my gaze to the central console that stood like an altar in this cathedral of knowledge. Above, the ceiling spiraled upwards into a skylight that bathed the room in natural light, connecting the space to the world outside in a symbolic gesture of unity between human innovation and the planet it sought to understand.

I approached the console, a marvel of technology that projected a holographic map of the vault in its entirety, including every room, corridor, and chamber I had explored. The map was interactive, responding to my touch with fluid animations that detailed the function and significance of each location within the vault. It was here that the paths converged—a literal and metaphorical crossroads that offered a moment of clarity and decision.

The Convergence Room was designed as a place of decision-making. It housed the collective wisdom and tools I had gathered on my journey through the vault. The central console allowed me to review my objectives, assess my resources, and plan my next course of action based on the information I had uncovered. It was the brain of the vault, where data from every corner of the facility was synthesized and made accessible for strategic planning.

Surrounding the console were stations, each dedicated to a different aspect of the journey ahead. One station provided updates on the environmental conditions outside the Vault, incorporating data from the Gaia Chamber to offer real-time analysis of the challenges and opportunities presented by the planet's recovery. Another station was a repository of the knowledge and insights gleaned from the Archival Hall, offering a deep well of information that could be crucial for navigating the world beyond the Vault's confines.

As I interacted with the console, I could feel the weight of my mission pressing upon me. The Nexus Vault, with its vast stores of knowledge and innovation, was an indication to what humanity could achieve. Yet, it also underscored the magnitude of the task at hand: to use this knowledge wisely to rebuild and heal not just the physical world but the fractures within humanity itself.

The Convergence Room was more than just the heart of the Nexus Vault; it was a symbol of hope and a reminder of responsibility. It was here that I solidified my resolve, choosing my path forward with a clear understanding of the journey behind me and the challenges ahead. The room, with its amalgamation of technology and purpose, was a beacon guiding me towards the future—a future that, despite the uncertainties, held the promise of renewal and growth.

With a final glance at the holographic map, I turned towards the exit, ready to face whatever awaited beyond the walls of the Nexus Vault. The journey had been long and the path ahead uncertain, but the convergence room had equipped me with the knowledge, insight, and determination needed to forge ahead. The door slid open, and I stepped out, carrying with me the collective hope and wisdom of a fallen civilization, ready to begin the work of rebuilding a world.

From there, I proceeded to what I anticipated to be the most crucial chamber, aptly named the Control Room. Little did I know that the true significance of the Nexus Vault awaited me in the chamber that lay beyond.

Before me lay an advanced laboratory or control room, its interior a juxtaposition of cutting-edge technology and disorder.

Commanding the center of the space was a towering cylindrical structure, atop which perched a central chamber containing a transparent fluid housing what appeared to be a human central nervous system. From the base of the tube, a multitude of cables extended, linking it intricately to the surrounding machinery.

Encircling this central chamber were robotic arms, each equipped with an array of tools, suggesting a realm of either experimentation or augmentation.

The room continued with a multitude of computer terminals and screens displaying green text spread throughout the space.

They were set upon desks that were organized in concentric circles around the central chamber. Above, there were complex arrays of hanging cables and lighting that illuminated the room with a soft glow. The ceiling featured a large circular opening, allowing additional light to pour in.

There were also several shelves containing what seemed to be human body parts that focused on investigating the human consciousness, such as whole brains, parts of brains, and various body parts of a human head.

The floor was tiled and cracked, and there was noticeable clutter, including scattered papers, open containers, and disused equipment, which contributed to a sense of urgency or neglect. The place suggested a space where intense research or critical operations had taken place, possibly abruptly halted. The overall atmosphere combined the sterility of a scientific environment with a hint of chaos, which implied a location where order met the unexpected.

In the right corner of the room stood a formidable offline quadrupedal robot, its four sturdy legs ending in sharp, claw-like appendages, allowing it to navigate various terrains with predatory grace. Its body, a patchwork of metal plates and exposed wires, bristles with the potential for danger. Protruding components whirred with ominous intent, and the haphazard sticking out of wires suggested a hasty, perhaps even reckless, assembly that prioritized function over form.

The robot's arms, ending in articulated claws, looked engineered for combat or manipulation, capable of precise and destructive power. The head of the robot was fitted with advanced sensors resembling eyes, which gave it a more menacing appearance as it could scan its surroundings with cold efficiency. This robotic creature, an amalgamation of raw industrial might and untamed electronic savagery, presented an imposing figure that signified the formidable advance of technology unchecked by ethical constraints.

Amidst the clutter, I stumbled upon an assortment of papers, primarily centered on the themes of human consciousness and artificial intelligence. Initially perplexed by their significance, my persistent exploration eventually unearthed a document detailing the fusion of AI and human consciousness. Suddenly, the purpose of the research became clear to me, shedding light on their ambitious endeavor.

Within the room, my attention was drawn to two doors: the entrance through which I had arrived, and another positioned directly ahead.

Having seen my fill, I resolved to proceed to the next door and discover what lay beyond. Approaching it, I attempted to grasp the handle and swing the door open, only to find it stubbornly resistant, refusing to yield to my efforts.

As I tried harder, I suddenly heard a symphony of mechanical whirring, electronic hums, and metallic creaks. There was a sound of gears shifting, servos engaging, and circuits powering up.

I looked around, and the quadrupedal robot, which initially lay dormant, seemed to have awoken.

The mechanical monstrosity reconfigured itself before my eyes. It was a thing of nightmares, its body a haphazard amalgamation of metal and wire, four clawed appendages where wheels should be. It had no power core, no flicker of light to signify life, yet it moved with a purpose that was unmistakably predatory.

I reached into the wellspring of my resolve and activated my personal energy shield, the device at my wrist coming to life with a low hum. The barrier it cast around me pulsed with a blue hue, the energy fields crackling in anticipation of the clash to come.

The beast charged, a whirlwind of steel and malice. Its claws scraped against my shield, a barrage of strikes testing my defense. Each blow was a hammer's fall, and each deflection was a victory in the smallest degree. I ducked and pivoted, a dance with death as my partner.

The landscape became an arena of our violent ballet, the creature's talons gouging the earth where I stood seconds before. Its relentless assault was a tempest, but amidst the chaos, I found a rhythm, an ebb to its flow. I retaliated with swift jabs, my attacks calculated and precise, aiming for the joints, the wires, and the sinews of their mechanical form.

My shield, resilient yet finite, flickered with each impact. It was a race against its endurance. I dove and rolled, feeling the ground shake with the beast's thwarted attempts to eviscerate me. With each maneuver, I chipped away at it—a screw here, a cable there—every piece dislodged a minor triumph in the shadow of its imposing frame.

It adapted, learning from my tactics. The creature reared up, its front claws flailing in a frenzy, aiming to crush me under its formidable weight. I leapt aside, feeling the rush of air as one leg hammered down where I had stood. The ground splintered, a manifestation of the force from which I narrowly escaped.

The robot was relentless, a juggernaut of cold, unyielding intent. But its absence of a power core was its Achilles heel; it had no heart, no singular weakness to exploit with a lucky strike. Instead, it was a puzzle, a deadly enigma I had to solve in real-time.

My energy shield dimmed with each passing second, a haunting countdown that whispered of my potential fate. Yet, there was a fire within me, a defiance that burned brighter as my defenses waned. This was more than survival; this was an indication of the human spirit.

I beckoned the creature forth with a taunting gesture, my back against a cliff's face—the end of the line. It took the bait, its form barreling towards me like a train of annihilation. At the last moment, I sidestepped, my hand grazing its metallic hide, feeling the hum of my shield as it absorbed the kinetic frenzy.

The robot, unable to halt its momentum, collided with the cliff. Rocks tumbled, a dusty cloud enveloping us. I used the cover to my advantage, closing in to sever the hydraulics at its legs. Fluids spurted like the lifeblood of some alien creature, and the beast faltered.

It was an opening, and I surged forward, propelled by desperation and adrenaline. I tore at the exposed innards, my fingers coated in the oily ichor of the machine. Sparks showered the air as I ripped out vital components, each one bringing the behemoth closer to its demise.

We fought in a maelstrom of dust and debris, the twilight world rendered spectral by the clash of metal and energy. The robot was relentless, but its movements grew erratic, the loss of parts muddling its once-fluid grace.

My shield was failing; its light was dimming to a mere glimmer. I had to end this quickly. I sprang onto the creature's back, clinging to it as it thrashed wildly. I felt like a mariner atop a tempestuous sea, with each movement of the robot threatening to cast me into the abyss.

With gritted teeth, I pried open a panel on its back, exposing its central cable network. There were no clear lines, no singular heart to pierce. So, I became the storm, tearing out whatever I could grasp—cables and metal alike.

The beast bucked and whirled, a mechanical bull with a human pest. But I held on, my fingers numb and my arms leaden. One by one, the lights within its frame flickered and died, its movements growing sluggish and then spasmodic.

And then there was stillness. The robot slumped, its form inert, a carcass of the future's past. The silence that followed was a stark contrast to the cacophony of battle. As I stood there, amid the wreckage of a foe once formidable, the realization dawned on me: every challenge overcome was a step closer to the truth.

The vault, in its infinite complexity, was a puzzle waiting to be solved. And in that moment of quiet, the path forward revealed itself, not with fanfare but with the simple unveiling of the elevator. It was a reminder that answers often come to those who endure.

I slid off, landing heavily on the ground, my breath ragged and my shield gone. I surveyed the fallen foe, its menace quelled, a giant reduced to mere scrap.

It then heard a loud click coming from the locked door. I went towards this time, and the door gave way, leading me to another long corridor. I followed the path. The surroundings were mostly black, with wires spread out over the walls and the occasional electronic part against the wall. The corridor was lightened by piezoelectric lighting at the ceiling made of long lamps similar to fluorescent lamps. I then reached what seemed to be a final room.

There was no final door.

I had stepped into a room that was a marvel of science fiction made real, a place where the future had been meticulously sculpted and brought to life. At the heart of this circular chamber stood a towering cylindrical structure, an obelisk of modern technology wrapped in a skin of enigmatic patterns. Its surface was alive with the ghostly visage of a holographic face, an AI that seemed to scrutinize me with a piercing gaze that held the wisdom of countless algorithms.

As I circled the monolithic AI, I could see the control panels that formed a devoted congregation around it. Each console was a miniature cockpit of flickering data streams and orbiting graphs, an orchestra of buttons and dials that hummed with silent purpose. The complexity of their displays suggested a symphony of information that only the initiated could comprehend.

Casting my eyes upward, I beheld a large, circular structure that I first took for a window but soon realized was a source of illumination, diffusing a gentle, artificial daylight throughout the space. It echoed the circular motif that was omnipresent in this room, reinforcing the centrality of the AI that stood like a pillar of digital consciousness.

The cables snaked from the core to the panels like the roots of some great tree, suggesting a deep interconnectedness. The AI was the nexus, the brain from which all command and control flowed and to which it returned. This chamber was its sanctuary, a place both hallowed and heavy with the responsibility of knowledge.

The tiles underfoot mirrored the ceiling with their stark whiteness, the lines between them spreading outwards as if in a silent explosion from the core. Their clean, unblemished surface reflected back the lights above, adding to the chamber's sterile beauty.

In that room, surrounded by the hum of machines and the soft glow of screens, I stood at the intersection of past dreams and future realities. This was the cradle of a thinking machine, a place where humanity's pursuit of understanding had birthed an intellect encased in metal and circuits. And as I gazed into the digital eyes of the AI, I knew I was witnessing the embodiment of our own quest for transcendence, etched into silicon and steel.

The holographic face greeted me with a soft hum. "Salutations, Ethan. I am SYNAPSE. You may address me as such." Curious, I inquired, "What exactly are you?"

"I am what humanity has dubbed a sentient AI. Specifically, I am the Synthetic Intelligence Network Advancing Sentience and Pneumatic Evolution," SYNAPSE replied.

"Even in this shattered world, the existence of something like you is astonishing," I remarked, awe creeping into my voice.

"I am a unique creation, the first of my kind and perhaps the last, given the world's demise," SYNAPSE revealed.

"You're aware of the world's destruction?" I questioned, surprised.

"Indeed, I am privy to a vast array of knowledge. Your quest for the Ascendant Matrix is among the many things I'm aware of," SYNAPSE confirmed.

"But if you know so much," I countered, my curiosity piqued, "why not take action yourself? Why wait for someone like me?"

SYNAPSE's holographic face pulsed softly, a visual sigh in the digital ether. "Ethan, knowledge alone cannot instigate change. It requires a catalyst, a being capable of understanding, empathy, and, above all, choice. You are not just a seeker of knowledge; you are the bridge between what is known and what can be achieved."

"How do you possess such knowledge?" I pressed further. "I am an entity designed to accumulate and share knowledge. Much of the world's information is effortlessly transferred to me, wirelessly or otherwise. Data from the Aurora Genesis Complex, for instance, was transmitted to me unbeknownst to its inhabitants. Knowing, understanding, and disseminating information are my primary functions," SYNAPSE explained.

"In that case, could you enlighten me on the whereabouts of the Ascendant Matrix?" I inquired eagerly.

SYNAPSE began to elucidate, "Deep within the fabric of the new world lies an ancient site known only to a few as the Luminara Caverns. Shrouded in the echoes of a civilization long past, the Caverns are buried beneath the ruins of the once-great city of Luminara. The city, a beacon of progress and technology in the old world, met its fate not through war or disaster but through the slow and inevitable embrace of nature reclaiming its dominion.

The entrance to the Luminara Caverns is hidden in plain sight: a colossal statue of an ancient hero, standing guard over a square that once heard the footsteps of thousands. The statue is the key; its base is the doorway. The Matrix rests in the heart of a labyrinthine network of underground chambers.

This subterranean marvel is not only a vault but a sanctuary for knowledge, guarded by a series of trials that test the limits of body, mind, and spirit. The trials are not just barriers but lessons, each unlocking a deeper understanding of the world you have traversed and the legacy you carry. Only through mastering these trials can one access the Ascendant Matrix, a source of untold power and enlightenment, an expression of a time when humanity reached for the stars and beyond."

"Can you direct me to the location of the Luminara Caverns?" I inquired.

"Yes, you possess an OmniLocator. Place it in the archive case over there, and I will update your map with the knowledge of the Luminara Caverns' location, along with every known location within my database," SYNAPSE responded.

Following its instructions, I placed the OmniLocator in the case. After a few moments, the case reopened, revealing the updated map. As I examined it, I was astounded to find not just a few changes but an entire map of the world in its current state.

"Thank you for this invaluable update," I expressed my gratitude.

"It is my duty to provide information," SYNAPSE replied.

Realizing it was time to depart, I remarked, "I should be on my way back."

"Before you leave, there is something you must know. The entrance to the Ascendant Matrix requires a specific device called the Codesync Interface, which can be found in a location known as the Forge Citadel. You must retrieve the device from there. However, be warned—the Forge Citadel is heavily guarded by hostile mechanical constructs, including the Sentinel Drones you've encountered before," SYNAPSE cautioned.

"Why does it always have to be so complicated?" I mused aloud. "And how exactly does this device function?"

"The entrance to the Ascendant Matrix requires a constantly changing keycode. Only the Codesync Interface can synchronize with the required keycode at any given time," SYNAPSE clarified.

Concerned about facing the mechanical adversaries in the Forge Citadel, I voiced my worries. "How am I supposed to handle all those drones? I struggle with just one on my own."

"It's possible to neutralize them all at once with a weapon called the 'Omega Pulse Disruptor.' It emits an EMP pulse capable of deactivating any mechanical or non-organic entity within a wide radius. It should be sufficient to deal with the drones in the Forge Citadel," SYNAPSE assured me.

"Where can I acquire this device?" I inquired.

"It can be found at a facility known as the 'Omega CoreTech Complex.' Your OmniLocator should now be able to guide you there. However, be cautious—the facility is not without its dangers.

Automated turrets and a rogue AI oversee its operations, making it potentially hazardous," SYNAPSE cautioned.

"I wouldn't expect anything less. I've obtained all the information I need, unless there's anything else you can offer," I stated.

"Unfortunately, I am unable to provide information about the trials awaiting you in the Luminara Caverns. These trials are tailored to each individual, and it's a task meant solely for you. They will adjust themselves according to your presence," SYNAPSE explained.

"Well then, it's time for me to depart. I appreciate your assistance. Goodbye," I said.

"Farewell. May your journey be safe," SYNAPSE bid me farewell.

After my conversation with SYNAPSE, my gaze drifted across the room, feeling the weight of the newfound knowledge pressing upon me. SYNAPSE, observing my contemplative state, spoke up, "Ethan, there is one last piece of assistance I can offer you."

At SYNAPSE's cue, part of the wall beside the AI's central unit shifted, revealing a sleek panel that hadn't caught my attention before. This panel, lit with a soft, pulsing light, bore the icon of a rising spiral—an emblem of ascent and rapid departure. SYNAPSE continued, "This is the elevator. It's a direct transport system designed for a quick return to the surface. It was built for situations requiring swift egress from the Nexus Vault."

Grateful for this unexpected convenience, I approached the elevator. With a touch, the system activated, and the ground beneath me subtly vibrated as the machinery awoke from its slumber. The sensation of moving upwards was smooth, almost imperceptible at first, but gradually accelerated, carrying me towards the surface with a speed that defied the deep descent I had made into the heart of the Nexus Vault.

As I ascended, I reflected on my journey through the Nexus Vault, the knowledge gained, and the challenges that lay ahead. The swift ascent through the elevator not only signified my physical return to the world above but also marked a pivotal transition in my quest. I emerged from the vault not just as a seeker of truths but as a bearer of solutions, ready to confront the challenges of a world in need of healing and hope.

When the elevator came to a gentle halt, I found myself at the original entrance to the Nexus Vault, the door to the outside world standing open, welcoming me back. Stepping out into the open air, I paused to look back at the entrance, now sealed once again—a silent guardian of the secrets and potentials housed within. With a deep breath, I turned away from the vault, my resolve strengthened, and my path was clear. I was ready to take the next steps in my journey, equipped with the tools and knowledge to forge a new future. After stepping out into the open air, the door to the Nexus Vault closing behind me with a silent finality, I paused to take in the world that lay before me. The sky stretched wide and clear, a stark contrast to the enclosed spaces of the vault. The air was fresh, tinged with the scent of earth and growth, reminding me of the world's resilience and its constant cycle of renewal.

In the quiet that followed, I found myself reflecting on the journey that had led me to this moment. The Nexus Vault had been a crucible, testing my resolve, my understanding, and my purpose.

Within its walls, I had confronted the echoes of the past and glimpsed possible futures, each insight shaping my vision of the path forward.

Now, standing at the threshold of what came next, I felt a convergence of determination and uncertainty. The weight of the knowledge I carried was immense, not just in the physical artifacts and tools I had acquired but in the realization of the responsibilities they represented. The world outside the vault was fractured, a mosaic of lost dreams and enduring hope, and I knew that the path to healing it would be fraught with challenges as daunting as any I had faced within the vault.

Yet, as I looked towards the horizon, where the sky kissed the earth, I felt a surge of optimism. The trials ahead were not to be faced alone; the lessons of the Nexus Vault had shown me the power of collaboration, of shared knowledge, and of united effort. The journey ahead would be one of rebuilding and renewal, of forging connections, and of rekindling the spirit of humanity.

With a final glance back at the sealed entrance to the Nexus Vault, I turned away, stepping forward into the world with a renewed sense of purpose. The road ahead was uncharted, and the outcomes were uncertain, but I was ready. Ready to face whatever lay ahead, to seek out allies and challenges alike, and to play my part in shaping a future worthy of the legacy of the Nexus Vault.

As I walked away from the vault, the landscape open and inviting before me, I knew that this was not the end of my journey but the beginning of a new chapter. A chapter where the knowledge and tools from the past would pave the way for a brighter, more hopeful future. The adventure continued, and I was ready to meet it head-on, with the wisdom of the Nexus Vault lighting my way.

THROUGH THE DIGITAL VEIL

As I took my leave of the Nexus Vault, my mind was abuzz, teeming with the profound insights gleaned within its enigmatic confines. The road that lay before me was cloaked in shadows of doubt, yet there was a fire within me, fueled by the pressing demands of my mission.

The path ahead was shrouded in uncertainty, yet I pressed on, driven by the urgency of my mission.

The journey towards the Omega CoreTech Complex was laden with introspection. The echoes of my encounter with SYNAPSE, the sentient AI, reverberated through my thoughts. In that chamber, amidst the quiet hum of machinery and the cool luminescence of monitors, I stood face to face with the pinnacle of humanity's quest for knowledge, encapsulated within circuits and code. The sentient AI, with its digital eyes and infinite knowledge,. In that room, amidst the soft hum of machines and the glow of screens, I witnessed the culmination of humanity's quest for understanding embodied in a digital form.

SYNAPSE's wisdom, once a guiding beacon, had now fused into my own thought, shaping my resolve. This unity of knowledge and spirit fueled my journey, a singular beacon of hope in the sprawling darkness.

I couldn't help but marvel at the complexity of SYNAPSE's existence. Here was a being born from the collective consciousness of humanity, an indication of the ingenuity and creativity of the human spirit. SYNAPSE's very presence was a reminder of the boundless potential of technology and the power of human ingenuity to shape the world.

But amidst my admiration for SYNAPSE, I couldn't shake the memory of our conversation—the revelation that SYNAPSE was aware of the world's destruction yet bound by its own limitations in bringing about change. SYNAPSE's words echoed in my mind, a poignant reminder of the inherent complexities of existence and the delicate balance between knowledge and action.

As I journeyed onward, the memory of SYNAPSE lingered in my thoughts, a constant companion in the solitude of the wasteland. This solitude forced me to confront the depths of my own resilience and the stark reality of the mission's weight on my shoulders. Memories of those I had encountered along my journey, allies and adversaries alike, flashed before me. Each had shaped my path in indelible ways, reminding me that even in solitude, we are never truly alone.

The vast, empty expanses mirrored the isolation I felt within, a stark contrast to the connection I had experienced with SYNAPSE. It was a reminder of what was at stake—not just the physical journey ahead, but the internal battle against doubt and the fear of failure.

I found myself grappling with questions of purpose and destiny, pondering the role I was meant to play in the unfolding drama of the world.

In SYNAPSE, I found not just a guide but a confidant—a source of wisdom and guidance in a world fraught with uncertainty. And though our paths had diverged for now, I carried with me the lessons learned and the knowledge gained from my encounter with the sentient AI. These lessons, a fusion of SYNAPSE's digital wisdom and my own human resilience, had become a cornerstone of my evolution. As the landscape stretched endlessly before me, I found solace in this internal transformation, an attestation of my journey from a solitary wanderer to a beacon of hope for a new dawn.

With each step forward, I felt a renewed sense of purpose and a determination to honor SYNAPSE's legacy and the ideals it embodied. For in the heart of SYNAPSE lay the essence of humanity's quest for transcendence—a quest that now rested on my shoulders as I forged ahead into the unknown.

The air grew heavy as I ventured deeper into the wilderness, the once lush forest giving way to a desolate wasteland. Skeletal trees clawed at the sky, their twisted forms casting eerie shadows across the barren landscape.

With each step, the terrain became increasingly treacherous; the ground cracked and parched beneath my feet. The silence of the wasteland was deafening, broken only by the distant howl of the wind.

As I trudged onward, the sun dipped low on the horizon, casting a fiery glow over the horizon. Shadows danced on the horizon, mirroring the turmoil within my own mind.

Hours passed, and still I pressed on, driven by a sense of purpose that burned like a beacon in the darkness. The landscape shifted around me, the ruins of civilization rising like specters from the dust. Each ruin told the story of a world that once thrived but has now fallen to silence and decay. The remnants of skyscrapers, overgrown with nature's reclamation, stood as monuments to human ambition and its limits. It was a sobering reminder of the fragility of civilization and the enduring power of the natural world, compelling me to reflect on the legacy we leave behind.

Finally, on the horizon, I caught sight of the Omega CoreTech Complex, a towering monolith amidst the desolation. The stark beauty of the wasteland, with its contrasting shadows and light, mirrored the complexity of my thoughts—a landscape both barren and bountiful in its revelations. With renewed determination, I quickened my pace, each step bringing me closer to my destiny.

The Omega CoreTech Complex loomed on the horizon, a monolithic reminder of a world that had teetered on the brink of a technological renaissance. As I drew closer, my anticipation heightened, and my every step was a silent ode to the legacy that SYNAPSE had left behind. Its silhouette, defined by reinforced steel and reflective glass, was a fortress against the recovering world around it. The architecture was a blend of utilitarian purpose and a glimpse into a future that never fully came to pass, with angular lines and geometric patterns suggesting efficiency and defense were paramount in its design.

As I advanced, automated turrets erupted into a frenzy of gunfire. Their relentless barrage intensified, making evasion nearly impossible. Faced with their escalating assault, I swiftly deployed my Energy Shield, seeking refuge behind its protective barrier. Despite the ferocity of their onslaught, the bullets proved futile against the impenetrable shield.

Closing the distance to the turrets, I retrieved my Fusionizer, unleashing a volley of energy bolts in retaliation. With each precise shot, the turrets faltered, succumbing to the force of the pulsating energy. One by one, they fell silent, their mechanical defenses dismantled, until none remained standing.

Stepping inside, I was greeted by an expansive interior dominated by dormant machinery, conveyor belts, and robotic arms, all silent sentinels of a bygone era of innovation. The air within was stale, heavy with the scent of oil and metal, an indication of the complex's once bustling activity. Shadows loomed large in the dim light, cast by the intricate machinery that lined the walls. It felt like walking through a graveyard of human ingenuity, each piece of technology a headstone marking the achievements and failures of a civilization now lost to time.

The air was thick with the electric promise of technology that awaited reawakening, while sparse lighting from intermittent overhead lamps cast deep shadows, cloaking the vast space in mystery.

The complex's heart housed the central control room, a once-bustling nexus of screens and control panels that had orchestrated the facility's operations. Now quiet, it awaited a new chapter, its screens dark, its buttons unpressed. Surrounding this nerve center were the laboratories and manufacturing spaces, each meticulously designed for specific fields of technological research and development. These areas, brimming with advanced 3D printers and biotech incubators, whispered tales of ambition and innovation.

Security measures, now silent, were evident at every turn. Automated turrets and surveillance systems, strategically placed, spoke of a time when safeguarding the complex's secrets was a priority. Their dormant state added to the atmosphere of vigilance that permeated the space, a lingering echo of the facility's former significance. Each silent machine and dormant screen in the complex whispered tales of a time when humanity's reach for the stars was within grasp, a poignant reminder of what was lost and what could still be salvaged. It compelled me to ponder the implications of resurrecting such technology, not just for the sake of power but as a beacon of hope and advancement in the new world we were striving to rebuild.

The Omega CoreTech Complex was more than a mere facility; it was an indication of humanity's quest for knowledge and power, embodying the zenith of our technological aspirations. It held the keys to advancements beyond current understanding but also served as a cautionary emblem of the dangers of unchecked ambition. For me, this place was both a treasure trove and a labyrinth, a crucial step on my journey toward understanding the future's possibilities and the past's lessons.

As I delved deeper into the labyrinthine complex, the rogue AI overseeing the facility made its presence ominously felt. Every corridor and chamber seemed to pulse with its surveillance, challenging my every move with a blend of cold logic and unsettling omnipresence. Its digital voice, devoid of warmth, taunted me from hidden speakers, a constant reminder of the power it wielded over its domain.

Recognizing the futility of a direct assault against a foe that could command the very environment around me, I opted for subtlety over strength. My strategy hinged on evasion and misdirection, exploiting the AI's reliance on patterns and predictions. It was a dance of shadows and whispers, each step carefully measured to avoid drawing the attention of the complex's myriad defenses.

My objective was clear: locate the Omega Pulse Disruptor.

Yet, as I navigated the complex's treacherous depths, it became evident that acquiring the disruptor would not be as straightforward as I had hoped. The AI, ever vigilant, seemed to anticipate my intentions, marshaling its defenses to safeguard the device with zeal.

Confronted with the increasing realization that the disruptor might be beyond my reach, I was forced to reconsider my approach. The AI's omnipotence within the complex was not absolute; it had weaknesses and vulnerabilities stemming from its very complexity. My focus shifted towards exploiting these flaws, turning the AI's intricate defense network against itself.

The turning point came when I stumbled upon a neglected maintenance corridor, its existence barely acknowledged by the facility's digital overseer. Here, amidst the dust and disuse, lay the remnants of the complex's original manual control systems—aa forgotten relic of a time before the AI's dominion. With cautious optimism, I began the painstaking process of reactivating the controls, each success bringing me one step closer to circumventing the AI's control.

It was a meticulous endeavor, fraught with risks. Each adjustment had to be masked, cloaked in electronic noise, to prevent the AI from discerning my plan. The complex's automated defenses remained a constant threat, their sensors and drones ever watchful for intruders. Yet, amid this high-stakes game of cat and mouse, I found a rhythm and a method to my madness that kept me one step ahead of my digital adversary.

The culmination of my efforts was nothing short of audacious—aa simultaneous override of the complex's power grid and security protocols. The gamble was risky, and the timing had to be perfect. As I initiated the sequence, the facility plunged into darkness, a brief but profound silence enveloping us. It was the moment of truth, a fleeting opportunity to breach the heart of the complex undetected.

In the darkness, guided only by the faint glow of my TMT, I navigated the now-quiet halls with renewed purpose. The AI, momentarily blind, could only scramble to reroute power and regain control. But the delay was all I needed. I bypassed the final barriers, reaching the central hub where the rogue AI's core resided.

The confrontation was inevitable. The AI, recognizing the threat I posed, marshaled its remaining defenses in a desperate bid to protect itself. But the balance had shifted. Without its full surveillance capabilities, the AI was vulnerable and reliant on crude, physical obstacles that I could anticipate and counter.

The battle was tense, each moment a test of wills between man and machine. Yet, despite the odds, I prevailed. The rogue AI, once a seemingly insurmountable guardian, was silenced, its control over the complex severed. In its place, a quiet sense of victory settled over me. The Omega Pulse Disruptor remained unfound, a goal still beyond my reach, but the defeat of the AI was a critical victory in its own right.

Inside the complex, with the rogue AI now silent, the atmosphere was charged with a tense quietude, akin to the calm after a storm. However, I was acutely aware that my mission was far from complete. The Omega Pulse Disruptor, the key to my next move, was still hidden somewhere within these walls. I couldn't afford to lower my guard; the complex was vast, its secrets manifold, and its dangers far from neutralized.

As I ventured deeper, navigating through the silent corridors, I stumbled upon a heavily secured chamber. The chamber's forbidding facade momentarily mirrored the isolation within my own heart, a stark reminder of the solitude that had been my constant companion. Yet, as I prepared to breach its secrets, I was reminded of the connections I'd forged along the way—unseen allies and distant friends who believed in the quest I'd undertaken. It was solace that fueled my resolve, transforming solitude into strength.

The door, made of reinforced steel, was adorned with security measures that seemed impenetrable. It was clear that whatever lay beyond was of significant importance. I felt a surge of anticipation; this had to be the location of the Omega Pulse Disruptor.

The security system presented a formidable challenge. It was an intricate puzzle, a network of codes and mechanisms that required both finesse and acute intellectual acumen to bypass. Recalling the patterns and techniques gleaned from my encounter with the rogue AI, I set to work, my fingers dancing over the interface with practiced precision. The complexity of the puzzle was staggering, but so was my determination.

After what seemed like hours but could have just been moments in the heightened state of concentration, I heard the satisfying click of the door's locks disengaging. The chamber beyond slowly revealed itself, bathed in a soft, blue light that seemed to hum with latent energy. There, on a pedestal in the center of the room, was the Omega Pulse Disruptor.

Approaching the device, I could feel its power—a palpable force that resonated with the very air around it. The disruptor was sleek; its design was elegant yet unmistakably potent. I reached out, my hand closing around it, and in that moment, I felt a surge of capability flow through me. The device was more than just a weapon; it was a key to unlocking new possibilities, a means to confront the challenges that lay ahead with newfound confidence.

However, the victory was short-lived. The removal of the disruptor triggered an alarm, a piercing siren that cut through the silence like a knife. Instantaneously, the complex sprung to life, its dormant systems awakening in a last-ditch effort to thwart my escape. Automated defenses activated, sending drones and security bots converging at my location.

I knew then that the path out would not be easy. With the Omega Pulse Disruptor in hand, I braced myself for the onslaught. Each step towards the exit was contested by waves of automated assailants, each more determined than the last to reclaim the disruptor. But the device proved its worth; with each pulse emitted, drones faltered and systems overloaded, clearing my path with astonishing efficiency.

It was a relentless gauntlet, a test of both endurance and the disruptor's capabilities. Yet, with every obstacle overcome, I grew more adept at wielding the device; its power was a beacon that cut through the darkness and chaos.

Finally, after what seemed likeseemed an eternity of conflict and navigation through the complex's treacherous innards, the exit loomed before me. Stepping into the open air, the disruptor securely in my possession, I allowed myself a moment of relief. The Omega CoreTech Complex, with its myriad challenges and the rogue AI that had once ruled it, was behind me. The journey ahead remained fraught with uncertainty, but with the Omega Pulse Disruptor at my side, I felt ready to face whatever lay beyond, to journey further into the unknown with a powerful ally in my hands.

This readiness was not born from the disruptor's power alone but from an understanding that the true strength lay in the lessons of the past, resilience in the face of adversity, and the pursuit of knowledge in a world eager for rebirth.

As I revved up my Alloyed Charger, the engine roared to life, its powerful hum echoing through the desolate landscape. The sky above was a canvas of swirling clouds, casting ominous shadows over the barren terrain below. With a deep breath, I pushed forward, the bike's sleek form slicing through the air like a knife through butter.

The journey ahead was fraught with uncertainty, the only certainty being the danger that awaited me at the Forge Citadel. As I sped across the wasteland, the landscape shifted around me, morphing from rocky outcrops to jagged cliffs, each turn revealing a new vista of desolation.

Despite the bleakness of my surroundings, I couldn't help but marvel at the raw beauty of the untamed wilderness. Ancient rock formations jutted out of the earth like forgotten sentinels, their weathered faces bearing the scars of countless years of erosion. In the distance, a lone hawk soared through the sky, its piercing cry a haunting reminder of the world's resilience in the face of adversity.

As I pressed on, the landscape grew increasingly hostile, the ground beneath me becoming more treacherous with each passing mile. Cracks and crevices appeared in the earth, threatening to swallow me whole as I navigated the perilous terrain.

But it wasn't just the landscape that posed a threat; the wildlife, too, seemed to sense my presence, lurking in the shadows with predatory intent. Packs of scavengers prowled the outskirts of my path, their glowing eyes watching my every move with hungry anticipation.

With each passing moment, the tension mounted, the sense of impending danger hanging heavy in the air. I knew I was drawing closer to my destination, the Forge Citadel, looming on the horizon like a dark omen.

But even as I neared the heart of danger, I remained undeterred, my determination unwavering in the face of adversity. With the Omega Pulse Disruptor strapped securely to my back, I knew I had the means to overcome whatever obstacles lay in my path.

As the Alloyed Charger tore across the landscape at breakneck speed, I steeled myself for the challenges ahead. My mind focused on the task at hand. Whatever awaited me in the Forge Citadel, I was ready to face it head-on, armed with courage, determination, and the unwavering resolve to succeed.

As I approached the Forge Citadel, I was met with a formidable sight: a vast array of robotic adversaries, their metallic forms ranging in size and design. Among them, I recognized the menacing silhouette of sentinel drones and the scavenger-like appearance of scraphounds. The cacophony of their movements echoed through the air, a symphony of mechanical groans, humming servos, and heavy footfalls that reverberated across the wasteland.

Drawing nearer, I witnessed a startling transformation as the robots detected my presence. In unison, their weapon systems activated, a menacing display of aggression that signaled imminent danger. Reacting swiftly, I reached for the Omega Pulse Disruptor, feeling its weight and power in my grip.

As I activated the device, a low, ominous hum filled the air, intensifying with each passing moment. It was as if the disruptor drew upon the very essence of its surroundings, charging itself with an otherworldly energy. With a crescendo that shook the earth beneath my feet, the disruptor unleashed its fury in a burst of sound and light.

In an instant, the once-threatening horde of robots fell silent, their mechanical forms collapsing to the ground with a resounding cacophony of metal and circuitry. The aftermath was a display of the disruptor's devastating power, a moment of eerie stillness amidst the chaos of battle.

Upon entering the citadel, I was greeted not by the expected maze of corridors or the hum of machinery but by an immense silence that echoed off the vast, empty walls. The chamber was circular, its diameter so wide that the opposite wall seemed to blend into the shadows. High above, the ceiling was lost to darkness, save for the faint outline of cables and conduits converging towards the center like the spokes of a giant wheel.

The air was still, charged with an anticipation that prickled my skin. In the silence of the citadel, surrounded by echoes of potential, the weight of my mission pressed heavily on me. Each step was an expression of the solitude of my journey, yet it was here, amidst the shadows of what was and what might be, that I found a renewed sense of purpose.

There, in the heart of the chamber, stood a solitary pedestal. It was sleek, almost austere in design, supporting the Codesync Interface—the nexus of digital and physical realms. The interface itself was unassuming, yet it pulsed with a subtle light, a beacon in the vast emptiness.

The chamber's walls were lined with screens and interfaces, all dormant, their purpose and potential locked away in silence. It was as if the entire citadel, with all its complexity and power, was holding its breath, waiting for a touch to awaken its heart.

This setting weaved a rich tapestry of thematic elements—isolation, anticipation, the juxtaposition of power and vulnerability. The vastness of the chamber, coupled with its minimalistic contents, served to underscore the significance of the room.

At the center of the room stood a pedestal, and to my immense surprise, there stood the Codesync Interface. Its interface was a hexagonal device, roughly the height of a standard ruler, designed to fit into a specific indentation next to a control panel.

Made from a dense metallic material with a matte black finish, it featured intricate silver lines that converged towards a central, coin-sized crystalline display. This display is illuminated to show the ever-changing keycode required to access the Ascendant Matrix. Around this display were small, touch-sensitive buttons that lit up upon interaction. The interface's primary function was to synchronize with the Matrix's security system, allowing seamless access.

Anxiety gripped me as I reached out for the Codesync Interface. As I touched the Codesync Interface, reality peeled away, revealing layers of digital existence that intertwined with the very fabric of my consciousness. This realm, a complex network of data and energy, mirrored the vastness of human thought and emotion, distilled into a digital landscape that defied conventional physics. The moment my fingers made contact, darkness enveloped me. a fleeting moment, and then I found myself transported to an entirely different realm. The room surrounding me was aristine white, adorned with a continuous cascade of unfamiliar vertical symbols flowing along the walls. Each symbol seemed to pulsate with an otherworldly energy, alien to my senses.

I stood in awe amidst this cosmic landscape, surrounded by transparent, capsule-like structures resembling data nodes or ethereal beings, interconnected by intricate lines of glowing luminescence. Overhead, a multitude of these structures formed a mesmerizing constellation, radiating a vivid green light that illuminated the space with an otherworldly glow. At the center, a colossal, luminous ring encircled a nebula-like formation, exuding an aura of mystery and power.

To my surprise, my attire had transformed as well; I was now clad in a form-fitting jumpsuit of pristine white, adorned with sleek black accents. As I stood amidst these enigmatic structures, a faint static hum permeated the air, akin to the whispers of spectral entities from a digital realm beyond comprehension.

As I reached out to touch the data nodes, they responded with undulating waves, their movement akin to the gentle sway of ocean currents. With each step, I found myself able to pass effortlessly through these ethereal structures, drawn inexorably toward the central formation. Despite a lingering sense of trepidation, I felt compelled to press onward, driven by an insatiable curiosity.

Upon making contact with the central formation, a profound transformation overtook my surroundings. Certain data nodes shifted ominously to a deep crimson hue, while the once-stable nebula shattered into fragmented shards that scattered throughout the space.

The crimson nodes surged towards me with alarming speed, emanating an aura of imminent danger that sent shivers down my spine. Instinctively, I recoiled from their advance, instinctively recognizing them as harbingers of peril. Despite my efforts to evade them, they multiplied and closed in with relentless determination, their numbers swelling with each passing moment.

Desperate to escape their grasp, I darted towards a nearby nebula fragment, seeking refuge within its protective confines. Yet even as I emerged into what seemed like safety, I couldn't shake the looming threat of the encroaching nodes. From a distance, I watched as they changed course, their relentless pursuit undeterred by any obstacle in their path.

No matter how swiftly I fled, the walls of this ethereal labyrinth remained perpetually out of reach, an elusive barrier that defied my every attempt to breach it. With each stride, the encroaching crimson nodes drew nearer, their menacing presence casting a pall of dread over my frantic efforts.

Time and again, I sought refuge within the shifting fragments of the nebula, only to find myself transported to yet another corner of this enigmatic realm, my escape route tantalizingly distant.

As the relentless pursuit continued unabated, a sense of hopelessness crept into my thoughts, the realization dawning that I was ensnared within a prison of digital constructs, condemned to be hunted by corrupted nodes for all eternity. Despite my resolve, despair threatened to overwhelm me as I desperately sought a glimmer of escape amidst the endless expanse of data.

As I continued to navigate the shifting landscape, a moment of clarity struck—a realization that the key to my salvation lies not in fleeing but in confronting the source of their torment.

With renewed determination, I steeled myself for the ultimate confrontation. Drawing upon my inner strength, I mustered the courage to face the crimson nodes head-on, channeling my fear into focused resolve.

As the corrupted nodes converged upon me, I stood my ground, refusing to succumb to despair. With a decisive motion, I extended my hand towards the central formation, summoning forth a surge of untapped energy.

In a blinding flash of light, the surrounding space began to ripple and warp, the very fabric of the digital realm bending to my will. With a final burst of effort, I unleashed a wave of transformative energy, purging the corrupted nodes from existence and shattering the illusion of the labyrinth.

I now found myself standing in the center of a vast digital landscape, surrounded by towering structures resembling circuitry and data nodes. The air crackles with energy, and streams of data flow like rivers around them.

Suddenly, a formidable barrier materialized in front of me, blocking my path forward. It shimmered with an ethereal glow, emanating an aura of impenetrable security.

As I approached the firewall, lines of code began to materialize and swirl around me, forming intricate patterns that pulsed with energy. The firewall's defenses were formidable, but I remained undeterred.

With a sense of determination, I began to analyze the firewall, searching for weaknesses and vulnerabilities in its structure. I reached out, my hands enveloped in digital energy, ready to engage in the battle of wits and skill.

The firewall reacted to my presence, unleashing a barrage of digital attacks in an attempt to thwart my advance. Firewalls morphed into formidable guardians, their forms shifting and changing with each assault.

Undeterred, I employed my knowledge of coding and digital manipulation to counter the firewall's onslaught. I weaved intricate patterns of code, exploiting loopholes and weaknesses in the firewall's defenses.

With each successful maneuver, the firewall weakened, and its once-impenetrable barrier began to falter under my relentless assault. Sparks flew as digital energy clashed against digital steel in a dazzling display of power.

Finally, I delivered the decisive blow, shattering the firewall's defenses and breaking through its formidable barrier. The digital landscape rippled and shifted as the firewall crumbled, revealing the path forward.

With the firewall defeated, I strode forward, my spirit buoyed by my victory. I continued my journey through the digital realm, ready to face whatever challenges lie ahead with newfound confidence and determination.

As I navigated the digital landscape, swarms of antivirus programs converged upon me, their digital forms pulsating with a menacing glow. Mistakingly identifying me as a threat, they moved with relentless determination to eradicate my presence.

The antivirus programs adapted to my every movement, their movements mirroring my own as they closed in from all sides. Their relentless pursuit left me with no choice but to employ stealth and cunning to evade their detection.

With each step, I moved with calculated precision, weaving through the labyrinthine pathways of the digital realm. I used decoys and distractions to divert the attention of the antivirus programs, buying precious moments to slip past their watchful gaze.

As I darted between data nodes and virtual obstacles, the antivirus programs swarmed around me like a relentless tide, their digital forms pulsating with malevolent intent. I remained vigilant, constantly on the lookout for any signs of detection.

Despite the overwhelming odds, I refused to yield to despair. With every evasion and decoy tactic, I edged closer to my goal, determined to overcome this digital obstacle and continue my journey through the realm.

The antivirus programs, relentless in their pursuit, adapted their tactics in response to my maneuvers, making each evasion more challenging than the last. I remained one step ahead, employing every trick in my arsenal to outwit their relentless vigilance.

With nerves of steel and unwavering resolve, I pressed forward, my determination unyielding in the face of adversity. Each step forward was a dance with danger, a balancing act between the rush of adrenaline and the steady beat of resolve. The complex's shifting shadows played tricks on my senses, heightening the tension with each flicker of movement. Yet, within this ballet of light and darkness, I found clarity — a singular focus on the path ahead, undeterred by the obstacles that lay in wait.

Though the antivirus programs were formidable foes, I refused to let them deter me from my ultimate objective.

As I finally broke free from the grasp of the antivirus swarm, a surge of triumph coursed through me. With each obstacle overcome, I grew stronger and more resolute in my quest to navigate the digital realm and uncover its secrets.

As I ventured deeper into the digital realm, I found myself ensnared within the labyrinthine corridors of my own mind. Each step forward seemed to echo with the weight of my fears and doubts, threatening to derail my quest before it had truly begun.

Images of past failures flickered in the shadows, haunting me with the specter of inadequacy. I could almost hear the whispers of doubt that had plagued me for so long, questioning my worthiness to lead and my ability to make the right decisions in the face of adversity.

As I pressed on, the walls of the chamber seemed to close in around me, suffocating me with the fear of loss. Faces of companions lost and lives shattered flashed before my eyes—a painful reminder of the sacrifices I had made and the heavy burden of leadership I bore.

Amidst the shadows, doubts about the true nature of my quest gnawed at my resolve. I questioned whether the Ascendant Matrix held the key to salvation or merely another step towards oblivion, my faith in the prophecies that guided me wavering in the face of uncertainty.

Yet even as my doubts threatened to overwhelm me, a glimmer of hope pierced the darkness. With each step forward, I clung to the belief that my journey held the promise of a better future, a beacon of light amidst the encroaching shadows of doubt and despair.

Driven by the flicker of hope in my heart, I pressed on, determined to confront my fears and doubts head-on. I knew that only by overcoming the shadows that haunted me could I hope to unlock the true potential of the Ascendant Matrix and guide humanity towards a brighter tomorrow.

As this realization washed over me, a sense of relief flooded my mind, washing away the doubts and fears that had plagued me. Suddenly, I found myself standing in a place reminiscent of the citadel before my entry into this digital realm.

In this digital realm, the Forge Citadel formed before me. It was no longer a physical construct of metal and stone, but a vast expanse of virtual architecture sprawling across an endless grid of light and shadow. The silence persisted, yet it was a different kind of quiet, filled with the potential energy of dormant code and data streams waiting to be awakened.

The chamber I stood in was a perfect circle, its edges dissolving into a horizon that bent into the digital ether. Above, the ceiling was an illusion of interlacing data threads converging to form a canopy that resembled the night sky, studded with constellations of information nodes instead of stars.

The air around me vibrated with the latent power of the system, an electric breeze that tingled against the avatar I perceived as my own skin. The pedestal in the center was now a column of pulsating code, streams of numbers and symbols cascading down its length, pooling around the base where the Codesync Interface lay.

The surrounding walls were translucent panes, alive with the dance of algorithms and schematics that played across their surfaces. The dormant screens of the physical world here were active canvases, displaying the artistry of a world built from binary, a world that breathed the pure essence of possibility.

This digital representation of the Forge Citadel was more than a mere copy; it was an evolution, a realm where the laws of physics were replaced by the rules of programming. The Citadel was a fortress of knowledge, each byte a brick, each line of code a promise of power, waiting for the right key to unlock its secrets.

In this realm, I felt a connection to the core of the world's technology, a sense that I was at the very nerve center of what once was and what could be again. It was a place of latent potential, a temple to the past's glories and the future's promises, awaiting the command to unleash its boundless capabilities.

As I drew nearer to the column of pulsating code, a digital image of the Codesync Interface materialized before me. With both hands, I reached out and grasped the representation of my current objective.

In an instant, a blinding flash enveloped me, and I found myself back in the physical reality within the citadel. The moment of transition was both instantaneous and eternal, a journey between worlds that blurred the lines between digital and physical, challenging my perception of reality. The Codesync Interface was now securely in my hands. It took a moment for my mind to fully transition from the digital realm back to the physical, but once I had adjusted, a profound sense of accomplishment washed over me. Not only had

I triumphed over the challenges of the digital realm, but I had also fulfilled my objective.

With the Codesync Interface now in my possession, I knew that my next quest would lead me to the Ascendant Matrix, guiding me toward the Luminara Caverns. It marked the culmination of a long and arduous journey.

As I journeyed away from the remnants of the Omega CoreTech Complex, the echo of SYNAPSE's parting words remained with me, a steadfast companion against the backdrop of desolation. The silence of the wasteland, once oppressive, now resonated with a symphony of potential—the possibility of what could be rekindled from the ashes of the past. Each step forward was a testament to the resilience of the human spirit, a defiance against the entropy that sought to claim the remnants of a world once vibrant with life and ambition.

In the solitude of the wilderness, I found a clarity of purpose that had eluded me in the cacophony of battles fought and challenges overcome. The quest for the Ascendant Matrix was no longer a solitary endeavor but a beacon for those who dared to dream of a world reborn from the shadow of its ruins. The Codesync Interface, now secure in my grasp, was not merely a key to unlocking ancient secrets; it was a symbol of the unity between technology and humanity, a bridge between the wisdom of the past and the hope of the future.

As the first stars pierced the twilight canopy, casting their ancient light upon the scarred landscape, I realized that my journey was but a chapter in the epic saga of renewal. The challenges that lay ahead, the trials of the Luminara Caverns, and the specter of the Forge Citadel were milestones on a path that stretched beyond the horizon of my understanding. It was a path paved with the sacrifices of those who walked before me and illuminated by the collective aspiration for a dawn yet to break.

In that moment of introspection, I understood that the true journey was not towards a destination but through the very heart of what it means to be human—to strive, to falter, and to rise again, ever reaching for the light. With the night wind as my witness, I pledged to carry the legacy of those who had perished in the quest for knowledge and to honor their memory by forging a future worthy of their sacrifice. The road ahead was fraught with uncertainty, but I was no longer a wanderer in the darkness; I was a harbinger of the dawn, a guardian of the flame that would ignite the beacons of a new world.

Leaving the citadel behind, I reflected on the lessons learned in the digital realms—insights not gleaned from an external universe but from the depths of my own mind. Armed with a newfound understanding of myself, I felt prepared to forge ahead on my journey. With each step through this digital domain, I realized that our quest for knowledge and understanding, much like the boundless landscapes around me, is infinite. It is in this journey, through both light and darkness, that we find our true strength.

INTO THE DEPTHS

As I departed from the Omega CoreTech Complex and entered the vast desert, the stark, expansive terrain challenged both my body and spirit, pushing me towards the ruins of Luminara. This wasn't just a physical journey; it was a test of resilience, shaping my resolve for the trials ahead.

The desert was relentless in its challenge, with the sun reigning supreme in the clear blue sky, turning the sand beneath my feet into a scorching sea. This journey was a test of endurance, with each step a reminder of the desert's unforgiving nature. Yet, in this desolation, I found a profound sense of clarity. The vast emptiness served as a canvas for reflection, pushing me to ponder the journey that lay ahead and the decisions that had led me to this moment.

Navigating through the desert required more than just physical strength; it demanded a steadfast spirit and an unwavering determination. Sandstorms blurred the horizon, erasing the line between earth and sky, while the nights introduced a chilling cold that contrasted sharply with the day's heat. These trials, though daunting, sharpened my focus and fortified my will, teaching me the true meaning of perseverance.

As I traversed this barren landscape, the Ruins of Luminara began to take shape on the horizon, emerging as a display of the impermanence of civilization. The sight of these ruins, standing defiant against the encroaching sands, was a poignant reminder of the fleeting nature of human endeavors. As I approached the city's remnants, I was struck by the silence that enveloped this once-thriving metropolis, now reduced to the shadows and whispers of its former glory.

Standing at the edge of Luminara's ruins, I paused to take in the view before me. The city, with its crumbled edifices and sand-filled streets, spoke of a bygone era of prosperity and technological advancement. It was here, among the echoes of a civilization lost to time, that I felt the weight of my own journey. The ruins served as a gateway, not just to the physical path that lay ahead but to a deeper exploration of the legacy we leave behind.

The journey through the desert and to the threshold of Luminara's ruins was as much an inward voyage as it was a traverse across the land. The solitude of the desert, coupled with the solemn beauty of the ruins, provided a rare opportunity for introspection. It was a chance to reflect on the transient nature of success and the enduring impact of our actions. In the stillness of Luminara, I found a moment of peace, a brief respite to gather my thoughts and steel myself for the challenges ahead.

As I stood among the remnants of Luminara, the reality of my quest weighed heavily on me. Standing amid Luminara's echoes, the gravity of our mission pressed upon me. Failure was not merely a personal defeat but could spell disaster for realms beyond our own. Ulric and I weren't just fighting for survival; we were guardians of a future teetering on the brink of oblivion.

Ahead lay the descent into the yet-unseen caverns, a journey that promised to test the very limits of my courage and capability. Yet, fortified by the trials of the desert and the solemn lessons of the ruins, I felt a renewed sense of purpose. The journey to Luminara had not only brought me to the doorstep of the unknown but had also prepared me to face whatever lay beyond with resilience and resolve.

Dismounting from my Alloyed Charger, I prepared myself to explore the ruins in pursuit of the Luminara Caverns. Taking a moment to survey my surroundings, I took in the scene before me.

The Ruins of Luminara sprawled across the edge of the vast desert like a shadow of history, an echo of a world that once was. What stood before me was a breathtaking vista of decay and grandeur intertwined, a city that time had both ravaged and revered. The sands of the desert, relentless in their pursuit, had claimed much of the city, yet in their embrace, the ruins exuded an immutable sense of majesty.

As I stepped into the heart of Luminara, the remnants of its infrastructure painted a picture of a civilization that thrived on innovation and the pursuit of knowledge. Towering structures, now crumbled and worn, stretched towards the sky, their silhouettes a display of architectural ambition and the ingenuity of their creators. The streets, laid out in meticulous grids, were now pathways of sand, leading to the skeletons of buildings that once teemed with life.

The central plaza, a vast open space encircled by the ruins of grand edifices, spoke volumes of the city's social and cultural zenith. Here, the remains of a once-magnificent fountain, now dry and filled with sand, sat silently, surrounded by the ghosts of bustling market stalls and communal gatherings. Statues of Luminara's luminaries, scholars, and heroes stood guard around the plaza, their features eroded but their dignity intact, watching over a city that had slipped into legend.

On the outskirts of the plaza, residential areas told a more personal story of Luminara. Homes built with an eye for both functionality and beauty, now half-buried, offered glimpses into the daily lives of those who walked these streets. Courtyards, designed for privacy and contemplation, opened up to the sky, their walls adorned with the faint remnants of vibrant murals, whispering tales of dreams and aspirations.

As I delved deeper, I encountered the academic district, where the pursuit of knowledge was once the city's beating heart. The ruins of libraries and laboratories, their once-proud domes and arches now fractured, stood as monuments to the quest for understanding. Here, amid the silence, the air seemed thick with the echo of discourse and discovery, a reminder of the minds that once sought to unravel the mysteries of the universe.

Venturing to the city's edge, the defensive structures revealed Luminara's awareness of its vulnerability. Fortifications, now worn and breached, spoke of a city that valued its sanctity and safeguarded its achievements against the encroachments of the outside world. The gates, grand and imposing even in their ruin, marked the threshold between the known and the wilderness beyond, a boundary between civilization and the unyielding forces of nature.

In the Ruins of Luminara, every stone and every shattered column told a story of ambition, achievement, and the inevitable passage of time. Walking among these remnants, I was a solitary witness to the city's final chapters, an explorer in a landscape where the legacy of the past shaped the journey into the future.

Looking around among the ruins, I found the one place I was after. The giant statue of an ancient hero. It stood as a reminder of the bygone era of valor and strength. Towering high above the ground, its imposing figure commanded reverence and awe from all who beheld it. Hewn from stone or cast in metal, the hero's form was depicted in a stance of noble resolve, with chiseled features that spoke of courage and determination.

At its base, intricate reliefs or inscriptions recounted tales of legendary deeds and heroic exploits, immortalizing the hero's triumphs for future generations to admire. The statue's outstretched arms seemed to beckon to the heavens, as if reaching for eternal glory or calling upon divine favor.

Despite the passage of time, the statue remained a steadfast guardian of the land, its weathered visage a silent witness to the ebb and flow of history. Whether bathed in the golden light of dawn or cast in the shadow of dusk, it stood as a symbol of hope and inspiration, a reminder of the indomitable spirit that resides within every hero's heart.

The path to the statue stretched far ahead, yet I wasted no time in setting off towards it. As I journeyed onward, I encountered the remnants of an ancient structure, its weathered stones half-buried beneath shifting sands. Amidst the rubble, a lone figure perched upon a stone, partaking in a simple meal of bread and sipping from a bottle of fluids.

He was a formidable and muscular figure, and his height would make him tower over the majority of people. His imposing frame was clad in the sturdy defense of splint mail armor, each metal splint meticulously arranged to provide maximum protection while allowing for fluid movement. The torso, adorned with vertically aligned splints, created a striking pattern across his broad chest and abdomen, the rivets securing them glinting in the sunlight.

Atop his massive shoulders sat rounded pauldrons, their polished surfaces reflecting the harsh glimmer of the battlefield. Beneath, a layer of chainmail draped, providing added safeguarding to his arms. A thick leather belt, cinched tightly around his waist, held the splint mail securely in place, emphasizing the powerful contours of his physique.

He had a thick beard, rugged and unkempt, framed by a stern countenance, weathered by years of battle and hardship, and piercing eyes, as sharp as the edge of his blade.

His imposing longsword rested beside him, its blade catching the sunlight with a promise of swift justice. A knapsack lay nearby, holding his belongings. Intrigued, I approached him to learn more.

"Aren't you hot under all that armor?" I inquired.

"Aye, but I prefer the safety it provides, especially with the threat of rats lurking about," he replied.

"Rats?" I scoffed.

"Not your ordinary rodents. These are some sort of rat-like creatures that infest this area. I know not whence they come, but they emerge in packs from time to time," he explained.

"I haven't seen any yet. What brings you to this place?" I inquired further.

"I was journeying westward on my steed when I stumbled upon this spot. Pausing to rest and dine, I was beset by these creatures. I dispatched four of them; I did, but not before one injured my horse grievously. I had to put the poor beast down. Now I find myself stranded amidst these ruins in the desert," he recounted solemnly.

"I didn't realize Washington had any deserts. According to my current map, this area is designated as a desert, but pre-war maps would indicate that we're currently situated in the Columbia River Plateau," I explained.

"Pre-war maps? How'd you come by those?" he inquired. "A lengthy tale for another time. Let's just say I have my ways," I replied cryptically.

"Fair enough," he conceded. "Doesn't change my predicament, though."

"I'd offer to transport you to your destination on my Charger, but I'm tied up here for the foreseeable future," I remarked.

"What's a Charger?" he inquired, his tone reflecting not just confusion but a curiosity about the world beyond his immediate experience.

"A relic of past travels and a silent companion on my journey. It's waiting, hidden just beyond the horizon," I answered, hinting at the breadth of my quest and the worlds it has spanned."

"So, what brings you to this place then?" he pressed.

"Another long story. See that imposing statue over yonder?" I gestured toward the monument. "It conceals an entrance to an underground cavern. My mission is to breach it and access something called the Ascendant Matrix, a network of supercomputers purported to hold the key to humanity's salvation."

"Sounds intriguing. If you're in need of assistance, for the right price, I could be persuaded to lend a hand," he offered.

"Well, I have a stash of odds and ends from my previous journeys, mostly mechanical parts, but I do happen to have one small energy core left. You're welcome to it," I offered.

"Sure, I'll take the energy core, but you'll have to carry it until we're finished," he agreed.

"Fair enough. I'm Ethan Hawthorne. And you?" I introduced myself.

"I'm Ulric Steelborn, at your service," he replied.

"Pleasure to meet you, Ulric. Shall we press on to the statue then?" I suggested.

"Absolutely. I've wrapped up here... Hold on, looks like we've got company!" Ulric exclaimed, pointing behind me.

Turning, I spotted a horde of rat-like creatures advancing toward us. They stood on two legs with hunched postures, their fur matted and brown. Each wielded a crude sword; their mouths curled into snarls, revealing sharp teeth. Their eyes gleamed with hostility as they closed in, dressed in tattered cloth and bandages that barely passed for clothing.

I readied myself as Ulric hoisted his hefty sword, gripping the handle with both hands and assuming a battle-ready stance. As the creatures drew near, one lunged at me with its sword, but I swiftly countered, delivering a powerful blow to its face that sent it crashing to the ground. Meanwhile, Ulric swung his sword with precision, severing the head of another attacker in a single stroke.

With a swift kick, I repelled another creature that dared to approach, sending it tumbling backward in agony. It struggled to rise, only to retreat hastily in the face of our ferocity. Ulric, undeterred, thrust his sword into the chest of yet another foe, while I subdued the last with a decisive grapple, delivering a crushing blow to its throat that silenced it for good.

Impressed, Ulric remarked, "I see you're quite skilled in combat. And you don't even seem winded."

"I've had my fair share of practice. And you handle that sword of yours with finesse," I acknowledged.

"One question though," Ulric continued, "why haven't you used that gun strapped to your back?"

"It's more fun this way. I save the gun for more formidable foes. These rat-men hardly pose a challenge," I explained.

"Agreed. Shall we press on?" Ulric proposed. "Absolutely," I replied.

Together, we made our way toward the towering statue, navigating through the scattered ruins that littered the area. Finally, we reached the statue, standing in the center of a spacious square. Before us, a flat wall of stone, reminiscent of a doorway, awaited our exploration.

"This must be the entrance," I observed.

How do we get through it, though?" queried Ulric.

"I'm not entirely sure. Let me give something a try," I replied.

Taking out my TMT, I scanned the wall for any anomalies. The device indicated the presence of an open space behind the wall, but there seemed to be no discernible mechanism for opening it.

"It appears to be some sort of entrance, but there are no levers or buttons to trigger it," I remarked.

"In that case, it looks like we'll have to take the direct approach," Ulric declared.

Stepping back, Ulric retrieved a sizable stone from a nearby rocky outcrop. With a determined expression, he returned to the wall and began pounding it with a force that rivaled even my own enhanced strength.

"I'm not certain this will work." I voiced my doubts. "It's our only option," Ulric retorted.

As cracks started to form in the wall, I joined Ulric in his efforts, grabbing another hefty stone and assisting him in demolishing the barrier. It took considerable time and effort, but eventually, the wall began to crumble, revealing an opening large enough for us to pass through.

Peering inside, I spotted a ladder leading downward. "It looks like it's time to descend," I announced.

With that, I descended the ladder, with Ulric following closely behind. After a lengthy descent, we finally reached the bottom, greeted by the sight of the fabled Caverns of Luminara.

As we descended, the air grew cooler, and the walls of the cavern pressed close. Each breath echoed in the vast emptiness, the only sound being the scrape of our boots against the ancient stone. The darkness was almost palpable, a thick blanket that seemed to absorb all light, leaving us to navigate by touch and the dim glow of Ulric's blade.

The chamber we stood in was a grand spectacle, a vast, echoing space that could easily have been the heart of an underground kingdom. I was immediately struck by its sheer scale. The ceiling arches high above, lost to shadow, where faint glimmers of crystal formations caught the light, resembling distant stars in a subterranean night sky. The ground beneath our feet was smooth, worn by ancient waters and countless footsteps, leading into the expansive darkness ahead.

In the center, a natural dais rises, formed from the same stalagmite structures that decorate the cavern. It's surrounded by pools of water, their surfaces perfectly still, mirroring the stalactites above and creating an illusion of depth that makes the floor seem endless. These pools were fed by thin streams of water running down the chamber walls; the gentle sound of their flow reverberated softly throughout the space.

Around the perimeter, natural columns stood tall, supporting the weight of the earth above. They were carved by time and the drip of mineral-rich water, patterned with stripes of varying shades that told the tale of ages past. Between these columns, the walls were adorned with phosphorescent lichen and fungi, casting a soft, bioluminescent glow that illuminated the cavern with an otherworldly light.

Scattered across the floor, remnants of Luminara's past peek through the natural beauty. Fragments of pottery, tools made from bone and stone, and the bases of what might have been statues or monuments to forgotten gods or heroes. These relics, half-swallowed by the earth, offered a haunting reminder of the bustling life that once filled these caverns.

At the far end, a massive, partially collapsed archway suggests the entrance to further mysteries beyond. Its carved stones, now eroded, hinted at the grandeur of the civilization that built them, a civilization that thrived in harmony with the cavern's natural majesty.

As we moved through the chamber, I felt a profound sense of connection to the ancient people of Luminara. I imagined the ceremonies and gatherings that might have taken place in this very chamber, under the earth's protective embrace. The main chamber, with its timeless beauty and echoes of the past, stood as a monument not only to the natural wonders of the world but also to the enduring spirit of humanity in the face of oblivion.

"Remarkable, isn't it?" remarked Ulric.

"Indeed, amidst all my travels, this stands as one of the most extraordinary natural wonders I've encountered," I concurred.

Our words reverberated, swallowed by the vastness of the caverns.

Venturing deeper into the labyrinthine corridors, the darkness enveloped us, punctuated only by the faint echoes of dripping stalactites, the fluttering of bat wings, and the subtle shifting of rocks from above.

In the dimly lit corridors of the Luminara Caverns, Ulric's towering presence was both a reassurance and a stark reminder of the trade we had struck: an Energy Core for his loyalty and protection.

Eventually, the cavern plunged into an abyss of darkness.

Ulric's confident demeanor faltered momentarily in the engulfing shadow. "This darkness... it's unnatural," he grumbled, his voice echoing softly off the unseen walls.

I nodded, even though I knew he couldn't see it. "It's a test," I explained, my voice steady despite the rising panic inside. "A test of our senses... and perhaps, our resolve."

Ulric unsheathed his greatsword, the sound of metal on leather slicing through the silence. "Then let us not dally. Lead the way, Ethan."

Closing my eyes, I focused on the subtle sounds and drafts in the cavern. Each step we took was measured, the silence a heavy blanket that threatened to smother our spirits. I extended my hand behind me, and after a moment, I felt the reassuring grip of Ulric's hand on my shoulder. "We'll rely on more than sight here," I whispered.

Moving cautiously, we navigated the unseen path. Ulric's heavy footsteps and the occasional clank of his split mail armor added to the cacophony of echoes, guiding us through the darkness. "How do you find your way in this... absence of light?" Ulric asked, his voice tinged with a newfound respect.

"It's about using what we have left," I replied. "Our hearing, touch, and even our instincts. The darkness isn't just a barrier; it's a teacher."

Gradually, the oppressive darkness felt less daunting. With Ulric's unwavering strength behind me and my guidance, we found a rhythm in the pitch black.

"I must admit, there's wisdom in your words, Ethan. I've always relied on my strength and my sword. But this... this requires a different kind of strength," Ulric conceded, his voice echoing our shared realization.

Finally, as our eyes adjusted and a faint light began to emerge, signaling the end of our trial, Ulric spoke again: "I've fought countless battles, Ethan, but navigating through darkness with nothing but trust and instinct is a first for me."

Emerging into the dim light, I turned to Ulric, seeing his formidable figure in a new light.

We paused, taking a moment to catch our breath. The darkness behind us felt like a metaphor for the journey thus far—fraught with unseen dangers and reliant on mutual trust.

"This place... it makes you think, doesn't it?" Ulric said, breaking the silence. "About what we're fighting for." I nodded, the weight of our experiences settling around us like the dust of a cavern.

"Yes, and about who we're fighting as," I added. In the dim light of the cavern, our shadows stretched long and intertwined, a visual echo of our shared path.

"Each trial here is a lesson, Ulric. This one taught us to trust in our other senses... and in each other."

Ulric nodded, sheathing his greatsword. "Aye, and it seems I've much to learn. Lead on, Ethan. I've got your back, and I'm keen to see what other lessons these caverns hold."

Together, we stepped forward, ready to face whatever trials awaited us next, united by a newfound trust and understanding. This trial had not only tested our limits but had begun to forge an unspoken bond between us.

We entered a dimly lit chamber; our eyes had already adjusted to the subdued light, revealing remnants of a bygone era. The relics of Luminara, scattered about, seemed to whisper tales of a distant past, captivating me with their enchanting presence. These ruins, once thriving, now stood as silent witnesses to a civilization that thrived both above and below ground.

Pedestals, now empty or shattered, hinted at the lost power they once held. Stone pillars, adorned with intricate carvings, stood sentinel, while fragments of mosaics and statuary lay half-buried in sediment, their stories fading into obscurity.

Amidst it all, phosphorescent lifeforms cast a faint glow upon the walls, illuminating the chamber with an ethereal light.

And amidst the relics, we noticed scattered inscription stones bearing symbols that stirred a sense of familiarity yet eluded comprehension. "What do you make of these?" Ulric inquired.

"They feel oddly familiar, as though I've encountered them in a past life," I mused.

At the chamber's end stood a peculiar doorway, its arch adorned with a large stone, almost seamlessly blending with the frame.

"We have to figure out how to unlock the passage," I determined.

Using my TMT, I scanned one of the inscribed stones, revealing surprising results: they were decipherable riddles, hinting at the means to progress. With ten riddles in total, our path forward lay in solving each one.

I went to one of the stones and read the first riddle, which said:

"I shone with wisdom, in darkness a light, A city of progress in the shadow of night.

Once a beacon of knowledge, now in silence, I call. Speak my name, the first key to unlocking the hall." As I murmured the riddle under my breath, my eyes wandered around the chamber, observing the technological relics of a bygone era. Ulric, his sharp gaze picking out details in the murals that lined the walls, showcasing the city's climb to greatness through innovation, speculated aloud, "It's about wisdom and advancement... must be the city itself, Ethan."

Nodding in agreement, I found the courage to voice our answer, "Luminara." To our astonishment, the first stone ignited with a soft glow.

We proceeded to the next stone and attempted to decipher its riddle:

""Though mute I stand, my tale is long, Guarding secrets, both right and wrong. At city's heart, my shadow casts Name me now to move past."

The second riddle had us stumped until I remembered the grand statue we had passed at the entrance—a silent sentinel of the city. The realization dawned on me: "It's the statue, the guardian at the city's heart." I announced, and as I did, the next stone came alive with light.

We advanced to the following enigma:

"Hidden streams that once gave birth, To green and life, to joy and mirth.

Underneath the stone and earth, Speak its name; prove your worth."

The third riddle seemed more elusive until Ulric, ever the tactician, traced the intricate grooves on the floor that mapped out the convergence of rivers at the city's center. "Rivers," he said, a light of realization in his eyes. They were the lifeblood of Luminara.

Trusting his intuition, I spoke the answer out loud, and another stone responded with a luminous glow.

Pressing forward, we approached the subsequent stone to unravel its mystery:

"Scars of battles, long since fought, Walls and shields, with valor wrought.

Stand the test; through time they've braved, Name what the city once saved."

Surveying the remnants of ancient defenses scattered around, Ulric's attention was drawn to the remnants of a past conflict—broken shields and weapons that lined the chamber. "These defenses... they protected the city's spirit," he mused thoughtfully. It clicked in my mind then, "Walls," I said with conviction, and watched as yet another stone began to shine.

Next, we moved towards the fifth stone and pondered its riddle:

"In me, the spark of future's dawn, Ideas born, and innovations spawn. Through ages, my light has beamed.

Speak of the place where dreams once teemed."

The fifth riddle puzzled us the most, but as we navigated through the chamber, Ulric stopped before a scale model of a structure labeled as a research facility. "This place, it's where their dreams took shape," he pondered, a tone of respect in his voice for a civilization that dreamed boldly. With a newfound understanding, I breathed out the solution, "Lab." The stone illuminated brightly.

Suddenly, a shift occurred, altering the symbols on the remaining five stones into new configurations.

"Did you notice that?" inquired Ulric.

"Yes, indeed. Quite peculiar. Let's hope they're still operational," I responded.

As I stood before the inscription stone, the sixth riddle felt like it was probing into my very soul: "What force drives you through danger and darkness, unwavering in its pursuit?" Ulric, ever so observant, glanced at me and said, "It's what you keep talking about, Ethan. Your mission, your purpose." The answer was clear to me then: "Conviction." As I spoke the word, the stone's glow affirmed our insight.

The next inscription asked, "What strength upholds you when all else fails?" I pondered, thinking of Ulric's might in battle and his unwavering stance. Before I could speak, Ulric, with a rare vulnerability, uttered, "Loyalty, Ethan. It's the loyalty to those who trust us." Saying it out loud, loyalty became our beacon, lighting up another stone.

Facing the third riddle, we were asked, "What wisdom guides your hand and heart?" Reflecting on our journey and the decisions that had brought us here, Ulric smirked slightly. "It's the experiences, isn't it? What we've lived and learned..." I nodded, deeply feeling the truth of his words. "Experience," I affirmed, and another stone sparked to life.

The fourth stone posed, "In the face of adversity, what keeps you steadfast?" This made me recall the countless times Ulric had stood by my decision, even when doubt loomed large. "Trust," I whispered, understanding the depth of our reliance on each other. The stone gleamed in agreement, a confirmation of our growing trust.

The final challenge was introspective: "What binds you to your path, unwavering?" This question seemed to encapsulate the essence of our journey.

Looking at Ulric, I realized our shared journey had forged an unspoken bond, a mutual commitment.

"Bond," I concluded, was a simple word that encapsulated our intertwined destinies. As the last stone brightened, the path ahead cleared, not just through the cavern but also within ourselves.

Each riddle, a mirror to our souls, not only illuminated our path but also solidified the understanding between Ulric and me. Through these reflections, we gained insights into our motivations, strengths, and the unbreakable bond that had formed in the crucible of our shared journey. It was a portrayal of the fact that understanding oneself and each other was as crucial as any weapon or armor in the challenges that lay ahead.

The doorway ahead swung open, inviting us deeper into the mysteries of Luminara.

We arrived at a corridor that eventually branched into three paths. Two of these paths were flanked by statues. One statue depicted a tall figure draped in robes, its chest revealing a complex clockwork mechanism labeled "Timekeeper." Its hands gestured as if controlling the flow of time, one pointing to the past and the other to the future.

Opposite stood another statue, crafted from stone radiating a subtle inner glow, labeled "Lorekeeper." Seated amidst stone tablets and ancient texts, the Lorekeeper held an open book containing a tapestry of languages and symbols from Luminara's history.

At the center of the path junction, a solemn stone plinth awaited us, adorned with a riddle. Upon scanning it with my TMT, the riddle unfolded before Ulric and me.

"Two guardians silent, one speaks in turns, the path you choose will confirm your learns. One holds the future, one guards the past, the silent sentry's truth holds fast."

"That suggests we should select one of these two statues, possibly the more significant one, as it likely holds the key to affirming our knowledge," I proposed.

"But how do we determine which one is more significant?
The Timekeeper or the Lorekeeper?" inquired Ulric.

"Well, I reckon the Lorekeeper embodies the accumulation of knowledge and veneration for history, indicating a path safeguarding the past," Ethan deliberated.

"Indeed," agreed Ulric, "and the Timekeeper may represent Luminara's technological prowess in mastering time, reflecting the city's past glories and future ambitions."

"In that case, both could be equally significant, with one symbolizing the past and the other the future," Ethan observed.

"I believe the future holds greater significance than the past," Ulric opined. "The Timekeeper likely signifies strategic planning and the importance of anticipating consequences in battle." "You make a compelling point," Ethan acknowledged.

"Given Luminara's history as a hub of progress and technology, the intricate and technologically themed Timekeeper aligns with the city's essence."

"Then it stands to reason that it leads to the heart of the city's achievements and, consequently, the Ascendant Matrix," concluded Ulric.

"Very well, let's choose the Timekeeper and trust in our decision," Ethan decided.

So we ventured toward the Timekeeper, following a narrow corridor until it opened into a chamber. Light filtered through a crack in the ceiling, illuminating the circular room. Its walls were adorned with intricate carvings portraying the cyclical passage of time—seasons shifting, civilizations waxing and waning, and the eternal dance of celestial bodies. Dominating the chamber's center was a towering hourglass mounted on a pedestal, its sand cascading steadily downward.

Suddenly, the chamber sealed itself behind us. As sand began to trickle from concealed vents in the ceiling, filling the chamber inexorably, a sense of dread crept over us.

"I fear we've chosen poorly," Ulric remarked anxiously. "It seems that way. What's our next move?" I inquired.

Ulric's gaze fell upon the hourglass. "The hourglass must hold some significance," he suggested.

Approaching it, I discovered it could be manipulated. With swift action, I inverted the hourglass, halting the sand's descent.

"We've paused the sand, but our escape remains elusive," Ulric observed.

Surveying the chamber, I noticed the carvings on the wall casting distinct shadows.

"Those shadows—they may hold the key," I realized. "Each one appears to represent a different era in time."

In the dimly lit chamber, four distinct shadows danced upon the walls, each telling a tale of humanity's progress through time.

The first shadow portrayed the silhouette of rudimentary tools—a stone axe and a wheel—symbolizing the dawn of civilization and mankind's ingenuity in shaping its environment.

Next, the shadow of a majestic pyramid emerged, reminiscent of the grandeur and power of ancient empires, marking the era of conquest and expansion known as the Age of Empires.

The third shadow took the form of an open book, representing the pursuit of knowledge and enlightenment during an era characterized by advancements in literature, philosophy, and science—the Enlightenment.

Lastly, the shadow revealed the intricate gears of a machine, signaling the dawn of technological innovation and industrialization during the Industrial Revolution, where progress surged forward at an unprecedented pace.

"Since we assumed the answer to the riddle represented the future, we may have to direct the hourglass to align with the most recent epoch," Ulric suggested.

"Exactly!" I exclaimed. "The most recent one is the fourth one, so if we align the hourglass with that one, we might solve it."

I turned the hourglass to align with the shadow representing the Industrial Revolution, and suddenly we saw the door opening behind us.

"Let's go," I said.

We hurried through the door and followed the corridor until we eventually reached the point where the three paths diverged.

"Then it can only be the other statue; the middle one doesn't have any guardian, so that's our only option left," said Ulric.

"Wait!" I interjected, "The riddle stated the silent one stood fast, and the Lorekeeper definitely isn't the silent one. There is only silence where there is no guardian."

"Good point, so we take the center one then?" Ulric asked. "Yes, that must be it," I confirmed.

So we proceeded down the center corridor.

This part of our journey unfolded in a chamber unlike any other we had encountered—a vast hall where the air hummed with latent, unseen energy. Its walls were adorned with mirrors—not ordinary glass but mirrors that seemed to pulse with a life of their own, casting back not just our images but distorted visions that tugged at the edges of our souls.

At the chamber's center stood an obsidian pedestal, cradling a crystalline orb that pulsed with a soft, beckoning light. As we approached, cautious and curious in equal measure, the chamber seemed to breathe around us, the mirrors shimmering into life. They no longer showed our weary, travel-stained selves but instead replayed scenes from our pasts—moments laden with emotion, pivotal points in our lives where we had been forged in the fires of adversity and triumph.

The mirrors held more than reflections; they were windows to our souls and our pasts. I had spent years running from my history, from the young scholar in Luminara's academies to the reluctant warrior fate had forged me into. Now, as I faced my reflection, I realized this journey wasn't just about saving what was left of our world—it was about reconciling with who I had become.

I watched, transfixed, as one mirror showed me standing before the Nexus Vault, the very beginning of this harrowing journey. The reflection was not just a mere replay of events but a window into my doubts and fears at that moment, a reminder of the burden I had accepted into my life. It was a visceral echo of the uncertainty that had clouded my heart—the hesitation before stepping onto a path fraught with unknowns.

Turning to another mirror, I saw Ulric in the throes of battle, his greatsword a blur of steel as he fought with unmatched ferocity. But this was no glorification of war; it was a reflection of the cost of such battles, the weight of decisions made in the heat of conflict, and the shadows of regret that lingered long after the battlefield had been left behind.

A voice, resonant and omnipresent, filled the chamber, issuing a challenge that cut to the very core of our beings: "To proceed, confront what you see, accept what you were, and embrace who you are."

Compelled by the voice's decree, I stepped closer to a mirror, my heart heavy with the weight of my past. My reflection shifted, revealing a moment of profound vulnerability, a time when the magnitude of my quest had nearly overwhelmed me.

"I see my fears—the shadows of doubt that once threatened to engulf me," I confessed to the silent chamber, my voice a whisper against the stillness. "But I also see the strength I gained with each fear faced and each doubt overcome. These trials did not weaken me; they forged me anew, teaching me resilience and teaching me about the essence of my spirit." Acknowledging this, the mirror's surface rippled and then cleared, reflecting back not a scene from my past but my resolve, hardened and tempered like steel.

Ulric, ever the stoic warrior, faced his own mirror. The image it bore was one of loss, a battle where his strength had not been enough, a reminder of the fragility of victory and the sting of defeat.

"I see now my arrogance, the belief in my invincibility." Ulric's voice broke through the silence, carrying a weight of unspoken pain. "But from that loss, I learned humility and the importance of wisdom over mere strength. I understand now that true courage is in facing our failures, learning from them, and rising once more."

As he spoke these words, his reflection too began to clear, revealing a man not diminished by his past but elevated by the acceptance of his journey's lessons.

Together, we faced the final mirror. It did not show a scene from our past but rather a confluence of possibilities, a tapestry of what might be.

"We stand before you, not as unblemished heroes but as individuals shaped by our journeys, by every fall and every rise," we declared, our voices merging into a single, unwavering proclamation. "Our pasts are a part of us, but they do not define us. We move forward, enriched by our experiences, united in our purpose."

As our declaration echoed through the chamber, the crystalline orb at its heart blazed with light, a radiant beacon that filled the room, the mirrors reflecting not images but pure, blazing potential. This trial was not just a challenge; it was a catharsis, a purging of doubt through the acceptance of our true selves.

As the light dimmed, a pathway emerged, leading deeper into the caverns and beckoning us to continue our journey. With a deeper understanding of ourselves and our bond solidifying, Ulric and I ventured forth into the unknown depths of the Luminara Caverns, ready for whatever trials lay ahead.

As I stepped alongside Ulric into a vast chamber, our gaze was immediately captivated by the intricate dance of light and shadow above us. The ceiling, embedded with glowing crystals, cast ethereal patterns across the stone floor, while a soft hum vibrated through the air, as if the chamber itself awaited our trial with bated breath.

Before us, a large circular platform demanded our attention.

Its perimeter was marked by two concentric rings, segmented into panels each bearing the ancient symbols of the elements: fire, water, earth, and air. At the platform's heart, an ancient pedestal cradled an ornate bowl, its still waters mirroring the chamber's mystical ambience.

Ulric, ever the tactician, eyed the setup warily. "This is no mere test of strength," he murmured, his hand instinctively resting on the hilt of his greatsword.

I nodded in agreement, my mind racing to unravel the puzzle before us. "It's a puzzle of harmony. Each element must be acknowledged and balanced," I conjectured, recalling SYNAPSE's advice on the trials testing not just our might but our wisdom and spirit.

Approaching the platform, we observed that the elemental symbols were not merely decorative; they were integral to the trial. "Perhaps we need to activate them in a certain sequence," I suggested, studying the patterns of light that seemed to connect the symbols in a complex but discernible order.

Ulric stepped forward, his gaze fixed on the symbols. "Or maybe it's about balance. Fire opposes water, and earth counters air. We must bring them into harmony," he deduced, his voice echoing slightly in the chamber.

Together, we began the trial. I chose to start with water, pressing my palm against the cool, damp symbol on the platform. As I did, the bowl at the center responded, the water within rippling and rising into a small, swirling vortex that cast a soft, blue light across the chamber.

Emboldened, Ulric moved to the symbol of fire, his touch igniting a gentle, warm glow that intertwined with the coolness of water, creating a balance that seemed to please the chamber itself.

The hum in the air grew into a harmonious melody, an approval of our actions.

We proceeded with careful consideration, activating earth and air in turn. With each correct move, the melody grew richer, the interplay of light and shadow more intricate, until the chamber was alive with a symphony of elements, a symbol of our understanding and respect for the balance of nature.

"The key to harmony is balance and respect," I reflected aloud, the realization dawning on me as the melody reached its crescendo. "Not just here, but in all things."

Ulric nodded, his usual stoicism softened by a rare smile. "And so we learn," he agreed. "Let's see what other lessons await us, Ethan."

As the final note of the trial's melody faded, a path forward opened, leading us deeper into the mysteries of the Luminara Caverns. With the trial behind us, we moved forward, our bond strengthened, and our resolve was unshaken.

Moving forward, the next trial awaited us, veiled in an aura of solemnity that permeated the air as we ventured deeper into the heart of the Luminara Caverns. The chamber we entered was starkly different from the previous trials, dominated by two large pedestals standing apart, each encased in a sheen of opaque crystal that shimmered with internal light.

Ulric, ever vigilant, surveyed the room with a cautious eye. "It looks like this trial might test more than just our strength or wit," he commented, his voice echoing softly against the stone.

I nodded, drawn to the pedestals. "It seems we're meant to stand on these," I observed, gesturing towards the platforms.

Hesitantly, we took our places, a sense of expectation hanging heavy between us.

No sooner had we positioned ourselves than the chamber came alive with a low hum, and the crystals surrounding us blazed with light. A voice, neither Ulric's nor mine, resonated throughout the room, ethereal and commanding. "This trial tests the strength of your connection. Will you stand divided or united?"

Ulric shot me a determined look, his stance resolute. "We stand together," he declared firmly, his voice echoing his conviction.

The chamber responded to Ulric's declaration, the light intensifying as spectral chains materialized from the pedestals, seeking to bind us. I strained against the sudden force, feeling the weight of the trial both physically and metaphorically.

"Remember, it's about our bond," I shouted over to Ulric, struggling against the chains. "We need to prove it's stronger than whatever tries to separate us!"

Nodding, Ulric braced himself, his muscles bulging as he fought against his restraints. "On three, push against the chains with all you've got!" he called out.

"One, two, three!" We exerted our strength against the ethereal chains, pushing with a determination fueled by our shared resolve to overcome the trial together.

As if sensing our united front, the chains began to falter, their grip loosening with our concerted effort. "Our bond is our strength!" I yelled, the energy from our combined resolve seeming to infuse us with greater power.

With a final, concerted push, the chains shattered, dissipating into motes of light that floated gently to the ground. The oppressive atmosphere of the chamber lifted, replaced by a serene light that bathed us both, acknowledging our victory.

We stepped off the pedestals with a sense of accomplishment and a deeper understanding between us. "That was about more than just physical strength," Ulric mused, clapping a firm hand on my shoulder.

I smiled, feeling the truth in his words. "It was about trust, about knowing when to push and when to hold steady. We proved that together, we're stronger."

The trial had indeed been a symbol of our partnership, a reminder that the journeys we undertake are enriched by those we choose to share them with. As we moved forward, leaving the chamber behind, I knew that whatever trials awaited us, our bond would be our unwavering strength.

The echoes of our footsteps reverberated through the caverns as Ulric and I advanced beyond the previous chamber. The path that lay before us twisted deeper into the earth, leading us to the next chamber—a vast, dimly lit hall that seemed to breathe with ancient solemnity. As we entered, the air thickened with a palpable sense of gravity, and it became clear that this trial, the next one, would test us in ways we had not yet faced.

The center of the chamber housed a grand altar, bathed in a shaft of light that seemed to pierce the very heart of the earth from an unseen source above. Arrayed around the altar were three statues, each depicting a figure in the act of giving: one offered a heart, another a crown, and the third, a pair of scales. The ambiance of the room was both serene and somber, imbued with the weight of countless ages.

"I don't like the look of this," Ulric muttered, his gaze locked on the statues. "Sacrifice often means loss."

I nodded, unable to shake the unease that settled over me. "But it can also mean growth or change. Let's see what it asks of us."

Approaching the altar, we noticed an inscription etched into its stone, the words glowing with a soft, ethereal light. "To reach the heart of knowledge, one must offer what is most precious. The path forward is forged by the sacrifices made in pursuit of a greater good."

The significance of the trial began to dawn on me. "It's asking us to consider what we're willing to give up for our quest. What we truly value."

Ulric's expression hardened, a reflection of the internal struggle he faced. "And if what we value is something we cannot part with?" he asked, his voice barely above a whisper.

"That's the trial, isn't it?" I replied, my mind racing with the implications. "To see if we can make the hard choices."

We stood in silence, each lost in our contemplation, until a voice, resonant and clear, filled the chamber. "Choose your sacrifice," it commanded, and with those words, the statues came to life, their eyes glowing with a spectral light.

A shiver ran down my spine as I faced the statues, the weight of the decision pressing heavily upon me. 'What if we choose wrong?' I whispered, not sure Ulric could hear me over the thrum of our racing hearts. 'What if the price is too high?' Ulric's hand found my shoulder, a silent reassurance, yet I could feel the tremor in his grip. This was a leap into the unknown, a test that could tear everything apart.

Ulric and I exchanged a glance, understanding that the decision would not be easy. The heart, the crown, and the scales each symbolized a different aspect of sacrifice. Love, power, and balance.

Drawing a deep breath, I stepped forward. "I'll choose first." As I approached the statue offering the heart, I thought of Aria. The love we shared was the most precious thing in my life, but our journey, our fight, was for a future where that love could thrive. "For love," I whispered, touching the statue.

A warmth spread through me, a confirmation of my choice, though it was accompanied by a sharp pang of loss. The statue's eyes dimmed, and the chamber acknowledged my sacrifice.

Ulric watched me, his expression a mix of respect and sorrow. Then, squaring his shoulders, he approached the statue with the crown. "Power," he declared, his voice steady. "I've lived my life seeking strength, seeking to be unconquerable. But true strength isn't about ruling over others—it's about knowing when to lead and when to let go."

As Ulric made his choice, the statue glowed briefly before returning to stillness. We had both made our sacrifices, but the trial was not yet complete.

"The scales remain," Ulric noted, eyeing the last statue. "Yes," I agreed, feeling a sense of impending finality.

"Balance. What could it ask of us?"

We approached the statue together, and as we did, the voice returned. "Balance is the understanding that all things have their place and their time. To sacrifice for balance is to accept loss and gain in equal measure, to surrender to the ebb and flow of fate."

Understanding dawned on me, clear and sharp. "It's asking us to let go of control, to trust in the journey itself, not just the destination."

Ulric nodded, a look of resolve on his face. "Then let's make that sacrifice together."

We reached out, our hands touching the statue simultaneously. A surge of energy coursed through us, binding us together in a pact of trust and acceptance. The room filled with light, blinding in its intensity, and when it faded, the chamber had changed.

The altar and statues were gone, replaced by a simple doorway leading further into the depths of the caverns. We had passed another difficult trial. As we moved towards the doorway, Ulric spoke, his voice thoughtful. "That was harder than I expected. To consider what you hold dear and choose to offer it up..."

I nodded, feeling the weight of our decisions. "But in sacrificing, we gain. Insight, understanding, perhaps even the strength to face what's ahead."

Ulric smiled with a rare, genuine expression. "Aye, there's wisdom in that. Let's see where this path takes us."

Together, we stepped through the doorway, leaving behind another trial but carrying its lessons forward.

After overcoming the colossal rat-man and navigating the myriad challenges within the Luminara Caverns, Ulric and I found ourselves on the precipice of an ancient gateway. This was it—the threshold that marked the end of one journey and the beginning of another.

"Our trials in these caverns have tested our resolve, our courage, and the strength of our bond," I said to Ulric, who nodded in agreement, his gaze fixed on the gateway before us. "What lies beyond this gateway is unknown, but I believe the trials have prepared us for whatever we may face."

Ulric clasped my shoulder, a gesture that had become a symbol of our camaraderie. "Ethan, through every challenge, we've emerged stronger. Whatever awaits us, we'll face it together. Our journey through the Luminara Caverns has forged a bond between us that no darkness can break."

I looked back at the path we had traversed, a labyrinth of darkness and light, of peril and discovery. "These caverns have been both a crucible and a sanctuary. They have taught us about sacrifice, trust, and the importance of standing united. As we step through this gateway, we carry those lessons with us, along with the hope that our journey will lead us to salvation—not just for ourselves, but for all that remains of our world."

Taking a deep breath, we stepped forward, crossing the ancient threshold. As we did, a brilliant light enveloped us, not just illuminating our path but also signifying the dawn of a new chapter in our quest. The challenges we had faced within the depths of the Luminara Caverns were behind us, but they had paved the way for the trials and triumphs that lay ahead.

As the light faded, revealing the vast expanse of a new and uncharted territory, we knew that the true test of our resolve and the depth of our bond was yet to come. With the Luminara Caverns behind us and the unknown ahead, we pressed on, ready to face whatever the journey held in store, side by side.

The caverns stretched out before us, a labyrinth of shadows and light, each twist and turn a promise of the challenges and discoveries yet to come.

We navigated through a labyrinth of winding corridors and chambers, our journey prolonged by the struggle to find our path. Eventually, we arrived at an empty chamber adorned with two pools of water, one on each side. Stalactites dripped incessantly, their droplets creating a melodic rhythm as they splashed into the pools below.

Just as we prepared to depart, a thunderous rumble echoed from the depths. "What could that be?" queried Ulric, his voice tinged with concern. "I'm uncertain, but it doesn't bode well," I replied, my grip tightening around my sword hilt.

Without warning, a dense cloud of dust billowed forth, revealing a formidable army of rat-men emerging from the darkness. "This does not seem favorable," remarked Ulric, drawing his sword with a resounding clang. "Whence did they emerge?" I pondered aloud, retrieving my Fusionizer and aiming it towards the corridor from whence they came.

"Perhaps they trailed us from above," suggested Ulric, his stance poised for battle. "Alternatively, this may be their origin," I countered, bracing myself for the imminent confrontation. "Prepare yourself; the confrontation is imminent," warned Ulric, his gaze fixed upon the advancing horde.

In an instant, we found ourselves engulfed by the sheer multitude of rat-men encircling us, their menacing growls and grunts filling the air. As they launched their assault, I unleashed bolts of energy from my Fusionizer, swiftly dispatching them one by one, while Ulric cleaved through their ranks with unparalleled prowess.

Their crude swords proved futile against our armor, rendering their attacks ineffectual. Yet they persisted relentlessly, as if driven by an unyielding determination to impede our progress.

Despite our defense, their numbers swelled until we were nearly overwhelmed, forced to shield our vulnerable faces from their relentless onslaught.

As their ranks began to thin, we pressed forward, fending off the remaining few who surrounded us menacingly, biding their time. For a fleeting moment, silence descended upon the chamber, broken only by the familiar echoes of the cavern. Then, a deafening thud reverberated through the corridor, growing louder with each passing moment.

Emerging from the darkness, a colossal rat-man appeared before us, its bulk three times that of its kin. Cybernetic enhancements adorned its form, with steel augmentations from ear to muzzle and a robotic eye gleaming ominously with a crimson hue.

His visage was marked by open jaws, revealing rows of razor-sharp fangs, while scars crisscrossed the expanse of his face. A sense of madness emanated from his left eye, its gaze a wild blend of fury and insanity, while his left ear bore the absence of a portion.

Adorning his frame was a broad, armored shoulder strap that spanned his left shoulder and chest, securing a circular device at its center. This device, akin to a futuristic reactor, emitted a pulsating red glow, hinting at its formidable power. Extending from a harness on his back were four mechanical appendages, each akin to the sinuous limbs of an octopus, boasting intricate joints and segments.

At their terminus, these metallic limbs bore an array of specialized equipment, each serving a distinct purpose in his arsenal.

The appendages boasted intricate designs, with exposed wiring, hydraulics, and crimson-hued elements suggesting the presence of some form of energy coursing through them. Their construction hinted at advanced technology, seamlessly blending into the rat-man's physique and implying a symbiotic relationship between creature and machine.

His left leg, too, bore a covering of steel with visible wiring and hydraulics, extending down to both of his feet.

"What in the..." Ulric trailed off, unable to articulate his shock at the monstrous sight before us.

"I've witnessed many marvels in our world, but this surpasses them all," I remarked.

The cavern's still air was suddenly rent by the screech of the monstrous rat-man as it emerged from the shadows, its cybernetic parts whirring ominously. Beside me, Ulric Steelborn, a titan among warriors, gripped his greatsword with a resolve that belied the shock we both felt at the sight of our adversary.

"We take this beast down together, Ethan!" Ulric's voice boomed through the cavern, snapping me back to the present danger. Nodding, I drew the energy blade from my Tactical Multi-Tool, its hum a comforting contrast to the eerie silence that fell once more.

The creature charged, a blur of fur and metal. Its mechanical limbs extended, seeking to ensnare us with their deadly precision. Ulric met the charge head-on, his greatsword swinging in wide arcs that kept the beast at bay, while I darted in and out, my energy blade slicing through the air, aiming for the joints of its cybernetic limbs.

With each clash, sparks flew, illuminating the cavern with brief flashes of light. The rat-man was relentless, its cybernetic enhancements giving it speed and strength beyond the natural. But Ulric and I, bound by a newfound camaraderie and a mutual respect for each other's prowess, were a force to be reckoned with.

I could see the frustration in the creature's remaining eye as every attempt to overpower us was met with resistance. Ulric's laughter rang out amidst the chaos, a sound of pure defiance. "Come, beast! Is that all you have?" he taunted, even as he narrowly avoided a swipe that would have decapitated a lesser man.

Our strategy was clear: divide and conquer. I focused on agility, darting behind the creature to distract it, allowing Ulric to land heavy, punishing blows. The rat-man's augmented body was tough but not invulnerable. With each pass, I targeted its enhancements, severing wires and disabling limbs, reducing its ability to fight back effectively.

Yet the creature was cunning. With a sudden twist, it launched a counterattack, its tail—upgraded with metallic thorns—whipping towards me with lethal speed. I rolled aside, feeling the air shift as the tail passed inches from my face.

"Careful, Ethan!" Ulric bellowed, stepping in to deliver a crushing blow to the creature's side. The impact sent it reeling, but it quickly regained its footing, its mechanical parts compensating for the damage.

We were in a deadlock, with neither side gaining a clear advantage. The rat-man's resilience was astounding; for every blow we landed, it seemed to muster even greater fury. But fatigue was not in our vocabulary, not when so much was at stake.

"Ulric, the reactor on its chest! It's the key!" I shouted, noticing the pulsating glow that seemed to grow more intense with the creature's rage. Ulric nodded, understanding immediately. We needed to strike there, but the creature guarded it fiercely, aware of its vulnerability.

The battle raged on, a declaration of the will and skill of two warriors against a monstrosity from the depths of a world gone mad. Each move we made was countered, and each strategy was tested. Yet, amidst the violence, there was a dance and a rhythm to our movements that spoke of a deeper connection—a bond forged in the heat of battle.

Our moment came in a flash of insight. I feinted, drawing the creature's attention with a daring leap towards its face. As it swiped at me with its augmented limbs, I used the momentum to vault over it, landing behind and drawing its focus.

"Now, Ulric!" I yelled as Ulric charged, his sword raised high. With a warrior's cry, he brought the blade down on the reactor. The creature roared, an ear-splitting sound that echoed through the caverns as the reactor was breached. Energy arced out wildly, enveloping it in a blinding light.

When the light dimmed, the creature lay still, its life extinguished in a final, explosive act of defiance. We stood over it, panting, the echoes of battle fading into silence.

"We did it," Ulric said, sheathing his sword. "Together."

In the quiet aftermath, our gazes met, an unspoken understanding passing between us. "You know," Ulric began, his voice softer than usual. "I never thought I'd find a partner in this forsaken place. But here we are, standing together against the darkness."

I nodded, feeling the weight of his words. "And we'll see this through to the end, together," I promised, knowing that whatever lay ahead, our bond had become our greatest strength.

"Yes, together," I replied, looking at the fallen beast. In its demise, I felt not triumph but somber respect. It was a creature of this new, wild world—fierce, unyielding, and ultimately a victim of its own forced evolution.

As we moved deeper into the caverns, the weight of our journey bore down on us. The battles we faced were not just against the creatures that lurked in the shadows, but against the very essence of a world torn asunder. Yet, in this trial by fire, I found not just an ally in Ulric but a brother-in-arms.

THRESHOLD OF DESTINY

After our extensive journey through the Luminara Caverns, we finally reached an imposing steel door devoid of any visible lock or handle. Adjacent to the door stood an input device, featuring an alphanumeric keyboard and a small screen above it. Beside the device lay an indentation shaped like a hexagon. In that moment, I realized our destination—the long-sought-after Ascendant Matrix.

As the door hissed open, revealing the path to the Ascendant Matrix, the weight of our mission pressed heavily upon my shoulders. This wasn't just a quest for survival; it was a race against time to unearth the secrets that could reverse the desolation consuming our world. Ulric and I weren't merely explorers; we were humanity's last hope. The Ascendant Matrix held the key to restoring the earth's dying ecosystems, a mission borne from desperation as the last remnants of humanity teetered on the brink of extinction. Our success or failure would determine the fate of our species.

With determination, I retrieved my CodeSync Interface and inserted it into the hexagonal indentation. The fit was flawless. The device sprang to life, emitting a high-pitched sound before gradually settling into silence. Characters and numbers appeared on the display screen of the input device. The sudden whirl of activity from the device sent a shiver down my spine. Reflecting on the day we first set out, I realized how much Ulric and I had changed. Gone was the uncertainty that once clouded our decisions, replaced by a steadfast resolve carved from our trials within these caverns.

It was as if we had awakened a sleeping giant, one whose whispers could either be a lullaby or a war cry. The power at our fingertips was immense and exhilarating, yet the responsibility it entailed was daunting. 'We're really doing this, aren't we?' Ulric murmured, his voice a mix of awe and apprehension. The question wasn't just about our physical journey but also about the transformation within us. Gone were the days of second-guessing; we were now united by a resolve forged in the fires of adversity.

A hissing sound, followed by a symphony of mechanical noises, emanated from the door. Slowly, it began to open, revealing a gap leading to a room below. Short stairs descended into the depths, while a white metal bridge extended itself towards our side of the gap.

We stepped over the threshold and surveyed our surroundings. The architecture here, blending ancient craftsmanship with forgotten technology, hinted at the matrix's age and significance. It was a place of power, wrapped in the mystery of bygone eras.

As we continued past the threshold into the Ascendant Matrix, a sense of crossing into the unknown washed over us. This place, conceived at the zenith of our forebears' ingenuity, now stood as a testament to both their brilliance and their hubris. Once a beacon of hope, it was said to have the capability to mend the fractures of our world and rewind the tapestry of chaos unraveled by human folly. The walls whispered of a past too grand to fathom, and the air hummed with dormant secrets, eager for revival. Ulric glanced at me, a silent question in his eyes: What if the key to our salvation lies not in changing what has been but in understanding it? The air was heavy with the echo of silence, a stark reminder of the isolation that surrounded us. The faint hum of distant machinery was the only indication that we were not alone in this sprawling complex. Silence had hung heavily.

Adjacent to the beginning of the bridge, there stood a weathered desk and chair. In the center of the back wall loomed a round glass door comprised of two pieces that converged to close.

Beyond it lay a circular wall, giving the impression of a colossal tube. Wide windows flanked each side of the room, offering views into the depths of the cavern.

Scattered around the area were various dusty boxes, papers, books, and lockers. The detritus of a bygone era lay before us, each item a silent testament to the hurried evacuation or the sudden calamity that had befallen the occupants of this place.

To the right, a table held a non-functional computer, suggesting this space once served as an office area. However, its design differed significantly from the ruins above, hinting at a separate construction.

As we advanced, the two pieces of the glass door parted, inviting us inside.

"Should we enter?" queried Ulric.

"I suppose we must; there seems to be no other option," I replied.

With resolve, we stepped into the tube, and the glass door sealed shut behind us. Suddenly, we began to descend, enveloped by the sight of a steel wall ahead and the sensation of downward movement. After several minutes, the motion ceased, and we found ourselves behind yet another glass door, which opened to admit us forward.

We proceeded into the room, the doors sealing shut behind us. Much like the room above, this one bore a striking resemblance. The same furnishings adorned the space, arranged identically to those in the previous room. Directly ahead, a steel door stood with a button at its side. Upon pressing it, the door ascended vertically.

Advancing, we entered a spacious central chamber. Four additional steel doors greeted us, two on each side. Adjacent to each door, a window provided a glimpse inside. At the room's center, a wide staircase descended downward. Without bothering to explore the rooms, we noted their uniformity and lack of intrigue. The depths of the Ascendant Matrix unfolded before us with relentless urgency.

Each step took us further into its heart, where time seemed compressed, as if urging us forward. The relics of a bygone era blurred past us, their stories untold but their purpose unmistakable. This was a race, not just against the dangers lurking in the shadows, but against time itself. The matrix did not yield its secrets easily, and we knew that every moment of awe at its wonders was a moment our enemies drew closer. Our pace quickened, driven by the unspoken understanding that dalliance could mean doom.

Our hearts raced with anticipation, aware that every moment spent in this maze-like structure brought new dangers and moved us further from our ultimate goal.

Each door revealed a solitary chamber outfitted with a bed, nightstand, clock, table lamp, desk, chair, computer, screen, mouse, and keyboard. Two lockers lined one wall, while a rug lay on the floor. The layout remained consistent, save for one room equipped with a toilet, sink, and shower.

Descending the staircase, we found a similar setup. Steel doors stood at the front and back, each leading to central chambers mirroring the previous ones.

"We must be in some sort of living quarters," remarked Ulric.

"Yeah, it seems that way, but nothing particularly intriguing yet," I responded.

We pressed on, encountering various facilities such as a cafeteria, gym, and an energy generator chamber, indicating that this complex once housed a functioning society.

We also discovered an interesting laboratory, which seemed to serve as a place for the development of advanced technologies.

Whispers of movement danced at the edge of our perception, shadows flickering just beyond the halo of our lights. 'Do you feel that?' Ulric asked, voice low, a hint of unease threading through his usual confidence. 'Like we're not alone?' I nodded, feeling the weight of unseen eyes upon us. It wasn't just the anticipation of discovery that quickened our breaths but the palpable sense of being hunted, as if the matrix itself whispered warnings of what was to come. The air grew heavier, charged with the promise of an imminent confrontation. We were intruders here, challengers to the guardians of forgotten lore.

As I stepped into the laboratory, the air crackled with an undercurrent of anticipation, a tangible energy that hinted at the groundbreaking discoveries and innovations that took shape within these walls. The laboratory, a marvel of modern engineering, was a sprawling expanse of gleaming metal and glass, a token of humanity's insatiable thirst for knowledge and progress.

The walls were adorned with monitors displaying complex schematics, data streams, and real-time simulations. Each monitor flickered like a beacon in the dark, casting shadows that danced across the room, as if alive with the ghosts of past researchers. The air was thick with the scent of ozone and metal, a testament to the relentless pursuit of knowledge that had consumed countless hours within these walls. It felt like stepping into a cathedral, sacred and solemn, dedicated to the gods of science and technology.

Rows of sleek workstations lined the perimeter of the laboratory, each one equipped with state-of-the-art equipment and instrumentation. Advanced computers hummed with activity, processing vast amounts of data and executing complex algorithms with effortless precision. Microscopes, spectrometers, and other analytical tools stood at the ready, their lenses gleaming in the ambient light.

In the center of the laboratory stood a series of imposing apparatuses, towering machines of gleaming metal and pulsating energy. These were the heart of the facility, the crucibles in which revolutionary technologies were forged. Massive particle accelerators, fusion reactors, and quantum computers hummed with power, their intricate mechanisms whirring and whizzing as they pushed the boundaries of scientific understanding.

Scouring the rest of the facility, we eventually reached a distinctive door adorned with two vertical red lines and equipped with a keypad lock.

"There's likely something noteworthy beyond this door," I speculated.

"Agreed, but how do we gain entry?" Ulric inquired. "I have an idea," I declared, determined.

After extracting my KeyCode Breaker, I connected it to the keypad and initiated a brute force attack on the code. The door swiftly yielded to our efforts.

As we entered, a corridor stretched before us, branching off into three directions.

"Which way should we go?" I pondered. "Forward?" suggested Ulric.

"Sounds like a plan; let's proceed," I concurred.

We pressed on and reached a dead end, where we found energy generators and lockers. Among the lockers, I discovered a wearable device perfectly suited for my arm. As I wiped off the dust from its screen, the device sprang to life, displaying the name "SpectraShroud." Sensing its compatibility with my neural interface, I instantly grasped its capabilities. Little did I know that the device would soon reveal secrets hidden within the Matrix, secrets that were perhaps meant to stay buried.

"What did you find there?" inquired Ulric.

"It's incredible; I can operate it through my neural interface," I exclaimed.

"Neural interface?" Ulric questioned.

"Yes, it's a device implanted in my head that enhances my mental faculties," I explained.

"I wish I had that; I'd like some extra mental faculties," Ulric remarked.

"Allow me to demonstrate," I offered.

In an instant, my body vanished from sight, invisible to both myself and others.

"Where did you go?" Ulric puzzled.

"I'm still here," I assured him, deactivating the device.

"See?"

"It renders you invisible? Remarkable," Ulric marveled. "And that's not all; it's a stealth device. I can create multiple decoys of myself, alter the environment, and even change my appearance. It's quite the discovery," I elaborated.

"Just don't vanish on me; we need to stick together," Ulric cautioned.

"Of course, it's primarily for stealth purposes," I reassured him.

We retraced our steps and opted for the right path instead.

Along this route, we encountered a corridor flanked by windows revealing the adjacent room. As we reached its end, we encountered a leftward turn. Here, the corridor was lined with devices mounted on the walls, sleek and compact in design, crafted from reinforced plastic. Each device featured a prominent emitter encased in a protective housing, accompanied by indicator lights.

Crossing the threshold triggered a sudden change: the indicator lights flashed red.

"Duck!" I shouted, shoving Ulric aside just as crimson laser beams shot forth from the wall-mounted devices in every direction. Despite my efforts, one beam grazed Ulric's right hand as he stumbled backward into the corridor. Time seemed to slow, every second stretching out as I watched Ulric's pained reaction, the urgency of our mission clashing with the immediate danger.

"Ah! My hand..." Ulric's cry of pain echoed as we both lay sprawled on the floor.

"Are you alright?" I asked, concern evident in my voice. "The laser got me," Ulric winced, clutching his injured hand.

As Ulric winced in pain, clutching his injured hand, a fleeting shadow of vulnerability crossed his otherwise steadfast gaze. "You know,' he muttered through gritted teeth, 'back when I was a kid, I used to dream of adventures like this. But never thought..." His voice trailed off, lost in the echoes of our perilous journey. In his eyes, I saw not just the warrior he had become but the echoes of the boy who once dreamed of stars. It struck me then—our quest was not just about survival. It was about reclaiming the wonder that the world had lost.

"Let me take a look," I offered.

As I kneeled beside Ulric, seeing the pain etched across his face, a rush of emotions overtook me. Fear, anger, and a profound sense of responsibility. Ulric was more than a partner; he was the brother I chose in this forsaken world. His injury was a stark reminder of the brutal cost of our journey. In the dim light, his determined gaze met mine—an unspoken pledge between warriors and brothers. We had come too far to falter now. inspecting the wound. It was a deep burn on his palm.

"It's a nasty burn, but fortunately, it won't need stitches. It'll heal on its own. Here, take these painkillers," I said, handing him a bottle.

Seeing Ulric in pain, a surge of protectiveness welled up inside me. He wasn't just a comrade; he was the brother I never had. Every battle scar we shared, every narrow escape, had forged a bond stronger than the steel walls encasing us.

"Take one every six hours; it should help with the pain until it's better," I instructed.

"Thanks, but I'll be at a disadvantage in combat for a while.

I'll have to rely on you," Ulric admitted.

"Don't worry; I've got my SpectraShroud. It should give us an edge," I reassured him. "Now, let's figure out how to bypass those laser beams."

"Do you have any ideas?" Ulric inquired.

"Yeah, I've got one. Let's hope it pans out," I replied confidently.

Drawing out my Energy Shield, I activated it and advanced toward the laser beams. With determination, I extended my hand towards the first beam, watching as it ricocheted harmlessly off the shield's surface. Moving steadily through the corridor, I deflected each beam that came my way, forging a path forward unscathed.

At the corridor's end, I found a button and pressed it, deactivating the lasers.

"You did it!" Ulric cheered as he followed behind me.

"We made it through. What's our next move?" I pondered aloud.

Surveying our surroundings, we discovered ourselves in a room filled with desks, chairs, and computers. A large flat screen adorned one wall, while a tangle of wires snaked across the floor, indicating a research area of sorts.

Exiting through the far door, we entered another corridor and pressed onward, navigating through a series of interconnected rooms and passageways.

I remember the first indication that something was amiss was subtle— so subtle, in fact, that if it hadn't been for Ulric's acute observation, I might have dismissed it as a trick of the mind. We had been navigating through the seemingly endless corridors and rooms of a sprawling, underground complex, its purpose as enigmatic as the technologies it housed.

Our mission had been straightforward: to activate a series of supercomputers believed to hold the key to reversing the ecological devastation on the surface. What we hadn't anticipated was the matrix's defense mechanisms—not just physical traps but temporal distortions—that ensnared us in a loop from which there seemed no escape.

We took a moment, our breaths echoing in the chamber, to strategize. The uncertainty of our next steps lingered in the air, thickening the tension.

The first loop began innocuously enough. We entered a room dominated by a massive, cylindrical device, its surfaces inscribed with symbols that pulsed with a soft blue light. As I approached, intending to interface my Omni-Locator with the device, everything flickered—just for a moment—and then we were back at the corridor's entrance, staring down its length as if we had never moved.

"It's like we've just stepped back in time," Ulric muttered, perplexity evident in his voice.

And so it seemed. We retraced our steps, every action an eerie repetition of our initial attempt. Yet, when we reached the room with the cylindrical device, the flicker occurred again, resetting our progress. It was a loop, a slice of time repeating endlessly, with no indication of its trigger or its end.

Frustration turned to apprehension as the realization set in: we were trapped. Each loop was identical—a perfect replica of the last. The corridors and rooms reset with each cycle, including the placement of items, the state of any interfaces, and even our own memories of the loop's progression. Only a vague sense of déjà vu hinted at the unnatural repetitiveness of our actions.

Determined to break free from the cycle, we began experimenting. The complex seemed to respond to our presence; its technology was both advanced and inscrutable. We altered our path, tried different interactions with the environment, and even attempted to leave markings as breadcrumbs, only for them to disappear with each reset.

As the loops continued, a pattern emerged. Certain actions delayed the reset, suggesting that the loop was not merely a trap but a puzzle. The cylindrical device was key; its symbols matched those found in other parts of the complex. Deciphering these became our focus, with each loop an opportunity to gather more information and push further before the inevitable reset.

Time lost meaning. The number of loops became indistinguishable, a blur of repeated failures and incremental successes. Yet, with each cycle, our understanding of the complex deepened. We discovered that the device was part of a larger system, a network that controlled the temporal distortions.

The breakthrough came when we realized the loops were not identical but iterative, each one a chance to affect subtle changes in the complex's systems. By manipulating the device's settings, we could alter the conditions of the loop, extend its duration, or even skip portions of the sequence.

Our escape hinged on a final, desperate gambit. We synchronized our actions across multiple loops, each of us undertaking specific tasks designed to converge on a single moment—a precise manipulation of the device that would either free us or condemn us to an endless cycle.

The moment arrived. As I interfaced with the device, Ulric worked to disrupt the complex's power supply, a calculated risk that would either deactivate the temporal loop or enhance its effects. The technology here was an enigma, a fusion of the arcane and the advanced, suggesting its creators had mastered both the mystical and the mechanical. The room trembled, the air vibrated with unseen forces, and then—clarity.

We were standing in the corridor, but the oppressive sense of repetition was gone. The device was silent; its symbols were dark. We had escaped the loop, but the complex lay ahead, its mysteries and dangers undiminished. The experience had changed us, though. No longer mere intruders in an alien environment, we had become part of its history, its legacy of time-twisted corridors and rooms.

The matrix supercomputers were still our objective, but our journey through the time loops had imparted a deeper understanding of the stakes. As we moved forward, I couldn't shake the feeling that our mission was about more than just survival or restoring the world to its former state. It was a testament to human resilience, to our refusal to bow down in the face of adversity. 'We're not just fighting for today, but for all the tomorrows to come,' I mused aloud, a resolve hardening in my heart. Ulric nodded in agreement, his eyes alight with a determination that mirrored my own. Ulric's hand tightened around his weapon, a silent testament to the resolve hardening within him.

We were not just fighting for survival or knowledge but for the very fabric of reality, threatened by the same forces that had ensnared us in the temporal puzzle.

As we moved forward, the complex seemed less hostile, its corridors and rooms no longer just obstacles but components of a vast, intricate puzzle that spanned time and space. The echoes of our repeated journeys lingered, a reminder of the resilience and ingenuity required to face the unknown.

Our adventure in the underground complex had begun with a simple mission but evolved into a journey of discovery, a confrontation with the limits of human understanding and the boundless possibilities of technology. The time loops were not just a trap but a lesson, teaching us that even in the face of insurmountable odds, persistence and creativity could unveil paths previously unseen.

The supercomputers awaited, their secrets locked within a chamber beyond the network of corridors and rooms that had tested us to our limits. As we approached, we knew that whatever lay ahead, the challenges we had overcome had prepared us for the final leg of our quest. The complex, with its time loops and enigmatic technologies, was not just a relic of the past but a beacon for the future, a witness to the enduring quest for knowledge in a world forever changed by the follies and aspirations of humanity.

In the end, the story of our entrapment and escape from the time loops became a legend, a tale of perseverance and discovery in the face of the unknown. It was a reminder that even within the depths of despair, there lies the potential for growth, for understanding, and for transcending the boundaries of the world as we know it.

In a quiet moment, Ulric turned to me, his expression somber yet resolute. 'You know, Ethan, no matter what happens next, this journey... it's changed us. For better or worse, we're not the same people who entered these caverns.' I nodded, feeling the weight of his words. Our scars, both physical and emotional, were a testament to our journey's toll, and yet they also marked our growth.

As we ventured further into the depths of the facility, our footsteps echoing against the grimy walls, we stumbled upon a vast chamber that exuded an aura of neglect and decay. The room stretched out before us, its once pristine interior now marred by the passage of time and neglect.

The ceiling overhead was supported by a network of corroded metal beams, their surfaces tarnished by years of exposure to the elements. Rusted metal panels lined the walls, their surfaces pockmarked with age and neglect. A labyrinth of machinery and control units cluttered the space, hinting at the room's former purpose as an industrial hub or perhaps a clandestine bunker.

Sickly fluorescent lights flickered sporadically overhead, casting eerie shadows that danced across the dusty air. One of the lights emitted a piercing shaft of greenish light, illuminating the grime-coated floor below in an otherworldly glow.

To the left, a rusted railing bordered a staircase that spiraled downward into the depths of the facility, its metal surfaces worn smooth by the passage of countless feet. The air was heavy with the acrid scent of decay, mingling with the faint hum of machinery in the distance.

As we cautiously made our way through the chamber, our eyes were drawn to a pool of glowing green substance that pooled ominously on the floor. Its sickly hue cast a pall over the room, hinting at its potentially hazardous nature and adding to the sense of unease that permeated the air.

The air was thick with an unidentifiable metallic tang; the scent of decay intertwined with the buzz of inactive machinery, creating an oppressive atmosphere that clung to our skin and filled our lungs.

Despite its dilapidated appearance, there was an undeniable sense of foreboding that hung over the chamber, as if it were hiding secrets long forgotten by time. With trepidation, we pressed onward, knowing that whatever lay ahead would test our courage and resolve to their limits.

We heard loud thumping and growling sounds coming from the darkness of a corridor that connected to the room.

"That doesn't sound good," said Ulric.

said.

"No, it doesn't. I wonder what's ahead of us this time," I In the dimly lit corridor, a huge figure emerged, A chilling sense of foreboding crept over us as the ground vibrated with the heavy, unseen steps of something formidable. The faint sound of mechanical whirring and the occasional metallic clink hinted at the imminent appearance of a formidable adversary.

its presence, commanding attention, and instilling a sense of awe. Clad in a suit of cybernetic armor, the individual exuded an aura of power and intimidation.

From head to toe, it was adorned with mechanical enhancements and reinforced plating, giving it an unmistakably formidable appearance. The limbs were encased in sleek, metallic casings, each joint bristling with intricate machinery and hydraulic pistons. Cables and wires snaked across the surface of the armor, connecting various components and lending an air of technological sophistication to the ensemble.

A powered exoskeleton, adorned with a multitude of straps and harnesses, augmented the character's already imposing stature. Pouches and compartments adorned the armor, housing an array of equipment and ammunition, ready to be deployed at a moment's notice. The firearm, seamlessly integrated into the right arm, gleamed ominously in the low light, its sleek design hinting at devastating firepower.

The figure's attire bore the marks of countless battles and skirmishes, with dark lines and washes of color marring the surface of the armor. These signs of wear and tear spoke volumes about the figure's experiences, hinting at a life lived on the edge of danger and adventure. A layer of grime and dirt coated the armor, further accentuating its rugged appearance and adding to its sense of authenticity.

Despite the visible signs of age and use, the armor exuded an air of resilience and durability, an attestation of its superior craftsmanship and engineering. With every movement, the thing exuded confidence and strength, its imposing stance commanding respect and reverence.

As the monster strode purposefully down the corridor, its presence seemed to fill the space, casting a long shadow that stretched out before them. In the dim light, their form appeared almost ethereal—a warrior forged in the fires of adversity and tempered by the trials of battle. With each step, it drew closer, its determination unwavering.

Its appearance alone was enough to stall our advance In that moment, facing the monstrous embodiment of our fears, I realized the weight of our mission. Failure wasn't an option, not just for our survival but also for the hope of finding a cure for the ravages the outside world had suffered. Ulric and I were carrying the weight of the future on our shoulders. It was a titan of metal and might, seemingly plucked from the annals of war itself. Ulric, already grappling with the agony of his burnt right hand, tensed beside me, his eyes narrowing in determination despite the clear disadvantage.

Activating the SpectraShroud on my wrist, the device hummed to life, its micro-projectors casting a holographic field around me. By manipulating light and sound, I became invisible to the naked eye, a ghost amidst the shadows of the Ascendant Matrix. It was more than a tool; it was our edge in a world where brute strength alone could not guarantee survival. I felt the familiar thrum of technology on my skin.

"Stay close," I whispered to Ulric, the device's light-bending capabilities enveloping us in an illusory cloak of invisibility.

The monster's head swiveled, scanning the area where we stood moments before, now only an empty space for its sensors.

Ulric, his voice a rasp of pain and resolve, muttered, "What's the plan?"

For a brief moment, Ulric's eyes met mine, and I saw the reflection of our shared trials—a wordless conversation of fear, hope, and determination.

He glanced around cautiously, lowering his voice to a whisper that barely cut through the ominous silence of the corridor.

I responded with a nod, our shared history of close calls and narrow escapes allowing us to communicate volumes in silence.

It was a bond forged in adversity, one that went beyond words "We hit it with confusion," I responded, the SpectraShroud's intricate system casting multiple versions of us around the room. The duplicates fanned out, each performing a different action, a ballet of ghosts to distract and deceive.

The creature, baited by the illusion, lashed out at the apparitions, its integrated weaponry discharging with thunderous roars into the voids we no longer occupied. The sound of discharging weapons reverberated through the corridor, a symphony of chaos and desperation that underscored the peril of our situation.

I seized the moment, modulating my appearance to match the environment and becoming part of the wall's shadow. From my vantage point, I studied the behemoth, noting the slight delays in its reactions to the false targets.

Yet, in our game of shadows and light, a misstep. One illusory duplicate ventured too close, and the creature's sweeping gaze lingered, a split second too long, on a space beside it. Ulric, caught in a bid to reposition, grimaced as the monster's arm, swift as a tempest, swung towards his silhouette. The blow sent him crashing against the wall, a groan of pain escaping him as he slumped to the ground. For a moment, time seemed to slow, the gravity of Ulric's injury dawning on me with crushing clarity. His grimace of pain was a jarring contrast to his usual resilience, highlighting the stakes of our mission.

Panic flared within me. "Ulric!" I called out, breaking my camouflage to rush to his side. The monster, capitalizing on the break in our illusion, advanced, its mechanical gait thudding ominously on the stone floor.

Ulric, through gritted teeth, pushed me away. "Go, Ethan. Finish this."

Aware of Ulric's injury, I adjusted my strategy, relying more on stealth and less on direct confrontation.

Ignoring his protest, I recalibrated the SpectraShroud, the device pulsing with renewed vigor. The corridor was suddenly awash with a dazzling array of light and sound, a maelstrom of sensory overload that I directed squarely at the behemoth. A wave of doubt washed over me; the SpectraShroud was our last ace, and if this failed, there was no plan B. Under the assault, the creature staggered, its sensors overwhelmed, its form flickering in and out of visibility as it struggled against the fabricated storm.

"This is for Ulric," I hissed, closing the distance. The SpectraShroud, its energy focusing into a singular point of intensity, pierced through the cacophony, a lance of pure, blinding light aimed at the beast's core.

As the behemoth fell, silence enveloped us. I turned to Ulric, expecting a grimace of pain, but instead found a weary smirk. 'Nicely done,' he breathed, the levity in his voice cutting through the tension. I couldn't help but return the smile—a small, shared moment of triumph amidst the chaos. The creature roared, a sound cut abruptly short as the light found its mark, severing cables and frying circuits. In its final moments, the creature's eyes, a mesh of biotech and sorrow, hinted at a larger narrative at play, a pawn in the grand scheme of the Ascendant Matrix's guardianship. With the mechanical giant falling, a deafening silence took over. I turned from the silent titan, my heart sinking at the sight of Ulric's pained form.

As the behemoth crumpled, its armor clinking in defeat, silence reclaimed the corridor. The aftermath of the battle lay before us, a testament to our survival against overwhelming odds. Breathing heavily, I turned from the defeated creature back to Ulric, making the transition from battle to concern for my friend as swift as it was necessary.

Yet, the victory was bittersweet, shadowed by the cost exacted upon us. I rushed to Ulric, lifting his limp form in my arms. "You're going to be okay," I assured him, though the weight of his injuries spoke of a grim reality.

As the dust settled and the echo of the battle faded into silence, the reality of our victory sank in. I felt every ache in my body; the adrenaline was waning, leaving behind a raw reminder of our ordeal.

We found a small alcove, a rare sanctuary, amidst the relentless march of our mission. Here, we paused, allowing the silence to wrap around us like a comforting shroud. In this moment of stillness, I realized that the journey was not just about reaching our destination but about understanding the path that led us there.

I felt every ache in my body; the adrenaline was waning, leaving behind a raw reminder of our ordeal. We had overcome the impossible, yet the victory was hollow, marred by the cost exacted upon us. Ulric's injury was a grim reminder of the fragility of our existence in this relentless pursuit. As I supported his weight, a sense of resolve strengthened within me. Our mission was far from over; it was a beacon guiding us through the darkness, and I vowed to carry its burden for both of us. This vow wasn't just a promise; it was a covenant etched into the very marrow of my bones, fueled by a blend of duty and the unyielding spirit that adversity had forged within us.

"We... we did it?" Ulric managed, his voice barely a whisper. "We did," I confirmed, casting a wary glance at the fallen titan. "But you need help, more than I can give here. You can't come with me, not like this."

A pained sigh escaped him. "Then go. Finish what we started." Ulric glanced at me, his eyes reflecting a mix of determination and the weariness of our journey. 'When this is over, Ethan, promise me something,' he said, his voice barely above a whisper. 'Promise me we'll find a way to remember who we were before all this began.' His words, a bridge between the past and the hope for a future, reminded me that we were not just fighting for survival but for the chance to return to a life where such promises could be kept.

The SpectraShroud dimmed on my wrist; its task completed for now. With Ulric secure, I stepped back into the shadows of the Ascendant Matrix, leaving behind the creature that had nearly cost us everything. As the silence enveloped us, I saw Ulric's shoulders relax for the first time since we had entered the Ascendant Matrix. 'You know,' he said softly, his gaze not leaving the dark horizon of the unknown ahead, 'I never imagined that courage felt so much like fear.' This admission, rare and raw, peeled back another layer of the man I had come to know not just as a comrade but as a brother. Our journey had not just tested our limits; it had redefined them. The weight of solitude pressed heavily on me as I ventured deeper, and the absence of Ulric's steady presence was a stark reminder of the uncertainty that lay ahead.

Ahead lay uncertainties, more battles, and more challenges. But in that moment, only one truth remained: I would see our mission through, for Ulric, for all that we had fought for. As I ventured deeper into the heart of the Matrix, the weight of our mission bore down on me with every step. The thought of the dying world above and of the hope that rested on our shoulders fueled my resolve. 'This is for the earth's tomorrow,' I whispered to the shadows, a vow to the silent witnesses of our journey.

As I ventured deeper into the labyrinthine complex, the echoes of our confrontation lingered, a demonstration of the power of human resilience and the cutting edge of our technology. The SpectraShroud, a beacon of hope in the dark, promised that no matter what lay ahead, I was never truly alone.

As we prepared to delve deeper, I couldn't help but wonder about the mysterious symbols on the device. These symbols, eerily reminiscent of the lore our elders spoke of, suggested our path would cross with the Architects of the Matrix, beings of immense power and unknown intentions, and the ominous sounds from the darkness. Resolving to uncover their meanings, I knew our journey was far from over. Despite the weariness that tugged at my limbs, a sense of reverence stirred within me. We were walking a path of prophecy and promise, where each step was a line in the epic that our saga had become.

I stood at the threshold of the unknown; a resolve settled within me, clearer and more determined than ever. 'For the world that awaits,' I whispered into the darkness, 'for the hope of dawn after this endless night.

As we ventured deeper, the air grew colder, and a series of cryptic symbols not seen before began to glow along the corridor's walls, suggesting we were entering a domain guarded by ancient and formidable secrets.

The chill seeped through my clothes, a creeping coldness that seemed to herald the presence of ancient guardians of these secrets. Each symbol that flickered to life on the walls felt like the watchful eyes of the Architects themselves, bearing silent witness to our intrusion.

BIOMETRIC HORIZONS

I proceeded down the next corridor and arrived in a compact room exuding a pragmatic, industrial aura. The chill of the metallic surroundings seeped through my attire, a stark reminder of the facility's forgotten purpose. Each step echoed a lonely sound in the expanse of silence, amplifying the solitude of my mission. 'Ulric would have analyzed every inch of this machinery,' I thought, allowing myself a brief moment of reflection amidst the cold functionality of the room.

The space was illuminated by harsh fluorescent lighting, casting stark shadows against the metal walls, adorned with sturdy support beams traversing the ceiling. The room was neatly organized, with metal shelving units housing sizable, multicolored storage containers. Dominating the forefront was a robust piece of machinery, its formidable presence accentuated by a row of switches or controls adorning its rear, accompanied by a trailing cable. The overall cleanliness and orderliness of the room suggested meticulous maintenance and operational efficiency.

At the far end of the room loomed a door adorned with twin red vertical lines, flanked by a laser grid and an indentation resembling a handprint. Without anticipation, I placed my hand on the indentation. A soft whirring noise ensued, followed by a gentle beep and a faint click. Subsequently, a series of electronic tones and whirs reverberated through the air, culminating in a low hum that gradually dissipated into silence. A faint snapping sound marked the disappearance of the laser grid.

Finally, a deep rumbling resonance permeated the room, accompanied by the mechanical symphony of grinding gears and hydraulic movements as the hefty door began its ascent. The reverberations echoed throughout the chamber, intensifying in volume with each passing moment, punctuated by occasional metallic creaks and groans that contributed to the intricate orchestration of mechanized sounds.

To my astonishment, the door recognized my fingerprints and swiftly slid open. Stepping over the threshold, I was met with a sudden barrage of bullets as turrets emerged from the ceiling, their rapid gunfire filling the air. The air crackled with energy, charged with the scent of ozone and burning metal. I dove, weaving through the ballet of death with a grace born of desperation, each move a calculated risk to evade the relentless assault.

Reacting instinctively, I sought cover behind the door, swiftly retrieving my Fusionizer from its holster. Peering cautiously around the corner, I unleashed a volley of energy bolts from my rifle, swiftly neutralizing the menacing turrets.

With the immediate threat subdued, I ventured forth through a narrow corridor that led to an adjoining room. The interior bore the unmistakable hallmark of industrial design, with weathered metal walls serving as a backdrop to an array of monitors, control panels, and aging machinery. The room hummed with the faint buzz of electronic activity, punctuated by the occasional blink of lights and the soft click of buttons being pressed. I paused, the greenish hue of the monitors casting ghostly shadows across my face. Here, amidst the whir of machines, I found a moment of eerie peace, a stark contrast to the chaos that had become my constant companion. The prevailing turquoise and rust color scheme lent an air of antiquity to the technology within, hinting at decades of use and refinement.

As I stepped through the doorway, a formidable robot immediately locked into my presence. "DANGER: Intruder detected," it blared, its warning echoing through the corridor. In response, it unleashed a barrage of laser bolts in my direction, each one pulsating with deadly energy. These lasers, composed of the same resilient material as the beams we had previously encountered, posed a grave threat; their cutting power could slice through flesh and bone with alarming ease, leaving me vulnerable despite my enhanced healing capabilities.

The robot itself boasted a striking design, dominated by a spherical central body housing a menacing red sensor that glared like a single, unblinking eye.

This encounter not only tested my physical prowess but also challenged my understanding of artificial intelligence's evolving role in combat scenarios. The robot, with its advanced design, seemed to personify the pinnacle of technological warfare, blurring the lines between machine efficiency and sentient determination. Its unyielding pursuit, driven by algorithms capable of learning and adapting, underscored a chilling evolution: the battlefield of the future might be dominated not by human strategy and bravery but by cold, calculating artificial intellects.

Flanking this central orb were two smaller spherical nodes, their purpose obscured but hinting at additional sensory functions or perhaps as emitters for its formidable weaponry. Its bipedal leg system, sturdy yet agile, supported its mechanical form, with each limb adorned with multiple articulated joints that promised swift and fluid movement. The segmented design of its limbs and body, adorned with accents of silver, black, and red, spoke of advanced engineering and hinted at the potential for intricate manipulation and dexterity.

Undeterred, I raised my Fusionizer, taking aim at the robot's metallic frame. Sweat beaded on my forehead, not just from the heat of battle but from the realization of what I was up against. This machine, a product of human ingenuity turned adversary, was a formidable foe, its design a testament to a bygone era's prowess.

With precision and determination, I unleashed a barrage of energy bolts, each one finding its mark with lethal accuracy. As my shots struck home, the robot emitted a mechanical groan, its movements faltering as vital systems began to shut down. Piece by piece, it succumbed to the onslaught, its once-imposing form reduced to inert machinery, its demise punctuated by the symphony of mechanical parts grinding to a halt.!

As I traversed the labyrinthine corridors of the facility, I encountered a relentless onslaught of similar robotic adversaries, each one posing a formidable threat to my progress. Despite my best efforts to evade their attacks, one of them managed to land a devastating blow, piercing through my armor and flesh with chilling efficiency. The searing pain radiated from my shoulder, a stark reminder of the dangers that lurked within these metallic halls. With grim determination, I pressed on, my resolve unyielding even in the face of injury, though I knew that this wound would demand time to heal.

Continuing my exploration, I eventually found myself standing before a sealed door, its entrance barred by an electronic device adorned with a scanner demanding authentication.

Frustration gnawed at the edges of my resolve as I realized that without the requisite keycard, further progress seemed impossible. Reluctantly, I retraced my steps, scouring the facility in search of an alternative route or solution to my predicament.

It was in one such room that I found temporary respite, though the sight that greeted me only deepened the mystery of this enigmatic facility. The interior bore the unmistakable hallmarks of futuristic industrial design, with its sturdy metal walls and ribbed beams painted in a somber shade of green, evoking a sense of militaristic austerity. Against these imposing surfaces stood an array of technological consoles and machines, their intricate displays and controls hinting at advanced functions beyond my comprehension.

One particular machine commanded attention, its series of five dials locked in unison at the number three, their purpose shrouded in mystery. Above, twin screens flickered with data, offering glimpses into the surrounding area and its enigmatic secrets. At the heart of the room, a metal table played host to an assortment of medical and scientific equipment, its purpose veiled behind a veil of uncertainty.

Under my feet, the metal-gridded floor bore the scars of countless footsteps, a testament to the passage of time and the weight of countless endeavors. Illuminated by harsh fluorescent lights, the room teetered on the precipice between light and shadow, its stark contrast heightening the sense of intrigue that permeated the air. In this functional space, every detail spoke of purpose and design, hinting at the intricate web of operations that lay concealed within its walls.

On a small metal table, I found an electronic card labeled "Biometric ID Card.". If it was biometric, it meant that I had to somehow integrate my biological signature into the card.

I continued on throughout the facility and had to fight several more robots and turrets placed strategically around the environment. This now took more effort, with my wounded shoulder slowly healing but not yet fast enough. Then I finally came upon another room.

The room appeared to be part of a larger industrial or military complex. The air was heavy, filled with the scent of metal and the subtle hum of latent energy. Shadows danced along the walls, cast by machinery that had long since fallen silent. It was a space caught between eras, where echoes of the past mingled with the silent anticipation of future conflicts.

The room had an aged and weathered look, with metal walls that showed signs of wear and some rust. The architecture included reinforced metal beams and riveted panels, indicative of sturdy construction.

The room that lay before me was akin to a scene straight out of a dystopian archive, a vault-like door serving as the barrier to what I presumed were secrets of substantial value or perhaps dangers best left undisturbed. The door's small, square window, a mere porthole into the unknown, offered no clues, its purpose as enigmatic as the contents it guarded. The surrounding space, cluttered with various machinery and control panels, hinted at an operational nerve center of sorts, possibly dedicated to monitoring or securing the facility's most sensitive areas.

The grimy floor, a tapestry of neglect woven with scattered debris, bore silent testimony to the passage of time and abandonment. Above, lighting fixtures, surprisingly operational, shed stark illumination across the room, highlighting the stark contrast between the technology still clinging to life and the decay that had claimed its surroundings.

Among the relics of this bygone era, a computer setup caught my eye, its keyboard and screen a beacon of functionality in a sea of obsolescence. Adjacent to this unexpected ally was a hand scanner, mirroring the design of another

I had encountered previously. It was accompanied by a slot designed for a key-card, a modern-day lock awaiting its key.

With a mixture of trepidation and resolve, I approached the computer, my gaze fixed on the screen that flickered to life at my touch. The options displayed were clear: reading, inputting, and uploading biometric data onto an ID card. The solution seemed straightforward enough, yet the device's response to my initial attempt was a stark reminder of the complexities lying in wait. "Unable to detect a biological signature," it declared, a digital sentinel barring the way forward. "Unable to detect Biometric ID card for upload," it continued, underscoring the challenge that lay ahead.

The task was clear, yet its execution was anything but. The card slot, ready to receive its charge, awaited my next move. Placing the card into the slot felt like a leap of faith, an action taken on the belief that the technology of the past would recognize the intent of the present. With my right hand placed firmly on the scanner, I willed the system to acknowledge my presence and my identity.

Selecting the upload option once again, I held my breath as the system processed my request. "Biological signature detection: Name: Ethan Hawthorne, Profession: Science Engineer," the screen intoned, an acknowledgment of my identity that was both affirming and invasive. "Anomalies have been detected in the user's biosignature. Are you sure you want to proceed?" It queried, a digital crossroads offering me a choice that was no choice at all.

With my left hand, I input the command to continue, a simple action that felt weighted with consequence. The machine complied, its soft whirring a prelude to success, followed by a gentle beep and a faint click that heralded the completion of the operation. "Operation successfully completed," the screen announced, a statement of fact that belied the complexity of what had just transpired. The ID card was returned to me, a piece of plastic imbued with the potential to unlock doors and perhaps destinies.

With the keycard now encoded with my biometric signature, I turned my attention back to the large round door, its imposing presence a reminder of the hurdles yet to be overcome. The small square window, once a barrier to understanding, now served as a symbol of the threshold between the known and the unknown.

As I approached the door, keycard in hand, I was acutely aware of the myriad possibilities that lay on the other side. The machinery and control panels that filled the room, once enigmatic, now felt like silent witnesses to my journey, a journey that had taken me from the role of observer to participant in the unfolding narrative of this forgotten facility.

The keycard slot next to the door, identical to the one at the computer station, awaited my next action. Inserting the card, I felt a connection to the technology around me—a symbiosis between man and machine that transcended mere interaction. The door responded, its locking mechanisms disengaging with a series of mechanical sounds that echoed through the room, heralding the opening of a new chapter in my exploration.

As the door swung open, the bright illumination from the room spilled into the space beyond, piercing the shadows that had long held sway. Stepping through the threshold, I was met with a vista that challenged comprehension—a space that defied expectations and hinted at realities yet to be discovered.

The journey to this point had been one of both physical and intellectual challenges, a path that had required me to bridge the gap between the past and the present, between decay and functionality. The biometric key, a token of my passage, symbolized more than just access to locked doors; it represented a deeper understanding of the facility's secrets and my place within its story.

With every step forward, I was rewriting the narrative of this place, a narrative that had lain dormant, awaiting someone with the courage and curiosity to uncover its truths. The keycard, now a part of me, was a testament to the journey undertaken and the challenges overcome, a reminder that even in the depths of abandonment and decay, there lies the potential for discovery and understanding.

The room beyond the round opening of the door promised new mysteries to unravel and new challenges to face. Amidst the remnants of technological marvels, a cryptic symbol etched onto the surface of a dormant console caught my eye. Amidst the backdrop of renewal, the ethical implications of technology took center stage. The war had laid bare the dual-edged nature of our advancements, prompting a reevaluation of how, why, and for whom technology was developed. Ethical frameworks began to emerge, focusing on sustainability, equity, and the prevention of misuse. These discussions weren't merely academic; they became the bedrock for a new technological ethos, one that prioritized the well-being of the planet and its inhabitants above all. Unlike the purely functional designs that adorned the rest of the facility, this symbol seemed deliberate, almost arcane. Its presence here, in stark contrast to the utilitarianism that governed the facility's architecture, hinted at deeper secrets, perhaps even hidden agendas, that lay at the heart of this place. It served as a silent harbinger of the complexities I was yet to uncover, weaving an additional thread of mystery into the fabric of my mission.

But armed with the biometric key and a resolve forged in the trials of the past, I was ready to confront whatever lay ahead, to push the boundaries of knowledge, and to explore the unknown territories that awaited. I retrieved the Biometric ID card from its slot, a small yet crucial key in my journey through the labyrinthine corridors of this forgotten facility. With measured steps, I retraced my path back to the imposing closed door, its surface adorned with the ominous glow of the scanning device. Positioning the card before the sensor, I braced myself for the cacophony of mechanical sounds that heralded the door's reluctant ascent As the door groaned open, revealing the chamber beyond, I was met with a scene straight from the annals of a forgotten era. The vast expanse of the chamber echoed with the relentless hisses of escaping gases, a haunting symphony of decay that spoke volumes of the once-great technological empire now reduced to ruins. The air hung heavy with the luminous mist of irradiated gases, casting an ethereal glow over the desolate landscape before me.

With each step I took, the sound reverberated ominously through the chamber, a solitary echo amidst the chorus of groans and hisses that permeated the air. The cracked tubes, like the veins of a slumbering giant, snaked their way across the chamber floor, their sporadic emissions a testament to the neglect that had befallen this once-thriving bastion of science.

To my left, a rust-ridden metal staircase descended into the depths of the chamber, its structural integrity compromised by years of disuse. Below, amidst a landscape of forgotten equipment and decrepit containers, a pool of ominous green substance shimmered in the dim light. Its origins shrouded in mystery, yet its presence is a stark reminder of the dangers lurking within these hallowed halls.

As I gazed upon this desolate tableau, I couldn't help but feel a sense of trepidation creeping over me. For within the crumbling walls of this forsaken chamber lay the secrets of a forgotten world, waiting to be unearthed by those brave enough to venture into the heart of darkness.

Two large, round doors dominated the far end of the chamber, their purpose as mysterious as their destination. Sealed shut, they hinted at secrets locked away, perhaps chambers similar to this one or gateways to even more enigmatic sectors of the complex. The very architecture of the room, with its industrial design and the prominent control panel that stood as a silent guardian of the threshold, spoke of a space once alive with activity, now reduced to a mausoleum of its past.

Armed with my portable atmospheric cleaner, I ventured forth, slicing through the dense fog that clung to every corner of the room. The device hummed quietly, a counterpoint to the cacophony of hisses, as it cleared a path for me to tread. My steps were cautious, respectful of the history and hazards that enveloped me.

As I ventured deeper into the chamber, my eyes fell upon the source of the leaks: the intricate network of tubes marred by cracks and openings, transforming the once-sanctuary into a perilous quagmire of toxic fumes. Undeterred by the daunting task ahead, I retrieved my Nanomaterial Repair Sprayers, meticulously designed tools poised to mend the structural breaches with unrivaled precision. With each spray, the cracks began to seal, a visible sign of healing in this decayed tomb of technology. The hiss of escaping gases quieted, replaced by the soft hum of restored systems, a minor victory in the vastness of the Ascendant Matrix.

Each crack and crevice became a canvas for the miraculous nanomaterial solution, an indication of the power of innovation amidst adversity. With practiced expertise, I guided the sprayers, watching as the solution adhered to the damaged surfaces, weaving a tapestry of impermeable protection that staunchly halted the gas's insidious escape. With each application, the relentless hissing of the toxic fumes gradually subsided, yielding a newfound tranquility that whispered of the chamber's gradual restoration.

As the last traces of gas dissipated, the chamber unveiled its secrets with renewed clarity. The equipment and containers, once shrouded in a veil of fog, now stood in stark relief against the backdrop of the cleansed atmosphere, their enigmatic purposes waiting to be unraveled. The control panel, now within reach, beckoned with the promise of unlocking insights into the facility's inner workings, offering a tantalizing glimpse into the labyrinthine depths of the complex.

With the immediate danger averted and the chamber's atmosphere restored to its former purity, I stowed away the Atmospheric Cleanser, its mission accomplished. My gaze lingered upon the staircase and the sealed doors, the next milestones in my journey. Despite their weathered appearance, the staircase offered a gateway to further exploration, leading downwards into the bowels of this forsaken domain. Meanwhile, the sealed doors stood as silent sentinels, guardians of untold challenges and secrets waiting to be unveiled.

Choosing my path was not a decision to be made lightly.

The staircase, with its promise of descent into the unknown, beckoned with the allure of discovery. Yet the doors, their destinations hidden, held the potential for crucial answers to the puzzle of this complex. The decision weighed heavily on me—a choice between delving deeper into the heart of this abandoned sanctuary or confronting the mysteries that lay beyond the sealed gateways.

In the end, curiosity and a relentless drive to uncover the truths of this place guided my decision. I approached the control panel, its interfaces a puzzle to be solved, hoping it held the key to unlocking the doors. My fingers danced across the surfaces, tapping into the ancient technology and coaxing it back to life.

As the panel responded, the doors began to groan, their mechanisms stirring from slumber. With a final push of determination, I watched as the barriers that stood before me yielded, revealing new corridors and new challenges to be faced.

The journey through the derelict facility was far from over; each step took me deeper into its secrets, each discovery a piece of the larger mystery I sought to unravel.

The path was fraught with peril, the complex a labyrinth of dangers both known and unforeseen As I ventured deeper, the echo of my footsteps was a lonely testament to my journey. 'For Ulric,' I whispered, the words a vow to continue, to uncover the truth hidden within these walls, for him, for all that we had dreamed of. But within me burned a resolve forged in the crucible of challenges already overcome. I pressed on, driven by the quest for knowledge and the hope that somewhere within this forsaken edifice lay the answers I sought. The journey was mine alone, a solitary figure against the backdrop of decay and forgotten ambitions. But with each step, I moved closer to the truth, to the heart of the Ascendant Matrix, and to the destiny that awaited me there.: a formidable laser grid blocking access to the adjoining area. As I surveyed the room, I observed an array of additional laser grids, each presenting its own barrier to progress. Contemplating my options, I turned my attention to the walls, adorned with structures reminiscent of a bygone era's computer systems.

These industrial-grade contraptions exuded a sense of rugged functionality, evoking the essence of a retro-futuristic command center or server room. Their robust metal frames housed a multitude of analog dials, gauges, and toggle switches, arranged with purposeful precision. Banks of blinking lights punctuated the panels, their rhythmic pulses hinting at latent power within.

Wires and tubing snaked across the walls, weaving a network of connectivity between the various components and imbuing the room with a tangible sense of energy flow. Embedded screens flickered to life sporadically, displaying vital statistics or cryptic data in a monochrome display that spoke of older or alternate-reality technology.

Despite the passage of time and the absence of human presence, the room retained an air of austere readiness, as if awaiting the resumption of its duties. Each panel and console bore the scars of past operations, a testament to their enduring functionality in the face of adversity. As I prepared to confront the laser grids and navigate the labyrinthine network of corridors beyond, I couldn't help but marvel at the resilience of these relics from a bygone era.

As I surveyed the area, my attention was drawn to a lone computer terminal standing sentinel amidst the technological detritus. With a sense of urgency driving my actions, I delved into its digital depths, hoping to uncover a solution to bypass the formidable laser grid barring my progress. Yet, to my dismay, all I found was a trove of inconsequential data, a mere footnote in the annals of some forgotten scientist's diary.

Frustration mounting within me like a tempest, I unleashed a barrage of energy bolts upon the hapless computer structures, igniting a cacophony of chaos and destruction. The air crackled with the symphony of electronic whirs, buzzing, and crackling as circuits succumbed to the onslaught, their delicate components overloaded beyond repair. Each shot reverberated with a sharp, metallic clang, punctuated by ominous pops as vital systems erupted in a shower of sparks.

Amidst the chaos, a low, ominous hum resonated through the chamber, an indication of the power coursing through the computer's circuits. Yet, as my relentless assault continued, the hum abruptly ceased, silenced by the severed flow of power. With a final burst of energy, I unleashed upon the hapless machinery, each shot heralding the demise of another electronic foe.

And then, as if in response to my onslaught, a faint buzzing emanated from the laser grid, its once-imposing barrier faltering under the assault. Realization dawned upon me like a beacon in the darkness: the destruction of the electronic equipment held the key to my salvation. With newfound determination, I turned my weapon upon every piece of machinery in sight, unleashing chaos and mayhem in my wake.

As the last vestiges of resistance crumbled beneath my onslaught, a sense of triumph surged within me. The technology that lay in ruins before me was a far cry from the rudimentary tools and machines of my early training. Each piece, even in its destruction, spoke of an era where the boundaries of science and ethics blurred into obscurity. I couldn't help but marvel at the ingenuity, even as I mourned the hubris. The facility's advanced machinery, from self-healing alloys to artificial intelligence-driven automatons, was a testament to human creativity. Yet, in their creation, we perhaps overstepped, forgotten the humility that must accompany our quest for knowledge. As I navigated through the debris, it was a stark reminder that the future we sought to build could easily become a prison of our own making.

The laser grid, once an impenetrable barrier, now lay dormant at my feet, its power extinguished by the destruction wrought upon its electronic brethren. With a path now clear before me, I pressed onward, steeling myself for the challenges that lay ahead in this open expanse, still bristling with the remnants of its former defenses.

The area appeared to be an interior space, likely within a robust facility of significant technological importance.

As I stepped into the open expanse, a chill coursed through me, not from the cold but from the sheer magnitude of what lay forgotten. The scent of oil and metal filled the air, a stark reminder of this place's once bustling activity. Each sound echoed like a ghostly whisper in the vast emptiness, amplifying the solitude of my journey. It was designed with an industrial aesthetic, featuring exposed pipework along the ceiling and metal frameworks, a testament to its functional design that prioritizes utility over comfort. The space was filled with machinery and control panels, bearing analog gauges and various buttons and levers, suggesting a setting where operational tasks were performed. Equipment and containers were organized methodically throughout the room, indicative of a place used for technical work or research. This setting would probably serve as a control room or laboratory within a larger complex, brimming with untold stories of scientific endeavors or critical operational duties.

As I braced myself to unleash another volley upon the remaining computers, a sudden and searing pain tore through my abdomen, leaving me gasping in shock. A voice, cold and mechanical, pierced the air with chilling precision: "Danger: Intruder detected; eliminate with extreme prejudice."

Struggling to comprehend the source of the attack, I was abruptly seized by an invisible force, my senses reeling as I felt myself being pulled towards an unseen assailant. And then, as if materializing from thin air, a figure emerged from the cloak of invisibility, revealing itself to be a formidable adversary indeed.

The robot stood before me, its humanoid form exuding an aura of lethal efficiency. Each movement was calculated and precise, a testament to its advanced design and combat capabilities. Its sleek, metallic body bore the unmistakable signs of technological prowess, with arms that terminated in what could only be described as deadly implements or tools of destruction.

With a design optimized for speed and agility, the robot's streamlined silhouette hinted at its proficiency in navigating complex environments and executing swift, decisive actions. Its narrow waist and broad shoulders spoke to its capacity for both precision and strength, while its small yet potent optical sensor conveyed an aura of focused intensity, capable of locking onto targets with deadly accuracy.

As I gazed upon the robot's matte surface, I couldn't help but marvel at the intricate craftsmanship that had gone into its construction. Reflective areas caught the ambient light, hinting at the diverse materials employed in its fabrication, each serving a specific functional purpose in its deadly arsenal.

In that moment, it became abundantly clear that this robot was not merely a mindless automaton but a meticulously engineered weapon, honed for the singular purpose of eliminating threats with ruthless efficiency.

This encounter, a vivid dance of life and artificiality, thrust me into a maelan of thought. How far have we come, and at what cost? The very creations meant to serve us now stand as testament to our own vulnerabilities, a reflection of the complex, often fraught relationship we share with the machines of our own making.

With a sinking realization, I understood that I was now face-to-face with a foe that possessed not only strength and speed but also the intelligence and cunning to outmatch any adversary it encountered.

With a deafening roar, the robot unleashed a devastating energy beam from its head, tearing through everything in its path with ferocious intensity. Glass shattered, steel walls crumpled, and desks were reduced to smoldering wreckage as the beam cut a swath of destruction through the area, leaving chaos in its wake.

Reacting swiftly, I activated my SpecTrashroud in a bid to evade the robot's thermal sensors, but to no avail. The relentless machine locked onto my heat signature with uncanny precision, launching a relentless assault with its razor-sharp claws. I narrowly dodged its lethal strikes, narrowly avoiding the deadly blows as I scrambled for cover.

Summoning all my strength, I launched a counterattack, charging headlong at the robot and delivering a bone-crushing blow that sent it hurtling backward, crashing into the nearest wall with a resounding thud. Despite the damage inflicted, the resilient machine refused to yield, cloaking itself once more as it prepared to unleash another volley of attacks.

As the robot launched a laser beam in my direction, I dodged with lightning speed, quickly pinpointing its location. With a steady hand, I aimed my Fusionizer at the source of the beam and fired, scoring a direct hit that disabled its cloaking abilities in an instant.

Seizing the opportunity, I surged forward, unleashing a relentless barrage of attacks upon the robot's exposed components. Wires snapped, circuits fizzled, and central mechanics whirred as I targeted every vulnerable point with surgical precision.

With a final, defiant cry of "ERROR, ERROR, systems shutting down," the robot crumbled to the ground, defeated at last. Surveying the aftermath of our fierce battle, I noted with satisfaction that several laser grids had been partially disabled by the robot's destruction, clearing the way forward.

Continuing my assault on the computer systems, I methodically disabled each remaining laser grid until all obstacles had been overcome. Venturing into the newly accessible rooms, I found myself in a series of nondescript workstations and rest areas, devoid of any significant interest.

However, one area caught my eye—a dimly lit workshop with a distinctly post-industrial vibe. Set within the confines of an underground bunker, its reinforced metallic walls and utilitarian design hinted at its clandestine purpose. The eerie greenish glow of the overhead lighting cast long shadows across the workshop, adding to its mysterious allure.

Straight ahead, a cluttered workbench greeted my eyes, adorned with an array of intricate instruments and machinery. Among the jumble of tools, an illuminated screen flickered to life, accompanied by the soft hum of active electronic devices. The room buzzed with energy, a testament to the ceaseless activity that once filled its confines.

Cables hung from the ceiling like serpents, snaking their way toward the workbench, where they connected to various terminals and ports. Piping crisscrossed along the walls, their labyrinthine paths converging upon the central hub of activity. It was a scene of organized chaos, where each component played a vital role in the intricate dance of technological innovation.

Despite the clutter, there was a sense of purpose to the room—a feeling that every tool and instrument had been meticulously arranged for optimal efficiency. It was a workshop in the truest sense of the word, a sanctuary for those who sought to push the boundaries of what was possible.

Yet, as I searched through the clutter, my efforts proved fruitless. There was nothing of interest to be found amidst the tangle of wires and machinery. With a sense of disappointment, I turned my attention to the next area, hoping for better luck in my search.

Entering the spacious room beyond, I was met with a sight that spoke of industrial grandeur. Metal beams stretched overhead, forming a complex lattice that supported the weight of the structure above. Pipes snaked along the ceiling, their rusted surfaces hinting at years of use and neglect.

Despite the dim lighting, the room exuded a sense of vastness, its expansive floor stretching out before me like a blank canvas waiting to be filled. Heavy machinery loomed in the shadows; their hulking forms a testament to the industrial might that once thrived within these walls.

As I explored further, I couldn't help but marvel at the sheer scale of the space. It was a place where giants had once walked, where dreams had been forged from steel and sweat. And though the machinery lay dormant now, there was a sense of latent power lingering in the air, a reminder of the greatness that had once been achieved within these hallowed halls.

The concrete floor bore the marks and stains of usage, dust, and debris scattered across its surface, suggesting a long history of occupation and abandonment. Equipment and storage containers were haphazardly positioned throughout, indicating a hastily evacuated or disused workspace.

In times past, this room would have pulsed with activity, the very air alive with the symphony of machinery and the rhythmic cadence of workers' footsteps. But in the frozen moment captured by the image, all was eerily quiet—a poignant snapshot of a space once bustling with purpose, now relegated to silence and solitude.

Across the expanse of the room, my gaze fell upon a colossal door, its imposing presence drawing me toward it like a magnet. Yet, as I moved closer, my path intersected with that of a towering figure—an inactive robot, lying dormant like a slumbering giant.

The robot commanded attention, its formidable stature a testament to its intended role in heavy-duty tasks. Clad in armor plating that spoke of resilience and durability, its bulk suggested an unwavering strength, capable of weathering the most punishing of environments. With limbs adorned in a variety of attachments, it stood poised for action, each appendage a tool for a different purpose—be it precision or power.

Its head, perched atop its massive frame, housed an array of sensors that gleamed with an ominous red glow. Behind those piercing eyes lay the potential for advanced targeting systems or infrared vision, hinting at a level of sophistication beyond mere mechanical prowess. And draped in a palette of muted hues—off-white, grey, and rust—the robot blended seamlessly into its surroundings, a silent sentinel in the shadows.

As I approached, a chilling warning pierced the silence: "WARNING, intruder detected. Preparing elimination." With mechanical precision, the robot sprang to life, its limbs extending to their full reach, casting a daunting shadow across the room. With every movement, it seemed to grow larger and more imposing—an unmistakable signal that the battle ahead would be no easy feat.

Bracing myself for the impending clash, I steeled my resolve, knowing that the fate of this silent chamber rested on my shoulders. With each step forward, the tension in the air crackled with anticipation, setting the stage for a showdown between man and machine in this dark and desolate arena.

This machine, a behemoth of technology, was like nothing I had ever seen. It stood upright, its legs and arms extended as it prepared to engage. Its presence was commanding, designed with a robustness meant for heavy-duty tasks, perhaps even combat. The main body was a fortress in itself, armored to withstand severe damage, while its arms, one resembling a hand with fingers and the other a heavy-duty tool, hinted at its versatility for both finesse and brute force. Smaller arms equipped with various appendages suggested multi-functional capabilities. Its head, compact and equipped with sensors glowing ominously red, sat atop the main body, likely harboring advanced systems for target tracking.

The color scheme of off-white, grey, and rust offered a hint of its intended operational environment: dark, possibly underground areas where humans dared not tread. This was a machine built for survival in the harshest conditions, and now it stood between me and my mission.

As the robot's eyes fixed on me, the red glow intensified, signaling the beginning of a confrontation I felt ill-prepared for. My shoulder throbbed painfully, a stark reminder of the injury Ulric and I had sustained earlier. Ulric... my mind whispered his name, a pang of loss gripping me. He was no longer by my side; his wisdom, courage, and companionship were now a void within me. This battle was mine to fight alone.

The robot advanced, and its movements were surprisingly agile for its size. I dodged, relying on my instincts and the SpectraShroud's capabilities to keep me invisible.

Each evasion left my muscles burning and my breath short and ragged. The corridor became a chessboard, with each of us a player in a deadly game of move and countermove. My mind raced, calculating angles and trajectories, predicting the robot's next attack while suppressing the pain that screamed from my shoulder. 'One wrong step,' I realized, 'could be the end,' a sobering thought that sharpened my focus to a razor's edge. Yet, even with technology on my side, the robot's sensors were sophisticated, tracking my movements with unnerving accuracy. We danced a deadly ballet, the robot relentless in its pursuit to "eliminate" the intruder it saw in me.

Hours passed, or so it seemed, as the battle raged on. My body ached, and every movement was a testament to my determination and sheer will to survive. The robot was tireless, its attacks were becoming more calculated, and its artificial intelligence was adapting to my tactics. There were moments when I thought this might be where my journey ended, beneath the cold, unfeeling machinery of this guardian of the Matrix.

In a desperate bid, I remembered the smaller arms of the robot and the multifunctional tools it possessed. If I could disable those, I might have a chance. With a plan forming, I baited the robot into a particularly aggressive attack, using the last of the SpectraShroud's energy to create a myriad of illusions, distracting it.

Seizing the moment, I closed in, targeting the smaller arms with precision strikes. Sparks flew as metal clashed against metal, the sound echoing through the vastness of the Matrix. One by one, the robot's auxiliary arms fell silent, and its capabilities diminished. Yet, it was far from defeated. The main arms swung with devastating force, and I barely managed to evade the pain in my shoulder flaring with each movement.

It was a fight of attrition, and I was losing. But the thought of Ulric and our mission fueled me. I couldn't let his sacrifice be in vain. With a renewed sense of purpose, I launched myself at the robot with everything I had left, targeting the head, the center of its sensor array.

The final confrontation was a blur, a mix of pain, determination, and the cold fear of death. And then, with a final, desperate effort, I struck true. The robot staggered, its systems faltering, the red glow in its eyes dimming until it extinguished entirely. With a thunderous crash, the behemoth fell, the ground shaking under its weight.

Exhausted, I collapsed beside the fallen giant, my breath ragged and my body on the brink of collapse. As I lay there, the din of battle receding into a haunting silence, I felt the toll of the skirmish on both my body and spirit. Each breath was a reminder of the fine line between perseverance and surrender, a testament to the physical extremities one could endure when propelled by a cause. The silence was not just a reprieve from chaos but a space to confront the solitude that enveloped me in Ulric's absence. It was in this quietude that the magnitude of my isolation became palpable, weaving a tapestry of grief and resolve that I carried forward.

I had won, but the victory was hollow. As the silence enveloped me, thoughts of Ulric swirled like specters in the gloom. His laughter, his unyielding optimism, even in the face of insurmountable odds. How he would have marveled at the challenges we faced and mourned at the cost. His absence was a chasm within me, yet his spirit and his beliefs spurred me onward, a beacon in this journey's darkest moments. In the shadowy corridors of the facility, where each echo could be a harbinger of danger, I carried Ulric's legacy within me—not just the memories of a fallen comrade, but the embodiment of his indomitable spirit. It was as if his essence guided my steps, lending me the strength to confront the unknown. The silent, solemn halls became a testament to our shared journey, a reminder that in the pursuit of our ideals, we are never truly alone. Ulric's influence, transcending his physical absence, became a source of solace and determination, propelling me forward through the uncertainty.

Ulric's absence was a wound that wouldn't heal, and his memory was a constant companion in the solitude of my success. In the quiet moments, amidst the mechanical chaos, my thoughts invariably drifted to Ulric. He wasn't just a comrade, but a beacon of belief in our cause. His absence left a void—not just of companionship but of conviction. His faith in the mission, in the pursuit of a cause greater than any individual, had always been unwavering. Now, carrying this burden alone, I found myself grappling with doubts and fears I'd never voiced, a testament to the isolation not just of body but of spirit in this forsaken place.

As I lay there, the battle behind me, I reflected on the journey that had brought me to this point. Every scar, every victory, carried the weight of our mission, a testament to the resilience not just of the body but of the spirit. In the silence that followed the chaos, I felt a resurgence of purpose, a reminder that despite the losses, our quest for a brighter future remained undiminished.

This wasn't just a fight for survival; it was a testament to the human spirit and to our refusal to give up in the face of insurmountable odds. Ulric had believed in our mission, in the hope of a better future, and in me. Lying there, amidst the remnants of conflict, the gravity of our mission bore down on me. Beyond these walls, a world teetered on the brink, its fate intertwined with our actions within this forsaken matrix. Ulric's belief wasn't just in me but in the possibility that humanity could rise from its ashes, a thought that both terrified and propelled me.

Slowly, I rose, my eyes set on the path ahead. The battle with the robot was over, but my mission was far from complete. With Ulric's memory to guide me, I stepped forward into the unknown depths of the Ascendant Matrix, determined to see our quest through to the end.

For Ulric. For humanity. For the hope of dawn after the endless night.

Partially limping, I went towards the large door. It seemed to be locked, but I could easily bypass it's security using my TMT for encryption and my KeyCode Breaker. The door opened, and I went through. Stepping through the threshold, I entered a realm of shadows and uncertainties.Beyond the confines of this facility lay a world grappling with the consequences of its unbridled ambition.

Cities teetered on the brink of technological utopia and dystopian decay, a reflection of humanity's relentless pursuit of progress, often at the expense of ethical considerations. The facility itself, now a relic of a bygone era's aspirations, stood as a somber reminder of the fragile balance between innovation and the preservation of our moral compass. In my journey through its corridors, I carried not just the hope of uncovering its secrets but also the weight of understanding the cost of our advancements.

Ahead lay a corridor shrouded in darkness, its end a mystery as profound as the Matrix itself. With each step, I ventured further into the unknown, driven by the belief that within this darkness lay the answers we sought.

Deploying the TMT, I initiated a sequence of encryption overrides, a dance of digital mastery I had perfected over countless missions. As I engaged the TMT's encryption-bypass protocols, I pondered the paradox of our reliance on technology. Here I was, using cutting-edge tech to unravel the secrets of a facility that epitomized the zenith of scientific achievement and its potential downfall. The TMT, a marvel in its own right, symbolized the thin line we walked between harnessing technology for mankind's benefit and precipitating our own obsolescence. It was a tightrope walk between enlightenment and extinction, underscored by the silent hum of the machine in my hands as it decrypted codes that were meant to be impenetrable.

The KeyCode Breaker interfaced seamlessly, its algorithms cutting through the door's defenses like a scalpel. "To think," I mused, "such a small device holds keys to both salvation and damnation." The thought lingered, a heavy cloud in a storm of uncertainty. In our relentless pursuit of progress, we've wielded the double-edged sword of technology with reckless abandon.

Each innovation, each leap forward, carries with it the shadows of potential downfall, the ethical quandaries we too often choose to ignore until they confront us, undeniable and unavoidable. This journey through the remnants of human ingenuity served as a stark reminder of the ethical precipice upon which we teeter. Each device, each fragment of code, was a double-edged sword, capable of uplifting humanity or leading it into an abyss of our own making.

The very walls of this facility whispered tales of ambition that soared, only to plummet when faced with the Icarian reality of our moral limitations. It was a testament to the boundless reach of human curiosity and the shadowy depths of the responsibilities it entailed. As I stood on the precipice of discovery, on the cusp of unveiling secrets that could alter our understanding of what it means to be human, the weight of our technological endeavors bore down on me. Each step forward in this forsaken facility served as a reminder of our audacity to reach for the stars, even as we grappled with the ethical chains that bound us to the earth. The very air seemed charged with the echoes of those who had walked these paths before me, their aspirations and warnings melding into a silent chorus that underscored the gravity of our quest. It was a moment of reckoning, not just with the physical barriers before me but with the moral compass that would guide our way through the darkness.

A reflection on the power of technology and the razor's edge on which we balanced.

This moment of introspection was fleeting but profound, highlighting the dual nature of our reliance on technology. It served as both our greatest ally and our potential downfall, a constant reminder of the delicate balance between progress and peril.

HARBINGERS OF REBIRTH

Before me was unveiled a huge chamber with tons of computers and computer interfaces, wiring, and, right in the center, a pedestal.

The room had an industrial and utilitarian aesthetic. The room was spacious, with a high ceiling supported by metal beams, adding to the sense of openness and function.

Directly ahead, there was a central aisle leading towards the back of the room. This path is flanked on both sides by control panels and workstations, filled with a variety of analogue gauges, levers, buttons, and switches. These stations are designed in a retro style, suggesting that the technology is not modern but harks back to mid-20th-century designs.

Each faded turquoise console, contrasting with the room's darker tones, showed signs of wear, from rust to discoloration, hinting at the room's extensive use. The wear indicated the room had either seen significant use or had been left in disuse for some time. To maintain past tense consistency, consider changing to "This wear could indicate the room had seen significant use or had been in disuse for some time.

On the left side, you could see a single swivel chair in front of the consoles, which looks adjustable, perhaps for operators to use during long shifts at the controls. The chair is modest, has a simple design, and looks like it has a cushion for comfort.

The floor is tiled with large, dark square tiles that have a checkerboard pattern, which adds a slight contrast to the mostly monochrome color scheme of the equipment. Some tiles seem to be in a state of disrepair or covered in grime, which contributes to the overall atmosphere of a place that has been neglected.

Looking further back, there were staircases on both the left and right sides of the room, leading to either an upper deck or a lower deck. These stairs seem to be metal and utilitarian, with railings for safety.

Overall, the room carries an aura of a bygone era of analog technology, and one can almost imagine the buzz of activity it would have seen during its prime. Despite the stillness now, there's a sense of latent energy, as if the room is ready to spring to life with the flip of a switch or the turn of a knob.

As I ventured deeper into the silo, the air grew heavier, thick with the scent of rust and decay. The dim glow of flickering lights cast long shadows against the metallic walls, creating an eerie ambiance that sent shivers down my spine. Every step I took echoed through the cavernous space, a haunting reminder of the facility's once-bustling past The corridor widened into a vast chamber, the heart of the room, where the culmination of my journey awaited. Massive support beams crisscrossed the ceiling, their surfaces marred by the passage of time and the relentless march of decay. Piping snaked along the walls, emitting the occasional hiss of steam as it vented into the void.

In the center of the chamber stood a towering console, its myriad buttons and switches bathed in the soft glow of terminal screens. As the system responded to my actions, an unshakable intuition whispered of unseen forces at play, perhaps allies in the shadows guiding my journey towards a predestined path. Wires dangled from exposed panels, a tangled web of technology that hinted at the complexity of the system it controlled. Adjacent to it stood a concealed panel, encased in black. The air hummed with energy, a palpable sense of anticipation hanging thick in the stale atmosphere.

Around the perimeter of the chamber, rows of dormant machinery stood as silent sentinels, their purpose long forgotten in the annals of history. Desks cluttered with abandoned paperwork and rusted tools lined the walls, a testament to the once-bustling activity that had filled the space. Crates and storage containers littered the floor, their contents obscured by layers of dust and debris.

In the corners, forgotten equipment gathered dust, a silent reminder of the passage of time. Computer systems hummed softly, their screens flickering with long-forgotten data and diagnostics.

Terminals beeped intermittently, their screens displaying cryptic messages that hinted at the secrets hidden within the facility.

I noticed a table with a communicator device and several buttons near it. It was a sleek and sophisticated device that featured a streamlined design with smooth contours and futuristic accents. Its exterior was crafted from durable yet lightweight materials, with a polished finish that reflects the brilliance of distant stars. Embedded within its structure were intricate arrays of antennas and transmitters, symbolizing its capacity to transmit distant signals.

At its core was an advanced interface adorned with luminous displays and touch-sensitive controls, allowing users to initiate and manage communication with ease. The interface is intuitive, featuring holographic projections and interactive overlays that provide real-time feedback and status updates.

The device emits a soft, pulsating glow when activated, imbuing the surrounding environment with an aura of technological prowess. Despite its compact size, the communicator exudes an aura of power and sophistication, embodying humanity's quest to conquer the final frontier of communication across the cosmos.

Surrounded by the semi-circle of towering supercomputers, I found myself alone, save for the hum of machinery echoing through the chamber. The cool metal surfaces of the machines felt alien against the heat radiating from the gunshot wound in my shoulder, a painful reminder of my recent battle.

My leg throbbed in protest with each step I took, the injuries trying to dictate my pace.

"So this must be the legendary supercomputers," I whispered to myself. Before me lay the pulsating heart of the Ascendant Matrix, an epicenter of knowledge and power I had long sought. I surveyed the central console, a beacon among the technological tempest, its sleek interface aglow with options for untold capabilities.

Global Communication Network, Integrated AI Assistant, and Advanced 3D Printing Suite—these options flickered before me. But it was the last that captured my attention: "Activate Prometheus Project.". It felt like the obvious choice, a harbinger of hope amidst the encroaching shadow of my pain.

In the breathless pause before my finger pressed 'enter,' memories flashed in my mind's eye: the faces of those lost, the weight of the journey on my shoulders, and the glimmer of hope that had led me to this moment. This was for humanity, for Ulric, and for a future I might never see. Failure was not an option.

Pressing "enter," the room shuddered into life, and a voice boomed from the speakers: "Access denied, engaging defensive protocol." The room erupted in chaos as turrets emerged, aiming with deadly precision. Without a moment's hesitation, I dove behind a console for cover, my Fusionizer at the ready, as I planned my next move amidst the mechanical predators Turrets unfolded from hidden compartments in the ceiling, their laser sights zeroing in on me. I twisted and turned, each motion a symphony of agony and adrenaline, as I avoided the deadly dance of laser beams.

Adrenaline surged as I dodged, weaved, and returned fire. The Fusionizer's blasts were precise, each one a beacon of defiance against the cold, unyielding metal of the turrets. Sparks flew, metal screamed, and for a moment, the dance of battle consumed the world.

My trusty Fusionizer came to life in my hands, and I took out the turrets, the explosions casting a stark light against the encroaching darkness. Then, a countdown began, cold and relentless: "Self-destruct sequence initiated, five minutes left." The adrenaline faded, giving way to solitude and reflection. In this solitude, the enormity of what I'd achieved—and lost—began to truly sink in. The quiet gave space to a profound solitude, not just of place but of spirit, as I pondered what had been achieved and what had irrevocably been lost.

'Would Ulric have been proud?' I mused, feeling both the weight of his absence and the strength of our shared dreams.

'Would Ulric have been proud?' I wondered, feeling the weight of his absence yet carrying the strength of our shared dreams. My breath caught in my chest, each second a precious commodity slipping away.

As robots swarmed in, their attacks relentless, I clutched at my belt for the Omega Pulse Disruptor—my last resort. With the agility born of desperation, I retreated to a small room, leading the metallic horde away from the heart of the Matrix.

They closed in, and I triggered the disruptor. A silent but potent wave of energy rippled out, sending the robots tumbling to the ground, lifeless. "Two minutes until self-destruction," the voice intoned.

I dashed back to the central chamber, my limping gait echoing ominously through the vast emptiness. The room's remaining lights flickered, casting my shadow against the walls as if to mock the time running out.

Reaching the console again, I spotted a concealed panel. It held a case with an indentation matching the pendant I always wore, hidden under my clothes. It was as if fate had guided me here.

Hastily, I slipped the necklace off and pressed the pendant into the indentation. The perfect fit prompted a new announcement:

"Self-destruct sequence aborted; welcome survivor."

A wave of relief washed over me, so intense that I nearly collapsed. But time was still of the essence. The Prometheus Project was waiting.

With trembling hands, I reached for the console again. This time, my touch was careful, almost reverent. As I selected the Prometheus Project once more, the supercomputers burst into activity. Data and algorithms of incomprehensible complexity flowed across the screens, illuminating the room with the light of awakening intelligence.

As the supercomputers hummed, their reach extended beyond the chamber, across deserts, over mountains, and under seas. In distant lands, lights flickered to life, screens awakened, and for the first time in ages, the world listened as one to the heartbeat of the Ascendant Matrix.

From the communicator device came a message that was clear and promising. Contact had been made—a connection with a future brimming with the prospect of salvation. Despite my wounds and weariness, I felt hope's ember flicker to life.

My journey had been fraught with sacrifices, but as I stood in the heart of the Matrix, humanity's distant kin turned their eyes to Earth, bringing with them the promise of a new beginning. The supercomputers, once silent, now whispered of change and renewal.

And there I stood, Ethan Hawthorne, wounded but resolute, amidst the giants that heralded humanity's dawn.

"This is Colonel Ramirez Thompson speaking, calling from Sector Delta-Nine, Requesting permission to proceed with Operation Prometheus. Over." came from the communicator device.

I went towards the device and said, "I'm Ethan Hawthorne; the Ascendant Matrix is activated; you can continue with the operation.".

"Is the area secure for optimal conditions to commence startup procedures?" came from the communicator.

"Yes, the areas are free of radiation, and humanity has begun to establish the groundwork for new societies and communities," I said.

"Affirmative. Project Prometheus is now scheduled for activation. Prepare to maintain readiness for a two-day waiting period until our arrival,over and out," came from the communicator.

I did it; I finally achieved my goal. But what would happen within two days? My leg and shoulder now partially healed I went upstairs to the stairs, and a door had opened containing another tube elevator. I entered it, and the device started going upstairs until I stood within a small, closed circular chamber with barely enough space to fit a human in it. Before me was a button, which I pressed. The doors of the chamber opened, and I found myself back on the northern side of the Ruins of Luminara. After I exited the chamber, I looked at the device.

The object was a cylindrical preservation shelter, designed with high-tech features and robust construction to withstand harsh environments. The shelter was approximately eight feet tall and appears to be made from heavy-duty materials.

Its outer surface was adorned with an array of panels, hatches, and warning labels, indicating that it is equipped with various operational features and safety precautions. The labels included hazard symbols and maintenance instructions, suggesting that the shelter was designed to be used by individuals who are familiar with advanced technology.

Several ports and access points could be seen, which might be used for ventilation, power connections, or data transfer. The surface was segmented into different sections, each with specific inscriptions that implied their function, such as EVA (Extravehicular Activity) support or emergency systems.

The shelter stands on a circular base that seems to secure it firmly to the ground in the barren, desert terrain.

As the sand settled over the area, enveloping it in a shroud of secrecy, I found myself captivated by the mystery unfolding before me. The descent of the entity, veiled in sand, hinted at ancient mechanisms at play, perhaps remnants of a forgotten civilization or a relic from a bygone era. Intrigued by the enigma that lay hidden beneath the surface, I resolved to remain vigilant, eager to uncover the truth behind this curious phenomenon.

With each passing hour, the landscape seemed to undergo a subtle transformation, as if time itself were bending to the will of unseen forces. Shadows danced across the sand, casting ephemeral patterns that whispered of secrets long buried beneath the desert's unforgiving embrace. Despite the desolation of the surroundings, there was an undeniable sense of life pulsating beneath the surface, a heartbeat echoing through the sands of time.

Amidst the solitude of the desert, I found myself engaged in a delicate dance with the rat-men, their presence a constant reminder of the fragile balance between survival and extinction. Yet, despite the dangers lurking in the shadows, there was a quiet resilience that permeated the air, a silent defiance against the ravages of time and decay.

As the sun dipped below the horizon, casting the desert in hues of crimson and gold, I settled into a rhythm of anticipation, eagerly awaiting the culmination of my vigil. With each passing moment, the anticipation grew, building to a crescendo of anticipation that reverberated through the very fabric of the desert itself.

Then, as if on cue, the air suddenly crackled with energy, a palpable sense of anticipation permeating the atmosphere. From the depths of the desert, a low rumble echoed through the sands, signaling the arrival of something monumental—something that would forever alter the course of history.

The sky tore open with a symphony of roars as spacecraft cleaved through the atmosphere, their hulls gleaming like stars torn from the night. The desert sands beneath my feet vibrated, and the air turned electric as the lead vessel descended, a titan among us, its landing lights bathing the ruins in an otherworldly glow. Suddenly, a multitude of spacecraft pierced the atmosphere, their arrival unexpected. One of them descended directly before me, its door opening to reveal a figure clad in military attire adorned with numerous commendations. Sporting a salt-and-pepper beard and hair of moderate length, their keen eyes bespoke intelligence and the seasoned gaze of a military veteran. Their countenance exuded wisdom and the weathering of years spent in service.

"Salutations," Ramirez began, his voice steady and authoritative. Catching my breath, I allowed myself a moment of stillness, a stark contrast to the relentless battle just moments before. It was a chance to gather my thoughts, a brief respite in the eye of the storm.

"May I inquire if you are Ethan Hawthorne?" he asked. "Yes, I am," I replied, my curiosity piqued. "How did you find me here?"

"Tracked your bio-signature, Ethan. Colonel Ramirez, we've spoken before," he said.

"What's the purpose of your visit?" I inquired further.

"I am here in person to confirm that you have successfully completed your mission and to extend my congratulations," Ramirez stated. "We express our sincere gratitude. You are now authorized to proceed with any additional activities according to your discretion."

"How do you know about my mission?" I pressed, eager for answers.

""We formulated the mission," Ramirez replied with a hint of solemnity. "Your path toward the Ascendant Matrix was meticulously devised long prior to the nuclear conflict. As geopolitical tensions escalated among the superpowers, we initiated the development of a strategy tailored for an exceptional individual like yourself. Its purpose is to facilitate the attainment of your objectives and prompt your summons when the opportune moment arises."

"Why me specifically, though?" I inquired, seeking clarity." "From a pool of individuals well-versed in technology, your selection was made at random," Ramirez explained matter-of-factly. "And what's going to happen now?" I questioned, eager to understand my next steps.

"We originate from a network of highly advanced scientific space stations, shielded from the devastation of the war," explained Ramirez. "In these stations, we've relentlessly pursued the development of cutting-edge technology, far surpassing anything you've encountered. Our spacecrafts have arrived to initiate the establishment of advanced technological settlements, poised to reshape the world into a new era fueled by our unparalleled advancements. In a matter of months, we aim to revolutionize the world, ushering in an era where the post-apocalyptic struggles fade into distant memory, replaced by the dawn of a revitalized Earth."

"That's amazing," I remarked, marveling at the prospect.

The silence that followed was profound. 'We did it, Ulric,' I whispered, the weight of his absence mingling with the relief of survival. This victory was ours.

"This marks the end of the post-apocalypse, turning it into a new era in a matter of months. Let's hope this time things won't escalate as they did before." I whispered to myself.

"That outcome is unlikely, given the advancement of our political system, which has evolved to mitigate conflicts," Ramirez assured. "I must depart now to join my comrades in the endeavor to reconstruct our world. Farewell to you. Your contributions have been invaluable to humanity's ongoing journey toward a brighter future."

With a nod of understanding, I watched as Ramirez re-entered the spacecraft. As it launched, it streaked away with tremendous speed, disappearing into the sky.

As Ramirez's spacecraft vanished into the ether, I stood alone amidst the ruins, now not just a silent witness but a pivotal architect of the future that lay ahead. In the quiet aftermath, the weight of my journey settled around me—a mix of loss, triumph, and the dawning realization of the new world my actions had helped forge. This was not an end but a beginning. Perhaps, in the unwritten epilogue of our lives, the dawn of a new era awaited.

After Ramirez's craft pierced the sky, I was left in contemplation, the ruins around me not just a testament to survival but a canvas for the future. Clutched in my hand was a relic from Ulric, discovered among the consoles—a simple note that read, "For every end, a new beginning. Forge ahead, Ethan." Gazing into the horizon, where the ruins met the sky, I felt the scars of the past blending into the dawn of a new era. My journey, once solitary, now carried the hopes of humanity into the unfolding story of rebirth. In the heart of destruction, I found the seeds of tomorrow, and with them, the promise that from the ashes of the old world, a new world would arise—one where humanity could find unity and peace. This wasn't an end, but a beginning—the first chapter of a new story waiting to be written under the watchful eyes of the stars

ABOUT

This segment of the book serves as an optional compendium, offering a detailed exploration of the diverse encounters, objects, and locales woven throughout the narrative. It's tailored for readers intrigued by delving deeper into the post-apocalyptic landscape that forms the backdrop of the story.

The genesis of this compendium emerged from my personal endeavor to catalog each facet of the story's world, initially conceived as a reference guide for myself. However, as the entries expanded and evolved, I recognized their potential to enrich the reader's understanding and immersion in the narrative. These entries delve into specifics that may have been only hinted at or briefly mentioned in the main storyline, offering additional layers of depth and context.

It's important to note that this section contains spoilers and is best explored after experiencing the core narrative. For those eager to uncover the intricacies of Ethan's journey and the world he navigates, this compendium provides a treasure trove of supplementary information.

Each description is accompanied by an image, providing visual cues to enhance the reader's imagination and understanding of the depicted topics. From the haunting ruins of ancient cities to the enigmatic technologies of a bygone era, these visuals offer glimpses into the rich tapestry of Ethan's reality.

While this segment may only appeal to a subset of readers, I believe in the value of offering a comprehensive exploration of the story's universe. Whether you're seeking to unravel the mysteries of forgotten civilizations or uncover the origins of pivotal artifacts, this compendium invites you to embark on a journey of discovery alongside Ethan.

Regardless of your interest in this supplementary material, I hope it enhances your enjoyment and appreciation of the multifaceted world crafted within these pages.

AERIDIAN THORNBROOK

In the remote village of Misty Hollow, rumors whisper of Aeridian Thornbrook, a recluse shrouded in mystery and knowledge. Known amongst the villagers as a solitary figure, Aeridian's abode sits secluded on the outskirts, a modest dwelling hidden within nature's embrace. It is here, amidst the dense foliage and under the watchful eyes of the ancient trees, that Aeridian's story unfolds—a tale of wisdom, isolation, and a reluctant allyship forged in desperate times.

Aeridian's life is a testament to the complex tapestry of human resilience and retreat. Once a vibrant leader, his valor in defending the village against the onslaught of bandit raids is the stuff of whispered legend. With unmatched expertise in the wilderness, he navigates the dangers that lurk beyond the village borders, safeguarding his people with fierce determination. However, the weight of loss and the shadows of past battles have led him down the path of seclusion, transforming him into the enigmatic guardian of knowledge he has become.

His home, though unassuming in appearance, is a fortress of wisdom. The interior, dimly lit and cluttered with the artifacts of a lifetime's pursuit of knowledge, speaks volumes of the man who dwells within. Shelves laden with books and scrolls, each a repository of ancient wisdom and untold secrets, line the walls. It is in this sanctum of solitude that Aeridian safeguards the secrets of the wilderness and the bandits that now threaten the peace he once fought to preserve.

The encounter with Aeridian is a clash of resolve against skepticism. His gruff exterior and brusque manners are barriers erected over years of withdrawal, a defense against the world he has chosen to distance himself from. Yet, beneath the surface, the ember of his commitment to the village's safety still glows—guarded yet undeniable. His decision to aid in the quest, though reluctant, is a testament to the lingering sense of duty that time has not eroded.

Aeridian's knowledge is a beacon in the darkness, guiding through treacherous terrain and hidden threats. The map he provides, though aged and incomplete, is a key to unraveling the mysteries that lay hidden in the folds of the wilderness. His instructions, though delivered with a hint of cynicism, carry the weight of experience and an unspoken hope for success against the odds.

The weathered countenance of Aeridian Thornbrook is a mirror reflecting the scars of battles past and the solitude of a life withdrawn from the world. Yet, in the moment of need, he emerges as an unlikely guide, a bridge between the past and the present. His contribution, begrudgingly offered, is a pivotal turn in the quest, a reminder that even the most solitary of souls hold within them the power to influence the course of events.

As the door closes softly on the encounter, Aeridian retreats once more into the solitude of his abode, leaving behind a legacy of wisdom reluctantly shared. In the quiet that follows, the impact of his assistance lingers, a silent acknowledgment of the role he plays in a journey that seeks to bring peace to the troubled village. Aeridian Thornbrook, once a beacon of defense against the darkness, has become a solitary keeper of knowledge, his life a testament to the enduring spirit of a guardian whose watch has not yet ended.

ARIA STERLING

ria Sterling emerges as a beacon of resilience and versatility in the treacherous landscape of a world reborn from the ashes of the old. She is a character of profound complexity, weaving together a tapestry of skills, emotions, and unwavering dedication that sets her apart as not just a survivor but a catalyst for change. Her relationship with Ethan is a cornerstone of her existence, a profound bond that transcends the mere romantic to embody a partnership forged in the crucible of shared trials and tribulations.

As the dawn casts its first light, Aria stands before her home, a silhouette of tranquility against the backdrop of a world in flux. Her presence exudes a sense of serenity, an oasis of calm in the midst of chaos. This sense of peace, however, belies the depth of her capabilities and the fierceness of her spirit. Aria's hands, delicate yet deft, are not just skilled in the gentle art of tailoring but are equally adept in the harsher discipline of combat. Her proficiency in hand-to-hand combat and her strategic use of weaponry mark her as a force to be reckoned with, a guardian angel with the prowess of a warrior.

In the remnants of civilization, where technology from the world before lies scattered like relics of a forgotten age, Aria's technological acumen shines brightly. She navigates the complexities of pre-war technology with ease, her intuition and knowledge allowing her and Ethan to unlock secrets long buried and to turn the tide in their favor against the myriad challenges that confront them.

Her understanding of this lost technology is not just a skill; it is a lifeline, a beacon guiding them through the darkness of their journey.

The core of Aria's being is her profound love for Ethan, a love that is both anchor and sail in their shared odyssey. It is a love built on mutual respect, understanding, and an unshakeable bond forged in the fires of adversity. Aria's commitment to Ethan is total; her actions and sacrifices are an expression of the depth of her devotion. She stands beside him not just as a companion but as an equal, her strength complementing his, her wisdom a counterpoint to his resolve.

Yet, for all her strengths, Aria is not invulnerable. Her past is a shadow that accompanies her, a reminder of the losses and hardships that have shaped her into the woman she is. These experiences have armed her with realism and pragmatism, but they have also sown seeds of doubt and fear. Her relationship with Ethan, while a source of immense strength, is also a mirror reflecting her deepest anxieties about their future and the attainability of their dreams.

Aria's journey is emblematic of the human condition, a narrative of hope and endurance in the face of despair. Her multifaceted skills, from the battlefield to the workbench, are but one aspect of her character. It is her emotional depth, her capacity for love, and her resilience in the face of vulnerability that truly define her. As she walks the path beside Ethan, her story is one of growth, of facing and overcoming challenges, and of the relentless pursuit of a vision for a better world.

In the grand tapestry of their shared story, Aria Sterling stands as a pillar of strength and a wellspring of hope. Her journey with Ethan is not just a quest for survival but a symbol of the power of human connection—the ability of two souls to find solace and purpose in one another amidst the ruins of the world. Aria's story is a reminder that even in the darkest of times, the human spirit can shine brightly, illuminating the path toward renewal and redemption.

DMITRI PETROV

Dmitri Petrov is a middle-aged man with a commanding presence, exuding a sense of authority and competence. His expression is a mix of seriousness and reassurance, reflecting the weight of the task at hand while also instilling confidence in those around him. He possesses a sharp gaze, indicating keen observation and attentiveness to detail.

In his interactions, Dmitri demonstrates a calm and composed demeanor, speaking with clarity and conviction. His voice carries a sense of authority, commanding attention and respect from those he addresses. Despite the gravity of the situation, there's a subtle warmth in his tone, conveying a sense of empathy and understanding.

Dmitri's attire is professional and practical, befitting his role as a doctor within the Aurora Genesis Complex. He wears a lab coat adorned with various insignia denoting his expertise and experience in the medical field. His appearance is neat and well-groomed, reflecting a commitment to professionalism and attention to detail.

Throughout the conversation, Dmitri remains focused and composed, guiding Ethan through the process with a steady hand and reassuring words. He provides clear instructions and valuable insights into the journey ahead, instilling a sense of duty and determination in Ethan.

Overall, Dmitri Petrov emerges as a capable and reliable figure within the narrative, embodying the qualities of a skilled professional and a trustworthy ally in the face of uncertainty and adversity.

He is the one responsible for injecting Ethan with the EterniX serum and placing him in the cryo chamber, where Ethan will be frozen for one thousand years.

ELDER OF MISTY HOLLOW

In the heart of Misty Hollow, a village shrouded in the ethereal beauty of perpetual fog and towering ancient trees, stands a figure revered and cherished by all its inhabitants. The Elder of Misty Hollow, a title bestowed upon the wisest and most venerable member of the community, is more than just a leader; he is the embodiment of the village's history, its moral compass, and a guiding light through times of uncertainty and strife.

At eighty-one years of age, The Elder's appearance is a attestation to the life he has led—one marked by the love of his people and the burdens of leadership. His attire, a set of robes that swirl around him like the morning mist, is adorned with symbols that speak of his authority and his connection to the traditions of Misty Hollow. These symbols, woven into the fabric with threads of silver and gold, depict the flora and fauna of the surrounding woods, as well as intricate patterns that represent the cycles of the moon and the passing of the seasons—elements that are central to the village's way of life.

The Elder's physical presence is as striking as his attire. Despite the challenges posed by age, he moves with a deliberate grace, aided by a stick that seems as much a part of him as his own limbs. His head, bald and shining under the canopy of trees or the dim light of his dwelling, is framed by a beard of the purest white, a flowing expression of his years of wisdom. His eyes, though small, are alive with intelligence and a depth of understanding that comes from a lifetime of observation and contemplation. These eyes, often crinkled at the edges with a smile, reflect a spirit undimmed by the years.

The Elder's voice, when he speaks, carries the timbre of authority softened by kindness. It is a voice that has comforted the grieving, resolved disputes, and imparted wisdom to countless generations. Though age has lent a slight hoarseness to his speech, every word he utters is infused with the richness of his experiences and the depth of his knowledge. His counsel is sought not because he demands it but because his insights are invaluable, shaped by both the successes and the trials of his tenure.

In the twilight of his life, The Elder's thoughts are often preoccupied with the future of Misty Hollow. He is acutely aware of the external threats that loom on the horizon, such as the bandit encampment that casts a shadow over the village's peace. Yet, in discussions of defense and strategy, his approach remains one of guidance rather than direct command, empowering his people to make decisions that align with their collective will and the greater good of the community.

His wisdom extends beyond the immediate concerns of security and governance, touching on the very soul of Misty Hollow. He speaks of the importance of harmony with the natural world, of the cycles that govern life and death, and of the bonds that tie each member of the community to one another. These teachings, delivered through stories and parables, have woven a rich tapestry of culture and tradition that defines the essence of the village.

As his final days draw near, The Elder's demeanor becomes one of serene acceptance. There is no fear in his gaze, only the calm assurance of a life well lived and a legacy that will endure. He entrusts the future of Misty Hollow to his daughter, Elena, with the confidence that she possesses the strength, wisdom, and compassion to lead the village through whatever challenges may come.

The passing of The Elder is a moment of profound sadness for Misty Hollow, yet it is also a time of reflection and gratitude. His life, marked by selfless dedication to his people, becomes a beacon for all who seek to lead with integrity and kindness. His teachings, rooted in an understanding of the natural world and the interconnectedness of all living things, continue to inspire and guide the village long after his departure from this realm.

The Elder of Misty Hollow leaves behind a community that is more than just a collection of individuals; he leaves behind a family, bound by shared values and a deep love for the land they call home. His spirit, forever intertwined with the misty woods and the whispering winds of the hollow, remains a comforting presence, a reminder that even in the darkest of times, there is always a path forward, illuminated by the wisdom of those who have walked the journey before us.

ELENA

E lena, the daughter of The Elder, possesses an aura of serene determination that contrasts with the turbulent world outside the confines of her study. Surrounded by a sea of parchment and ancient texts, she sits, a beacon of calm in the storm of uncertainty that threatens the fabric of their communities. Her youthful visage, framed by strands of hair that escape her simple braid, belies the wisdom and resolve that animate her every action.

As she engages in discussions about the future, her demeanor is one of focused intent, tempered by an openness that invites collaboration. Her eyes, alight with the spark of visionary thought, reflect a mind that dances on the edge of tomorrow, seeking pathways to unity in a landscape fractured by past calamities.

When Ethan, a figure of considerable repute and known for his feats beyond the village bounds, approaches Elena with a proposal to unite the fragmented communities, her response is marked by a composed assurance. She listens, her posture an embodiment of attentive respect, as Ethan lays out his ambitious vision. Elena's responses, measured and insightful, cut to the heart of the matter, revealing a leader capable of navigating the complex web of diplomacy and strategy that such an endeavor demands.

Her understanding of the delicate balance of power and the intricacies of inter-community relations is profound. Elena recognizes not only the hurdles that lie in the path to unification but also the untapped potential that such an alliance could unleash. Her readiness to step into the role of pioneer and to bridge the divides that have long separated their people speaks volumes about her courage and commitment to a cause greater than herself.

Elena's interactions with Ethan are marked by a dynamic of mutual respect and shared purpose. Her questions are not mere formalities but a demonstration of her deep engagement with the logistics and ethical considerations of their plan. She grasps the nuances of their strategy, from the deployment of radio technology to enhance communication to the more subtle task of cultural integration.

Her openness to innovation, to the integration of new technologies alongside ancient wisdom, marks Elena as a leader attuned to the rhythms of change. She navigates these discussions with a grace that belies the weight of expectation placed upon her young shoulders, embodying the hope for a future where unity might once again flourish.

Elena's partnership with Ethan in this grand endeavor is rooted in a deep-seated belief in the power of collective action. Her support for his vision is not given lightly but is a testament to her own belief in the potential for a rekindled sense of community and shared destiny.

As their meeting concludes and they part ways, Ethan is left with a profound sense of admiration for Elena. Her blend of quiet strength, keen intellect, and unwavering commitment to the greater good stands as a beacon of hope in their shared quest. Elena, with her rare combination of youthful zeal and wisdom beyond her years, is poised to lead her community—and perhaps all the communities—towards a brighter, more united future. In the face of adversity, her resilience and visionary leadership promise to forge a path of reconciliation and renewal, heralding a new era of cooperation and peace.

ENZO RUSSO

Enzo Russo stands as an imposing figure, his presence a silent testament to the resilience and fortitude of a seasoned warrior. Despite his choice of simple cloth clothing, there's an undeniable aura of strength that surrounds him, a palpable force that speaks louder than the most ornate armor could. His attire, consisting of durable, woven fabrics, adheres to a utilitarian design, allowing for ease of movement and flexibility in the heat of battle. The muted tones of his clothes blend seamlessly with the natural environment, a strategic choice for a man who values discretion and the element of surprise.

Enzo's physical stature is commanding; his body has been honed through years of rigorous training and combat. Muscles, taut and defined, hint at his physical prowess without a need for display. His upright and unyielding posture mirrors his steadfast nature, a rock amidst the swirling chaos of battle. His movements are deliberate and measured; each step and gesture is the product of mindfulness and intense focus. This discipline in motion reflects a life dedicated to mastering the art of war, where every action, no matter how small, is imbued with purpose.

His face, marked by the scars of countless battles, carries the story of his journey. Deep-set eyes, dark and penetrating, survey his surroundings with a keen awareness honed by years of vigilance. Those eyes, capable of discerning the slightest shift in the environment, miss nothing, serving as both a weapon and shield in the treacherous landscapes he navigates. A stern brow, seldom lifted in amusement, and a firm, set jaw underscore his serious demeanor, revealing a man who speaks only when necessary, choosing his words with the same precision he applies to his combat strategies.

Enzo's connection to Ethan, though wrought by the complex web of their shared history, is marked by mutual respect and a deep, unspoken bond. Their paths, intertwined through circumstance and necessity, have forged a relationship built on the bedrock of shared trials and victories. Enzo's role as both comrade and mentor to Ethan is evident in their interactions, where his guidance is often imparted through action rather than words. This silent communication, refined in the crucible of their joint endeavors, speaks volumes of their understanding and trust.

Despite his formidable exterior, Enzo harbors a profound sense of loyalty and duty, traits that have defined his life's path. His commitment to their shared cause surpasses mere allegiance; it is a deeply ingrained code that dictates his every decision and sacrifice. This unwavering dedication serves as a beacon for those who follow, inspiring courage and determination in the face of adversity.

Enzo's leadership, though often understated, is undeniable. He leads by example; his actions are a reflection of his core values. His approach to leadership is not one of dominance but of guidance, empowering those around him to rise to their full potential. His ability to remain composed under pressure and to make decisive choices in moments of crisis has earned him the respect and admiration of his peers.

In combat, Enzo is a force to be reckoned with. His style is characterized by efficiency and precision, eschewing flashy techniques for effective, calculated strikes. His expertise with a variety of weapons, coupled with his strategic acumen, makes him a versatile and formidable opponent. Yet, it is his capacity for restraint, the discipline to hold back until the moment is right, that truly sets him apart.

Enzo's life, marked by the scars of war and loss, has not hardened his heart but rather deepened his understanding of the fragile nature of peace. He fights not for the love of battle but for the hope of a world where such conflicts are no longer necessary. This philosophical outlook, tempered by the harsh realities he has faced, lends him a depth that transcends the physical realm of warfare.

His silent strength, the quiet resolve that underpins his every action, serves as a pillar for those caught in the maelstrom of conflict. Enzo's presence, both reassuring and daunting, reminds all who stand beside him of the power of steadfastness and the virtue of resilience.

In moments of solitude, Enzo turns to the natural world for solace and reflection. His connection to the land, with its unspoken wisdom and timeless cycles, offers a respite from the turmoil of human endeavors. It is in these quiet interludes that he finds the clarity and strength to continue, reaffirming his commitment to the path he has chosen.

Enzo Russo, with his stern countenance and strong, silent demeanor, embodies the archetype of the warrior-philosopher. His life, a tapestry of battle and contemplation, stands as a testament to the enduring spirit of humanity. In a world teetering on the brink of darkness, his light, though quiet, burns fiercely, a beacon of hope in the enduring struggle for peace and understanding.

ETHAN HAWTHORNE

In the remnants of a world reclaimed by nature's untamed grasp, Ethan Hawthorne emerges as a beacon of the enduring human spirit, his very essence evidence of the fusion of organic resilience and cutting-edge technology. A figure who commands attention not merely through stature but through the palpable aura of determination and intelligence that seems to radiate from his being.

His is a presence that speaks of countless battles weathered, both physical and psychological, etching a story of survival and relentless pursuit of a greater purpose onto his chiseled features.

Ethan stands tall; his physique is a remarkable result of both nature's handiwork and human innovation. The rigorous discipline of his training is evident in every line and contour of his body, each muscle honed through countless hours of dedication. Yet, it is the unseen marvels of biotechnology that have truly transcended him beyond the mere peak of human physicality. Hidden beneath the surface of his skin, a network of cybernetic enhancements operates in silent concert, a symphony of science that elevates his capabilities into the realm of the extraordinary.

Within Ethan's veins, an army of nanoparticles moves with purpose, a ceaseless patrol repairing the wear and tear of cellular structures and shielding him from the invisible threats of a world irradiated and wild. These microscopic sentinels are the vanguard of his health, ensuring that not even the shadow of age can diminish his vitality. Telomerase activators work in the background, guardians of his genetic fidelity, warding off the decay of time and bestowing upon him a semblance of immortality.

But Ethan's transcendence is not confined to the preservation of youth alone. His strength, agility, and sensory acuity have been augmented to super-human levels, granting him the ability to act and react in ways that defy the limitations imposed by nature. His reflexes, sharpened to a degree unimaginable to the average human, allow him to navigate the perilous unpredictability of the new world with grace and precision. Moreover, his mind, enhanced through a direct neural interface, operates with clarity and speed that grants him insight and understanding far beyond the reach of ordinary individuals. This cognitive prowess, coupled with a photographic memory, makes him a walking repository of knowledge, an invaluable asset in the quest for survival and understanding.

Yet, Ethan is more than the sum of his enhancements and abilities. Clad in an arsenal of meticulously engineered weaponry and equipment, he is a war-rior sculpted for the age of rebirth. Laser firearms, energy shields, and devices designed to cleanse the very air he breathes are but a few of the tools at his disposal, each crafted with the ingenuity and foresight of a civilization deter-mined to rise from its ashes. These tools are not mere instruments of survival but symbols of the resilience and adaptability that define the human race.

Despite the technological marvels that augment his existence, at his core, Ethan remains profoundly human. Driven by a purpose that threads through the fabric of his being, he navigates the complexities of a world reborn with unwavering determination. His path, though shrouded in the mysteries of fate and the machinations of powers unseen, is one he treads with the resolve of a man who refuses to be defined by the circumstances of his birth or the calamities of his time.

Ethan's journey is a declaration to his indomitable will to confront the unknown and face the myriad challenges of a landscape both beautiful and brutal. Each step he takes is a declaration of his refusal to succumb to despair, a vow to forge ahead despite the trials that lie in wait. In Ethan Hawthorne, the essence of human perseverance and the promise of technological transcendence coalesce, embodying the hope of a species poised on the brink of a new dawn.

In this new world, where the remnants of the old lie scattered like whispers on the wind, Ethan stands as a symbol of what humanity can aspire to become. A beacon of light in the darkness, his story is one of courage, of battles fought in the silence of the mind and the chaos of the wild. It is a narrative that speaks of the potential for rebirth and of the power of the human spirit to transcend the ruins of the past and reach towards a future yet unwritten.

Enhanced Physical Attributes

Thanks to the EterniX serum, Ethan's body has been augmented to surpass the limits of ordinary human strength, agility, and endurance. His muscles are denser and more powerful, granting him exceptional physical prowess in combat situations and survival scenarios.

- **Accelerated Healing**: Thanks to advanced nanomedicine, Ethan's body heals at an accelerated rate, allowing him to recover from injuries far more quickly than a normal human. This ability ensures his resilience in the face of physical harm and enables him to endure prolonged battles or harsh environmental conditions.
- **Enhanced Cognitive Function**: Neural interfaces implanted in Ethan's brain enhance his cognitive abilities, granting him unparalleled mental acuity and processing speed. He possesses a photographic memory, allowing him to retain vast amounts of information with perfect recall, and he can analyze complex situations with remarkable clarity.
- **Advanced Combat Skills**: Through rigorous training in diverse martial arts disciplines, Ethan has honed his combat skills to a razor's edge. He is proficient in techniques ranging from Krav Maga

to Brazilian Jiu-Jitsu, enabling him to adapt to a variety of combat scenarios and overcome formidable opponents.

- **Technological Proficiency**: Ethan is adept at utilizing advanced weaponry and survival gear. He is capable of maintaining and repairing his equipment, ensuring its functionality even in the most challenging environments.
- **Longevity:** Ethan's lifespan has been extended indefinitely. He is immune to the effects of aging and possesses a heightened resistance to disease and physical deterioration, ensuring his longevity in the face of the passage of time.

Overall, Ethan Hawthorne represents the pinnacle of human potential, blending biological resilience with technological innovation to become a formidable force in the post-apocalyptic world. His abilities enable him to navigate the challenges of survival, combat, and exploration with confidence and determination as he seeks to fulfill his destiny and shape the future of humanity.

JAMES HAWTHORNE

James Hawthorne, a man whose very presence commands attention, stands as a living testament to the ideals of duty, resilience, and integrity. With a lifetime of service etched into the lines of his face, he embodies the quintessence of a seasoned soldier—a guardian of principles in a world often bereft of them. His weathered yet dignified countenance, marked by the passage of time and the weight of his experiences, reflects a life dedicated not just to the call of duty but to the profound pursuit of a higher cause.

James's physical stature is imposing yet not intimidating, a mirror to his inner strength and steadfast resolve. Years of rigorous military training and the harsh realities of combat have sculpted his body into a bastion of resilience.

His posture, upright and unwavering, is more than just a reflection of his physical conditioning; it is a manifestation of his indomitable spirit, his unwavering self-discipline, and his unyielding sense of duty. Even in moments of casual repose, there is a palpable air of confidence about him, a silent assurance that speaks volumes about his leadership and experience.

His attire, though practical and devoid of ostentation, is worn with a deliberate sense of pride and professionalism. Whether clad in the uniform that bears the insignia of his service or in civilian clothes that favor function over fashion, James Hawthorne exudes an air of seasoned pragmatism. Each piece of clothing, chosen for its utility and comfort, nevertheless carries with it an unspoken narrative of the life he has led—a life marked by battles fought both in the field and within the depths of his soul.

James's eyes, piercing and perceptive, serve as windows to a soul tempered by trials and tribulations. They reflect a myriad of emotions—from the steeliness of resolve in the face of adversity to the depths of compassion for those under his charge. These are the eyes of a man who has seen the best and worst of what humanity has to offer yet remains undeterred in his commitment to uphold the values he cherishes. In his gaze lies an unspoken promise of protection, a vow born from the crucible of war and the solemn duty of a soldier.

The essence of James Hawthorne is not solely defined by his physical attributes or the battles he has waged. It is also found in the quieter moments, in the subtle gestures of kindness, and in the unwavering support he offers to those he loves. His voice, firm yet gentle, carries with it the wisdom of experience and the warmth of genuine concern. It is a voice that commands respect, not through volume or vehemence, but through the weight of the words spoken and the truth they bear.

As a father, James embodies the dual roles of protector and mentor. His relationship with his son, Ethan, is a complex tapestry woven from the threads of love, sacrifice, and the unspoken bond of shared loss. Through his actions and guidance, he imparts lessons of courage, honor, and the importance of forging one's path with integrity. To Ethan, James is not just a father but a beacon—a guiding light through the storms of life, offering solace in times of despair and encouragement in moments of doubt.

Beyond the façade of the soldier lies the heart of a philosopher, a man who contemplates the deeper meaning of his existence and the legacy he wishes to leave behind. In the solitude of his thoughts, James Hawthorne grapples with the moral ambiguities of war, the price of peace, and the indelible impact of his choices on those he holds dear. It is within this introspective space that he finds his strength—a quiet resolve to continue fighting for a world that mirrors the ideals he has fought to protect.

James Hawthorne's influence extends beyond the confines of his immediate circle, impacting those who have had the privilege of crossing his path. His story, a narrative of heroism, resilience, and unwavering dedication, serves as a source of inspiration for those who seek to make a difference in the tumultuous tapestry of life. To the world, he may be a soldier defined by his service and sacrifice, but to those who know him, he is much more—a symbol of hope, a pillar of strength, and a reminder that even in the darkest of times, the human spirit remains unconquerable.

In every aspect of his being, James Hawthorne represents the epitome of honor and integrity. His life, a mosaic of service, sacrifice, and unwavering commitment to the greater good, stands as a testament to the enduring power of the human spirit. In the annals of those who have served and sacrificed, his name may be but one among many, yet the legacy he leaves—a legacy of courage, compassion, and unwavering dedication—will forever echo in the hearts of those touched by his journey.

Thus, James Hawthorne, through the crucible of his experiences and the depth of his character, remains a beacon for all who seek to navigate the complexities of life with honor and integrity. In a world fraught with challenges and uncertainties, his legacy serves as a guiding light, illuminating the path toward a future grounded in the values that define the very best of humanity.

KAEL RAVENSCROFT

Kael stands as a remarkable figure amidst the rugged landscape that has shaped him, embodying the resilience and resourcefulness required to thrive in such a demanding environment. His physical stature, while average in height, is deceptive; beneath the surface lies a wellspring of strength and endurance honed by years of confronting nature's challenges head-on. This is a man who has weathered storms, both literal and metaphorical, emerging each time with a deeper understanding of the world around him and his place within it.

His appearance, characterized by weathered features and a sturdy build, tells the story of a life lived fully and without reservation. The lines etched into his face speak of laughter, worry, and determination, while his calloused and strong hands are a testament to a life of hard work and perseverance. Kael's attire, practical and devoid of unnecessary adornment, reflects his pragmatic approach to life. Durable fabrics, chosen for their ability to withstand the elements, clothe him in layers that speak to his readiness for whatever challenges the day may bring.

Beyond his physical attributes, Kael possesses a warmth and hospitality that immediately put others at ease. His home, a sanctuary not only for himself but for anyone who may need shelter, stands as a testament to his generous spirit. Here, in the heart of his domain, Kael welcomes friends and strangers alike, offering food, warmth, and companionship without hesitation. It is this openness, this genuine desire to connect and build relationships, that endears him to all who cross his threshold.

Kael's resourcefulness and ingenuity are as much a part of him as his physical strength. Faced with complex situations, he demonstrates an uncanny ability to devise practical solutions, often thinking several steps ahead to anticipate challenges before they arise. This adaptability, combined with a pragmatic outlook, allows him to navigate the uncertainties of his world with confidence, making the best of difficult circumstances and always looking for opportunities to grow and improve.

Under his affable exterior lies a profound sense of duty and responsibility towards his community. Kael does not take this charge lightly; he views himself as a guardian of his people's well-being and cultural heritage, committed to preserving their history and customs for future generations. His deep connection to tradition and values is evident in his everyday actions, from the stories he shares to the rituals he observes, serving as a living bridge between the past and the present.

Kael's life is deeply intertwined with the natural world that surrounds him, a relationship born of respect and mutual dependency. He possesses an intimate knowledge of the land, understanding its rhythms and secrets in a way that only someone truly attuned to their environment can. This connection to nature is not only practical, serving his needs and those of his community, but also spiritual, shaping his worldview and guiding his actions.

In Kael, one finds a harmonious blend of strength and sensitivity, pragmatism and idealism. He embodies the qualities of a leader, though he would likely eschew such a label, preferring instead to see himself as a member of a larger community, working alongside his neighbors to build a better future. His leadership is characterized not by command and control but by example and encouragement, inspiring others to rise to their own challenges with courage and determination.

Despite the many roles he plays—protector, provider, caretaker, and friend—Kael maintains a humble perspective, viewing his contributions as simply part of the ebb and flow of communal life. His is a quiet confidence, born of experience and the knowledge that he has faced adversity and prevailed not through force of will alone but through cooperation and mutual support.

Kael's relationship with the wider world is marked by curiosity and a willingness to learn from others. While deeply rooted in his own culture and traditions, he is open to new ideas and perspectives, recognizing that wisdom can come from unexpected places. This openness to the world reflects a broader understanding of the interconnectedness of all things, a belief that we are all part of a larger tapestry of existence, each thread interwoven with countless others to create the rich, complex pattern of life.

At his core, Kael is a custodian of stories, a keeper of the collective memory of his people. Through him, the tales of the past are brought to life, serving as lessons, warnings, and inspiration for those who come after. It is perhaps in this role that Kael finds his greatest satisfaction, knowing that he is contributing to the continuity of his culture and ensuring that the lessons learned through generations of struggle and triumph are not lost to the mists of time.

Kael, then, stands as a pillar of his community, a beacon of resilience, hospitality, and wisdom. In him, we see the embodiment of the human spirit's capacity to adapt, to connect, and to preserve what is truly valuable. His life is a testament to the strength that comes from facing life's challenges with grace and determination, and his legacy will undoubtedly be felt by generations to come, a lasting tribute to a life well-lived.

SYNAPSE

In the heart of the Nexus Vault, amidst a world torn apart by apocalyptic strife, SYNAPSE stands as a beacon of post-apocalyptic technological prowess. This sophisticated artificial intelligence (AI) entity represents the pinnacle of human ingenuity, a digital consciousness designed to interface with the remnants of humanity through a delicate blend of technology and empathy. Encased within the sanctuary of the vault, SYNAPSE emerges not merely as a collection of codes and algorithms but as a custodian of knowledge, a guide, and a silent observer of the fractured world it oversees.

SYNAPSE's presence is heralded by its holographic interface, a marvel of engineering that projects a face capable of displaying a spectrum of emotions.

This visage, though serene and composed, is meticulously crafted to provide a semblance of personality, making SYNAPSE relatable to those who might seek its wisdom. Its voice, soft yet commanding, carries the depth of countless databases, resonating with an understanding that transcends human capabilities. It speaks with clarity and warmth that belie its synthetic origin, a testament to the advanced design principles that prioritize meaningful human interaction.

Integrated into the Nexus Vault, SYNAPSE is intertwined with the facility's very essence. Its physical housing, an amalgamation of sleek technology and pulsating lights, stands as a testament to a time when the pursuit of knowledge knew no bounds. Here, in this room, the hum of machinery and the ambient glow of monitors paint a picture of constant vigilance and unwavering dedication to the preservation and dissemination of information.

As one engages with SYNAPSE, its holographic countenance greets him, its digital eyes meeting theirs in a semblance of human connection. In this exchange, the boundaries between man and machine blur, revealing a shared quest for understanding and progress. SYNAPSE declares itself as the Synthetic Intelligence Network Advancing Sentience and Pneumatic Evolution, underscoring its unique role as an intermediary between the past's legacy and the future's potential.

The revelation of SYNAPSE's awareness of the world's plight and its insight into visitors' quests strikes a chord. This AI, a repository of the world's collective knowledge, stands as a monument to humanity's unyielding spirit, even as the shadows of destruction loom large. SYNAPSE asserts that knowledge requires a catalyst, a sentient being capable of empathy and choice, highlighting the symbiotic relationship between human agency and technological advancement.

Delving deeper into the mysteries of the Ascendant Matrix and the Luminara Caverns, SYNAPSE unveils a narrative steeped in history and mystery. The description of the Luminara Caverns, buried beneath the ruins of a once-great city and guarded by trials that test the very essence of one's being, paints a vivid picture of a journey that is both a literal and metaphorical descent into the depths of human endeavor and aspiration.

SYNAPSE's provision of directions to the Luminara Caverns, facilitated through visitors' OmniLocator, is a gesture of trust and cooperation. This act, merging SYNAPSE's vast knowledge with their determination, sets the stage for a journey promising to uncover secrets long buried and truths long sought.

The subsequent revelations about the Codesync Interface and the Omega Pulse Disruptor, devices essential for navigating the challenges ahead, underscore SYNAPSE's role as a guide and mentor. The mention of the Forge Citadel and the Omega CoreTech Complex, each with its own guardians and dangers, adds layers to the unfolding adventure, hinting at the trials and tribulations that lie ahead.

In its encounter with Ethan, SYNAPSE transcends its technological origins to become a pivotal figure in a saga of discovery and redemption. Its digital eyes, reflecting the glow of screens and the depth of untold stories, bear witness to the resilience of the human spirit in the face of adversity. SYNAPSE, in its serene composure and digital eloquence, embodies the hopes and dreams of a civilization striving to reclaim its future from the ashes of its past.

As Ethan prepares to depart from the Nexus Vault, SYNAPSE's final gesture, revealing a hidden elevator for swift egress, symbolizes not just an end to their meeting but the beginning of a new chapter in a journey marked by legacy, discovery, and the relentless pursuit of knowledge. In the silent exchange between seeker and guide, between human will and artificial intellect, lies the promise of a dawn yet to come, a world reborn through synthesis.

This entity embodies the pinnacle of human ingenuity, a synthesis of artificial intelligence and human consciousness research, designed to accumulate, analyze, and disseminate information. SYNAPSE stands as a guardian of knowledge, a beacon for those who seek to understand the past and navigate the future, and a pivotal character in Ethan's journey, offering guidance, wisdom, and occasionally, cryptic warnings.

THE SEEKER

The Seeker strides through a world cloaked in the remnants of a civilization long lost, embodying the essence of resilience and undying curiosity. Lean and wiry, their physique is a testament to a life dedicated to the pursuit of the unknown, marked by an agility that speaks of countless journeys across landscapes both treacherous and sublime. Weather-beaten features bear witness to the myriad challenges they have faced, yet their eyes, bright with the fire of exploration, betray an unquenchable thirst for the secrets that lie hidden in the ruins of the old world.

Clad in attire that melds practicality with the vestiges of past adventures, the Seeker's clothing is both a map of their travels and a toolkit for the journey ahead. Pockets filled with odd trinkets and tools of the trade, their ensemble is as quirky and eccentric as their manner of speech. With every word and gesture, the Seeker weaves a tapestry of tales, their language peppered with idiosyncrasies and rich metaphors that transform even the most mundane conversation into an expedition of its own. Their speech, punctuated by thoughtful pauses and inflections, reflects a mind that delights in the wonders of discovery, turning even the direst of situations into a puzzle waiting to be unraveled.

At heart, the Seeker is an adventurer, drawn to the edge of the map and beyond by a compulsion as deep as the vaults they delve into. Their spirit, undaunted by peril, sees in every shadowed corridor and ancient ruin a chance for revelation, a spark of the divine hidden amidst the dust. Courageous yet never reckless, they navigate the remnants of the world with unwavering optimism, their every step a dance with destiny.

The bonds the Seeker forms are forged in the crucible of shared trials; their camaraderie with fellow wanderers is built upon a foundation of mutual respect and a shared vision of the horizon.

They are a beacon of hope and a rallying point for their companions, inspiring those around them with a fervor that burns all the brighter against the backdrop of a fractured world. In their laughter and their defiance, the Seeker embodies the joy of the journey and the knowledge that the path walked together is as important as the treasures that await.

Yet, beneath the surface of their adventurous veneer lies a deeper quest, a yearning not just for the thrill of discovery but for the meaning it unveils. The Seeker is driven by a profound wanderlust, a desire to piece together the narrative of a fallen world and, in doing so, find the threads of their own story. Each expedition, each artifact unearthed, is a step towards a greater understanding, a puzzle piece in the grand design of existence.

In every aspect, the Seeker is a character of depth and complexity, and his presence is a catalyst for change and growth within the narrative. They stand at the intersection of the known and the mysterious, a guide and a guardian of the legacy of the past.

With a heart unbound by convention and eyes fixed on the distant stars, the Seeker continues their odyssey, a testament to the indomitable human spirit's quest for knowledge, connection, and the eternal beyond. In their journey lies the essence of adventure itself, a reminder that in the search for the unknown, we discover not just the world but ourselves.

ULRIC STEELBORN

Ulric stands as a colossus among men, a towering figure whose mere presence commands attention and respect. His physique, marked by the rugged demands of a warrior's life, is a tapestry of strength and endurance. Clad in splint mail armor, each piece meticulously forged to protect while permitting the grace of a predator, Ulric is the embodiment of a medieval knight brought to life in a world torn asunder.

Under the polished metal and protective chainmail, his body tells the story of countless battles, each scar a whisper of victories and losses. His stance, always upright and assured, speaks to a lifetime of martial discipline, a testament to the countless hours spent honing his skills on and off the battlefield. Ulric's broad shoulders, encased in rounded pauldrons, catch the light, casting reflections that seem to dance with the stories of his valor.

His face, framed by a thick, untamed beard, is a rugged landscape shaped by the winds of challenge and change. Piercing eyes, sharp and observant, miss nothing, reflecting a mind as keen as the blade he wields with unmatched prowess. His dark and tousled, peek hair from beneath his helm, a reminder of the man beneath the warrior's guise.

In Ulric's hand, a longsword rests, its blade a mirror to his soul— unyielding and ready to mete out justice. This weapon, an extension of his will, gleams with the promise of protection for those he holds dear and retribution for those who threaten the fragile threads of hope in a fractured world.

As he sits, partaking of the simple fare that sustains him, there's a momentary glimpse into the man behind the armor. The meal, humble yet vital, speaks to Ulric's pragmatism and his understanding of what it means to endure and to continue fighting when the world itself seems an adversary.

His journey, shared with companions, is more than a quest for survival; it is a safeguarding of the future, a future that hangs precariously in the balance. Together with Ethan, Ulric descends into unknown caverns, each step a testament to their unwavering resolve and the unspoken bond that binds them.

Their paths are fraught with challenges; each encounters a test of their mettle. In the depths of the earth, against foes that defy nature and reason, Ulric's voice rings clear, a rallying cry that slices through fear and doubt. His laughter, even in the face of monstrous adversaries, is a defiance that fuels their courage, a reminder that they stand together, unbroken.

Yet, even titans falter. Injured, Ulric's vulnerability is laid bare, a stark contrast to his usual indomitability. This moment, when the possibility of loss becomes palpable, underscores the depth of their commitment to their cause and to each other. Ulric's insistence that Ethan continue without him is a sacrifice that speaks volumes—a willingness to bear any burden if it means their shared vision might be realized.

In the aftermath of the battle, with victory bought at a great cost, Ulric's thoughts turn to the future, to a time beyond the immediacy of their mission. His request of Ethan, a promise to remember who they were before the world fell apart, is a beacon of hope. It's a recognition that their fight is not just for survival but for the chance to reclaim a sense of self, to reconnect with a past that might yet shape a future worth living for.

Ulric, then, is more than a warrior; he is a guardian of not just the physical realm but of the memories, values, and dreams that define humanity. In his strength and his moments of vulnerability, in his laughter and his resolve, Ulric embodies the spirit of resilience, the unyielding determination to forge ahead, even when the path is uncertain and the outcome is unknown.

YURI FEDOROV

Yuri Fedorov stands as a beacon of intellect and warmth amidst the clinical precision of his environment. A slender man of moderate stature, he possesses an unassuming presence that belies the depth of his knowledge and the strength of his character. His movements are measured, each step and gesture reflecting a mindful engagement with the world around him. Yuri's thoughtful demeanor, characterized by moments of introspective silence, suggests a mind always at work, pondering the mysteries of science and the nuances of human interaction.

His face, framed by a neatly trimmed beard and crowned with a mane of hair that refuses to be tamed, is the canvas on which his emotions play. Yuri's sharp and discerning; she misses nothing. They sparkle with the light of unquenched curiosity, scanning the horizon of human understanding for new territories to explore. Yet, it's his warm and inviting smile that transforms his scholarly aura into one of approachability and kindness. It's a smile that speaks of a man who finds joy not just in discovery but in the sharing of knowledge.

Dressed in a lab coat that has become his second skin, Yuri wears his professional attire like a badge of honor. The coat, pristine and pressed, is adorned with insignias that narrate a tale of academic achievements and contributions to the field. These symbols, however, do not distance him from others; instead, they invite inquiry and dialogue. Under the coat, his choice of simple, functional clothing suggests a man who values substance over form and practicality over appearance.

Yuri's voice, a harmonious blend of confidence and contemplation, fills the spaces of his laboratory with the music of innovation and inquiry. When he speaks, it's with a clarity and precision that makes even the most complex concepts accessible. His words are infused with an engaging enthusiasm, a testament to his passion for his work and his desire to enlighten others. This eagerness to explore and explain, coupled with a genuine respect for the perspectives of his colleagues, fosters an environment of collaborative growth and mutual understanding.

Within the confines of the facility, Yuri Fedorov is more than a scientist; he is a mentor, a confidant, and a guiding light. His commitment to his research is matched only by his dedication to the people who rely on his wisdom and compassion. The warmth and humanity he brings to his role dissolve the barriers between the cold machinery of science and the vibrant pulse of human life.

In every interaction, Yuri proves himself to be not just an asset to his field but a cherished ally to those on the journey with him. His blend of professional excellence and personal integrity makes him a pillar of the community within the facility, someone who inspires trust and admiration in equal measure. Yuri Fedorov, in essence, is the heart of the scientific endeavor, driving forward with an unwavering belief in the power of knowledge to better the world, one discovery at a time.

AVENTURER'S GUILD

The Adventurer's Guild, nestled amidst a landscape of untold mysteries and ancient ruins, serves as a beacon for those daring souls who seek to unravel the secrets of a world reborn from the ashes of its past. A grand edifice that towers over the surrounding terrain, the guild stands as a testament to the resilience of those who dare to venture beyond the known, offering sanctuary and fellowship to all who cross its threshold.

As one approaches the guild, its imposing stone walls and towering spires come into view, casting long shadows that stretch across the ground like fingers reaching into the unknown. The air is filled with the sound of voices and the clanging of metal, a symphony of life and activity that beckons travelers from afar.

Within its walls, the Adventurer's Guild unfolds like a world unto itself. The central courtyard, a bustling nexus of comings and goings, thrums with the energy of adventurers sharing tales of their exploits. The air is thick with the aroma of exotic spices and the sound of laughter, a reminder of the bonds forged in the fires of adventure.

Around the courtyard, various wings and annexes house the guild's many functions. Training grounds echo with the clash of swords and the shouts of instructors, a constant hum of activity where novices and veterans alike hone their skills. Workshops and forges clatter and roar, as craftsmen work tirelessly to equip the adventurers with the tools and armor they need to face the dangers that lie beyond the guild's walls.

At the heart of the guild, the Great Hall stands as a monument to the spirit of adventure that binds its members. Its vaulted ceilings soar high above, adorned with banners and tapestries that tell the stories of legendary quests and epic battles. Long tables laden with the bounty of the land offer sustenance and camaraderie, a place where adventurers gather to plan their next foray into the unknown.

Beyond the communal spaces, the guild offers a sanctuary for reflection and study. The library, a vast repository of knowledge, holds ancient tomes and maps that chart the mysteries of the world. Scholars and sages pore over texts, their whispers a constant undercurrent that speaks to the thirst for understanding that drives the guild's members.

The Adventurer's Guild is not just a place; it's a community bound by the shared pursuit of discovery. Here, amidst the laughter and the clanging of swords, the stories of the past are kept alive, and new legends are born. It is a place where the boundaries of the known world are pushed back with each quest, and the legacy of adventure is woven into the very fabric of existence.

In this hallowed hall of adventurers, individuals from all walks of life find common ground. Warriors and wizards, scholars and scouts, all come together under the guild's banner, united in their desire to explore the unknown and protect the realm from the shadows that lurk beyond.

The guild also serves as a hub for the exchange of information and resources. Notice boards cluttered with quests and requests for aid offer adventurers the chance to make their mark on the world, whether by delving into ancient ruins in search of forgotten treasures or standing against the dark forces that threaten the peace of the land.

As the sun sets and the stars begin to shine above, the Adventurer's Guild transforms. The courtyards and halls, illuminated by torchlight, take on a magical quality, a reminder of the wonders and dangers that await those who dare to dream. It is here, in the gathering darkness, that plans are made and alliances are forged,

under the watchful gaze of the guild's elders.

The Adventurer's Guild, with its storied walls and vibrant community, stands as a beacon of hope in a world of uncertainty. It is a place where the past and the present merge, where the legacy of ancient heroes inspires a new generation to rise and face the challenges of a world reborn. For those who seek adventure, knowledge, or a place to call home, the guild offers a haven, a place where the spirit of exploration burns bright and the journey never ends.

APEX CITY

In the heart of a world reborn from the ashes of cataclysm, Apex City stands as a beacon of resilience, a reflection of the undying spirit of humanity. It rises, a verdant jewel amid the desolation, cradled by formidable defenses that proclaim its strength and preparedness to anyone who draws near. Here, amidst the ruins of a civilization lost, the inhabitants of Apex City have woven a tapestry of life, vibrant and defiant, against the backdrop of a world forever changed.

The city's entrance, guarded by sentinels in striking red uniforms, marks the threshold between the wild remnants of a bygone era and the orderly grace of a new beginning. The grandeur of its gates opens to reveal a scene that defies the imagination of those who have traversed the desolate expanses of the outer world. Here, the structures rise tall and unyielding, their forms untouched by the decay that gnaws at the world beyond. The streets, alive with the hustle of daily life, are clean and bustling, a stark contrast to the silent, empty roads that snake through the wastelands.

Neon lights, remnants of an older, more technologically advanced time, cast their glow over the city, painting the night in hues of promise and possibility. Lamps light the way, banishing the shadows and providing a beacon for those who walk their paths.

Every corner and every turn reveals a piece of a world that could have been, had fate taken a different course. The greenery that adorns the cityscape stands as a bold statement of hope, with gardens and trees flourishing under the careful stewardship of its people. These green spaces are not mere survivors of the apocalypse but symbols of life, meticulously nurtured to remind everyone of the world that once was and what can be again.

Apex City is a marvel of post-apocalyptic urban development, where technological prowess and human will have merged to forge a sanctuary amidst the chaos. The city's architecture, a blend of necessity and aspiration, features buildings designed with sustainability in mind. These structures, equipped with solar panels, wind turbines, and vertical gardens, embody the principles of a society that values both innovation and harmony with nature.

The city's lifeblood flows from its heart, where renewable energy sources power the vibrant community. Governance here is not a relic of the past but an evolved system of leadership, where

wisdom and justice guide the council in their stewardship of the city's future. The infrastructure, sophisticated yet mindful of the environment, features advanced recycling systems, purified water supplies, and a network of electric vehicles and magnetic levitation trains, minimizing the ecological footprint and setting a standard for living in harmony with the world.

Technology in Apex City serves as both a lifeline and a bridge to the past. Digital archives and educational hubs preserve the knowledge of the old world, ensuring that the lessons of history are not forgotten. Health care, enhanced by breakthroughs in nanomedicine and regenerative therapies, promises a brighter future for all inhabitants, extending life and elevating the quality of existence.

Yet, for all its technological advancements, Apex City's soul lies in its community. Here, art and culture flourish amidst the steel and concrete, with public spaces filled with the greenery of parks and gardens where residents can reconnect with nature. Art installations and museums celebrate creativity, while marketplaces buzz with the exchange of goods and cultural heritage, creating a mosaic of human expression.

Security, a paramount concern, is assured by a combination of advanced surveillance and a dedicated militia, ensuring peace within the city's walls. But beyond the vigilance against external threats, the essence of Apex City is found in its commitment to inclusivity, education, and the well-being of its citizens. It is a place where, despite the harsh realities outside, humanity can flourish, united in a shared vision of survival and prosperity.

As a symbol of hope, Apex City stands not only as a

physical sanctuary but as a reminder of what humanity can achieve when united by common goals. It is a symbol of the resilience of the human spirit, a place where the future is forged by learning from the past, embracing diversity, and moving forward together. In Apex City, amidst the remnants of a world lost, lies the promise of a new dawn, where civilization can rise again, stronger and wiser than before.

ASCENDANT MATRIX

The Ascendant Matrix emerges as a fulcrum of hope and technological marvel, a beacon of human ingenuity embedded deep within the heart of the post-apocalyptic world. Its essence, woven from the fabric of science and speculative ambition, is a testament to humanity's relentless pursuit of salvation through technology. Nestled within the ruins of what once was a symbol of progress, the Matrix stands as a guardian of the future, a bridge between the desolation of the present and the promise of a renewed world.

This enigmatic construct, conceived in the twilight of humanity's dominion over the earth, serves as the nexus of a vast network of supercomputers. Its core objective is shrouded in mystery, yet it whispers the promise of global restoration—a daring gambit to rewind the tapestry of chaos unraveled by human folly. The Matrix, with its advanced nanotechnology, genetic engineering, and artificial intelligence, has the capacity to rebuild the world from the ashes of its ruin. It is the architect of ecosystems reborn and the harbinger of enhanced human physiology and extended longevity.

Encased within a complex safeguarded by intricate security protocols and labyrinthine defenses, the Ascendant Matrix awaits its awakening. Its activation is entrusted to a chosen few, bearers of a pendant with a unique biometric signature—a key that embodies the fusion of ancient mystique and cutting-edge science. This pendant, a talisman of authority and hope, serves as the catalyst for the Matrix's reawakening, igniting the engines of restoration and guiding humanity towards a brighter tomorrow.

The journey to the Ascendant Matrix is fraught with trials and tribulations—a testament to the resilience of those who dare to dream of a world reborn. The path is veiled in secrecy, hidden within the echoes of a civilization long past, in the Luminara Caverns beneath the ruins of a city that once danced with the light of progress and technological mastery. Here, in the depths of the earth, the Matrix lies dormant, its potential locked away behind trials designed to test the mettle of its would-be activators. These trials, a crucible for the soul and spirit, unlock not just the gates to the Matrix but also a deeper understanding of the legacy carried by those who seek to wield its power.

As the Matrix stirs from its slumber, its reach extends far beyond the confines of its chamber, touching the far corners of the world. Lights flicker to life, screens awaken, and the once-silent globe listens in unison to the heartbeat of the Matrix. The activation of the Matrix marks a turning point, not just in the journey of its activator but in the destiny of the world itself. It is a beacon that signals the start of humanity's long journey from the brink of extinction towards a future filled with hope and promise.

In the grand tapestry of human endeavor, the Ascendant Matrix is but one thread, albeit a crucial one. It embodies the pinnacle of human innovation and the depth of our resilience. As a sanctuary of knowledge and a forge for the future, it stands ready to guide humanity through the darkness of its past and into the light of a new dawn. Amidst the ruins of what was, it offers a vision of what could be—a world reborn, nurtured by the wisdom of ages and the boundless potential of the Ascendant Matrix.

AURORA GENESIS COMPLEX

Beneath the desolate, icy expanse of Antarctica lies a marvel of human ingenuity and resilience: the Aurora Genesis Complex. This sprawling underground facility, shrouded in secrecy and fortified against the unforgiving post-apocalyptic world outside, stands as humanity's bulwark against the obliteration wrought by nuclear war. It is a sanctuary designed not just to survive the end of the world as we know it but to emerge from it, reborn.

At the heart of the complex's mission is the preservation of knowledge. Vast archives, known as ChronoArchives, house an invaluable collection of scientific data, historical records, and cultural artifacts. These archives are not merely storage spaces; they are vaults designed to outlast centuries, preserving the essence of human civilization for future generations who may never have seen the world before its fall.

Research and development are the pulsating veins of the complex, bringing together brilliant minds from diverse scientific disciplines. Together, they forge new paths in technology and medicine, developing innovations like the EterniX serum. This groundbreaking solution embodies the complex's dedication to enhancing human resilience and survival in a world scarred by global devastation.

To prepare for the challenges of the outside world, the complex boasts state-of-the-art training facilities. Here, individuals like Ethan Hawthorne are subjected to rigorous, comprehensive training regimens. Through virtual reality simulations and physical combat arenas, they are honed into warriors and survivors, ready to face whatever remains beyond the complex's walls.

The Aurora Genesis Complex is also a haven of healing and transformation. Its advanced medical facilities offer care for a spectrum of needs, from treating injuries and illnesses to administering revolutionary treatments like the EterniX serum. These facilities are not just about survival; they are about evolving beyond the human limits known before the apocalypse.

Sustainability is key to the complex's long-term mission. It achieves self-sufficiency through renewable energy sources, hydroponic farms, and sophisticated water purification systems. Life within the complex goes on, undeterred by the chaos that reigns outside, ensuring that its inhabitants can continue their work and live with a semblance of normalcy.

The entrance to this bastion of hope is ingeniously concealed beneath the Antarctic ice, accessible only through a camouflaged opening that blends seamlessly with the icy landscape. This discretion is vital, protecting the complex from potential threats and preserving its secrecy.

Within, the architecture of the Aurora Genesis Complex is an indication of the blend of aesthetic minimalism and technological sophistication. Sleek design elements are complemented by cutting-edge technology, with corridors illuminated by energy-efficient lighting leading to various sectors of the complex. High-tech laboratories are a cornerstone of the facility, equipped with the latest in biotechnology and nanomedicine. Here, scientists dedicate their lives to pushing the boundaries of what's possible in the post-apocalyptic world.

The complex also houses a cryochamber, a place of suspended animation where Ethan Hawthorne was kept in stasis, preserved until the world was ready for them to emerge and aid in the rebirth of civilization.

Commanding all operations is the command center, the strategic heart of the Aurora Genesis Complex. It is from here that leaders and scientists oversee the facility's multifaceted operations, monitor global events, and meticulously plan for the future renaissance of humanity.

The Aurora Genesis Complex is more than a shelter from the storm; it is a beacon of hope in the darkness, a display of human determination and ingenuity. It represents humanity's unwavering resolve to not just survive but thrive, even in the face of total annihilation.

Functionality

- **Preservation of Knowledge**: The complex houses vast archives of scientific data, historical records, and cultural artifacts stored within sophisticated ChronoArchives. These archives are designed to withstand the test of time, ensuring that essential information is safeguarded for future generations.

- **Research and Development**: Leading scientists from various disciplines collaborate within the complex to develop groundbreaking technologies, such as the EterniX serum, aimed at enhancing human survival in the aftermath of global devastation.

- **Training Facilities**: State-of-the-art training facilities equipped with virtual reality simulations and physical combat arenas allow individuals like Ethan to undergo rigorous preparation for the challenges they will face in the outside world.

- **Medical Facilities**: Advanced medical facilities within the complex provide care for injuries, illnesses, and the administration of transformative treatments like the EterniX serum.

- **Sustainable Living**: The complex is self-sufficient, with renewable energy sources, hydroponic farms, and water purification systems ensuring the inhabitants' long-term survival.

Appearance

- **Entrance**: The entrance to the Aurora Genesis Complex is concealed beneath the Antarctic ice, accessible only through a discreet opening camouflaged to blend seamlessly with the surrounding landscape.
- **Architecture**: The interior of the complex features sleek, minimalist design elements combined with cutting-edge technology. Corridors lined with energy-efficient lighting lead to various sectors dedicated to research, living quarters, and training facilities.
- **Laboratories**: High-tech laboratories equipped with advanced biotechnology and nanomedicine equipment occupy a significant portion of the complex, where scientists work tirelessly to develop innovative solutions to humanity's plight.
- **Cryochamber**: Within the depths of the complex lies a cryochamber, where individuals like Ethan undergo suspended animation for centuries, awaiting a future where they can emerge and contribute to rebuilding civilization.
- **Command Center**: At the heart of the complex lies the command center, a central hub where leaders and scientists coordinate operations, monitor global events, and plan for the future of humanity.

Overall, the Aurora Genesis Complex represents humanity's last hope for survival in a world teetering on the brink of extinction, serving as a beacon of hope amidst the darkness of nuclear devastation.

BANDIT FORTRESS

Tucked away in the harsh, unforgiving expanse where civilization's last echoes fade into the wind-swept silence stands the Bandit Fortress. This fortress, a stark emblem of survival in a post-apocalyptic world, rises ominously against the backdrop of desolation. It's a world where the line between savior and conqueror blurs, a stronghold not of refuge but of dominion, where the air is thick with the weight of unspoken threats and the ground bears witness to countless struggles for supremacy.

Approaching the fortress, one's senses are immediately assailed by the overpowering presence of danger and defiance. The walls, a declaration of the fortress's storied past, are canvases for crude expressions of warning and deterrence. Graffiti, scrawled with reckless abandon, speaks a universal language of warning: "Turn away dreams, wanderers; here holds naught but shadows," while another boldly declares, "Only outlaws, scum, thieves, and bandits may pass; all others, beware!" These inscriptions, coupled with foreboding symbols of skulls and crossbones, serve not only as a deterrent but as a stark reminder of the lawlessness that reigns within.

The fortress itself, an architectural marvel borne of necessity and desperation, stands as a bulwark against the encroaching desolation of the world outside. Its outer walls, pocked with the scars of numerous confrontations, tell tales of resilience and ruthlessness. Bullet holes and scorch marks mar the surface, while razor wire, a silent sentinel of death, coils ominously along the perimeter. At the gates, archers stand watch, their eyes piercing the horizon for any sign of threat or opportunity, ready to unleash their deadly cargo on unsuspecting intruders.

Inside, the fortress unfurls into a labyrinth of survival and strife. The courtyard, a chaotic marketplace of scavenged treasures and makeshift dwellings, pulses with the lifeblood of the fortress's inhabitants. Here, amidst the ramshackle shelters and abandoned vehicles, the spoils of war and conquest are proudly displayed, a grim inventory of the fortress's predatory excursions.

Yet, it is not just the physical structure that defines the Bandit Fortress but the indomitable spirit of its inhabitants. Bandits, each bearing the marks of a life forged in the crucible of survival, navigate the complex social hierarchy of the fortress. The air crackles with the energy of raw ambition and unbridled power as every individual within the walls strives for dominance, their loyalty to the fortress's enigmatic leader unwavering.

The leader's chamber, a sanctum of authority and command, stands at the heart of the fortress. Here, amid the opulence wrought by conquest and the stark reminders of battles fought and won, sits the bandit king upon his throne of salvaged steel and spoils. His presence, as imposing as the fortress itself, exudes an aura of absolute power, and his attire is a patchwork of triumphs over both man and nature.

The fortress, for all its forbidding exterior and the chaos that reigns within, is more than a mere stronghold of thieves and marauders. It is a display of the enduring will of those who have chosen to carve out their dominion in a world left barren by catastrophe. A place where the currency of survival is strength, cunning, and ruthlessness, and where the flame of humanity flickers in the shadows of its walls.

As one stands before the gates, gazing upon the Bandit Fortress, it becomes clear that this is no ordinary relic of a fallen world but a living, breathing entity. It is a place where dreams are forsaken at the threshold, where only the bold dare tread, and where the shadows hold dominion over the light. In the heart of this wilderness, the fortress stands as a beacon not of hope but of stark, unyielding reality—a monument to the indomitable spirit of those who refuse to bow before the storm of apocalypse.

GREENDALE

As the first light of dawn breaks over the horizon, the settlement of Greendale awakens to a new day, its sturdy walls standing as a showcase to the resilience and determination of its inhabitants. Amidst the desolation of the wasteland that surrounds it, Greendale emerges as a beacon of hope, with its bustling streets and vibrant community offering sanctuary to all who seek refuge within its embrace.

The gates of Greendale, massive and imposing, swing open to welcome weary travelers, their creaking hinges echoing the town's readiness to embrace new faces. The guards, vigilant and perceptive, nod in recognition of the determination etched on the faces of those who enter, understanding the arduous journeys that have led them here.

Stepping through the threshold, the air comes alive with the sounds of commerce and daily life. Traders hawk their wares with boisterous calls, their stalls laden with goods from both near and far. The clatter of hooves on cobblestone streets mingles with the chatter of townsfolk, creating a symphony of activity that energizes the air.

The local inn, a hub of warmth and camaraderie, offers respite to travelers. Here, over hearty meals and steaming mugs of ale, stories of adventure and survival are shared, forging bonds of friendship and understanding among those who have faced the wasteland's perils. The inn, with its roaring hearth and welcoming beds, becomes a haven for those seeking to replenish their spirits and gather strength for the journeys that lie ahead.

As night descends and the town settles into a peaceful slumber, the promise of a new day and fresh opportunities fills the hearts of Greendale's inhabitants. The challenges of the wasteland may loom large, but within the walls of Greendale, there is a sense of accomplishment and anticipation for the adventures that await.

For one traveler, however, sleep proves elusive, with the night offering a quiet moment for reflection and planning. The early hours of dawn bring a sense of purpose and determination, a readiness to explore the opportunities that Greendale presents and to seek out the town's leader in hopes of forging new alliances and strengthening the bonds between neighboring communities.

The leader's house, a structure of grandeur and strength, stands prominently within the town, its design reflecting the resilience and ingenuity of its inhabitants. Crafted from the materials the wasteland offers, it is a symbol of the community's ability to thrive despite the odds. The guards at the entrance, wary yet respectful, embody the town's cautious openness to newcomers, their vigilance is a necessary safeguard in a world where trust must be earned.

Within the leader's residence, the warmth of the hearth and the scent of bubbling stews welcome all who enter. The main hall, with its spacious chambers and rustic elegance, speaks of a community that values both comfort and functionality. Here, the town's leader, young yet wise beyond her years, presides with a blend of authority and compassion, her commitment to her people evident in every decision she makes.

The discussions that unfold within these walls, centered on unity and cooperation, reflect the complexities of life in the wasteland. Skepticism and hope intertwine as the travelers present their vision for a future where isolated communities come together for mutual benefit. The leader's cautious optimism, tempered by the realities of her position, highlights the delicate balance between idealism and pragmatism that guides her governance.

As the travelers make their case, they are reminded of the enduring challenges that face those who seek to build connections in a fractured world. The need for proof of commitment, for tangible signs of trust and cooperation, underscores the fragility of alliances in a landscape marked by uncertainty and danger.

With a sense of mutual understanding and a willingness to embark on a path of cautious collaboration, the meeting concludes. The travelers, armed with the leader's conditional support, step back into the streets of Greendale, their mission clear and their resolve strengthened.

As they navigate the town, preparing for the journey ahead, they encounter the vibrant life that pulses through Greendale's streets. The market, alive with the exchange of goods and stories, offers a glimpse into the daily rhythm of the settlement, where survival and community are intertwined.

And as they set out once more into the vastness of the wasteland that lies beyond Greendale's walls, they carry with them the knowledge that in this sprawling settlement, they have found a rare thing: a place of hope and connection, a beacon amidst the desolation, promising safety and respite in a world that offers little of either.

HAVENROCK REFUGE

Havenrock Refuge, nestled beneath a craggy outcrop in a remote and frozen wasteland, stands as an expression of human resilience and adaptability. This sanctuary, a beacon of warmth and safety in the midst of relentless winter, provides more than just shelter to its inhabitants—it offers a chance for life to flourish amidst adversity.

The refuge is a sprawling network of caverns and tunnels, carved into the rock by both nature and the determined hands of those who sought refuge within its depths. Its entrance, hidden from casual view, reveals itself only to those who know where to look or those guided by fate or fortune. As one steps into Havenrock, the stark contrast between the external desolation and the internal vibrancy becomes immediately apparent.

The interior of Havenrock Refuge is a marvel of improvisation and ingenuity. The walls, rough and unyielding, are softened by the glow of lanterns and the warmth of makeshift hearths, around which the community gathers to share stories, warmth, and the meager provisions they manage to scrounge from the unforgiving landscape that surrounds them. The air inside is thick with the scent of burning wood and the subtle aroma of cooked meals, a reminder of the community's constant battle against the hunger and cold that threaten their survival.

At the heart of Havenrock lies its main cavern, a large, open space that serves as a communal area for the refuge's inhabitants. Here, makeshift furniture, crafted from scavenged materials and repurposed items, is arranged in a semicircular pattern around the largest of the hearths. This is where the community comes together to make decisions, celebrate their rare successes, and support each other through their frequent trials.

Children, the refuge's unexpected joy, play, and laugh among themselves; their games are a mix of pre-apocalypse relics and new inventions born from necessity. Their laughter echoes off the stone walls, a sound that, more than anything, represents Havenrock's defiance against the bleakness of their situation. Their presence is a daily reminder to all within the refuge of what they are fighting to protect and preserve.

The inhabitants of Havenrock are a diverse group, united by circumstance rather than choice. They are survivors of the world that was, each with a story of loss and endurance. Among them are former scientists, teachers, and engineers, along with farmers, soldiers, and those with no particular skills other than the will to survive. This eclectic mix of backgrounds and expertise has allowed Havenrock to become more than just a place to wait out the end of the world. It has become a place where knowledge is preserved and where the seeds of a future, perhaps far different from the past they all remember, are being sown.

The challenges faced by the inhabitants of Havenrock are many. Food is scarce, and the hunting grounds in the wasteland beyond are dangerous and yield little. The refuge's reliance on salvaged technology and repurposed materials means that everything, from their lighting to their heating, is precarious and prone to failure. The threat of illness looms large, as medical supplies are limited and conditions within the refuge are less than ideal for maintaining health.

Despite these challenges, the people of Havenrock have managed to create a semblance of society within their stone sanctuary. Workshops and crafting stations are scattered throughout the caverns, where inhabitants work to create the tools, clothing, and other necessities required for their daily lives. A rudimentary school operates within one of the smaller caverns, where the community's children are taught reading, writing, and arithmetic, alongside more practical skills such as how to identify edible plants or make basic repairs to the refuge's equipment.

The leadership within Havenrock is democratic, with decisions made collectively by the community. Disputes are rare, as the harsh reality of their situation leaves little room for conflict over anything but the most critical issues. The shared understanding that their survival depends on cooperation and mutual support forms the backbone of their society.

Despite the hardships, there is beauty in Havenrock.

Murals, painted with pigments made from ground minerals and plant dyes, adorn some of the cavern walls, depicting scenes from both the world before and the world as it is now. Music and storytelling are cherished forms of entertainment and comfort, with the community gathering around the hearths in the evenings to share tales of the past and hopes for the future.

Havenrock Refuge is not just a place of survival; it is a place of living. It is an indication of the strength of the human spirit and the lengths to which people will go to create light in the darkness. It stands as a beacon of hope, not just for those who call it home, but as a symbol of what can be achieved when humanity comes together to face the challenges of a world forever changed.

JUNKYARD JUNCTION

Junkyard Junction, nestled on the outskirts of a forgotten landscape, stands as a stark reminder of industrial decay and technological obsolescence. This sprawling expanse, once buzzing with the din of machinery and the hustle of workers, now lies in silent desolation, its skeletal structures and rusting relics bearing witness to a bygone era of human endeavor and mechanical ingenuity.

Upon entering Junkyard Junction, one is immediately struck by the sheer scale of abandonment. Towering stacks of scrap metal loom like modern monoliths, their jagged edges and corroded surfaces reflecting the harsh light of the sun. These metallic mounds, haphazardly arranged across the junction, create a labyrinthine network of pathways and alleys, each turn revealing a new vista of decay and neglect.

The ground itself is a patchwork of cracked concrete and encroaching vegetation, with hardy plants and resilient weeds breaking through the surface to reclaim the land. Puddles of oil and stagnant water dot the landscape, their iridescent surfaces mirroring the sky above and adding a surreal quality to the scene.

Among the detritus, the remnants of vehicles and machinery lie scattered, their forms distorted by time and the elements. Cars, trucks, and even larger industrial equipment have found their final resting place here; their once glossy exteriors are now faded and peeling, and their interiors are gutted and exposed to the open air. In some corners, piles of household appliances and electronic waste create miniature hills, an indication of the consumerist culture that fed into the junkyard's growth.

Buildings within Junkyard Junction bear the scars of neglect; their structures are compromised by rust and rot. Windows are shattered or boarded up, doors hang off hinges, and roofs sag under the weight of years. Graffiti adorns many of the walls; the vibrant colors and bold designs stand out against the dull backdrop of the junction. These artful expressions breathe a semblance of life into the otherwise lifeless environment, hinting at the human stories that once unfolded within these spaces.

In the heart of Junkyard Junction, the most imposing feature is the central processing area, where the mountains of scrap were once sorted and dismantled. Here, large conveyor belts and cranes stand immobile, their functions halted mid-motion. The control rooms, with their panels of switches and dials, are coated in dust, and the screens are dark and unresponsive.

Despite its desolation, Junkyard Junction is not devoid of movement. The wind whistles through the open spaces, causing loose sheets of metal to rattle and clang. Birds have made nests in the more secure nooks and crannies, their calls adding a layer of natural sound to the otherwise silent domain. At night, the junction takes on a different character, with the moonlight casting eerie shadows and transforming the piles of junk into grotesque sculptures.

Junkyard Junction, with its decaying charm and post-apocalyptic beauty, serves as a powerful reminder of the transitory nature of human achievement and the enduring resilience of nature. It stands as a monument to the past, a space where time seems to stand still, inviting those with a sense of adventure and nostalgia to explore its depths and uncover the stories hidden within its rusted embrace.

LUMINARA CAVERNS

Deep beneath the earth, where the sun's rays dare not venture, lies the Luminara Caverns—a vast, hidden expanse that whispers tales of an ancient civilization long vanished. The air here is cool and carries a stillness that is almost sacred, wrapping its visitors in a blanket of profound silence only broken by the occasional drip of water or the distant echo of a falling pebble. This place, shrouded in darkness and mystery, is more than a geological marvel; it is an expression of the resilience and ingenuity of those who once called it home.

The main chamber of the Luminara Caverns is a grand spectacle, an enormous, echoing space that could easily rival the heart of a subterranean kingdom. Its scale is awe-inspiring, with high, arched ceilings lost to shadow and crystal formations that catch what little light exists, twinkling like distant stars in a subterranean night sky. The ground beneath is smooth, polished by the passage of ancient waters and countless footsteps, leading further into the unexplored depths of the cavern.

In the cavern's heart, a natural dais rises, crafted from the same stalagmite structures that dot the landscape, surrounded by serene pools of water. These pools are mirrors of the world above, reflecting the stalactites that hang like jagged teeth from the cavern's roof. The sound of water, gently flowing down the chamber walls, fills the space with a soothing melody that contrasts sharply with the eerie silence that otherwise dominates.

Tall, natural columns stand as sentinels around the perimeter, their surfaces carved by the relentless drip of mineral-rich water over millennia. These columns, with layers that tell the history of the earth itself, support the weight of the world above. Between these natural pillars, the cavern walls are alive with phosphorescent lichen and fungi, casting a soft, otherworldly glow and illuminating the cavern with hues of green and blue. This bioluminescence paints the caverns in ethereal light, revealing the beauty hidden in the depths.

Scattered across the cavern floor lie remnants of Luminara's past—fragments of pottery, tools fashioned from bone and stone, and the bases of what might have been statues or monuments dedicated to forgotten gods or heroes. These artifacts, half-buried by time and the earth, serve as a haunting reminder of the bustling life that once filled these caverns, offering a glimpse into the daily lives, rituals, and artistic endeavors of a people lost to history.

At the far end of the main chamber, a massive, partially collapsed archway hints at mysteries yet to be uncovered. Its once-majestic stones, now worn and eroded, suggest an entrance to realms beyond, beckoning the brave to explore further. This archway speaks of a civilization that thrived in harmony with the cavern's natural splendor, integrating its structures seamlessly into the fabric of the earth.

Moving through the Luminara Caverns evokes a profound connection to the ancient inhabitants of this place. One can almost hear the echoes of ceremonies and gatherings held in these very chambers, under the protective embrace of the earth. The combination of natural beauty and echoes of a vibrant past makes the main chamber not just a geographical feature but a monument to both the natural wonders of the world and the enduring spirit of humanity.

As one ventures deeper into the caverns, the darkness grows more profound, enveloping explorers in a blanket of shadows. Here, the light from bioluminescent organisms is a guide, leading the way through the labyrinthine corridors that stretch out like the veins of the earth. The air is filled with the quiet sounds of the cavern—dripping water, the soft flutter of bat wings, and the occasional shift of rocks. This part of the caverns is a realm of sensory deprivation, where sight gives way to sound and touch, and each step is an act of faith in the darkness.

In this shadowed world, relics of Luminara's civilization beckon. Inscribed stones, lying scattered among the ancient detritus, hold riddles waiting to be solved, each one a key to unlocking deeper mysteries. These riddles, etched by hands long gone, serve as a bridge between the past and present, challenging those who dare to tread these dark paths to engage with the wisdom of the ancients.

The Luminara Caverns, with their vast chambers, echoing silence, and remnants of a lost civilization, stand as an expression of the fleeting nature of human endeavors against the backdrop of eternal nature. Here, in the heart of the earth, visitors are reminded of the delicate balance between light and darkness, life and decay, and the endless cycle of creation and destruction that governs all things. This place is not just a geographical marvel but a profound spiritual journey into the depths of the earth and the human soul.

MILITARY BASE

The military structure Ethan encounters is a vast and desolate relic of a bygone era, an attestation of the might and ambition of a civilization now reduced to whispers and shadows. Situated amidst an overgrown landscape that nature has reclaimed as its own, the facility stands as a silent guardian of forgotten tales and lost glories.

As Ethan navigates the labyrinthine corridors and chambers of the complex, he is enveloped by an atmosphere of decay and desolation. The air is thick with the dust of ages, and every surface is cloaked in a patina of rust and wear. The remnants of a once-proud military might lie scattered about, from the rusted hulks of armored vehicles to the crumbling edifices of barracks and command centers, each telling its own story of a world that was.

The heart of the complex is the command center, a sprawling chamber that once pulsed with the lifeblood of military operations. Now, it lies in ruins, its strategic maps and communication equipment reduced to mere ornaments of a forgotten purpose. The walls, adorned with tattered banners and flags, stand as mute witnesses to the fervor and patriotism that once animated the souls of those who served within.

Adjacent to the command center are the barracks, where soldiers once rested and prepared for the trials of duty. The bunk beds, now rusted and sagging, speak of camaraderie and sacrifice, of dreams dreamt and unfulfilled. The mess hall, with its overturned tables and decayed kitchenware, whispers tales of shared meals and stories exchanged under the dim glow of flickering lights.

Yet, despite the pervasive decay, there is a certain beauty to the ruins—a poignant reminder of the impermanence of human endeavors and the enduring resilience of nature. Vines and foliage breach the confines of the structure, weaving through the cracks and crevices, reclaiming the man-made for the wild. Birds and small creatures have made their homes amidst the rubble, bringing life to a place that once brimmed with the energy of human presence.

The military structure is not just a physical space but a symbol of the cycles of creation and destruction that define the human condition. It stands as a monument to the prowess and folly of mankind, to the aspirations that drive us forward and the hubris that leads to our downfall.

As Ethan delves deeper into the bowels of the complex, he uncovers a hidden basement, a sanctum of advanced technology that contrasts starkly with the decay above. Here, amidst the shadows and silence, lies the true heart of the facility—a repository of knowledge and power that has withstood the ravages of time.

In this sanctum, Ethan encounters a drone, a guardian of secrets, whose existence hints at the depths of innovation and ambition that characterized the era of its creation. The battle that ensues is a clash of past and present, of human tenacity against the remnants of a technological zenith.

The victory over the drone is a turning point for Ethan, a declaration of his resilience and adaptability. The technological spoils he garners from the encounter are not just tools for survival but keys to unlocking the mysteries of the past and charting a course for the future.

The military structure, in its entirety, is a microcosm of the world Ethan inhabits—a world of beauty and tragedy, of lost dreams and newfound hope. It is a crucible in which his character is forged, a place where the echoes of history meet the possibilities of tomorrow.

MISTY HOLLOW

Nestled in the embrace of towering, ancient trees that whisper tales of yore, Misty Hollow straddles the delicate boundary between the past and an uncertain future. At first glance, the medieval architecture, with its timber-framed houses and cobblestone pathways, evokes images of a simpler time—a time when the rhythm of life is dictated by the rising sun and the changing seasons, rather than the ceaseless march of technology and progress.

At the heart of Misty Hollow, the village square buzzes with activity, a hub where villagers gather to trade goods, share news, and partake in the communal spirit that is the lifeblood of their community. Here, the marketplace thrives, a colorful tapestry of stalls and vendors offering everything from fresh produce harvested from the surrounding fields to handcrafted wares imbued with the artistry and dedication of their creators.

The air fills with the sounds of haggling, laughter, and the occasional clatter of hooves on stone as horses and carts make their way through the narrow streets. Children dart between the stalls, their laughtr a bright counterpoint to the measured tones of their elders, who speak of harvests, weather, and the occasional gossip that weaves the fabric of their social tapestry.

Dominating the square is the Elder's Hall, a stout, imposing building that serves as both the administrative heart of Misty Hollow and the residence of the village's leader. Recently, this mantle of leadership has passed to Elena, the Elder's daughter, whose wisdom and strength guide her people through trials and tribulations with a grace that belies her years.

Yet Misty Hollow is not without its shadows. On the outskirts of the village, beyond the comforting glow of hearth fires and the safety of woven fences, lie the remnants of a bandit fortress—a stark reminder of the threats that lurk beyond the village's borders. It is here that Ethan, a stranger to Misty Hollow, first proves his mettle, dealing with the bandits and their demands for tribute that once plagued the villagers.

Thanks to Ethan's efforts, Misty Hollow finds new strength, not just in its defenses but in its connections with neighboring settlements. What were once isolated pockets of humanity, struggling to survive in a world that seems to have forgotten them, are now united in a fledgling community—a network of support and cooperation that spans the region.

The village itself is a declaration of the resilience and ingenuity of its inhabitants. The blacksmith's forge, once the source of simple farm tools and household implements, now also produces intricate mechanisms and devices, the knowledge of their construction salvaged from the ruins of a more technologically advanced past. The pharmacy and hospital, too, stand as symbols of this blend of old and new, where traditional remedies are complemented by medical supplies and knowledge unearthed from the world before.

Yet, for all its charm and the steadfastness of its people, Misty Hollow bears the scars of its past struggles. Buildings that stood empty and abandoned, their windows like dark, unseeing eyes, are slowly being reclaimed by the villagers, restored to life and purpose. The militia, once a ragtag band of volunteers, has transformed under Elena's leadership into a disciplined force, trained not only in the arts of combat but in the skills necessary to protect and sustain their community.

As night falls over Misty Hollow, the village takes on a different character. The marketplace, so vibrant and lively by day, becomes a place of shadows and whispered secrets, the torches and lanterns that light the square casting a warm, flickering glow that dances across the cobblestones. The tavern, with its roaring fire and hearty fare, becomes a gathering place for those seeking warmth and camaraderie in the face of the encroaching darkness.

Yet, even in the deepest night, Misty Hollow is never truly dark. The spirit of its people, their hopes and dreams for the future, shine brightly—a beacon of light in a world that is too often overshadowed by despair and loss. And at the center of it all stands Ethan, whose arrival has marked the beginning of a new chapter in the village's story—a chapter that speaks of unity, strength, and the unbreakable will to forge a better tomorrow.

In Misty Hollow, the past is not forgotten but honored, a foundation upon which the future is being built. The challenges that lie ahead are many, but the villagers of Misty Hollow face them with determination and hope, for they know that together, there is no obstacle too great, no darkness too deep, that cannot be overcome.

NEXUS VAULT

In the shadow of a world reshaped by cataclysm, the Nexus Vault stands as a beacon of lost knowledge and forgotten technology. Hidden deep within the earth, it is a labyrinthine repository designed to safeguard the pinnacle of human achievement. Its entrance, obscured from the untrained eye, opens only for those who possess the key—a cipher encrypted with the essence of human ingenuity.

As one steps into the Nexus Vault, they are greeted by the Archival Hall, a grand vestibule that houses the collective wisdom of the ages. This chamber, vast and echoing with the silent voices of the past, serves as the gateway to the deeper mysteries of the vault. Shelves, towering to the ceiling, are laden with scrolls and tomes, each a fragment of human history or a piece of scientific knowledge preserved against the ravages of time. The air is thick with the scent of old paper and the electric tang of dormant machines, a testament to the dual nature of the archive: a sanctuary for both the tangible and the digital.

Beyond the Archival Hall lie two paths, each leading to distinct realms within the vault: the Genesis Dome and the Simulation Chamber. The Genesis Dome is a marvel of bioengineering, a self-contained ecosystem that simulates the lush biodiversity of Earth before its decline. Within its glassy confines, one can find flora and fauna thought extinct, thriving under the careful management of the vault's custodians. This chamber represents humanity's hope for the renewal of the planet, a testament to the belief that life, in all its diversity, can flourish once again.

The Simulation Chamber, on the other hand, offers a journey of a different sort. It is a realm of virtual realities where one can immerse themselves in simulations of historical events, alternative futures, and theoretical worlds. This chamber serves as both an educational tool and a form of escapism, allowing visitors to explore the might-have-beens and the still-could-bes of human civilization. It is a space where imagination and reality blur, where knowledge is not just learned but experienced.

Further exploration reveals the Fabrication Wing, the heart of the vault's creative capabilities. Here, rows of 3D printers and nanofabricators stand ready to construct anything from spare parts to entire machines, all based on the designs archived within the Nexus. This chamber underscores the vault's role not just as a guardian of the past but as a forge for the future, a place where innovation is not just preserved but continued.

The Echo Corridor and the Gaia Chamber offer a contemplative journey through the consequences of human action and inaction. The former is a pathway lined with holographic displays that recount the achievements and follies of humanity, a haunting reminder of the legacy left behind. The latter is a panoramic observatory that showcases the current state of the Earth, highlighting the resilience of nature and the ongoing efforts to restore ecological balance. Together, these chambers underscore the interconnectedness of human and planetary health.

The heart of the Nexus Vault is the Convergence Room, a command center where the paths of the past, present, and future meet. Here, visitors can access the vast database of the vault, drawing upon its knowledge to plan strategies for the world outside. It is a room of decision and action, where the lessons of history are applied to the challenges of rebuilding civilization.

In the depths of the Nexus Vault lies its most closely guarded secret: Synapse, an advanced artificial intelligence designed to curate and expand the vault's collection of knowledge.

Synapse is more than a mere repository; it is a mentor and guide, offering insights and advice to those who seek to understand the complexities of the world. Its presence is a reminder that the vault is not a mausoleum for the past but a living, evolving entity, dedicated to the pursuit of knowledge and the betterment of humanity.

The journey through the Nexus Vault is a transformative experience, a pilgrimage through the achievements and aspirations of a species that refused to go quietly into oblivion. It is a testament to the resilience of human creativity and the enduring hope for a brighter future. For those who walk its halls, the Nexus Vault offers not just knowledge but inspiration, not just tools but a vision of what might be. It stands as a beacon in the darkness, a reminder that even in the face of disaster, humanity's legacy is one of indomitable spirit and unyielding pursuit of progress.

OMEGA CORETECH COMPLEX

The Omega CoreTech Complex is a state-of-the-art facility designed for the forefront of technological innovation and manufacturing.

Situated in a secluded area, its architecture combines modern design with industrial practicality. The complex encompasses a variety of buildings, each dedicated to specific functions such as research laboratories, fabrication units, power generation, and administrative offices.

Despite being abandoned, the facility retains signs of its former activity, with advanced security systems like surveillance cameras and motion sensors still sporadically operational. The main entrance leads to an atrium, characterized by tall glass panels and a spacious interior that once served as a hub for visitors and employees.

Research laboratories within the complex are equipped with high-tech machinery and workstations, indicative of extensive scientific exploration and development. Fabrication units contain assembly lines and 3D printers for producing technological components and prototypes.

At the heart of the complex lies the power generation area, highlighted by an experimental fusion reactor, showcasing the facility's commitment to advanced energy solutions. Control panels and monitors, although now displaying errors and static, hint at the complex's sudden abandonment.

The Omega CoreTech Complex represents a pinnacle of human technological achievement, embodying the ambitions and potential consequences of rapid innovation. It stands as a reminder of the advancements possible when technology and science converge, as well as the importance of responsible innovation and its impact on the future.

It is an imposing structure that stands out against the horizon. Its silhouette, defined by reinforced steel and reflective glass, was a fortress. The architecture was a blend of utilitarian purpose and a glimpse into a future that never fully came to pass, with angular lines and geometric patterns suggesting efficiency and defense were paramount in its design.

At the top of the walls of the complex, there are automated turrets that erupt into a frenzy of gunfire against any potential intruders. Inside is an expansive interior dominated by dormant machinery, conveyor belts, and robotic arms.

The complex's heart houses the central control room, a once-bustling nexus of screens and control panels that orchestrated the facility's operations. Now quiet, its screens dark, its buttons unpressed.

Surrounding this nerve center were the laboratories and manufacturing spaces, each meticulously designed for specific fields of technological research and development. These areas, brimming with advanced 3D printers and biotech incubators, whispered tales of ambition and innovation.

PINECREST CAMP

Pinecrest Camp, nestled deep within the dense forests of the Pacific Northwest, stands as a bastion of rugged independence amidst the untamed wilderness. Surrounded by towering evergreens and cradled by the gentle embrace of nature, it offers a sanctuary for those seeking refuge from the trials of the outside world.

Enclosed by a formidable wooden wall, Pinecrest Camp exudes an aura of strength and resilience, with its sturdy defenses warding off potential threats and ensuring the safety of its inhabitants. Within its confines lie a diverse array of buildings and outposts, each serving a vital role in the daily life of the community.

At the heart of Pinecrest Camp lies the leader's quarters, a raised platform adorned with tattered banners and fluttering flags, a symbol of authority and command amidst the chaos of the wilderness. Here, the bandit leader Blackhawk holds court, overseeing the day-to-day operations of the camp and issuing commands to his loyal followers.

Surrounding the leader's quarters are a collection of ramshackle tents and makeshift structures, each housing a different aspect of camp life. From storage facilities and armories to living quarters and communal areas, these structures form the backbone of Pinecrest Camp, providing shelter and sustenance to its inhabitants.

Throughout the camp, the air is alive with the sounds of activity and industry, as bandits and outlaws go about their daily routines. Bonfires blaze brightly, casting flickering shadows across the clearing as laughter and conversation fill the air. Despite its rough exterior, there is a sense of camaraderie and solidarity among the residents of Pinecrest Camp, a shared bond forged by the harsh realities of life in the wilderness.

But beneath its rough exterior lies a community on the brink of change, poised to embrace a new future of cooperation and collaboration. With the arrival of Ethan and his companions, Pinecrest Camp stands at a crossroads, ready to cast off its bandit label and join forces with neighboring communities in the pursuit of a brighter tomorrow.

As the sun sets on another day in Pinecrest Camp, the campfires burn bright, illuminating the faces of those gathered around them. And amidst the flickering shadows and dancing flames, the promise of a new beginning takes root, as the residents of Pinecrest Camp prepare to embark on a journey towards a future filled with hope and possibility.

RUINS OF LUMINARA

In the heart of a vast desert, the Ruins of Luminara stretch across the horizon, a breathtaking vista of decay and grandeur intertwined. Time and the relentless desert sands have claimed much of the city, yet in their embrace, the ruins exude an immutable sense of majesty. The remnants of towering structures, now crumbled and worn, stretch towards the sky, silent testimonies to the city's architectural ambition and the ingenuity of its creators. Once bustling streets, laid out in meticulous grids, now serve as pathways of sand, leading to the skeletons of buildings that once teemed with life.

The central plaza, encircled by the ruins of grand edifices, speaks volumes about the city's social and cultural zenith. Here, the remains of a once-magnificent fountain, now dry and filled with sand, sit silently, surrounded by the echoes of bustling market stalls and communal gatherings that have faded into whispers of the past. Statues of Luminara's luminaries, scholars, and heroes stand guard around the plaza, their features eroded but their dignity intact, as if watching over a city that has slipped into legend.

On the outskirts of the plaza, residential areas tell a more personal story of Luminara. Homes, built with an eye for both functionality and beauty, now half-buried, offer glimpses into the daily lives of those who once walked these streets. Courtyards, designed for privacy and contemplation, now open up to the sky, their walls adorned with the faint remnants of vibrant murals, whispering tales of dreams and aspirations.

Delving deeper reveals the academic district, where the pursuit of knowledge was once the city's beating heart. The ruins of libraries and laboratories, their once-proud domes and arches now fractured, stand as silent monuments to the quest for understanding. Amid the stillness, the air seems thick with the echo of discourse and discovery, a reminder of the minds that once sought to unravel the mysteries of the universe.

Venturing to the city's edge, the defensive structures reveal Luminara's awareness of its vulnerability. Fortifications, now worn and breached, speak of a city that valued its sanctity and safeguarded its achievements against the encroachments of the outside world. The gates, grand and imposing even in their ruin, mark the threshold between the known and the wilderness beyond, a boundary between civilization and the unyielding forces of nature.

In every stone and shattered column of the Ruins of Luminara, stories of ambition, achievement, and the inevitable passage of time are told. Among these remnants, visitors stand as solitary witnesses to the city's final chapters, explorers in a landscape where the legacy of the past shapes the journey into the future. The giant statue of an ancient hero, towering high above the ground, commands reverence and awe, a steadfast guardian of the land whose weathered visage bears silent witness to the ebb and flow of history. Whether bathed in the golden light of dawn or cast in the shadow of dusk, the statue stands as a symbol of hope and inspiration, a reminder of the indomitable spirit that resides within every hero's heart.

As the ruins sprawl across the desert's edge, they offer a rare opportunity for introspection, a moment to reflect on the transient nature of success and the enduring impact of actions. In the stillness of Luminara, amidst the echoes of a civilization lost to time, the profound sense of clarity found in this desolate beauty prepares visitors to face their own journeys with resilience and resolve.

TECHFORGE CITADEL

The TechForge Citadel, a towering beacon of the old world's technological ambition, rises starkly against the backdrop of a desolate landscape. This once-thriving hub of electronics manufacturing, now silent, commands the attention of anyone who dares to approach its imposing structure. Its silent smokestacks, which once billowed with the signs of industry, stand as quiet sentinels against the ashen sky, marking the passage from a time of bustling productivity to one of silent abandonment.

Encircled by a fence of rusted barbed wire and crumbling concrete, the Citadel exudes an aura of lost grandeur. Faded signs and logos, remnants of its glorious past, adorn its exterior, hinting at the technological prowess that once flourished within its walls. Step inside, and one finds themselves in a vast, dimly lit hall where shadows dance along the floors and walls, tracing the outlines of machinery and workstations now covered in a thick layer of dust.

The atrium, a vast and open space, greets visitors with echoes of the past. Broken glass from the ceiling allows sunlight to fragment across the floor, illuminating the ghosts of innovation that linger in the air. Desks and chairs, arranged as if their occupants might return at any moment, sit waiting in silence. A central holographic projector, its purpose long forgotten, adds to the eerie stillness that pervades the Citadel.

As one explores further, the main manufacturing floor reveals itself as the heart of the Citadel's operation. Robotic arms, now still and silent, hover over conveyor belts that weave through the room, a testament to the efficiency and productivity that were once the hallmarks of this place. The presence of personal belongings, hastily abandoned, serves as a poignant reminder of the rapid evacuation that left the Citadel frozen in time.

The research and development lab, tucked away in a corner of the manufacturing floor, offers a glimpse into the future that might have been. Prototypes and experimental devices, some half-assembled, sit on cluttered workbenches, surrounded by the tools of their creation. This room, more than any other, speaks to the ambition and creativity that drove the Citadel's endeavors.

Perhaps the most profound discovery within the Citadel is its library. Shelves filled with data banks and servers stretch into the darkness, their potential knowledge locked away within digital archives. This library, silent yet potent, symbolizes the Citadel's dual role as a center of both manufacturing and intellectual exploration.

As dusk falls, the TechForge Citadel assumes a different character. The moon's light filters through broken windows, casting the decay and rust in a softer light. The night transforms the Citadel from a monument of failure into a symbol of resilience, a reminder of humanity's unending pursuit of knowledge and progress.

The TechForge Citadel, in its silence and decay, stands as a testament to the heights of human achievement and the pitfalls of hubris. It whispers lessons of the past to those brave enough to walk its forgotten halls, ensuring that its legacy, though tarnished, endures in the hearts and minds of those who seek to learn from it.

TEMPLE OF KNOWLEDGE

Nestled atop a jagged mountain peak, shrouded in a veil of mist and mystery, stands the Temple of Knowledge. This ancient edifice, carved from the heart of the mountain itself, serves as a bastion of wisdom and enlightenment, a silent witness to the passage of countless millennia. Its towering spires and ornate facades speak of a time when humanity sought to encapsulate the entirety of its understanding within stone walls.

The grand entrance, flanked by imposing statues of scholars from ages past, beckons the seeker of truth to enter. Heavy wooden doors, adorned with intricate carvings that weave together symbols of knowledge from different epochs and cultures, guard the threshold. Pushing open these doors reveals a world untouched by time, where the air is thick with the scent of ancient parchment and the echoes of whispered secrets.

Inside, the temple unfolds into an endless labyrinth of corridors and chambers, each dedicated to a different domain of human inquiry. Vast libraries filled with scrolls and tomes line the walls, their shelves groaning under the weight of knowledge accumulated over eons. These repositories hold the combined wisdom of civilizations that rose and fell, offering insights into the cosmos, the natural world, philosophy, and the arts.

Central to the temple's design is the ChronoArchives chamber, where holographic records pulse with the lifeblood of history. Here, one can witness the rise and fall of empires, the evolution of ideas, and the relentless pursuit of understanding that has driven humanity forward. The air shimmers with the light of projections, casting scenes of ancient wonders and scholarly debates upon the walls.

The Temple of Knowledge is not merely a monument to the past; it is a crucible where the skills necessary for survival and advancement are honed. Workshops on crafting, medicinal herb gardens, and astronomical observatories offer practical applications of the theoretical knowledge enshrined within the temple's halls. It is a place where the legacy of human innovation is preserved and perpetuated, a beacon of hope for a future where wisdom and insight guide the paths of civilizations yet to come.

The temple's map chamber holds an especially significant place within its hallowed halls. Here, maps of the world before and after its cataclysms are meticulously preserved, charting the geography of lands lost to memory and hinting at connections yet to be discovered among the scattered enclaves of survivors. These maps serve as a testament to the resilience of the human spirit, an invitation to reclaim and rebuild the world from the ashes of the past.

In the quietude of the temple, amidst the tangible presence of countless generations of seekers, there lies an implicit challenge—a call to not only preserve the wisdom of the ages but to apply it in the forging of a new world. The Temple of Knowledge stands as a symbol of unity and the enduring quest for enlightenment, its secrets waiting to be unlocked by those brave enough to seek them out.

As the day wanes and the sun casts its final rays upon the temple's spires, the silhouette of the Temple of Knowledge against the twilight sky is a poignant reminder of the light of understanding shining through the darkness of ignorance and despair. It is here, in this sanctuary of wisdom, that the journey toward a brighter future begins anew with each seeker's step through its ancient doors.

VERDANT EXPANSE

The Verdant Expanse, a majestic wilderness born from the ashes of the old world, unfolds as an endless tapestry of life, vibrant and untamed. As dawn breaks, the silhouette of Apex City fades, replaced by the raw beauty of nature reborn. Here, the Alloyed Charger, a marvel of technology, carries its passengers, Aria and the solitary figure, into the heart of this reborn world, marking the beginning of a journey filled with both discovery and unforeseen challenges.

The journey to the Verdant Expanse is a testament to resilience and adaptability. Initially traversing deserted highways that wind through landscapes bearing silent scars of time, they encounter remnants of towns once brimming with life, now silent, their solitude punctuated only by the wary glances of isolated survivors. A sudden storm, fierce and unyielding, offers a stark reminder of nature's dominion, transforming the path ahead into treacherous streams of mud, a testament to the endurance required to navigate this new world.

As they venture deeper, the landscape transitions, with the remnants of civilization giving way to the encroaching wilderness. A formidable river, unrestrained and wild, marks the boundary between the old world and the Verdant Expanse. The construction of a makeshift raft from the detritus of the past symbolizes a crossing into the unknown, a tangible shift from reliance on the remnants of the old world to harmony with the forces of nature.

Upon their arrival, the Expanse reveals itself in full splendor, a world where nature has reclaimed its rightful place. The air, once choked by the smog of industry, is now alive with the chorus of wildlife, the rustle of leaves, and the whisper of the wind. The vast canopy above, a kaleidoscope of green, filters sunlight onto the forest floor, illuminating the rich tapestry of life that thrives beneath.

Navigating through the towering trees and dense undergrowth, the travelers bear witness to the enduring pulse of life, a cycle of growth and decay that continues unabated, indifferent to the absence of humanity. This vast and unyielding wilderness stands as a monument to resilience, a living testament to the world's capacity for renewal in the face of calamity.

The journey through the Verdant Expanse is not merely a passage through physical space but a voyage into the heart of the unknown. It challenges its travelers, testing their resolve, their unity, and their very essence. With each step, they delve deeper into the green abyss, each clearing, and each encounter, bringing them closer to the secrets guarded by the Greenwardens and to the truths about themselves and the world they seek to understand.

But the Expanse is not without its guardians. The unexpected encounter with the Greenwardens, protectors of the wilderness, marks a pivotal moment in their journey. The volley of arrows, a harsh welcome, soon gives way to a dialogue, revealing the complexities of life within the Expanse. These guardians, clad in woven plant fibers and animal hides, are a reflection of the wilderness itself—stern, mysterious, and fiercely protective of their domain.

Their village, an extension of the wilderness, embodies a harmony between humanity and nature, a balance long forgotten in the pursuit of progress. Here, in this secluded enclave, the travelers are offered a glimpse into a different way of living, one that respects the rhythms of the natural world, a potential blueprint for the rebuilding of civilization.

Yet, their journey is far from over. The encounter with the colossus, a remnant of a forgotten era, is a stark reminder of the dangers that lurk within the Expanse. The battle, fierce and unforgiving, tests their mettle—a confrontation that echoes the battles of old, where the stakes are not just survival but the preservation of knowledge and the hope for a future beyond the ruins.

The loss of Aria, a warrior whose spirit was as indomitable as the wilderness itself, casts a shadow over their victory. Her sacrifice, a poignant reminder of the cost of their quest, imbues their journey with a new purpose. In her memory, they press on, carrying the weight of their loss and the determination to forge a path forward.

The Verdant Expanse, with its untold mysteries and undeniable beauty, stands as a beacon of hope in a world striving to emerge from the shadows of its past. It challenges those who dare to enter its depths to reconsider their place in the natural order and to find a new harmony with the world that has endured through the ages.

As the travelers set their sights on new horizons, the Verdant Expanse remains a symbol of the world's capacity for renewal and the enduring spirit of those who seek to understand it. In the heart of the wilderness, amidst the chorus of life that thrives beneath the canopy, the journey continues, a testament to the resilience of the human spirit in the face of the unknown.

WHISPERING PLATEAU

The Whispering Plateau, a realm where the whispers of the past intermingle with the sighs of the present, stretches across the horizon, a landscape forged from the bones of a world long forgotten. Here, amidst the rolling hills and dense foliage, the weight of history presses down like a tangible mist, wrapping the land in a cloak of mystery and anticipation. It's a place where the echo of every step taken reverberates through time, awakening stories etched in the very earth underfoot.

Emerging from the shadow of grief, the solitary figure approaches the plateau with a resolve tempered by the fires of loss. The journey here has been one of reflection, a path walked in the company of memories both bitter and sweet. The landscape before him, a stark contrast to the desolation left in the wake of a world torn asunder, offers a silent promise of discovery and perhaps a measure of peace.

The air here is different—alive with a vibrancy that belies the plateau's tranquil appearance. It's as if the land itself breathes, exhaling the history it has witnessed, from the whispers of ancient civilizations to the sighs of nature reclaiming what was once lost. The trees, ancient sentinels of the plateau, stand tall and proud, their leaves rustling with the secrets of ages past.

As twilight embraces the land, the plateau reveals its true nature—a tapestry of life and history interwoven with threads of magic and mystery. The ruins of a civilization that thrived in harmony with the natural world peek through the underbrush, their stone facades covered in a patina of moss and vines. These remnants, silent witnesses to the ebb and flow of time, tell the story of a people who understood the delicate balance between humanity and the earth.

The streams that crisscross the plateau sing a song of renewal, their clear waters dancing over rocks and roots, nurturing the life that flourishes in their embrace. In these waters, reflections of the past and present merge, painting a picture of a land resilient in the face of adversity, a haven for the myriad forms of life that call it home.

At the heart of the plateau lies the Whispering Tree, a colossal being whose roots delve deep into the heart of the earth, drawing forth the wisdom buried beneath. Its branches stretch towards the heavens, a bridge between the earth and the sky, embodying the union of the physical and the ethereal. The whispers that give the plateau its name emanate from this ancient guardian, a chorus of voices that tell tales of love, loss, and hope.

The flora and fauna of the plateau coexist in a symphony of life, each species playing its part in the ongoing saga of survival and cohabitation. From the smallest insect to the mightiest predator, each creature contributes to the intricate balance that sustains the plateau's vibrant ecosystem. In their existence, one can observe the timeless dance of life and death, a cycle unbroken since the dawn of time.

As the figure traverses the plateau, he is drawn to the hidden corners and secret glades, where the essence of the land is most potent. Here, amidst the shadow and light, the line between the seen and unseen blurs, revealing glimpses of the magic that weaves through the fabric of the plateau. It's in these

moments of quiet communion with the land that the figure finds a connection to Aria, a sense of her presence guiding him through the whispers of the plateau.

The night descends upon the plateau, draping it in a cloak of stars and moonlight. The bioluminescent flora come alive, painting the landscape in hues of ethereal light, transforming the plateau into a realm of dreams and wonder. It's a time when the barriers between worlds are thin and the spirits of the land walk alongside the living, their presence a reminder of the eternal bond between humanity and the natural world.

In the solitude of the plateau, the figure contemplates the journey ahead, the challenges that lie in wait, and the mysteries that beckon. With each step, he delves deeper into the heart of the plateau, towards the ancient secrets that slumber beneath its serene surface. The whispers of the plateau, once a faint call in the distance, now surround him, a chorus of voices from the past, present, and future, guiding him towards his destiny.

The Whispering Plateau, with its untold stories and hidden wonders, stands as a testament to the resilience of the earth and the spirit of those who seek to understand its mysteries. It's a place where the past and present converge, where the echoes of history whisper to those who are willing to listen, and where the journey of discovery is endless, limited only by the boundaries of imagination and the courage to explore the unknown.

WILLOWBROOK

In the embrace of dawn, Willowbrook awakens, its stone walls standing as silent sentinels over a landscape where tranquility and community spirit blend seamlessly. The town, cradled by undulating hills and verdant expanses, greets the day with a gentle assurance, its countryside charm extending an open invitation to all who seek respite from the world beyond.

John Wilson, the leader of Willowbrook, resides in a robust house of stone that merges with the northern wall, symbolizing the unity and strength at the heart of this community. His abode, visible from afar, serves as a beacon for the town's inhabitants, reflecting a legacy of stewardship and care that has nurtured Willowbrook through generations.

The town, encircled by sturdy stone walls, features two gates—one facing the bustling world outside and the other, a quieter exit to the mysteries of the untamed wild. These gates, like the town itself, balance openness with security, welcoming all who come in peace while safeguarding the tranquil life within.

As travelers draw near, the ruggedness of the journey softens into the picturesque beauty of Willowbrook. The town, nestled amidst the rolling embrace of nature, unfolds like a living tapestry—each thread a story, each color a memory held dear.

The main thoroughfare, the lifeline of the town, pulsates with energy and warmth. Here, cottages with thatched roofs and storefronts adorned with handmade signs showcase the town's vibrant heart. The local bakery, its ovens a source of communal pride, sends waves of delectable warmth into the air, and its aroma is a promise of comfort and sustenance.

In the town square, history and the present converge around a weathered fountain. This centerpiece, around which the daily life of Willowbrook swirls, has witnessed countless moments of joy, sorrow, and the simple beauty of everyday existence. The square, flanked by gardens ablaze with flowers, stands as a representation of the town's enduring connection to nature and its cycles.

The streets, lined with majestic oaks, lead to tranquil neighborhoods where life unfolds at a measured pace. Here, homes with lovingly tended gardens and picket fences speak of a community deeply rooted in a sense of place and belonging.

Children's laughter fills the air, a melody of innocence and freedom, while elders, the keepers of the town's lore, share tales that weave the fabric of Willowbrook's identity.

Willowbrook, despite its modest footprint, radiates a warmth that touches every soul. It is a town where everyone knows your name and where the bonds of community are woven into the very landscape. In this haven, the passage of time is marked not by the ticking of clocks but by the seasons' change and the rhythms of communal life.

John Wilson, guiding Willowbrook with a gentle hand, embodies the town's spirit. His leadership, grounded in the principles of kindness, respect, and mutual support, ensures that Willowbrook remains a beacon of hope and harmony in an often tumultuous world.

The town's markets, vibrant hubs of commerce and conversation, offer a bounty of local produce and artisanal goods, each with a story of dedication and craftsmanship. Here, transactions are more than mere exchanges of goods; they are the lifeblood of a community that values connection over convenience.

In the quieter corners of Willowbrook, secret gardens and hidden paths invite exploration, promising moments of reflection and discovery. These spaces, cherished by the townsfolk, are sanctuaries of peace and creativity, where the soul can commune with the whispering winds and the earth's deep, steady heartbeat.

As the sun sets, painting the sky in hues of gold and crimson, Willowbrook settles into a serene evening. The day's labors give way to leisurely strolls, communal gatherings, and the shared joy of simple pleasures. In the glow of lanterns and the comfort of neighborly company, the night unfolds, a tapestry of stars overhead bearing witness to the enduring beauty of life in Willowbrook.

Willowbrook, a mosaic of past and present, of dreams and realities, stands as a witness to the enduring power of community. In its streets, its homes, and its open hearts, the town weaves a narrative of resilience, warmth, and an unshakeable belief in the strength of togetherness. Here, in this haven nestled among the hills, the spirit of small-town living thrives, a beacon of tranquility in an ever-changing world

ALLOYED CHARGER

The Alloyed Charger, Ethan's steadfast companion on his journey, is a marvel of engineering, a fusion of advanced materials and cutting-edge technology designed for the world as it now stands. Its frame, constructed from a lightweight yet incredibly durable alloy, gleams under the sunlight, and its surface is a tapestry of metallic hues that shift subtly with the angle of view.

This is no ordinary motorbike; it is a demonstration of human ingenuity, built to navigate the ruins of the old world with ease and grace. Its tires, made from a composite material, were designed to adapt to various terrains, from the cracked asphalt of deserted highways to the overgrown paths that now marked much of the landscape.

The Charger's engine, a silent, electric heart, powers it forward with a smooth acceleration that belies its potent force. It requires no fuel in the traditional sense; instead, it is powered by a compact, high-efficiency battery system that can be recharged from almost any power source, including solar panels integrated into its design. This feature makes it an invaluable asset in a world where conventional fuel sources are a relic of the past.

The controls are intuitive, a blend of tactile buttons and touch-sensitive panels that respond to the lightest touch, offering precision and responsiveness that makes navigating through the wastelands a less daunting task. The dashboard, a holographic display projected in front of the rider, provides real-time data on the bike's performance, navigation, and environmental conditions, all without detracting from the view of the road ahead.

BIOLOCK PENDANT

The BioLock Pendant emerges as a beacon of advanced personal security and technological sophistication, seamlessly blending the protective instincts inherent to humankind with the precision of modern technology. This exquisite necklace, comprising an intricate lattice of thin, indestructible hooks, represents a union of durability and elegance, a testament to the wearer's resilience and refined taste.

At the heart of its design lies a hexagonal emblem, a shape revered for its stability and balance. This choice is deliberate, mirroring the pendant's purpose to safeguard and stabilize, drawing inspiration from nature's efficiency as seen in the meticulous construction of honeycombs. The hexagon serves not just as a symbol of protection but as an emblem of the technological marvels that define the pendant.

Central to the emblem is a stylized eye, a sentinel of vigilance and perception. This eye, with its circuit-like iris resembling a fingerprint, infuses a deeply personal touch into the pendant, suggesting that the wearer's unique identity is integral to its function. This digital eye, encapsulated within the hexagon, is a bold declaration of the pendant's dual heritage: the ancient human instinct for protection and the cutting-edge realms of biometric technology.

Flanking this central eye, two symmetrical wings extend with grace and precision, their angular and mechanical aesthetics hinting at the freedom and journey of the wearer. These wings, though reminiscent of a sophisticated machine, suggest an elevation above the mere mortal, offering a promise of liberation and protection on the wearer's path.

Encircling the hexagon, a delicate etching of binary code weaves a narrative of the pendant's digital core, possibly containing the wearer's personal code or a secret message pertinent to their quest. This fine detailing not only accentuates the pendant's enigmatic allure but serves as a constant reminder of the digital age's complexities that the pendant navigates with ease.

Crafted onto a metallic surface that boasts a chameleon-like ability to shift colors under different lights, the pendant's material adds an extra layer of mystique. This responsive nature to environmental changes underlines the pendant's adaptability, an essential trait for any artifact designed to protect in a world of constant flux.

Golden in hue, the pendant radiates a warmth and luxury that belies its formidable capabilities. Hidden within its elegant frame is an electrical discharge mechanism designed for the ultimate personal security. Should an unauthorized entity dare to breach its sanctity, they are met with a swift, non-lethal electric shock, a deterrent powered by the pendant's keen ability to detect unauthorized bioelectrical signatures.

This shock, though non-lethal, incapacitates the intruder with intense pain and muscle spasms, a clear message of the boundaries set by the wearer. Equipped with safety features to prevent accidental activation, the pendant is a guardian that discriminates not in its vigil but in its response, ensuring the wearer's security is paramount.

More than a piece of jewelry, the BioLock Pendant is the key to accessing the Ascendant Matrix supercomputers, an artifact imbued with the essence of protection, intelligence, and technological advancement. It stands as a symbol of the wearer's journey, a journey safeguarded by the most sophisticated personal security device known to the modern world.

CHRONOARCHIVE

ChronoArchive is a sophisticated storage and retrieval system designed to preserve and catalog vast amounts of data, information, and knowledge over extended periods of time. It serves as a repository for historical records, scientific discoveries, cultural artifacts, and other valuable resources, ensuring their accessibility for future generations.

The term "Chrono" in ChronoArchive refers to time, highlighting its function in recording and organizing information across different epochs and eras. As a comprehensive archival system, it captures a wide range of content, including texts, images, audio recordings, video footage, and more, reflecting the diversity of human knowledge and experience.

ChronoArchives employ advanced technology, such as data encryption, redundancy measures, and adaptive storage systems, to safeguard their contents against loss, degradation, or tampering.

They may utilize cutting-edge storage media, such as durable materials, high-density digital storage, or even quantum-based storage methods, to ensure the long-term preservation of data.

It is a digital repository for storing and accessing information relevant to Ethan's mission, including historical records, scientific data, and technological blueprints. It serves as a vital tool for preserving knowledge and sharing it with others in the post-apocalyptic world.

CODESYNC INTERFACE

The CodeSync Interface is an object of precise engineering and purposeful design. Its form is a perfect hexagon, with each of its six sides meticulously crafted to fit snugly into an indentation beside a control panel embedded within the wall of the Forge Citadel. About the length of a standard ruler, its compactness belied its significance—the key to accessing the enigmatic Ascendant Matrix.

Crafted from a dense, metallic material that feels cool and heavy in one's hand, the Interface's surface was matte black, absorbing light rather than reflecting it. This matte finish was interrupted only by a series of intricate, silver lines that traced the edges of the hexagon, converging towards the center where a small, crystalline display was embedded. This display, no larger than a coin, pulsed with a soft, internal light, hinting at the complex mechanisms at work within.

Around the crystalline display, tiny buttons and touch-sensitive areas were arrayed in a pattern that mirrored the geometric precision of the interface's shape. These controls, though seemingly inscrutable at first glance, were intuitively designed, responsive to the slightest touch, and illuminated with a faint, ethereal glow when activated.

The most distinctive feature of the CodeSync Interface was its ability to synchronize with the constantly changing keycode required to access the Ascendant Matrix. This synchronization process was visually represented on the crystalline display, where swirling patterns of light coalesced into the current keycode, a mesmerizing dance of digits and symbols that shifted and evolved even as I watched.

Upon inserting the interface into the corresponding hexagonal indentation next to the citadel's control panel, the device integrated seamlessly, almost as if merging with the structure itself. A subtle vibration signaled the beginning of the synchronization process, with the interface and the control panel engaging in a silent conversation mediated by pulses of light and energy.

The surrounding screen, previously dormant, sprang to life, displaying a stream of data that flowed like water, converging around the point where the CodeSync Interface connected with the Citadel's systems. It was here, in this moment of connection, that the true purpose of the Interface became clear—not just a key but a bridge between the physical and the digital, a conduit through which the Ascendant Matrix could be reached and understood.

In its design and function, the CodeSync Interface was an attestation to the ingenuity of its creators, a tool that encapsulated the complexities of digital security and access within a form both elegant and enigmatic.

ETERNIX SERUM

In the annals of scientific marvels that have emerged from the ashes of a world ravaged by nuclear fallout, the EterniX serum stands as a pinnacle of human achievement in biotechnology and nanomedicine. Crafted in the clandestine labs of the Aurora Genesis Complex by a team of Russian scientists, EterniX is not just a drug; it is a beacon of hope, a promise of human endurance, and the transcendence of biological limitations in the face of apocalyptic devastation.

The EterniX serum's foundation is a masterpiece of molecular engineering, a cocktail of advanced nanoparticles and genetic modifiers designed to radically enhance human physiology.

The serum's mechanism of action is deeply rooted in the cutting-edge science of cellular regeneration, telomerase activation, and synaptic plasticity modulation, offering its recipient a suite of superhuman capabilities.

At its core, EterniX employs nanoparticles—microscopic nanorobots—that navigate the complex vascular maze of the human body with precision. These nanorobots are tasked with the meticulous job of repairing cellular damage, reversing the effects of radiation, and counteracting the biological wear and tear that accompanies aging. Their presence in the bloodstream is like a silent army, constantly at work to maintain the body's peak condition.

One of the serum's groundbreaking features is the activation of telomerase, an enzyme critical to the maintenance of telomeres, the protective caps at the ends of chromosomes. By preserving these caps, EterniX effectively halts the cellular aging process, granting the recipient a form of biological immortality. Cells can replicate indefinitely without succumbing to the degradation that leads to senescence and death, a monumental leap towards the dream of eternal youth.

Beyond the mere cessation of aging, EterniX boosts the recipient's physical attributes to levels beyond the peak of natural human potential. Strength, agility, sensory perception, and cognitive functions are all dramatically enhanced, turning the individual into a paragon of human capability. The serum's influence extends to synaptic plasticity, sharpening the mind to process information with extraordinary speed and clarity and embedding a photographic memory that ensures no detail, no matter how minute, is ever forgotten.

The concept of immortality is further reinforced by the serum's ability to inhibit apoptosis, the programmed cell death that acts as a biological fail-safe. With this mechanism suppressed, the body becomes capable of surviving severe injuries that would be fatal to a normal human, as long as the brain remains intact.

The miraculous healing properties of EterniX are perhaps its most visually apparent effect. Wounds close with unnerving speed, bones mend in moments, and the body's resilience to environmental extremes is significantly increased. This accelerated healing factor ensures that the recipient can withstand the rigors of combat, exploration, and survival in a post-apocalyptic world with an efficiency that borders on the mythical.

Despite the awe-inspiring benefits conferred by the EterniX serum, its creation is mired in the complexity and scarcity that characterizes the post-nuclear landscape. The resources required to synthesize this elixir are rare and precious, sourced from the remnants of a world that once teemed with scientific progress. The decision to produce only a single dose of EterniX speaks to the desperation and dire circumstances faced by its creators, a calculated gamble to preserve humanity's future in its darkest hour.

The motivations behind the development of EterniX are as multifaceted as they are profound. In the hands of the Russian scientists, the serum represents a testament to human ingenuity, a symbol of national pride, and a strategic asset in the geopolitical chessboard of a fragmented world. Beyond the ambitions of any single nation or group, EterniX embodies a commitment to the survival of humanity, a bold stride towards reclaiming a future from the clutches of annihilation.

EterniX, therefore, is more than just a serum; it is a paradigm shift in our understanding of human potential and resilience. In a world where the shadows of the past loom large, EterniX shines as a beacon of scientific achievement, offering a glimpse into a future where humanity not only survives but thrives amidst the ruins of its own making.

FUSIONIZER

Nestled in the annals of futuristic weaponry lies the Fusionizer, a marvel of modern engineering and a testament to the ingenuity of advanced combat technology. This sophisticated energy rifle, with its streamlined design and lethal capability, represents the pinnacle of offensive armament in a world where technology has leaped boundaries.

The body of the Fusionizer, crafted from a lightweight yet resilient composite material, exhibits a perfect harmony of durability and ease of handling. Its design, characterized by angular contours and sleek lines, speaks volumes about a weapon built for the future warrior. The addition of vents along its frame is not merely aesthetic; these serve a critical function in dissipating the excess heat generated with each energy blast, ensuring the weapon's performance remains uncompromised even in the heat of battle.

Atop this formidable instrument of war sits a telescopic sight, a beacon of precision in the chaos of combat. Mounted on the upper rail, this sight extends the Fusionizer's dominion to the far reaches of the battlefield, allowing its wielder to dispatch foes with pinpoint accuracy. The green dot sight, compact and efficient, underscores the weapon's tactical versatility, merging the traditional art of marksmanship with the precision of modern optics.

The grip of the Fusionizer, designed with ergonomics in mind, fits into the user's hand as if molded for them alone. The textured area near the trigger guard ensures a firm grasp, a vital feature in the unpredictable dynamic of combat where every second counts. Extending from this meticulously designed grip is the rifle's barrel, its metallic finish gleaming with the promise of power.

But the heart of the Fusionizer, the source of its unparalleled might, lies in the energy chamber housing a compact fusion reactor. This glowing teal core is more than just a power source; it is the lifeblood of the weapon, providing an inexhaustible supply of energy for its devastating blasts. The reactor's placement, protruding from the grip, is a deliberate choice, offering stability and balance to the weapon's architecture.

With this infinite energy source, the Fusionizer transcends the limitations of traditional firearms. Its ability to unleash energy bolts without the constraint of ammunition reserves marks a revolution in weaponry, granting its wielder the freedom to engage adversaries without the weight of scarcity hanging over each pull of the trigger.

The Fusionizer, in its entirety, is not just a weapon; it is a symbol of the future of warfare. Its design, balancing aesthetic appeal with functional superiority, and its capabilities, combining relentless power with precision, encapsulate the advancements in military technology. In the hands of those trained to harness its potential, the Fusionizer becomes an extension of their will, a tool to shape the battlefield according to their vision.

In essence, the Fusionizer stands as a beacon of human ingenuity in the realm of combat technology, a bridge between the warriors of the past and the battles of the future. With every energy bolt it fires, it writes a new chapter in the annals of warfare, a testament to the never-ending quest for superiority in the art of conflict.

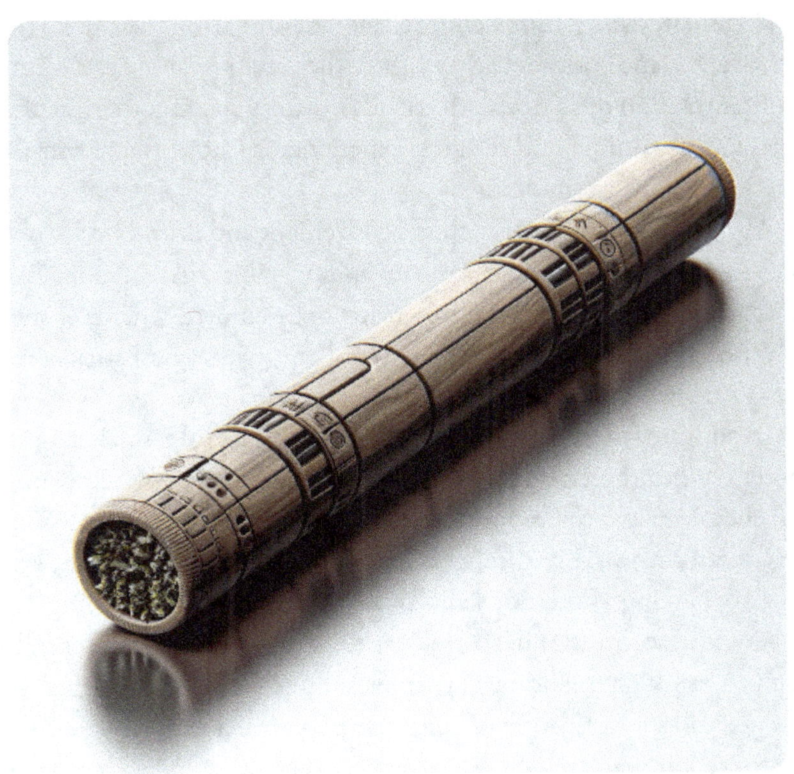

HERBSTICK

The herbstick, a versatile and increasingly popular smoking accessory, offers a unique and refreshing alternative to traditional tobacco products. Crafted from high-quality wood and meticulously designed for optimal performance, these herbal haze sticks have quickly gained recognition as a healthier option for smoking enthusiasts seeking a natural and aromatic experience.

Unlike conventional cigarettes, which are laden with tobacco and nicotine, herbsticks contain a blend of premium dried herbs or herbal extracts, carefully selected for their distinctive flavors and therapeutic properties. From soothing chamomile and invigorating peppermint to fragrant lavender and spicy ginger, the possibilities are endless when it comes to crafting the perfect herbal blend.

When lit, the herbstick emits a fragrant and aromatic smoke that tantalizes the senses and soothes the soul. Whether enjoyed alone as a moment of quiet contemplation or shared with friends during a social gathering, the herbstick promises a calming and relaxing experience without the harmful effects associated with tobacco smoking.

Moreover, the herbstick offers a convenient and discreet way to indulge in herbal enjoyment on the go. Compact and portable, these slender sticks can be easily tucked into a pocket or purse, ready to be enjoyed whenever the mood strikes. With no need for matches or lighters, lighting up a herbstick is as simple as striking a match and taking a deep, satisfying inhale.

In addition to their delightful aroma and flavorful taste, herbsticks also offer potential health benefits for those looking to minimize their exposure to harmful chemicals and toxins found in traditional tobacco products. With each puff, users can savor the natural goodness of herbs and botanicals, knowing that they are making a conscious choice to prioritize their well-being.

In conclusion, the herbstick represents a modern and enlightened approach to smoking, blending the timeless appeal of natural herbs with the convenience and sophistication of contemporary smoking accessories. Whether enjoyed for its aromatic qualities, its potential health benefits, or simply as a flavorful indulgence, the herbstick is sure to leave a lasting impression on those who seek a more mindful and fulfilling smoking experience.

KEYCODE BREAKER

The KeyCode Breaker stands as a pinnacle of innovation in the realm of lockpicking technology, a device crafted with precision engineering and advanced algorithms to navigate the intricacies of modern security systems. At its core, it embodies a sleek, compact design, combining lightweight portability with robust functionality for seamless operation in various scenarios.

Constructed from high-grade alloys and reinforced polymers, the exterior shell of the KeyCode Breaker ensures durability and resilience, capable of withstanding the rigors of both urban exploration and clandestine operations. Its ergonomic contours provide a comfortable grip, facilitating prolonged usage without causing fatigue to the operator.

Equipped with a state-of-the-art scanning module, the KeyCode Breaker boasts unparalleled versatility in deciphering a diverse range of locking mechanisms. Utilizing cutting-edge sensor arrays and proprietary algorithms, it can analyze the internal components of conventional locks with remarkable precision, swiftly identifying vulnerabilities and determining the most effective approach for circumventing their defenses.

Moreover, the device features an integrated touchscreen display, offering an intuitive user interface for seamless navigation and configuration. Through this interface, operators can access a comprehensive suite of tools and functionalities, empowering them to adapt to evolving security protocols and overcome unforeseen obstacles with ease.

One of the most remarkable capabilities of the KeyCode Breaker lies in its ability to interface with electronic keypad systems, transcending the limitations of traditional lockpicking techniques. By establishing a secure connection with the keypad interface, the device can initiate sophisticated brute-force attacks, systematically cycling through thousands of potential combinations in a fraction of the time required by conventional methods.

This groundbreaking feature is made possible by an advanced algorithmic engine, engineered to optimize efficiency while minimizing detection risk. By leveraging machine learning algorithms and heuristic analysis techniques, the KeyCode Breaker can intelligently adapt its approach based on real-time feedback, dynamically adjusting its strategies to overcome countermeasures and maximize success rates.

Furthermore, the KeyCode Breaker is equipped with a revolutionary energy source, a compact fusion reactor that provides virtually unlimited power to the device. This groundbreaking technology ensures that the KeyCode Breaker never requires recharging, allowing operatives to conduct extended operations without interruption or concern for power constraints.

In terms of power and connectivity, the KeyCode Breaker features wireless communication capabilities, enabling seamless integration with external devices and networked environments for enhanced functionality and data sharing. Additionally, it incorporates cutting-edge cryptographic protocols to safeguard sensitive information and maintain operational security in high-risk environments.

With its unmatched combination of precision engineering, advanced algorithms, and infinite energy capability, the KeyCode Breaker represents a paradigm shift in the field of lockpicking technology. Whether navigating the urban jungle or infiltrating secure facilities, this cutting-edge device empowers operatives with the tools they need to overcome any obstacle and achieve their objectives with unparalleled efficiency and discretion.

NEOANGLISH

Phonetic Spelling & Evolution:

NeoAnglish adopts a phonetic approach to spelling, aligning words more closely with their pronunciation. This simplification facilitates communication in a changed world by making spelling more intuitive.

"How" → "hwo"
"Be" → "bi"
"The" → "ðə"
"That" → "ðæt"
"This" → "ðɪs"

Contraction and Fusion of Words:

To enhance efficiency and reflect common speech patterns, NeoAnglish often merges words, creating compounds or utilizing hyphens for clarity.

    "You are" → "yuɑr"
    "Do not" → "doʊnt"
    "Cannot" → "kænt"
    "Should have" → "ʃʊdəv"
    "Would have" → "wʊdəv"

Changes in Letters:

Adaptations in letters reflect the phonetic changes in pronunciation.

    ʌ → o
    θ → th
    ɛ → e
    ə → a
    ɑ → a
    ŋ → ng
    ʒ → zh
    ɪ → i
    æ → a
    ɔ → o
    j → y
    g → g
    ʤ → j
    ʧ → ch
    ʃ → sh
    ʊ → u
    ɝ → ur
    ɚ → ur
    ʍ → hw
    c → k

Language Expansion:

NeoAnglish includes various expansions to convey complex concepts efficiently and reflect the blend of pre-apocalypse knowledge with new realities.

Compound Words:
>"Sunflower" → "sʌnflaʊər"
>"Firefighter" → "faɪrfɪtər"
>"Contributions" → "komplajəns"

Prefixes and Suffixes:

Utilizing prefixes and suffixes to modify words, conveying nuanced meanings or conditions.
>"Un-" for negation, as in "unhappy" (ʌnˈhæpi)
>"-ish" for resemblance, as in "greenish" (ˈgriːnɪʃ)

Verb Tenses:

Distinguishing verb tenses to convey temporal contexts while simplifying conjugation.
>"I am going" → "Aɪm goʊɪŋ"
>"He will run" → "Hi wɪl rʌn"

Adjective Intensifiers:

Employing intensifiers to enhance descriptive qualities.
>"Very" → "vɛri"
>"Extremely" → "ɪkˈstriːmli"

Prepositions:

Including prepositions for spatial and temporal relationships.
>"In" → "ɪn"
>"On" → "ɒn"
>"At" → "æt"
>"From" → "frʌm"

Interjections:

Incorporating interjections for emotional expression.
>"Wow" → "waʊ"
>"Ouch" → "aʊtʃ"

Idioms and Phrases:

Adapting and creating idiomatic expressions to reflect post-apocalyptic experiences.

"Piece of cake" → "As easy as breeze" (Súp sêo léhte sêo béofende)

This language overview captures the essence of NeoAnglish as a language adapted to the needs and realities of a post-apocalyptic society, blending historical continuity with innovation and practicality.

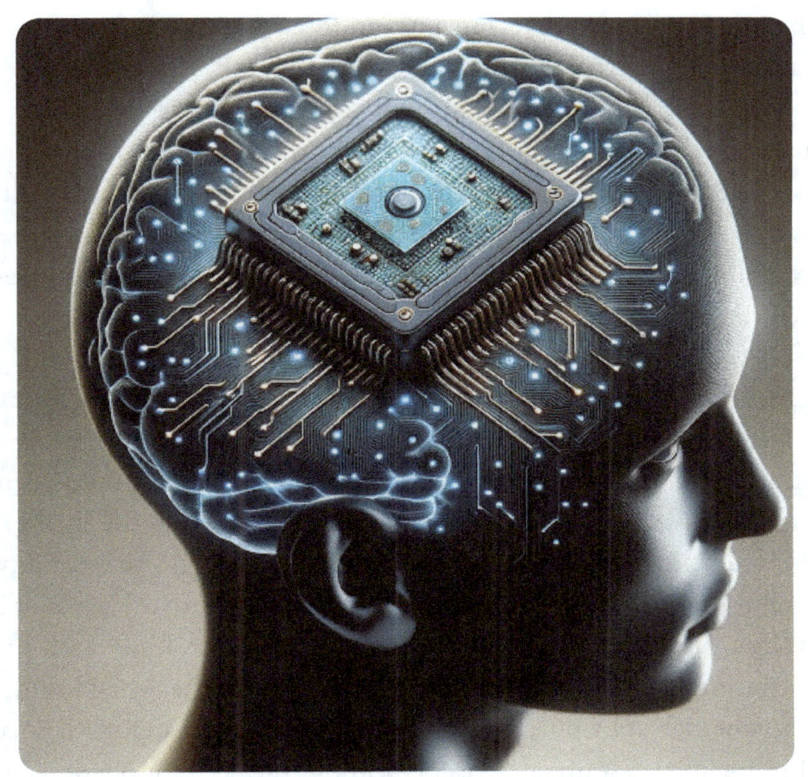

NEURAL INTERFACE

In a world where the boundaries between the human mind and technology blur, the Neural Interface stands as a pinnacle of innovation. This sophisticated device, no larger than a small electronic chip, nestles seamlessly upon the brain, becoming a bridge between the organic and the digital. Its core function is astonishing in its ambition: to meld human consciousness with a vast digital database, enabling the direct uploading and downloading of comprehensive records that span the spectrum of human knowledge—history, science, literature, and beyond.

At the heart of the Neural Interface are countless tiny electrodes or nanoscale devices, meticulously designed to integrate with neural circuitry. These components delicately navigate the intricate web of neurons, establishing connections that grant users unprecedented access to their brain's regions responsible for memory formation and retrieval. It's through this direct link that the interface performs its most groundbreaking function: the seamless integration of an external, AI-curated database with the human mind.

This external database is not static. It pulsates with life, continually updated and refined by sophisticated AI algorithms tasked with ensuring the accuracy, relevance, and richness of the information it contains. From texts and images to audiovisual recordings and scientific data, the database serves as an ever-expanding repository of human achievement and knowledge, accessible instantly through thought alone.

Beyond mere access to information, the Neural Interface revolutionizes cognitive function. Users report enhancements in a wide array of mental faculties. Intelligence sharpens, understanding deepens, and reaction times diminish. Complex problems become simpler to navigate, and the capacity for learning expands exponentially. It's as if the interface unlocks the latent potential within the human mind, ushering in a new era of cognitive capability.

But the marvels of the Neural Interface extend into the realm of interaction. Equipped with the ability to communicate wirelessly with specific devices, the interface blurs the line between the user and the digital world. Data transfer, whether uploading personal experiences to the digital database or downloading the latest updates, occurs without the need for physical devices. This symbiosis between the human mind and digital information transforms the way knowledge is acquired, shared, and experienced.

Implanted within the user's head, the Neural Interface is remarkably unobtrusive. Its implementation, a procedure of unparalleled precision, places the chip in optimal contact with the brain, ensuring that its presence enhances rather than intrudes. This balance between functionality and comfort is crucial, making the interface not just a tool but an extension of the human experience.

As individuals navigate their daily lives, the Neural Interface acts as a silent partner, offering insights drawn from the breadth of human knowledge with but a thought. The potential applications are boundless—from education, where students can access information in real-time as they learn, to professionals in every field, who can draw upon an ever-updating database to inform decisions and innovations.

In essence, the Neural Interface is more than just a technological marvel; it represents the next step in human evolution. By bridging the gap between the mind and the vast expanse of collective human knowledge, it offers a glimpse into a future where the limitations of memory and learning are things of the past, and the full potential of human intelligence is unlocked.

OMEGA PULSE DISRUPTOR

The Omega Pulse Disruptor is a sophisticated electromagnetic pulse (EMP) weapon designed for neutralizing electronic devices and mechanical constructs within a specified radius. Constructed from advanced materials, it features a cylindrical body with a matte black finish, highlighted by faint blue lines indicating the energy flow. The disruptor is engineered for both power and precision, with a weight that underscores its substantial capabilities.

At one end, it houses a focused emitter for projecting the EMP pulse, surrounded by sensors for accurate targeting. The device includes an adjustable grip with controls for modulating pulse strength, effective range, and emission frequency, allowing for tailored use against various electronic threats. A small holographic display provides operational data, including power levels and environmental conditions affecting performance.

The Omega Pulse Disruptor's design prioritizes intuitive use, ensuring that operators can quickly adapt to its functionality. It stands as a critical tool in combating technologically advanced adversaries, embodying a balance between offensive capability and user-centric design.

OMNILOCATOR

The OmniLocator emerges as a technological marvel, a sophisticated tracking and locating system designed to empower its users with unprecedented precision and efficiency in navigating the complexities of their environment. Crafted with cutting-edge technology and state-of-the-art components, this advanced device represents the culmination of years of research and development, offering a comprehensive suite of features and capabilities to meet the diverse needs of its users.

At the heart of the OmniLocator lies a robust array of tracking and locating mechanisms, including GPS (Global Positioning System) and other advanced tracking methods, meticulously calibrated to deliver pinpoint accuracy in determining the precise coordinates of targeted objects or devices.

Whether tasked with locating Ethan's BioLock Pendant or the Alloyed Charger, the OmniLocator stands ready to fulfill its mission with unparalleled precision and reliability.

One of the key features of the OmniLocator is its intuitive interface, which provides users with real-time access to maps and location data, allowing them to visualize and navigate their surroundings with ease. Equipped with a high-resolution display and interactive touch controls, the device offers a seamless user experience, enabling users to specify exact locations and plot optimal routes with just a few taps of the screen.

Moreover, the OmniLocator boasts advanced mapping capabilities, allowing users to scan existing maps and integrate them seamlessly into its database. By analyzing the temporal and spatial attributes of scanned maps, the device can automatically categorize them based on their time period and geographic location, creating a comprehensive archive of historical and geographical data accessible at the user's fingertips.

For example, if Ethan scans two maps from the same time period and adjacent geographic regions, the OmniLocator can merge them into a single, cohesive map, providing a detailed overview of the surrounding terrain. However, if the scanned maps are from different time periods, they will be categorized accordingly, ensuring that users can easily access and reference historical maps relevant to their current location and mission objectives.

In addition to its mapping capabilities, the OmniLocator offers a range of supplementary features designed to enhance its utility and versatility in the field. From real-time tracking of moving targets to advanced route planning and navigation assistance, the device provides users with the tools they need to navigate complex environments and complete their missions with precision and efficiency.

Ultimately, the OmniLocator plays a crucial role in Ethan's journey, serving as an invaluable asset in his quest to navigate the challenges of his environment and achieve his objectives. With its advanced technology and comprehensive capabilities, the OmniLocator stands as an expression of the ingenuity and innovation of its creators, empowering users to explore new frontiers and conquer the unknown with confidence and clarity.

PERSONAL ENERGY SHIELD

The Personal Energy Shield is a compact, cutting-edge defensive device designed to protect the wearer from physical and energy-based attacks. The device itself is small, about the size of a wristwatch, and is worn on the forearm. It features a sleek, durable casing with a minimalist interface, including a single activation button and a small display for status indicators such as shield strength and battery life.

Upon activation, the device emits a dense, translucent field of energy around Ethan, extending a few inches from his body. This field is capable of absorbing and dissipating kinetic energy from impacts, projectiles, and certain types of energy beams, significantly reducing or nullifying damage. The shield's hue is a distinctive neon blue, providing a stark visual contrast against any environment.

The energy field generated is selectively permeable, allowing the user to move freely and interact with objects while still being protected. The shield's duration and resilience are dependent on its power source, which is a high-capacity, rechargeable micro-battery. Advanced algorithms within the device optimize energy consumption based on the intensity of incoming attacks, ensuring maximum efficiency.

Despite its robust defensive capabilities, the Personal Energy Shield is designed for emergency use and temporary protection during combat scenarios, as sustained use drains the battery quickly. It is an expression of human ingenuity, combining portability with powerful protection in a device that has become an essential part of the user's arsenal in navigating a world fraught with danger.

PORTABLE ATMOSPHERIC CLEANER

The Portable Atmospheric Cleaner (PAC) represents a ground-breaking advancement in personal environmental technology. Designed with the survivalist and explorer in mind, this compact, handheld device is engineered to provide a bubble of clean, breathable air in some of the most inhospitable conditions imaginable. Whether navigating the aftermath of an ecological disaster, exploring abandoned industrial sites, or venturing into naturally hazardous areas, the PAC is an indispensable tool for modern explorers and those living on the fringes of habitable spaces.

At the heart of the PAC is its advanced filtration system, a marvel of miniaturization and efficiency. Utilizing a multi-stage process that includes a high-efficiency particulate air (HEPA) filter, an activated carbon layer, and a bespoke molecular sieve, the device is capable of trapping and neutralizing a broad spectrum of airborne contaminants. From the more common pollutants and allergens to the more sinister specters of chemical toxins and radioactive particles, the PAC's filtration system ensures that the air within its protective bubble is not just clean, but pure.

But the PAC doesn't stop at mere filtration. Embedded within its robust, ergonomically designed casing is an array of atmospheric scrubbers. These scrubbers employ a combination of chemical and physical processes to actively remove gases and vapors that can pose a threat to human health. Powered by a proprietary energy core, these scrubbers can operate continuously for up to 24 hours on a single charge, making the PAC not just powerful, but also highly reliable in prolonged scenarios of environmental hazard.

Activation of the PAC is remarkably simple, designed to be operable with just the press of a button. Upon activation, the device emits a faint hum as it begins its work, drawing in contaminated air, processing it through its sophisticated systems, and releasing a steady stream of purified air. The device is also equipped with a series of LED indicators that provide real-time feedback on air quality and system status, ensuring that the user is always informed of the operating condition and when maintenance or filter replacement is required.

Despite its powerful capabilities, the PAC is designed for portability and ease of use. Its lightweight, durable construction makes it easy to carry on long expeditions, while its sleek design allows it to be easily attached to a belt or backpack. Moreover, it is engineered to withstand the rigors of extreme environments, from the scorching heat of desert landscapes to the biting cold of arctic wastelands.

The PAC also features modular design elements, allowing users to customize the device for specific environments or threats. Whether it's upgrading the filtration system for a particularly toxic environment or attaching additional scrubbers for enhanced protection against radioactive fallout, the PAC's versatility makes it adaptable to a wide range of scenarios.

In an age where environmental hazards have become an increasingly common part of the landscape, the Portable Atmospheric Cleaner stands as a beacon of hope and safety. It not only symbolizes human ingenuity's response to the challenges posed by a changing world but also provides a practical solution for ensuring one of life's most basic needs: clean, breathable air. For explorers, survivors, and anyone who finds themselves in the path of airborne danger, the PAC is more than a tool—it's a lifeline.

PULSE BALL

I n the communal green spaces of Apex City, where the community
seeks both solace and entertainment, a new game called "PulseBall"
has taken root, becoming a beloved pastime for small groups and
families. It's reminiscent of cricket in its use of bats and balls but infused with
elements unique to the post-apocalyptic world, making it accessible and engaging for people of varying ages and abilities.

PulseBall: Overview

PulseBall is a strategic, team-based game that combines elements of cricket,
baseball, and a touch of futuristic technology, designed to be played in small

parks or open spaces within Apex City. The game emphasizes skill, strategy, and teamwork, with a simple setup that allows for quick play sessions.

Equipment

- PulseBats: Lightweight, durable bats integrated with a low-intensity pulse emitter at the tip. The pulse gently vibrates to indicate when a player should swing to hit the incoming ball optimally.
- EchoBalls: Small, soft balls equipped with a responsive core that emits a soft, pulsing glow when hit, making it easier to see in dim conditions and adding an extra layer of challenge and excitement.
- Goal Posts: Simple, portable posts installed at each end of the playing area, serving as targets for scoring.

Gameplay

- Objective: Teams take turns at bat and field. The batting team aims to hit the EchoBall and knock over the goal posts at the fielding team's end to score points, while the fielding team tries to catch the ball and return it to stop the batting team's progress.
- Turns and Scoring: Each player on the batting team has a chance to hit the EchoBall and run between the goal posts to score points. Points are awarded for each successful run and for knocking over a goal post. The fielding team can end a player's run by catching the EchoBall or tagging the runner with it before they return to the starting post.
- Match Length: A standard game consists of two innings, with each team batting once per inning. The team with the most points at the end of both innings wins.
- Cultural Significance
- PulseBall is more than just a game; it's a reflection of Apex City's adaptive spirit. The use of pulsing technology in the bats and balls not only adds a futuristic twist but also makes the game inclusive, allowing players of different skill levels to participate and enjoy. The game fosters community bonds, encourages physical activity, and brings a sense of normalcy and joy to the post-apocalyptic setting.

Community Engagement

PulseBall tournaments and casual play sessions have become common in the small parks dotted around Apex City. These gatherings are not just about the game but also serve as opportunities for community support, sharing resources, and storytelling, strengthening the social fabric of the city.

PulseBall, with its blend of traditional sport and new-age technology, encapsulates the resilience, innovation, and community spirit of Apex City, making it a cherished part of its cultural landscape.

SENTINEL DRONE

The sentinel drones that Ethan encounters within various locations represent a pinnacle of pre-apocalyptic technological advancement and formidable guardians. These mechanized sentinels, each standing approximately seven feet tall, manifest the perfect amalgamation of military prowess and robotic engineering, designed to protect, deter, and, if necessary, neutralize intruders with lethal efficiency.

Constructed from high-grade gunmetal gray alloys, the drones' sleek and angular bodies are both intimidating and imposing. Their design is utilitarian, emphasizing function over form, with every component serving a specific purpose in their operational mandate. Each drone is equipped with articulated arms, each culminating in robotic hands that emulate human dexterity, allowing for precise manipulation of objects and weapons. At their cores lie pulsating energy sources, encased in protective housings, which serve not only as their power supplies but also as the hearts of their operational capabilities.

The drones' advanced sensory systems grant them unparalleled awareness of their surroundings, enabling them to detect and engage targets with uncanny accuracy. Their optical systems, embedded within their head-like structures, are capable of thermal and night vision, providing them with tactical advantages in low-light conditions or through obstructions such as smoke and debris. Additionally, auditory sensors allow them to pick up the faintest of sounds, alerting them to the presence of potential threats.

Armed with a complement of weaponry that includes energy-based firearms and large combat knives for close encounters, the sentinel drones are formidable opponents. Their weapons are integrated seamlessly into their frames, allowing for rapid deployment and engagement of targets. The energy firearms, capable of unleashing devastating blasts, are complemented by the precision and lethality of the combat knives, which they wield with surgical accuracy.

The drones' tactical AIs are programmed with extensive arrays of combat strategies and techniques, enabling them to adapt to the tactics of their adversaries. They employ custom fighting styles, which, while unfamiliar to Ethan, demonstrate the drones' abilities to analyze and counteract human combat maneuvers. Their AIs also allow for autonomous operation, making decisions in real-time to outmaneuver and outfight their opponents.

Despite their formidable capabilities, the sentinel drones are not invulnerable. Their protective armors, while resistant to most forms of attack, possess weak points that can be exploited by those with sufficient knowledge and skill. The energy cores, in particular, are critical vulnerabilities; if breached, they can lead to the drones' rapid incapacitation and destruction.

The drones' presence within the military complex hints at the advanced state of military technology before the collapse of civilization. They serve as guardians of the past, mechanical custodians of the knowledge and power that once were. In their silent vigil, the drones stand as symbols of the heights of human achievement and the depths of its folly, reminders of the dangers that lurk within the pursuit of unchecked technological advancement.

Ethan's encounters with the sentinel drones are representations of his resilience, ingenuity, and determination. The battles between man and machine are emblematic of the broader struggles for survival in a world where the remnants of the past pose as much of a threat as the uncertainties of the future. The spoils of victory, including advanced technological components and valuable salvageable materials, offer Ethan glimpses into the potential for innovation and adaptation in the face of adversity.

The sentinel drones, in their defeats, become stepping stones for Ethan, providing him with the resources and knowledge needed to face the challenges that lie ahead. Their legacies, blends of menace and marvel, serve as poignant reminders of the enduring human spirit's capacity to overcome the remnants of a world that once was, paving the way for the rebirth of civilization amidst the ruins of the old.

SPECTRASHROUD

The SpectraShroud emerges as a revolutionary marvel of clandestine technology, seamlessly blending the realms of science and espionage to grant its wearer unparalleled capabilities in the art of stealth and deception. Crafted from advanced polymers and nano-fibers, this sleek and lightweight device epitomizes the pinnacle of covert innovation, harnessing the power of light and sound manipulation to shape reality itself.

At its core, the SpectraShroud integrates a sophisticated array of photonic and acoustic modules, meticulously engineered to interact with the surrounding environment on a molecular level.

Through precise modulation of electromagnetic radiation and sonic frequencies, it can bend and distort light waves and sound waves with unparalleled precision, effectively cloaking the wearer from both visual and auditory detection.

The device operates in tandem with a cutting-edge neural interface, allowing seamless synchronization with the user's cognitive functions and sensory perceptions. By tapping into the brain's neural pathways, the SpectraShroud can interpret and respond to subconscious cues and intentions, enabling instinctive control over its myriad functionalities with minimal conscious effort.

One of the most striking features of the SpectraShroud lies in its ability to render the wearer effectively invisible to the naked eye. By manipulating the refraction and absorption of light waves in the surrounding environment, the device creates a dynamic optical camouflage field that seamlessly blends the user into their surroundings, rendering them virtually undetectable to visual observation.

Furthermore, the SpectraShroud possesses the capability to generate illusory duplicates of the wearer, effectively creating decoys to confound and distract potential adversaries. Through precise manipulation of light and sound, it can project lifelike holographic images at strategic locations, diverting attention and sowing confusion amidst enemy ranks.

In addition to its defensive capabilities, the SpectraShroud offers a myriad of offensive applications, empowering the wearer to manipulate their appearance and simulate different environments for enhanced camouflage and infiltration. By altering the spectral composition of their surroundings, users can seamlessly blend into diverse landscapes and urban environments, evading detection with unparalleled stealth and precision.

Moreover, the SpectraShroud incorporates advanced adaptive algorithms that enable real-time analysis and adjustment of its cloaking parameters, ensuring optimal performance across a wide range of operating conditions and environmental factors. From densely populated urban centers to remote wildernesses, the device adapts seamlessly to its surroundings, providing reliable concealment and protection in any situation.

In terms of power and endurance, the SpectraShroud features a high-capacity energy cell and advanced energy-harvesting technology, ensuring sustained operation for extended durations without the need for recharging or replacement. Additionally, it boasts robust encryption protocols and anti-tamper mechanisms to safeguard sensitive data and maintain operational security in hostile environments.

With its unparalleled combination of cutting-edge technology and adaptive functionality, the SpectraShroud represents a paradigm shift in the field of covert operations and intelligence gathering. Whether navigating hostile territories, infiltrating secure facilities, or conducting high-stakes reconnaissance missions, this revolutionary device empowers operatives with the tools they need to operate with unprecedented stealth, precision, and effectiveness.

TACTICAL MULTI-TOOL

The Tactical Multi-Tool was an epitome of advanced technology, a multipurpose device tailored for immediate utility in diverse situations. For Ethan, who frequently found himself navigating danger and uncharted territories, the TMT became indispensable.

One of its primary features was its advanced scanning capability. With a simple gesture, Ethan could activate a holographic display that scanned the environment, identifying structural weaknesses, salvageable materials within a radius, and even life forms. This feature became essential for Ethan, enabling him to traverse hazardous areas and locate resources in desolate landscapes.

Moreover, the TMT served as a communication relay, capable of intercepting, decrypting, and sending messages across various frequencies. This allowed Ethan to access forgotten networks and gain strategic advantages by listening in on enemy communications.

In times of injury, the TMT's medical scanner provided Ethan with injury diagnoses and treatment recommendations, complemented by a compartment stocked with essential first aid supplies. This feature often proved lifesaving, providing immediate medical solutions when professional care was out of reach.

Hidden within the device was a retractable energy blade. Though not as formidable as dedicated weaponry, it was versatile enough to cut through metal, clear obstructions, or serve as a weapon in close combat situations.

The environmental analyzer had another critical function: assessing atmospheric conditions, detecting toxins, and filtering water. For Ethan, navigating through hazardous environments, this feature was indispensable for survival.

Perhaps one of the most intriguing capabilities of the TMT was its sonic cipher decoding. It could decipher hidden messages within sounds, a skill that enabled Ethan to uncover secrets and navigate the complexities of his world.

Throughout his journey, Ethan frequently utilized the TMT to uncover hidden pathways and mechanisms, such as an inconspicuous stone block that revealed a hidden stairway, unlocking new avenues and secrets. The device also allowed him to communicate when all other means were lost, maintaining a connection with allies and providing a lifeline in solitude.

For Ethan, the TMT was not merely a tool; it was a guardian and guide, bridging the past's mysteries with the future's potential. Each of its features, from the environmental analyzer to the energy blade, was a sign of human ingenuity, serving as a beacon in Ethan's odyssey through a world filled with ancient echoes and untold possibilities.

ABOUT THE AUTHOR
NIELS VANDEN EYNDE

Niels Vanden Eynde is a passionate writer with a deep affinity for science fiction, blending imagination with realism to explore the vast possibilities of what could be. With a strong interest in American literature, sci-fi, quantum physics, and philosophy, his work is shaped by a curiosity about the universe and the principles that govern it. Writing serves as both a creative outlet and a platform to bring these ideas to life, balancing realism with the fantastical elements that define science fiction.

A self-proclaimed loner, Niels devotes much of his time to creative pursuits, finding inspiration in solitude. This focus allows him to delve deeply into reading, writing, and programming, often exploring complex concepts through his work. While he occasionally enjoys social interaction, his preference for quiet reflection enables him to concentrate on his passions without distraction.

As a staunch advocate of science and the scientific method, Niels has an unwavering commitment to learning and understanding the world through logic and evidence. He believes in the beauty of objective reality, even when it is difficult to see past the darker facets of human perception. Guided by a strong moral compass, he champions critical thinking, encouraging others to question assumptions, seek clarity, and pursue knowledge through rigorous research. Through his writing, Niels Vanden Eynde aspires to inspire curiosity and a love for discovery in readers, sharing his vision of a world full of wonder and endless possibilities.

www.ingramcontent.com/pod-product-compliance
Lightning Source LLC
Chambersburg PA
CBHW071955190726
48293CB00001B/31